PRESUMED GUILTY

PRESUMED GUILTY

SCOTT TUROW

GRAND
CENTRAL

NEW YORK BOSTON

Grand Central Publishing
Hachette Book Group
1290 Avenue of the Americas, New York, NY 10104
grandcentralpublishing.com
@grandcentralpub

First Edition: January 2025

Grand Central Publishing is a division of Hachette Book Group, Inc. The Grand Central Publishing name and logo is a registered trademark of Hachette Book Group, Inc.

The publisher is not responsible for websites (or their content) that are not owned by the publisher.

The Hachette Speakers Bureau provides a wide range of authors for speaking events. To find out more, go to hachettespeakersbureau.com or email HachetteSpeakers@hbgusa.com.

Grand Central Publishing books may be purchased in bulk for business, educational, or promotional use. For information, please contact your local bookseller or the Hachette Book Group Special Markets Department at special.markets@hbgusa.com.

Library of Congress Cataloging-in-Publication Data
Names: Turow, Scott, author.
Title: Presumed guilty / Scott Turow.
Description: First edition. | New York : Grand Central Publishing, 2025.
Identifiers: LCCN 2024025669 | ISBN 9781538706367 (hardcover) | ISBN 9781538771082 (large print) | ISBN 9781538706398 (ebook)
Subjects: LCGFT: Detective and mystery fiction. | Legal fiction (Literature). | Novels.
Classification: LCC PS3570.U754 P68 2025 | DDC 813/.54—dc23/eng/20240621
LC record available at https://lccn.loc.gov/2024025669

ISBN: 9781538706367 (hardcover), 9781538706398 (ebook),
9781538771082 (large print), 9781538774441 (signed edition),
9781538774434 (special signed edition)

Printed in the United States of America

LSC

Printing 1, 2024

For six wonderful parents

Ben & Rachel

Liz & Gabe

Jason & Eve

With love and thanks

I.

Gone

1

Gone

September 13, 2023

Aaron has disappeared. It has happened before and, despite my recent hopes, it will probably happen again. Everybody realizes that. Except his mother.

"Do you think he's okay?" asks Bea, pronounced like the letter B. Thirteen months ago, as a gift of sorts for my seventy-fifth birthday, Bea agreed to marry me, although she's been reluctant since then to set a date.

Late last night, while we were sleeping, a hellacious storm blew in from the north. The concussive power of the thunder doubled as it ricocheted off Mirror Lake, on whose shore we live. After a boom like an artillery round rattled our windows, I felt Bea rise—and a few minutes later tumble back into bed with a cheerless weight that let me know that Aaron was not home. Up for the morning, she's just checked again, hope against hope, with the same result.

"Of course," I answer about Aaron, doing my best to look convincing. "You know him. He's probably by himself out in the woods."

"But how did he get there?" Now that she asks, this is a troubling question. Since Aaron's felony conviction a year and a half ago, after he was arrested with enough cocaine and meth to mean real trouble, his driver's license has been suspended. More important, the terms of the strict probation he agreed to in order to get out of the Skageon County jail after four months there require him to live in our house and stay in close touch with us. Aaron, we both know, could teach classes at the university level in how to get in your own way. And yet, this is the first time since he moved in that he has 'gone dark,' as he likes to put it, turning off his phone and voicemail, relieving himself of what he often finds the most onerous responsibility of civilization, the obligation to communicate.

I ask Bea whether her ex has heard from their son, and she says she hasn't tried Lloyd yet. She did speak to her own father, but Joe, who is close to Aaron, claimed to have no idea concerning his grandson's whereabouts.

"Do you believe him?" I ask, and Bea's face is mobile for an instant with her customary skepticism of her father.

"Probably," she says. For a second, we ponder one another in silence, until she asks, "We don't have to call the judge yet, do we?"

'We,' as she knows, is euphemistic. The sentencing judge, Morton Sams, thought that I, as a former judge myself, and someone who still needs his license to practice law, would understand my duty to the court if Aaron steps out of line.

"Not yet," I tell her. "It's one night. It could be anything. Maybe whoever's car he was in broke down. He'll turn up soon."

Before now, I would have said that Aaron has done well. He attends meetings faithfully, avoids the drug-addled crew who resembled the undead that he was living with before his arrest, and even found a job he loved. He was working for Galore, a party planner in the swanky summer enclave of Como Stop nearby, doing all manner of commercial art, everything from banners to designing invitations. But with the annual retreat of the seasonal residents, he was unexpectedly laid off last week. The support groups Bea attends emphasize how precarious sobriety is for someone like Aaron who is new to it. Now the unspoken probability that he has relapsed, and the dark complications that would invite, including the risk of a significant prison sentence, has turned his mother's fabulous amber eyes into lakes of misery.

At these moments I am impressed by the occasional cruelty of motherhood with its consuming anxieties that seem to have no expiration date. Bea often admits that until she and Lloyd adopted Aaron at birth, she regarded herself as laid-back. Instead, her worries multiplied at once, as people she would never have suspected drew back at the sight of an infant in her arms who was, by some uncertain proportion, Black.

Until now, the new year that functionally commences in the US after Labor Day had fallen into a satisfying rhythm, after a languorous summer. I had returned my attention to the legal work I've done for the last decade, as a mediator and arbitrator—basically a privately paid judge—and Bea had survived the avalanche of administrative crises that befall a grade school principal at the start of every year. Ecclesiastes was not correct when he proclaimed that there is nothing new under the sun, but one of the comforts of this age is that there is less.

I have resided up here in what is called the Skageon Region for fourteen years. We are a bit more than one hundred miles north-northwest of Kindle County, where I had always lived before: Son. Student. Husband. Father. Prosecutor. Judge. A dutiful and generally successful existence. But that life collapsed under the impact of a series of numbing calamities that began with the death of my wife and culminated in a prison term for me, which ended unexpectedly when the prosecutor suddenly conceded I was innocent.

After my release, I planned to hide out up here for a year or so. I had no wish to explain myself to anyone and figured I'd wait long enough that people would forget to ask. Instead, I realized that aside from my son and granddaughters, whom I see once or twice a month, there was nothing in Kindle calling me back. The prospect of a new start in a very different place, where remaining solitary seemed more natural than antisocial, was appealing. Here I could recover at my own pace.

The Skageon Region contains a sort of variety pack of American life. At the western end is the magnificent Como Lake, whose clear waters run seven miles long and three across and more than two hundred feet deep. On its shore, every summer since the late nineteenth century, the rich at leisure have gathered, baronial families who would arrive by train from as far away as New York City to spend a few idyllic

months in the vast mansions that hulked along the lake. The nearby
place, where the railroad came to a halt, was called Como Stop, a name
that stuck as the town developed. Today Como Stop has roughly ten
thousand full-time residents, and maintains a distinctly upscale vibe,
with coffee shops and brew pubs and the kind of stylish stores selling brightly colored ladies' wear and home décor items familiar to
well-to-do suburbs. Sixty miles east, in Carroll County, the old worn-
out city of Kweagon, which was once the home to a US Motors plant,
holds block after block of empty storefronts and dilapidated housing
for the struggling communities of color.

Between the extremes of those two towns is where Bea and I and
fifty thousand other people dwell. Outside Como Stop, shopping centers and townhouse developments have sprung up, principally serving
those who toil in the many large warehouses and distribution centers
along the interstate. Moving east, the rich land in the Skageon River
Valley is given over to family farms, where dairy cows swish their tails,
and corn, soybeans and alfalfa, as well as several kinds of fruits and
vegetables, rise and fall. Here and there the large fields are broken up
by the few remaining swaths of primary growth forest. On our side of
the county, the footprints of the glaciers pushed the land into rocky
formations with ponds and small lakes forming in the low spots.

It was the dream of a second home in that area, a place where we
could swim and boat with our son, that first brought me and Barbara,
my deceased wife, up here almost forty years ago. These days, fer-
tilizer runoff leaves many of the local bodies of water eutrophic and
rimmed in green algae, but we discovered Mirror Lake, sourced by
subterranean creeks that percolate up through cleansing layers of lime-
stone. The business of being a prosecutor, as I was then, gives you a
proctologist's view of humanity. I wanted a haven for my family, away
from the turmoil of the city and the anxieties of my job. For once,
Barbara and I agreed, and we bought a small cabin at the rear of the
property I now live on. (There's a story there, too, but I'll take them
one at a time.) From May to late September, whenever I had a break
between trials, we'd come up on the weekend, living in our bathing
suits and striking up comfortable friendships with our neighbors.

I enjoyed the sense of reprieve and over time looked forward especially to Sunday mornings, when Nat and Barbara usually slept in, and I could ride my bike the three miles to Mirror, the little town nearby, where I was able to find a copy of the Kindle County *Tribune* at a local gas station. A billionaire commodities trader had purchased the *Trib*, determined to turn it into a national paper. The Sunday edition now had the heft of a phone book, and provided a whole day's reading with its expansive coverage of news and culture.

After my exile up here, I continued that habit but eventually found that periodically the station was sold out. Eventually, Ravi, the proprietor, told me that despite his protests, his distributor was delivering only a single copy of the Sunday *Tribune*. I started getting up earlier and earlier to snag it.

One Sunday, I walked in a little before seven a.m., and there was a shorter woman in front of the cashier. Her back was to me, her springy black hair banded in a ponytail, but I could see that she had 'my' copy of the paper in her hand, while she awaited change from Dema at the register. When the woman turned, I was deeply struck—yes, she was very attractive, at least by my lights, with those yellowish eyes that stood out like beacons in her darker complexion. But it was what passed through her face instantly that took hold of me, a bolt of intelligence, self-confidence and humor. Of course, she could tell at once from my crestfallen look why I was there.

She hesitated only a second and then asked, 'What's your favorite section?' I was startled, but said, if I had to pick, it would be the front pages, featuring world and national news.

Later in the day, I came back from fishing to find that section of the paper stuffed into my mailbox. The fact that she recognized me was not all that surprising. Since my life had once made headlines, I was fairly notorious around Skageon, and my address was in the phone book.

The next weekend I left her a note at the gas station that thanked her for her generosity, but informed her I was henceforth conceding the paper to her, having now taught myself how to access the digital edition (which apparently was the billionaire's new strategy to turn a profit). After my release from prison, I had started a largely clandestine relationship with the widow, Lorna Murphy, who lived in the large lakeside house that fronted my cabin, but we had both moved on by

then. I was dating occasionally, and considered whether it was wise
to add another flirty line or two, asking my competitor, for instance,
about *her* favorite section—but I decided against it. A woman with
that kind of natural spark was almost certainly married or attached,
and even if that weren't the case, I was, from the looks of it, about
thirty years older than she was. More to the point, I decided, was the
fact that she had delivered the front section to my mailbox without a
note or card, a clear signal that she was not inviting further contact.

Now and then, when I was filling up at Ravi's, or visiting Mirror's
one sparse grocery store, she'd cross my mind, but there were no further sightings. I accepted the judgment of fate, realizing that, as so
often happens, she would likely turn out to be not half as interesting
as she'd appeared in that initial moment.

2

Mansy Potter

Mansy Potter—Mansfield Potter IV—is the best friend I have in these parts. We met when we were both appellate court judges, and once I ran into big trouble, he was a stalwart, who denounced the charges against me, purely on faith. We have lunch together every Wednesday, usually at Trixie's, a stylish café with excellent food, on the eastern edge of Como Stop.

For the half-hour drive, I shortcut down a series of two-lane roads. Time, in the country, passes differently. In Kindle County, for decades I commuted by bus or ferry and began my workday at once, concentrating on the briefs and motions I carried in my briefcase. Now, although I often drive considerable distances, I'm more at leisure. Sometimes there are phone calls with my son, Nat, sometimes a podcast, or an audiobook, or conference calls regarding an arbitration. But more often I enjoy the meditative zone I find myself in on a straight road with little traffic, where I can relish the liberty of existing in open space, absorbing the simple poetry of the country landscape. The land rolls gently and the farm fields, rising against the horizon, look like a quilt. The soybeans are going from green to gold, the feed corn is still standing, its withering leaves looking like arms lowered in disappointment, and the early harvest of other crops has left either yellow stubble or, where the earth has already been turned, the rich black of the loam that somehow looks almost good enough to eat. Sometimes on a high point, a substantial farmhouse will command the distance, often a trilevel McMansion, in contrast to the five-room clapboard bungalows the locals bought from the Sears catalog a century ago.

My visits with Lorna aside, I was keeping to myself when I moved up here. I first accepted Mansy's invitation for lunch as an act of loyalty. I assumed—correctly—that he needed company in the wake of the death of Kathleen, after fifty-three years of marriage. As time went on, however, it was Mansy who became the person with a mission, determined to lure me back into the practice of law.

When I arrived in Skageon, I viewed the law the way the lapsed regard their forsaken faith. But with Mansy's prodding, I became intrigued with the idea of accepting court appointments as the lawyer for criminal defendants too poor to pay an attorney. I thought I'd bring a unique perspective, as someone who'd been the accused, and a piece of me enjoyed the ironic prospect of achieving a kind of repertory role in the criminal justice system. Prosecutor. Judge. Defendant. And now defense lawyer. Except for the clerk who calls out 'Hear ye' to start each session, I would have played every speaking part in the courtroom.

Mansy, who still exerts considerable political power in Skageon County, was quick to help, but I liked the work less than I had anticipated. My clients were all guilty, which I had expected, but their plights did nothing to lift my spirits. They had stumbled through life, each of them. Their crimes were one more thing at which they'd failed in the course of an existence in which hindrance and struggle were constant themes.

'I have another idea for you,' Mansy said several months later when I sheepishly reported my disappointment. Since leaving the state supreme court, he'd been working as an arbitrator and mediator, through a big outfit down in Kindle County. He had more work than he wanted and thought he could direct the overflow to me. Thanks to the start Mansy gave me, I'm now able to handpick my cases.

When I arrive at Trixie's, I am surprised to see Mansy standing beside a two-top, in the midst of what looks to be an intense conversation with his second son, Harrison, who is called Hardy everywhere but on his official letterhead. Like his father a generation before him, Hardy is the Skageon County Prosecuting Attorney. My first guess, given the look of gravity between the two men, is that Hardy has encountered a substantial obstacle in his campaign for reelection next year, a problem which requires his father's seasoned advice. Almost a head taller than his dad, with dark hair and eyes in a family of blonds, Hardy is holding his lunch check, so I take it that he bumped into his dad after dining with other companions.

Standing by the glass case that holds the cash register, I look around the restaurant aimlessly, rather than seeming to spy on the Potters' conversation. Trixie's has the peppy feel of a chain, new construction with exposed rafters and skylights, but the food is strictly home cooked. Every week now the crowd is thinner. The weather remains mild, but most of the folks with houses in Como Stop have kids and grandkids back in school and have resumed their usual routines in Kindle County or Milwaukee.

Mansy finally notices me. He waves me forward while Hardy heads out, brushing past me with a somewhat reluctant smile that suggests he remains deeply preoccupied or is even less pleased than usual to see me.

"Sorry," Mansy says, taking his seat and motioning me toward mine. "Family issues."

Like his son, Mansy, even at the age of eighty-three, remains a handsome fellow. I have often tried to figure out why the WASP elite in this country look so good. To some extent, I think, it must reflect their long hold on power, meaning they set—or were taken to embody—aesthetic standards in their own image—tall, blond, blue-eyed, athletic. And of course, for generations they married their own kind, so that the towheaded children seem to come forth like they were issued from a stamping plant. Whatever the reason, Mansy is a Rockwell figure, with a full mane of white hair parted to the side and going just a trifle yellow near his scalp. Below his thick white eyebrows, a somewhat prominent nose dominates his well-proportioned features. His cool-blue eyes still hold the light of a fierce intelligence.

"No intention of prying," I say, "but is Charmaine all right?" Hardy's wife has MS and uses a wheelchair these days at times.

"Fine," Mansy answers. "The MS is stable, but Charmaine doesn't need a lot of stress, and my screw-loose granddaughter is providing plenty, as usual."

I decide 'What now?' is a trifle impolite. Mansy's manners are flawless and I'm always trying to emulate his genteel manner. When he speaks, his voice modulates like a radio announcer's and he exhibits artful tact, a sort of perfect pitch for knowing what can be well expressed and what can't, what people will hear and take to heart, rather than ignore.

"Mae has disappeared," he says. "She said something about camping, but slipped out of the house and is on radio silence. Won't pick up her phone or answer messages."

I'm sure my face betrays me, and Mansy's expression darkens.

"Aaron too?" he asks. When I answer yes, he takes a second to ponder and then says what we're both thinking: "Too coincidental."

Neither family will receive this as good news. Bea regards Mae as the principal cause of Aaron's troubles. It's certainly true that on his last arrest, the one that landed him in jail for four months, he was holding drugs Mae had purchased. It infuriated Bea that Mae wasn't even questioned, but the sheriff's deputies here, like cops in many other places, extend some professional courtesy to the elected prosecutor and his family. Besides, as Aaron pointed out to his mother, he was the one who was driving loaded.

Aaron and Mae have been an item since junior high, with fiery breakups and quick reunions becoming frequent toward the end of high school. After he was released from jail, I thought Aaron had sworn not to see her.

"We hadn't even heard they were back together," I tell Mansy. Aaron, especially since he's gotten sober, is generally honest. He prefers not to answer, rather than lie. But with him, Mae is a tender subject.

Mae is both brilliant and uncommonly beautiful, even by the standards of her fine-looking family. A white blonde, tall and slender, she has the angelic features of the kind of young women who were on shampoo bottles in my youth. She actually tried for a while to make it as a model in Manhattan after she dropped out of college. Long before this summer's cinematic extravaganza, her hair and figure inspired comparisons to that iconic doll.

"Think they're eloping?" Mansy asks out of nowhere.

"Jesus. El*op*ing?" I had immediately assumed that the two of them were in a tent, enjoying an ecstatic orgy of sex and drugs. "Does Mae talk about that?"

"No, it just came into my head," Mansy says, although I suspect he is being discreet. "It's the kind of crazy impulsive thing they both would do. Certainly her."

"That marriage wouldn't last a month," I declare. "And I sure wouldn't send china as a wedding gift. It would all end up shattered against the walls."

I'm not completely positive how Mansy would react to a Black grandson-in-law. I suspect he'd need a second to hitch up his britches and then accept it in stride. Charmaine and Hardy would be another matter. They would never ascribe their reservations to skin color, but the racehorse breeding of the Potter family has been impeccable, and I imagine they tried to inculcate the idea of 'marrying well' since Mae was at a young age. In Skageon County, the Potters are accepted as one of the few dynastic families, and have long played the role of benevolent aristocrats. The original family fortune was made in the nineteenth century by digging sphagnum moss, and was expanded into forestry, real estate and banking. The children have gone off to elite educations in the East or Midwest and then returned here, where they attend church with everybody else and do their business honorably.

"Would it be an imposition, Mansy, if I asked you not to say anything about Aaron to Hardy just yet?" Hardy's attitude toward Aaron is similar to Bea's feelings for Mae, but the power of his elected position makes him far more threatening. Whenever Aaron has had his scuffles with the law, Hardy has claimed to have removed himself from deciding his daughter's boyfriend's fate. But Hardy is in many ways his father's polar opposite, and seems to make up for his lesser abilities by adhering to lower scruples. It would not be unlike him to offer some kind of winking direction to his chief deputy, who now would be the one to decide whether to move to revoke Aaron's probation, if he's violated its many strict terms. "I'd like to give him a day or two and see what kind of shape he's in when he gets back here."

Mansy lowers an eyebrow and asks, "You think he's using again?"

"I hope not," I say. The fact is that substances seem to have been a large part of Mae and Aaron's relationship from the start. Even at thirteen, they were drinking Hardy's vodka and watering the bottles, and occasionally stealing some of Charmaine's pills.

"He's been sober quite some time now, hasn't he?" Mansy, who comments often about his unsuccessful effort to discipline himself with alcohol, regards sobriety as a substantial achievement, as do I.

"I thought he's been doing fabulously," I answer. "He's got a sponsor in Kweagon, Reverend Spruce, he really admires."

"Oh yeah. Donall Spruce. Never said a good thing about me, but he's an honest man." Mansy gives his head a shake at the thought of the Reverend. "Has Joe heard from Aaron?" he asks, referring to Bea's father.

"Bea says he's denied it to her, but she never really believes him. I think I better lay eyes on Joe," I tell Mansy. "If push comes to shove, he'll lie to me anyway, but it's harder for him to do it face-to-face."

With the worrying subject of Mae and Aaron pretty much exhausted, we find, after another couple of minutes, that we've fallen back into the usual meandering flow of our luncheon conversations. Since each of us held public office for years—Mansy was a state senator, then served three terms as the elected PA for Skageon County, before running for the bench—politics is an inevitable topic, especially since we get the opportunity to joust with one another. We don't agree about some national issues, like how to address climate change or tax policy, but our discussions are tempered by the recognition that these are matters far beyond the control of either of us. Our views have no more impact than a fan shouting instructions to the batter at a baseball game.

We also share a lot of local information, which, truthfully, is not much more than gossip. These are small towns, where people's lives tend to intersect in multiple ways. Frequently, the news is about who has moved away, especially the young people, who often go off for college and find themselves educated beyond the level of available local employment. Bea also often comes home from the teachers' lounge with tales of sexual intrigues, but Mansy is too gentlemanly to get into extended discussion of those topics. And certain other subjects are generally banned as well, since we have adopted the same three rules Mansy says he follows with his golf buddies. One, no discussion of physical ailments. A few years older than I, Mansy has a slightly longer list of complaints, but the truth is that both of us have enough friends who've passed by the wayside that we count ourselves among the blessed. Two, no grousing about the women in our lives. Mansy now has two female friends he sees regularly. Naturally, I have some curiosity about how this arrangement works in practice, but Mansy is not the kind to welcome any inquiry into the details. Third, no more than five minutes on grandchildren, including bragging—a rule observed in the breach today with our extended talk of Mae.

That news remains enough in mind that it requires no transition as we are winding up for me to return to it.

"And you'll keep the stuff about Aaron between us for a day or two?" I ask again.

"Of course," Mansy answers. "Speaking to Hardy wouldn't be productive anyway. You could probably see he goes off like a Roman candle whenever Mae gets out of hand. And frankly, he needs to focus on his campaign. He's gotten a late start as far as I'm concerned."

Hardy has a primary opponent for the first time, a state senator named Madison van Ohne, who is running at him from the right.

Out in the parking lot, Mansy and I are smiling as we part, promising to be in touch if either of us gets further word about the missing pair. But I have no doubt we're each leaving far more worried than we were when we arrived.

3

Text Aaron

As I expected, the news I deliver when Bea returns from school—that Aaron is probably with Mae—induces a pained reflex. She leans forward with her slender hand gripping her forehead and shielding her eyes.

"Her mission in life is to bring him down, it really is," she says. This is a clear exaggeration. Mae's antic behavior most often strikes me as intended to harm herself more than anybody else. And it was Aaron who became an actual addict. But that does not prevent Bea from declaring, "Honestly, sometimes I just wish the earth would open and swallow that girl."

After dinner, I can hear Bea on the phone with a couple of Aaron's closest friends. She taught virtually every kid who grew up in the Mirror district while they were in grade school, and no matter how insolent they've become—and a lot of these kids still seem to need a solid smack—they answer her respectfully. But nobody knows much, with the exception of Cassity Benisch, Aaron's bestie, who plays her cards close but, after a long pause, answers yes when Bea asks if Aaron is with Mae.

Bea passes another restless night. In the morning, I can see that the agony of being the parent of an addict, which she has not felt for close to a year and a half, has returned with its harrowing effect. The numbers say that most teen addicts eventually become productive adults. The problem is keeping them alive long enough; the year after rehab is the most tenuous. Aaron already failed once, after his first arrest while he was a college freshman, but having gotten this far now, he supposedly has a solid chance. Thus there is a special agony in finding that all the hopes raised by months of disciplined behavior may now be wasted, bringing us to the brink of disaster.

As she's headed out to school, Bea stops by the garage door.

"Will you text Aaron, please, and warn him?" she asks. "Tell him you're going to have to call the judge if we don't hear from him."

The point of this is lost on me, since none of her own messages have been delivered, all seemingly pending somewhere in the cloud.

"I'll take that under advisement," I say, trying to avoid an outright no. "But Mansy did make the point that we ought to talk to Joe. If anybody knows anything, your father does. If we haven't heard from Aaron by tonight, we should probably go over to the VFW to have a word with him."

"Me too?" Bea generally prefers to deal with her father only in Aaron's company. When they are alone, she sometimes cannot contain her rage. Throughout her childhood, he was an abusive drunk who battered her mother and terrified his children.

"I just think if he knows where Aaron is, he'd have a harder time looking both of us in the eye and lying."

Bea seems to accept my logic, but still issues a shudder before heading out the door.

I work until lunch, enjoying a half sandwich of gravlax we cured ourselves with a salmon I caught last week during the spawning run. I've just finished when the house phone rings. It's the landline that comes free with our Internet.

"It's Gert," the woman says, a voice always enlarged by the rattle of phlegm from years of smoking. Gertrude Gevorgian is Aaron's probation officer. "Where's Aaron? I've been calling his cell for an hour."

Now I'm in a spot. Addicts often take their families down with them, and so I know better than to lie for Aaron. But saying he's AWOL will only create a crisis—for him, because that might jeopardize his probation, and also for me, since I'm supposed to be his keeper for the court.

"He's camping. Gloria laid him off last week, so I think he's trying to get some headspace."

"Camping? How'd he get there?"

"I think he went with Mae Potter." Gert knows what this means as well as anybody else, but she takes an unexpectedly long time to react.

"Yeah, someone said that," she answers finally. "But I need to see him. I want him to come in now."

That can only mean she wants a random drug test.

"He knows he has a meeting with you Monday," I answer.

"Before that," she responds.

"He doesn't seem to have cell coverage right now."

"He didn't leave the county, did he?"

"He knows the rules, Gert. I'm sure they're just up north. It's a black hole when you get close to Marenago County."

Gert is normally laid-back—too laid-back if you ask a former prosecutor—and so her insistence is strange. I promise I'll text him.

Afterwards, I sit in the living room, facing the rock fireplace, chunks of local granite that rise impressively to an eighteen-foot ceiling, while I try to decode this call. In the sixteen months since Aaron's release, this is the first random Gert's imposed, at least so far as I know. But that fact joins in significance with Gert's acknowledgment that she had heard that Aaron was with Mae. After another instant for reflection, I realize that Mansy gave me the low end of what I'd asked for yesterday, twenty-four hours—but not a moment more. Then he told Hardy and Charmaine. And Hardy, even though he supposedly has nothing to do with Aaron's case, immediately got Gert to jerk Aaron in. I don't know if by drug-testing Aaron, Hardy means to test his daughter, too, or if, more likely, he's looking for a way to put Aaron back inside and keep him away from Mae.

But I honor my promise to Gert—and Bea. I pick up my phone.

'Aaron,' my text says. 'Please. If I don't hear from you

today, I'll have no choice about contacting Judge
Sams.'

Unfortunately, this is not an idle threat. Gert will tell the judge
shortly what is going on, so I can't fall far behind her in carrying out
the promise I gave him sixteen months ago.

Unless Aaron shows up shortly, tomorrow will be a very unhappy day.

4

Dr. Housley

It was Mansy who decided that I should sit on a public body that was basically his brainchild, called the School Policy Legal Review Council. Even then, in 2016, there were serious scraps that were basically political over what kids should and shouldn't learn. Up in Glenville, which is right across the river from Wisconsin State, and is in temperament not all that different from Berkeley, there was a campaign to reform the teaching of US history by barring all laudatory reference to slaveholders like George Washington and Thomas Jefferson, as well as hardcore racists like Woodrow Wilson. The critics wanted any text or library book, no matter how old, that did not mention these deprecating facts about those former presidents to be removed from the shelves.

In our neck of the woods, an insidious fellow named Aloysius aka Ralph Proctor, who was the pastor of a vast evangelical congregation just outside of Mirror, which Aaron's dad, Lloyd, and his new family attended, had initiated yet another of his whispering campaigns. Pastor Proctor had the outward manner of Fred Rogers and refused to associate himself publicly with anything that might foster controversy. But a small cohort of his most devoted acolytes were demanding the removal of 'smut' from local school libraries, meaning any book that made even a remote reference to people having sex outside of marriage or to queer life.

Mansy, a moderate to the core, had gotten his many old friends on the county board to pass an ordinance requiring the review councils to examine all these proposed changes before they could be implemented. The councils would be composed of three retired judges who would simply render an opinion on whether any proposed change 'complied with existing law,' which was code for the First Amendment. To ensure the doctrinal neutrality of the councils, at least one of the three members was supposed to come from the opposite political party of the other two. Since Democrats are in short supply in Skageon County, Mansy was eager to press me into service.

'People don't want a convict on their school board,' I told him.

'Convict my ass,' said Mansy. 'You'll need a better excuse than that. The only thing about your case that people here remember is that Sandy Stern got the Kindle County Board to pay you four million dollars to settle your civil suit after you were exonerated, which is about two million dollars a month for the time you spent inside. Most folks here say they would have done it for half that price.'

'But they still remember.'

'Listen, everybody on that board is going to have the same first name: Judge. Nobody will get beyond that. Just give me a freaking year to get all the hoo-ha settled down. After that, everybody who comes off the bench will be happy to do a job with a nice title and no work.'

I was too indebted to Mansy to refuse, and so when I showed up for the first meeting of the Council for Districts 64 and 65, meaning eastern Skageon County, I was startled and amused when the principal of Mirror Elementary School stood to introduce herself. Beatrix Mena Housley, PhD, whose school was under frequent attack, was my winning rival in the Sunday newspaper competition at Ravi's. I thought there was a sly smile the first time she looked my way. Knowing my name all along, she had been far ahead of me.

The council met four times a year, and Dr. Housley was required to respond frequently. In a perverse way, I was disappointed to discover that she seemed to be exactly the person I had imagined in the service station. She was poised and nimble-witted, and a study in patience with the small cadre of objectors, the same three people, who had several new books to denounce in each meeting. Bea adhered to a simple standard, namely whether any change would encourage or limit a child's curiosity. She had done her research and could show that every one of the challenged books was in a majority of the school libraries around the state, not to mention thousands across the country. And she had initiated a system in her school by which any parents could present the school librarian with a list of books they didn't want their child to browse or borrow.

There was no denying that Dr. Housley was attractive with a capital A. But in addition to everything that had discouraged me a few years before at Ravi's, there was now an insuperable barrier: As a member of the council, I exercised clear supervisory authority over her, which obliged me to act as if she were no more alluring than a doorstop.

Nonetheless, I listened carefully when people talked about her. As a principal, she had a large fan club, and was viewed as energetic, imaginative and dedicated. From the occasional remarks about her personal life that arose in passing, I gleaned that she was divorced, and heard no reference to a current partner, for what little that might mean. A few times, because this is America, people also mentioned that she was the single woman with a Black son, which was passed on as something interesting or revealing.

I kept my distance from her normally, afraid of what I might betray, but I did make small talk with her a couple of times before meetings and found her relaxed and witty. I once asked if she was possibly named Beatrix after the author of *Peter Rabbit*, which I thought would be oddly fitting for a grade school principal. I got a big laugh, but she said her mom, a German immigrant, dead for more than fifteen years, had christened Bea with her own mother's name.

The council served on a calendar-year basis. My last meeting in January of 2017 included introducing the three judges Mansy had corralled to replace us. When we adjourned, I found that Dr. Housley had left her purse and coat next to my parka. I no longer believe that was an accident.

'So you're done,' she said, as she put on her parka, which, God save me, required briefly projecting her chest. 'I'm sure you're relieved.'

'You made the job easy,' I told her.

'And I'm really grateful for your support. I felt like you always got it.' She smiled. 'Stay in touch,' she said, and then, after a thoughtful instant, added quietly, 'Call me sometime.'

Her tone was matter-of-fact, but those gemstone eyes of hers, the color of citrines, fixed on me directly. I was impressed by her finesse, which was leagues beyond me. I could tell that in high school she'd been one of those cute, flirty girls who was completely devastating and who still knew where she stood on the ladder of desire. I was stopped cold by the reality that this moment that had been no more than a futile fantasy had unexpectedly arrived. I could do no better than to stammer out, 'Really?' and then nearly sank to the floor in shame.

She laughed out loud, but at least she seemed to take my disbelief as a compliment of sorts. 'Yes, really,' she answered.

I've always been a sucker for self-confident females, perhaps because they leave less work to me, and I recovered quickly enough to ask if she had time for a drink then. We walked together to the center of town a couple of blocks, down to the Cummin Inn, where we found seats at a high-top and each ordered a light beer.

I told her how well I thought she'd done all year, killing her antagonists with kindness, and she laughed at the thought.

'That's because I'm forty-seven years old,' she said, 'and I'm still trying to figure out how to be confrontational.'

At the mention of her age, I squinted a bit.

'You know, I'm going to be seventy soon.'

She squinted back, well-intended mocking.

'You look like you're still in good shape.'

I was, I thought. I was in my canoe every morning, even when the temperature required a wetsuit. When the lake iced over, I cross-country skied in the nearby forests. I felled trees and chopped wood, and handled all the hauling that a boat and dock required. I'd kept my mid-length prison beard, which had gone mostly grey, like my hair, which was now a good deal longer than in my judging days. Physically, I was doing well. It was just my soul that still required repair.

'No telling how long it stays that way,' I said. 'I'm probably past my best-by date.'

She laughed heartily. She laughed a lot, I could see, a generous, unhindered sound I found hugely appealing.

'Well, I'm not looking to purchase, Rusty. I haven't done very well as a long-term customer. But I've lived here all my life, not that I always wanted to, but I pretty much know everybody—at least everybody I want to know. And there aren't a lot of guys around who'd ride their bike six miles back and forth just so they could read the Sunday paper. Which might be interesting for a change.'

I asked what she meant about not always wanting to live here.

'I think I'm kind of a city girl who never got around to leaving the country.'

'And how did that happen?'

'Well, you know, you're twenty-one, you don't know what's right. After graduation, my sorority sisters all wanted to get jobs in the Tri-Cities so they could hit the bars four times a week and meet guys. I knew how old that would get. I always adored my mom, and was afraid to leave her alone with my father, which, frankly, had nearly kept me from going away for college. And I loved Lloyd in a young-love kind of way. He was nice and kind. He was the nicest boy I'd ever met, which was a big contrast to the guy I'd dated through most of high school, who was gorgeous but moody and sometimes actually mean. Lloyd was ready to get married. His parents are super religious so there was no thought of just moving in together.'

I actually knew Lloyd Housley. He was a former deputy county sheriff who'd given up police work and become an HVAC contractor. I was one of his customers, but despite the same last name, it had never crossed my mind that Bea and he had ever been together. In my view, they weren't a natural match. I learned in time that the high school boyfriend she was referring to was Hardy.

'You can do worse than kind,' I said.

'Right. You can. Maybe if the rest of life is great, that's enough. But ten years later, frankly, we had nothing in common. I mean, I don't want to bore you talking about my divorce. The point is that I was happier alone. I loved the part of the day after I got Aaron in bed when I could feel myself for a little bit, roam the Internet or read. When Lloyd and I split, I was convinced I was going to move down to Kindle County. But Lloyd got together with Camille, his new wife, pretty quickly, and I could see he was already feeling challenged to spend the time he wanted to with Aaron. Joe, my dad, was—shock of my life—a great grandfather. I didn't want to take Aaron away from either of them.'

So she was stuck and unfulfilled. That would be nearly twenty years now. I chose the brief silence that followed as the time to add another discouraging detail.

'I've been in prison. Did you know that?' I wondered if she was thinking that an ex-con might provide a little of the taste of urban life she felt she was missing.

She reared back, squinting again.

'Is this like a negative sell?' she asked.

'Hardly,' I answered. 'I'm just trying to avoid any unpleasant surprises.'

'Rusty, this is a small town. You think there's anybody in Mirror who doesn't know your background? Mansy says you were framed. Like they actually made up evidence because the prosecutor had some lifelong grudge against you.'

My large settlement from Kindle County has cemented that impression, which is why my lawyer, Sandy Stern, encouraged me to sue in the first place. I told her, like anyone else who's ever asked, that Mansy's story was, in the largest sense, true. Beyond that, I have nothing to say. One question leads to the next, and some I will never answer.

With the new mood and the low light, I took an instant to scrutinize her. She was definitely pretty, which is always a good start. She had her Native grandmother's high cheekbones, but she kept herself in an unstudied way, with sparse makeup, and her springy black hair spreading around her face. I'd already noticed that her curves had been a little softened by age, but her shape remained appealing. And there were those devastating eyes that I loved studying at close range, an outer circle that was almost yellow, with an orange ring surrounding her irises.

When we parted back at the school parking lot, she seemed very pleased with herself. Knowing her as I do now, I've realized that it required more gumption than I'd understood at the time for her to approach me. I'm sure she had armored her heart for some kind of rebuff, but she understood why I might forever hesitate on my own.

When I got home, I lay in bed with a book and discovered I couldn't sleep. There was no anxiety, but it was as if I was attached to some hot-air balloon that wouldn't let me sink below consciousness. I dozed only a little and was up to watch the sun rise on the lake. Knowing she had to rise early for school, I texted her at six thirty to ask about dinner on Saturday night.

Unlike our talk at Cummin Inn, where we got the serious stuff out of the way, we spent the evening laughing. She told me more about Aaron. I knew Mae, of course, through Mansy, and I'd seen her with her boyfriend. He had purple hair at that stage and rings in both nostrils and was almost as beautiful as she was. But it was late in the conversation before I squared that circle.

At that time, Aaron was almost sixteen and Bea talked about him with the shrewd irony that suits the parent of any teenager. Yes, he was a pain in the ass a lot of the time, but sooner or later the light bulb would turn on and he would realize that he was not the first human being ever to be young. I told her that Nat had been plenty of trouble growing up, depression and drugs, not the background you might necessarily guess for a man who's now a highly regarded law professor and a dedicated husband and father. That night, Bea talked about everybody in her life—Aaron and Joe and Lloyd—with a sane humor, which like so much else about her, I found completely beguiling. We weren't even halfway through our entrées when I looked up at her and said, apropos of nothing, 'I'm having a wonderful time.'

She stopped, her glass of Chardonnay aloft, before she quietly answered, 'Me too.'

She was so much more attractive than any woman I had met up here that I couldn't understand why some man hadn't planted himself on her front porch like a foundling, begging her to take him in. I'd already been through enough first dates with women who seemed great and who, with a few more meetings, proved to have serious issues. A warning voice within told me to keep my heart on a leash, but the truth is that I was already lost to her by then.

We talked until they were beginning to put the chairs up on the tables. Afterwards, I walked her to her car in the lot behind the restaurant. When we arrived, I leaned down and kissed her. No matter how old-fashioned it makes me, I had found in my sporadic dating life that there is a shocking intimacy to a first kiss, to erasing the physical boundary that normally exists between two humans. She received the caress with a huge smile, grabbed my coat and kissed me once again, before disappearing behind her car door.

The aftermath of that kind of evening, the excitement of the felt connection, left me feeling like a steak coming off the grill, the radiance and high heat lingering even in the cold. But that kiss had resolved itself into a more single-minded reaction. I was close to seventy years old and turned on like a teen. The winter cold had no effect. Instead, my reaction was so emphatic that I needed a minute before I could comfortably take a seat behind the wheel of my Tundra.

Driving home, I reviewed the evening and tried to calculate my next move, cautioning myself about letting the physical hunger that now engulfed me lead to an unwise forwardness. But that, as it turned out, was not a needed worry.

The next morning, I received a text. 'Want to read the paper?'

She was at my door in ten minutes. She had the *Tribune* under her arm, but no clothes at all under her long puffer coat. When she left, so she could prepare dinner for Aaron after he'd spent Sunday with his father, it already pained me to say goodbye to her.

5

Joe

By dinnertime, there is still no word from Aaron. Bea texted around two to say she had been dragooned for a dinner meeting of the county Principals' Roundtable, which is debating, again, whether the proper solution for trans kids is to build a separate restroom. I am left to make dinner for myself. These days, Bea favors a vegetable-heavy diet, so I take advantage of her absence to grill a pork chop on the Kamado oven on the back deck, which is a fancy-ass barbecue with a thick ceramic shell, on which I like to believe I am some kind of master.

At 8 p.m., I have not heard from Bea yet, which is not completely surprising. The restroom issue is always turbulent, since even the few fifth or sixth graders wondering about their gender don't agree with one another on this question. Accepting the need to locate Aaron by tomorrow, I head off on my own to get a word with Bea's father.

I tend to join my future father-in-law for a beer every few weeks. Bea and Joe frequently can't get through a brief phone call without fireworks, so I accept the obligation to make a status check on an eighty-four-year-old man who insists on living alone, despite a terminal

illness. As only Bea has license to say, Joe has been promising to die of
cancer within the next three months for close to four years now.

After a lifetime of abuse, Joe has stopped drinking. He likes to
say he did it to be a role model for Aaron, but Bea is quick to point
out that abstinence was virtually required after several fainting episodes caused by the interaction between alcohol and lomustine, which
has been administered from time to time for his lung cancer. A few
months back, we lit a candle to celebrate Aaron's first year of sobriety, and Bea cooked a nice dinner. Joe was invited and Aaron asked
innocently about how they'd celebrated landmark events in his mother's household. She immediately recalled the bender Joe was on that
caused him to miss her high school graduation.

Joe has been Aaron's transportation when he attends NA meetings
in Kweagon, and Joe seems to have absorbed some of the lingo.

'That's because I was an alcoholic,' he said in quick answer to Bea,
'and so I was an asshole.' Joe had trotted out that line a couple of
times before in response to accounts of other outrages decades ago—
his beatings of Willi, Bea's mom; his DWIs; the paychecks he squan-
dered. He tosses off the words as glibly as an advertising slogan. This
time Bea could not contain herself.

'Dad,' she said, 'you got the tense wrong. You're supposed to say,
"I *am* an alcoholic." ' She paused. 'And "I *am* an asshole." '

Wrath was not a good look for Bea, and completely out of keeping
with her steady kindness to everybody else. Aaron murmured, 'Come
on, Mom,' in evident disappointment, while she was completely flattened by the sight of a weak old man departing from the table close
to tears. Bea sat there with her face in her hands, realizing yet again
the intense emotional hazards presented by her relationship with her
father. It's like one of those hideous medieval torture devices in which
each arm was shackled to horses that then galloped in opposite directions: venting her rage versus feeling choked by it.

I'm sure a psychologist would see my bond with Bea as seethed
in the same stew of fury, longing and regret we each grew up with
as the child of a violent alcoholic. From the time I was six or seven, I
spent at least one night a week locked with my mother in the bedroom
she no longer shared with my father, while he toured the rest of the

apartment screaming drunken curses at the enemies he'd left in Serbia. Inevitably that led, by a logic apparent only to him, to his destruction of some keepsake my mother prized—a small china figure, a shawl of her grandmother's. Yet unlike my father, whom I had not seen for years before he died in a mobile home in Arizona, Joe ultimately developed a redeeming quality: He has turned out to be a remarkably attentive grandfather to Aaron. That in turn has forced Bea to maintain a steadier relationship with him than she'd otherwise prefer, monitoring her father's medical care and enduring dinner with him once a week.

No reasonable person who knows Joe would dispute his daughter's view that he is a completely impossible human being. Cantankerous and wildly opinionated, he evidences little loyalty to the truth. He finds it demeaning to say thank you for even a great kindness, and displays little interest in any conversation that isn't about him. But unlike his daughter, who has spent a lifetime suffering Joe's limitless shortcomings, I cannot keep myself from a grudging admiration of the man.

Joe grew up tough. His dad was a Mexican migrant who came to the Skageon River Valley every summer to pick—strawberries first, then, in succession, cucumbers, tomatoes, raspberries, apples, and finally pumpkins. In one of those fields, he met Joe's mom, a full-blooded member of the Winnebago Nation. (In recent decades, the Ho-Chunk, as they've rebranded themselves, have become the proprietors of a chain of hugely successful casino-based resorts. Anyone who has at least one Ho-Chunk grandparent is eligible to receive an annual stipend from the gaming profits, more than $14,000 last year. Joe, whom no one had ever heard acknowledge his ancestry, signed up eagerly, then, in his usual dodgy way, claimed to have done it only so Bea, a cash-strapped single mom, would receive a grant too.)

The oldest of his parents' six children, Joe moved around the country harvesting with the rest of the family until he was eight or nine. Then Skageon County insisted that the migrant kids here after Labor Day—the time of the raspberry crop—had to be enrolled in school. Joe was placed in foster care when his parents moved on later in the fall to Louisiana to pick pecans. After reuniting for a few summers, Joe maintains he lost complete track of them. Bea's mom believed that Joe, characteristically, had outraged his family somehow.

Sturdily built but never taller than five four, Joe was an all-state wrestler in the 113-pound weight class at Skageon Consolidated High, but in those days no one ever talked about scholarships or college for kids like him. He eventually enlisted in the army, rather than get drafted, and was sent to Germany, where he met Bea's mother, Wilhelmina. Willi, a curly-haired dishwater blonde, was a full head taller than her husband. He re-upped, expecting to stay with his wife and newborn son in Mainz, and instead was shipped to Vietnam, where he became one of the first tunnel rats, smaller men who cleared the underground networks that had been dug by the Vietcong over decades. Encounters down below with the enemy often required hand-to-hand combat to the death. Joe returned with a Bronze Star, but it's long been hidden away. Instead, Joe will tell anyone who asks how much he hates the US military. 'They poisoned me, the army. Forcing young men to kill or be killed while you can feel the other fella's breath on your face? What happens to you after that?' Out of complete contempt for their father, Bea's only sibling, her older brother Fritz, made a career with the army.

When Joe returned from service in 1967, he found a job on the line at US Motors in Kweagon. He had become a leader in the union in 1987 when US was bought by Chrysler, which decided to close Joe's plant. Joe led a series of wildcat actions. Depending on who you talk to, Joe is either a hero, for forcing Chrysler to grant wide-ranging benefits to all employees, or a villain because the senior guys, Joe included, retired early with full pensions. After that, Joe, who'd always farmed a small piece, bought the 100-acre farm he's worked since 2005, which was where Bea and Aaron lived after her divorce.

Joe's favorite watering hole is here at the VFW outside Mirror. I too am a member, by virtue of my time in the Army Reserves, although I am basically an impostor, since I chose the Reserves years later to avoid the same traumas Joe experienced in Nam. Given that Joe no longer drinks, and despises the military, it might seem peculiar to show up at the VFW almost every night, but he's here to argue with anybody who praises our armed forces, even if he has to face down the entire room on his own. It's just Joe.

When I ask after him, the bartender, Sallie, the heavyset widow of a soldier killed in Iraq, working tonight in a flowered blouse and bike shorts, says Joe hasn't appeared yet. I've called him several times and even stopped by the farm, but it's typical of Joe that he treats the telephone as a one-way instrument. He answers only when he likes but reams you out for missing his call.

I settle at the bar, exchanging an agreeable nod with a couple of the men here I know only by sight. The people in this part of the county are principally farmers and folks whose jobs depend on related pursuits— combine repair, for example, or feed sales. All of them tend to keep to themselves, since farming by its nature is a self-reliant endeavor. What- ever mingling occurs takes place in the country taverns.

Except for the big flagpole out in front and the notation that iden- tifies this as Post 4549, the VFW resembles the other bars in these parts, an old two-story farmhouse converted decades ago, with a rut- ted parking lot and a flickering Schlitz sign out front. The barroom is dim, with knotty pine paneling and various apparatuses along the walls, including an Internet jukebox, poker machines, and a bowling game, sixty years old if it's a day, where gamblers aim a stainless-steel puck down the lacquered ash alley toward the plastic pins.

I like meeting Joe here, because it gives me an opportunity to eavesdrop on a world I still don't know well. There is a lot of talk about crop prices and what the local co-op or distributors are paying, and the virtues of some of the direct-to-market selling a few farmers have been attempting through the Internet. Luke Combs is singing loudly from the sound system, while the TVs over the bar are muted, one on ESPN, the other on Fox News. This is the land of the angry white men you're always hearing about, who feel ignored and dissed by the people in charge.

Right now, a fellow named Muller Wirzer is lamenting the dog he had to put down yesterday. Muller's immense belly strains the buttons of any shirt he wears, and he refuses to wear sunblock, which means his face and bald head are red well into November. About two years ago, I got into it with Muller. I try not to answer when the talk turns to politics, since most of the people here ignore the ranting, not so much because they disagree, but because it violates the privacy they treasure. But on that night, I'd had one more beer than usual, and couldn't stifle a response to Muller, who was going on loudly about how inflation was running wild because of all the money Biden was spending on food stamps and Medicaid. 'But not the Covid relief payments you got for lost crops, right, Muller?' He was furious with me, but a couple of months later, when I needed help getting my boat out of the water while the lift was out of service, Muller was in the team of guys who showed up at my house.

I am listening attentively to Muller's stories about Rufus, the dog, who'd come from a shelter in rural Kentucky after being used to train fighting animals. His teeth had been filed down to keep him from defending himself, and his hide and muzzle were deeply scarred. Muller says there was not a day when he couldn't see the depth of Rufus's gratitude for his new home in the dog's eyes.

I notice only now that Joe has taken a seat on the stool next to mine.

"Beer?" he asks me and signals Sallie for a Lite for me and his Heineken Zero.

"Where have you been?" I ask. "I went by the farm on my way here."

"I must have been closing up the Harvestore," he says, referring to the big blue metal silo he uses to store the alfalfa hay he bales in June and sells to his neighbors in the fall. Munchie next door needed silage because of the recent drought conditions, far too dramatic to be overcome even by the heavy rains two nights ago. Still, the downpour had left Munchie's lower field a mess.

"Mud was like quicksand and damn near sucked the tenny runners off my feet." In his shorts, Joe gestures to his bare legs. I have always found Joe's calves remarkable, thicker at the midlines than his knees, with the vasiform shape of the supports in the stone railings you see outside public buildings. Tonight his white athletic shoes are caked in brown all the way over the laces, and after coming straight from the farm, there are orangish streaks of dirt on his old UAW Local 646 T-shirt. A thick line of black soil is ground in under his fingernails.

"Two point three inches in an hour that night," he adds, "damn near a record." The weather is one of the few topics besides himself Joe's always ready to discuss. Of course, weather around here is more than a curiosity. Rain and sun and wind are the variables that control most livelihoods and, these days, the subject of frequent lament. Too hot, too wet, too dry, it's all just crazytown, although there's seldom talk about the causes. It's just the shit luck of farmers, the guys here say.

"Well, I wanted to ask you about Aaron," I say.

Mention of his grandson will reliably seize Joe's attention, and he turns his broad face toward me. Even as a young man, Joe was a long way from good-looking, with a wide nose, pockmarked skin and a permanent squint. His old face is deeply weathered, but after a summer in the sun it shows a gorgeous depth of coppery color.

"What about him?" Joe demands.

"He's been gone three days now. He won't answer his mother's calls or texts. It looks like he's turned his phone off."

"Good for him. He's a grown man, ain't he? My damn daughter, she'd love to have one of those drone planes keeping an eye on him. She wants that cellphone to be a leash."

"He's on probation, Joe. We're responsible for knowing where he is."

"The hell," says Joe. "Let the boy breathe."

"Any notion of where he headed?"

He looks straight at me, a fearless level look from his small black eyes.

"No idea," he says. I am convinced until he adds, "And I wouldn't tell you if I did. If he has two hairs goin the wrong way, you'd tattle to that turd of a judge, wouldn't you?"

"We all agreed to that, Joe, as a way to get him out of jail."

"I didn't agree to none of that. And I'm not worried about him, neither."

"Well, we're pretty sure he's with Mae Potter."

Beside me, I feel Joe tense.

"Well, that's trouble," says Joe.

"A little more worried now?" I ask. Joe has no fear of contradicting himself, even in the breadth of a single sentence.

"I thought he'd finally decided to have no truck with her," says Joe. "That's what he needs to do, once and for all. I think that girl can whistle 'Yankee Doodle' with her pussy, something like that. Somethin amazing that's got him in a trance."

"I don't think it's Yankee Doodle that he's interested in." Vern, the guy beside me, who's been pretending not to listen, can't stifle a laugh.

It's easy to say that Aaron's bond with Mae is all about sex, especially since that's what so many males are thinking about around her.
She's a beauty and a flirt and seems to welcome that response. But
there's always been something powerful between Aaron and Mae that
goes well beyond the merely carnal.

"Joe," I say, "if you know where he is, you need to give him a
message—"

"Nuh-uh," says Joe. "No clue. He said a couple days back he
might go up north like he likes to do, since that asshole laid him off.
Not a word in advance, because she was afraid he might not work
fourteen hours a day if he knew. Just how they do in Como Stop." Joe
has always had a union man's distaste for the well-to-do.

"But if you hear from him—"

"Yeah, I know," says Joe. "E.T. phone home. I got it."

I ask how he's feeling and let him complain for a minute about
his doctors, whom he treats as yet another enemy force determined to
strip the last joy from his life. On the way out, I circle toward Muller's
end of the bar and tell him quietly that I'm sorry about the dog.

Once I'm in the parking lot, I feel my phone lurch in my pocket. I
assume Bea has come home and wants to know if I'll return in time to
lay in bed and watch an episode of *A French Village*, which we've been
streaming. Bea enjoys the show, especially because it offers the rare
chance to practice the French she mastered in high school and college.
She loves to tell me whenever the subtitles have omitted a nuance she
deems essential. I keep promising that if she ever stops kicking the
can down the road on our wedding, we'll take a honeymoon in Paris.
Since a couple childhood visits to Germany to see her mother's family,
Bea has not been overseas and, despite her mastery of the language,
has never so much as taken a single breath in France. We both know
I'm trying to tempt her.

But the message is from Aaron, addressed to his mother, his father
and me.

        'Just got to recharge my phone. Sorry. OTW
        back. Home tomorrow.'

6

Aaron Does Not Return

September 15–16

Aaron does not return the next day. Bea comes back from school earlier than usual, and surges through the door, more upbeat than she's been in days.

"Where is he?" she asks.

When I shake my head, she stops in place.

"Did he call?" she asks.

"No call," I say, "no text." And of course, no email, a form of communication that Aaron and his age peers treat like a dead language. She falls into a chair.

"Please," she says. Please not the nightmare-land we were living in a couple of years ago, when Aaron never failed to disappoint. She sits, silent and unmoving, for a few minutes, then pours herself a glass of wine and drifts down to the lake, where, from the broad windows of the living room, I can see her on an old park bench at the water's edge, staring at the placid surface. I do not have the heart to remind her yet that we have a social obligation tonight, hosting a long-delayed dinner for Bea's deputy principal, Daria Lucci Zabatakis, to celebrate Daria's fiftieth birthday. Instead, I decide to grant her a half hour alone.

I lived in this house, four bedrooms and all, by myself for several years after I acquired the place from my erstwhile lover, Lorna Mooney. Guilt-racked after telling me she was moving to California to marry someone else, she had offered me the place at a price I would have been foolish to refuse.

In response to Lorna's announcement—her engagement and the house in the same agonized soliloquy—I chose my words with care. I didn't want to say out loud that I was actually relieved, but I steadily maintained that her price essentially turned the house into a magnificent gift. Yet Lorna's sons had moved on after their father's death, and Lorna couldn't imagine returning with her new husband while her former lover was living immediately behind her. Matt had left her oodles, and the new guy was also loaded. I, by contrast, could not ultimately forsake the chance to live with the view that for decades I had coveted. From our cabin, Barbara and I could glimpse only a fragment of the lake when our spring chairs were positioned just so on our front porch and the trees were bare of leaves.

I dwelled here for a few years, relishing the sight of the lake, serene in every season but a different shade each day, before I realized that the architecture of the house itself is not much to my taste. It was solidly built but getting older when Matt and Lorna bought it more than two decades before with the intent to knock it down and start again. They never got that far, because Matt's business, like many contractors, was always cash-starved. The place is 1960s construction, which was a kind of dead zone in American design. The style is neither Modern nor rustic. The living room ceiling rises at a steep slant to make way for the impressive rock fireplace, and Matt made a smart choice by blowing out the wall that separated that space from the dining area and kitchen. But I don't care for the thick mullions that turn the wall of windows facing the water into a checkerboard of two-by-three-foot panes, or the 1960s efficiencies elsewhere, like hollow-core doors, lower ceilings and walls of skimpy drywall. Bea and I talk about a significant renovation after we get married, but like our elusive wedding date, that is, so far, no more than talk.

By six thirty, Bea has dressed and put on a game face, and we are on our way to Como Stop. We rarely make plans for Friday nights, when Bea is characteristically exhausted by the school week, but our date with Daria has been postponed so many times, starting with the pandemic, that both couples have sworn a blood oath to show up in the posh dining room of the Hotel Morevant on the shore of Como Lake. Daria is probably Bea's closest friend locally, although their intimacy doesn't rival Bea's relationship with Neba Malone, Bea's BFF since their freshman year of college.

Bea and Daria also met in college, during the second semester of Bea's senior year at Wisconsin State. After Neba graduated early, Bea moved into her sorority house, where Daria and she were matched as roommates since they were both Education majors. When Bea became the principal in Mirror decades later, she recruited Daria to join her. Raised in a strict Italian home outside Kindle County, Daria can do a more convincing impression of the tough disciplinarian the kids sometimes require, and, in addition, has a knack with budgeting.

She is also a perfect companion for tonight, since she is relentlessly entertaining and generally relieves everybody else of the need to make conversation. She speaks at the speed of a bullet train, dropping frequent one-liners that fly past so fast you get only limited time to laugh. Her husband, Nick, a quiet CPA, nods and smiles, but rarely interrupts.

We are home by ten thirty. Bea, of course, has rushed into the house to find, a full day after last night's text, that there is still no sign of Aaron. She imparts a lifeless kiss and announces she is turning in. I did not call the judge this morning, because I expected Aaron to show up any minute. Saturday or not, tomorrow I am going to have to track down Morton Sams.

I doze off in my recliner while simultaneously reading and watching a West Coast football game. I finally wake myself enough to go to sleep in our bed, only to feel, a few hours later, the sudden movement of Bea's departure. I struggle to depart the floating craft of sleep but finally manage and find her with her hand still on the kitchen light switch. At the breakfast bar sits Aaron, who has been picking at a cold chicken breast I grilled a couple nights back. His other hand is over his eyes in the sudden glare.

Aaron is a striking young man, who I've always thought bears a considerable resemblance to Julian Bond, the activist and poet who used to get a lot of attention in the press decades ago. Ordinarily careful about his appearance, he looks somewhat rummaged tonight. His T-shirt is grimy and for some reason he's stepped out of his jeans, which are heaped in the doorway, while he sits on a highbacked kitchen stool in his briefs. After getting shorn to a prison buzz, he's taken some pleasure in his hair, worn in a stylish high and tight, a low 'fro with shaved sides, the top recently dyed chartreuse, but he hasn't noticed a twig enmeshed a few inches above his eyes. A streak of mud cuts across his throat, near his tattoo. Lloyd, Aaron's father, regards body ink as an insult to the deity, but Aaron outflanked his dad a few years ago by having a six-inch gothic cross, outlined in blue, inscribed from the corner of his jaw almost to his shoulder. Lloyd could not complain, knowing that for Aaron, it was a sincere gesture. Since childhood, Bea says, Aaron has been steadfast in his faith. Bea herself is suspicious of all organized religion, save the Church of George Lucas, meaning she feels some Force, larger and more inscrutable than mere human intelligence can fully comprehend. Sadly I, by contrast, have never really experienced the presence of a higher being.

"Aaron, where the hell have you been?" she asks.

He sighs and finally says that it's a long story.

"Well, we'd like to hear it," she answers. "Except for a one-line text, we haven't seen or heard from you since Monday. It's Saturday now."

"Barely," he answers. He licks his fingers and presses the plastic top back onto the container. Then he climbs down from the stool. He is tall and lean. Dressed, he appears insubstantial, but when he's in his skivvies, you can see he's ripped. "I'll tell you tomorrow. Right now, I'm just wasted. I need to crash."

He takes a step toward the doorway and his mother cuts him off.

"No," she says. "*No.* We're all going to treat one another with respect. That's what we said when you moved back in here. We promised the judge you'd stay in touch—or go back to jail. *Where* were you?"

This is as harsh as I've heard Bea be with Aaron, certainly since he's lived here. She usually relies on the fact that Aaron, like any child, knows when she's angry. In those moods, she tends to guilt him with practiced patience. Aaron's grey eyes linger on his mother now. I can see he's still thinking about stonewalling her.

"I was camping up north."

"And how did you get there?" Bea says. "You didn't ride your bike."

"I was with Mae."

Bea studies her son, rolling her jaw unconsciously. At least he's telling the truth.

"I thought you and Mae were done with one another."

"We are now," he says.

"What happened? And why were you with her in the first place?"

He exhales deeply and takes a step back to perch his hind end on the stool.

"We were talking about getting married," he says. I realize immediately that Mansy's remark about eloping did not come out of the blue. It was probably something Mae's mom had shared as a deep dark secret. But I had not repeated that to Bea, understanding how panicked she'd have been by the notion. Now, she's reduced to gap-jawed silence for a second.

"*Married*? You're thinking of marrying Mae Potter? Talk about a beautiful mess. I don't understand you, Aaron. I thought you realized how toxic this young woman has been for you."

"I never said she was toxic. You said she was toxic, and I didn't bother to fight. But, legit, it's not going to happen, Mom, so, you know, chill. I'm done with Mae. But if you want to see why I didn't say where I was going, look in the mirror."

Subdued by this remark, Bea requires an instant to think.

"Were you using?" she asks.

"Negative, Commander."

"Was Mae using?"

"Look. Mae's gone. Forever. So you shouldn't care what Mae was doing. We had a fight. We always have a fight, but this, you know, it was a mega fight, like clash of the titans. And we're done. Done done. Can I go to sleep now?"

He slides again toward the door.

Silent until now, I mention Gert and he nods.

"I saw her text. I told her I was on the way back, but I was hitch-hiking so I didn't know when I would get here." Without driving privileges, Aaron often hitchhikes when he's going a distance too long to bike and Joe is unavailable to chauffeur him. But his remark confuses Bea.

"Mae didn't have her car?" she asks.

"Hey, Mom. Hear what I'm saying. We had this humongous fight. I was not going to sit in a vehicle with Mae for two hours while she ranted. And she probably would have pulled some power play and refused to drive back. So I thumbed. Only it wasn't like hitching between Mirror and Como Stop, where a lot of people recognize me. Up north, there weren't a lot of folks wanting to stop for a Black guy on the side of the road."

Oddly, race is something Aaron almost never mentions when he's talking to his mother. I don't know if it's a product of Lloyd's ironclad insistence that being Black is never an excuse for anything, or the fact that Aaron thinks that for all his mother's earnest empathy, she will never fully understand. But it's one of those freighted subjects, like a few others, that is rarely addressed between them.

"I got rides eventually. But it like took forever. Last night I slept in a culvert. Tonight, I'd already snuck into a KOA, just to get running water, but there's like a gas station/grocery just outside the gate. My debit card was pretty much flatlining, but I was so hungry that, around ten, I walked to the store to buy like a Slim Jim and I ran into Arden Mack from high school. He's driving for a food delivery service—you know, on contract, in his own car. It was like torture sitting next to all those pizzas he was picking up and dropping off, but we got to Mirror about one and I walked from there because he had to make a delivery in Como Stop. So you know, it sucked. The whole time. But my life does, right?"

The note of occasional self-pity is one of Aaron's least attractive traits. In his deepest depressions, he will tell you how things have gone against him from the start, when his birth parents didn't have a place for him. There's been a lot less of that since he entered the program with Reverend Spruce. Now he can see both Bea and me react to his remark, and he raises a hand.

"I'm just wasted," he says. "And I've got to get up in like four hours. I promised Brice I'd help him." His buddy Brice paints houses in the summer months and needs Aaron's assistance with a backlog of jobs that is pressing now that the days of good weather are dwindling. "And we have to stop at the Potters at some point, so I can return Mae's phone." He's taken the device from his back pocket to show us.

Bea asks, "What are you doing with her phone?"

"It's a story."

"I'll take it," she says. "I have a meeting in Como Stop in the morning. I'll drop it over there and save you boys the time."

This is purely fictitious. Tomorrow is Saturday and we've already agreed to head the opposite direction to an excellent farmer's market in a town called Granger. Just like me, Aaron sees through her immediately, realizing that his mother is simply trying to keep him away from Mae. He issues the tiny smile that is often his response, even when he thinks something is screamingly funny.

"I got it, Mom," he says. "And I promise you, *promise*, you will never see Mae with me again." A long sober look comes over him as he processes the gravity of that vow. He then knocks on the wall in parting and heads down the hall to his room.

Bea slides close and whispers, "What did you think of that?"

"Jesus, Bea," I say. "What part? I don't think he was using, if that's what you mean."

"No," she says. "*Married*? And done with her? I'll believe it when I see it."

"He seems pretty certain," I answer.

"And her phone? Why does he have her phone?" she asks.

"Let's go to sleep, Bea," I answer. "You can ask him about all of that tomorrow." I take her hand and say what I surely mean. "Right now, I've had enough."

7

Fire

September 16

T he bedroom I have shared for the past three years with Bea looks out on Mirror Lake. It sports the same floor-to-ceiling windows as the living room, including those thick mullions whose look I don't care for. For the sake of the view, Lorna never bothered with window treatments, and I followed her example. The moon fractured on the lake and the profuse color of the sunsets are regular sights that sometimes make my heart like a quick bird flying through my chest.

Rising with the first light is not a problem around here on the weekdays when Bea is up early for school. On the other hand, since Aaron moved in, having no curtains on the bedroom windows has sometimes limited our privacy. Generally, he does not sleep well, and frequently when I've been roused in the middle of the night, I see his slim silhouette on the dock, where often he is sneaking a cigarette.

And it is smoke that wakes me—and fire. I sit straight up and eventually realize that Aaron is standing over the stone firepit in the rear yard, with flames doing their tortured dance. There is so much wrong about this scene, starting with building a fire at 4 a.m., that I put on a pair of jeans and a T-shirt and head out. The one sign of the dwindling summer is the new coolness at night. I'm barefoot and my toes are chilled in the settling dew.

Primitively fixated on the fire, Aaron is too preoccupied to notice me until I am only a few feet away.

"Fuck," he says. "I woke you up. I should have thought of that. Man, I really wasn't trying to be a dick. I'm just so, you know—" He can't find the words and I mutter something more kindly than I actually feel.

"I thought you were exhausted," I say.

"Like *so* tired," he answers. "I don't know if I slept two hours next to the culvert. I was sure the cops would roust me, you know, Black vagrant or something. I need sleep so much, man, it hurts. But you know how sometimes it feels like there's a floor underneath you that you can't sink through?"

That sounds like he might be coming off something, but I keep that thought to myself. The test Gert will run on Monday will catch most anything.

Instead, we stand side by side at the fire, enjoying the heat and its mystical attraction. But even in the sporadic light, I can see the weight of weariness and worry on him.

"I've just got Mae on the brain," he says, "you know, like going round and round. I'm so big mad and disappointed. I guess I never felt before that we'd totally for sure reached the end. So I just wanted to, you know, come out here and get done with all this stuff. Turn the page."

In the fire, when I finally look down there, I recognize his backpack and sleeping bag.

"Those are expensive items, Aaron."

"Tell me." His laugh is a kind of murmur. "But you want to hear a story, man? You will not believe how totally fucked up this is."

I nod a bit to show he has my full attention.

"Like, we went out there with this kind of understanding. We were going to get away and unplug. You know, turn off the phones. Just be into one another and talk this marriage thing through. Not get married today. But like, how could we get there? What had to happen and like what had to change?

"And instead, we didn't even have the tent up on Tuesday, and Mae won't do anything but take selfies and videos of herself. She's got a new thing: She's going to become some kind of influencer on Insta and TikTok. Like all of the sudden. Which I thought frankly was kind of pathetic and juvenile. I expected her to stop after a while. But she didn't. So I finally was like, 'What the fuck, man, that's not why we're here,' and she promised to cut it out, and an hour later, she's posing again with these stupid cutie-pie expressions. By the third day I finally flipped out. I grabbed the phone out of her hand and just kept walking. I didn't even turn around for my backpack. I was just done, finally, *so* done. She ran after me screaming and going on about her phone and trying to snatch it back. I just kept moving."

"Where were you?" I ask casually, hoping desperately he hadn't left the county.

"Harold's Woods," he says. Far northern corner of Skageon County. Good news. "I'd walked about an hour from the park, and I was probably still a mile from 47, where I figured I could catch a ride, and I hear a car jetting down the dirt road behind me. I know even without seeing the Subaru who it is. I went ripping into the woods right there. There was no path or anything. I got all these scratches as I was crashing through the buckthorn." He points to the inside of his arm. "But she saw me, I guess. She skids to a halt there and starts yelling. I'd gotten her up that morning to take the path to the Point to see the sunrise, and she'd thrown on this jeans microskirt and a tank top, so the way she was still dressed, she couldn't follow me into the brush. Instead, she's calling me names and daring me to come out. Finally, she goes back to the car. She's got my backpack and is yelling that she'll trade it for her phone. I'm about fifty yards away, crouched behind a rock, watching her. And you know, it was legendary stupid to leave the pack behind, especially the sleeping bag, because I'd realized by then that no way was I catching enough rides to get home that night. And I've got like zero cash, so I need the clothes and stuff in my pack, but I'm thinking like, No, I can't. I can't. I'm done. I know if I come out to talk to her, we'll just start in again, it will be completely cray again in no time. So I stay put.

"Finally she shouts 'Fuck you' about a thousand times and then throws the backpack down and like straddles it. And I'm like, What now? But pretty soon I see she's got her thong in her hand, and she's kind of scooching around peeing all over the thing. She takes another minute to scream, I mean shriek at the top of her lungs, until she gets back in the car at last.

"I was afraid she'd double back, so I didn't come out. The mosquitoes, that deep in the trees, I was like a tasty treat for all of them, but finally, after another twenty minutes, I was sure she was gone for good. My pack—I mean it's completely disgusting. And it reeks. Like she peed pure ammonia. But you know, I need the thing. I can't even imagine what I'm going to say about the smell, if I finally get a ride.

"The sleeping bag was soaked, which was partly why I had such a bad night yesterday."

Because of the light of the fire, I can't see much of the lake about thirty yards from us, but there's a fresh wind off the water. Owls, a mated pair I never see, but whose gentle hootings often make their way into my sleep, are calling to each other now.

"That's quite a story," I say. "About Mae." I hold my breath and ask, "Was she straight or high when that happened?"

"She'd been like completely baked for a day and a half by then," he answers, truly downcast. It's a second before he raises his eyes to see my look and adds, "Not me. Like I'd said really clearly before we left, 'No drugs.' But she still brought shit. I really felt swindled, man." As a step to maintaining his sobriety, Aaron's probation also requires him not to associate with drug users. "Not just because she didn't give a shit about what she'd promised. But I'd been hoping for the good Mae. The good Mae, man, there's nobody else I know like that, not even close. It's kind of why I've been so totally hung up on her."

I just nod.

"Did you ever get like that with somebody?" he asks. "You know— just can't shake free?"

"Me?" I ask. Only so it nearly destroyed me, I think. Twice, actually. But I just answer yes.

"And what happened?"

I've never shared much of myself with Aaron. He's somebody else's kid, and was a troubled one at that by the time he arrived under our roof. I am also a little shy of a subject I've never spoken about in detail with his mother. But he's never really asked for this kind of help before. And I'm willing to come through for him, not only because he's the center of the world to someone I love, but because I've always been convinced there is real good in this young man. So I go on, with the firelight licking over both our faces, like a shifting mask.

"Truth? I got so carried away that I basically lit a fuse to my whole life, so that after the explosion I could only find a few random pieces here and there. Not to mention the so-called collateral damage to the other people who got absolutely mauled in the process. Nothing good," I say. "I have nothing good to say for myself."

I look back on that man, Rožat K. Sabich the younger, as a madman. That's not a euphemism either. I was out of my mind. Utterly desperate. Whoever I was in those moments with those women was the person I otherwise had no chance of being, someone on a thrill ride that would take me out from under the dark weight of my own life. Whatever Aaron had going with Mae—first love, pure love, big love—is miles more noble than my obsessions, which were nursed in secret.

"But I can tell you this straight from the heart. If you don't go back to her, Aaron, if you really close the door on that part of your life, it will get better. Slowly. It's like any other wound. It will heal. If you don't keep reopening it. And yeah, I hear you. Mae's not ordinary. Granted. And I won't bullshit you. Maybe there's a piece of what you had with her that you're never going to have again. But consider the cost. Really. Somebody who will literally pee on your stuff, and you in the process? Somebody that ferocious and destructive? Way better to say goodbye."

I get a long look in response. Then he worries his chin a little bit.

"Yeah but, like even now, I want to help Mae. Help her be, you know, not so extra, man. I think I can and she thinks I can. That's always been a part of it. If she would ever let me."

"Aaron, when I was young, I always thought what older people said to me, it was fake somehow, especially when they told me, 'I know how you feel.' But I do know how you feel. Barbara? Nat's mom. She was like Mae in some ways. Super bright. And beautiful. But full-on

nuts. I did some really bad things to her, and she did even worse stuff
to me, and we split. And then she tried to commit suicide. And I
thought, That's my son's mother, I should take care of her. And that
was like tying my leg to a big iron anchor and thinking I could swim.
I nearly drowned instead. So I envy you. Because you're way ahead
of me. That is, if you realize what I should have, that you can't love
somebody back to sanity, or save them when they don't want to be
saved—if you accept that and don't go back."

"Won't happen," he says. "Lockdown guaranteed." He nods looking into the fire, until it seems his mind has drifted to something else
and, as sometimes happens, he musters a tiny furtive smile. "But one
person who won't think twice about Mae? My mom. She straight-on
hates her."

"Hand to God, Aaron, I don't think that's true. She just doesn't
like what happens when you two are together. You don't bring out the
best in each other."

"I don't know, man. There's some ripping good shit between Mae
and me, and always has been. And my mom won't see it, so she can
never understand what's been so hard for me."

Ironic or not, some of the nicest things I ever heard said about
Mae came from Bea, who'd taught Mae in third grade. She described
an unusually precocious, charming little girl, adored by everybody,
classmates and teachers. She loved being the center of attention, like
a lot of kids, but she knew how to coax it from people, rather than
simply demanding they pay heed. She wrote a play and the music—
much of it admittedly lifted from songs she heard on FM—and got
her whole class to perform it, while Mae sang at the piano, off-key but
exuberant. 'You see that,' Bea said to me a while back, 'where a happy
high-achieving kid gets to adolescence and is like a tire that goes flat.
Charmaine's illness may have been part of it, I guess. You never know.
Life is so chancy.'

Watching Mae has always reminded me of a leaf turning on the
breeze, drifting without any predetermined direction, but graceful,
nonetheless. She often dresses entirely in white, which has struck me
as a subtle statement, but may only be an effort to match her frothy
light straw-colored hair, which is always blowing around her face.

Observing Mae, I have wondered, if I were Aaron's age, how long it would take me to realize she is deeply unsettled. She has a lot of easy charm with everyone, but the occasionally forced gestures, her emphatic laughter, the way her hands fly around her, have seemed to conform to somebody else's idea of how she should behave.

Even so, like everyone else, I've been struck by Mae's smarts. I know her principally through Mansy's and Aaron's stories about her, but she often impressed me in our sporadic face-to-face contact. When Bea and I had just started our romance, I came over one Friday night while Aaron and a group of his high school friends were on the back porch of the apartment Bea was renting. The kids were hooting and yelling at each other about some young man, a sailor they'd met on a trip into Kweagon. One of the females insisted he was not in uniform, which left her no way to explain why she thought he was in the navy. At that point, Mae came into the kitchen for water.

'Don't you think,' Mae asked me, as she stood by the tap, 'you can tell so much about people by the details they notice, what they think is important and then sticks in their memories? It like tells you *every-thing* about them.'

I didn't answer, because I was so struck. It was not something I'd ever articulated to myself.

"But truth, with my mom?" Aaron says now. "That went two ways. Mae always talked a lot of shit about her, too."

"What kind of shit?"

"Oh, you know. I thought she was so cool and, you know, moral, and she wasn't."

"Anything more specific?"

"She was vague. I always thought she was bullshitting." He looks away.

For a kid who's been in his share of trouble, Aaron is a bad liar. But I'm not going to press. Like a lot of manipulative people, Mae knew how to spread the currents of discontent, relishing the sense of power it imparted.

Whatever Aaron suspects or doesn't want to say silences him. I turn toward the house, then pause and gesture to the fire.

"Make sure that's out, please, before you go back in."

"Sure sure," he says.

I look at him, my would-be stepson, and drift back to put my arm around him. It's been decades since Nat was this age and I embraced a young man this way. His solidity, like a well-constructed house, communicates a strength in Aaron I otherwise seldom feel. He's built for survival and has already surmounted a good deal. With any luck this will be another passage from which he emerges better set for the future.

"It'll be okay," I say.

"I don't know," he answers. "Sometimes I have this feeling in the pit of my stomach, like how do I actually go forward? Why did I do that anyway? And then I remember that there was no real choice. I will never be who I can be if I don't get away from Mae."

His mother and his grandfather would nod enthusiastically. 'He gets it now,' they'd say. 'He's stumbling but will find his footing in time.' I tell him again that it will be okay, then head inside.

8

Jazz

Because of my wee-hours rendezvous with Aaron at the firepit, I end up sleeping in. It is a luxury I seldom allow myself, and my body always seems to exult when I wake up with the rare sensation of being completely rested. I slip on a pair of sweatpants and arrive barefoot in the kitchen to find Bea working over the stove. On the weekends, she takes over as chef. She is far more skilled than I am and frequently likes to tackle recipes she's read about that require considerable preparation. For tonight, it's a Jamaican chicken, made with spices she found at a shop in Como Stop. Right now, she's getting ready to marinate. As she stirs what's in a bowl, she tells me that Aaron, on his way out early this morning, promised to be home for a late dinner.

Now that I am awake, Bea turns up the music on the speaker system. I settle with a cup of coffee, while jazz piano, the standard musical accompaniment of our life together, floats like silver confetti from above. Willi, Bea's mom, was playing piano in a jazz trio in a small club when Joe met her. Willi taught Bea for years, although Bea claims she never became her mother's equal. The tracks Bea prefers are laid down by musicians she adores, like Keith Jarrett or Kurt Elling, or lesser-knowns Bea has introduced me to, like Art Hodes, whose fluid blues surrounds us this morning. I do not understand what I am listening to, not the way Bea does. Sooner or later, I get lost trying to fathom the improvisations. But that doesn't frustrate me. Because when I moved up here after the catastrophic disappointments of my life in Kindle County, I wanted to experience something very different than what had gone on for the sixty years before, and in every precise piano note, I hear the sound of a desire fulfilled, of my refusal to subside into old age defeated.

Listening as she works, Bea now lifts her spoon unconsciously and, as Hodes works through a passage she likes especially, strokes the air emphatically on every downbeat. Matt and Lorna added two skylights over the kitchen, and midmorning an intense beam illuminates her. Seeing her there, spotlit and restored by Aaron's return to the upbeat self that is her default setting, my heart stirs as it does a couple of times a month. I swell with gladness and gratitude that after all my blundering I have ended up here, with this remarkable woman, kind and smart and beautiful, who takes joy in her life, and in me as an essential part of it.

Before Lorna Murphy, my erstwhile lover, departed for good from Mirror Lake, she insisted on taking me out to dinner, yet one more unneeded apology for falling for somebody else. The lawyers and bankers had passed papers on the house sale hours before, and a huge moving van had squeezed up and down the gravel drive, headed, with all of Lorna's worldly goods, to Palm Springs. It was late fall and the elegant dining room at the Morevant, where we ate with Daria and Nick last night, one of the two fancy hotels that adjoin one another along the shore of Como Lake, was uncomfortably quiet in the waning days before its seasonal closing. We were seated by the large windows that look down on the huge sloping lawn, dotted with white Adirondack chairs.

My dinner out with Lorna was an unaccustomed event. During the eighteen months or so I had seen Lorna romantically, she had been reluctant about being together in public. I had never probed her hesitation, but I assumed she feared the uncertain reactions of her sons, if they found out she had taken another man into their father's bed. In truth, there was always a good deal I did not fully comprehend about Lorna. I didn't understand why she had started writing to me after I was indicted, or why it had become an exchange of three or four

letters a week while I was inside. Her first communication, sent after
the charges became public, expressed absolute faith in my innocence
and sympathy about having the sorrow of losing a spouse, which she
knew firsthand, multiplied by this kind of Kafkaesque horror. It later
seemed that by a logic only she could understand, her expression of
empathy had somehow implanted the idea that I was the right guy
with whom to put her toe in the water again, now that Matt was three
years gone. Of course, my circumstances at the time made it unlikely
that she'd ever be called upon to turn that thought into action, and
I've always wondered if the long odds against anything actually occurring might have been what tempted her to entertain these notions
initially.

But the second I was released, she put aside whatever hesitations
she felt. As a starter relationship, it did the job for both of us, always
conducted with kindness and appreciation and emotional limitations.
I never, for example, spent the entire night. But it was all good enough
until she'd bumped into one of Matt's former business partners in
Palm Springs. I think her new marriage is happier than her first one,
and in our occasional emails, she always thanks me for getting her on
the way.

Lorna is a tall woman—an inch taller than me—with elegant long
hands and a full hairdo that cleverly adds dimension to her narrow face.
On this night when we were bidding farewell to one another, she finished her second Old Fashioned and had ordered a third—her drinking
was one of several things that I felt set a boundary on our long-term
prospects—and squared back to look at me. She'd been blathering
about Lorne, her intended. Yes, they were Lorne and Lorna, a coincidence so awkward that it might have stopped some other couples cold,
but which they took as a sign of destiny. She held the sweating glass to
her cheek and said, 'But what is it *you* want, Rusty?'

She meant what did I want in a future partner, assuming there was
ever to be such a person, which I doubted.

I wound my head around, as if the mere conjecture made me
dizzy, and said, 'I just want to be happy, Lorna.'

'Then you should look for somebody who's happy, don't you
think?'

This seemed a bit simplistic to me, and in that—may the Lord forgive me—typical of Lorna, but over time, the evident good sense of her suggestion became clearer and clearer. Why should someone as glum as I am double the trouble by hooking up with somebody else with a heavy heart? As my relationship with Bea blossomed, it occurred to me several times that I had, consciously or not, taken Lorna's advice.

Bea is a willfully happy person who schooled herself, probably since childhood, on concentrating on the parts of life that deserve celebration. Her warmth, the way she embraces the world and the people who inhabit it, inspires my endless admiration, even though I can seldom drop my guard enough to enjoy things the way she does. I do not mean that she is naive or immune to aggravation. Aaron has turned her into a fretful mess, too often, and at school her patience is tried a hundred different ways, by everything from meddlesome bureaucrats to her problem teachers, who are, for the most part, tenaciously problematic, marginal performers and maximum complainers. But there is rarely a day when she loses track of her fundamental joy in the children who are her responsibility or fails to find a moment of hilarity in their random declarations, so sincere and so wrong as they build their understanding of the world ("Mrs. Housley, it looks really nice the way you've started dying your hair a little grey").

I have found over time that her joy in simple things has done a lot to moderate my grim disposition—her wonder at the tree frogs clinging on the porch screen, or the wild turkeys wobbling stupidly as they amble along down near the dock in the late afternoon, or the exotic growths, like ghost pipes, she brings back from the County Preserve that adjoins our property. My favorite moments perhaps are when the mood suddenly strikes her and she'll spend half an hour or so improvising melodies and riffs on Willi's old upright Steinway, which we moved into the living room when we began sharing this house. Without warning, Bea's light laughter will reach me a room or two away, as she delights herself unexpectedly with one of her own innovations.

Yet even today, I am not certain that we would have ended up under the same roof if Covid had not forced our hands. We were deeply enmeshed by then, spending most of our free time together, and well past the point of acknowledging we were in love (no matter how much trouble that declaration had spelled for me in the past). But we'd hung on a precipice for about a year, both having learned by sad experience that relationships were perishable, and each of us uncertain whether we were willing to sacrifice our treasured independence to make a longer-term gamble on one another. Then the disease closed down the world, Bea's school included. Aaron supposedly was on his own. The imperatives the virus gave us were clear: Either put our thing on pause, or cocoon together while we held other humans at a distance.

It proved a great bet, as far as I am concerned. But Bea remains reluctant to put down her final chip and agree to a wedding date. She is emphatic that her hesitation is not about the difference in our ages and the chance that she will end up as a nursemaid as I head into final decline. Given the fundamental satisfaction she finds in caretaking roles, I am inclined to believe her. Instead, her logic seems on the order of 'If it ain't broke, don't fix it.' My desire to take this step, which I could never have imagined until recently, is born of lawyerly considerations. I am likely to be gone long before her, and as my wife, Bea can inherit my judicial pension and enjoy the tax-free use of all my assets, including this house, for the rest of her life. (Whatever is left when she passes would go to my granddaughters, since Nat and Anna could never spend everything Barbara, thanks to her father, placed in trust for our son.)

In the face of those advantages, I expect her to relent eventually, although I sometimes think it will take a serious health crisis affecting me to push her over the line. For now, I refuse to quarrel about it, since that would only disrupt a life I savor.

After an afternoon spent on errands—two farmer's markets and a trip to a fabric store in Como Stop—we find ourselves, as we often do, on the old park bench down by the shore, watching the sun set over Mirror Lake. We try to do this whenever the weather and our schedules permit. We have a beer or a glass of wine and share whatever seems worthwhile. Often though, we subside to silence, enjoying the steadiness of our connection, the way we seem to be breathing in time. A couple of weeks ago, at the end of August, a Super Blue Moon, a giant copper coin, crept into the horizon a few degrees north of the setting sun and rose with its perfect glow into the darkening sky. We had been reading about the phenomenon, which is supposed to be repeated only once before 2037. I am not generally morbid, but it dawned on me that it might take a bit of luck for me to be around to see the one fourteen years on. In the moment I didn't mind. I sat beside Bea, a woman I should have been dreaming of always, our hands webbed and the two of us otherwise unspeaking, knowing I had arrived at a place of peace in my life I had always yearned for.

While Bea heads up to work on dinner, I stay behind to pull my canoe closer to shore. I will be in charge of grilling Bea's preparation on my Kamado oven on the deck. I am trudging uphill to light the fire, when I hear the pealing of the house phone. That generally means a friend who was in my life before the cellphone era or a jerk ignoring the Do Not Call List. She is still on the line when I arrive in the kitchen.

"I'll ask, I'll ask, I promise," she says, then replaces the handset with a somewhat nettled look. "That was Charmaine," she says, referring to Mae's mother. She says that, as promised, early this morning Aaron dropped Mae's phone over at the Potters' house, a huge place on a wooded hillside a couple of miles outside Mirror. "But she says he ran off before she could ask him any questions."

"What questions?"

"Well, for one thing," Bea says, "Charmaine tells me that Mae isn't home yet."

Bea's fine eyes stay on me with a deeply uncertain look, almost as if by reading my reaction she will understand her own. And she's right: I'm surprised. The news, as it settles in, feels odd, and therefore slightly ominous. "Charmaine tells me she called Aaron's cell all day, but he never answered. That's why she phoned here, hoping she could catch him. I explained he's been up on a ladder all day and probably got no chance to call back."

I nod. That might even be true.

"I really didn't know what to tell her," Bea says, "except to repeat what Aaron said about their fight. Talking it over, Charmaine and I thought maybe Mae was driving around trying to find him." There are countless routes between here and Harold's Woods, about two hours north and east. "But I still didn't know how to answer when she kept asking me why Aaron had Mae's phone."

"I have some idea about that." I tell her in a few strokes that Aaron couldn't sleep and that we ended up around the firepit talking. She is hungry for every detail of this conversation and is not easily put off, even when I say that I prefer she ask Aaron directly.

Fortunately, he comes through the door from the garage at that point. He is in his underwear again and his socks, having left the rest of his paint-smeared garments outside. He simply stares at his mother when she tells him Mae isn't home.

"That's fucked up," he says. He'd taken it for granted that she'd been back since late on Thursday.

"Do you think there's any chance she's driving around trying to find you?" Bea asks.

"Maybe," he answers. "I'm sure she wants to talk me out of cutting the cord. But three days? She should have given up by now."

We are all silenced for a second by that puzzle.

"Aaron," I say. "Did Mae have a lot of stuff with her? Drugs?"

"*Drugs?*" says Bea, then flaps her hands in exasperation. "Of course."

"Not me, Mom," Aaron inserts quickly, pointing at her.

"Did she have a lot?" I repeat.

"Bet," he says. "I didn't even want to see it, but Mae's never short."

Given Mae's rage, as he described it, I could see her going back to the tent and staying high for quite a while. I ask him if that's possible.

"Possible," he says. He thinks that over and nods again and repeats, "Yeah, very possible."

Bea is still on her own track.

"Charmaine is very worried, Aaron, because she can't reach her daughter. Because you took her phone. I don't understand why you did that."

"Because I was next-level pissed," he says. "Because I'd believed what she said for, like, the one-millionth time, and for like the one-millionth time she didn't mean it. Or remember it. And instead, every second she was basically stepping around like a ballerina in front of her phone, or else watching the videos and editing them. So, okay, should I have grabbed it? Not really. But it felt like exactly what she deserved. So sorry, not sorry Charmaine is worried. Because if Mae had her cell, she wouldn't answer her mother's calls anyway. Or her father's. She wasn't speaking to them most of the time, as it was."

I am impressed that he is literally speaking of Mae in the past tense. I'll probably never know everything that transpired out there, but it was something that seems to have produced a real change.

"Aaron, you really need to call the Potters before you go to sleep," Bea says.

"Ugh," he says. "Never gonna happen."

"Why?"

"Because they're going to want me to tell them why she's not home and I don't know a freaking thing for sure. And I'm definitely not saying that she's probably in a tent stoned out of her skull. Not a whole lot of positives coming from that."

We settle in for dinner but haven't been at the table for more than twenty minutes when Aaron excuses himself. He promised to hang out tonight with his best friend, Cassity Benisch, who lives in town. She has a young child who's asleep by now, meaning she can't come for Aaron, as she often does. As a result, he has a long bike ride to get there and wants to get started now.

He's smart enough to compliment the meal as he picks up his plate, but still heads off, ignoring his mother's dissatisfied look.

9

Hardy

September 17

Late Sunday afternoon, while I'm in front doing the fall pruning of the lilacs, a huge black SUV with the heft of something that might be driven by Darth Vader steams up the gravel driveway. The speed alone catches my attention. I am startled and then, with a glance, I know who it is: the mighty prosecuting attorney for Skageon County, Harrison Potter.

Because of my affection for Mansy, I have tried for a long time to like his only living son, but Hardy and I got off to a bad start. He was the deputy prosecuting attorney on the one case I ended up trying during my brief stint as a defense lawyer. My client was the staff accountant for the local Chevy dealership who messed with the books so she could embezzle close to $60,000. As is often true in indigent cases, Della Kmiec was a figure of pathos rather than evil. In her early fifties, two hundred pounds overweight and the married mother of three, she became convinced that an ex-con fifteen years younger than she was desperately in love with her. She stole the money for him, so he could supposedly care for his elderly mother. Naturally, he spent every penny on drugs.

Hardy took a hard line and offered Della three years on a plea. I was convinced her sentence wouldn't be much worse after a trial. Hardy was infuriated, but I gave him a run for his money in front of the jury by showing she'd kept careful records and had plans to repay the amounts she'd pocketed from her deferred profit sharing. After two full days of deliberations, they convicted her anyway. Judge Sams—the father of the current Judge Sams—fulfilled my prediction and gave her eighteen months, rather than the five years Hardy wanted by then.

The anger that is part of the contest Hardy and I had is pretty routine in criminal practice and usually becomes, a decade later, the subject for some laughter. But Hardy has never warmed to me. On first meeting, he can evince a smiling frat-boy manner, as if you're both in on the same joke, but at least with me, the bonhomie doesn't last long. I'd see him now and then around town, or when Mansy included me in some event, and he generally treated me with indifference. After I started living with Bea, he became surlier. He's like that with her too. Bea says Hardy hasn't ever really forgiven her for dumping him in favor of Lloyd as their senior year of high school was drawing to a close.

Perhaps the worst thing I can say about Hardy is that he seems to have learned nothing from his father. Not being as smart as Mansy is hardly his fault; I don't know many people who are. But he seems to have deliberately eschewed his father's polish. Where Mansy is reserved, quiet-spoken, and says little that does not seem to have been considered, Hardy is brash and something of a loudmouth. And he lacks his father's balanced style as a public servant. Hardy is always hard-line and is relentless about maintaining his office's conviction rate, an attitude that can sometimes foster corner cutting by the county sheriff's deputies and state troopers who investigate his cases.

Despite that, he is facing his first real primary race. A state legislator, Madison van Ohne, is running at him from the right. She says the prosecutor's office is an old boys' club—definitely true—and virtually a sanctuary center for local undocumented migrants—definitely false. The migrants Hardy deals with are mostly farmworkers who get stupid drunk on the weekends and crash borrowed cars into phone poles and the RFD mailboxes that line the country roads. Many of the local farmers depend on these workers to maintain their operations, and now and then, in less serious cases, Hardy's office pleads them out without informing ICE.

Mansy has asked me to publicly endorse Hardy for reelection, and I will, since Hardy is the less bad choice. Nobody around here will give a damn about what I say, and that seems to include Hardy, who is unsmiling when he catches sight of me. He puts one foot on the driveway and stands to speak to me from inside the car door of his huge vehicle. Without any greeting, he asks, "Is Aaron here?"

I tell Hardy that Aaron has been at work since eight that morning. "Where's that?" he asks.

"I don't really know, Hardy." My teeth are on edge already with the tone of interrogation. "Do I take it Mae isn't back yet?"

"No," he says. He gets out fully now and slams the door too hard. "Mae isn't back yet."

He's wearing a white shirt, open at the collar, and a blue blazer. He may have been at a campaign event or at church, listening to Pastor Proctor, which is one and the same as far as I'm concerned, since the pastor controls thousands of votes. Hardy is a deacon in the congregation.

As unpleasant as Bea finds Hardy, she acknowledges that his life, like his father's, is overshadowed by tragedy. Hardy's older brother, Mansfield V, called Mark, had come back to Skageon after Yale Law School, made buckets of money in business, then seemed destined to exceed his father in political life. He was thirty-eight when he was called up on a reserve deployment to Afghanistan and killed by an IED right before his year there was up. After Mark's death, Hardy had the opportunity—or the obligation—to occupy the large void left.

He's a big man and fit. That was one thing he had on Mark, I'm told. Harrison is a better physical specimen, a couple inches taller, a more skillful athlete, with the thick-browed handsomeness of a leading man. He looks terrific on his campaign posters and by reputation has also leveraged his physical advantages more directly, since he is a notorious fuckaround. I often hear gossip about him when I am sitting with Joe at the VFW. The joke is that women seeking work at the

PA's office send a photograph rather than a résumé. Charmaine has long pretended to know nothing.

I have never been certain that people up here are truly friskier, or if there's just more talk about it in a small community where it's harder to keep secrets, especially if your last name is Potter. Bea tends to favor the first theory. 'There aren't many restaurants. It's thirty miles to a movie and ninety to a concert venue. People drink for recreation and when they drink...' Her hand shoots off into space.

'Sex to relieve the boredom?' I ask.

'Sometimes.'

'But everybody's so religious.'

'That's why. Because they need forgiveness.'

Referring now to Mae, I ask Hardy, "Can we help?"

"Help?" he asks. "Sure. You can tell me what kind of asshole decides to leave a young woman in the wilderness without a phone or credit cards." 'Wilderness' is of course an exaggeration. Governor Harold State Park is a large tract of primary growth forest, oak and hickory and walnut, more than a thousand acres, but with trails and campgrounds. Then again, I noticed the little adhesive silicone pocket on the back of Mae's phone, when Aaron held it up the other night, but I didn't register that Aaron had left her not only without communication but also money. I understand why Hardy is upset. But he's also done a lot to irritate me in this conversation, and standing on my drive and calling the young man who lives here an 'asshole' has me stifling an impulse to ask Hardy to leave. I still have the large garden shears I was using in my hands, and I notice that I've raised them unconsciously. I lower them a bit, before I reply.

"They had a hellacious fight, Hardy. For a change."

"That's no excuse."

"I'm not making excuses, Hardy. I'm telling you what happened. We both know they have an exceptional talent for pissing each other off." This may apportion too much blame to Aaron, who is far quieter and more mild-mannered than Mae, but then again, I hear only his side of the story. "It was bad enough that he says it's really the end."

"I wish," he says.

"We agree," I say. "It's probably the best thing for both of them."

"Aye to that," he answers. "Looking back, I always wish I'd told her to stay away from him the first time I saw them flirting at Young Life, while I still had some sway with her."

I can feel my brow contract. What else could Hardy have known on first sight, except that Aaron's Black? He understands my reaction and is quick to correct me.

"Like mother, like son," he says.

I'm completely startled by the remark and the idea that a grown man is still nursing his high school heartbreak three decades later. Yet I know firsthand that Hardy is the kind to bear a grudge.

"Where were they anyway?" Hardy asks.

"Up north, I think."

"In this county?"

I take a beat on that. "From what I'm told."

"Like where? Aren't you supposed to know his whereabouts at all times?"

I consider my answer.

"I believe they were somewhere near Harold's Woods, Hardy."

"Were they out there getting high?"

"Hardy, did you come here to trick-bag somebody or because you're concerned about your daughter? They were camping. And I don't think Aaron was using. But he has a drop tomorrow, so we'll both find out for sure." 'We'll both find out' is meant to let him know that I'm convinced that Gert didn't jerk on Aaron's leash without Hardy's encouragement.

"I told you why I'm here," he says. "I want to know what the hell he was thinking."

"From what he's said, Hardy, Mae had a full tank of gas and he expected her to drive straight home."

"Only she didn't," Hardy says. "She had a wreck somewhere, or she's sitting in a ditch. Or God knows what else."

"Did she have road service?"

"Of course she had road service. She doesn't have a damn telephone, Rusty."

He got me on that one. I try a softer tone.

"Hardy, we understand why you're concerned. We'd feel the same way. We'll all be relieved when Mae turns up."

He pulls a mouth and opens his car door, shooting a finger in my direction.

"Tell Aaron to call me," he says again, then throws the car in gear and circles around to head out. Yet again, I decide there's not much to like about that man.

Aaron comes in from the garage just as we are finishing dinner, but he gets no farther than one step inside before his mother stops him. He says he declined Brice's offer of a pair of coveralls because he thought that would be too hot over his clothes, but his jeans and shirt are spattered everywhere with white paint, and he has in hand the coveralls he'll wear tomorrow. Bea sends him to use the outdoor shower by the stairs from the shore. When Aaron returns, I describe Hardy's visit, which I had skipped when Bea returned from coffee with one of her younger teachers. I preferred not to disturb the tranquility of our glass of wine by the dock.

"Aaron," his mother says, "did you really leave her out there without money too?"

He takes a second to recall.

"Nn-uh," he says. "She used her cards for gas and groceries. So I hit an ATM and gave her my half in cash."

"Wasn't the money with the phone?" I ask. His grey eyes stay on me a second. Perhaps he's a little taken aback that I'm quizzing him.

"Her father gave her too many credit cards. She keeps cash in her back pocket."

"Okay, well, Hardy wants to talk to you," I tell him. "But do me a favor. Log a call to Cap first."

"Cap?" Bea asks, an instant before her son. Casper Sabonjian was the lawyer who worked out Aaron's plea deal eighteen months ago.

"Hardy's upset," I say, "and angry at Aaron. You'd be better off getting Cap's read on the whole situation before you let Hardy grill you. I'm pretty suspicious that Gert whistled you in because Hardy gave her the signal."

Bea says, "I thought legally Hardy can't have anything to do with Aaron's case."

"My love," I reply, "someone as sweet and trusting as you should be a grade school teacher."

Aaron has a taste for cheap irony and laughs out loud, while Bea pokes me in the side. But when we're alone later, she says, "Do you really think he needs to go as far as calling Cap?"

"Bea," I say, "I don't know everything that happened out there, and I don't want to know, because I'd rather not hear something I'd be expected to report."

"What are you afraid of?"

"I don't know, Bea," I answer. I don't want to mention what I still regard as likely, namely that he was using with Mae, because that would set Bea off. "Suppose they weren't actually in Harold's Woods but had left the county? I can give you a million more examples. Let him talk to somebody who can hear everything and evaluate any risks."

"Doesn't it make him look guilty of something, if he involves a lawyer?"

"It makes him look like somebody on probation who doesn't want to go back to jail."

"I just don't like the way this whole thing is developing," she says. "It feels weird."

"It'll be fine," I say. "Mae will show up tomorrow and everybody will settle down."

But the truth is that I share Bea's apprehensions. It is part of Mae and Aaron's odd magic that their relationship has often served to make everybody connected to them tense. And I agree with her. It just feels weird.

10

But Mae

B ut Mae is not back on Monday. That evening, Charmaine calls Bea again, just as we have finished dinner. I am rinsing the plates and filling the washer when Bea grabs the phone, so I pick up only a limited part of her end of the conversation.

"I was hoping you had good news," I hear Bea say at one point. When the call ends a few minutes later, Bea comes to fill me in.

"Charmaine is beside herself. They're upset they haven't heard from Aaron. She wants to know if Mae said anything that might give him any idea where she is."

Aaron is out for the evening, babysitting for Brock, the two-year-old son of his friends Cassity and Brice, who do not live together, much to Brice's dismay. Cassity is taking night classes at Skageon CC to become a CNA, as the initial step in a nursing career. Brice needs his evenings to tend to his business, including picking up the paint and supplies for the next day's work. So Aaron, who loves children—a likely legacy from his mother—has volunteered for Mondays to relieve them both.

Bea, usually early to bed, insists on waiting up for his return. We watch her French show in the living room, but she is not translating occasionally, so I know it doesn't have her full attention.

"Aaron, really," his mother says, almost as soon as he is through the door, "if you have any inkling where Mae is, I know the Potters would appreciate hearing it."

He's in his nighttime biking gear that makes him look like he's in a school play about space invaders. He wears an optic reflective vest, the kind you see on highway workers. His helmet is festooned with several plastic blinkers, and mounted on the top on a steel crosspiece is a 2000 lumens bike light I bought him for Christmas. In truth, it was a gift not only to him but his mother, who worries about the risks on the road posed by the drunken patrons headed home from the taverns at night.

He stands still, assessing Bea's request, then nods to show he's heard her, and heads down the hall to his room. I can tell he's feeling a bit harassed about a situation that is completely out of his control. I'm surprised when he returns to the living room a few minutes later to address us from the doorway.

"Want to know what I really think?" he asks. "I kind of figured it out this afternoon up on that ladder. It's Mae being Mae. She knows everybody's worried about her by now, and she wants to make me look bad."

On the pale sofa, Bea has turned to see him over her shoulder, and now rotates further, with one leg beneath her.

"I don't understand," says Bea. "How does that make you look bad?"

"Weren't you just telling me that the Potters are pissed at me? And really worried? She wants everybody asking me, 'Where is she, where is she, what did you do with her?' She's getting even."

"Charmaine didn't say, 'What did Aaron do with her?' Why would you even think that?"

"Oh, come on, Mom. That's the whole point of what Mae's up to."

He turns heel and departs again. Bea faces me then.

"Is he making any sense to you?" she asks quietly.

"Some," I answer. "Maybe he's a little paranoid, but he's right that the longer this goes on, the more accusatory Charmaine and Hardy are going to get. And Mae can be pretty inventive and dramatic."

"I hope he doesn't say that to anybody else," she says. "It sounds cold-hearted. And paranoid, like you said. Hardy and Charmaine are terrified and they have reason to be. It was idiotic to leave her out there without credit cards or a phone."

In the morning, not long after Bea departs for an early meeting at school, Brice's car crunches up the drive. As usual, he gives a quick honk to let Aaron know he's out there, but it's a few minutes before Aaron emerges from his room. I'm in the kitchen, quaffing a sports drink after my canoe trip around the lake at sunup.

Aaron lingers at the front door, clearly weighing something.

He finally says, "My dad just called. He wants me to stop over at the sheriff's substation in Granger and talk to the cops about Mae."

"Did you speak to Cap?"

He frowns. "No."

"Well, I don't like to get between you and Lloyd. But my advice is to talk to your attorney before you go running to the police station."

Aaron makes a face. "He's going to charge me, right?"

Aaron has a substantial debt to his parents for the accumulated legal fees they paid Cap for representing Aaron on both of his arrests. He gives Lloyd and Bea something out of each paycheck, but he's also trying to save for art school.

"Aaron, you need to discuss this entire situation with a lawyer who can hear the whole story, every little detail. And for many reasons, that shouldn't be me. I don't believe Cap will charge you a lot for a consultation. But whatever it is, I'll pay for it. I think it's that important." In general, I have steered clear of offering Aaron money. Neither of his parents likes it. And I learned a long time ago that with an addict, the safest answer is no, when they request financial help. It's a sign of how far Aaron has come that I feel comfortable making this gesture, but I add that it would probably be better to keep it between us.

In response, he puts on a slightly pained expression. But I am pleased when he calls Bea later to tell her he has an appointment with Cap. Joe will be driving him. She tells Aaron that we'll keep dinner for both of them.

When they return, Aaron says he isn't hungry, and heads straight to his room. Joe takes a seat at the table, waiting, as usual, to be served. Bea gets him a bottle of the nonalcoholic beer, which Aaron also drinks occasionally, from the fridge, while I ladle up a bowl of the vegetarian chili I made for dinner.

"Any idea what Cap said?" Bea asks him quietly.

"Yeah, don't talk to nobody about none of this," says Joe.

I tell both of them that is exactly what any decent criminal lawyer would say.

Bea asks her father, "Did Aaron tell you that he's got this theory that Mae is hiding out so that people start asking Aaron what he did to her?"

"He didn't do nothing to her, Beatrix," Joe says immediately. Among the many things Joe does that drive his daughter mad is giving her birth name a decidedly American pronunciation, 'BE-ah-tricks,' rather than the German way Willi intended, with the last syllable as 'treeks.'

"I know that, Dad. But Aaron thinks Mae wants to stay away long enough that people get suspicious of him. Then she'll ride in at the last minute, so he's grateful to her for saving him."

"Sounds just like her," says Joe. Since the Potters are richer than anybody else, Joe has special contempt for them. And as far as he is concerned, Mae, with all the hurts she's periodically done to Aaron, deserves to be on a wanted poster.

"I don't know," says Bea. "That notion still makes no sense to me. She's been gone more than a week. How has she gotten by that long with just the seventy-five dollars Aaron gave her?"

"For one thing," I say, "she's got the tent. And her sleeping bag. And whatever food they bought." In the last few days, the weather has been mild—and dry—so staying outside would present no problem. "And nobody says she had only seventy-five dollars. That's what Aaron repaid her. God knows what she had in her pocket to start."

"People their age don't carry cash," Bea says.

"But she's a Potter. Some families just believe in always having money for an emergency." Mansy usually has several hundreds in his wallet when we divide the check for lunch.

Bea's face narrows with her growing doubts about the entire situation. Lawyering up is contrary to her customary openhanded way of dealing with other people. It shows too little empathy for the Potters. Not to mention reinforcing suspicions about Aaron.

Wednesday morning, just as I've settled in to work, my cell rings, showing Cap Sabonjian's caller ID.

"I've called the sheriff's office and the PA's," he says, "and told them both that Aaron is eager to answer all their questions, just as soon as he gets a non-use letter." A non-use letter means that instead of invoking his constitutional right to silence, Aaron will cooperate, provided that nothing he says can be used against him criminally, which in this case would include a probation revocation proceeding.

I pause for a second, trying to read through Cap's maneuver. He's probably just being careful, as every defense lawyer should be. The results of Aaron's drop for Gert will not be back until tomorrow, but Aaron continues to say it will be no problem, and a non-use letter wouldn't protect him from a dirty drop anyway, since that involves acts, not statements. But like most local members of the criminal defense bar, Cap doesn't trust Hardy or his office. Hanging around with a drug user—the PA's daughter or not; being out of touch for seventy-two hours—there are a lot of infractions Aaron would admit to that a determined prosecutor could use for a probation revocation, if Aaron didn't get a letter before the interview. So I think I understand why Cap set these terms. But there's also the chance that Aaron acknowledged something to his lawyer we haven't heard yet that might implicate him in a more serious situation.

Cap then gets to his retainer, which I figured to start was why he was calling. He wants $3,000, meaning he expects to spend no more than ten hours on this, including the consultation he already had. I like Cap, who was in his last days as Skageon County state defender during the time when I was volunteering to take assigned defense cases from the court. He was a knowledgeable teacher whenever I needed his assistance, as I often did. The next year, he went into private practice, after his pension fully vested, trying to feather his nest a little in advance of retirement. Given his long experience, he's pretty much become the go-to defense lawyer in the county on the little paying criminal work there is up here. Most often he's representing the well-to-do residents of Como Stop who are pulled over on DUIs with some regularity during the summer, and a few Kindle County gangbangers caught delivering drugs.

Aaron got busted his first time not long after Bea moved in with me. Covid had closed the dorms at Wisconsin State, but he'd remained in Glenville. He was sleeping on a friend's floor and supposedly finishing work for a studio art class, when he tried to buy a considerable quantity of Ecstasy and psilocybin from an undercover cop. Cap was my immediate recommendation to Bea and Lloyd to serve as Aaron's lawyer. Hardy removed himself from the case and let his chief deputy deal with Cap, who convinced her to reduce the charges to a misdemeanor, with a stipulation that Aaron's guilty plea would be erased if he completed a rehab program and avoided another conviction for five years. Given the quantities involved, it was an outstanding arrangement for Aaron, a golden opportunity that he ultimately flushed away.

The one collateral consequence of Aaron's deal was that Cap could not get the university to deviate from its fixed policy that anyone convicted of a drug offense was suspended for a year. Bootless, Aaron was soon cascading downhill and probably started messing then with meth and opioids. There were no jobs to be found, but he refused to move in with us, and we heard from him only sporadically. One report we received consistently was that he had often been seen with Mae Potter, who had returned from the small liberal arts college in Iowa she'd been attending, like generations of Potters before her. Bea's initial theory was that Aaron was consorting with Mae only because she could afford to buy all the illegal substances either of them wanted, but if she was lending Aaron money, it was not enough to meet his habit. One night in December 2020, we came home and our 50-inch LCD TV had been taken right off the wall in the living room—the sight was a little like meeting a six-year-old with missing front teeth. It was then that Bea realized that her engagement ring from Lloyd, which she'd been looking for for several weeks, had not been simply misplaced. We installed a safe and changed the locks on the doors. Lloyd heard from friends in law enforcement that Aaron was dealing, but the warnings Lloyd and I both tried to deliver were pointless. Aaron stopped taking our calls, and several months passed without any of the older adults in his life having contact with him. Even old friends like Cassity claimed not to be hearing from him.

The one time we needed to find Aaron, Lloyd again relied on some former buddies from his days as a sheriff's deputy to determine his son's whereabouts, but it was I who had to go give Aaron the word that his grandmother, Lloyd's mom, was in hospice, where Lloyd was sitting vigil. Aaron turned out to be sharing the company of a few anorexic-looking meth heads in a prefab apartment complex on the outskirts of Como Stop. The buildings had been erected on the cheap decades before as housing for the service workers employed in town. I knocked on the door I'd been directed to, and one of the zombified residents, a young woman who was almost shaking as she stood in the doorway, simply disappeared when I said Aaron's name. The reek of a litter box that had gone too long without attention hit me as soon as I took a single step inside. There was a large hole in the living room wall, probably the result of a fist—or even a head—slammed against it. And there was every kind of debris strewn all over the green indoor-outdoor carpet—beer bottles, plastic wrappers, crackers and candy and other food ground underfoot. When Aaron finally appeared, he was sallow, and his eyes looked completely wild. He mustered no visible response when I told him about his grandmother, who, in truth, had never warmed to her adopted grandson. He just said 'Okay' before he closed the door on me.

Things came to their predictable end around Thanksgiving of 2021, when Aaron's elderly Saturn, a high school graduation gift from Joe, was observed wobbling at about 15 mph down both sides of Center Street in Como Stop. The cops who pulled him over found Mae in the passenger seat and Aaron's pockets full of drugs, which were actually Mae's, including four vials of coke.

Aaron was held in the Skageon County jail with bail of several hundred thousand dollars. Cap advised us to 'leave him there.' He'd been to this picture show a hundred times before, and this was the time and place, he said, where young folks like Aaron decided which way their lives were going to go. Lloyd had no trouble with the tough love approach, but Bea agonized. I had no vote and wavered in my own mind. The jail in Skageon County was not like Kindle County's, which at its worst was sometimes comparable in its horrors to Abu Ghraib. But it was not going to be confused with summer camp either, with more than a few gang members who'd wandered up from Kindle County or over from Kweagon confined there. The level of actual violence was low, and Aaron is big enough to present a challenge to the usual jailhouse thugs, but I feared that it would be a hardening experience for him, because the threat of harm never goes away.

After he had been inside for four months and had gotten serious about the substance program run by Reverend Spruce, Cap felt it was time to make a motion to reduce his bond. It required, to say the least, a fair amount of discussion between Bea and me when Cap proposed taking Aaron into our house. Cap was certain Judge Sams would deem the home of a grade school principal and a former judge a suitably stable environment.

As soon as Cap came up with this idea, I knew two things: One, I did not want to run a rehab program in my household. And two, I had no choice. I knew better than to tell a mother to choose between me and her child, but I'd already been through the rearing of one troubled young man. I liked to hold up Nat to Bea as an example that a combination of patience and discipline, as well as a lot of psychotherapy and antidepressants, could reclaim a kid sucked into a maelstrom of drug use, depression and—far the most frightening part of it—suicidal thoughts. But I also looked back on that as a private hell, a period when I lived most days fighting off my perpetual anxieties that Nat would perish in a car crash, or from an overdose, or be discovered after having electrocuted himself in the bathtub, as he once witnessed Barbara about to do. I was also certain that Aaron would drive a permanent wedge between Bea and me when I was forced to report him to Judge Sams after he fucked up again, which I fully expected.

But until now, my worst fears have been unfounded. I expected to reside with a sullen, uncooperative man, resentful of having been ordered to live like a child again with his mother. While Aaron has never pretended to like the arrangement, both Cap and Judge Sams drove home the point that he should be grateful to us, and most of the time he seems to remember that. He consents to sit down for a meal a couple of times a week, although his participation in the conversation is limited. But that admittedly has always been Aaron's way. He abides by the curfew Judge Sams set for him, and answers his mother's questions about where he's going and who he will be with briefly but directly. Leaving aside his recent disappearance, he's done everything right, and overall seems to be a vastly different human being, who emerged from the jailhouse as a real adult. Bea and I both think it's no coincidence that for the first year after Aaron's release, while he found a solid footing, Mae was gone, moved to New York to try to make it as a model.

Now I promise Cap that I'll put a check in the mail to him today. But I have one more thing that's bothering me, and I try to calculate an artful way to put this.

"Cap, I know better than to ask what Aaron told you. But he's been saying something recently that's started to bother me a little. He has this theory that Mae is hiding out so that people will suspect him of having done something to her."

"Okay," says Cap, giving no sign whether he heard that from Aaron or not. "And what about that?"

"Well. As I've thought it over, there's a little tiny piece of the old prosecutor in me that's a bit fearful that he's laying down a kind of anticipatory defense."

"Go ahead," Cap says.

I pause a second, embarrassed to be confessing my worst fears out loud.

"I don't really believe this is what's happening, but somebody else, not Aaron, but someone who did harm to that young woman—wouldn't that person need some kind of excuse for why she hadn't returned, maybe to slow the start of an investigation, and certainly to explain why he didn't seem worried about her, if it turns out something bad happened?"

"I see," says Cap. "And you want to know whether I've heard something or know something that might make me worried along those lines?"

"I guess," I say.

"Well, you were right to start. I won't tell you what my client told me."

"Understood," I say.

"But Rusty," he says. "Think about this. You've been around this game a long time. And I'm sure you know enough to realize that any defense lawyer who had any reason to suspect or fear something like that—I mean, not just me, *any* defense lawyer."

"Yes?" I ask.

"That defense lawyer would be asking for a much, much bigger retainer."

11

Lunch

On Wednesday morning, before Cap called, I'd had a disconcerting conversation with Bea as she was walking out the door for school. She had on a print shirtwaist dress that looked especially becoming and a little more makeup than usual, because she has a meeting today with other local principals and the state superintendent of education, a man she'd gone out with several years ago. I took the opportunity to tease her a little, which provoked the usual frustrated pout at the thought I might be jealous. The truth is, I'd met this fellow once for a few seconds, and to my mind, he proved again that single, middle-aged women don't get much to pick from.

'Would it be weird if I cancel lunch with Mansy?' I asked, as she stood there holding the leather tote she uses to haul materials back and forth from school.

'Why would you cancel lunch?'

'He's got to be upset about Mae. It's ten days since her parents have seen her.'

'You're guys, aren't you? You don't talk about your feelings. Tell him we're worried, too, and ask him if he thinks Wisconsin State has a chance on Saturday against Iowa.' Although Wisconsin State lies across the state line on the other side of the Skageon River, fifty miles north, WSU, especially its powerhouse football team, is a local obsession at this time of year. That is more than a matter of geographical proximity. Decades ago, to settle a serious legal dispute about the amount of water the university was drawing out of the river from its pumping station, which sits on the bluffs on the Skageon County side, the state of Wisconsin agreed that all Skageon County residents would be treated as in-state students for purposes of admission and tuition at WSU. That is why Aaron started there, and why Bea studied there for both her BA and the doctorate she completed in the subsequent summers while she was, in her own words, 'waiting to get pregnant.'

I shook my head dubiously at Bea's suggestions, but she persisted.

'Don't you think it's weirder if you cancel? It will look like you're afraid to face him, as if it's really Aaron's fault somehow that she's not back yet.'

I'm not convinced, but Bea had gotten this much right—Mansy is too good a friend for me to run for cover. If nothing else, I decide, I should go and express our concerns and sympathy in person.

I arrive at Trixie's a few minutes late. It was a slower trip today, something I should have figured in advance. In harvest season, huge pieces of farm machinery are often on the back roads, being moved between fields—enormous green combines or huge tractors, puffing black wisps of diesel as they chug along at 18 miles per hour, and presenting the existential challenge of rural life, namely passing in the lane reserved for oncoming traffic.

Even on first sight, Mansy wears his worry. He's not quite as upright and his eyes have the bruised look of sleeplessness. More telling, a certain tension emanates from the way he holds himself. Usually, Mansy is as relaxed as a boiled noodle—he has a sweetly ironic manner that reads as, 'I'm old, I've seen it all, and for the most part, everything turns out okay.'

"I'd ask how you are," I say, as soon as we're seated, "but I can guess. We all wake up every morning hoping to hear Mae's checked in."

"It's a worry, Russ. A real worry. You try to stop your imagination from going to dark places, but that's not easy."

This is delicate, as I anticipated. Wild as she is, Mae is close with her grandfather. She was named for him, in fact, and for all their differences, they sometimes deem each other kindred spirits, sharing the same special intelligence.

"Mansy, believe me, I understand being worried and upset. We are, too, and it has to be unimaginably worse for Mae's family. But because I'm not family, I might have more perspective. Mae Potter is the only person I've met in the Skageon Region who I think might be as smart as you. I can remember when Aaron and she became an item in high school. It was maybe sophomore year and she was already taking some classes at WSU. And she sat at the dinner table explaining a paper she was writing for a History of Science class, contrasting the phlogiston theory to the current belief in quantum waves. I'm still trying to grab hold of that one.

"But we both know people that brainy are often pretty independent-minded. And she's not afraid of drama either. So the one comforting element to me is that it's Mae, who might be up to something unexpected. She's the person who figured out how to get a cow up on the roof of the high school as a senior prank."

His mouth rolls around. I was hoping for a lean smile when I mentioned the cow. One thing I won't say to Mansy, but which has increasingly preoccupied me, is the reality that people disappear all the time, leaving no word where they have gone. I actually looked on the net and found that it's about 600,000 Americans every year who simply quit on the life they have been living with the suddenness and finality of a worker on an assembly line who shouts something obscene and drops their eye shield and gloves right where they stand and walks off the job forever. Thousands of men and women go on business trips and never return home. Housewives depart with the iron still plugged in and scorching hot, as if pressing one more shirt will permanently erase their souls. Almost all of these people turn out to have come to no harm, but that discovery often does not take place for years. After Aaron called it quits with Mae, after her failures—first in college, then in modeling in New York—Mae may be thinking, 'Screw this all, time for something new,' a mindset that virtually commands no contact with the world she's left behind.

"Well, frankly," he says to me, "I'd be taking a lot more comfort if Aaron hadn't lawyered up."

"He's on probation, Mansy."

"That doesn't mean he shouldn't answer questions. In fact, he has to, doesn't he?"

"Not unless they've revoked the Fifth Amendment recently. Gert can ask him questions like 'Where were you?' and 'Who were you with?' but she already has. She knows he was camping with Mae."

"Where?" asks Mansy.

"I told Hardy the other day, that I thought they were near Harold's Woods."

"Jesus Christ, Rusty. That's more than five percent of the county by land mass. That barely helps. Aaron should sit down and respond to a few basic questions about where they were and what happened."

"I'm not his lawyer, and I didn't make the decision. But I know Cap says Aaron will be happy to do just that if he gets a non-use letter."

"Why does he need a freaking non-use letter?"

"Because he's got a good attorney who doesn't want to see his client in a probation revocation proceeding."

"And why would his probation get revoked?"

'Because your son's a jerk' is the correct answer, but I take a second. Mansy and I argue all the time, playing like two dogs who tumble around practicing their fighting skills by feigning bites. On those occasions we're both grinning throughout. There are no smiles here. Instead, I decide to channel Bea.

"I think for the sake of our friendship, we should talk about something stupid like whether Wisconsin State has a chance against Iowa. Just know, we feel for all of you."

Mansy's old face is still while he considers what I'm saying. Beside us, a couple of nicely dressed middle-aged women are looking over at our table too often to be merely checking on their surroundings. People have heard a lot by now. We're providing the drama in their day. Mansy, to my dismay, is not ready to give up this subject.

"I'll tell you why I wouldn't give him a non-use letter," Mansy says. "What if he says he choked her and left her in a ditch?"

I ponder remaining silent or, alternatively, trying a passive approach, just saying, 'I understand, I understand,' a kind of rope-a-dope until he punches himself out, figuratively speaking. But I don't think either will go well. He's a lawyer at the core, and so answering him as lawyers do, appealing to what passes as reason, seems the best choice.

"Mansy, you know as well as I do that there are several answers to that. First, what are your goals here? Do you want to find Mae or punish Aaron? Second, if something as horrible as that had really happened, the investigators would find plenty of evidence against him, despite the letter. And third and most important, Aaron isn't going to say anything like that, because it didn't happen. They had a fight. He went out there to be with her for the first time in a long time with great hopes, thinking they would talk seriously about their long-term prospects together, and instead she wouldn't do anything but pose for pictures of herself she could post. So he grabbed her phone and hitchhiked home. That was stupid, but you know Mae can figure out how to infuriate just about anybody. It's sort of her superpower."

"You're telling me Aaron hasn't said anything to you that's worried you even a little bit about what happened between them?"

We are at the fork in the road. It's his family against my family. I lie a little.

"Absolutely, that is what I'm telling you."

"Then he doesn't need a non-use letter," Mansy snaps. He's leaning forward, motioning at me with a butter knife, chewing on a piece of bread and talking at the same time. That is completely unlike the courtly gent I'm accustomed to, who was taught almost from infancy not to speak with his mouth full. This is as upset as I've ever seen Mansy, but it's inevitable that I am also starting to feel a bit provoked.

"You think so?" I ask. "What if Mae was skulled half the time and one of the conditions of his probation is to stay away from drug users. Just as a hypothetical."

"If he was using, his probation *should* be revoked."

"I didn't say *he* was using. I said maybe she was. His drop will be back today, but he's utterly serene about it."

"How else would he act, if he wants to be able to say the test is wrong?"

I close my eyes for a second. He's not going to give any ground.

Too late, I'm seeing that I should have taken my own counsel, not Bea's, who is far from objective and who is putting a priority on protecting Aaron.

"Mansy, let's just drop this. Again: I understand why you're upset."

"No, you don't. Because you don't know what I know. Hardy's already gotten the State Patrol involved and they've checked all the hospitals in northern Skageon. There are no patients matching her description. They've talked to every tow service and the two Subaru dealerships and no one's seen the vehicle. She had this Internet security system on the car, but of course she forgot to renew it, and it's dead. There are troopers searching the campgrounds in northern Skageon even as we speak, but there's no sign of her yet. Hardy's next step will be to get the FBI involved. And he's going to go to the press in the hope that somebody's seen her and will speak up. This is a damn serious situation, Russ."

Now that I'm trying to see it his way, I realize that hospitalization or automobile failures don't come close to exhausting the frightening scenarios. Angry at Aaron, Mae could easily have wandered into a bar to find a little substitute male attention and ended up catching the eye of the ever-present law enforcement nemesis, Mr. Stranger Danger. There's a lot to be afraid of. And I should have recognized what those fears would ignite for Mansy. This is a man who's already lost the two people in the world he was closest to, his wife and his oldest son. They say your strength declines as you age, and that includes your emotional wherewithal. Old men weep when young men act like stones. Mac still carries the banner for the Potter family into the future. Mae's older sister, Harriet, a shy woman, is now at home with two babies in a Denver suburb. Mark had two sons, but they are both special needs kids. The grandchild most able to impact the outside world as Mansy has and thus fulfill his legacy is Mae. And so Mansy has tried hard to believe what parents so often do—she'll grow up, she'll straighten out, she'll gain control, and she'll be fabulous. I wouldn't bet against that either. And it's why the thought of losing her, too, approaches the unbearable for him.

I try to offer what I can.

"I know she didn't have her credit cards, but have they looked at her ATM withdrawals before she left? Aaron repaid her for groceries and gas, but he thinks she might have been carrying a lot more cash."

That is what Aaron said, when I asked him this morning, as we were passing through the kitchen at about six forty-five. Mae, he says, has been taught to never leave the house without a hundred dollars in twenties folded in her back pocket.

I can see Mansy hasn't considered this. I would hope that might pacify him a little, realizing his granddaughter may not be quite as helpless as they've feared. But he's in one of those moods where he's too agitated to be calmed.

"You see," he says. "You're making my point. That's just the kind of thing we would have known a few days ago, if Aaron would answer questions instead of listening to Cap and you and stonewalling us."

"Mansy, if Mae was the one on probation—and we both know she could have been," I say, referring to when Aaron was arrested while they were together, "you'd think it was good lawyering, not stonewalling."

"Mae wasn't an addict. Or driving under the influence. Don't act like Aaron got treatment he didn't deserve."

I, of course, wasn't complaining about the way Aaron was treated. I was asking him to think about how easily the tables could be turned, if Mae had been dealt with less favorably. But I take a beat. This man is my friend and he's suffering.

"Mansy," I say. "This is my fault. I should have thought about this more carefully and known how worried you'd be and canceled lunch. I apologize. I didn't come here to upset you further."

I'm hoping with that much offered, he'll sit back and wave a liver-spotted hand past his face and say something like, 'Okay, okay, what about State's chances?' Instead, the cool look remains in his glacier-blue eyes. I finally stand, because there's really no other choice.

"Mansy, please tell Charmaine and Hardy again that we're thinking about them every minute. Everybody in my house who prays is praying for good news soon. I hope all of this is behind us next week."

Something enters his expression, doubt or regret as he realizes how much of his ordinary life, the mundane pleasures he's accustomed to, are already being lost in the flood of fears raised by the current situation. Looking down, I see the old man he rarely appears to be, his lower jaw circling minutely, no longer subject to conscious control. He flips up a hand in a dismissive farewell gesture and with no more said, I go.

12

Trouble

On Saturday, as I'm returning from a long bike ride, cruising downhill on Lake Road toward our house, a sight ahead makes me stand on the pedals and sprint. Aaron is at the foot of our driveway. A green Charger is parked across the mouth of the graveled way, and Aaron is in conversation with two people, who I recognize at once as officers of the State Patrol. One is a Smokey in uniform, the other a plainclothes officer in a blue blazer. The state troopers are referred to as Smokeys, even by themselves, because of their broad flat-brimmed grey felt campaign hats, very much like the ones also worn by US Park Rangers, including, most famously, the cartoon character I was inexplicably smitten with as a child, Smokey the Bear. As I get closer, I can see that the Smokey has a notebook in her hand, meaning the plainclothes officer is taking the lead.

"Whoa, whoa, whoa," I say as I skid in sideways, clenching my handbrakes.

Aaron and Brice clearly finished early today, meaning they'd completed painting on the current house and will set up elsewhere tomorrow. His mountain bike rests on its kickstand. He's in the shorts and

T-shirt I presume he was wearing under his coveralls. His hands are spattered with white and robin's-egg paint and there is what appears to be a shoebox under his arm.

"What is this?" I ask.

"Who are you?" the plainclothes agent asks me at once. The trooper, in her grey blouse and charcoal trousers, has a nameplate over her right pocket—'A. Martinez'—but the 'special agent,' as the State Patrol detectives are called, wears nothing to identify herself. She's dressed like Hardy was on Sunday, her blue blazer over an open-collar starched white shirt, along with carefully pressed grey slacks. A couple years ago, in a rebranding effort reminiscent of a fast-food chain trying to convince everybody to eat the same old hamburger, the state police were redubbed the State Patrol. This move, in the wake of George Floyd's murder, was clearly intended to send the message that they are a more professional outfit than, say, the worst big-city police departments. I will grant them that, too. In my experience, the state cops, by whatever name, display polish and discipline and good training.

In line with that, the plainclothes officer's appearance is almost frighteningly precise. Despite her grimly determined expression, she's very pretty, with a small straight nose, even features and wide eyes, but there are no pheromones emitted. Her vibe is all business, even aggressively so. She has a short bob that's been sprayed unyieldingly into place and a smartly shined pair of black kitten heels.

"I was about to ask you the same thing," I answer. "But I'll go first. My name is Rusty Sabich. I'm a few months away from becoming Aaron's stepfather. His mother and he live with me here. This is my house and you're blocking my driveway. May I see your credentials now?"

She measures me coolly, then reaches to her inside pocket. This is Lieutenant Vanda Glowoski. Lieutenants do not ordinarily conduct on-street interviews.

"Well, Lieutenant Glowoski and Trooper Martinez, Aaron's lawyer has told the PA's office that Aaron does not want to be interviewed concerning Mae Potter, unless you have a non-use letter for him. So if you don't, and you're trying to speak with him, I'm afraid this conversation is over."

"Are *you* his lawyer?" the lieutenant asks me.

"I *am* a lawyer," I answer.

"Well, he can decide for himself then, can't he, Aaron here?"

I could debate, but to shortcut matters, I turn to Aaron and say, "Aaron, do you want to talk to these officers without a non-use letter or your lawyer present?"

"Nope," he answers.

"You're just making yourself look guilty," Glowoski says.

I could say, 'Of what?' but there's a larger point.

"Lieutenant, I think you know better than to try to continue an interrogation when an interview subject says he's following his lawyer's advice and declining to speak. And I suspect you already knew what Aaron's lawyer had said while you were hiding wherever you were, waiting for Aaron."

"No lawyer called our office," she says.

"Lieutenant, this is how police agencies get themselves in big trouble. By trying to be cute with the rules. If anything came of this, then your cellphone records and your text messages would be subpoenaed, and we'd find out what you knew and what you didn't. I was a prosecutor for years, and I'd be very very surprised if you came out here without talking to the PA's office first. Did you?"

Glowoski's eyes are sharp as darts. She doesn't answer.

"Okay, Lieutenant," I say, "you're blocking my way into my home. If I have to ask you to move your vehicle again, it's going to be with my cellphone out while I record myself doing that."

The other officer, the Smokey, Martinez, huffs in disbelief at what a jerk I am but follows when Glowoski slowly returns to the Charger. From behind the wheel, she lowers her window and leans out to address us again.

"I don't understand what he's hiding," she says.

"And I don't understand what's so hard about providing a non-use letter, but you and I are just not going to understand each other. I'm sure Sabonjian will be talking to the PA's office on Monday morning."

Glowoski takes off with a rocket start, exploding dust and gravel. Aaron and I then walk our bikes up the drive side by side. I meant what I said to her—I don't comprehend their reluctance to give Aaron the non-use letter so he can answer all their questions. One reason to hesitate would be what Mansy said, the fear that Aaron will confess to something horrible whose prosecution could be complicated by the letter. Whenever I've turned that possibility over in my mind, I have felt a little wrinkle of apprehension that the authorities actually have a solid reason for that concern.

"Have you heard anything about them talking to other people?" I ask.

"Hell, yeah," says Aaron. "They sort of jumped Cassity at home a few days ago."

"They did? How did you find out about that?"

"She called me when she saw the police car pull up outside. I told her to talk to them. I wish Cap would let me do it, too."

Overall, the State Patrol and the PA's office have been doing a clever job of steadily increasing the pressure on Aaron, hoping that he capitulates to an interview, no holds barred. As Mansy foretold, Hardy has skillfully chummed the waters with the media. On Thursday and Friday, Mae's picture was everywhere—TV news, websites, even the front page of the crummy advertiser given away at the grocery store. The prosecutors made sure that the reports said consistently that Mae was last seen in the company of her friend Aaron Housley. Last night Aaron was supposed to attend a party with Brice but chose to stay home. I know people are asking him questions wherever he goes, because the same thing is happening to Bea, both at school and around town. She has a rote answer, that we're all hoping and praying Mae reappears soon. But the response Aaron's been advised to give—'I'm not supposed to talk about this'—is bound to sound suspicious, especially when he's talking to friends he's known his entire life.

Thursday night, Bea's cell rang and before she answered she looked at the caller ID and told me it was Lloyd. Aaron's dad is a quiet-spoken guy and hard to rile, but I could hear him screaming on the phone across the room. Bea let him go on a few minutes and then hung up without a word in response. Afterwards she said he'd used that term again, 'stonewalling,' and said that Aaron was making it so Lloyd was starting to feel shunned by customers and at church. Things between Aaron and his dad had gotten a little frosty before all this began, because after his release from jail, Aaron refused to resume his practice of attending church with Lloyd and Camille, as he had done every Sunday since his childhood, when he was in Mirror. They'd go to Pastor Proctor's 10 a.m. service and then have a large meal at home, as people often do around here, referred to as 'Sunday supper.' After that Aaron played with his three younger stepsisters. These days Aaron's church attendance is limited to occasions when Joe is willing to drive him into Kweagon to hear Reverend Spruce preach.

In response to the increasing fuss about Mae, Aaron has been spending more time alone drawing, sitting out by the dock with Cray-Pas or in his room doing pen and ink. I saw a portrait of Mae, seemingly rendered from memory, when he left open the 18-by-24-inch spiral-topped artist's pad he's been toting about.

Since his social life is on hold, Aaron agrees to join us at dinner tonight. With the hours after sundown getting noticeably cooler and starting to color the leaves, the water temperature of Mirror Lake is falling, meaning the walleye fishing has improved. Bea, who's very skillful with a spinning rod, landed a four-pounder from the canoe late this afternoon on a glidebait. She was a beauty, with those goggle eyes that looked like they'd been glued to the side of her head. As is true with most fish species, the bigger walleyes are females and, in Bea's opinion, better eating. We all heap praise on the fish who gave her life for our meal.

We're joking agreeably, when Aaron interrupts abruptly by saying, "What if I go out looking for Mae?" By now, even Aaron seems to be checking his phone periodically, in hopes that Mae's reappeared or at least made her whereabouts known.

Bea gives me another of her help-me looks and so I respond first.

"Aaron, the State Patrol and the FBI are looking for her all over three states. What could you add?"

"I know, but people are always like, 'Aren't you worried about her?' I feel like I have to do something."

"Because people expect you to?" asks Bea.

"Sort of. I mean, mostly because maybe she'll hear that I've kind of joined the posse and that might make her show herself."

"Aaron," I say. "Are you starting to worry that Mae isn't okay?"

He responds with an elaborate shrug in which even his hands leave the table.

"Kind of," he says. "I mean, it's a lot by now, right? I think all kinds of shit." He casts a quick look at his mom, who is frowning. Bea still prefers that the dinner table be a haven for polite language. "Sometimes I think maybe she's checked into like an ashram. There's actually one in upper Michigan I heard her talk about. But still, basically Mae is pretty much main character. So she's probably enjoying all the attention and sticking it to me." Recently, Aaron seems convinced that Mae has bought a Tracfone and a phone card and is enjoying the details of the search for her from afar.

"But yeah okay, I worry now and then, you know, that something bad happened to her. She was pretty out of her mind when I left. But Hardy wants to make it like she's this snowflake trapped in the wilderness, and that is just so much bull. The dude who thought he could jump Mae would be the one tapping out. Truly, you don't want to mix it up with that woman." During her time in New York, Mae got involved in MMA training, principally as a workout. After her return, she opened a studio in Como Stop, pitching it as a facility to train other women in self-defense skills, but Hardy ended his financial support for the venture because of the drop-off in revenue over the winter months. "But I still feel like I should be doing something to track her down, just so she's not the one calling all the shots."

"The police will tell you immediately, Aaron, that if you want to help, the first thing to do is sit down for an interview, without a letter. And I'm more and more convinced that's a bad idea. I don't think there's anybody in the PA's office who means you well."

First thing Monday, I call Cap Sabonjian to report Glowoski's visit on Saturday.

"What the hell is going on over in the PA's office?" I ask.

"Funny you should ask," says Cap. "I had a long heart-to-heart with Gert on Friday." Gert, Aaron's probation officer, worked with Cap when he was SD—the State Defender—and she is married to another Armenian, a cousin of Cap's. "She didn't talk out of school, but I could read between the lines. I think there's a lot of push and pull over in the PA's office and that they're kind of running around bumping into each other. Gert made me think that you're right that Hardy is not keeping his distance from the matter. He didn't like the time-served deal we made for Aaron eighteen months ago, thought there should have been some pen time added, and he's riding herd on Helen"—Helen Langerschutz is the chief deputy PA who is supposedly in charge of Aaron's case—"and kind of blaming her for all of this. They were fit to be tied when Aaron's drop came back clean. They actually sent it out for a second analysis."

"Gert told you this?"

"Not that I'm supposed to repeat it. The bottom line is that Hardy thinks Aaron is a wrong kid and wants him off the street one way or the other. And he's afraid a non-use letter is a trick that will get in their way." I'd largely figured this. Occam's razor. That's the simplest explanation for why they've resisted the letter.

"I was thinking about this whole thing last night," Cap says. "My gut feeling, Rusty, is that Mae will turn up this week. Don't ask me why. If she's making a point, she's been gone long enough to do that. Otherwise, she's decided to disappear and might be out of pocket for quite some time."

That possibility, which appears increasingly realistic as the State Patrol turns up no trace of her, would be bad for everyone—the Potters to start, but also Aaron and Bea. A dark cloud could hang over all of them for as long as Mae is unaccounted for. Aaron would probably decide to leave Skageon when his probation is over six months from now.

On Tuesday and Wednesday, I am in Minneapolis, arbitrating a business dispute between siblings. The older brother, who was president of the company that had been left in trust for the entire family, basically looted the enterprise for years. He is such a greedy unapologetic jerk that by the last day of the proceedings I think I'm going to spring out of my chair at the conference table to choke him. Predictably, he shakes his head vehemently throughout my ruling, which on every significant point goes entirely against him.

I drive back on Thursday and arrive in the late afternoon. I've just taken a stew of root vegetables out of the freezer for dinner, when Cap's name appears again on my cell.

"I'm not trying to have you do my heavy lifting," he says, "but it would be better to talk to you first. Kerwin Silko just called me. Do you know Kerwin?"

"The reporter? He was working for AP last I heard."

"Still is. He was trying to confirm a tip about Mae Potter."

"They found her?" I feel ready to sing. Until Cap takes an audible breath.

"Well, if Ker's source is right, they just discovered her remains up in Marenago County at Ginawaban."

"Oh my God," I say. I crash under a waterfall of fear and sadness.

"Her Subaru was in the brush at the base of a utility road. There were a lot of drugs on her. The deputies think she was stoned and took a wrong turn. First impression is that she's been dead a couple of weeks. Kerwin was racing around to confirm this, but odds are it will be on the news tonight."

"I'm so sorry," I say before I hang up.

Bea is not home yet, and I sit in the living room, trying to compose the words I'll use to tell first her and then, far worse, Aaron. But beyond them, my mind goes to Mansy. This will kill him. This will be the third strike that will turn out the lights in a long, good life. I don't know if he'll ever forgive me for telling him Mae may have been acting out. I think of Charmaine, dealing with so much already. I feel even for Hardy.

I say a word of prayer for Mae, as good as an agnostic can offer, and then go to make myself a drink to await whoever comes first through the door. Yet as I sit there, I begin to unpack the colliding feelings I had at first, focusing finally on an icicle of fear that ran me through once I registered where Cap said Mae's body had been found. Ginawaban is the largest wilderness area in the state. Joe often took Aaron there when he was young, and it became Aaron's favorite refuge during his last high school years whenever he wanted to be alone, as he frequently did. I have heard him say a couple of times now that he plans to head straight there the day his probation ends.

13

Again: Gone

September 28–29

E ventually, I call Bea. At this hour in the late afternoon, she is usually in her office, responding to phone calls and emails. She does
not pick up, so I send a text saying she needs to come home right now.
I want her to be the one to tell Aaron. I think that's what we would
both prefer. Every fifteen minutes or so, I check the Patch, a site which
is the best local news source for the Skageon Region, but the story has
still not broken when Bea enters from the garage. She stands a foot
inside the threshold in her fawn-colored puffer vest and looks at me
and says, "What?"

She receives the news in silence at the breakfast bar, then turns to
stare out the window over the sink. I can see her tongue feeling around
inside her mouth, as if her lips have gone numb, which is possible.

"What can we possibly say to Charmaine and Hardy?" she finally
asks. Yet with a few more remarks, I can tell that she has realized
what I have, that, whether or not it makes complete sense, Aaron
is going to bear some of the blame for Mae's death because he left
her far from home, upset and addled by drugs, with no means of
communication.

Aaron told us this morning that after today, Brice will be caught up on his painting jobs and that this will be their last day toiling together. He expected to work until sundown at about six fifteen to be sure they finish a house in nearby Eastlake. Just as Brice's car crawls up the drive in the sinking light to drop Aaron, I get a breaking news notice from the Patch, but I wait to read it until we have shared what's happened with Aaron.

There is an element of comedy to his appearance as he comes in from the garage. At his mother's request, Aaron has changed every night before entering the house, putting on a variety of old clothes she leaves out there for him. Tonight he's in a pair of Bea's old sweats that don't even reach the top of his socks as he stands there shoeless. His face and hands and upper chest look like the paint-spatter works by Jackson Pollock. But when he catches sight of our expressions his face drops and he says the same thing as Bea: "What?"

I'm not sure Aaron, at the age of twenty-two, has lost anybody central to his life since Willi passed when he was three. As Bea speaks to him, saying again and again, "I'm so sorry, Aaron," his eyes circle around and his speech seems to falter, but what I see most on his face is all the confused tenderness of what sometimes transpired between Mae and him, which has been all but lost in the last couple of weeks.

When he finally speaks, it is a total non sequitur.

"How could they just find her?" he asks.

I have no idea what he means. How could she be found so suddenly after weeks of searching? But I suspect that Aaron cannot help arguing with the facts, insisting that this makes no sense and thus must be a mistake and, in the end, untrue.

We have been at the dining table and I repeat what I was told and then think to examine the story in the Patch, which has picked up Kerwin Silko's piece for the AP. The three of us huddle together as I hold my phone at arm's length so that we can all read. A hiker saw a taillight glinting and informed a county sheriff's deputy on patrol, who hiked down the steep road. The piece does not mention the drugs they found on Mae, but does say she was apparently under the influence and took a wrong turn on the road approaching the one parking area in Ginawaban. The body is scheduled to be removed by

EMTs and will be sent to the police pathologist in Kindle County, who is more experienced in examining remains in a state of advanced decomposition.

The rest of the piece recaps the search for Mae and says she has not been seen in two weeks, since she parted with a former boyfriend after a quarrel. For the first time, Aaron's name is unmentioned.

He takes the phone from me and slowly reads the item again by himself, then stands. He looks back and forth between Bea and me.

"What do I do?" he asks. I don't know if he's asking about the gestures of condolence or whether he can safely speak to the police now, to which the answer, by the way, is no. Hardy will only be more vengeful.

"Wait," says Bea. "We all need to gather ourselves a little."

But he isn't listening. His eyes have abruptly gone vacant, much as his mother's did, and his breathing seems to have quickened. It's coming home, the truth of it.

"She's dead," he says. He grabs his forehead and turns quickly to go to his room, but he is soon howling behind his door.

Bea and I both drink more than normal, wine for her and whiskey for me. Around eight, I remember the stew I defrosted, but neither of us cares to eat. She warms some for Aaron, but when Bea knocks on Aaron's door with a plate, he does not answer. We clean up briefly and then do what we were doing before, sitting together in silence. Now and then my mind goes to Mansy, but I suspect right now I may be the last person he wants to see.

We sleep fitfully. After an hour of trying unsuccessfully to fall off, Bea gets up to take a pill, and she is out solidly when I hear Aaron rooting around about four a.m. I sit up in bed, expecting to see, through the mullions, the familiar sight of him smoking on the dock, but he's not there. Then I hear the garage door and the cough of a car starting.

By the time I get outside, I can see only the taillights of Bea's 4x4 most of the way down the drive. I go back in and grab my cellphone from the night table, but there is no answer from Aaron, not even a pickup for voicemail. I try to stifle my groan. He's done it again, gone dark. This young man doesn't need Hardy or anyone else to make trouble for him, because he does such a great job of it himself.

I am never going back to sleep, but I decide not to rouse Bea, in the hope that Aaron just needed to sit out on some remote ledge and watch the sunrise and will return when he's cleared his head. But that doesn't happen.

About five forty-five, Bea comes into the kitchen, heading straight to the coffee pot. At this moment, when the emotional pathways seem jumbled, my feelings don't run down the channels of the expected, and I am startled by a sudden stroke of desire as I view her, fetching in her sleepwear, short shorts and a T-shirt. It takes her a second to notice me. She crawls out of bed every morning at 5:30 and tries not to wake me until she leaves.

"What?" she asks yet again.

After I tell her of Aaron's departure, she can't keep herself from going to the garage to see for herself.

"What is *wrong* with him? What is *wrong*?" she asks when she returns. "Why does he do things like this? Mae is dead and he blames himself and so he is deliberately placing himself in harm's way. I'm sure he'll drive a hundred miles an hour until the police stop him."

She is again at that peak of frustration, unable to quell her love and unable to save Aaron from himself. This is the point when a lot of parents let go. But that will never be Bea. At this moment, it is hard not to see her life as one where she will always be buffeted by desperate love and tireless regrets. I wonder suddenly what that means for me.

"Maybe he just needs some time to think, Bea. Remember. He's spent the last couple of weeks hating her. Maybe he wants an hour or two to remember he loved her."

"He could sit out on our dock and do that."

I let Bea take my car to school. By seven thirty, my cellphone on the kitchen table seems to be a live animal, buzzing and jumping around with the inflow of texts and calls. I can only imagine what is going on with Bea. I decide to answer no one. The Patch item has been updated somewhat, saying that the State Patrol are heading the investigation and noting that the family is expecting to have a private burial as soon as the body is released. The piece is accompanied now by the same high school graduation picture of Mae that I've seen dozens of times in the last ten days, a gorgeous young woman smiling with the confidence of a queen.

About nine a.m., I call Mansy. He doesn't answer, but I leave a voicemail, one of dozens he's probably received already. "I cannot tell you how sorry I am. So so sorry." The rest of it, the mea culpas, will have to come in person when he is more willing to hear me than he is likely to be today. I still have not fully recovered from the brutal edge he showed in our last encounter, even though better sense had long told me it was there. You don't succeed in politics, even in local races in a rural county, without knowing how to throw an elbow when need be.

I leave the same message for Charmaine and, after a second's hesitation, for Hardy. I'm afraid that out of sheer orneriness he is going to pick up, so he can say, 'I told you so, I told you she was in trouble, I told you she was in danger,' and of course, 'I told you he never should have left her alone.'

But he doesn't, and I speak the same message of condolence that I've left for his father and his wife, sounding perhaps too practiced, which by now I am.

Around noon, I get a call from Joe. It's the third or fourth time he's tried to reach me, and I decide I am finally ready to deal with whatever unexpected and inappropriate response he's likely to deliver.

"Bea around?" he asks. That means she hasn't picked up at school, which is routine when he phones her there. I explain that she is at work, and he says, "When she gets home, you two might want to come over here and pick up her car."

Bea returns at four, not long after the class bell, which means she is escaping.

"Half the people over there are giving me the death stare. It's like I killed Mae. And nobody did that. Except Mae. She might have crashed herself deliberately. But people are still looking for someone to blame. A couple of parents came in to talk about their kids, and I knew damn well they were just gawking, like the people who rush out to see a fire burning down their neighbors' house."

I finally tell her about Joe.

"Oh Jesus," she says. That's beyond her limit, to have to deal with her father too. "So Aaron went over there and took off in Joe's truck?"

"That's what I'm guessing. I imagine Aaron asked his permission."

She hasn't drawn the obvious inference yet, that borrowing Joe's pickup means Aaron won't be returning soon. He knew his mom and I could spare our cars less easily than Joe, who always keeps some old jalopy in the barn that he tools around in when the truck is covered with the dirt of farming or in the shop with its frequent alternator issues.

It's about twenty minutes to Joe's hundred-acre piece on County Y. He's got about six outbuildings on the property, all steel prefabs, and a stand of pine trees that never got planted, just sort of blew over here about fifty years ago when everyone thought they could make a bundle growing Christmas trees. His tractor is parked in back of the house, much as the occupant of this house a century ago might have tied up his horse.

At the north end of the property, a good mile and a half away, is the Little House. To start, it was a kind of lean-to, where the farmer or his livestock could take shelter in storms. Making up for yet another outrage, Joe decided to add walls and plumbing and a Franklin stove so Willi could play the piano out there at all hours. But by Bea's accounts, the peace the gesture was meant to buy did not last long, and the Little House was soon the place where Joe slept in the wake of one of his and Willi's epic brawls. She always took the worst of it, but not before delivering a few blows from which the satisfaction seemed to outweigh the bruising that came next. When Bea and Aaron moved into the Little House as a temporary refuge after she left Lloyd, Joe put up some drywall to split the single bedroom into two small ones for each of them.

Bea knocks on the door of her parents' home but doesn't go in after Joe answers. She seldom enters the house since her mother died, a little like Persephone in Hades, refusing hospitality. Bea's grievance with her father is akin to a spring with an underground source; it will never run dry. I would have thought that past fifty she would have just exhausted herself with the sheer intensity of the emotions, but I'm wrong. She will never forget, never forgive. Then again, I never forgave my father either, who could have taught even Joe a thing or two about cruelty.

Bea is standing beside her Jeep, while she talks to her father.

"Did you actually give him your truck?" she asks.

"Said he needed to get away."

Bea lights into Joe with that unique fury. In moments like this, I understand why she treasures the steady flow of positive feeling between us. I'm not sure she realized how much she had always craved that until she finally found it. Lloyd is a good man, but not capable of exhibiting his emotions or, frankly, even understanding them. And he was a better choice than what followed him. From the vague descriptions I've received, most of her boyfriends after her marriage were like Hardy—temperamental jerks who were quick to wound her. For Bea, like me, we are a triumph, proof that if you live long enough you can figure out how to do better.

"Jesus," she says. "Jesus, what is wrong with you? Hardy's been doing everything he can to make trouble for Aaron, and you give Aaron a truck so he can speed around with a suspended driver's license?"

"Boy looked like he needed some time. Asked to borrow a sleeping bag and some gear."

"Sleeping bag?" she says. "He has his own sleeping bag." I still haven't shared all the details about that fire, feeling that was Aaron's business to tell, not mine.

Joe shrugs. Shrunken by age, he can't be more than five two now, and stands there with his metal cane in a pair of bib overalls. The hair he lost during chemo, which was thick and intensely black even as he approached eighty, always probably his most attractive feature, came back grey and patchy. He still mourns aloud the loss of that head of hair occasionally.

"Well, now we have to try to find him before the police do."

"Oh bullshit, Beatrix. You tell me why the police are going to bother with a young man sitting on a rock on Tornado Ridge and keeping company with his own thoughts."

For Joe, of course, who lost his license frequently during his drinking years, suspended driving privileges are nothing more than a warning to stay away from spots where the police are likely to be.

"Is that where he was going?" I ask. "Tornado Ridge?"

"Didn't ask and wouldn't want to know. Wasn't my business. And I doubt he had much idea when he left here. Just needed to be with himself. Without his mother or the Potters breathin down his neck."

"Damn you, Dad," she says. "You never really get what's going on. This is a tragedy. A tragedy. And we need to try to keep it from engulfing Aaron too."

"How's it a tragedy?" Joe asks. "He couldn't break with that girl. And she was nothing but bad for him. Don't tell me you didn't feel that way, because I know you do."

"That doesn't mean I need to revel in her death. When you've taught as long as I have, you know there's no way to tell how a kid will turn out."

"Age six or ten? Maybe. When they're twenty-two? Bad is bad by then."

"Fritz was worthless until he went into the army. You know that. And look at him now." She's referring to her brother. Fritz entered the army back in the day when judges gave young men that alternative to a conviction for lesser crimes. Fritz had vandalized the house of a boss he hated. But he loved the military, the more so because of how much his father detested it. At the end of his hitch, he chose a reserve deployment, used the GI Bill to pay for college, and returned to active duty for Officer Candidate School. Now a full-bird colonel, Fritz commands US forces on several bases in South America and expects to get his star before retirement.

When it comes to his father, though, Fritz is remorseless. They have not spoken in forty years, even though Fritz phones or emails Bea at least once a week. Fritz has vowed to return to Skageon County only when he can see his father in a coffin.

"Fritz? That's your idea of turning out good?" Joe asks.

"I'm making a point, Dad, about how young people grow up."

"And so am I. I ain't pretendin to be all kinds of broken up cause that girl killed herself one way or the other. She'da caused trouble the rest of her life. Some fella would be unlucky enough to marry her and drink her poison. Maybe she'd have popped out a kid or two and delivered the world a couple more humans broken for life. I'm sorry and all for the Potters, at least as sorry as I can get when that crew is involved. But no matter how coldhearted it sounds, this may be the best that's ever happened to Aaron."

"I hope you didn't say that to Aaron."

"Neh, but he wasn't very happy with what I did say. I told him, 'You don't want to hear this right now, but I'm going to tell you the rock-hard truth. You'll forget about this girl. That's how it goes. The living care only about the living. It's the nature of things. And the ones who're dead, they're dead. Dead yesterday is pretty much the same as them who died with the dinosaurs. You'll find out. And you'll just stop thinkin about them.'"

"Jesus, Dad, what a shitty thing to say to him."

"Well, it's true, Bea. When Wilhelmina died, I could barely breathe, but now days pass before she even crosses my mind."

Given the inflamed state she's always in with her father, adding this about her mother, on top of the news about Aaron, so enrages Bea that for a second she can't move. She's stock-still, with her eyes wrenched shut. For Bea, Willi is ever-present, the source of everything Bea counts as worthy in herself. Finally, Bea emits a huff of exasperated sound and shakes herself like a dog coming out of the rain. She gets into her car without another word to her father or me and speeds off. We both watch her go.

"Was that the end of it between you and Aaron, Joe?"

"Pretty much. He put me in my place a little. You know how he does. Gets you in just a few words. After I said all that about the dead being gone, he says, 'Well, I'm not going to stop thinking about her, Joe. And I won't stop thinking about you either when you're not here.' Damn near started cryin."

We part company there and I point my own car toward home, a minute or so behind Bea. That anybody in Joe's life could bring him close to tears remains a shock to Bea. As she tells the tale, she was not speaking to her father when they brought Aaron home, because Joe had told her, with some ugly words, that she was courting a world of trouble by adopting a Black child. But the first time she put the baby in Joe's arms, he did not want to lay the boy down.

Willi was killed in a freak accident, when a huge branch severed
from a tree and crashed onto her car. It was from a lone white oak,
majestic and probably three hundred years old, that overhangs the
driveway and gives the place a postcard look as you approach. A bough
was severed by the cyclone-force winds of a blizzard that was on the
way in. Willi had been racing along the interior road to herd the cows
they kept then back to the barn.

One of the reasons Bea had moved into the Little House was
because Willi was already looking after Aaron while Bea was teaching. The horrible blow of Willi's death was deepened for Bea by the
practical burden of quickly finding daycare for Aaron, not easy in the
Skageon Valley. Instead, Joe volunteered to look after the boy. For
the next couple of years, until Aaron started kindergarten, Aaron was
with Joe during the day, whatever he was doing—strapped beside him
on the tractor, handing over tools when Joe fixed the farm machinery,
riding out to survey the four fields, learning which cows were ornery
and the ones whose noses he could pet while the milker was attached.
Aaron was virtually inconsolable once he was told, on the eve of starting school, that he would no longer be spending the days with his
grandfather, and so Joe became the one, even after Bea and Aaron
moved to her own apartment, to take the boy back and forth every
school day. Often, Bea returned home to find Aaron on a kitchen
stool, eating a snack and listening attentively while Joe delivered one
of his interminable lectures, much of it utter nonsense.

How does a man who decades before had transformed his marriage
into a periodic cage match and left his children quailing at dinnertime
each day from the violence he might do when he came through the
door—how does such a man, past sixty years of age, find himself smitten with an infant and forever attached to him? It is a mystery, but one
to me that has always held some of the wonder of life. One answer is
that when Aaron was born, Joe's drinking had slowed somewhat. In
time, he was also known to mutter, when he held Aaron, about 'us
dark men,' a remark that drove Bea up the wall. Joe, in fact, was of the
melting pot generation, and never spoke a word of Spanish, nor would
he acknowledge his Native ancestry—until the Ho-Chunk started
handing out money.

On the one occasion that Bea has asked me if I have any explanation for Joe's transformation with Aaron, I shared an idea that had
grown obvious to me—that Joe had been laboring all his life with love
stillborn inside him, emotions whose expression was inhibited by fear.
A child, innocent born, had delivered none of the rebuffs that had
quickly hardened him against other people.

The suggestion left Bea intensely agitated with me. It took me a
long time to understand why. The day Aaron graduated high school,
she had watched Joe and Aaron together and suddenly dissolved
into tears. Joe had just made a gift to his grandson of the old auto,
the 'barn car' he kept before the current Escort, the 2002 Saturn in
which Aaron later was arrested and which now sits on blocks in one
of Joe's outbuildings until Aaron regains his license. Aaron was close
to delirious when Joe handed over the keys. His father's son, Aaron is
rarely demonstrative, and it caught all of us by surprise when he not
only hugged his grandfather but literally lifted him off the floor. Joe's
laughter in response had the freedom of a cascading brook.

And Bea cried. As we walked back to her car, she was still trying to
recover, a knot of Kleenex crushed to the middle of her face.

'I just don't understand,' she said finally, confessing what I'd
slowly come to suspect. 'I just don't understand why he could never
spare just an ounce of that for me.'

14

Search

I thought Bea was merely being emphatic, as she often is with Joe, when she said we have to find Aaron before the police do, but when I get home, she is already preparing to set out. I quietly remind her that our state, running from the environs of Kindle County in the south to the north woods, is close to 80,000 square miles, not to mention the nearby parts of Wisconsin, but she says she simply cannot stay home waiting for bad news.

She adds, "I don't expect you to come along."

"I'll come," I say after a second. The omen of Mae's death, of danger striking unexpectedly in the same territories Bea will be exploring, is too clear to let her go on her own. More to the point, after a moment's thought, I realize that this is a great time to get out of Skageon County. With the start of October this weekend, the traditional fall market will open in Como, the last occasion when many of the summer residents will be lured back. Everybody strolls around with a cup of hot cider, buying bags of apples and stylish local crafts. We would run into lots of friends, and the conversations inevitably would turn to Mae and the Potters and, eventually, Aaron.

Additionally, since Sunday will be October 1, Bea would ordinarily make her quarterly trip to Reverend Proctor's megachurch, which she regards as more or less an obligation of her job. He would mourn Mae from the pulpit and afterwards many worshippers would ask Bea about her son, whom they've known for decades. If he has not returned, those questions would be difficult to answer.

On the other hand, it's far from obvious where we should search. For Aaron, being alone with his thoughts inevitably means outside. Beyond that, who knows? Ginawaban is Aaron's favorite outdoor destination, but since Mae's body was found there, it's likely that police officers will still be examining the crash site, making it the wrong place to show up for a young man violating his probation—assuming Aaron is thinking at all. Lacking any other information, we decide to try the spot Joe spoke of, Tornado Ridge, at the far northeast corner of the state, on the assumption that Joe didn't mention it simply as an off-the-cuff example. Tornado, the state's highest point, is where Aaron once spent six weeks in a nature camp he loved. Given the vistas there, it would be a fine place for solitary contemplation. We throw cosmetics and a change of clothes in a duffel and head north in my Tundra.

Considering the hour, I want to get as far as we can before darkness makes the unknown country roads, with their occasional hairpin turns, more treacherous. But as always seems to happen on County JJ, we get stuck behind a car that would be called an antique in the city, a 1996 Cutlass Supreme. At this hour, there is just enough oncoming traffic, racing through the hilly terrain toward home on Friday night, that it's hard to pass. The Cutlass has rust holes in its fenders that look like they have been chewed by some metal-eating moth, and the taillights on both sides are held on with duct tape. Worse, the engine doesn't seem to have been rebuilt, and the vehicle tops out at forty on a road where everybody else is doing sixty-five. But it's not uncommon out here to see a car that might have been junked long ago in Kindle County still on the road. Farmers are by nature frugal, and many people in the Valley are challenged to make ends meet. When I'm sitting at the VFW with Joe, a lot of the guys on the barstools beside us follow the same routine he did years ago, working full-time jobs in the warehouses and tending their small farms in hours stolen just after sunrise or before sunset.

Once I finally get past the Cutlass, which proves to be driven by an old gent whose nose is just about touching the steering wheel, we make good time for an hour, before full darkness settles in. The shock of the last twenty-four hours has left both of us weary, and Bea starts looking on her phone for a place to stop. The most appealing alternative is a country B&B about fifteen miles ahead, where the male couple who run it are also said to be outstanding cooks. Bea finds they have a room left, which is our luck. Next weekend, when the fall colors start to peak, there's a waiting list.

Upon arrival, the proprietors, Dack and Gary, have put food aside for us, since their dinner service has been over for some time. We eat alone in the Victorian kitchen, all the pine woodwork, floors and cabinetry, restored to the original orangish shade. With the excellent hunter's stew, our hosts have provided a complimentary bottle of Pinot Noir that Bea and I drink freely.

Back in our quaint little room with a brass four-poster and tons of antique tchotchkes, Bea comes to me immediately, full of creature need. I don't know if she's propelled by too much wine, or gratitude that I have come with her on this quest, or is simply retreating to the place of refuge in herself that physical pleasure often provides, but I find that the lust that visited me at 5:30 a.m. is easily reignited. Our lovemaking is more prolonged and passionate than it has been in a while, a welcome reminder of our bond amid the current turmoil.

I was very pleased to learn at the start of our relationship that Bea exults in sex, something I never found especially easy to predict about the women I dated. The physical heat, which I was overjoyed to experience again as seventy approached, has eased of course, but never disappeared. We were not far along in our relationship before it dawned on me that someone who relishes the physical act in the unbounded way Bea does hadn't lived the life of a nun for the two decades before we met. But overall we seem to share a compact that the past is just that: past, gone and for the most part forgotten, not worth discussion except for the marks it may have left on the present. She told me about two men, including the state superintendent of education,

who still had a minor role in her professional life. And probably as a
test of sorts for me, she shared the fact that about ten years ago, she'd
been involved with a woman. It was a worthwhile experience, she said,
because it demonstrated to her that a completely fulfilling relationship
could never be a matter of will alone. For my part, before we became
too deeply embroiled, I felt obligated to confess that my married years
had included two entirely consuming affairs. I expected that news to
excite some concern, but instead she shrugged and said, 'Yeah, I've
been the other woman.' At this stage, we've both lived awhile, with
the primary meaning of what's gone before being that it brought us to
one another.

   We are up early. Our hosts set the coffee pot for 6:00 a.m. and left
a plate of homemade scones beside it, and we are on the road by seven.
Bea plays her jazz, and we proceed otherwise unspeaking, buoyed by
the sense of union lingering from last night.

   After driving another hundred miles north, we find the fall leaves
here, three hours from home, are at their most vibrant in the heavy woods
that side the road. It is an utterly clear autumn day, where the trees stand
out like movie figures against a green screen. Bea turns off the music and
we drive with little conversation, nudging each other periodically when
we see a stretch of trees that looks like it was painted by a designer. My life
in Skageon is simpler. Work no longer possesses me like a curse, and perhaps as a result, the pleasures I take feel deeper. Away from the city, you
face nature more directly, and necessarily with more respect.

   As we cross into northern Marenago County, the swells of land
are steeper. The change in climate and elevation means different vegetation, the deciduous trees, with all their fine color, giving way here
and there to stands of conifers. A century ago, logging was a central
industry here and in the regions to the north in this part of the state.
The buildings visible through the branchless lower trunks are often
log construction, looking like the pioneers are still present.

   Further ahead we reach the southernmost aspect of what geolo-
gists call the Canadian Shield. The hills get high enough to be called
mountains by flatlanders like me and the soil is noticeably orange from
deposits of iron. As we begin the ascent to Tornado Ridge along a
twisting road, the traffic slows as we join a line of vehicles. The name,

Tornado Ridge, is a bit of a misnomer, because twisters seldom strike here. Rather, it's due to the fact that people taking in the magnificent views have from time to time witnessed the lethal storms spinning their sinister way through the valley below. Access to the actual peak is solely by foot, meaning that if Aaron is here, we'd find Joe's F-150 in one of the two parking lots on the east and wide sides of the slope. We don't. We check the nearby nature camp, but it is closed for the season, behind locked gates, then return to the Tornado parking lots in case we missed Aaron somehow. For half an hour, Bea stands at the base of the trails, asking people who've made the descent if they've seen someone like her son. She receives a disdainful look or two when she mentions that he's Black. By 1 p.m., Bea decides we should head home.

"Thank you for doing this," she says, once we're underway. "I know you thought it was ridiculous. I had to try." She is quiet then, trying to envision what will happen next. "He might drive around for a day or two and never get stopped, right?"

"Unless he does something to call attention to himself, Bea, that's what's most likely to occur. He may even be home by the time we get back there." I'm being cheerful for his mother's sake, although I know a young Black man is still more apt to get pulled over.

We agreed to ignore our phones, filled with messages about Mae, when we departed and have both been good to that promise, except for Bea's periodic efforts to reach Aaron. Right now, I don't want to speak to anyone from Skageon. But we're reliving the movie from two weeks ago: If we reach Monday morning with no sign of Aaron, my first call at 8 a.m. will have to be to Gert and Judge Sams.

Bea knows the same thing. It's how it is with Aaron, periods when we seem to be out for a pleasant stroll, then suddenly fall through a booby trap into the pit of doom. I'm tired of it. Granted, Mae's death, particularly when Aaron has some remote responsibility, is a special circumstance, but I'm going to tell him without humor that the next time he disappears, I won't be searching for him with Bea. I'll leave the job to the police.

"I ask what's wrong with him," Bea says suddenly, breaking a long silence in which she clearly was entertaining similar thoughts. "But I know this is all my fault."

"Your fault?" I ask, although I heard similar self-recriminations periodically when Aaron was in jail.

"For being so arrogant or naive to think I could raise a Black child in a place like Skageon County and that he wouldn't be the worse off for it. Let alone as a single mother."

"You were married when Aaron came to you."

"I knew there was a good chance Lloyd and I wouldn't make it. I mean, we'd spent enough time on fertility treatments that I tried to convince myself that when we finally had a child, we'd be fine. But I knew how different we had become. He and his parents were really drinking Ralph Proctor's Kool-Aid, and I didn't think police work agreed with him—he was developing too thick a hide. I remember staring at myself in the mirror more than once after Neba had talked to me about this baby, and asking myself if I was really ready to handle the daily burdens of child-rearing on my own. I knew that might happen."

"Okay," I say. This is a more candid version than I've heard in the past about how Bea ended up alone with Aaron. But she's always been at pains to emphasize that whatever people think, her split with Lloyd did not reflect any reluctance on his part about becoming a parent. He's done well as a divorced dad. When I arrived on the scene, with Aaron a difficult teen, Lloyd still spoke to his son every evening. And from Aaron's infancy, Lloyd and he were together Sundays, starting with church. Lloyd's problem is not so much his bond with Aaron as his wife's. Camille is a petite, pretty, utterly humorless woman, rigid as a ruler. The Reverend Proctor's niece, Camille, fresh from college, had captivated Lloyd within months of his separation from Bea. They were married less than a year later. Camille accepts Aaron as a fact of life, but he holds no place with her remotely like her daughters'. After Aaron's first drug arrest, Camille would not even let him in the house, and the inevitable disruption between Aaron and his dad, who sided with his wife, almost surely played some role in the downward spiral Aaron was soon on.

"But I was just an idiot about race," Bea says. "If we loved this child—and I knew how much we would—what else would he need? No wonder he prefers to be alone. Because that's how I let him grow up, alone, with no one completely like him around."

"What did Neba think about a Black boy growing up in a place like Mirror?" Neba had been raised in Madison, one hundred fifty miles away, where her mom practiced as an ob-gyn and her father was a history professor, so she knew the area.

"I'm sure I talked about it with Neba. But the truth is, how much did either of us know? She's never been white, and I've never been Black."

Neba Malone and Bea were randomly assigned as freshman roommates in the dorm at Wisconsin State, and bonded in a way that's hard to duplicate if you're not in late adolescence and a newly sprung fugitive from your parents' home, on the journey to your essential self. Their friendship remains intense. On the West Coast now, Neba tends to call late, and they talk for hours, more or less costing Bea a night of sleep.

When Bea and Lloyd concluded they were not going to get pregnant naturally, they decided on adoption, rather than undergoing the agonies of in vitro, for which they didn't really have the money anyway. Aware of that decision, Neba called Bea to announce that there was going to be a baby available in her family. Bea was thrilled, but she also sensed a challenge in the offer. Here was your adored Black friend asking if you could find the same love for a Black child of your own. Bea was certain they could—so was Lloyd, who is serious about the equality of all God's children—but under the circumstances she gave little thought to anyone's reactions but their own.

"I was *so* excited that I didn't even read much about transracial adoption until we had him and I confronted the reactions when we were out with him. It wasn't exactly hatred I felt coming off those people who saw Aaron, so much as this ingrained belief that this child just didn't belong here."

As a condition of the adoption, Aaron's birth parents required that Bea and Lloyd know next to nothing about them, except a bare outline of their circumstances Neba was allowed to share. They had separated and filed for divorce, but were driven back together months later, when he was hospitalized for an illness that first appeared fatal. In a series of long, tearful deathbed meetings, their love reignited, and after he made a surprising recovery, they determined to go forward together. Yet there was an issue. She was pregnant as the result of a casual encounter. Her husband regarded it as certain doom to try to start over by raising another man's child. After much anguish, they agreed she would give up the child at birth and have no subsequent contact with the baby.

Looking at Aaron, I've always guessed he has biracial ancestry, but in America it's often hard to tell anymore. When Aaron, a few years ago, defied Bea and Lloyd and paid for one of those genetic testing services, he found potential cousins on each side who identified as white and Black.

"Once I started reading," Bea says, "every book and article said the same thing: Make sure you raise your child around other kids of his race. But how was I going to do that in Mirror, let alone on Joe's farm, once Lloyd and I split?"

Once or twice a month after the separation, Bea would spend the weekend in Milwaukee, where Neba had a tenure-track appointment in the History Department at Marquette. Aaron loved her daughters, but they were too much older to be peers. And then Neba got a job she could not pass up at one of the Claremont Colleges in California. When Aaron was eight, Bea sent him to what he refers to as 'Black camp.' He was homesick throughout and found most of the campers from big cities alien, with more than a few ridiculing him as too white. For better or for worse, he has grown up in Skageon, frequently one of only a handful of Black kids. Leaving aside Clement Morse, the son of a restaurant owner from Como, who moved to Minneapolis when they were in eighth grade, Aaron has not made close African-American friends there. Ironically, the Skageon County jail provided his first experience with a large number of Black men, who more or less welcomed him.

"When he was little, he seemed to be race-blind. I wanted him to recognize that he shared something with Neba's kids, but he didn't seem to. Not when he was three. Joe is so dark anyhow, I'm not sure he even understood what I was talking about. I don't think I heard him use the word 'Black' until he was five. I tried to reinforce that, but it was a struggle. It feels completely wrong to tell a child 'You're not like me in an important way.' I've always wanted to get into my Ho-Chunk ancestry, for instance, but I've hesitated, because that would be another thing that would exclude Aaron. It's all crazy-making. Because I knew that if we'd adopted a white baby, we'd give him an unwavering message that skin color absolutely must not matter in how you relate to other human beings."

Lloyd, by contrast, was never comfortable focusing on race. Yet even he, ardently pro-police, taught his son in Aaron's early teens about the precautions he needed to adopt in any interaction with law enforcement. 'Yes sir.' Hands always in sight.

I'm in no position to tell Bea she is wrong about her son and the impact on him of being a Black kid in a largely white environment. But the source of any human's troubles is rarely singular. Adoption by itself is a crisis for many children. And his parents' divorce was surely traumatic. Yes, Aaron, like any other Black person, has endured frequent episodes of racism, whether it's been something as overt as being the one kid followed by security guards when he was with friends at the mall, or more subtle expressions like the schoolmates who could not contain their amazement when they found out he couldn't sing or didn't care all that much for basketball. But the same forces that drove Aaron into himself might also have spurred his passion to make art. I appreciate that Aaron is saying something important to his parents— and himself—by preferring to speak his piece to God in a Black church thirty-five miles away. But isn't that exactly what Bea has always believed he needs?

"You did your best," I tell her, as we are getting close to home. That is what I told myself regularly during Nat's difficult years. "What else can any parent do, especially someone like you who gave Aaron your full attention every moment you could? He's been loved and knows it. But in this country, is there such a thing as being completely well-adjusted about race?"

We reach Mirror a little before seven. Darkness, earlier each night now, is starting to fall, and so even a few blocks away from the house, I can see the lights through the woods, including the multicolored flashing from several spinning beacons atop the vehicles. At first, I'm sure that Danil Jerlow, our elderly neighbor, has had another health crisis requiring the assistance of paramedics. Yet as soon as I pull into our driveway, I can see several cruisers at the house ahead. With that, I finally notice that a police vehicle again is parked straight across the gravel drive, blocking our way. I pull up a bit and roll down my window to speak to a young deputy who has already raised a hand to stop us. He's wearing body armor and a helmet, SWAT gear, and carries an automatic rifle. It's pointed at the ground, but overall he's a shocking sight at the gateway to our own home.

"You can't go in there," he says.

"Because?"

"Sheriff's business. This isn't a spectator sport."

"I own that house."

He licks his lips. "Well, you still can't go up there."

I decide to be obnoxious.

"Deputy, one of us spent close to twenty years as a judge, and unless I'm wrong it's not you. What kind of country do you think it would be if I had no right to be present while the police run all over my property? Can you please get your commanding officer down here?"

He turns away and, after walking a few steps, speaks into the radio mounted at his shoulder.

"What is this?" Bea whispers. "What's happening?"

I believe I know, but I don't want to tell her until I'm certain. The truth is that I'm quite unstrung. I can feel the physical signs of panic—tingling fingertips, difficulty breathing—and some amazement about how absolutely stone-brained I've been about the other potential meanings of Aaron taking off as soon as he knew Mae's body had been located. Now I'm afraid the police are executing a search warrant on our house.

15

With Warrant

September 30

A uniformed Skageon County sheriff's deputy, a sergeant named Dom Filipini, who shows up at the VFW now and then, strolls slowly down the drive, careful on the gravel footing. He's got a little middle-aged belly, but he's reasonably fit, with a pleasant look. He's hatless, so you can see the full head of dark hair that flows back thickly above his brow, and the badge on his grey uniform catches the light when he passes the squad car across our driveway. His heavy gun belt, with his service weapon, cuffs and flashlight, imparts a slight roll to his gait.

Beside me, Bea whispers his name and says he and Lloyd joined the force at the same time.

"Bea," he says, when he reaches us. "Judge." He nods. He's never called me anything but Rusty before. "I've got the warrant right here. We knocked but there was no one home."

IN THE SUPERIOR COURT,

COUNTY OF SKAGEON

SEARCH WARRANT

No._23CR866_____

To any sheriff, constable, marshal, police officer, or any other peace officer in the County of Skageon:

Proof, by affidavit, having been made this day before me by Lieutenant Vanda Glowoski, a detective employed by the State Patrol, that there is substantial probable cause for the issuance of the search warrant pursuant to Penal Code Section 1524, you are there-fore commanded to make search at any time of the day, good cause being shown therefor, the premises, including all rooms, safes, storage areas, containers, surrounding grounds, trash areas, garages and out-buildings assigned to or part of the residence located at 2474 Lake Road, in township of Mirror, for the fol-lowing property, to wit: all personal effects that may belong to Aaron Russell Housley, including clothing, shoes, outerwear, camping gear, papers, documents, writings, electronic devices including telephone, cell-phone, tablet, computer and all other effects that may bear the fingerprints or DNA of Aaron Russell Housley, and if you find the same, or any part thereof, to bring it forthwith before me at the Superior Court of the County of Skageon, or retain such property in your custody, subject to the order of this Court, pursuant to Penal Code 1536.

Given under my hand this 30th day of September, 2023.

_____

MORTON SAMS, Junior
Judge of the Superior Court of Skageon County

When I'm done, Bea takes the paper from me and reads herself. She doesn't get far.

"A search warrant!" She's not quite yelling. "How do they just get a search warrant?"

I hold up a hand. The less we say the better right now, when we don't know exactly what is going on. But I am certain of one thing. I'd rather not tell the cops that we've spent the last twenty-four hours searching for Aaron.

Bea, however, is not easily contained.

"Dom, does this mean you think Aaron committed a crime?"

"Can't say just yet," he replies.

"Sergeant," I say, "does that mean you don't know the answer or would prefer not to say?"

He simply shakes his head in response. Forty-eight hours after discovering her body, they've probably received initial autopsy results on Mae. But the officers would also have an arrest warrant if they had a real case on Aaron. They're here looking for evidence.

"I'd like to come up to watch," I say. "I think that's our right."

"That's fine. Just stay out of the way. We don't have that much more to do. I have a couple of questions when we get there."

As soon as Dom turns back to instruct the young deputy to slide the cruiser out of the way, I whisper, "Don't say anything. Nothing."

In my Tundra, we inch up the drive, letting Filipini trudge ahead of us. The slow pace gives me a chance to dial Cap with my free hand, but the call goes to voicemail. Hardly a surprise on a Saturday night.

Up top, we find that our front door has been broken open. The jamb has come loose and is splintered top to bottom, while, in a demonstration of the sturdiness of our dead bolt, a jagged chunk of wood still surrounds the lock. The door has been removed from its hinges and leans against the coat closet in the entry.

"Did anybody try the handle, Dom? We don't lock it." I take hold of the brass knob and turn it freely to demonstrate. Filipini is wordless for a second. We both know what happened. The deputies, with an opportunity rare in Skageon, were eager to use their battering ram and waited only seconds after knocking. That instrument, looking a little like an air-to-ground missile, including its military drab color, lies on the floor beside the door. The thing weighs more than two hundred pounds and requires at least three officers to swing it.

"That's on me," he says.

About half the cops I ever met, embarrassed this way, would just tell me to go fuck myself, so I give Dom props.

Inside there are about eight deputies striding through the house in an urgent manner. Like the deputy below, they remain in their bulletproof vests and helmets, but several assault rifles are parked beside the doorway, as if they were umbrellas. Even the tiniest police departments have all this defense hardware courtesy of the Law Enforcement Support Office in DOD, and, as with the battering ram, the cops can't wait to use it. Did they really expect a shoot-out on Mirror Lake?

The entire dining table is covered with items they've collected. Every piece of clothing from Aaron's closet is heaped there, all his shoes and his laptop. Bea's computer and the desktop from my office are also part of the collection. I notice that Aaron's big Strathmore drawing pad is here, the one where he did all his recent sketches of Mae.

Bea is hovering close to me. In my early days as a deputy PA, I drafted a lot of search warrants and frequently came along for their execution, when legal questions were anticipated about the scope of the judge's order. And there was an occasion, decades ago, when my life went completely sideways, and I watched a pack of searching officers, several of whom I'd worked cases with, turn Barbara's and my house upside down. So what I'm witnessing is of my realm—and it feels otherworldly anyway. But for Bea, this is a nightmare awake: people with military gear and weapons zooming through her intimate space, picking up her property like it's their own. Her face is rigid and her eyes are large in absolute terror.

Filipini emerges from the kitchen in the company of Lieutenant Glowoski, and the two of them approach us. We're still standing not far from our front door. Dressed for action, Glowoski is in uniform today. Her bulletproof vest is unzipped, and she doesn't wear a helmet. Her hairdo is too perfect to be subjected to headgear very often, I suspect. She delivers a terse nod when she sees me.

"Where is Aaron?" she says. "The warrant includes searching him too."

I grab Bea's hand as I hear the first murmur of a response stirring from her.

"I don't think that's what the warrant says, Lieutenant. But I have a more important question. Can you promise us that neither Bea nor I are suspected of any crime?"

"Well, how can I say that?" she asks. "I don't know yet what-all you might be hiding."

Cop-think. Guilty until proven otherwise.

"Until you can give us assurances on that point, Lieutenant, I'm sorry but neither of us will be answering any questions. Not right now."

I'm somewhat amused by the speed with which I've flipped into defense lawyer mode, a role in which I have barely any practice.

"No clue where he's gone?" Glowoski asks.

"Lieutenant, I just said we're not answering your questions. If I recall, you and I had another conversation a week ago about continuing an interrogation after someone's invoked their rights."

"Is that what you're doing, Judge? Invoking your rights? We've called Aaron several times now and he won't pick up. Why is that?"

Her sidekick, Martinez, quite a bit shorter, appears and lifts her face to whisper to the lieutenant, but I take Bea's hand to lead her to the far side of the living room, so we're out of the way. I direct her to an easy chair and gently push her down.

"Rusty, I don't understand," she whispers. "What does this mean for Aaron?"

I mouth, "Later," and touch a straightened index finger to my lips.

In the meantime, I see a deputy beginning to bag some of the items that were collected on the dining table. I stride forward and ask her if she'd mind getting Lieutenant Glowoski.

"Yep," Glowoski says when she arrives, and places her hands on her hips.

"Lieutenant," I say, "I can't agree to let you take either Bea's laptop or my desktop." I tap on each item. "I know for certain that Aaron has never used either device." I don't explain further, but Aaron doesn't have our passwords, which were changed when he touched bottom a couple of years ago, in order to make it less attractive for him to steal this equipment. What is on both machines, I say to Glowoski, is a lot of material both Bea and I are obligated by state law to protect, documents from my work that are covered by court confidentiality orders, and in Bea's case, student records whose disclosure outside the school is prohibited.

Narrow-eyed, Glowoski listens and then says, "I thought the cat had your tongue." She turns to her smaller sidekick, Martinez, who seems to be following Glowoski around, and the lieutenant tells her, "Pack it all up."

I raise my hand.

"Let's have a discussion with Judge Sams before you do that. I'm sure you have a way to reach him."

I imagine that on Saturday night, Morton Sams is having dinner at the country club and is on his third martini. I'm not sure he'd be a lot of good to the cops or me.

"And assuming you get a specific order from Judge Sams to take this stuff," I say, "which I don't expect, I'll need to have a conversation with the PA's office so we can agree on a minimization procedure."

I would wager a good sum that Glowoski has never dealt with minimization, which limits the intrusion into privileged material. It requires a so-called taint team, a separate group of prosecutors unconnected to this case, to go through everything first to remove anything potentially protected before turning the rest over to investigators. I suspect the Skageon PA's office has neither enough lawyers nor the experience to do that.

Glowoski gives me a long nasty look, then tosses her head in disgust, but walks away. I cross the living room immediately, because Filipini has just approached Bea. As I get there, he is asking, "Bea, do you have any plastic rope around here anywhere? White? Maybe out in the garage?"

She's still slow and agitated, but shakes her head decisively.

"Not in the garage," she says. "I was searching for my gardening hand tools last week and looked through everything. The only plastic rope I know about is down by the dock."

I explain that our small runabout and my canoe are both tied up there with plastic rope. There may be some extra line down in the storage box too.

"I may need the rope from the boats," Filipini says.

"There's no way to secure them, if you take all the rope, Dom. I'm going to end up having to swim out to the middle of the lake to drag them back tomorrow. How about if you cut a sample off of each line now, and I'll buy some more rope in the morning and you can take what you want then?"

Filipini screws up his mouth for a second and then lowers his voice.

"I don't think she'll go for that." He doesn't turn to look over his shoulder at Glowoski. "But I'll ask." He goes off in her direction.

Three deputies emerge from our bedroom and dump two arm-loads of clothing on the far end of the table. It's all mine, stuff Aaron's never touched. I have an impulse to tell them that, but then decide not to push my luck with another objection. Cap can file a motion for return of property in the morning. In the meantime, I can buy myself an outfit at Target, when I get more rope.

Filipini has joined the lieutenant, speaking to her a few feet away from me in the kitchen. I don't catch every word, but I can overhear most of their conversation. I look in the other direction so they pay no attention to me. Glowoski is asking Dom if his guys went over the garage, and the sergeant says they looked there for the camping stuff. Filipini then adds, "I've known this woman thirty years. They say it's not there."

"We need all the rope they have," Glowoski answers, but to my surprise agrees that Dom only needs samples from the lines securing the boats. She asks him to mark the lines, however, so we can't change out the rope overnight.

The remaining deputies gather around the dining table and begin to place the items they've collected in large clear plastic bags. They use a separate bag for each room they searched and write the location in permanent marker, adding the date.

After a few more minutes, they seem ready to go and begin hauling the bags out to their vehicles. At that point I hear the door from the house to the garage scraping open. I move that way and see Glowoski down the hall, coming through that doorway with a large coil of white rope in her hand. She fixes me with a black look, but that is not the part that bothers me. Like Bea, I have no memory of that rope being stored in the garage.

Filipini is the last of the officers to leave. Before that, he helps me get the broken door back on its hinges. It won't quite close over the fragment around the dead bolt, but it will keep out some of the cold.

Before he goes, Dom looks at me and asks, "What the hell happened with that rope, Rusty?" I know we ended up embarrassing him, but I sigh and pass an open hand before me, as if to say I've had enough, which in fact I have.

Once he's gone, I return to Bea, who's in a blue easy chair that came from her apartment. She's normally comfortable there. Still in her puffer vest, she's turned to stare at the lake.

"They're gone," I say.

"Tell me this is going to be okay," she says.

I smile weakly and shrug. "I want to," I say.

I get up to look around the house. It will take a long time to put things back together. A couple of the search scenes I was at as a PA were ransacked as thoroughly as if by professional burglars, with everything ripped off the shelves and out of drawers and scattered on the floor. This is better than that, thanks again, probably, to Filipini. But all our books have been displaced, unshelved and stacked on the floor, and the electronics throughout the house have been disconnected and moved aside. Bea's portion of our closet is undisturbed, as is her dresser, but the clothing of mine they didn't take is all heaped on our bed.

Cap calls back while I'm in the bedroom. I return to the kitchen, where Bea has moved, and put the phone on the breakfast bar so Bea can hear Cap on the speaker.

"Oh shit," he says, when I tell him there's been a search. "Did you keep Aaron away from them?"

"He wasn't here," I say, and then explain how we've spent the last twenty-four hours.

"Oh, how fucking stupid can he be?" asks Cap immediately, then pauses to check his temper. He goes silent, and I know he's realizing what I finally did, that there may be a much more troubling reading of Aaron's disappearance. He won't say that, though, with Bea on the phone, and like me, he's probably reluctant to believe it. "Let's keep our fingers crossed that he shows up before the police demand to see him to get DNA and fingerprints."

I take a photo of the warrant and text it to Cap while we're still on the phone.

"Does this mean what I think?" I ask Cap. "About Mae? Something turned up in her autopsy?"

"Maybe. But it could also be that they're off on some funky manslaughter theory, that Mae crashed because she was drugged, and they think she got the stuff from Aaron. You don't need to let your mind go to the scariest places yet. Aaron has a recent drug conviction. They wouldn't need much more than that to establish probable cause that he might have supplied her."

Aaron's clean drop when he returned from his trip with Mae cuts strongly against that theory, but then again, the PAs could have told Judge Sams only what they wanted to. Like me, Cap takes some heart from the fact that the officers arrived without an arrest warrant. Whatever suspicions they have about Aaron, when they busted through our door, they were still looking for proof to confirm them. And Cap can make no more sense than I of them looking for a rope. What connection could that possibly have to Mae crashing her car at the bottom of a utility road?

"I'm going to try to get hold of Helena in the morning," he says, referring to the chief deputy PA, who is supposedly in charge, "but I may not reach her on a Sunday. Come Monday, we'll know a lot more. I'll have some work to do. But let me know the minute you hear from Aaron."

With that reminder, as soon as Cap rings off, Bea picks up her phone, which has been on the table beside her. I know just from her expression that there is still no word from her son.

16

Another Warrant

October 1–2

W e spend Sunday morning putting the house back together. Bea is flattened. I ask if she'd like music—I could stand the calming background of an artfully struck piano—but she is definite when she says no. She wants to be sure she can hear her phone on the breakfast bar, to which she returns hastily every time the device bleats with an incoming call or text. It is never Aaron. Except for a call from a teacher who is going to be out tomorrow, she sends everything to voicemail.

Around eleven a.m., Cap phones.

"Well, I reached Helena," he says. "She had nothing to say. 'Sorry we missed him last night.' Like they'd come by with a plate of cookies."

"No indication why they were searching?"

"Zero. She wants me to bring him in for questioning, naturally."

"What did you say?"

"I didn't answer her. But we'll never do that. My shoulder is sore already from telling Aaron to keep his mouth shut." He means his shoulder is sore from patting himself on the back. "Imagine where this mess would be, if they had a statement from him they could twist around. Which reminds me. Has that knucklehead shown up yet?"

I tell him no.

"Rusty," he says, "you know what the cops and prosecutors will make of it if they find out he's bolted. They'll assume he's guilty of something, even if they have no evidence now. What the hell is he thinking?"

"You know him, Cap. He's to himself. When he was first in jail in Skageon, the inmates were in seg most of the time because of Covid, and you told me he was the only client you had who didn't belly-ache about spending so much time alone. I think he's processing this death." I offer the same speculation I shared with Bea early on Saturday, that after trashing Mae for two weeks when she didn't reappear, he's contending with both guilt and the lost love he was trying to renounce.

"Well, he better turn up soon," Cap says.

"We understand," I answer.

A little after noon, when I have pretty much gotten our bedroom and my closet back in order, I pass through the living room and suddenly notice two Smokeys in uniform standing on the sloping lawn behind the house that leads down to the water. I stare at both of them for a second, and the one who catches my eye remains eerily impassive. I head to the slider to ask them what the hell they are doing, but something strikes me, and I backtrack to the front door. Through the glass panes beside the door, cracked but still intact, I spy three cruisers in the gravel circle beside the garage, two tan cars with the new State Patrol logo, and another in the grey of the Skageon sheriff's police. Glowoski, once more in her blue blazer, is leaning against the fender of one vehicle with a handheld radio, but it is Dom Filipini who is proceeding slowly up the walk. I maneuver the door open.

For the tiniest second, we just face each other. I can tell this is big trouble.

Dom removes his billed hat before he steps into the house. As I realized yesterday, he's a true gentleman.

"I have a warrant for Aaron's arrest," he says.

It takes a second for me to speak, and then I ask to see it.

The arrest warrant has been issued by the superior court in Mare-nago County, where Mae's body was discovered. All the worst words are there, the ancient terms still trapped in state law like amber: "...did, with malice aforethought, trespass with force and arms upon the person of Mae Cheryl Potter and did thereby commit the crime of murder in the first degree."

Not unsurprisingly, at least not for me, the lawyerly calculations gather promptly, a strand of order arising from the emotional swim within. This is not some strained manslaughter theory about Aaron feeding Mae drugs. This is Murder One. They're saying Aaron decided to kill her and then did it.

I have had my share of these moments, maybe more than the next person, when you know that life is suddenly and irretrievably altered. You will never return to the normal you knew when you woke up. And that is true now for Aaron—and for Bea. This moment, these charges, will cleave a permanent divide in their lives as surely as if a fault had opened in the earth they were standing on.

But I survived. I was changed, and not for the better, but I am here. And Bea will be here too. That is more a prayer in this moment than a certainty. But it is what I fervently want to believe.

"Is he here?" Filipini asks.

"He's not, Dom. But I know you can't take my word for it. Especially after yesterday." I'm talking about the rope, and he understands.

"Neh," he says. "Once we got a chance to think about it, we all believed what Bea and you said about the garage. Even the lieutenant. But on an arrest warrant, we gotta look."

"I understand," I say and stand out of the way.

He motions over his shoulder. Two young deputies, a man and a woman, who were lurking just out of sight, suddenly appear and swiftly pass both of us as they head into the house. Filipini follows and I say before he's out of earshot, "Dom, we just kind of got the house back together."

He nods diligently as he proceeds back to supervise.

I realize only now that Bea has been observing in silence from about twenty feet away, having emerged from the kitchen. She comes forward now and takes the paper from my hand.

After a second, she cries out like she's been stabbed. She turns one way then the other and finally crumbles into the nearest chair in the living room. She's sobbing. I stand beside her, rubbing her back. The drugs, the torment—I went through all of that with Nat. But not this. Something like this brought down on your child is the worst thing you can imagine.

From where I stand, I have a view straight down the hallway to our bedroom, and I can see the two troopers who have literally propped our bed in the air on the rear legs of the frame. Under beds. In closets. Behind large furniture. That's where the wanted hide.

Filipini is back in a second.

"Bea," he says, "when was the last time you saw Aaron?"

"Dom, please," I answer. "I know you have a job to do. But there are eight billion people on the face of the earth you can interrogate to build your case. Doesn't simple decency say you should skip his mother?"

"We'll get a subpoena, Rusty."

"I know that, Dom. And we'll deal with that when it comes to pass. But right now—" I just wind my head around like it's on a spring.

"Okay," he says. "But he wasn't here last night, while we were searching. And we had two deputies sitting on the place in case he came back. Which he didn't. This doesn't look very good for him, you know. We find Mae's body and he disappears. What does that say? He's only going to make it worse, if we have to conduct some kind of manhunt."

"Dom," I say, "you're preaching to the choir."

"Dominic," Bea says suddenly, "my son didn't kill Mae. This is ridiculous."

I grab her shoulder. She'd gotten control of herself briefly, but she breaks down again after this declaration and covers her face with both hands.

"I'm sorry for you guys," Dom says. "I truly am. You *and* the Potters. It's a nightmare for all of you."

In another second, the deputies are done and file past us without a backward look. Dom, with his cap still in his hands, starts to follow, then turns to me.

"I'll call Lloyd to tell him," he says, "so Bea doesn't have to. He should be home from church by now."

As soon as the police are gone, I phone Cap. He is ominously silent in response, then says, "Marenago County, huh?" The meaning of that hadn't fully dawned on me. These charges have been brought in another county. This isn't Hardy being a hothead or a jerk. Another prosecutor without a dog in the hunt evaluated the evidence and said, 'Murder One.'

By now, I've realized it's the rope—that's why they didn't have an arrest warrant yesterday, but returned with one today. That's why Filipini said that, with time to think, they realized that Bea and I were telling them the truth when she said there was no rope in the garage. Because neither of us put it there. Aaron did. I could lash myself, because this is a forceful demonstration of the enduring wisdom that in a situation like this you don't say one word to the cops. The briefest and most innocuous and most truthful answer has ended up making Aaron's situation dramatically worse.

I share all of that with Cap, who, normally garrulous, is suddenly reluctant to speak. He's thinking this through. As a defense lawyer, the abiding lesson is that your clients will always disappoint you. And so, he's probably explaining to himself how this is possible. A quiet kid like Aaron, someone who rarely shows his emotions—how much rage is there stopped up within him, a rage which Mae, uniquely manipulative, would be able to uncork?

As a final thought, Cap repeats what Filipini said, that it would be infinitely better for Aaron if he showed up and surrendered, but there's no other point to that than thinking out loud. Aaron is beyond our control. That's why this has happened, I suppose.

Cap and I click off then, and I take a second to wonder, as Cap seemingly did, how Aaron might have done this. I'm not convinced. Not at all. Aaron has his failings, many, but I've never seen violence in him. If Mae and he were on some behavior-altering chemical—PCP, for example—maybe. But his drop was clean. Then again, how many disbelieving parents and loved ones, sincerely shocked and hoping against hope, did I encounter as a prosecutor? Their faith in the defendant was almost always misplaced.

The day wears on. I feel painfully isolated. The news is probably spreading, but no one will call, because what can they say, what consolation can they offer that will not seem to condone what Aaron has supposedly done? Bea has placed herself again at the breakfast bar and has remained there, immobile for periods. Every twenty minutes or so a new bout of weeping commences. It's like dealing with a sudden death, the slow, creeping process of absorbing the reality.

Now and then, when I pass by, she confronts me with her grimmest thoughts.

"His life is over," she says. "He can be proven innocent a hundred times and he'll always be an accused murderer."

"Have you considered who you're talking to?" I answer after a moment.

"It's different. You were established and respectable. And framed. He'll always be guilty in the eyes of everyone around here."

"Bea, there is life after. Yes, he may need to move away, same as me. But our job right now is to stay on Aaron's side. Everybody else can be against him. Until he tells us to give up, we should hold on to our hopes."

"I'm not giving up," she says, with a decidedly belligerent edge.

The next time she decides to speak, she asks, "Can he get bail? After they arrest him?"

Her question takes it for granted that Aaron will soon be found. But I'm not sure. If it's as bad as it might be, if he'd actually done harm to Mae, then he'd know that the cops' initial belief that Mae died in a car wreck was wrong. And that the mistake provided him with a window to run. He knows a lot more than most people about how to survive in the wilderness. If this is as bad as it appears, he may be a fugitive for some time.

But if that's not the case, then Cap has good reason to want to locate Aaron and bring him in. Cap might even have a chance to try to negotiate bail before Aaron surrenders. But assuming instead that the cops end up successfully hunting Aaron down, I know that even Superior Court Judge Sabich, a man who existed thirty years ago and faced these questions all the time—even he, Judge Rusty, would never grant bail to someone like Aaron. A convicted felon who's accused of a violent crime while on probation is rarely regarded as a good candidate for release, let alone a guy who ran. But I answer Bea's question by saying I don't know.

"So maybe not?" she asks. "So maybe I never get to hug my son again?" She's imagining the worst: conviction, sentencing, incarceration. I tell her there is a long way from here to there. Right now we need to take it one day at a time.

Around three p.m., her phone buzzes and she answers after staring at the screen. It can only be Lloyd.

"I know," she says. "I know."

After listening, she says, "It didn't happen, Lloyd. I realize," she says, "I realize. We need to believe in him. More than ever." She listens for another minute, shaking her head the entire time.

It dawns on me that I should call Joe. And Nat. Joe does not pick up, which is what I would expect on a Sunday afternoon when he is at the VFW watching football. I just don't want somebody bushwhacking him with the news, but I reject the thought of going over there to tell him, since it would mean leaving Bea alone.

I step outside to phone Nat.

"It's bullshit," my son says at once. He and Anna and the girls are the leading members of the Aaron fan club. Drug use, even addiction, is something Nat understands from experience. He takes it as a phase of growing up. Murder is not a possibility. We spend a minute trying to figure out what to tell my granddaughters, who might see something come across a screen or on social media. Next, Anna and he will text Bea to say that they are here for her—and for Aaron. I thank him, because I know she will not be getting messages like that often enough.

When I return through the sliding door, Bea gives me a stark look and shares her latest dark thought: "He's going to kill himself."

I take a second. It is true that in his worst moments, Aaron is likely to lament in the fashion of Romeo that he is fortune's fool. Everything goes against him. And if he is falsely accused, this will seem the most monumental example ever of the fact that he cannot win. But suicide?

And then again, there is the other side, that he really did do this, that he murdered Mae in some fit of passion, that he came home pretending that wasn't so, because that, naturally, was what he most wanted to be true. Now, with that facade fallen, he will be destroyed by shame. That happens: the spouse-killer who turns the gun on himself. But I won't go there. I find myself no more willing than I was a couple of hours ago to grant the basic assumption of this line of reasoning, that is that Aaron killed her.

"I don't think that will happen," I say.

"Did you think *any* of this was going to happen?" she asks. Again it sounds like she is casting blame, instead of welcoming my support.

"It won't happen," I repeat.

An hour or so later, Bea comes in to tell me that she's texted Daria, her deputy principal, to say that Bea will be taking a personal day. I have stuff scheduled too, for tomorrow, a few calls. I'll push them in the morning.

As soon as the sun is down, Bea says she is taking a pill and going to sleep. I heat some soup from a can, drink whiskey until I'm tired enough to fall in beside her, but I'm up by five a.m. and decide that I'm going out in my canoe. I am on the water for sunup a little before seven. It's getting colder, in the high forties, but the chill, the space and the isolation do me good. I gather myself around various simple mantras that will plot the way forward. Deep breaths. Live through the moment. Go on to the next.

I have padded into the bedroom and am peeling off my wetsuit when my phone, still on the night table, vibrates like a rattler's tail. I assume it's Joe, who I never reached. But I see Cap's caller ID.

"They arrested Aaron at Ginawaban, where Mae's body was found. I can't imagine what the hell he was doing there, but you and I both know what a prosecutor will say." Hiding evidence, is what they'll say. With reason, too. My own conclusion on Friday as we prepared to search for Aaron was that a guy breaking the terms of his probation by driving would never go near Ginawaban, where there were still likely to be police—as, indeed, there were, apparently. Meaning something about the scene there, something left behind perhaps, required Aaron to take a considerable risk. If he was even thinking about risks. But with this news, I find my faith in his innocence, which seemed to be holding firm, suddenly weaker.

"Oh shit," I groan.

"They want to have the initial appearance this afternoon. As soon as I can get up there. Figure one o'clock in the courthouse in Portage."

"We'll be there," I say.

I stand beside the bed staring at Bea, contemplating the dearness of her form, the spray of crinkled brown hair that surrounds her on the pillow, a well-turned calf that has escaped the covers. She fell asleep half dressed, wearing an apricot-colored T-shirt from a Springsteen tour that she often puts on at night, but below she's still clad in the old hemmed cargo shorts she had on for the job of reordering the house. In her anguish, she probably lacked the will or energy to prepare for bed and simply sprawled there, where the sleeping pill took her down sooner than she expected. Watching in this instant, I am sabered the most deeply yet by the pity I feel for her.

I thought my conversation with Cap might wake her, but she has not stirred. I can wait another hour before we'll have to leave for Portage.

I'm about to exit the room when she speaks behind me.

"I'm up," she says. "I've been awake since you went out. I've just been pretending that if I don't open my eyes, I won't have to face all this." Her lids rise then, and those tawny eyes, now marked by rivulets of red from all the weeping, fix on me. Today they bear a new light, the harder gloss of a gem. It is as I feared and as I hoped. She will get through this. But something has been subtracted from her soul, for today, perhaps forever.

"Where is it," she asks, "we have to go?"

17

The Initial Appearance

October 2

W hat in the Jesusfuck is goin on over there?" It's Joe who's finally called back, while we're scrambling around to get ready to depart for Portage. "The State Patrol just left here sayin Aaron's been arrested for murder."

"The State Patrol?" I ask. "What were they doing with you?"

"Well, the boy was sittin in my truck when they got him. They showed up here thinkin I was gonna say he stole it. There's something in court at one p.m. Any chance I can hitch a ride with you?"

Fortunately, I am on speaker, so I merely look to Bea, who squeezes her eyes shut but finally nods.

When we arrive at Joe's, I get out to help him up into the back seat of the Tundra, a complicated operation given his height and the weakness of one of his legs. I must hoist him by the elbows. As soon as he's settled, he starts swearing again about Aaron's situation.

I interrupt to get Joe's account of his encounter with the police. So far, Joe shows no real signs of dementia, but his reporting is generally distorted by his need to turn every happenstance into mythology, with Joe in the hero's role.

"Some state troopers with the Smokey hats show up at my door askin where's my pickup. I kinda stare out at the garage and act like, 'Sonofabitch, it was here last I looked.' Didn't get off on the right foot with them cause of that.

"'Well, we know you're lyin,' they say, 'cause we found your truck up in Ginawaban and the driver had the key. Did you let anybody use it?'

"I could tell right then I was cornered, but I kept up and said, 'Maybe the tenant farmer, Abel took it.'

"'Listen,' they say, 'we're gonna ask you a third time, and if you don't tell us the truth, we're takin you to jail. Did you let somebody use your truck?' After a minute, the younger one, who was taking notes, says, 'Here's a hint. Do you know Aaron Housley?'

"'Oh, Aaron,' I say, and carry on a little like I just remembered. 'Yeah, I let him borrow the truck. He come by early in the morning Friday and asked to take it for a few days. Just found out that his girl-friend, if that's what you want to call her, the Potter girl, had turned up dead and he wanted to get some time alone to take that in. He gets that from me. Something bad happens and I'm just like, Leave me the hell alone, I need to think about this. When my wife died, I sat in that barn out there for two days before I even let my kids know.'"

Bea, who's turned in her seat to listen to her father, interjects sharply, "You didn't tell them that you barely think about Mom these days?"

"What in the hell are you talking about, Beatrix? I think about your mother all the time."

I reach over to take her wrist and ask if we can please stay with Joe's meeting with the State Patrol. She complies, but frumps around in her seat, facing the windshield so she doesn't have to see her father. Every-thing she was saying on Friday, about how foolish he was to let Aaron have the truck, has been borne out, not that Joe would ever admit that.

"Anyway," Joe says, "they went over that with me several times. 'Did Aaron steal the truck?'

"'No, I handed him the keys.'

"'Did you know his driver's license was suspended?'

"'Well, now you bring it up, I remember, but I didn't think about that at the time. Kid was upset. He's my grandchild, so what else would I do?'

"Asshole asking questions, the older one, kind of smirked when I said 'grandchild,' you know, cause Aaron's Black, and I said, 'Listen, I love that boy like my own breath, couldn't love him more if I give birth to him myself, so don't be smilin or any of that shit, cause cop or not, I'm gonna have to knock your block off.'

"Guy got kind of riled, but his partner, the younger one, sticks in, 'He doesn't mean anything by that. We didn't realize you were the grandfather, that's all.'

" 'I am. And how is Aaron?' I ask. 'Have you seen him?'

" 'Well, first you answer our questions. Did you know he wasn't supposed to leave Skageon County?'

" 'Not sure as how I did.'

" 'Well, did he drive this truck of yours ordinarily?' As if I wouldn't realize that was a trick question so they'd have something else on him.

" 'Nah,' I say, 'I'm old and useless, so I been drivin him around.'

" 'And did you know his license was suspended?'

" 'Told you I knew that, but I didn't think about it.'

"They got so interested in trying to back me off that load of crap that they never asked how he got to my door at five a.m. Must have thought he hitchhiked or a friend dropped him off.

"Finally, they told me he'd been arrested for the girl's murder. And I told them straight up, 'That is just the biggest stinking pile of bull-pucky I ever heard of. That boy just don't have any violence in him. He's stopped deer hunting cause he can't stand to see the silly critters die. That's how he is. He didn't murder no one. No one.'

"They look at me, like, Okay, now we know for real that you're his grandfather, talking like that.

"They told me there was going to be this hearing this afternoon, then they mentioned that my truck wasn't starting. I guess that's how they got Aaron, cause the damn alternator conked out again, and he was just sittin there."

I go over the story with Joe a few more times. For Aaron, of course, it would have been a lot better if the cops didn't know he'd taken off not long after Mae's body was found. Joe would have been happy enough to lie, I'm sure, especially for Aaron, but because he's Joe and never bothered to call me back yesterday, he didn't understand the situation.

After that, we drive largely in silence, except for Joe's occasional

monologues about weather events in the towns we're passing. Bea eventually has enough of that and puts on some Harold Arlen vocals, recorded
when he was older, quiet and even soulful renditions of his normally
happy songs. We are on the same route Bea and I drove on Saturday, but
in the current funereal mood, none of us seems to take much pleasure
from the pageantry in the forests we pass after a couple hours on the road.

Casper Sabonjian is a tubby little guy with a full head of grey hair. His
belly is big enough that in profile he almost resembles the person carrying the bass drum in a marching band. Cap is always carefully groomed,
appearing in court in a nicely tailored suit that has enough fabric that
he can fasten the center button on the jacket to hide his full contours,
although the expensive clothing lends him a slicker urban air. To com-
pensate, Cap's courtroom style is to be everyone's best friend. I'm sure
that shtick wore thin with the prosecutors in Skageon County long ago,
but in Marenago, where I suspect he seldom practices, it is opening
night. When we arrive, he is leaning on the rail, chatting up the judge's
docket clerk, whose nameplate identifies her as Moriah Moses.

As soon as Cap notices us in the rear of the courtroom, he hustles
back, shaking hands with each of us. He then draws us into a corner to
confer. The prosecutor—the prosecuting attorney himself, not some
deputy, which is a sign of the gravity of the case—gave Cap a copy
of the affidavit Glowoski swore out in support of the complaint and
arrest warrant. The affidavit covers only a couple of pages. Cap has
secured photocopies for both Bea and me, but there is not a lot of time
to study it, because he says the judge has been waiting only for the
arrival of the defendant's family, who might be needed when today's
proceedings reach the question of bond. Even with a quick perusal, I
realize that the spare document is devastating.

The centerpiece of the allegations is the Kindle County police
pathologist's autopsy of Mae's remains. Based on the advanced decomposition when the doctor first examined the body, she estimates the time
of death as approximately two weeks earlier, on or around September 14.
Concerning the cause of death, however, the pathologist is more precise. Mae died by strangulation. Furthermore, the ligature mark around
Mae's throat is characteristic of a nylon rope, like the one found in our

garage. Rope fibers recovered at various locations, including in Harold's Woods in Mae's Subaru and on the floor of Aaron's closet, have all been identified, after microscopic examination, as consistent with that rope.

I am trying to read through the affidavit a second time, since I found comprehension challenging, but I feel Bea's eyes on me. She is entirely without expression, but she whispers, "This is bad, right?"

"I've read worse," I answer. And I mean it. Fiber evidence is nowhere as certain as DNA or fingerprints. And I know from experience that an autopsy on a body that has been basically rotting in a hot car for two weeks has its own challenges that will make it hard for the pathologist to testify that her conclusions are free from doubt. On the other hand, the purpose of an affidavit at this stage is only to outline enough evidence to show probable cause justifying Aaron's arrest. Very often the most damning proof in the prosecutors' hands will not be mentioned, to avoid it being challenged in court before trial.

Cap interrupts to urge us to take seats, so the proceeding can get started. He informs Moriah, the clerk, that we are here, and almost at once Aaron is walked in from the holding cell beside the courtroom by a female court security officer who grips his arm. For good or ill, Bea has already witnessed her son in a courtroom in handcuffs and a jail jumpsuit—this one a deep blue. I know it is a sight she prayed never to see again, but it must be less shocking as a repeat performance. Looking thin in the gaping coveralls, Aaron, whose hands and ankles are chained together, shuffles toward the podium to join Cap. As soon as Aaron, almost a full foot taller than his lawyer, is beside Cap at the rostrum, Aaron turns and peers into the gallery, in the hopeful way of a third grader at a class performance. He quickly focuses on us in the second row and manages a weak smile of recognition.

Now the clerk bangs the gavel to announce the arrival of the judge, the Honorable Wendy Carrington. Judge Carrington, a shorter person, ascends the bench from a doorway immediately behind her tall black leather chair, an entrance that presumably leads to her chambers down the hall. The so-called Main Courtroom we are in is a jewel, a relic of Marenago County's bygone era of prosperity. When the building was erected in the 1880s, here just south of logging country, all kinds of hardwood were easily available. The walls are wainscoted and the two rails that separate the witness stand, bench and clerk's area, and then partition the well of the court from the spectators' area, are both gentle arcs, plainly hand carved. Given the meaty grain of the wood and its pale ocher color, I believe it's sycamore, which would cost a pretty penny today. A lot of natural light comes through the large double-hung windows on the left, and the ceiling, a full two stories overhead, is coffered, with a geometric design on the beams and large globe fixtures with brass fittings suspended every few feet.

The prosecutor, accompanied by Lieutenant Glowoski, emerges from a side door. He steps toward the podium in a tweedy suit too heavy for the season. He's a middle-sized man about my age. He looks like he's been at it for a lifetime, as if he is worn out by the righteous anger he has been required to summon in the name of justice. When he turns to the gallery to see who has shown up—probably scanning for the Potters—you can see he has some disfiguring dermatological condition that reddens his entire face and leaves it marked by boil-like lumps, one of which is even brighter than the rest and crowned by a dot of blood. And there's something sour in his demeanor. His grim expression does not yield, even when he nods in greeting to the judge. He gives his name for the record being made by the court reporter as Hiram Jackdorp, representing the people of Marenago County.

"Casper Sabonjian," Cap replies, "appearing specially for the defendant, Aaron Housley."

It is the judge, seated on a bench a good five feet above the courtroom, framed by the American and state flags behind her, who unexpectedly seizes my attention. She's well past fifty, with a pleasant round face, a pointed nose and mid-length hairdo that parts on one side. I know her. That's my first thought. But from where? The CPU spins more slowly these days, although sometimes I like to think that's only because there are more people to remember. But what comes back through time is a strongly positive impression of her. Good lawyer and good person.

"What does 'appearing specially' mean?" Bea whispers.

"It means basically that Cap's only here for purposes of this one hearing. He hasn't been retained yet." For a murder case, Cap is going to ask for a large amount to represent Aaron. Bea is yet to ask about the costs of what is ahead, and I haven't thought much about that either, but it is going to be crushing financially for Bea and Lloyd, more than enough to wipe them out. I will offer money, as I did last time Aaron was in trouble, and it will be harder for them to say no now.

Cap is a clever lawyer, and he takes control of the proceedings. An initial appearance is to inform the defendant of the charges against him and to decide on bail. Cap, however, says the affidavit is ridiculously conclusory, with many of the alleged results of the autopsy open to question. Furthermore, the affidavit makes no mention of Mae's widely reported drug use and the role it played in her death. Accordingly, Cap demands that the probable cause hearing Aaron is entitled to under the law begin immediately. The prosecutor gives his grey head a weary shake and reminds the judge that the same law allows the prosecution ten days to prepare. The judge agrees.

Cap knew that, too, and he undoubtedly realizes, as I do, that the hearing, which would offer Aaron his first chance to test the evidence against him, will never take place. The PA will ask the grand jury to return an indictment in the next few days, which, in the eyes of the law, suffices as a determination of probable cause.

But Cap uses his attack on the affidavit to support his request to the judge to set a reasonable bail. This young man, he's suggesting, is being held on flimsy proof, and if he can't get an immediate evidentiary hearing, then the judge should allow him to bond out. He points to us in the gallery and says the family will do everything it can to assist the defendant in coming up with whatever is required.

Jackdorp, the prosecutor, responds, "Well, I don't know Mr. Sabonjian here, Judge, but he must have a sideline as a comedian. The defendant is on probation in Skageon County on his felony conviction eighteen months ago for possession of distribution-size quantities of controlled substances. One condition of his probation is that he is not supposed to leave that county. But he was arrested here. He was dangerously intoxicated at the time of his prior arrest, and so, with his conviction in that case, his driver's license was suspended. But he clearly drove himself from his grandfather's place to Ginawaban. So the idea that this court could impose conditions that this defendant would obey—well, Judge, history is against that. That's just for starters. He disappeared from his home as soon as he heard the decedent's body had been found. And where was he arrested but the site where the remains were recovered? It's not much of a stretch, Judge, to conclude he arrived there to tidy up the murder scene, before anyone realized that's what it was, a crime scene, rather than the site of an accident as investigators initially believed. So the defendant also appears to be a flight risk, and quite likely intent on obstructing justice.

"And lest any of us forget, he's here charged with first-degree murder, where the presumption has to be strong that he could endanger other people in the community."

The prosecutor, Jackdorp, has done an efficient job of demonstrating why bail is out of the question. But Cap keeps fighting, and I'm impressed that the judge is patient enough to let Cap have his full say. By now, I've recalled how I met her. We were on a panel together organized by the state supreme court roughly twenty years ago to discuss the legal ramifications of a proposal, then gathering support in the state legislature before its eventual passage, to do away with the death penalty. I was chief judge of the appellate court in Kindle County and she, as I recollect, was the state defender up here, although she'd been a deputy PA before that. Including the afternoon I spent beside her and a couple of phone conversations to prepare, our association lasted no more than a few hours, so we are barely acquaintances, but I came away certain she was an excellent lawyer and a good-natured human being—sharp, funny, highly intelligent and eminently sensible. As she denies the bail motion, she refers to the matter as 'my case' and grants Cap permission to bring the subject up again in the future if that's warranted. I take it that up here in Marenago County, the superior court follows the tag-you're-it approach to judicial assignment on criminal cases, meaning the judge randomly drawn to handle the initial appearance presides over the case until its conclusion. If I've got that right, it's the first good thing to happen to Aaron in the last few days. Wendy Carrington is not likely to fundamentally change the ultimate outcome, but at least Aaron will be treated fairly on the way there.

The judge then sets the matter over for a week for the probable cause hearing that everyone knows is unlikely to happen, and with that bangs her gavel and retreats. Aaron is whisked from the courtroom by the bailiff, leaving Bea on her feet, with one hand raised futilely toward her son.

Cap in the meantime has come to join us. He says Aaron will be allowed visitors at the jail until five, which is a clear relief to Bea. But first, Cap wants to talk to us and suggests a diner across the street. I suspect Cap will discuss his retainer. Joe needs to get over to the sheriff's office, attached to the jail, to find out about his truck.

The diner, the Lamp, is your standard American joint, with booths of crimson pleather, and wagon-wheel fixtures overhead that cast tremendous amounts of light. The food must be decent, because it is crowded, with what appear to be local business types—merchants and insurance agents and real estate agents—finishing lunch. The loud burble of conversation suits Cap fine, allowing us more privacy. He hunches over the table to be heard.

In response to Bea's questions, he says that we will find Aaron doing relatively well. He was bewildered, Cap says, and adamant about his innocence. Bea takes that part with visible relief, while Cap and I both know that at this stage, most defendants don't say anything else.

Cap then changes the subject.

"Listen, I don't know how to say this, so I'll just come out with it. I can't go any further with this case. You need another lawyer. Except for my prior relationship with Aaron and you, I wouldn't even have driven up today."

Bea and I are both stung. Cap gave no indication of this when I spoke to him this morning. Bea softly asks, "Why?"

"There are a lot of reasons. I've been trying to concentrate my practice around Como, so I don't have to drive all over the damn state. My back can't take it. More important, I haven't had a murder trial in my entire career. I represented that Slutsky boy years ago who killed both his parents, but that case, and the few other first-degrees I've had, they were just long plea negotiations. If Aaron sticks to his guns and goes to trial, then you'll need somebody who's done all this before, cross-examined pathologists and whatnot. You shouldn't want your boy to be my teachable moment."

You can tell from Cap's affect, the pace with which he's speaking and the fact that he's doing his best not to look toward us, that he feels guilty. The reasons he gave, especially his lack of critical trial experience, seem good enough on their face to justify his decision, which leads me to conclude that there's another factor that he finds somewhat embarrassing.

"It's Hardy, right?" I ask.

Cap jolts a little like I'd stuck him with a pin, but after a second, he nods.

"Like I said, I want to do most of my work in Skageon County. And I have to have a reasonable relationship with the PA. And we all know Hardy. If I defend the man he thinks killed his daughter, he'll hold it against me forever. Somebody from up here won't face that issue."

I ask Cap if he has other names to suggest. And he promises to work on that first thing tomorrow.

I can tell that Bea is reeling—for the last three days, the bad news never stops—and we sit with Cap only a few more minutes, using the schedule at the jail as an excuse to leave. We exit the Lamp and stand on the corner outside. A cold wind, the precursor to the rain that Joe says will be coming, ending the hot, dry period of the last couple weeks, has kicked up and Bea's hair lifts off her neck like a curtain in the breeze. She zips her vest to her throat.

"I thought defense lawyers take on all cases, even ones that will make them unpopular," she says.

"Don't kid yourself, Bea. They need to earn a living, like everybody else. But it doesn't make any difference. If Cap never tried a murder case, he isn't the attorney we want anyway."

"Well, how do we find another lawyer? You don't just open the phone book and look under Murder, do you?"

I laugh at her, whether she means to be funny or not.

"I still know half the lawyers in the state," I tell her. "There are a dozen terrific attorneys in Kindle County I can think of off the top of my head." I keep to myself my instant recognition that anybody with an urban shine won't play well up here. The contempt that residents of the rural parts of the state feel for the city seems worse than it ever has been in my decades of coming up to Skageon County. Even Sandy Stern, who defended me, probably the best defense lawyer I ever saw in action, would not sell well up here with his Latin accent. And he's long retired anyway.

Yet for now, I fold her hand over my forearm and direct her toward the jail a couple blocks away.

"We'll find someone great," I say. "I promise."

18

Jail

Public attitudes toward crime and criminals being what they are, jails are not meant to be comfortable or welcoming. Thus, in its starkness, the Marenago County Correctional Center would be considered an architectural success. But on a scale that starts at the bottom with the urban hellholes like the Kindle County Jail as I experienced it on visits starting in the late 1970s, Marenago appears somewhat better than average. It occupies the rear half of a single-story cinder-block structure that is shared with the Marenago County sheriff's Portage substation. The building sits incongruously in the midst of a residential block of trim white frame houses.

We wait for Aaron in the whitewashed vestibule on a backless wooden bench that has probably been here for decades. Beside us are the small brown metal lockers where I placed my cellphone and wallet and where Bea left her purse, containing the same items. The correctional officer, who functions as a receptionist, a young woman whose black hair is pulled back severely, sits behind a sheet of bulletproof glass adjoining a walk-through metal detector. She busies herself with paperwork and occasionally answers the phone. A couple of calls produce a smile of such delight that it seems almost impossible from the baleful woman we've been dealing with. When we arrived, she asked for the nature of our relationship with the inmate, explaining that would determine the site of our visit with Aaron. Once Bea answered, the jailer gave her a searching look. My instant suspicion was that she was seeking signs of what Bea had done wrong to raise a murderer.

After about ten minutes, she calls out, "Aaron Housley," although no one else is seated in the waiting area, and stands to motion us toward the metal detector. The nameplate on her uniform blouse reads 'Crawford.'

I go through the magnetometer first and she pats me down briskly, then does the same with Bea. Then Crawford speaks into a handheld radio she's carrying, and a buzz opens the steel doors before us. We enter a bleak institutional hallway, a white tunnel, notable for the absence of decoration of any kind on the walls—not a picture, or a frame, no graphics. Outside, I hear shouting and it takes me a second to realize that some of the inmates are in the interior courtyard that functions as an exercise space, probably playing basketball.

Crawford uses one of the innumerable keys rattling off her belt to open another steel door and points us inside. This is the inmates' dining hall. Aaron is seated on the far side of a long stainless-steel table, and he smiles warmly when he sees us. This is how having been inside before helps. He shows no sign of the hobbling fright I experienced in my first days in confinement.

"Can I hug him?" Bea asks Crawford.

"No ma'am," she says. "No contact. You can pat his hand for a second when you sit down, but only a second."

Aaron cannot rise to greet his mother because the chain connecting his handcuffs and leg irons has been locked to a stout iron loop cemented into the floor. Bea and I take the steel bench opposite Aaron's at the picnic-style table.

"Mom," he murmurs when she takes his hand.

The jailer quickly instructs, "Enough," and Bea withdraws her touch with an obedient nod that fills me with sudden pathos. Even a mother's love is now under control of the state.

"I didn't do this, Mom," Aaron says then, even before Bea has unzipped her vest. "This is just insane."

In this moment, I wish I had more experience as a defense lawyer. In my three cases, only the woman who had embezzled from her boss claimed to be innocent, because of her recordkeeping, but she didn't really believe it. Whenever she denied responsibility, she developed a living form of rigor mortis, except for the way her eyes jumped around like bugs. I never represented any of the higher-order crooks I prosecuted who had actually given thought to getting caught and thus had prepared themselves. I am desperate to believe Aaron, as I know Bea will be. But I also recall the months after his first arrest, when he regularly made forceful denials to his mother that he was using, declarations that soon proved to be wildly untrue.

But whether or not his claim now is honest, I raise a hand to caution Aaron against any further comments about his case. Officer Crawford has exited, but another CO, a tall blond guy with a military-style crewcut, stands at a metal door in the rear, with his hands behind his waist as he gazes into space. I explain that whatever the guards overhear Aaron say can be used against him in court. Only his visits with his attorney are truly private.

That reality means that Bea cannot ask her son the many questions that are boiling over in her. What were you thinking running off like that? What were you doing in Ginawaban? How did they end up arresting you there? What's the story with that rope? Instead, I ask Aaron about the facility, which he says isn't bad. He has his own cell, and is sure he will be housed alone, because there is only a single steel bunk hanging from the wall, where he unfolded his bedroll. There is a day room with a TV, where the inmates say they are allowed a couple hours to watch football on the weekends. Overall, there are twenty-two cells, only sixteen currently occupied. So far as Aaron can tell, seven or eight of those men are here for nonpayment of child support or repeated episodes of drunk driving that prevent them from bonding out quickly. One guy, a career burglar, in for breaking into a grocery warehouse, admits to having been in several jails and says Marenago is probably the best of them. The food is decent, no maggots in it, like happened now and then when he was in a facility in Michigan. A lot of potatoes, but you can get worse. The only complaint he voiced, along with a couple of the other men, is that the jail gets pretty cold in the winter. The drive to save fossil fuels in Marenago County apparently begins here.

We have to tell Aaron about Cap. He takes the news with one of those beaten-down victimized shrugs that instinctively sets me on edge: Naturally, my lawyer is deserting me. For poor me, nothing ever goes right.

"Well, who's going to be my lawyer?" he asks.

I repeat exactly what I told Bea, that I still know countless lawyers around the state, and we'll find someone outstanding.

"Not Black," he interjects. The statement is shocking to Bea and to me. For a second, neither of us can manage a response. "I know there are plenty of great Black criminal defense lawyers, Rusty," Aaron says.

"Plenty," I add. I've always been proud of the fundamentally meritocratic nature of the trial bar, where clients make their choices based on a record of good results, and where African-Americans succeeded, even when other sectors of the bar or society were closed to them. Going back decades, the mob chieftains, who knew what was what when it came to criminal prosecutions, consistently chose a Black lawyer, Sherm Crowthers, to represent them. Sherm was hands-down the best trial lawyer in Kindle County when I started out, especially for the kind of violent crimes that got prosecuted in the superior court, although Sandy Stern soon outshone him on white-collar work. Sherm eventually went on the bench and in time to the federal penitentiary for bribery, where he died of cancer.

"But I'm the only Black guy in here," Aaron says. "And you know, I've got a tiny window in my cell, and I swear to God, I haven't seen a single Black person walk by in the street. I mean, it's *white* up here. If there are two African-Americans looking across the courtroom at the jury, I don't think I'd have a chance."

I don't regard Aaron as particularly savvy or strategic. His naivete is often endearing. But he's lived enough to understand being Black, and I immediately recognize he has a point. It's not that every juror up here would hate Aaron on sight. But even if it's just one or two out of the twelve, he'd start out with virtually no chance of acquittal.

"And what's that going to cost anyway?" Aaron asks. "The lawyer?"

Oddly, he is the first member of his family to raise this question. Since we've left Cap, I've recognized that there is another alternative.

In Kindle County, the most experienced defense lawyers on murders are either the state defenders or veterans of that office. As a twenty-two-year-old, Aaron is an independent entity and is broke enough to qualify as indigent and thus to receive free representation. I know nothing about the SD's office up here, but I'll wager a small sum that murders are pretty rare, meaning that group has no more experience trying this kind of case than Cap.

Eventually, we leave that subject and get on to other questions Aaron has that are no easier to answer and will need to be addressed to his lawyer in the end. Can he write a letter of condolence to the Potters? Has anyone informed Gert, his probation officer, about where he is, and if so, what happens with that case? As the conversation goes on, it's clear to me that Aaron is assuming his circumstances now are akin to the period when he was confined in Skageon: It might take a while to work things out, but he's going to get out of here. He shows no recognition of the peril that he may be inside for the rest of his life. Now that Bea is with her son, she too is suddenly buoyant. I realize that it's mostly an act for his sake, but I also have a suspicion that the sight of Aaron, clearly unharmed, the same man who left her house four days ago, makes her feel more optimistic. She remains sunny throughout our time with Aaron, occupying the last few minutes with amusing stories of the kids at school.

Joe is in the waiting area when we emerge. Bea and I agree to walk around for half an hour to give him a chance to see his grandson. We set out from the jail and head toward the center of town. Portage was built on the land bridge between the Marenago River and Sly Creek, one of the sources of the Skageon, that wanders for miles, no wider than a ditch but deep enough to provide outstanding fishing, including a few trout in the spring. I make a mental note that this might be a good spot to take my granddaughters next season for some shore casting, a less dangerous form of angling, since the younger one, Briony, remains a menace with a hook swinging at the end of her line in the small confines of my boat.

Beginning more than a century ago, these river towns thrived with industries related to the logging areas a hundred miles north. Those good times are still apparent in the number of brick buildings that remain. Back then, the big business in Portage was a foundry along the Marenago, where they manufactured papermaking machines. These days, the factory, with its unfaced masonry and its roof of triangular shapes that resemble a row of incisors, has been converted to riverside apartments and a small arts center. But that, alas, is as far as renewal got in Portage. The main street, a row of flat-faced two- and three-story red and brown brick structures that once held ground-level stores and offices overhead, now shows For Rent signs outside many of the up and downstairs spaces. Portage is still the county seat, which drives a small amount of business, especially for the lawyers, but the limited commerce here these days serves the surrounding farms. The largest employer is a tractor and parts dealership called XYZ Supply, housed on the other side of town in an ugly prefab metal building with a shiny rimpled roof.

There is a pretty little park a block from the jail, and for the last few minutes of our wait for Joe we sit on a bench. In the aftermath of our visit, Bea has crashed again as she processes the harsh sight of Aaron sitting casually in chains. For a few minutes we subside to silence. The day has left us both with a lot to process.

Out of nowhere, Bea says, "You know who should be Aaron's lawyer?"

"Who?" I ask.

"You," she says.

I actually laugh out loud.

"That's a terrible idea, Bea."

"Why?"

"About a million reasons. No attorney who knows his butt from a basketball represents a family member."

"Well, he's not your family. Not legally. You're really just getting to know him."

"Bea, he lives in my house. And I'm in love with his mother. I'd never have the professional distance a good lawyer needs to provide objective advice. That's one problem. And I don't have the right background. I've had all of one trial as a defense lawyer. Which was for embezzlement. Not murder. And that was a decade ago."

"But how many murder cases did you try as a prosecutor? Or preside over as a judge?"

"It's different, Bea. The roles are different. Do you think the referees in the NBA can hit a three-point shot, just because they've been on the court to see a thousand go in? Cross-examination, which is where defense lawyers have to shine, is a skill you need to practice to stay sharp. Defending a murder case is like performing brain surgery. Would you want somebody fiddling around inside Aaron's skull who'd never done that before, and hadn't even been in an operating room for years? I'm not qualified."

"Do you know what qualification you do have? You understand what it's like to be charged with a murder you didn't commit."

It's a problem, not a virtue, when the lawyer identifies too much with the client. But I skip that point, since there is so much else wrong with her suggestion.

"Besides, Bea, the judge or the prosecutor—either one of them or both—will probably object. I'm too close to the situation. I might even be a witness."

"What kind of witness?"

The unmentioned details about what Aaron was burning the night he returned are the first thing that crosses my mind.

While I'm thinking about that, Bea adds, "And do the judge and prosecutor get to pick the defense lawyer?"

They don't. She's right about that much. The defendant's choice of counsel is a constitutional right, so long as certain rules are respected. But overall, she's clearly wrong. I close my eyes and breathe, until I can put a name to the apprehensions that swelled in me as soon as I realized she was entertaining this thought. What scares me most is that it's a kind of magical thinking. Having found someone to give her so much of what she always needed emotionally, some weird cross-wiring in her heart has given her the idea that he can also prevent what is clearly shaping up to be the worst thing to happen in her life. And I can't, of course. I'll fail. And we'll never recover from her disappointment. I try to explain that.

"Bea, there's another reason not even to consider this, because it would end up tearing us apart, you and me. I'll stop being the man who loves you and I'll become the man who sent your son to prison."

"But think how much more I'll love you if you win," she says. She can't keep up the deadpan for long. Her smile, even if momentary, is a relief to me, a sign she realizes after a brief discussion that her proposal is a laughing matter. Yet in that, I'm soon disappointed.

"Rusty, think about it," she says as we start walking back to the jail, our arms around each other like strolling high schoolers. "Promise me you'll think about it."

I shake my head again, but say no more, knowing it won't be productive.

When we reach the facility, Joe has just emerged from the steel door leading to the cellblock, and his face is shining with his tears. I've never seen the old guy cry, even after his cancer diagnosis, and the sight bruises my heart.

"I couldn't say it in front of the boy," says Joe, "but all the time I was back there thinkin, 'Dear God, why did you have to let me live to see this?'"

Joe was more collected when Aaron was confined after the arrest in Como Stop that led to his conviction. But he regards drugs as an out-and-out plague, especially after what he saw them do to some soldiers in Vietnam. More important, he knew damn well that Aaron was guilty, and probably thought what a lot of people did, that a little bit of jail was going to kick some sense into the kid—which, frankly, until recently, is exactly what seemed to have occurred. But this, murder, it's life, it's Aaron's life for something Joe believes instinctively his grandson didn't do.

"We gotta get him outta here," Joe says.

Bea and I have no answer to that.

"I tell you what," says Joe. "How about I just say I killed her and let them go after me?"

Bea's mouth parts slightly. Her constantly hard-hearted look, when she regards her father, instantly transforms into something approaching adoration.

"I've actually been thinking the same thing," she says.

'Insane,' the word Aaron used to describe the charges, apparently applies to all of us. The desperation of the situation is filling the brains of both of them with nutso ideas. First me as Aaron's lawyer. And now this.

"All you'd accomplish with those stories," I say to them, "is that you'll each get a cell next to him. The defendant's mother? What parent wouldn't say, 'Do it to me instead?' Or his grandfather with terminal cancer? The prosecutor's going to say immediately, 'What's he lose by taking the blame?'"

"That's the point," says Joe. "Can't do nothin to me that God isn't gonna do soon enough."

Unlike the other members of his family, Joe's faith is purely situational. He seems to think about God only when the deity is useful.

"No, that *is* the point, Joe. Mr. Jackdorp would laugh himself silly."

"I'd do it anyhow," Joe repeats.

"And no one would believe it. An eighty-four-year-old guy with a cane strangles a fit young woman who was eight inches taller than him and trained in martial arts? It's the same for both of you. At your heights"—Bea is no more than five three, but by now she's probably an inch taller than her father—"you'd have needed to bring a ladder even to get a rope around her neck."

"Believe me," Bea says, "when I talk about what she was doing to my son, I could be convincing."

"And how'd you find her to kill her up at Ginawaban or wherever? Neither one of them, her and Aaron, were answering their phones."

Bea has no response. I can see tears welling in her frustration. For a second, a mad second, she thought there was an exit from this dungeon.

"Well, she called me," Joe says.

"Is that so?" I ask. "Aaron had her phone. Which will show no record of her contacting you. I'm touched. By both of you. And at the right time, Aaron should know you each love him so much you wanted to do even *this*. That will mean a lot to him. But I'm sure a million parents in this situation have had the same instinct. And there's a reason it never happens."

We are rescued from this discussion, because Lloyd enters the jail vestibule. Lloyd is now a big lump, six five and certainly over three hundred pounds. He has always been massive, a great football lineman in his day, and unusually broad. I remember being impressed by his hands the first time I met him, when he showed up to fix my furnace, which had conked out in the middle of the night. His hands and fingers were literally twice as wide as mine, but he handled the tiny screws he needed with impressive dexterity. I like Lloyd. He has the gentle confidence of some big men who approach most human interactions with nothing to fear. He is soft-spoken and kind, just as Bea says he was in high school.

She comes forward to hug him. I've never seen any physical tenderness between them before. They are invariably respectful of one another, good exes, but she's right to think that no one else is quite as devastated as the two of them.

Like so many business owners these days, Lloyd is short on qualified help and could not see his way clear to attend the first appearance on short notice, but he came as fast as he could when Bea let him know about the opportunity to visit. We brief him now. When he hears about Cap, Lloyd says, "Doesn't Aaron qualify for the public defender?" To me that means he's already been talking about the potential cost of a defense and Camille has protested. She's not sacrificing her daughters' college educations for an addict and murderer.

That's a bad omen. The magnitude of what Aaron is charged with is going to overturn everything in our lives, disorder all relationships. All the sympathy in the justice system is reserved for the families of murder victims, but the experience is as bad, or even worse, for those who love the accused. Like the jailer who took a long look at Bea today, everyone else is inclined to assume the lovers, the children, the parents of the defendant deserve their suffering. They end up devastated by the combined weight of scorn and loss. I know all of this, have witnessed it a hundred times before, and at close range twice, but it is the oncoming locomotive in a nightmare you have no power to stop. For the first time, a lifeless feeling crowds my chest that I recognize as the initial stirrings of despair.

19

Aaron's Lawyer

October 3–6

I spend the entire day on Tuesday working on getting Aaron good counsel.

I start with Cap, who has some feelers out, he says. When I tell him who Bea wants, he has the same reaction as me. He laughs out loud.

"Well, the price would be right," he says, once he's done chuckling. "And it's not completely ridiculous. No one ever forgets how to try a case."

Cap is right in a way. The experiences of trial are burned into me like a brand. Now and then, in my dreams, I still find myself on my feet making objections. By my own judgment I was a good prosecutor. Steady and competent. And always well prepared. Yet I nurture no illusions that my success in that role would translate to the other side of the courtroom, especially in light of my one effort a decade ago. Prosecutors—public employees with nothing obvious to gain from making false accusations—start out as truthtellers in the eyes of most juries. But I lacked the charisma of someone like Sandy Stern, which helps the best defense lawyers overpower the prosecution's natural advantage.

"We both know Aaron could do a lot better," I tell Cap. He doesn't differ, but as we talk it's far from obvious who that superior choice might be.

Like me, Cap thinks a lawyer from the city will get off to a very bad start with a jury in Marenago County. The jurors will be quick to think he or she is talking down to them, even if they're not.

But finding a country lawyer with the right experience will be difficult. Murders are relatively rare in Skageon and all but unheard-of in Marenago County. The last murder case tried in Portage took place eight or nine years ago. The defense lawyer was the state defender herself, who got a manslaughter from the jury, rather than the first-degree conviction Jackdorp was seeking. That's the good part. The bad is that the SD was Wendy Carrington, the judge in Aaron's case, who is clearly unavailable.

As for the current SD, Rita Nova, Cap has spoken to her and she all but begged him to find retained counsel. No one in Rita's office has tried a murder. More than that, the county has cut her budget three years in a row, meaning she has only skeleton staffing. If she and her two assistants give Aaron's case the priority it will require, all the other work of that office will come to a halt.

The other group of likely candidates, former deputy PAs in Jackdorp's office, are also unavailable. Jackdorp long ago promulgated an ethical rule preventing former criminal prosecutors from taking defense cases for five years after leaving. The rationale—and it's not all baloney—is to ensure that those lawyers don't end up on the other side of cases they had some contact with as prosecutors. The time also provides a breathing space for everyone before the newly minted defense lawyer faces off against the deputies and cops they worked beside. But after half a decade, most former deputies have gravitated to civil work or established practices in other counties. Even following that period, Jackdorp doesn't care to see his former deputies across the courtroom in major cases.

"Is that because he's sentimental about them?" I ask the one former Marenago deputy PA, Tim Blanc, who's willing to take a few minutes to educate me. Blanc finds my question hilarious.

"It's because he wants to win," Blanc answers.

After thirty years in office, Jackdorp is the biggest political power locally and is known to bear a grudge. Former deputy PAs who, for instance, have thoughts of becoming a judge, as most former prosecutors do at times, would imperil that hope by opposing him in a case like this.

It's clear I'll have to cast a wider net. Cap has an evidentiary hearing later this week and needs to concentrate on that, leaving the search to me. On Wednesday morning, I call at least a dozen lawyers I know, looking for names, ending with a conversation with Sandy Stern. Retired more than five years, Stern is doing relatively well in assisted living, although he is mourning the sudden death of the girlfriend he found there. He comes up with a lawyer in Indiana, Darren Forester, who sounds perfect when I get him on the line. Forester is country all the way, with a distinct twang, and he's one of those lawyers whose whole life is trying cases, civil, criminal, arbitration, dog bite to murder. But he's much in demand. His hourly rate is fit for New York City. More to the point, he's starting a civil antitrust case next week that he says "may last the rest of my life." By the time it ends and he picks up on the many matters he will have to ignore in the interval, he projects as much as eighteen months will pass before he would be available for Aaron's trial. If Aaron could get bail, that might be okay, but neither he nor the judge would agree to that kind of delay with Aaron behind bars. In places like Marenago, without a large criminal backlog, defendants who are jailed without bail are pushed to trial quickly. The reason, with which I've always agreed, is that someone presumed to be innocent shouldn't endure prolonged confinement without a judgment on their guilt.

By Friday, I am feeling pressured. Aaron's preliminary hearing is scheduled for Monday, and Cap is reluctant to show up. I still expect the State to return an indictment and obviate the proceeding, but that will only heighten the need to find another lawyer. On a custody case, Judge Carrington may well set a trial date as soon as Aaron comes to court to enter his formal plea of not guilty at the arraignment.

Mae's death has already attracted a lot of publicity, and the same is likely to be true of the trial. Somewhere in the Midwest, there's a good young lawyer who'd like to build a reputation as a defense attorney by taking this case. But after putting out the word to everybody I can think of, that ambitious attorney still has not appeared.

I reluctantly accept that we are going to have to go with somebody from Kindle County, and I phone Nat early Friday for ideas about younger lawyers down there I'm not acquainted with. I explain the situation, including the fact that Bea has only grown more imploring each day that I take up the defense.

"And you're thinking about it?" my son asks.

"Of course I'm not thinking about it, Nat!" I detail the many reasons I regard this as a bad idea for Aaron and for me, including the incalculable damage it is likely to do to my relationship with Bea.

"Have you asked Aaron?" my son says. "If I was him, I'd probably think you were the best alternative. Like you say, a city lawyer will have a hard time up there, and you've got more experience on murders than anybody else you're going to find in Skageon or Marenago County."

"I *am* a city lawyer," I say.

"No, you're not. Not anymore. You're completely woodsy. You've got the beard now and the hair."

"What's wrong with my hair?" I ask, only kidding. He's right that it hangs over my collar these days.

"You know what I mean. You understand how to talk to people up there. What not to say and how to put things in their terms. I think you're not a bad idea."

"You're *not* helping, Nat." Purely as a makeweight that is not convincing even to me, I point out that taking up this defense would come at a cost in Nat's own household. Anna, Nat's wife, whom he first met when she was my law clerk—another long story there—has become a bang-on success as a big-firm litigator. She is an excellent mom, but the law beats its wings over her life like a flying dragon. Her travels, which have resumed after the pandemic, create the episodic need for me to come to Kindle County to help out with the girls.

"We could figure it out," he answers.

"Well, I don't want you to have to. I called you for the names of good young defense lawyers down there who I might not know."

He has several ideas. I'm too embarrassed to tell him that for sound reasons Aaron doesn't want a Black lawyer—Nat and Anna are both vigilantly anti-racist—which my hasty Internet searches as we speak shows is true of half the attorneys he names.

Before we hang up, Nat says, "Dad, the main issue is what's best for Aaron. But if you're holding off because this will harm your relationship with Bea, I'm not sure you're looking at this the right way. If you say no, and Aaron gets convicted, then you'll have a problem anyway, won't you? I mean, every time Bea goes to Rudyard"—the state maximum security prison—"to visit, won't she be wondering what would have happened if the smartest guy she knows had taken the case?"

"I'm hardly the smartest guy she knows. I could name a dozen other people, including you."

"You understand my point. She's got complete confidence in you. And preserving that relationship— I never thought I'd see you this content. Anna too. I think the Bea factor, that says do it. She'll always be grateful you put the rest of your life on hold to try to save Aaron."

Once I hang up, I dwell for a second in a whirlpool of emotion, angry and frustrated and also somewhat scared by the magnitude of the responsibility my son wants me to accept. But that is a point in itself. How much of my reluctance is because I'm scared to fail, rather than dubious about my competence?

As Nat suggested, there is one person who holds the deciding vote and who can, if I'm lucky, shut down this entire discussion. I decide to take the two-hour drive to Portage. Aaron is allowed visitors every afternoon, an hour each. Bea and Joe and Lloyd have been coordinating, and I check to be sure my timing won't conflict with any of them.

Once I arrive, I tell Officer Crawford that this is an attorney visit, and show her my bar card. She places me in a small white cubicle, where improbably there are black scuff marks that run halfway up the wall, looking as if they were left by the heels on someone's shoes. My first thought is that a defense lawyer was struggling, while held in a head lock by a client, until she or he was rescued by the guards.

The advantage of calling this an attorney visit is immediately apparent, not only because we can meet in private but also because Aaron is brought in uncuffed. He is surprised to see me, given our meeting site. He probably expected Cap.

A CO is outside the door, peering in occasionally through a small square window.

"So is this about the lawyer thing?" he asks.

"It is," I say.

I explain what his mother has proposed, and some of the reasons that I've been loath to agree.

"I can't be objective, Aaron, as your lawyer should be, not given my relationship with you, and of course, your mother."

"You mean, because you're going to tell her what I say?"

"No!" I answer emphatically. "I would never tell her or anybody else what you've said, Aaron, unless you specifically instruct me to. Even I know that much."

"But like even if I tell you that I'm guilty?"

My heart stalls, but I answer, "Especially that."

"Well, I'm not," he says, "so that won't be an issue."

I hold up a hand. I don't want to discuss the details of what happened, not yet.

"I wouldn't care, Aaron. I promise you that too. I'd fight like hell for you, no matter what."

"But I'm innocent. And I'll never plead. If you're my lawyer, you better know that. I want a trial."

This is the same thing Aaron told Cap, but I know that time in confinement and the anxiety of not knowing the future often softens that kind of determination. And my experience in this system still slows my willingness to put full faith in his denials. The internal logic of most defendants seems to be that convincing other people you're innocent is the next best thing to it being so.

"And are you going to charge us?" he asks.

"Of course not."

"So nobody goes broke, right? Not my mom or dad?"

"Aaron, don't let money drive this. We'll figure out the finances, your mom and dad and me, if we find the right lawyer."

"Okay," he says. He drums his fingers on the small table. "Okay, let me think about it."

"Take your time." I assume he means over the weekend, but as soon as I stand up, he says, "I like it. This is good."

I'm startled and find myself saying, "May I ask why?"

"Respect, man. You're great at law. Everybody says you're great at law. That's what Mae's grandfather and father told her. And I trust you, Rusty. Half the guys inside, whether I was in Skageon or here, they hate their lawyers, more than the cops or the prosecutors. The attorneys make them scrape up money they don't have—you know, ten thousand dollars—and as soon as they hand it over, the lawyer says, 'Plead guilty.' It's a complete scam as far as the men in here are concerned."

As I told Nat earlier, he's smarter than me and correctly predicted Aaron's likely view.

"Well, there's a little more to this," I say. "And I still need to convince myself."

He draws back slightly. "Don't pull the rug out, man. You come all this way to ask me and then you're gonna say you won't do it anyhow?"

I smile at him. He's got me there.

"The judge and the prosecutor also have to sign off, Aaron. Especially the judge. And if they agree, she'll need to question you in court, so you can't come back later and say you didn't understand what you were getting yourself into with me."

"Do I have to tell her that you can't carry a tune when you hum around the house?"

Aaron's humor is like a lurking assassin that comes out from hiding with no warning. He delivers these lines without smiling. After a quick look at the door and sensing the jailer nowhere near, I reach out and take Aaron's solid form in my arms, even though it's a vivid demonstration of why I should not proceed.

Afterwards, I go back to the park I sat in with Bea. It's a bright day, with the first real feel of cold in the air. Up here, even in the time of global warming, snow is probably no more than a month away. I'm wearing a wool overcoat but reach into my pocket for the neck warmer that's in there. The seasonal winds are beginning to strip the trees of leaves. And the overcast day shows some of that dungeon grey that will last for months.

Whenever I think this through, I get dizzy with the many ways it can go wrong. But there is one hard truth I always come back to. I love Beatrix Mena. She puts a circle of peace in the center of my life. I love Bea, and I am too old to start again or to hope this can be recreated. I am desperate not to lose her and I probably will anyway, for the many reasons I've already figured out. But Nat is right. I am damned if I do. And more damned if I don't.

So will I actually do this? Maybe. I still don't want to answer for certain. But I realize that I have experienced the first moment when I think I could say yes.

The Marenago County courthouse is a gorgeous relic of the rich past. The two towers reach five stories, the one on the north housing a large 150-year-old clock that's still bonging on the hour. The bricks are set off by alternating greystone blocks at the corners, and the small portico has red wooden geegaws over the entry, which also ornament the sides of the two carved pillars. The outer window casings throughout are painted the same red.

I trudge up to the second floor, where the PA's office is located. From inside the foyer, I can see Jackdorp in his expansive office, turned sideways in his desk chair as he speaks on the phone, with his chin raised high, making me think he must be issuing an edict of some kind. I ask the receptionist if he might have a minute, and a few moments later she ushers me inside. Jackdorp's office reflects his three decades in power. The walls are thick with photos of Jackdorp in the company of various personages, governors and legislators. There's one with him shaking Reagan's hand. In the upper right there is a group picture where I'm pretty sure I see Mansy Potter. The corners of the room on either side of his large Empire-era desk are occupied by two busts on pedestals, Greek or Roman figures I don't know enough to name.

When Jackdorp rises, I extend my hand. His skin condition looks no better up close, and he appears older than his movements in court suggested. His face is well creased, in some places virtually corrugated like cardboard. His grey hair, about half gone, is neatly parted on the side.

"I'm Rusty Sabich, Mr. Jackdorp. I'm a lawyer down in Mirror and—"

"I know who you are, Judge," he interrupts. There is nothing pleasant in this acknowledgment. No matter how many people have washed away all suspicions about me in the shower of money in which Kindle County bathed me, there will always be some, especially in the law enforcement community, who won't accept the idea that I was wrongly accused. For people like Jackdorp it's an article of faith: The State never gets things completely wrong. To him, I'm a guy who probably got away with murder.

I tell Jackdorp I may become Aaron's lawyer. As I would have predicted, he plays his cards close to the vest. He listens to me with a studied absence of expression and says only, "Not my business, is it, who represents the damned defendant?"

"Well, I want to be sure you have no objection."

"I'm not going to give this the Good Housekeeping Seal of Approval, if that's what you want." He's afraid I'm trying to trick him, so that after a trial, Aaron would be able to blame him for what proved an unworkable arrangement. I see what he's like. Defense lawyers are untrustworthy turds, with whom you keep your business brief and formal. I repeat again that I'm only trying to give him an opportunity to say so, if he sees a problem.

"Do whatever the hell you like," he says tartly. "But if you're going to be the lawyer, you probably want this."

He hands over the indictment. Although the charging document was expected, the caption, 'People versus Aaron Arthur Housley,' still adds a sluggish beat to my heart.

"Returned this morning," he says.

I take a minute to scan it. Two counts. Murder and obstruction of justice. Then I page back. Count one, the murder count, says Mae was killed in Skageon County at Harold's Woods. It's Count two, the obstruction count, involving hiding the body and tampering with the crime scene, that supposedly took place here in the northern part of Marenago County, near Ginawaban. The US Constitution says that defendants should be tried where the offense occurred, but if related crimes charged in the same indictment happened in different counties, either is legally proper. Yet given the Constitution's command, it's customary that charges are brought—and the trial is held—at the site of the more serious offense.

"A little odd to choose venue here, isn't it, if she was murdered in Skageon?"

"Where her father's the prosecutor? I thought Aaron's defense lawyer would be pleased."

"And if I'm not?"

"Tough luck," he says, with no hint of humor. "It's my choice. Look at the law."

His brusque manner doesn't land well.

"I know the law, Mr. Jackdorp," I answer. "If I proceed as Aaron's lawyer, I'm sure you'll find that I have a lot of shortcomings in that role. Knowing the law won't be one of them. That was my job for a long time."

We stare, unblinking, across his large desk. Not off to a flying start, I'd say.

I finally speak, telling him I'd like to run this by Judge Carrington as well. He calls out the door to ask his assistant to find out if 'Wendy' is in. She is, and we head to the first floor, where Judge Carrington's chambers are located, immediately behind her courtroom. Her space, anteroom and private office, is equivalent to Jackdorp's, but far more sparsely decorated. There are lots of photos of her daughters and husband on the credenza behind her desk.

I was right. She recognized me. As we enter, the judge gets up and offers her hand with a warm grin. She's been working in chambers in a cream blouse and a straight navy skirt, casual attire but proper, which is probably her manner at all times. Her reading glasses hang from her neck by a chain croaky. She doesn't seem to have aged much from my memory of her. She has to be late fifties now. If she's greying, it's been dyed away, and she's a bit thinner. When we did that panel, as I recall, she was no more than a year past the birth of her second child, who must be the one in a Cornell sweatshirt in several photos.

"So nice to see you, Judge," she says. She seems to mean it. Of course, she was the state defender when I was released from prison, with the prosecutor saying, 'I made a big mistake.' The entire defense community in the state exulted and thought of me as a bit of a hero.

The contrast in their attitudes toward me, Jackdorp's and the judge's, supports an intuition that there are many areas where they don't see eye to eye. Certainly, there seems to be a little coolness between them. When she turns to Jackdorp, she simply nods and says, "Jack," and points both of us to armchairs in front of her desk.

I explain what brings me, careful to note that Aaron lives in my house with his mother, who I'm engaged to marry. I also say that I haven't fully set aside my own misgivings, but that Aaron, at least on first blush, wants me to do this.

"Well," she says. "Let me think about it a bit. But my first reaction is like Jack's. It's the defendant's constitutional right to have the lawyer he wants, unless there's some obvious professional problem. Which I don't see right now. Mr. Sabich isn't a witness, is he?" she asks Jackdorp.

"Not so far as I know," he answers. It's dawned on me already that signing on as Aaron's lawyer will keep me from routine questioning by the police. I have no regrets they won't hear about that fire.

Mulling for a second, Judge Carrington adds that any trial witnesses who know about my personal relationship with Aaron must be cautioned against mentioning it, to prevent the jury getting the impression that I'm vouching for my future stepson.

"And unfortunately," she adds, "I won't address you as 'Judge' in front of the jury. That wouldn't be fair to the State either."

"Of course," I answer.

She looks to Jackdorp and me. For now, neither of us has more to say.

"All right, let me know, Judge, when you make your final decision. If you want to go forward, I'll take a look at a couple of cases, just to be sure I'm not missing something. And I'll want to admonish your client on the record, so he can't claim later that he was disadvantaged by this arrangement."

"Understood," I say.

"Well, good," she says and stands. She wishes me a safe drive home and then adds a remark, at which I notice Jackdorp briefly wince.

"It would be a pleasure," she says, "to have you in my courtroom."

20

My Decision

On Saturday, about eleven a.m., I am heartened to receive a text from Mansy, asking if I have the time to meet for coffee later this afternoon. That seems like a good start to reestablishing our relationship. My best guess is that he wants to plot a path past the twin horrors of Aaron's indictment and Mae's death, deciding what contact we might have and what we won't talk about.

We meet at a corner table in a little place called Coffee &, a bakery and coffeehouse in Como Stop that excels in both departments. It's an upscale competitor with Starbucks. The outstanding sweets are baked on the premises, and the beans are roasted in a giant stainless-steel cauldron that dominates the interior and fills the place with magnificent aromas. The tables are brown granite.

I'm there a few minutes before Mansy and come to my feet when he arrives. Finding his eye, I shake his hand and say again how devastated we were by the news of Mae's death and how heartbroken we are for all of them. That neatly skips subsequent developments.

In response, Mansy looks away and shakes his white head.

"It's hit me pretty hard. I mean, Mark. And Kathleen. But this is the worst. The circumstances..." he says. And doesn't finish. Now that I'm with him, I note an uncharacteristic lack of focus in those ice-blue eyes, as if a news crawl were at the bottom of the screen on whatever he's witnessing in the present. Mansy regards complaining as unworthy, so I know the little bit he has allowed himself to say averts what is in reality an ocean of pain.

Bea and I had debated whether to attend Mae's funeral—we both decided yes was the correct answer—but the Potter family opted for a private service graveside. There will be a celebration of life at some undetermined date—probably after Aaron's case is resolved, I suspect, when the attendees will fully understand the circumstances under which Mae died.

We both order only coffee, and once it arrives, Mansy settles into the topic that apparently motivated his request to meet.

"Thanks for coming out," he says, a dispiriting remark. I am sad to think that things between us have unraveled to the point that he feels he must express gratitude about something he's always known I would do automatically. "I need to put a question to you."

"Anything, of course."

"I've heard a rumor that seemed unlikely to me, but I wanted to ask you directly. Is it really true that you're thinking of filing an appearance in Aaron's case?" 'Filing an appearance' is legalese for becoming Aaron's trial lawyer. I'm surprised, naturally, by how fast the news has spread.

"I was going to give you the courtesy of letting you know, once I made up my mind," I say, vamping quickly. This is a stone lie. Informing Mansy never occurred to me, amid the many other worries. But he takes me at my word.

"Well, I'm relieved to hear that," he says, "that you were going to discuss this with me. Because if I can say it, Rusty, I can't comprehend how you would even be giving this idea serious consideration."

I smile a little. "Love makes you do crazy things."

The understated humor that is always part of the currency between us doesn't seem to hit well.

"Well, you'll forgive me, but it *is* crazy. This is Bea's idea?"

"I think 'obsession' is a better word."

"Have you explained to her that you're not the only good lawyer in the state?"

"Many times. But finding an adequate replacement is not as easy as you might think. For one thing, I'll work cheap," I say.

"You can afford to pay legal fees."

"I can, but Aaron and Bea and Lloyd can't, and it would be a bitter pill in a bad situation to take my money."

"Still," he says. "You can't have your intended running the defense. So it sounds like you're off to a bad start. And I'm not sure you really understand what you're getting yourself into. You're not going to have a good time."

"With my almost-stepson's life in my hands? That occurred to me already." A few feet away, the steam machine hisses as it froths a cappuccino. The pleasant odor of cinnamon is persistent as people drink hot apple cider or pumpkin spice latte. Just as was the case at our last lunch, I've noticed we are occasionally gathering some second looks from other customers. "Mansy, is it all right if I ask how you heard about this? I still haven't put anything in writing."

He takes a beat. There is an elderly twitch that's started showing minutely around his mouth. The evidence is mounting every minute of how Mae's death has run him over.

"Jackdorp called Hardy late yesterday afternoon."

I nod. It's no surprise that Jackdorp and Hardy, PAs in adjoining counties, are in communication. Besides, Hardy is the victim's father. Still, it's a little off-key for Jackdorp to be so quick to discuss a matter in which Hardy is supposed to have no say.

Mansy continues. "Someone might have made you think that Aaron's going to have a great advantage with Wendy Carrington as the judge. It's true that there's a lot of bad blood between Jack and her. Wendy hated working for Jack so much that she volunteered to become the SD, not a natural path for most prosecutors. And then she was such a stickler and pain in the ass that Jackdorp actually told her he'd support her if she ran for judge. She blamed Jack when another former PA entered the race, and she might even have been right to think he arranged that without his fingerprints showing.

"But apparently, he's cuffed her around enough that she thinks twice before giving him an excuse for more. He's been a presence in that county a lot longer than her. Most of your jurors will have voted for Jack several times. I'm told he just makes faces at the jury when he finds her rulings problematic. And he gets a lot of backing in the appellate court. He's mandamused her twice and won." 'Mandamus' means that the appellate court took the extraordinary step of correcting Judge Carrington even while a case was still going on in front of her.

"Seems like you know Hiram Jackdorp pretty well, Mansy."

"Of course I do. He's been the Republican chair up there for more than twenty years. I sat on the state central committee with him. I won't pretend that I have great affection for him. The man doesn't seem to have much need of friends. With him it's like cuddling a cactus, and I'm still not convinced he's really mastered how to smile. But you shouldn't think Wendy will make things easy for Aaron. Jack will run the show up there. He always does. And he's no liberal. You know that maxim that a prosecutor should strike hard blows but fair? Jack takes the first part to heart. That stuff about fairness—that's the defense lawyer's job."

I can't fully stifle a laugh, because Mansy's formulation is true of many prosecutors, particularly the bad ones.

"Don't get me wrong. He'll color inside the lines," Mansy says. "He got his fingers burned on a *Brady* violation by the supreme court when I was up there." That means Jackdorp failed to turn over evidence favorable to the defense, which the US Supreme Court has long said is an essential ingredient of a fair trial. "But it won't be service with a smile."

"I appreciate the warning," I say, although I don't. No lawyer worth his salt should be deterred because the guy on the other side is a jerk.

Mansy says, "I would think one of Jack's former deputies who worked in his office would be a much better choice for Aaron. Someone Jack would at least be cordial to. And whom the jurors might even recognize."

I explain how Jackdorp roadblocks the lawyers who worked for him from showing up across the courtroom.

"I see," says Mansy. His brow condenses as he mulls these unexpected facts.

"Look, Mansy. You're not telling me something I don't know by suggesting there's a better lawyer for Aaron somewhere. But I've been SOL in finding that person." I briefly describe the obstacles to finding Aaron other qualified counsel. "You're probably acquainted with every courtroom lawyer in this part of the state. I'm sure you don't want to appear to be helping Aaron—"

"I certainly don't."

"But if you know the right person, write the name on a piece of paper with no return address and leave it in my mailbox. We'll talk to him or her at once."

Mansy makes a small wave over the stone table. He's not going to take on that problem.

"Mansy, I won't offend you by telling you that Aaron is innocent."

"Please don't," he says.

"I know it's early. But so far, simply from the feel of things, I think there's a chance he may be. So it's essential he be well represented. This isn't a case where he just needs somebody to take his hand and escort him to the penitentiary gate."

Mansy frowns openly.

"Well, we hear it's a solid case. But Rusty, let me make this easy. As a matter of personal privilege, as a friend, a longtime friend, and one who has done you a favor or two, find someone else."

His plainness surprises me and I don't answer.

"I don't like to be melodramatic, Rusty, but if you proceed, it will be the end of our friendship."

"Forever?" I ask abruptly, sounding to myself like a wounded teenager.

"Without question."

"Can you explain?"

"Look, a case like this—you're going to put the victim on trial. You'll say not only that Aaron didn't kill her, but that there were a lot of other people who would have wanted to."

"I haven't even thought about what the defense will be."

"I have. And I'm not going to be happy sitting in that courtroom watching someone I counted as my close friend slinging mud at a young woman I'm in despair about losing."

I have a feeling that this is like Mansy's inkling that Mae and Aaron might have eloped. He knew something he wasn't willing to share then, and he knows enough about Mae to realize that the defense he outlined is inevitable.

"Promise me you'll think about this," he says.

"That's what I've been doing all week. But out of respect—and love—I'll add what you've said to the brew, before I make a final decision."

He leans a little closer and speaks softly. He gives me the first small smile I've seen today.

"Decide right, Rusty. Please."

With that, he stands and, despite my protest, throws down a $20 bill to cover the check. Then he goes off. His arthritic hip, the one that hasn't been replaced, is clearly bothering him more than ever, because he moves now with a distinct hitch.

I sit, waiting for this meeting to settle out within me. I don't know how long I remain here, largely still, but what gathers in me is deepening sadness and increasing agitation.

My first conclusion is about Mansy. I return in memory to the sense of doom I had a few days ago when Dom Filipini showed me that warrant for Aaron's arrest and I realized that life will never be the same. Mansy, a precious friend who has been one of the pillars of my revival here in Skageon—he is likely gone from me for good.

I feel deeply for Mansy. I wouldn't trade places with him—or Charmaine or Hardy—even for a minute. But there is something ugly going on. The fact that Jackdorp called Hardy as soon as I left the courthouse—that speaks volumes. Because it demonstrates that it is no accident that this case will be tried in Marenago County, rather than here. That was a decision the two PAs made in consultation. Perhaps they gave some thought to the conflict in Hardy's dual position as prosecutor and father of the victim. But in that kind of circumstance, it would not be unusual for Jackdorp to ask to be appointed by the state supreme court to try the case here. Hardy and Jackdorp agreed on Marenago because a jury up there is more likely to convict Aaron.

In the last twenty-four hours I have thought more than once about Aaron's remark that once he got a hundred miles north of Skageon, there were far fewer drivers who would pick up a young Black hitch-hiker on the side of the road. That, I suspect, is what Hardy explained to Jackdorp—that if this case were tried here, there would probably be three or four jurors whose children or grandchildren were in Bea's school and who in most instances think highly of her. There easily could also be one or two who over the years have encountered Aaron, who, despite his troubles, has always been a quiet but likeable kid. A few might also have heard gossip about Mae and her sometimes-antic misbehavior. State law, even-handed on its face, gives the prosecutors a choice of where to bring this case, and so they will deviate from cus-tom in order to deprive Aaron of the natural advantage of being tried where he lives.

So the Potters have a clear agenda, one that cannot be concealed even by Mansy's graciousness and charm. The family's suspicions of Aaron grew in the weeks before Mae's body was discovered, when Aaron returned and she did not, when he followed his lawyer's advice and refused to answer questions. Those suspicions have now solidified into a diamond-hard certainty that he is guilty. Over the decades, I have seen this frequently with the families of murder victims. In their grief, they need a hasty explanation to make sense of their loss. And thus, for them, emotion demands that Aaron be swiftly tried and imprisoned. And that is now their mission.

Mansy came to this meeting with a long list of selling points he delivered with his usual polish: 'The prosecutor will truss you on his altar for ritual slaughter.' 'The judge won't help you.' 'You aren't up to this professionally.' 'If you proceed, we won't be friends.' The Potters would prefer a walkover to a fair trial. In their view, Jackdorp made a serious mistake yesterday in saying he won't oppose my representa-tion. Because, in his regard for me, Mansy fears I might actually excel.

Mansy used a word that grated when I heard it and which places these recent maneuverings in their proper light: 'Privilege.' For a cen-tury and a half, the Potters have run things in Skageon County like benevolent potentates. And by the judgment of most people, includ-ing me, they have done a decent job of it. They pose a worthy contrast to the ham-handed politicians I grew up watching in Kindle County, with their foxy smiles as they employed a steady motto—'Where's mine?'—and turned public office into a personal treasure chest.

But because the Potters have been somewhat self-sacrificing, when the moment arises, when their personal needs become paramount, they take it as a matter of right—of privilege—to ensure those needs are met. Hardy, not really up to family standards, was nonetheless installed as the local prosecuting attorney, because Mark died and making Harrison PA tempered Mansy's terrible loss. And now the Potters' desires demand that the prison cell clang shut as swiftly as possible behind Aaron for decades, even the remainder of his life. And with their manipulations they are implementing a disturbing calculus, which says that justice for Mae is far more important than justice for him.

So I will do it. I will be Aaron's lawyer. I will do it, because I can reluctantly see I am the best choice available, a judgment that Mansy, unwittingly, has confirmed. I will do it, because it provides the best chance to preserve Bea's love. I will conquer my own fear of failing. And I will fight passionately for Aaron. But I will also do it because the calling that has been mine throughout my adult years as an American lawyer stands on a first principle, albeit one that has not always been applied to humans Aaron's color. But win or lose, I will accomplish this much for myself. I will say to the Potters, and to Bea, to Joe and Lloyd, to God, in case He or She is looking in, and to myself, that the life Aaron was granted, and along with it, the limitless future he was endowed with, which is now in peril—that life is worth every bit as much as the troubled one Mae Potter so sadly lost.

II.

The Prosecution

21

Opening for the People

February 6, 2024

"Ladies and gentlemen," he says, "my name is Hiram Jackdorp and I am the elected prosecuting attorney for Marenago County." Mansy is wrong. Jackdorp can smile. He does it briefly as he comes to take up his position at a respectful distance from the jury box. For a second, he stands there in silence in a grey wool suit that is probably decades old, a middle-sized man with an old face and bad skin, and a greying mustache trimmed above his lip. As Mansy warned me, everybody in the jury box looks to Jackdorp with clear regard. He has played the role up here for decades of an avenging Old Testament God—unsparing, and uninterested in excuses from those who cross the line. I am yet to encounter anyone around town who speaks of Jackdorp fondly. But he does what must be done, as they see it. Without Hiram Jackdorp, life as they know it would veer toward chaos.

Jackdorp's only job as a lawyer has been as a prosecutor, and I suspect he will be good at it. After giving his name, his pleasant expression evaporates and he reverts to his standard courtroom manner, irretrievably grim, as he introduces Lieutenant Special Agent Vanda

Glowoski, who occupies the other chair at the prosecution table. Predictably, she is perfectly coiffed with rigid posture and a bright new manicure, her orderly beauty drained of all appeal by her taut manner.

"With the lieutenant," he continues, "it will be my sad duty to present to you the evidence which will prove beyond a reasonable doubt that on September 14 of last year, this young man, Aaron Housley—" Jackdorp turns then and gestures literally with the back of his hand at Aaron. My stepson-to-be, my client, is seated beside me in a royal blue suit whose purchase became Bea's obsession, hoping to make the perfect impression on the jury. We wanted a garment that would show Aaron was respectful of the process—and thus the jurors—without pretending to be someone he wasn't, for example by imitating me. His facial jewelry—nose ring and earrings—was taken from him by the jail. He's been allowed to grow his hair out to a medium length, in order to hide the prison haircut that would show he's in custody, but the chartreuse topping is long gone. I am in a far more conservative outfit, albeit the standard costume I have always donned for trials— midnight blue suit, white shirt, muted red tie—hoping to send a sub- liminal message of abiding patriotism.

Before Jackdorp started, I told Aaron, 'You're not going to enjoy his opening, but he's going to point at you, and when he does, be sure to look right back at him without hostility, but also no shame, no fear.' Aaron does a good job of that right now.

"—that Aaron Housley murdered by strangulation the victim in this case, a beautiful bright lively young woman named Mae Cheryl Potter, this young woman." A fifty-inch monitor is angled toward the jury box from a position near the witness stand and it comes to life for the first time with a color photo of Mae. It is one of her headshots from her brief time as a model. Her mouth is parted in laughter, her blue eyes full of dancing light. Her head is tilted upward, and one hand is behind her ear, playing with one of her loose curls. Jackdorp's choice of this picture is considered. It's not a photo taken at church. It concedes that this was a young woman who liked her fun. "The evidence will show beyond a reasonable doubt that Aaron Housley did that, and because of that, he must now be found guilty and pay the price. You swore an oath to follow the law. And that, I am sad to say, is what the law requires."

We are back in the main courtroom, that jewel of carved sycamore. I discovered during pretrial hearings that the acoustics in here rival those of a concert hall, meaning there is no need for the booming stentorian tone I first adopted decades ago in the auxiliary courtrooms of Kindle County, where the totalitarian architectural style seemed to flatten voices. In his firm voice, Jackdorp is as perfectly audible to me as he would be in a pair of earbuds.

Aaron is seated to my left at the defense table, which by tradition is the one further from the jury. Positioned to my immediate right is my investigator, Susan DeLeo. I hired her the same day I parted unhappily with Mansy in Como Stop. Susan was the staff investigator for the SD's office in Skageon County, and had impressed me with her help on cases I handled a decade ago. I lured her out of retirement, with the prospect of a paramount experience, working on a well-publicized murder trial. She is dressed in what I regard as her personal uniform, a fringed rawhide jacket and matching skirt, with an array of turquoise jewelry, including several rings. Her hairdo is even more attention-getting, a rainbow-striped Mohawk pasted stiffly up the center of her otherwise shaved head. I have never felt free to ask what meaning she gives to all of this, whether she, for instance, is honoring Native ancestry, or simply doesn't want to dress like most other people.

For today at least, with the drama of openings, the courtroom pews are full. Beyond the rail, in the front row they share with at least a dozen journalists, the families sit, each on their 'sides' of the courtroom, a ghoulish echo of the wedding that Aaron and Mae momentarily contemplated. The Potters—Hardy, Mae's older sister, Harriet, on a brief visit from Colorado, and Mansy—are right behind Jackdorp's table. On our side, Bea, worn with worry, sits directly behind her son. Aaron's dad, Lloyd, is beside her. In my occasional dealings with Lloyd of late, he frequently appears spaced-out, unable to accommodate the fact that after his time in law enforcement this is happening to anybody in his family. Charmaine and Joe were here for jury selection, but as forthcoming witnesses, they will be barred from listening to the evidence until their testimony is complete. Bea leaned across the rail to touch my shoulder before the jury was called in this morning, a welcome instant of connection in a circumstance where those moments have become far less common.

"Just to outline briefly, the evidence will show that the defendant Housley and Mae had an on-again, off-again personal relationship that dated back to junior high school. Sometime in early September last year, Housley asked Mae Potter to marry him, and they had gone off for a few days together in isolation, revealing their plans to no one in advance, so that they could talk seriously about his proposal. At least that is what he believed. But once they got to Harold's Woods in northern Skageon County, a favorite campground of the defendant's, Mae refused to pay attention. Instead, she was principally interested in taking photos of herself, selfies and videos, since she hoped to become something called a 'TikTok Influencer.'" He shakes his head minutely and adds, "Don't expect me to explain that one." Many of the jurors, watching carefully, grin, an uncomfortable sign to me that they are already with him. "The evidence will show you that by the morning of September 14, Mr. Housley had had enough of that. He grabbed Mae's phone from her in the parking area of Harold's Woods, where a physical fight broke out between them. That fight continued and intensified so that sometime in the next two hours Aaron Housley strangled Mae Potter with a white nylon rope—this one—from a position behind her in her 2022 Subaru." The long loop of white rope recovered from our garage has sat on the prosecution table, unexplained until now, when Jackdorp picks it up. It's contained within a thick transparent plastic envelope, sealed with orange tape marked 'Evidence.' Now he weighs it in his hands, as if he can feel its sinister energy. "The indictment further alleges that after Mr. Housley killed Mae, he drove her car, with her remains inside, about ninety miles north up here to Ginawaban and disposed of the SUV and her body by crashing the vehicle at the bottom of an old utility road and hiding it behind some of the broken brush. That conduct led to the second charge in our indictment, obstruction of justice." On the screen, Jackdorp displays a photo of Mae's silver Subaru as it was discovered under heavy vegetation.

"Now, as you look across the courtroom at Aaron Housley, you may be thinking that he appears like a nice enough young man. But you will learn that he was under a court order—"

"Objection!" I shout on pure instinct and rocket to my feet.

The most protracted legal fight Jackdorp and I had prior to trial was about whether he could make any reference to Aaron's felony drug conviction. If the defendant doesn't testify, his criminal record is usually barred from evidence. The law reasons that jurors who learn about a prior offense become more likely to convict the accused just for being a bad person, rather than based on the proof concerning the crime for which they're currently on trial.

Jackdorp maintained that it was proper to introduce the conviction, because an important part of his evidence against Aaron is that he disappeared when he learned that Mae's body had been found. And the inference that he was fleeing from imminent prosecution is stronger when it's buttressed by the fact Aaron was under a court order not to leave Skageon County and not to drive.

The judge ultimately split the baby, ruling that Aaron's prior conviction be barred from evidence. But the jury could be told that he was under an agreed court order which, for unspecified reasons, set various restrictions on his activities. I was initially unhappy with the ruling, feeling that the jurors would be quick to assume that those limitations reflected a conviction of some kind. Susan laughed that off. 'They'll assume it was drunk driving. Around here, half the people on the jury have been pulled over for that.' Either way, the intent of the judge's ruling was to prevent the very implication Jackdorp just gave to Judge Sams's prior court order, that Aaron is some kind of bad kid.

Now the judge sustains my objection, with a furious look at Jackdorp, but I still ask to be heard outside the jury's hearing. We all move to the side of the judge's bench farther from the jury box, where she can lean down to confer with the attorneys. The defendant has the right to listen in, and I have encouraged Aaron to join us at the sidebar, as long as he avoids looking bored. With her courtroom full of spectators, Wendy Carrington has made a mild surrender to vanity and has a new haircut and a lot more makeup than she has worn to date. On the occasions I've seen her in the corridor behind the courtroom in her judicial robes, I've noticed that, since she is only a little more than five feet, the black fabric reaches almost to her ankles.

"Your Honor," I say in a hushed voice as soon as everyone is assembled, "I have to move for a mistrial," meaning I am asking for the trial to stop right now. I explain what the judge already knows, namely that she had prohibited Jackdorp from trying to draw implications about Aaron's character from the court order he violated.

"On the contrary," Jackdorp answers, "you said, Judge, that I couldn't refer to the defendant's conviction. I didn't." It is all he can do to keep from smirking.

Beneath her dark straight bangs, Wendy Carrington studies Jackdorp with a look that broils with hatred. His violation of her ruling is so blatant that it seems calculated to get her to lose control and perhaps to undermine herself immediately in front of the jury.

"Mr. Jackdorp, you understood completely the very limited purpose for which I agreed to admit that evidence. Mr. Sabich, your motion for a mistrial will be taken under advisement," meaning she's going to think on it for an undetermined time. "Mr. Jackdorp, if you continue to defy me, then I will not only grant a mistrial motion, but assuming I decide the case can be tried again, part of my order will require the appointment of a special prosecutor, to prevent any reoccurrence."

She nods curtly. Jackdorp says again with the barest sincerity that he thought he was abiding by the letter of her ruling. His real purpose, I've decided, was to let both me and the judge know who is actually in charge. If anything, the distaste between the prosecutor and the judge, as I've watched it play out in the various pretrial proceedings, is even fiercer than I'd anticipated.

The judge addresses the jury once everyone has returned to their seats.

"Ladies and gentlemen, let me tell you right now, you are going to hear some evidence that at the time of the alleged offenses, Mr. Housley was under a court order which he had agreed to, and which prohibited him from engaging in certain activities. You are not to speculate about why that court order came into being. You certainly may not infer from that evidence anything about Mr. Housley's character. In other words, what Mr. Jackdorp just tried to tell you, that the order shows that Mr. Housley is not a nice young man, that is not true. You gave your word by the oath you took to follow my instructions. And I am instructing you now that you cannot consider that evidence for that purpose. Take that thought out of your heads. That's not what it means or was intended to mean. Mr. Jackdorp knows better.

"Now and then, the lawyers for both sides are likely to make mistakes, to say things they shouldn't have. The other side will object and I will rule. That is a normal part of the trial process. Sometimes it will happen that the law or my prior rulings were very clear, and you may see me become quite irked with the lawyer who made the objectionable remark, as I'm sure was obvious to you in the case of Mr. Jackdorp's comment. That, too, happens in trials occasionally. All right, Mr. Jackdorp. Proceed."

I wonder how all this will land in the jury box. Angering judges is generally not the way for trial lawyers to burnish a jury's opinions of them. But Jackdorp has the advantage of his long standing in this community. During jury selection, the judge agreed to excuse several potential jurors who were personally acquainted with Jackdorp—including his minister. Further, as Mansy reminded me months ago, the simple odds say most of the people in the jury box have voted for Jackdorp several times and approve of his job performance. He is now in his seventh term as prosecuting attorney.

Overall, in the war of impressions that is every trial, I think Jackdorp may have won this first round. Given all the agitation, the jurors are quite likely to conclude that there is something significant about that court order, which they are not being told.

Jackdorp returns to his place six or seven feet from the jury box.

"Well, I apologize to the Court for that misunderstanding. But the evidence will show you the defendant was under a court order and that he defied it. He was not supposed to drive. But he did. Numerous witnesses, including his own grandfather, will tell you that. He wasn't supposed to leave Skageon County. But after he heard Mae Potter's body had been found, he did. He was up here over at Ginawaban, far from home, when the police finally arrested him. We'll talk about why he returned to what was, in a fashion, one of the scenes of the crime."

In the face of all this talk about his untoward behavior, I have felt my client periodically tense. Generally speaking, Aaron is well suited temperamentally to carry out the standard advice for a criminal defendant, which is to display no reaction to the evidence and to remain calm before the jury, even, if possible, self-confident. With Aaron, my concern is that he might take things too far and appear entirely aloof, and at the worst moments, dangerously out of touch.

During the last months, I have tried to pay close attention to Aaron and the toll all this is taking on him—his long confinement, the weight of being charged with a terrible crime, or the bizarre reality that twelve strangers off the street will decide the course of the rest of his life. Although I have focused on him more clearly than when my reactions to him were mediated largely by my concerns about his mother, he is in some ways more obscure to me than ever. Certainly, if anything, the months of isolation from friends and family seem to have reduced his already subdued affect and caused him to sink further into himself. He's listened patiently when Susan and I have met with him to discuss the evidence, but judging by his frequent vacancy, I doubt he is taking much of it in, and clearly prefers not to dwell on the facts of the case. He can answer questions, smile when it is called for, and seems generally—even troublingly—remote from any anger.

Yet this morning, I found him almost buoyant. Standing outside the lockup, the room with a small cell beside the courtroom, where Aaron will be confined during the brief intervals when court is not in session, I gave him my game-day speech, repeating pointers he's heard several times before. At the end, I put my hand on his as it gripped one of the cell bars.

'Listen, I don't know how this is going to turn out. But I know I'm prepared. Susan and I couldn't have worked any harder. You're going to get a good defense.'

He nodded several times, then showed me one of his tiny unexpected smiles.

'You want to know what I think?' he asked. 'This will seem really weird to you. But I'm pretty sure I'm going to be like you. I'm walking out of here.'

The fact that I made a heroic rise from very similar circumstances has undoubtedly fused my bond with Aaron. He never has to ask if I understand what he's going through. But his prediction brought a flutter of despair to my chest. Despite some obvious flaws, the case Jackdorp will be presenting against him is coherent and entirely plausible.

By now, Jackdorp has returned briefly to the podium, which he's rotated to face the jury box, to take a quick glance at his notes.

"Now I would like to discuss with you in more detail the evidence you are going to hear. I'm sure Mr. Sabich across the courtroom, when it's his turn to talk to you, is going to tell you that our evidence, the People's evidence, is merely circumstantial." He wags two fingers in the air to make quotation marks and accompanies it with a trifling smile. "At the end of the case the judge is going to tell you that circumstantial evidence can be regarded by you as just as convincing as direct evidence"—he again raises his hands to act out the punctuation—"meaning what somebody saw or heard. Why? Well, if the path out your window is clear when you go to sleep, and covered with snow when you wake up, you know it snowed overnight. The snow on the path is circumstantial evidence of the weather. And if the snow is fresh when you wake up, and there are shoeprints in the snow several hours later, then the circumstantial evidence tells you without any doubt that somebody walked down that path. You didn't see the person. But you know someone passed by, and you know it beyond a reasonable doubt.

"Now, as it happens, there is going to be quite a bit of testimony in this case about actual shoeprints. And they will prove to be just like the prints you might see out your window in the snow. There won't be eyewitnesses who saw Aaron Housley kill Mae Potter. But those shoeprints, and the testimony of the pathologist and other forensic experts, and the proof about that rope I showed you, also very important—all that so-called circumstantial evidence, will prove just as clearly as any eyewitness what happened to Mae Potter."

Jackdorp, who is now strolling a bit, nods sagely, as if agreeing with his assessment of how clear the jury will find the evidence.

"Now, this sad tale starts on September 12 last fall, when the defendant Housley drove off with the victim, Mae Cheryl Potter, in her 2022 silver Subaru Outback, an SUV for those of you unfamiliar

with it. You will hear from Mae's mother, Charmaine Potter, that
Aaron had recently asked Mae to marry him. Before they left on September 12, Aaron told a friend of his, Cassity Benisch, who you will
also be meeting in this courtroom—Mr. Housley told Cassity that he
and Mae intended to camp for a few days, where they had agreed to
give their full attention to their possible marriage, and for that reason
to turn off their cellphones.

"The next time Cassity heard from Aaron was late on September 14.
She asked how it had gone with Mae, and he answered, using a barn-
yard term, that the trip had turned out badly. He said that despite
their agreement to turn off their phones, Mae was completely focused
on taking selfies and uninterested in talking about their marriage.
Finally, on the morning of September 14, in frustration he'd grabbed
her phone and left her behind. He hitchhiked straight home, he told
Cassity, although he acknowledged that as they spoke he still had a
distance left to travel, because it had been harder than he expected
to find rides. You will hear evidence showing you that what Aaron
Housley said to Ms. Benisch—that he had hitchhiked straight back to
Mirror starting September 14—that was untrue.

"So what is the true story of what had happened to Mae Potter?
You will learn that on the early morning of September 14, a man
named George Lowndes parked in one of the lots at Harold's Woods.
He was there to accompany his wife for an early morning hike on her
birthday, and they had arrived a bit before eight a.m. They reached
the head of the eastern trail, not far from the parking lot, when they
realized that Mrs. Lowndes had left her water bottle in their car, and
Mr. Lowndes walked back to get it. When he did, he saw two young
people at the far end of the lot. One was a tall young man, who, from
his hair and complexion, Mr. Lowndes thought was probably African-
American. The second figure was a tall blond young woman. The
young man was holding something over his head. She was shouting at
him, jumping to reach what he held, which he kept moving away from
her. Finally, according to Mr. Lowndes, the male pushed her down.
She got back up and started screaming again. Mr. Lowndes will tell
you that he was a little concerned about what he was witnessing, but
Mrs. Lowndes was waiting and so he went on to meet her.

"When Mr. and Mrs. Lowndes were done with their walk, about two hours later, they returned to the little gravel parking area. Mr. Lowndes visited the restroom. As he was on the way back to his car, a silver SUV—remember my description of Mae's car—came tearing out of the lot. Mr. Lowndes had to jump out of the way, and the SUV went right by him. Inside, he saw a single passenger, an African-American male driver, who closely resembled the young man Lowndes had seen tussling with the blond female.

"So what had happened to the young woman Mr. Lowndes observed in the midst of that argument Mr. Lowndes saw starting to turn physical? What occurred in the two hours that the Lowndeses were off on their birthday hike? The evidence will show you. It will show you that Mae Potter was strangled to death right inside the car by that young African-American male.

"After Mae did not return home from her trip with Aaron, state investigators began looking for her. They spoke to Cassity Benisch, who told them that Mr. Housley had said Mae and he had been camping in Harold's Woods from September 12 to 14. On September 24, the officers went there to see what signs of Mae they could find. You might recall that on the night of September 12, there had been a weather event, a band of fierce storms that had pounded our entire part of the state with almost two and a half inches of rain. After that, we had a couple weeks of unusually hot dry weather. So the investigators who went to Harold's Woods found a lot of dried mud near the campsite they concluded Mae and Aaron had used. And ground into that mud they discovered quite a few white nylon fibers, consistent with having been shed by a nylon rope.

"What you will learn is that Aaron Housley had bought a white nylon rope while he was with Mae." Back at the prosecution table, Jackdorp again lifts the white skein from our garage. "He'd bought it at a Home Warehouse about ten miles away from Harold's Woods on September 13. You'll see the notation for the purchase on Mr. Housley's debit card statement, and you will see the receipt, this receipt." Jackdorp has it in a plastic envelope and stands before the jury, using a squat finger to point out the lines he then reads. " '09/13/23 2:12pm 50ft white nylon rope.' We'll even present the closed-circuit footage from the camera behind the cashier, so you can see Mr. Housley with this white rope in his hands.

"You will learn that Mae's body was found in her car two weeks later, up here in Marenago County at the Ginawaban wilderness area, crashed into the woods at the foot of a wash sometimes used as a utility road. The body was lying across the front seat, with her head under the dashboard on the passenger side. All over the passenger seat, investigators found white nylon fibers, matching this rope.

"Dr. Rogers, an expert pathologist who works with the Kindle County Police Department, conducted the autopsy on Mae's body, which, very frankly, was half-rotted at that point. Despite that, Dr. Rogers will tell you that she uncovered several significant pieces of proof. First, there was a black mark around Mae's neck, the kind of mark, she will say, that is characteristically left by strangulation when the blood vessels in the neck get cut off. She will tell you that the pathologists who study these things are often able to judge from those black strangulation marks what the killer had wrapped around the victim's neck—a bedsheet, a belt—but in this case she will tell you that the strangulation marks on Mae Potter are characteristic of a plastic rope. She will tell you her hands were constricted beside her throat in a way known to accompany violent death. There were white plastic fibers, matching that rope, under her remaining fingernails and many on her neck. There were shoeprints on the dashboard of Mae's car, which an expert on such matters will identify as clearly coming from the boots Mae was wearing. Dr. Rogers will explain that if Mae was being strangled from behind, she could have resisted by pushing her feet against the dashboard. Other experts will tell you that there was plenty of DNA from Aaron Housley in the back seat of the car where the strangler would have been positioned.

"Now, you remember I told you that before Mae's remains were found, investigators had been to Harold's Woods to examine Mae and Aaron's campsite. In addition to the white nylon fibers matching the rope I've shown you, they discovered several items Mae had seemingly left behind—cosmetics and a tank top and some underpants drying on a bush, all of which her mother will tell you were Mae's. Lieutenant Glowoski will testify as a police expert that leaving those kinds of things behind is typical of someone else packing up Mae's belongings. In the mud at that campsite they also found clear impressions from Mae's boots. And they also discovered prints from the kind of sneakers Aaron Housley owned.

"You remember, I suspect, that I said you would hear a lot about shoeprints, and that will come from the State Patrol impressions expert. Before her testimony, you will learn from Aaron's grandfather, an older gentleman named Joe Mena, who will testify—he'll tell you he had bought Aaron a new pair of Nike sneakers several months before. And the footwear expert will give you a detailed explanation about the resemblance between those very sneakers and the impressions she examined in the mud at Harold's Woods. You will also learn that was not the only place where prints consistent with Aaron's sneakers turned up. On microscopic examination, there proved to be a shoeprint from that style of Nike sneaker on the blouse Mae was wearing when she was killed. Dr. Rogers will say that print was likely caused by the murderer placing his foot on her shoulder to gain leverage as he was strangling her from behind. And in another patch of dried mud, this one at the bottom of the utility road in Ginawaban, where Mae's body was discovered—there beside the Subaru containing Mae's remains, distinctive prints from the very kind of Nike sneaker Aaron owned were also identified."

Having told the jury that the shoeprints in this case would be like the shoeprints in the snow in his example about circumstantial evidence, Jackdorp now stands stock-still and lets his eyes roam across the jury box to let them absorb the significance of what he has just said.

"Now, how did Mae's Subaru end up at the bottom of that rough little road up here in Marenago County, when I've told you she was murdered roughly a hundred miles south at Harold's Woods? Here's what the evidence will say about that. Remember, George Lowndes saw the young African-American male driving the vehicle out of the parking lot at Harold's Woods. Another kind of evidence you'll hear about in this case are the records of cellphone tower connections. When you use a cellphone, even when it's merely turned on, it connects to nearby cell towers, information that is then captured by your service provider. And we will introduce records of the cellphone connections from Mae's phone and Aaron's phone—important evidence in both instances.

"Now we know, just as Aaron told Cassity, that when Mae was at Harold's Woods, she did not turn off her phone. One reason we're certain is because of the photos and videos she posted to social media on September 12 and 13 and 14, all identifying her location as Harold's Woods. We'll show you those images. Very cute young woman, full of life, that's what you'll see. But after roughly eight a.m. on September 14, when George Lowndes saw the young man and woman struggling over something he was holding over his head—after that, the posts cease. And the cell tower records show Mae's phone was turned off at 9:06 a.m. You are probably not surprised to learn that Aaron Housley's fingerprints are all over that phone—including the on/off button. Without power, the phone no longer connects to the towers and there is no longer a record of Mae's location.

"And Aaron's phone? Aaron's phone, which had been powered down for days, with the voicemail turned off as well—that phone comes back on for a few minutes on September 14. The first time it connects to two cell towers about thirty miles north of Harold's Woods. Why? Not to make a call. Coincidentally, one comes in to Aaron's phone then, lasting only seconds, but the woman on the other end has told police she'd dialed a wrong number. Instead, what Aaron's phone shows is that he was using a navigation app, as drivers often do, for a few minutes. And you will also see, about two hours after George Lowndes saw that African-American male tear off in the silver SUV, a photo from a tollbooth not far from Ginawaban, which clearly shows that vehicle. So although Cassity will tell you Aaron claimed he'd headed straight back to Mirror, hitching south, the tower records show he had in fact gone north. North is the direction that the tollbooth photo will show the Subaru was traveling. And north is where Mae's body and the Subaru were found here at Ginawaban, beside a shoeprint from the kind of sneakers Aaron Housley owned.

"Now, given everything I've said, you can understand why investigators were eager to find Aaron's shoes, which would allow the shoeprint expert to say not simply that all those shoeprints—in the mud at Harold's Woods, and on Mae's blouse, and beside the Subaru—were left by shoes just like Aaron's, but rather to declare with scientific certainty that the impressions were made by Aaron's very sneakers. And so on September 30, after Dr. Rogers's autopsy results were known, a search, pursuant to a warrant issued by a judge, was conducted of the house where Aaron lived with his mother and her boyfriend. But those Nike sneakers were not there. Nor was he wearing them when he was arrested. The Nike sneakers have never been found.

"And there were other items you'd expect to discover that weren't there when the investigators searched. Aaron's backpack that he used to go camping with Mae? Never located. His sleeping bag? The same.

"But that search of Aaron's residence uncovered other evidence. In the closet of Aaron's room, where he kept his clothes, white nylon fibers corresponding with our rope—they were recovered from the carpet on the closet floor, although none of the clothing hanging there had any rope fibers on them." Jackdorp pauses and squints and turns his head at a curious angle, a good job of indicating that there is something fishy about what he's just described, although in an opening statement he can't say that out loud.

"But what *was* found, ladies and gentlemen—" He approaches the jury box, so they know that something good is coming. "What *was* discovered in the garage was a white nylon rope." He goes back to the prosecution table and lifts the coil again. "This rope. And there's some interesting evidence about this rope. One of the sheriff's deputies who was leading the search had known Aaron's mother for many years, and he asked her, with her boyfriend who owned the house standing right beside her, if there was any white plastic rope in the house, perhaps in the garage. 'Not the garage,' she said. She knew because she'd been looking around for gardening tools the previous week.

"Now, the evidence will give you no reason to think that Aaron's mom, who is sitting there in the front row, no reason to believe she or her boyfriend were lying to the officers when she said there was no rope in the garage. The evidence will show that's what she honestly believed. But what did Lieutenant Glowoski find stuffed in a carton at the back of a storage cabinet in the garage, behind several other boxes? This white nylon rope, the kind of rope that left a little blizzard of fibers in Mae's car, the same kind of rope whose fibers were on Mae's clothes and under her fingernails. Aaron Housley was the only other person who lived in that house and had access to that garage.

"The other charge against Aaron Housley besides murder is obstruction of justice. That means exactly what it says—that he engaged in various acts with the plain intent of avoiding justice, to keep the justice system from catching up with him—that he hid or destroyed important evidence and fled when he realized he was in danger of getting caught.

"Now, of course, the evidence of obstruction may also be considered by you in connection with the murder charge, and it's very important evidence of that crime as well. These are not the acts of an innocent person."

I stand up. "Judge, I've been biting my tongue and letting Mr. Jackdorp speak his piece to these folks, but he's arguing, Judge. He's veered into closing argument."

"Sustained. Mr. Jackdorp, both Mr. Sabich and I have given you considerable latitude in your opening. Your job is to tell the jury about the evidence you expect to introduce. I don't want to hear anything that sounds like a closing argument, and your last remarks and several before it certainly do."

Jackdorp shrugs. In these moments, despite his stiff personal demeanor, he has a kind of art, and the way his shoulders shift says it all: What can you do with these people, who are being silly sticklers?

"All right, well let me tell you one more thing about the evidence of this obstruction charge. Aaron Housley learned late on the night of September 28, 2023, that Mae's body had been found at the bottom of that utility road. The initial impression of the first trooper on the scene, who found drugs in Mae's pocket—" Jackdorp draws himself straight up and lifts a finger. "Oh," he says, as if he has not waited strategically to reveal this fact until the jury's sympathy for Mae was well formed, "that is something I should have mentioned earlier. The evidence will show you that Mae Potter was a drug user, that she'd been using plenty of drugs—cocaine and fentanyl—while she was out camping with Aaron Housley. And when the first trooper found her remains he reached into the pocket of her jeans in an effort to identify the body, which was too bloated and decomposed to be certain it was

Mae's, and found tablets of fentanyl. And so his initial conclusion, which was reported in the papers, where the missing persons hunt for Mae Potter had been well publicized—the initial conclusion was that Mae had been high on drugs and taken a wrong turn and crashed and died.

"At that point, no one was talking about murder. No one knew it was murder, except, of course, the murderer. But hours after Aaron Housley heard that Mae's body had been found, he took off. He went to his grandfather and borrowed his truck—even though Aaron was under a court order not to drive. He told his grandfather, and I quote, 'I've got to get out of here.' And he did. He turned off his phone and voicemail again, which meant the cell towers would not record his location. And he still had not come back two days later when Dr. Rogers's conclusion that Mae had been murdered was reported publicly and a warrant was issued for Aaron's arrest. Instead, a manhunt ensued. And where was Aaron Housley arrested? At Ginawaban, where Mae's body and her car had been dumped. And what was in the flatbed of that vehicle in which Aaron Housley was arrested? A shovel. A hand truck for moving stuff around. Notable items to bring to a site the murderer alone would realize was almost certain to eventually be searched for clues."

I get back to my feet to object again that Jackdorp is engaged in argument, trying to make inferences from the evidence, rather than simply stating what it will be. Judge Carrington agrees.

"The last remark about what the murderer would realize is stricken. I think you better wind up, Mr. Jackdorp."

He looks down to the floor, as if trying to contain himself.

"Well, the judge says I have said enough about the evidence the People will be presenting to you. It may turn out that I've misstated one or two things as the trial progresses. If so, forgive me. But we have made no mistake, I promise you, on the fundamental point: The evidence in this case will show you beyond any reasonable doubt that Aaron Housley murdered Mae Potter, that he committed the crime of obstruction of justice hoping to avoid getting caught."

For the first time, Jackdorp has slowly migrated from the prosecution table toward ours. With the white rope still in his hands, he stands over Aaron, solemnly shaking his old head. Aaron again responds as I hoped. He looks up to Jackdorp fearlessly and holds the man's eye. And something about that response takes Jackdorp aback. I've assumed he is prepared to end by delivering a stinging line or two directed to Aaron, but now, rather than continue the confrontation, he turns away. The conclusion to what I know has been an excellent opening statement gets cut short. He faces the jury and thanks them for their attention and goes to sit down.

22

The Defendant's Mother

February 6

Because of the degree of publicity in this area about Mae's murder, Judge Carrington summoned 125 potential jurors to be sure we could find twelve who seemed earnestly capable of ignoring what they'd heard from the news or as gossip. As a result, jury selection was protracted and ended only early this afternoon after a day and a half.

My hope was that Jackdorp would make quick work of his opening, allowing me to deliver my own before court adjourned for the day. The theory among trial lawyers, not necessarily validated by any research I'm aware of, is that you want to have the last word before any breaks, during which impressions of the case may harden. That's especially so with openings, which are critical in shaping jurors' views. But once Jackdorp finishes, Judge Carrington gavels court to a close after telling the jury not to talk about the case among themselves or speak to others or take in any reports about the trial.

The court security officer who is in charge of Aaron today, an elderly former sheriff's deputy named Rolly, comes to collect him to transport him back to the jail. I promise Aaron a visit tomorrow after court, but I am pressed tonight. After Jackdorp's opening I need to rethink parts of what I planned to say in reply.

While Aaron has turned to place his hands behind his back to allow the jailer to cuff him, he looks at me and says, "You were right. I didn't enjoy that." A smile, like a thief, sneaks through the edges of his mouth, reflecting his perpetual taste for irony. I think he means to show me that he is bearing up. But Jackdorp did an impressive job, and Aaron's crack leaves me worried again that he is not fully absorbing what is happening.

After collecting our files, Susan and I sit down outside in my Tundra, which has sometimes doubled as a mobile workspace. Susan retired from the Skageon State Defender's Office so that her husband Al and she could buy a farmette in the northern part of the county. Her proximity, about thirty miles from Portage, was another reason I hoped she'd be willing to work on the case. Even so, during trial every waking minute is precious, and so I expect her to spend many nights with Bea and me in the little house we rented nearby. She stayed there last evening so we could continue studying the data she'd assembled for jury selection. As a result, I agreed she could go home tonight to see her husband and check on the organic pigs and poultry Al and she raise.

She gives me several thoughts about responses to Jackdorp, all of them astute as usual, and then I see her off on her Sportster 1200 Custom. She has donned her motorcycle gear in the ladies' room in the courthouse, entrusting me with the rawhide outfit that I will hang in my car and return to her in the morning. She is prepared for temperatures like tonight's, in the teens, because her helmet, jacket and leather leggings are heated, plugging into 12-volt outlets on her Harley.

Whatever doubts I have about Aaron's choice of counsel, I have none about the investigator. Susan is as smart and resourceful as the best detectives I worked with. She also exhibits an intense commitment to ensuring Aaron gets a fair trial, working hours every bit as long as mine. Yet for everything she brings to this job, Susan's principal identity is clearly as a self-described biker chick. Now in her late fifties, she has no intention of giving it up, and on their free weekends, she and Al ride with as many as seventy others in a frightening herd, most of the men on their enormous roaring Harleys with long hair flying behind their do-rags.

Before trial, Susan asked me to think hard about whether I wanted her sitting beside me at the counsel table, knowing very well how people sometimes react to her appearance. I was still considering her offer when I visited Jackdorp's office. I was there to collect documents, and the receptionist, an older woman with heavy cheeks and grey curls, said, 'Your gal got them already.'

'Susan? Our investigator?'

' "Investigator"? Is that what she is? I've seen her hereabout now and then for years. Hard not to remember her with that cockscomb on her head.'

I took a point from the conversation. Living in far northern Skageon County, Susan is often in Portage, the nearest town, generally to visit the Tractor Supply. As Jackdorp's receptionist proved, her look makes her memorable, meaning many of the jurors will recognize her. Maybe she's a nut, walking around like that, they'd think—but she's their nut. Anything that marks Aaron's defense team as local will be beneficial, for the reasons I've been aware of from the start.

It is a little after seven when I return to the shabby house Bea and I have rented. She is seated in the living room on a wing chair, which she's pulled close to the window, although there is next to nothing to see in the country darkness. After balancing the costs, we decided to take a six-month lease on this small house just outside of Portage, rather than pay three times as much for long stays at one of the chain motels twenty miles away on the interstate. Situated at the front of a large farm, our place feels more garage than house. There is a narrow living space, where Susan and I each have our laptops, and two tiny bedrooms—Susan sleeps in the smaller one when she needs to stay over—as well as a galley kitchen and a single bathroom.

The house has an irretrievably grim air. There is not a single overhead fixture, and at no time of day does the sun come directly through any of the small windows. The ceiling of dropped acoustical panels is low enough that I have to stifle the impulse to duck whenever I walk in. At night there is a surprising amount of traffic noise as semis go roaring by along our road, apparently a well-recognized shortcut to the interstate. The walls have some kind of smutty layer that made it seem like a prior occupant might have built a fire, which is probably exactly what occurred. About a month ago, we had one of those stretches of climate-catastrophe cold when minus 12 was the high for the day, and even with a space heater and a heavy sleeping bag, I discovered that it's possible to be too cold to sleep.

It was Joe, when he first looked the place over, who quickly figured out what it was intended for, namely housing farm workers in season. There are probably three or four families in here at the height of the summer.

Bea's initial confidence that we could brighten the house up has proved largely misplaced. Whatever slick is on the walls made them impossible to paint. We bought a truckload of furniture at Goodwill in Como Stop, where the inventory included a lot of nicer pieces, since many of the summer residents refurnish often and shuck what they're tired of after the season. We could not resist a living room set that is very comfortable but further cramps an already small space. Bea has hung a few family photographs, but there seems less point without Aaron here to see them.

She does not stir as I enter, continuing to stare out. She promised to cook and there are appetizing smells from the kitchen, but I notice on the coffee table in front of her a wine glass and a bottle of white that is half-empty. When she finally faces me, it is with a harrowed look.

"I didn't realize how it would sound," she says. "I mean when Jackdorp sewed it all together. I lived through most of it. But I never connected it all in my brain."

I set my briefcase down and come closer.

"That rope," she says, "everything about it—having it, hiding it. That's what's going to convict him, isn't it?"

I understand. Aaron had a good reason to buy the rope, but we may have a hard time proving it. And even so, that doesn't mean he didn't use the rope to kill Mae the next day. No matter how many alternative scenarios I construct, they all conclude with Mae dying with that rope around her neck. And the evidence will place it in a single living person's hands once it left the store.

"It's not good for Aaron," I say. "But it's not all as bad as Jackdorp says." I remind her of the limitations on fiber evidence, which I've explained before. "And I'm still not sure how Jackdorp is going to argue that Aaron hid or destroyed stuff like his shoes or his clothing or his backpack, and then stuck the actual murder weapon in a cabinet in the garage. That still doesn't make any sense."

Bea looks long at me, her eyes unmoving and darker than normal.

"Tell me you think he didn't do it," she says.

One of the advantages of the role I've taken on is that I don't have to bother myself much with the ultimate question. My job is to poke holes in the State's evidence, and that is where my full attention has been focused. I think we have some things to work with.

"I'm his lawyer, Bea. I want to assume he didn't do it."

"Does Susan think he did it?"

"She has the same attitude as me, but deep down, I think we both still have some feeling that he may be innocent."

"Because?"

"There are ways the evidence doesn't really hang together. But most of it is what comes off Aaron. He just doesn't read like a guilty person."

"But sometimes you don't feel like that, right? You think he's guilty."

"Sometimes," I answer.

I lean over to hold Bea, but she feels somewhat wooden in my embrace, not indifferent, but unable to respond. Every now and then, we have shared tender moments, when we cling to each other like people on a life raft. Before I left for court on Monday for jury selection, Bea hugged me. She told me I looked handsome. I have absorbed minor trims to my beard and hair, but don't want to lose a rural look.

'No matter what,' she said, 'thank you for doing this. I had no idea what I was really asking for. The work? I probably took years off your life.' Yet the kiss that followed felt obligatory.

As I tried to tell her repeatedly, preparing Aaron's defense has not been good for our fortunes as a couple. There are a million reasons why, which I could only sense before, but now recognize plainly. At home in Mirror, she returned at night wanting a reprieve from the persistent atmosphere of accusation she faced at school. But it was no refuge to come home to me. I cannot shelter her from her intense anxieties about what might happen to her son, because I may be his doom, an inept defender who smooths the way for Jackdorp to secure a life sentence. Instead, the sight of me reminded her of the two-ton meteor hurtling toward her world. I no longer can provide the distraction she needs at those moments, no anecdotes about my daily life, because for months now my daily life has been consumed by Aaron's case. And worst, the intensity of those efforts has lessened my focus on her when she needs me most.

Between us there are now boundary issues. As hungry as she has sometimes been to know about the evidence, I will not talk to her at length about my impressions of it, because those are confidential matters which Aaron generally prefers I not share with her. He doesn't want to talk about that on her visits, when he prefers to have the company of his mother, not another member of the defense team.

And on my side, the damage to the relationship is no less steep. Bea can no longer be a complete partner to me. She can't empathize about the immense burden I am bearing with this young man's life in my hands, because as she sees it, undoubtedly correctly, the emotional toll is greater for her. In consequence, I get little of what has often been the most magical thing about her, namely her intuitive understanding of my needs from moment to moment.

Our intimate life has suffered. Naturally. And we both look the worse for what we are separately enduring. She's lost weight because she is too overwrought to eat. Despite the war she used to consistently declare on an extra ten pounds only she saw in the mirror, she does not look better. Her trips up here to visit Aaron have absorbed all the time in which she might have exercised. She is haggard with worry. There are now more lines, more sagging, more grey, less color, and a nearly complete loss of her joyful light.

I, by contrast, am beginning to resemble the Michelin Man. I have put on at least twelve pounds, because the refrigerator is my one refuge when I am working, and also because I am drinking more, especially late at night, as a pathway to sleep.

Our inevitable minor conflicts are treated with less patience, meaning they can become wounding. When Susan and I first started scouting potential rentals, I asked Bea if we wanted a place big enough for Joe to stay too. He has driven back and forth from his farm virtually every day since Aaron's arrest so that he can spend the allotted hour with him at the jail, and I know he will not miss a second of the trial, once he is off the stand. But Bea responded to me with wrath and a paralyzing look.

'What?' she asked. 'Are you *trying* to think of a way to make an unbearable experience even worse?' She had never adopted a tone that harsh with me, and for a second, I felt like she had channeled Barbara.

Mindful of that, I try now to summon tenderness and calm when I answer her about Aaron's guilt. I remind her she is his mother, whose first job is to believe in him. She nods in a dutiful way. I know she will recover. Bea would not recognize herself without fully embracing Aaron. Even if the day comes when he reverses field and admits his guilt, sooner or later Bea would find her way back to him. In that, I envy Aaron.

For me, however, this conversation spells a difficult night ahead. I had wanted to eat dinner, touch up my opening for a bit, then have a drink or two and get a full night's sleep. But now I see that I must reevaluate everything I was going to say, and provide some genuine refutation to Jackdorp's presentation. For many reasons, all of them sound, defense lawyers in their openings try not to promise to introduce specific evidence.

But I cannot imagine what the impact of Jackdorp's opening was on the jurors if, even briefly, it has swayed the defendant's mother.

"Rusty," Bea says. "Rusty. Please wake up. Wake up."

My first thought, as I rise toward the outer world, is that there is an intruder, or the sound of one lurking outside. Bea is sitting straight up in her T-shirt and has turned on the cheap gooseneck reading light on her bedside table, whose sudden glow is momentarily blinding. The clock there says 4:06.

"What?" I ask. "What's wrong?" I press myself upright as well.

"I just remembered something," she says. She is rigid with the urgency of this memory, but for some reason can't quite look at me. "You need to hear this. *I* put that rope on the shelves in the garage."

"You did?" I blink. My thinking feels incredibly slow. Outside, a semi rumbles by, the noise always unusually loud against the utter silence of the country. Miles away, you can hear the rolling clatter of the freight trains barreling through town at this time of night.

"I brought it home from school. We'd used it to rig a backdrop for the kids' spring show. I brought it home and put it in a box of extra supplies."

I've seen the carton, stuff needed on a seasonal basis. It's Bea's so I never gave it more than casual attention, but I certainly don't recall the rope.

After another second, I realize she is lying to save her son.

"Bea, you can't say you just remembered something like that."

"But I did," she says. "I did. I mean, I knew they found a rope when they searched, you always told me that, but I never saw what they took. I thought you meant a much shorter piece, because I was imagining it, you know, what it would take to choke her. I never realized it was a big, long roll like Jackdorp was parading around in court. Every time he did that, I got this sick feeling, because I knew something was wrong. But it just came back to me while I was asleep. *I* put the rope there."

"Bea, it's too late for this."

"Why?" She looks at me directly for the first time.

"I told you a long time ago. You're his mother. You can't try to shoulder the blame for him. No one would believe it."

"I'm not shouldering blame. It's true. It's the truth. I just remembered."

It's obvious why she would say this. The idea might even have started with my remark that it makes no sense that Aaron would bring the rope home, especially when Jackdorp wants to argue that Aaron hid the other evidence. Bea is a smart woman, brilliant actually, and evaluated what she heard in court today and has cleverly assessed the impact of what she wants to claim. All those fibers Jackdorp was talking about that he said 'match' our rope—if what Bea is saying now were true, it would make him look like an idiot, because the supposed matches would actually be to a random piece of junk, stored away long before Mae died. Even more important, if Bea put the rope there, it would mean that Aaron didn't—and that what I referred to earlier as 'the actual murder weapon' was just something left over from a grade school show.

But what happened then to the rope the jurors will see Aaron buying at Home Warehouse? That's yet another reason that Bea's new memory, no matter how welcome it is to her, would never hold up.

"Bea, you already told Dom Filipini that there was no rope in the garage." Early on, to avoid any situation where I was a potential witness, I informed Jackdorp that we wouldn't dispute what Dom would say about his conversation with Bea—or my apparent agreement. But once Bea testified and contradicted herself, Jackdorp would be well within his rights to demand I take the stand and describe how certain Bea was when she spoke to Filipini. That is the ultimate nightmare for any defense lawyer, having to testify against his client, but I doubt Judge Carrington would save me after I promised her that would never happen.

"Rusty, who knows what's really in every dark corner in their garage? I wasn't thinking. There were police officers turning my house upside down. I was panicked. Anyone would be panicked. The jurors will understand that."

They will understand exactly one thing: that any mother would do this for her son. But it means she's convinced he's guilty—that's how they'll see it, that she's certain that they, the jury, will never let him go. In an odd but very true way, Bea, too, will have turned herself into a witness for the prosecution.

Clearly, I am going to have to talk her out of this, by explaining how much damage she'll do to Aaron's chances, no matter what she thinks. But I am not going to spend hours arguing with her when I have to give my opening at 9 a.m.

"Bea, we're not going to thrash this out right now. If you were going to testify, that wouldn't be for a week at least, after the prosecution rests and we decide whether to offer a defense. So let's just both think this through for a while."

"I thought you might want to use it in your opening statement. That's why I woke you up."

I explain how delicate it is for a defense lawyer to promise the jury any evidence in his opening. But it's obvious that she's deeply disappointed by my reluctance—and, worse, has clearly read my disbelief.

"Rusty, it's what happened." She looks at me for a long time and says, "I don't lie to you, Rusty. You know I don't."

With each second, she pushes more chips into the center of the table and now has gone all in, even as I see clearly how this lie will ultimately doom us as a couple. Because she is putting saving Aaron ahead of her relationship with me. And because, when I refuse to let her testify, it will always be the reason, in her mind Aaron was convicted.

"Bea, I need to sleep. We have a full day in court tomorrow."

There is not a chance in the world that I will sleep another second, but I need to end this exchange and preserve whatever presence of mind I can to deliver my opening.

"I don't lie to you," she repeats.

I decide not to answer. Rather, I quietly ask her to turn off her light. I lie down again in a bed we now occupy as different people.

23

Opening Statement for the Defendant

February 7

W ell," I say, as I amble to the same spot where Jackdorp stood
to start, remaining silent a bit longer. It's a stage entrance,
waiting to be sure I have the jurors' full attention. This is the first
moment I've faced this bunch eye to eye, and I try to project my positive feelings about them as a group. Both Susan and I thought we did
surprisingly well during jury selection, the process in which the judge
and then the lawyers interview potential members individually, before
deciding whether to exercise one of the small number of 'peremptory
challenges' each side is granted by law to bar someone they just don't
like. Including two alternates expected to be dismissed when deliberations start, there are fourteen people seated in the sycamore box, in comfortable padded armchairs, below the large windows. They are for the
most part who our jury consultant, Damon, a law school pal of Nat's gra-
cious enough to offer his advice for free, told us to expect in Marenago
County, that is, older white folks. In outlook, most are probably somewhat old-fashioned, because farmers live a life governed by fundamentals
that have not really changed since agriculture began millennia ago.

"He made it sound pretty bad for Aaron, didn't he, Mr. Jackdorp, the elected prosecutor? I'm sure you're wondering what we can say, Aaron and I, about all that. The judge already told you more than once, Aaron doesn't have to prove anything. The burden of proof, of coming forward with evidence, and evidence so substantial that it convinces you beyond a reasonable doubt—that *heavy* burden remains on Mr. Jackdorp from start to finish, not on us. Under our Constitution, by pleading not guilty, Aaron gets to say in answer to the charges brought by Mr. Jackdorp, to the government he's part of"—I drop my voice to try to sound like a thug on television—" 'Oh yeah? That's bull. Go prove it.' "

As I hoped, I get a small smile from a couple of them, including Mr. Alvin Smith, an elderly farmer, a serene gentleman, completely bald except for a neat fringe of white hair. He is the lone juror who's been coming to court in a coat and tie. He was also the only Black face in the jury pool. According to Damon, who was steeped in demographic data, one resident in fifty in Marenago County is African-American. Although Mr. Smith is a registered Republican, Jackdorp tried to use a peremptory on him, but bungled the legal requirements established by the US Supreme Court to inhibit the nationwide practice of prosecutors—me included, frankly—who back in the day used to challenge all Black jurors when another African-American was charged.

For jury selection, Damon assembled a huge interactive database, compiled from public records like voter and real estate tax rolls and census tracts. Yet Damon had one frank warning: No matter how many happy interracial couples we saw on TV commercials, in Marenago County Aaron's race might count heavily in the minds of some jurors. As one measure, Damon pointed to election returns that showed Black candidates here consistently run about three points behind other office-seekers from the same party.

To find the most open-minded jurors, Damon gave us certain benchmarks—gross stereotypes, frankly. We agreed to seat four registered Democrats, and eight jurors who spent some time in college—significantly higher percentages in both categories than in the county in general. We also chose five veterans, because they inevitably served beside African-Americans. Aside from Mr. Smith, we seated two other people of color, an Asian woman who runs the local Chinese restaurant with her husband, and a man named Gomes, who we took to be Latino.

"But let me say one thing to start, one important thing about what Mr. Jackdorp told you: He's wrong. He's wrong in the large sense, because the evidence will *not* convince you beyond a reasonable doubt that Aaron took the life of Mae Potter. And he's also wrong because you will often find that the evidence will not turn out as he led you to believe. Not in every aspect, of course. There are many facts in this case that we—Aaron and Susan and I—have no argument about. But you will see that at a number of critical points there are gaps or contradictions in the government's evidence. And you will also learn that whether he wanted to or not, Mr. Jackdorp in some instances was misleading you. Let me give you a quick example."

In state courtrooms, the common parlance is to refer to the prosecution as 'the State,' or as Jackdorp prefers, 'the People,' but the jurors won't know what's standard practice and so Damon suggested referring to 'the government,' a word that in Marenago carries negative connotations.

"I don't know how many times I heard Mr. Jackdorp say that the fibers found in various locations—at Mae and Aaron's campsite, in her car, on her clothing—he said they 'match' this rope." With that, I go to the prosecution table and pick up the white coil from our garage. Jackdorp has already tied an exhibit label around it, calling it People's Exhibit 1. " 'Match,' " I repeat. "What you will find out is that this rope and the fibers are both made from a material called 'nylon 6.' But nylon 6, it turns out, is everywhere. There's an endless list of things manufactured from nylon 6—clothing, outdoor furniture, toothbrushes and brooms, parts of your car, and, more relevantly perhaps, camping equipment, including some sleeping bags and backpacks. You literally can't get away from nylon 6.

"As a result, no fiber expert in the world, even one who works for the government, like a number of the experts Mr. Jackdorp intends to call—no expert will come here and testify that as a scientist he can say conclusively that the source of any of the fibers in this case was *this* rope. I repeat: No matter what you heard the prosecutor tell you, not one single little filament from the campsite or the clothing or the car will be positively identified as coming from this rope." From a couple feet above, I release the coil from my hands so that it thunks loudly on the prosecution table. Then I nod toward the jury box, where I see several of them sitting back with knotted expressions. We've scored.

"That's just one example. Wait until I get to the shoeprints, which Mr. Jackdorp compared to the footprints you might see out your window on a snowy morning. But before I go on to that and other matters, let me pause to reintroduce myself."

My instinct a decade ago was that by becoming a criminal defense lawyer, I would learn things about the justice system I never could otherwise, and that suspicion has been confirmed a dozen times as I've prepared for trial. I never fully recognized before how steeply the road rises against criminal defendants. Jury research shows that 80 percent of jurors make up their minds about a case after openings and never change it. Yet the defense is always hamstrung at this point. If Jackdorp's case blows up on him—and we know a couple of weak points already—the defense will rest without offering evidence. And so the worst thing I can do is promise proof I may never deliver, because then Jackdorp's failure to establish what he said he would will seem no worse than mine.

Nevertheless, I can fudge a little and talk about Aaron's background, stuff he'd testify to, without explicitly promising the jurors that they actually will hear from Aaron. They won't, if I get my way. Putting Aaron on the stand is a bad idea for several reasons, starting with the reality that his felony drug conviction would be admitted on cross-examination, because in the eyes of the law a felony draws his credibility into question.

And I also won't be telling the jury that the defense will be calling expert witnesses to challenge the State's. We didn't hire any, both because they are too expensive and because the ones I interviewed agreed with most of the general conclusions of the prosecution's experts.

But Bea's reaction—her feeling after listening to Jackdorp that her son will be convicted—demonstrated, even before she woke me, the dire need to forcefully answer Jackdorp's presentation. Harping on reasonable doubt and the burden of proof, the standard fare of defense openings, won't do it. And so I have decided to come out swinging, hoping to use the mistakes Jackdorp made by overstating the fiber and shoeprint evidence to diminish him as a truthteller in the jury's eyes.

"To remind you, my name is Rusty Sabich and I am proud to stand before you to represent this young man, Aaron Housley." I have returned to the defense table behind Aaron, one hand on each of his shoulders. "Proud, I say, because there is truly no higher calling for any lawyer than to speak on behalf of the wrongly accused." The judge clears her throat meaningfully. I have come close to vouching for the innocence of my client, which lawyers may not do, but I think it's a fair response to Jackdorp's self-congratulations about the nobility of his duty as a prosecutor.

"Let me tell you a little bit about what the evidence will show concerning Aaron that you didn't hear from Mr. Jackdorp. He grew up in the town of Mirror, one county south. His mom, who's the principal of the local grade school, is there, as you know, in the front row. His dad, a former police officer, is seated beside her. Aaron's grandfather, Joe Mena, will be called by the government as a witness, but you will see him right there afterwards. Aaron, you will learn, is blessed with a fine supportive family into which he was adopted at birth."

Seated just for today where Joe will be in time, on the other side of Bea, are my two granddaughters, Minerva and Briony, twelve and ten, both lean and black-haired. My contact with the two of them for the last six weeks, as trial prep has hit high gear, has been confined to Sunday Zooms, instead of the two or three in-person visits I would normally have made, as auxiliary babysitter or as fan of their ice hockey matches or musical recitals. Their father, my son Nat, is on the other side of Briony. Forty-seven now, Nat still has the pretty-boy looks that so closely resemble his mother's that there are always instants when I feel like I am seeing a ghost.

Everybody in Nat's family adores Aaron, particularly the girls, for whom he has played de facto camp counselor whenever they've come up to Mirror—canoeing with them, fishing with them, singing songs with them and, in the snowy season, tobogganing with them down the hill onto the frozen lake, all three shrieking at the top of their lungs. My granddaughters learned two years ago that Aaron was in jail, which in their household provided a teachable moment about the dangers of drugs. But parents and daughters are united in regarding the murder charges against the man they know as laughable, and the girls were eager to be here to show their support.

They have also come for my sake. It is not lost on Nat—or me—that this is almost certainly the last opportunity any of them will have to see me perform in a courtroom. So Nat rescheduled his classes today and took the girls out of school, although Anna, who had to travel to St. Louis today, wisely insisted that they should hear only my presentation, and not Jackdorp's. Minnie, my older granddaughter, has her hand entwined with Bea's, as they comfort one another.

"Aaron finished high school, started college," I say, "but quit to follow his talents as an artist, which was how he had been employed, as a graphic artist, until shortly before the events of this case. You may see him drawing now and then, while he listens to the proceedings. That's more or less his way of thinking. It's not that he's bored or not deeply concerned about what's happening.

"The evidence will show you that Aaron has always been a bit of a loner. But he is very close with the friends he's been able to make, and that certainly included Mae Potter. They were one another's first love. They met in junior high, sort of Romeo and Juliet, love at first sight, and dated throughout high school. It was, as first love so often is, wild and passionate and crazy. They argued fiercely and broke up and almost inevitably came back together. There was something very special between them. You will hear a lot about Mae Potter in this trial, and not all of it, I'm afraid, will be flattering. I apologize to you and to Mae's family for that. The process of finding the truth sometimes requires shining a light in some ugly dark corners. But I would ask you to hold one thing in mind throughout this case. Whatever you hear about Mae, Aaron Housley knew the best of Mae, the brilliant, funny, loving woman she could be, especially when she was with him. He loved her and always will. He is as heartbroken by her death as any person in this courtroom.

"But there were other sides of Mae, too. Her mood could shift in instants. She could become unthinking and unkind, even cruel. She was often in emotional turmoil. And she had a serious problem with drugs, as Mr. Jackdorp finally remembered to mention to you. Mae was using cocaine and fentanyl heavily during the time Aaron and she spent in Harold's Woods, which, by the way, is one reason Aaron had to drive her car, whatever the court order said. What the evidence will establish, however, is that even though Mae was high most of the time they were camping, Aaron was not. You'll learn that tests performed when Mae first failed to return home showed absolutely no sign of drugs of any kind in Aaron's bloodstream.

"As almost always happens, Mae's drug use worsened her behavior. She was more and more erratic, meaner and ever more undependable, and often treated the people she was close to like her worst enemies, which some inevitably became. As a result, down in Skageon County there were a fair number of individuals who, to be blunt, hated Mae Potter's guts."

I have warned myself in advance that throughout the proceedings, I will need to stifle my impulse to look over to the Potters. Their reactions—whether tears or beams of pure hatred trained on me—will only distract me, and I don't want my eyeline to provide any further encouragement to the jurors, who are bound to view all the Potters with keen sympathy. But just to get the worst out of the way for my own sake, I steal a glance toward Mansy. His grey head is bowed and his face in his hands. At the sight of his obvious suffering, I quickly turn away.

"As I keep reminding you, the evidence will *not* prove to you that Aaron killed Mae. He didn't do that. Someone else did. We do not have to establish who actually strangled Mae—if she was in fact strangled. That's not the job of the defense. We don't have to solve the crime that the prosecution and law enforcement have failed to solve. But why they failed? The evidence will give some ideas about that.

"One thing you will learn is that Mae's father is Harrison Potter, who, like Mr. Jackdorp, is an elected prosecuting attorney, down in Skageon County, where I'm from. The law enforcement community, as you may already know, is relatively tight-knit. And so the unexplained disappearance of Mae Potter last September, daughter of a local prosecuting attorney, produced a pretty dramatic response from the start, with sheriff's deputies and the State Patrol and even the FBI all searching for her. And that urgency about finding Mae heightened

into a virtual panic state about locating her killer, once the cause of
her death finally became known a few days after the discovery of her
body.

"Now, Mr. Jackdorp mentioned Lieutenant Special Agent Glowoski,
who is sitting right there." I turn to acknowledge Glowoski. Like
Susan on my side, the lead investigator is always permitted to remain in
the courtroom, whether she will testify or not, because she's regarded
as part of the legal team. True to form, Glowoski scowls as soon as
I say her name. "Mr. Jackdorp said he will call her as a witness, and
what you will see when she testifies is that this was an investigation,
which from the very start considered only one suspect, Aaron Housley. The efforts Lieutenant Glowoski led were aimed almost exclusively
at gathering proof that Aaron did it, with no thought of other possible
perpetrators, including the many people I mentioned who, to put it
bluntly, hated Mae. And as a result, there were errors, serious errors,
one after another. So please listen carefully. Not just to take note of
those mistakes. But also because there will be some clues, I suspect,
about who actually committed the crime, clues the State Patrol and
others had no interest in pursuing.

"Now let me turn back to a more detailed discussion of the evidence. As Mr. Jackdorp conceded, what he outlined is a circumstantial
case. And I'm sure you remember Mr. Jackdorp's little story about
circumstantial evidence, how if you see fresh snow on the path outside
your door, and then footprints in that snow a few hours later, you
know someone has walked down your path. Yes, true enough. Because
you can draw only one conclusion from that evidence.

"But let me give you another example about circumstantial evidence, which is more like the circumstantial evidence in this case. One
of the blessings of living here in Marenago County, or even down
south in Skageon, is looking at the sky on a clear night. Those of us
who are lucky enough to pass our days up here, miles and miles from
the smog and dirt of any city—we see a magnificent abundance of
stars. Looking at the brightest star, the North Star, I was taught as
a boy that if you trace a line from there through several of the stars
nearby, it will outline what we call the Big Dipper, a handle and a
bowl. The Greeks, thousands of years ago, looked at those very same

stars and thought what they saw was a figure they called Ursa Major, the Big Bear. Now, once you know to look for those shapes, you can trace them out in your mind. You can see a dipper. You can see a bear. And, in another mood, especially up here where the sky is thick with stars, you can see only a beautiful array that God set there to be appreciated in and of themselves with no other form in mind.

"You will see that the circumstantial evidence in this case is just like the night sky in Marenago. And if at the end you are saying to yourself, 'Well maybe it's a dipper or maybe it's a bear, or maybe they're just stars'—that, ladies and gentlemen, is far, far from proof beyond a reasonable doubt, that is far from the footprints in the snow outside your door.

"But Mr. Jackdorp chose to emphasize the actual shoeprints you will hear about, and he told you straight out why. Because when it comes to direct evidence of the critical events in this case, meaning live witnesses who can tell you what they saw or heard, when it comes to direct evidence, he has none. No one will mount the witness stand right there below the judge to testify, 'I saw Aaron Housley put that rope he bought around Mae Potter's neck.' Because that did not happen. No witness will say, 'I saw this murder'—if it was murder—'take place.'

"Mr. Jackdorp told you about people very close to Aaron who the government has subpoenaed here to testify: Aaron's best friend, Cassity Benisch, or his grandfather, Joe Mena. Cassity or Joe—neither of them will say Aaron so much as hinted that he had a role in Mae's death. Instead, both are going to tell you that Aaron was devastated when he learned about the passing of Mae, the only woman Aaron had ever loved in his young life.

"So Mr. Jackdorp has no direct evidence of the critical events in this case. But he said to you, 'Well, we've got these shoeprints and in the long run they're just as good as eyewitnesses.'"

"Objection," says Jackdorp. He saw that when I detailed his over-reach on the fibers, it had an impact on the jury, and he doesn't want me to deepen those doubts with the shoeprints, even though my bet is that he's unaware of the full extent of his problems. "I didn't say that."

"The jury will rely on their memory of what was said," says the judge. "Overruled."

"That's right," I say. "That's right. When you deliberate, you will be able to remind one another, and together you'll find that with the twelve of you working together, you have a nearly perfect memory of what has been said here. And in all events, it's your memory, not my memory or Mr. Jackdorp's, that matters. And if I mischaracterize what Mr. Jackdorp said, then I apologize. But I suspect when you search your collective memories, you're going to agree that Mr. Jackdorp made that comparison to the shoeprints in the snow and suggested that the footwear impressions in this case are as good as an eyewitness.

"Maybe when he said that, you scratched your heads a little. And you were wise to feel skeptical, because, ladies and gentlemen, the evidence will show you that the shoeprints in this case are *nothing* like the shoeprints in the snow. Instead, what those shoeprints are going to prove are the dangers of a circumstantial case.

"Now, as I said, there are some facts in this case that are undisputed. At some point Mr. Jackdorp will get up and read to you what's called a stipulation. That's Aaron and me agreeing that we don't need to waste your time or the court's time making the government try to prove matters that we know are true. Yes, you're going to hear that Aaron's fingerprints are on Mae's keys and her phone and the steering wheel of her car, that he drove and wasn't supposed to. And by the way, please don't get confused. Aaron is not on trial for violating court orders. He's not on trial for traffic violations. He's on trial for murder. If you want to convict him for driving when he was not supposed to, you're in the wrong courtroom.

"But we don't take issue with certain basic facts. Aaron and Mae went away for a couple of days alone to discuss the possibility of getting married. It was Mae, by the way, who proposed to Aaron, and I'll tell you at the end of the case why that might matter. But either way, they had agreed to give their full attention to each other as they talked about that prospect. No calls from home or friends, no texts. Alone together. Phones off.

"And as you heard Mr. Jackdorp admit, Mae didn't keep that promise. As I said, that was too often her way. And yes, Aaron was angry about that—he took time away to talk about the rest of their lives and instead she was striking poses and making faces for her camera. And yes, he got so angry that he took her phone away from her and left her there in Harold's Woods and hitchhiked home. He didn't kill Mae. He didn't dump her car and her body a hundred miles north in Ginawaban. The evidence won't convince you of either of those things.

"But Aaron certainly doesn't dispute that his grandfather Joe had made Aaron a gift of a pair of Nike sneakers, Nike Air Force 1 shoes to be specific, about ten months before the events of this case. The shoeprint expert, who like Mr. Jackdorp works for the state government, is going to tell you about the footwear impressions, as shoeprints are formally called, that were found at the campsite in Harold's Woods where Aaron and Mae stayed, starting September 12. She, the expert, is going to give you her opinion that some of those very complete shoeprints left in the mud in Harold's Woods closely resemble the soles of the Nike Air Force 1 shoes Joe bought for Aaron. I'll concede right now that those Nike Air Force 1 shoeprints in Harold's Woods were in fact from Aaron Housley's shoes. So never mind Mr. Jackdorp's concerns that the actual shoes can't be found, even though by the time we're done here, in all likelihood, there will be no mystery about what happened to Aaron's sneakers.

"But then the government, Mr. Jackdorp, goes from Harold's Woods to Ginawaban, a hundred miles away. As Mr. Jackdorp described the evidence, he may have made you think that the expert will say those Ginawaban prints—the grisly one on Mae's shoulder and the one near where her car crashed—were made by Aaron's shoes too. What he did not tell you, however, is that the prints in Ginawaban are partial impressions, tiny pieces of a complete print. The expert can say only that they share some of the characteristics of the distinctive soles of Nike Air Force 1s. As a result, neither she nor any other expert will be offering an opinion that the fragmentary prints found in Ginawaban are from Aaron's sneakers. If that sounds to you a lot like what I told you about the rope fibers—well, I'll let you draw your own conclusions about the reliability of what you heard from Mr. Jackdorp.

"Instead, I am telling you right now that the evidence is going to show you that it is highly likely that Aaron Housley did *not* make

either of the Ginawaban prints. Because there is a very important
fact that Mr. Jackdorp didn't mention. To be fair, it might even be
something Mr. Jackdorp doesn't know. The Nike Air Force 1 sneaker
is the most popular shoe ever sold in the US, or around the world for
that matter. During the three years before Mae died, which is about
how long those shoes last—during those three years there were about
thirty million pairs of Nike Air Force 1 shoes sold, and thousands
upon thousands purchased in our little neck of the woods up here. By
some estimates, one in every eight American males has bought a pair
of those sneakers at some time. And so what I expect the shoeprint
expert to tell you is that the fact that Aaron was wearing Nike Air
Force 1s when he left Mae in Harold's Woods, and the fact that whoever hid Mae's car in Ginawaban might also have been wearing that
kind of shoe—that is no more than a coincidence, and one that is not
especially significant. I expect the expert to concede that coincidence
means about as much as if the evidence showed that Aaron was wearing blue jeans in Harold's Woods and the person in Ginawaban was
wearing blue jeans too. A lot of people wear blue jeans—like several of
you folks in the jury box, right now. And a lot of people wear Nike Air
Force 1s, and that doesn't mean that any of them murdered Mae Potter." I then creep toward the jury box and briefly take a peek over the
rail, more a stage gesture than a real look. "I can't see for sure," I say
now, "but it wouldn't be a complete surprise if one of you was wearing
Nike Air Force 1s today."

My statement is better than a pure guess. In the hour before court,
Susan casually positioned herself by the front door to get a look at the
shoes worn by every person she recognized as a juror, and she saw the
Nike trademark, the swoosh, twice, meaning that my observation at
the worst won't be far from right.

But sure enough, as soon as I've spoken, a man in the back row—
Ritzenberger, I think his name is, a big round guy, midforties, with
knots of reddish hair—actually starts chuckling, and several of his colleagues around him laugh, too, as Ritzenberger points down at his
feet. I instantly feel happy enough to purr and raise my fist to my
mouth so I don't look like I'm gloating.

"At any rate, you understand my point now about the danger

of circumstantial evidence, of trying to see a dipper or a bear when there's really just a bunch of stars."

Deeply vexed, Jackdorp stands to say, "I think he's arguing now, Judge."

"I think so too," says Judge Carrington.

I've gotten away with a lot that I might not have been allowed in other courtrooms, but Jackdorp opened the door to this with his examples about the snow. However, there's no point in quarreling with the judge. I nod and say that I'm done with this subject. The shoeprints and the fibers offered the best chance to diminish Jackdorp's case, which sounded so convincing yesterday, and all in all it's gone about as well as it could have. I've taken some risks that Jackdorp's experts may eventually contradict me, but for now, when impressions matter so much, I've dented Jackdorp's armor as a truthteller. Judge Carrington, as many judges do these days, allows the jurors who care to make notes on pads the court provides, which will be left in the care of the court security officer overnight. All but two of the jurors accepted the pen and paper, and several have been writing, especially about the shoeprints.

"In fact, ladies and gentlemen," I say "there will be no direct evidence, no eyewitness testimony, no documentary or electronic evidence—no proof of any kind putting Aaron at Ginawaban any time near when Mr. Jackdorp is saying Mae's body was deposited there. All you will learn is that Aaron, two weeks later, *after* Mae's remains were discovered—after that, Aaron went to Ginawaban. Remember, please, what the proof will clearly show you. When Aaron left home on the trip that took him to Ginawaban, it was Friday, September 29. The news everywhere—on social media, on TV—said what law enforcement then believed, that Mae had been intoxicated, took a wrong turn and lost control of her car, dying when her SUV crashed at the bottom of that old road. There were no public reports about the autopsy saying Mae had been murdered until late Sunday. By that time the sheriff's deputy who arrested Aaron will tell you that Aaron had been stuck in a dead truck without a working radio, and with a phone that had run out of juice, meaning he had no way to know what was now newly being said about Mae's death.

"But despite that, Mr. Jackdorp tells you that Aaron went to Ginawaban to obstruct justice. Did you notice that Mr. Jackdorp

didn't name a single piece of evidence that Aaron supposedly dis-
guised or altered or hid at Ginawaban? There's no proof of that. All
the evidence will show is that Aaron, as loved ones often do, went
to pay his respects where he believed Mae had passed her last living
moments on earth."

I am nearing the end of my opening and pause for a second to face
the jurors. This will be my last chance to address them eye to eye until
my closing argument, when, the jury researchers would say, it may be
too late. From here on, I will steal only brief glances at the jury box.
It's another courtroom maxim that jurors don't like the lawyers studying their reactions to the evidence, which is apt to make them feel like
creatures in a zoo.

As I observe the group, I am struck by the subtle differences in
appearance from the juries I addressed decades ago in Kindle County.
It's not only that they are older and whiter. The conventional wisdom
is that the population on average gains two pounds for every hundred
miles north you go from Kindle County, and looking at these folks
you might say that two is low. And when I've gotten occasional smiles,
I've been reminded that orthodonture is less common up here.

Eight of the fourteen people in the box are female, because we
wanted moms. Two of the women, both in their seventies and sitting
beside each other, are somewhat dowdy and look like they may still be
putting their hair in curlers at night, and none of the females show the
sleek coiffure you see in places like Como Stop. Mr. Smith is in his tie,
and one man, a former CPA, has been coming in a corduroy sport coat,
but the other four men are in versions of what I call the Rural Uniform, burly fellows with woolly beards, in worn T-shirts and blue jeans
and seed caps that Moriah, the clerk, has instructed them to remove.
Yet as a group they have been attentive enough to me to give me hope.

I conclude with a quick tour through the staples of defense openings. I remind them that there are two sides to every story, and ask
them to suspend any judgments until they've heard all the evidence.
I echo the judge's reminder about Aaron being presumed innocent,
even now. And then I thank them for their service here, and for putting up with the questioning they went through by the judge and
Jackdorp and me.

"You are the fourteen people, chosen from all your neighbors who were first gathered here, that the judge and Mr. Jackdorp and Aaron and Susan and I decided were most able to render a fair verdict in this case, the fourteen people in whose hands Aaron and Susan and I have chosen to lay Aaron's future. We stand before you with trust and respect and confidence that when you've heard everything, you will find the government's evidence wanting, that you will recognize errors and gaps, that you will say, 'I just don't see it, it's just stars,' and you will find Aaron Housley not guilty."

After I finish, Judge Carrington recesses for an early lunch, in hopes of getting through the State's first two witnesses this afternoon. The court officer today, a gum-chewing female named Judy, takes Aaron by the elbow back to the lockup where he will spend the lunch break. When I turn briefly to the gallery, Bea is awaiting my glance and covers her heart with both hands. When she woke up, as I was on the way out to court to go over a few preliminaries with Susan, there was no mention of what she'd said last night about the rope, and for my own sake, I'd be more than relieved if the subject never comes up again.

After a brief exchange with Susan, I knock and ask Judy to admit me to the lockup. I want to brief Aaron on the first witnesses. We have a short conversation about what I expect while he's consuming the thin bologna sandwich he gets for lunch. I leave the lockup, promising Aaron that I will see him for a longer visit at the jail tonight.

Exiting the heavy door, I find myself completely alone in the courtroom where, only a few minutes ago, there was not an empty seat. Now that I'm by myself, I can feel my limbs still ringing from the high adrenaline of my performance. For a moment, as I consider the beauty of this room, even more evident without occupants, I am struck by the arc of my life. How odd, how utterly remarkable to find myself back in this arena, the focus of so much of my adult energies, but also the site of some of my keenest disappointments. When I told Nat years ago that I had asked Mansy's assistance with appointments as a defense lawyer, he was flabbergasted that I was even willing to set foot in a courtroom again. But there is no other place in my life like this, requiring the ultimate in concentration and fleet thinking.

I suppose what I've experienced here is akin to the thrill jocks get on the playing field, but for them there is no chance to repeat that at this age. Throughout my career, I've known men and women who thrive in court, who relish being the center of attention and the daily duel with their opponents. In my own mind, I've thought of those people as the real trial lawyers. I am no better than a journeyman who was never willing to say that I love being here. The anxiety leading up to trial has always been painful for me, and I've never come home from a trial day without brooding on some random question or remark that I fear might prove to be a pivotal blunder. But I am *alive* here, making full use of everything I have as a human, and that, after my slackened pace in recent years, is something just now I can savor.

24

Charmaine

Whether I like it or not, Jackdorp exudes a proprietary air in the courtroom. He has lived his role for decades, with a quietly determined approach. He rises in his heavy tweed suit, his face worked over by age, and looks directly at the jury in a fearless way. While I am sorry to say it, his complexion, hard to bear on first sight, works to his advantage. This is what the truth looks like, he is saying by standing there. It's not beautiful. It's just the truth. He has told the jury what the evidence will show and is now going to deliver with resolute discipline.

One of the great challenges in the prosecutor's job, as I learned decades ago, is not to, in the familiar phrase, 'chase rabbits around the courtroom.' Working against someone with the straight-ahead style of Jackdorp, a first principle of defense is to try to create distractions for the jury—those are the rabbits. Hiram Jackdorp, according to Tim Blanc, his former deputy, is of the school of prosecutors who do their best to pretend that the defense lawyer is not even there. His redirects, after my questioning of his witnesses, will be limited, even sometimes skipped entirely. He wants to say to the jury, by his responses, 'Who cares about this malarkey from the defense? I am keeping my eye on the ball and so should you.'

And so he starts his proof by calling Mae's mother, Charmaine

Potter, as his first witness. It's adroit, if not subtle. As exercises in narrative, prosecutions must be conducted with the directness of a popular television show, with tried and true themes likely to engage everybody in the jury box. Charmaine is first, in order to make tangible some of the incalculable damage done by this crime. A weeping woman in a wheelchair—she is the emblem of why Aaron must pay a heavy price.

Once Jackdorp gives her name, Hardy retreats to the courtroom doors in the rear and holds them open. Charmaine propels herself forward. Judge Carrington asks if she can testify from the witness stand and she answers yes, but Hardy and Mansy, who have accompanied her like an honor guard, help her slowly mount the stairs. Once Charmaine is settled, she issues a determined nod and both men retreat, neither with so much as a sidewise look at Aaron or me.

After getting Charmaine's name and address, Jackdorp marches forward.

"What is your relation to the victim in this case, Mae Cheryl Potter?"

"I'm her mother," Charmaine answers with considerable dignity, which slowly crumbles. Her lower lip quivers and she bows her head and grips the bridge of her nose with two fingers as she cries. It's not for show. I'd cry too in her position.

The judge intervenes and tells her to take her time. Charmaine, as my mother once did, has placed a hankie inside her sleeve and withdraws it to wipe her nose and eyes while she regains herself. From another prominent Skageon family, Charmaine was never quite as good-looking as her husband, with a pinched quality to her features, but she has always been well-kept. She wears a mauve suit of shiny silk, and a soft short do of mid-blond tones. Her makeup appears to have been applied with skill, but the toll of illness and her daughter's death has left her looking older than fifty.

When I first began to sift into the Skageon County community, I judged Charmaine to be a lot smarter than Hardy and often bitterly funny. Mae spoke of her mother as tough. Bea, of course, has known Charmaine most of her life and seems to regard her with a great deal of sympathy, not simply because of her illness, or even due to Hardy's relentless philandering. Bea sees Charmaine as the woman who caught the bullet that might once have been aimed at her. She is the person living a life that Bea knows would have left her screaming, not only because she is yoked to a true mediocrity, but because being a Potter, always seen and judged, requires a steady stoic affect in public. Charmaine did not always carry that off, even long before her diagnosis. With a drink or two, her tongue grew sharp.

She is, however, far better suited than Bea ever would have been to the role of a politician's spouse. Charmaine remembers names and seems positively delighted to make happy talk. When I first started living with Bea, she would greet me by taking both my hands in hers and saying the same crap every time, stuff like, 'We see a lot of Aaron around our place and he is such a wonderful boy.' I knew damn well that she had called the county sheriff a dozen times about his drug use. That was another thing Mae said about her mother: Charmaine is completely calculating.

In response to Jackdorp's questions, Charmaine reviews Mae's upbringing and achievements, especially in high school. Honor roll every semester. Letters in volleyball for three years. Senior choir. Young Life. Prom leader, as it's now called, instead of prom queen, which was Bea's title back in the day, when she and Hardy were the star couple, junior year.

"Do you have a photograph of Mae as she appeared in September 2023?"

It's another of Mae's modeling shots, part of her book, a bit more wholesome than the one Jackdorp showed during his opening, more as a mom might see her, with Mae joyous with laughter, a striking beauty with her blond hair cascading.

"And do you know the defendant, Aaron Housley?"

"Yes."

Before Aaron is ordered by the judge to stand and be pointed out, I agree to the identification.

Charmaine next says that Aaron and Mae dated on and off since junior high.

"And calling your attention to early September 2023, did you have a conversation with Mae about the defendant?" Jackdorp asks.

"She told me that Aaron had asked her to marry him."

I stand. "Your Honor, the prosecutor has chosen to elicit hearsay."

"Is that an objection, Mr. Sabich?"

"I'm making a point for the record."

Jackdorp glances back at me with the irritation I have already seen him display a few times when he doesn't understand what I am up to. Without Charmaine's testimony on this point, he probably will have no other way to establish that Aaron proposed, which is a building block in his argument that Aaron became crazed by disappointment in Harold's Woods. In his eagerness to slip this fact in through the vehicle of a distressed mother, he clearly gave little thought to the opportunity he was creating for the defense.

Charmaine then says she last saw her daughter on September 12. She disappeared sometime that day and did not answer her phone thereafter, although Charmaine and Hardy both left several voicemail messages.

"Did you see Mae at breakfast?" Jackdorp asks.

"Yes, but it was more like brunch," Charmaine says. "She wasn't much of an early riser. Lots of times she'd read or fuss on her phone all night."

"And when did you see your daughter next after that meal on September 12?"

"Never," answers Charmaine and, understandably, breaks down again, as Jackdorp knew she would. He pauses to allow Charmaine to recover.

"And after September 12, did you have any idea where she might have been?"

"Well, I heard some talk she was with Aaron. The defendant. That happened all the time when she went off with him, just, you know, going silent. So that made some sense to me, that that's who she was with."

Jackdorp then goes through another tear-jerking moment when Charmaine identifies a simple heart pendant that was found on Mae's corpse, just below the black mark left by her strangulation. I would love to object, but the truth is that Mae's remains were badly enough decomposed to leave some doubt it was her. Charmaine also says a thong the investigators found drying on a bush near the campsite and tubes of lipstick and eyeliner that had rolled down a slight incline all belonged to Mae.

"Did your daughter customarily keep track of these kinds of cosmetics?"

"She'd sooner walk out the door without her head. Those things were always in her pocket."

I steal a look at the jury. Several of the women are gripped, fully attuned to Charmaine, which is no surprise.

"Calling your attention to the defendant Housley, did you see him after Mae disappeared?"

"Yes."

"When?"

"Looking at the calendar, you and I have kind of figured out it was September 16. The bell rang about six o'clock in the evening and Aaron was at my door."

"And what happened?"

"He had Mae's phone. He just handed it over and said, 'Please give this to Mae.' He was gone before I could even ask him a question."

"And calling your attention to People's Exhibit 4, is this the phone the defendant Housley handed you?"

It's in a plastic evidence bag. She identifies the little glitter star that Mae had applied to the outside of the silicone pocket on the back of the case. That says something by itself.

"And before this occasion, had the defendant appeared at your door before?"

"Sure. I couldn't count the times."

"And what did he customarily do?"

"Well generally, he'd say hello to me, and ask how I was doing, and then ask to see Mae."

"And did he ask for Mae on this occasion?"

"No. Just handed me the phone and turned tail."

"And what was your reaction?"

"Well, the whole thing was real strange. I thought my daughter was with him, but he didn't even give me the chance to ask a question. I called after him, but he just went down the driveway and got in a car that was waiting for him."

"And he never asked anything about Mae?" Jackdorp repeats.

He already established that. I could object to the repetition, but there's no point. The jury's heard it, and it's Jackdorp's final point. He sits down.

As I stand, Susan offers a warning look. Beating up on a grieving mother in a wheelchair will not endear me to the jury. A gentle cross-examination often requires more skill than flagellating an obvious liar. And Charmaine without question is telling the truth. As I'm approaching the rostrum in the center of the courtroom, I ask if Charmaine prefers 'Ms.' or 'Mrs.' The latter, she says. 'Ms.' means her daughters.

"Mrs. Potter," I say then, once I'm settled at the podium with my legal pad, "under the circumstances, I take it there has not been a lot of direct communication between your family and the Housleys. So I want to begin by offering the deepest condolences of all of them, Bea and Lloyd and most importantly, Aaron. They are all heartbroken for your sake and for everyone else in your family."

This is a little bit of grandstanding to which Jackdorp could object, but he doesn't bother. If he thinks of it later, he will ridicule this moment in his closing as 'crocodile tears.' I can see Charmaine weighing a pointed response—which was the risk of beginning this way—but finally she just nods while maintaining a narrow look.

"Now, let me go to Mr. Jackdorp's last point, that Aaron didn't ask to speak to Mae when he returned her phone. Where did Mae park during those times when she was living at home? Was there room in the garage?"

"No, my husband likes his cars, so there was no space there. She usually kept her SUV in a little parking area just off our driveway."

"So anyone who knew Mae well would recognize that she was not at home, if her car wasn't in that area off the driveway, right?"

"Yes."

"And sadly, her car was not there on September 16, correct?"

"Sadly," she says.

I want the jurors to know there was a reason for Aaron's quick departure other than what Jackdorp will argue—an unwillingness to face the mother of the woman he'd killed.

"Now, you say Mae and Aaron had gone out for periods of time since junior high school. And they had many angry breakups, is that right?"

"Anyone who knew either of them could tell you that."

"And yet for all the anger, isn't it true that you never knew, based on what Mae told you or what you observed on your own—you never knew of Aaron becoming physical or violent with Mae?"

"I don't know about that," she says. "I'd need to think that over."

"Well, Mrs. Potter, when your husband—well, let's take a second with that. Your husband, the younger fellow who helped you to the witness stand, is Harrison Potter, Mr. Jackdorp's colleague as the elected prosecuting attorney in Skageon County, directly to the south."

"You know that," Charmaine says.

"But the jury doesn't, Mrs. Potter. What I said, that your husband, Hardy as he's called, is Mr. Jackdorp's colleague—that's true, isn't it?"

"Of course it is. But what's that got to do with anything?"

The judge intervenes then. "This is kind of a one-way street, Mrs. Potter. You answer the lawyers' questions. They can't answer yours."

Jackdorp gets up. "Well, I'll ask the same question as Mrs. Potter, Judge. What's Mr. Potter's job got to do with anything?"

"Is that a relevancy objection, Mr. Jackdorp?"

"It is."

Judge Carrington tilts her head and peers at me.

"Does this relate to issues concerning the investigation that you raised in your opening, Mr. Sabich?"

I say it does and she overrules Jackdorp, and I continue.

"Your husband got the sheriff's police and the State Patrol and even the FBI involved in looking for Mae—that's what he did, right?"

"We were worried about our child."

"We all would be, Mrs. Potter. But after this investigation began, a Deputy Rossiter came to talk to you on September 22, 2023. Do you remember speaking to him?"

"It's hard to recall now, I talked to so many of them."

I mark Rossiter's report as a defense exhibit and ask the judge's permission to stand beside Charmaine.

"And do you see here in Deputy Rossiter's first report that he said, 'When asked, Mrs. Potter said she had no knowledge of any physical violence between Aaron Housley and her daughter. They quarreled a lot, but she never worried Aaron might have hit Mae.' Do you see that?"

"Yes."

"And do you now remember telling that to Deputy Rossiter?"

"I suppose. But that was before we knew what had happened to her."

"Well, that's the point, Mrs. Potter. Before you knew that your daughter was dead or that Aaron was a suspect—before you knew that, you told this deputy that you didn't know of Aaron ever acting violently toward Mae."

"That's what I thought."

"Thank you. And last, I want to ask you about the testimony you gave that Mae told you that Aaron had asked her to marry him. Now first, may I ask how you reacted when your daughter shared that?"

"I said, 'Over my dead body.'"

Laughter breaks out from several points around the courtroom.

"And how did Mae respond when you told her that?"

"Oh, you know, how she usually would when Aaron and she were in one of their good spells. 'Mom, Aaron is the only person in the world who actually understands me.' Something like that. Something she'd convinced herself of."

"But you were angry about this idea of her marrying Aaron."

"Definitely. She would be throwing her life away."

I let that answer sit for a second. As far as the jury knows, there's only one obvious reason Charmaine would regard that marriage as the ruin of Mae.

"And if Mae had told you that this was actually her idea, would you have been even angrier?"

"That's not what happened."

"I see. Were you there, Mrs. Potter, when these two young people discussed getting married?"

"Of course not."

"So of your own firsthand knowledge, you don't know whether she proposed this idea or he did?"

"I know what Mae said."

"But would you have been even more irritated with your daughter if she admitted that she'd approached Aaron about getting married?"

"If that was what happened."

"Did Mae ever lie to you to avoid your anger or to look better in your eyes?"

"How do you mean?"

"Did Mae tell you, for example, that she was still attending college, when she'd dropped out six months before?"

"That was so we'd keep supporting her, if you want to know the truth."

"Well, were you angry when you found she had dropped out of college?"

"Of course. You never saw a child make more trouble for herself than that one."

"But the point, Mrs. Potter, without going through a blow-by-blow, is that Mae lied to you regularly, isn't that true?"

She takes a second to reflect, clearly hoping there is a way out.

"You could say that, I suppose."

"And she was often out of sorts with your husband and you, was she not? A lot of screaming in your house when Mae was around?"

Charmaine begins to cry again.

"She was my child. I loved her. We loved her. Hardy too. She was difficult and she seemed to enjoy making people angry at her, her parents most of all. But I loved her."

"Mrs. Potter, that is not in dispute here. It really isn't. No one is questioning your deep love for your daughter. But her behavior was getting more unpredictable and challenging, isn't that also true?"

"I guess."

"And as a matter of fact, Mae had gone to New York for roughly a year to try to make it as a fashion model, and that had come to a difficult conclusion, had it not?"

"Yes," Charmaine says, suddenly cold. She's afraid I know the story, and I do. Stuck for money, because she wasn't getting modeling gigs, due to the fact that her Breck-Girl looks were deemed 'too twentieth century,' Mae had made an audition tape for a porn producer.

Somehow Hardy heard about it and had to fly out to New York to pay the guy close to $100,000 to destroy all copies.

"But when you brought Mae back from New York, you got her to see a psychiatrist on a few occasions."

"Judge," Jackdorp says. "This is irrelevant."

"Your Honor," I answer, "that's why I pointed out that Mr. Jackdorp had chosen to introduce hearsay. I am entitled under the rules of evidence to impeach the hearsay declarant, meaning Mae Potter, with hearsay of our own."

The judge didn't understand my game during Jackdorp's examination, and she can't suppress a smile now.

"I'll permit a few more questions," she says.

"That didn't last long, her going to the headshrinker," Charmaine says.

"But she was diagnosed with borderline personality disorder, was she not?"

"That's what he said. I wasn't so sure about that."

Jackdorp is over there tapping his pencil. I'm sure he was fairly certain that he'd be able to keep this information from the jury.

"And to make this brief, as the judge asked, borderline people have difficulty regulating their emotions, and seem to have an uncertain sense of who they are and frequent difficulties in interpersonal relationships. Things like substance abuse and even suicidal behavior are common for such people. Did the psychiatrist explain something like that to you?"

"Something like that."

"And did he recommend a program of psychotherapy and medication?"

"Yes."

"Did Mae go into therapy?"

"She saw him a couple more times and said it was a waste. Hardy and I kind of agreed."

"Did she take the medication that the doctor prescribed?"

"Not so far as I know."

"Had Mae threatened suicide at times?"

Jackdorp stands up, angry.

"That's got to be irrelevant."

Judge Carrington's face is fixed in a thoughtful expression and she ultimately waves us to the sidebar.

"Is this still impeachment?" Judge Carrington whispers when we all arrive. She appears to be earnestly curious.

"This is the basic theory of the defense. That Mr. Housley had nothing to do with Mae Potter's death and that there's another explanation."

"But is the defense maintaining that this death was a suicide?"

"It's one of the possibilities."

"He's got to do better than that, Judge," Jackdorp interjects.

"I agree," she answers. "Will you follow up on this possibility with other witnesses?"

"Definitely," I answer.

She gives me a long look, weighing whether to warn me, as most judges would, that she will be keeping track of whether I follow through on that promise.

"All right, I'll allow it." Once we're all seated, the judge turns to Charmaine and directs her to answer the question.

"She said all kinds of stuff," Charmaine says and reddens again. The tears return, but now less in sorrow than anger. She points at me with a finger that seems somewhat bent by disease. "We know what you're doing here, Rusty. You're just trying to dirty her up. You want these people to think she was a terrible person, everybody in town hated her, even her parents, she was just this crazy girl, and who cares that she's dead?"

I'm entitled to strike that answer. But I know I'm on the verge of going too far with Charmaine, and I'm still pondering how to respond to her when Aaron hands me a note, the first suggestion I've gotten from him. It's not a question I would think to ask, but Aaron knows Charmaine far better than I do.

"Charmaine," I say, acknowledging the acquaintance that was obvious when she addressed me by my first name. "In your opinion, based on what you saw—did Aaron love Mae?"

"Mae said so."

"Aaron loved Mae even though she had these faults. Would you acknowledge that? People around town, many came to dislike her because she was so unpredictable. During the periods when she was not with Aaron, young men would come into her life and depart suddenly because they couldn't deal with her behavior. But the one person who always came back, the one person who seemed never to give up on her and who loved her, aside from your family—that one person was Aaron. Is that fair?"

"Loved her until he murdered her, I guess."

"Loved her," I repeat.

She doesn't answer and I sit down.

25

Cassity

Jackdorp's next witness is Cassity Benisch, Aaron's best friend. She steps into the courtroom looking more grown-up than I anticipated. She's in a black tailored suit. Her long ash-blond hair has been swept up behind her head, and she's wearing makeup, which I don't recall seeing before. Her appearance is so different that it strikes a note of fear in me, as if she will not be who I expect on the stand, even though my hope is that it's Jackdorp who will end up surprised.

It's a familiar saying that power corrupts. But in my experience, its corrosive effects are more wide-ranging. Power inevitably magnifies the weaknesses in a personality. A guy always regarded as deliberate becomes a CEO and wears out his welcome because he can't pull the trigger on important decisions. Jackdorp has a catalog of personal peculiarities that would be innocuous if he was just a rural lawyer handling wills and real estate closings, but which have combined to make him less effective as a prosecutor. One foible I wouldn't have thought much about is that Jackdorp prefers to live in a narrow zone. He's a small-town guy who'd rather not go anywhere else. He's interviewed Cassity by Zoom, according to what she's told me, because he didn't want to make the trip down to Mirror to meet with her in person. I've spent hours face-to-face with her and expect that to be an advantage.

And that is not the only way in which Jackdorp has hamstrung himself. His maneuvers to keep his former deputies from appearing across the courtroom have, I'm starting to see, come at a cost, because he hasn't faced the best competition. His straightforward manner shows little sense for nuance, and seems to take no notice of the usual courtroom chess match. And in a lot of the pretrial jousting, like what took place when he tried to exclude the Black juror, Mr. Smith, he has not seemed up-to-date on the law. Finally, I suspect he's not accustomed to taxing himself in the runup to trial. When I glanced his way, I seemed to have caught him flat-footed with how common Aaron's Nikes are. An unprepared prosecutor can lose a lot more cases than a great defense lawyer can win. All of that has gone to raise my hopes for Aaron a bit.

With Cassity, he leads her through the preliminaries, name and where she lives, and establishes that Aaron and she have been good friends since the fifth grade, when her family moved to Mirror from Milwaukee.

"And in September 2023, how often did you and the defendant Housley speak?" he asks.

"Most days."

"And did you talk on September 11?"

"Yes."

"And did he tell you that he was planning to be out of town?"

I stand. "Your Honor, I object to the leading," I say, referring to the fact that he's putting questions to Cassity that require a yes or no answer. Lawyers who've called a witness are expected to make open-ended inquiries. The attorney already knows what the witness is going to say and shouldn't steer the testimony to get what he expects.

"Judge, these folks have lives to get back to," Jackdorp says, gesturing to the jury. "They don't need to sit through a bunch of irrelevant twaddle."

"Your Honor," I respond, "no one wants to keep the jurors here unnecessarily. If Mr. Jackdorp is really that concerned about wasting time, he can dismiss these charges now and let all of us go home."

"All right, gentlemen," the judge says. "That's enough of the speaking objections. If you have a problem with what's going on, state the grounds succinctly. It's not an essay contest. Mr. Jackdorp, lay an appropriate foundation."

Jackdorp, as usual, shakes his head minutely, as if the judge and I are just difficult dopes.

"On the evening of September 11, 2023, did you have any contact with the defendant?" he asks.

"Yes sir."

"Where were you?"

"At my apartment."

"In Mirror?"

"In Mirror."

"And who was there?"

"Aaron and me, and my son, Brock, was asleep."

"And did you discuss his plans to be out of town?"

I get up again. "Your Honor—"

I don't need to finish. "Mr. Jackdorp," the judge says. "You know how this is supposed to be done. Ms. Benisch, tell us what was said and by whom."

"Well, Aaron told me I wasn't going to hear from him for a couple of days. I asked him why, and he didn't seem to want to say at first, and then he told me that he was going away with Mae. And I was like, 'Whoa, I didn't even know you guys were back together,' and he was, you know, a little embarrassed, but he said, 'Yeah, we're actually going to talk about getting married.'

"And I was like, 'Married! How many times have you told me how bad she is for you?'

"And he said, 'Well, that might be true, but I'm beginning to think I'll never get away from her, because I don't really want to. So maybe I should just make the best of it.'"

"That's what he said? That he couldn't escape from her emotionally?"

I object. "The question was asked and answered, and the jury certainly doesn't need Mr. Jackdorp's embellishments of the testimony."

"Sustained. Mr. Jackdorp, you can't go over the testimony with a highlighter."

He shrugs like he meant no harm. As usual, he's done exactly what he set out to and emphasized one of the most critical parts of Cassity's testimony: Aaron felt he'd never be free of Mae—at least while she was alive.

"He said he wanted to see if they could actually make a

commitment and stick to it. And then he told me this story about how he'd run into her at a party in Como the weekend before and he asked her for a ride home, because he can't drive, and instead she drove him around the back side of the lake, and you know, one thing led to another, and when they were laying in the back of the SUV, she said, 'You know, maybe we should just face facts and get married.'"

This was why Jackdorp was trying to lead Cassity, so he could get her to skip saying that it was Mae who had first suggested marriage, contradicting Charmaine. If it was Mae who was driving the idea of marriage, there's less reason to think Aaron would be galvanically angry when he saw it wasn't going to work out. Jackdorp takes a beat now over that small defeat.

"And did you have any further conversation about this planned trip with Mae?"

"He told me they'd agreed to, you know, just go away, and really talk about this and, I mean, concentrate on each other, even turn their phones off."

"Did he say where they were going?"

"Not then. I just knew they were going to camp for a couple of days."

"And when did you next speak to the defendant Housley?"

"It was a few days later. He phoned right after I got Brock in bed. Aaron told me he was on his way back. He said he wasn't with Mae."

Jackdorp presents her with a copy of her cellphone bill and establishes that the call had taken place late on September 14 at about 8:20 p.m.

"And did you ask him what had happened with Mae?"

"Yeah, he just said it had been a real shit show and he was done with her for good. He'd left her at a campsite in north Skageon and was hitchhiking home."

"Straight home?"

"He just said he was headed home."

"And when was the next time you spoke to him?"

"He called me later than I expected the next night."

"And what did he say?"

"He said he hadn't gotten very far and might be gone another day."

"Did you in fact see him the next day, September 16?"

"He came by for a second just to tell me the entire story. He said Mae was high the whole time. She didn't turn off her phone, like they said they'd do, because she had this new thing that she was going to become a TikTok influencer, so she was shooting videos of herself like every twenty seconds. He said he finally got so pissed, he just grabbed her phone from her and took off and thumbed his way back here."

"Did he say where they had been?"

"He said they'd been in north Skageon, in a state park called Harold's Woods."

"And did you observe his mood when you spoke to him on September 16?"

"He was still upset. I mean, Aaron's pretty flat, doesn't like to show his emotions. But he was definitely worked up. He said he'd been stupid and really believed they were going to talk about being together, and instead, you know, she was just Mae. Just completely into herself. He said he should have known better and now was totally done with her. He said there was part of him that was glad that it was finally over. But you know, I think there was another part that was still kind of heartbroken. That's what it looked like to me."

"Ms. Benisch, in succeeding days, did you become aware that Mae Potter in fact had not returned home?"

"Sure. I mean I heard that from Aaron."

"Do you recall when?"

"I mean, we talked every day. So the conversations kind of moosh together. He said that Hardy, Mr. Potter, was jumping in his shit because he'd left Mae 'out in the wilderness'—Hardy's words—without a phone. And Aaron was like, she had a lot of cash, she could buy a Tracfone in a 7-Eleven if she really needed to get a phone. He thought she was just being Mae, you know, acting out to get attention. She did that a lot. But you know, pretty soon the police and everybody were looking for her."

"And did you continue speaking to the defendant daily?"

"Yes."

"And as the days went on and Mae Potter didn't reappear, did he express any different attitude, compared to when you first spoke about her when he returned?"

"Well, he didn't want to talk about her. He was convinced that she would show up and was just trying to create a scene."

"But even when she had been gone for two weeks, did he express any concern for her?"

"Like I said. Mae could be pretty extra, and that's what he said."

"Did the defendant ever say he was in love with Mae Potter?"

"Oh God," she says. "A million times."

"But even though he said he loved Mae Potter, he expressed no concern about her well-being, even when she had been gone for more than two weeks?"

I object. The question again is argumentative, and the judge sustains me, but Jackdorp once more has made his point. He's crafty, naturally, well-versed in the standard courtroom tricks.

"Now, calling your attention to September 28, did you see the defendant again?"

"Is that when they found Mae's body?"

"That's what I'm referring to."

"Well yeah, he called to tell me about it. And then he came by that night."

"Did you talk about Mae?"

"It was all we talked about. I mean, he was a mess. He said maybe Hardy was right, that he shouldn't have left her out there. I'd never really seen him that upset. He kept saying he couldn't believe it. I couldn't either, frankly, so most of the time, we just sat there holding hands and crying."

"And did you talk to him the next day?"

"No. I called, but he wasn't picking up his phone by then. I haven't talked to him since, actually because he got arrested, and Rusty—you know, Aaron's lawyer—said I really shouldn't have any contact with him, because I was going to be a witness."

"But in the period before the defendant's arrest, from September 29 to October 1, when was the last time you had gone three days without speaking to Mr. Housley, leaving aside the trip with Mae?"

"I can't remember. Not often. I mean, sometimes he'd go on vacation with his family, or have sports trips in high school. But I mean usually, like when he went off with Mae, he'd tell me beforehand that I wouldn't hear from him."

"He didn't do that this time?"

"No. But like I said, I knew he was super upset."

Jackdorp turns on his heel and looks at me and says, "Your witness." He's close to preening. He thinks he cleaned my clock.

I start my questioning from directly behind the defense table. Aaron has watched Cassity's testimony with a hand over his mouth. He knows how hard exposing herself in public is for Cassity. In these settings, she tends to be quite shy.

"Ms. Benisch," I say and stop. "Is it all right if I call you Cassity? I think that's easier for both of us."

"For sure," she says.

"Now, you and I, Ms. Benisch, Cassity, we've spent a bit of time together talking about your prospective testimony, have we not?"

"A few hours, yeah."

"And did you also discuss your testimony with Mr. Jackdorp?"

"Yes."

"Now, did you tell Mr. Jackdorp that you had spoken with me?"

"No."

"Why?"

"Well, first I don't think it's any of his business. And second, he told me not to talk to you."

"Objection," says Jackdorp from his wooden chair. "I said nothing of the sort."

Wendy Carrington just stares down at Jackdorp. I don't even bother with an objection. Without taking her eyes from Jackdorp, the judge says, "Mr. Jackdorp's last remark is stricken." She then turns to the jury. "That's another of those things Mr. Jackdorp is not permitted to say. The lawyers are not allowed to be witnesses."

Jackdorp emits another beleaguered sigh.

"And I also object that whatever I said to her is irrelevant," Jackdorp says. Again, he hasn't bothered to rise to add that complaint. He's showing the jury that this judge isn't worth even a superficial effort at respect.

"Mr. Sabich?" asks the judge.

"Your Honor, any effort by the government to short-circuit the truth-finding process conforms to what I told the jury in my opening about the manner in which this prosecution has been conducted."

"I'll allow this briefly. Ladies and gentlemen, the lawyers are not allowed to try to keep the witnesses from speaking to the other side. Witnesses aren't the property of either party. Go ahead, Mr. Sabich. But let's not spend all day on this."

"What did Mr. Jackdorp say to you about speaking to me?"

"He said it would be better for me not to talk to you."

"And how did you take it when he said that to you?"

"It sounded like a kind of threat. That he'd make trouble for me up here or down in Skageon. I knew he was real friendly with Hardy."

Jackdorp sits there engaged in robust headshaking for the benefit of the jury. He might as well be standing up, saying, 'Untrue, untrue, untrue.'

My goal with this line of questioning is not merely to make Jackdorp look heavy-handed. I want the jury to understand what's about to develop, and why I may seem to know so much more about what Cassity has to say than Jackdorp does.

Cassity presents a familiar predicament for the prosecution. The Fifth Amendment prevents them from calling Aaron as a witness. So one of the best ways to prove what Aaron knew about relevant events is the testimony of people close to him whom he confided in. But they're close to him. Which means they're happy to help the defense, if they can.

That's particularly the case with somebody like Cassity, who has a lot more going for her than I once realized. Not understanding the depth of her friendship with Aaron when I first met her, I had taken her as another of his stoner friends, a judgment I made mostly based on her appearance. When she showed up, she was in a T-shirt in all seasons, sometimes stained, often braless, her long blond hair ratted into indifferent tangles. Her skin was still spotty and she was one of those people always talking out loud about losing weight and never doing it. She had started community college and stopped out when she got pregnant by her boyfriend, Brice, who worked in the giant Amazon warehouse near the highway. Cassity herself had seasonal employment, scooping ice cream in the summers and as a receptionist answering the phone at a local construction company.

But I've recently come to understand why Aaron kept a fast hold on her since virtually the first day she showed up in Mirror when they were eleven. There's a lot about her nature that's very much like Aaron's mom, a person with tremendous intuitive warmth. Cassity speaks of virtually everyone approvingly, with the glaring exception of Mae, whom she'd once counted as her best friend. She's a doting and patient mother with Brock, her two-year-old, even though, like most single moms, she's frequently exhausted. And with parenthood, she's begun to settle on real plans for herself. She's been reconsidering her reluctance to marry Brice, although by his own admission he fucked up badly the first time they'd made plans to get married after she'd become pregnant, when he got drunk at a party and slept with someone else.

She arrived in Mirror at a difficult time for most preadolescents, when the social order is starting to sort out and cliques are forming. Aaron was one of the few kids to welcome Cassity, and to some extent they have always regarded themselves as outsiders together. Her loyalty to Aaron has not flagged now that he is in trouble, and in fact, she has displayed some actual bravery by ignoring Jackdorp's veiled threats about speaking to me.

"Now I want to go through some details about your conversations with Aaron during the time leading up to and after the discovery of Mae's death and get at other elements of these conversations that Mr. Jackdorp didn't ask you about. Starting with the conversation on September 11, when he first told you he was going away with Mae. Had you been home all evening?"

"No."

"Where had you been?"

"I had a class at Como Community. I want to be a nurse's assistant. And I started my second semester. But my mom can't sit on Monday nights. Because she has sisterhood meetings. And Brice, Brock's father, in the summers he has stuff he needs to do at nights to get ready for work the next day. So Aaron had said, 'Okay, I'll sit.'"

"Aaron had babysat for your son that night?"

"Right."

"That's Brock, correct? How old was Brock at that time?"

"Just past two."

"And you regarded Aaron as a trustworthy sitter for your two-year-old?"

"They love each other. Brock calls Aaron 'Un.' He means 'Uncle,' but he still says 'Un.'"

"And how did Aaron get to your house?"

"That night he rode his bike."

"How far is your house from his?"

"Judge, really," Jackdorp interjects.

"Is that a relevancy objection, Mr. Jackdorp. If so, I sustain it. We're supposed to be talking about the conversation on September 11."

"All right, Your Honor. In that conversation on September 11, did Aaron tell you that he'd scheduled this trip with Mae to start on a Tuesday because he had this obligation to sit for Brock?"

Jackdorp objects again and the judge tells me to move on.

"Let's turn next, Cassity, to the conversations you had on September 14 and 15 about what had happened in Harold's Woods. Did Aaron describe any physical altercation between Mae and him?"

"Well, he said Mae went nutzoid when he took her phone. He said they'd hiked up the East Trail to see the sunrise, and she'd been taking videos of herself the whole time, after promising to stop, and he finally, you know, like on impulse grabbed the phone out of her hand when they got back. He told her he was out of there and started to get his pack and she literally blocked his way and was screaming, and so he just turned, stepped around her and left. He was done talking to her."

"Now, Mr. Jackdorp asked you about whether Aaron said he headed directly home when you spoke on September 14. What about when you spoke on September 15? Did he say anything about what direction he went?"

"Objection, hearsay," says Jackdorp. He's playing a prosecutor's game, picking and choosing between the things that Aaron said, introducing what he likes and claiming the rest is inadmissible. He might get away with that kind of thing with prosecution-oriented judges, but he's in the wrong courtroom now. Judge Carrington pages back through her notes and rules even before I can answer.

"Mr. Jackdorp. You opened that conversation on September 15."
A defendant can't avoid taking the stand and being cross-examined by
using another witness to relay his out-of-court statements, but once
the prosecution has chosen to discuss a particular conversation, the
rules say the complete exchange may be introduced.

Grumpily, Jackdorp takes his seat and Cassity answers.

"Yeah, he said he hitchhiked home, but when he left Mae at Harold's Woods and first got to 47, the road, he was so upset about her that
he actually stood on the wrong side and got a ride that took him twenty
miles in the opposite way he wanted to go before he realized it."

At this stage, I'm sure these details don't mean much to the jurors,
but Aaron's mistake, briefly going north rather than south, will prove
important.

"Now when you visited with him in person on September 16, did
you see any cuts or bruises on him of the nature that someone might
suffer in a physical fight or a car crash?"

"Nothing. He *told* me at one point that after he left, Mae tried
to find him and he'd hidden from her in the woods and got a little
scratched up just crashing through the bushes. But there weren't any
bandages or bruises or big cuts I saw."

I nod. When I pre-tried Cassity, the lawyer's term for rehearsing
the witness, Cassity made no mention of the scratches, which I'd have
been just as happy to skip. But that's trial. You can prepare, but it's all
going down live.

"Now, we know Aaron spoke to you often about his relationship
with Mae. What about Mae? Did you speak to her about Aaron?"

"Well, I mean, she was my best friend at one point. I mean my
best *girl* friend. So yeah, we talked about Aaron all the time."

"And over the years when you talked about their relationship with
Aaron or Mae, did you hear from either of them about any angry
breakups?"

"I mean like constantly. From both of them. I was always in the middle and I was like, 'I love you both, don't dish on the other one to me.'"

"And in describing these angry breakups, had either of them at
any point mentioned Aaron laying hands on her in an aggressive way,
hitting or, Lord forbid, choking her, anything like that?"

"Never. I mean, that's not how Aaron is with anybody."

"Do you in fact have an opinion, based on your observation of Aaron over many years, about his character for peacefulness?"

"I definitely have an opinion. He's not a violent person. At all."

"And can you give us any examples of that?"

If Jackdorp were better on the law, he could object at this point, and prevail. But for too many years, the law in Marenago courtrooms has probably been whatever he says.

"I mean, he was great at football, because he was so fast and could catch, but he quit after sophomore year because he didn't like that part of it, the violence. He said it was just getting to be the whole game. So he ran track instead. And there was one guy in high school, whenever he was wasted, he'd call Aaron the N-word, thinking he was being hysterical or something. And Aaron told him to stop, but this guy didn't and, I mean, this was somebody Aaron could have absolutely smoked, but he just walked away whenever he saw the guy. Because he said you can't do anything about people like that. You can't change them."

"And another thing, Cassity. Was this unusual for Aaron and Mae to go out in the woods by themselves?"

"No. I mean they did that pretty regular. Aaron said it really seemed to settle her down, being out in nature."

"And what about Aaron himself? Did he have any habit or regular practice about being out in nature, as you put it?"

"He loved it. I mean, Joe, his grandfather, had pretty much taught him all about that. And Aaron is an outdoor person. I mean, he'd go camp in the snow, which, I mean, that never seemed that fun to me."

Around the courtroom, several people laugh, including a couple in the jury box. One of the hair-curler ladies, Patricia something, has surprised me by showing a pretty lively sense of humor already.

"And what about when he was upset? Did he have any habit or practice?"

"Definitely. When something bad or extreme happened—like that N-word thing at school—he liked to go into the woods on his own. I mean, he just wanted to get away from people and be with his own thoughts and feelings, so he didn't have to humor or deal with anybody else. He told me a lot that that was truly the worst thing about not being allowed to drive. That he couldn't get off by himself."

"All right, thank you. And changing the subject, Cassity, do you know that Aaron has been charged with two crimes in this case and the second is obstructing the investigation that ensued after Mae disappeared? Did you know that?"

"Kind of."

"Well, I want to turn your attention to September 20. Did you have occasion to be interviewed by Lieutenant Glowoski, who is sitting at the prosecution table, and a State Patrol trooper who was with her?"

"Yes."

"What happened?"

"Well, they showed up at my apartment and asked to speak to me."

"And did you speak to them?"

"Sure."

"And before doing so, did you have any conversation with Aaron about talking to the officers?"

Jackdorp's up again. "Objection, Judge. I never asked about that meeting with the lieutenant, so it's beyond the scope of my direct. And whatever the defendant said is hearsay."

"Your Honor. First, the prosecution at the end of Ms. Benisch's examination offered evidence to support their theory that the defendant fled prosecution. So this responds to that. And the defendant's comments to Ms. Benisch are not hearsay, because they are offered only to show what Aaron said."

The age-old rule against hearsay evidence is not as complicated as some lawyers think. A witness, Cassity, is not allowed to testify that Mae, or Aaron, said outside of court that the sky is blue, if the point of the testimony is to establish the sky is, in fact, blue. But if you're trying to prove that Mae or Aaron *thought* the sky was blue, regardless of what color it actually was, then their statements are just another fact the witness observed.

Judge Carrington thinks about that. This is one of the hundreds of lesser judgment calls a judge has to make during a trial. She could say that the testimony is out of order now, and I have to bring Cassity back during the defense case, but she knows by now that would be a two-hour trip each way for a single mother. She says she'll allow my question, and I ask the court reporter to read it back.

"Yeah," Cassity says after that. "I saw the police car pull up downstairs. And I knew they were going all over asking about Aaron and Mae, so while they were on the way up, I called Aaron and I was like, 'What should I do?' "

"And what did he say?"

"He said, 'Talk to them. Tell them the truth. Don't play games. I've got nothing to hide. Don't get yourself in trouble for my sake.' "

"Thank you," I say. "Now the last subject I want to talk to you about, Cassity, is Mae and, frankly, her character."

Jackdorp pops up. "Well, here we go, Judge. More of this effort to dirty up the victim and blame her for getting killed."

This becomes another moment where Wendy Carrington delivers the death stare to Jackdorp.

"Mr. Jackdorp. I have cautioned both of you about speaking objections, and especially ones like you just made, which is nothing more than a closing argument. The next repetition by either of you will result in a finding of contempt. Mr. Jackdorp's last statement is stricken from the record. Jurors, please wipe that from your mind. I'll see counsel at the sidebar."

Jackdorp and Aaron and I trudge up to the far side of the bench. Aaron lagged at first. It turned out that he was working on a portrait of Cassity on his legal pad, a ballpoint pen drawing that strikes me as an impressive likeness, because so much of Cassity's flint is reflected. He gets like this, so engrossed by his drawing that he loses track of outward events, and I actually prodded him to bring him back. I'm grateful that I told the jury this might happen.

"What's going on, Rusty?" the judge says as soon as we're there. The informality is a little surprising and a sign that Jackdorp's continued unruliness is unsettling her. I've brought printed copies of cases with me and explain what the judge already knows, that even though so-called character evidence—evidence that somebody has a tendency to behave a certain way—is usually improper, that rule doesn't apply to the victim in a criminal case. And in this instance, not to put too fine a point on it, Mae Potter had a propensity to enrage people. And since the principal theory of defense is that someone else was respon-sible for her death, it is highly relevant to demonstrate that she was likely to have made many other people angry enough to kill her.

"Judge," says Jackdorp in response. "I've never heard of anything like this. He can't just insinuate and throw mud at the wall. If he's got evidence someone else killed her, fine, go ahead. But Mae's mom is right. He's just trying to sully Mae."

This is another juncture where a trial judge has broad discretion. She could say to me, 'You can't have a propensity to make people want to kill you,' or she could limit the evidence to instances of when some-one actually threatened to harm Mae. But this is why the conventional wisdom is for a trial lawyer never to piss off the judge—because a judge may become more inclined to give your opponent the benefit of the doubt, whenever she can. And she does now.

"Well, you explain to me, Mr. Jackdorp, if the rule says he's allowed to show a pertinent trait of the defendant, how her propen-sity to severely anger other people isn't such a trait in a case where the principal theory of defense is that someone else is the killer." Jackdorp looks away in a failing effort to think, which the judge cuts off, saying, "You may continue, Mr. Sabich."

We all return to our places. I squeeze Aaron's arm a little before he sits down. This is going to be good.

"Now, Cassity, I was about to ask you if Mae Potter had a reputa-tion for making people deeply angry with her."

"I'll say," answers Cassity. "You know they tell you, whatever it is, don't trash people who are dead. And Mae could be so sweet and kind. She really could. She was like truly one of the smartest, funnest people I knew. It could be a complete trip being with her. But then she could get in just the worst moods. The ugliest moods. She would tear peo-ple down in public to their faces. Or she'd promise to do something for them, something important, and then disappoint them. I mean, this is probably dumb, but I always thought she wanted to make other people hate her as much as she hated herself."

"Were you one of those people?"

"For sure."

"Was she your friend?"

"She was like my best, you know, female friend. At least, I thought she was, but, you know, toward the end of high school she just got like, you know, cray-cray. I don't know what else to call it. She'd ghost me at times. People would tell me really terrible things she'd said behind my back, and when, you know, I'd kind of confront her, she'd laugh about it. She wouldn't deny it."

"And did there come a point when you finally broke off relations with her?"

"Yes."

"And can you tell us what happened?"

"You know Mae had a lot of money, her family did, and for the first holiday season during the pandemic, I'd made these Christmas tree ornaments for me and my mom that looked like the Covid-19 molecule, you know, this green Styrofoam ball with these red pins with smaller red balls on top stuck in all over. And Mae saw it, and she thought it was so great, and she asked me to make like three hundred of them and said she'd send them out to people on their Christmas card list—you know, they had a big list because her dad was a politician—and she said she'd pay me ten dollars for each of them. And I really needed the money. I was just pregnant, and I was sick in the mornings and couldn't go to work, and that was when I'd broken up with Brice, my boyfriend. So I mean, paying me to make those ornaments, she knew that was a real lifeline. And I worked on them to all hours of the night and finished them two weeks before Christmas, and I brought all these boxes over to their house, and she was like, 'Oh, I don't want them. My father says they're tasteless and I can't send them out.' She didn't even ask me in. Just closed the door. Never even offered to repay me for what I'd spent on the materials. I just ended up with a credit card bill I couldn't pay. So that was that. I mean, she had issues, okay, but we all have issues, and who needs a best friend like that?"

"And were you aware of other instances where she'd deeply angered other people?"

"I mean, I couldn't count them. Like one thing she did more than once when she and Aaron weren't together is she'd go after other people's boyfriends, just because she could, because, you know, she was gorgeous and every guy was always crushing on her. I know three girls who stopped talking to her because of that."

There will be some grim moments during this trial, there have been already, but the ugly accumulated weight of these incidents has hushed the courtroom.

"Let me divert for just a second to something I should have asked before. But speaking about Brice, were Aaron and he friends?"

"Definitely. We all were. Like we hung out a lot as couples. When we were couples."

"And during the period Mr. Jackdorp talked about, after Aaron returned to Mirror on September 16, did you have occasion to see him with Brice?"

"Yeah, once." She explains that she had to talk to Brice about Brock during that period and found Aaron working with her ex, painting a house. "During the summer, Brice took jobs as a house painter to make some extra money for Brock. I mean, he's a good dad. But as he was getting to the end of summer, he had jobs piling up, and he needed help, and Aaron started working with him. Cause his job as an artist for this company in Como had ended. And one day I needed to talk to Brice about when he was going to take Brock that weekend. So yeah, Aaron was up on a ladder painting the other side of the Kitniks' house."

I've been waiting for Jackdorp to object and he finally does. What does house painting have to do with Mae angering people? I say it's something I intend to return to in the defense case, and the judge says we've heard enough about it now.

"All right," I say. "Let's go back to Mae and her propensity to make people angry. Within Mae's family, were there people she made intensely angry?"

"I don't know about all of them."

"How about her father?"

"Oh my God," Cassity answers.

Jackdorp rises. "Judge, what is this testimony? Is it occurrence testimony, because I don't hear her talking about anything that occurred." It's a lame objection, but it's clear that Jackdorp deems Hardy a sensitive subject, perhaps because of the mention of him I made in my opening.

"I'm about to get to what occurred, Your Honor," I say.

"I've already ruled, Mr. Jackdorp. Take a seat."

I turn back to Cassity. I crept closer to her when I got to the stuff about Mae, because I want to hold her eye and try to soothe her. Whatever hesitation Cassity feels about presenting herself in public, she was positively skittish about Mae's problems with her parents, because, quite simply, she didn't want to worsen what's already a hideous time for the Potters. I'd comforted Cassity by saying that the judge probably wouldn't let me get into all of it, and now she raises her dark eyes to me, like 'Really?' I answer with a tiny downstroke of my chin, hoping she understands this is necessary.

"Cassity, when you say Mae had a bad relationship with her father, during the period you were close to her, did you ever witness any of their disagreements?"

"I mean, Hardy, Mr. Potter, he's pretty, you know, buttoned up, but Mae could push his buttons like you wouldn't believe." She stops herself with a self-conscious smile. "Is that a pun?" she asks. "Anyway, there were times like, you know—veins bulging and screaming loud enough to shake the windows."

"Do you remember a specific occasion when they had these disagreements?"

"Well, there was kind of this crisis with Aaron and her, something happened, and the Potters wanted to get Mae out of town and back to college."

"When was this?"

"Say September of 2021. I'd kind of gone back to talking to her for a little while, you know, because she'd fallen all over herself apologizing, but then she left town without even saying goodbye. So I was done for good. Anyway, instead of college, Mae came up with this idea to go to New York and model. Things were supposedly opening up again there, a little, with the pandemic. And Hardy and Charmaine, they both were against it. And she said, Mae said, 'I'm going anyway,' and Hardy was like, 'I'll disown you, I swear, you'll never see another penny, you'll never set foot again in this house.'"

"And what happened? How did she end up going?"

"Well, like three or four days later, when I came over, Mae showed me a few images on her cellphone. And she had gotten hold of her dad's phone, and, you know, she knew the passcode, it was his birthday, and she'd taken screenshots of some of the texts, you know, even going back a few years."

"Good Lord." Jackdorp is up again. "Judge, the messages are hearsay. And how is this related to my direct examination?" This is another flailing objection. I'd be surprised if Jackdorp knows what's coming, but he's a courtroom cat who can sense danger.

"Judge," I answer, "I'll be happy to subpoena Mr. Potter's text messages, if that's what Mr. Jackdorp demands. But this relates to the principal theory of defense about who else had a motive to commit this crime. And I think I can finish with this subject with only a few more questions."

Wendy Carrington looks honestly confused. Like Jackdorp, she feels an omen about this testimony, and she also knows that making trouble for the Potters, a power throughout the state, is not a good way to advance her career. So it seems to take her a second to get herself in hand and deny Jackdorp's objection.

"A few questions," she says. "But unless we have the texts, I don't want any recitation of the specific contents."

"That's fine, Your Honor. Cassity, did you see the photos of Mr. Potter's texts?"

"Yes."

"Were they, in your opinion, revealing of Mr. Potter's personal life?"

"You could say that. Like extremely."

"Things he would not want to be widely known, in your view?"

"You could say."

"Would the messages you saw—would they have been damaging to Mr. Potter's family life, in your opinion?"

"For sure."

"Would they have been damaging to his professional life as the county's prosecuting attorney?"

"Definitely."

"And how about his political career? Would these messages, in your opinion, have damaged his reputation locally?"

"Well, you know, he was a church deacon, so yeah, I don't think that would have— I mean, one of the texts I saw, I don't think he would have been able to show his face around town."

Cassity has told me that Hardy had an affair with one of their high school classmates, Gwen Higgins. Gwen had her heart set on law school, and had pretty much begged Mae to help her get a part-time job in the prosecuting attorney's office in a gap year after high school. Within a few months of starting there, Gwen, who was thirty years younger than Hardy, was sleeping with him. Cassity said Mae was probably angrier with Gwen than her father, whose behavior she was long aware of.

"And what did Mae tell you she was going to do?"

"She said she was going to let her father know she had these texts and threaten him that if he didn't let her go to New York, she'd ruin his life, she'd tweet these out."

"And what happened?"

"Well, she went to New York."

"And as far as you know, at the time of her death, did she still have the photos of those texts?"

"As far as I know, yes. I mean, she might have promised him not to show them to anybody, but you know, how much could anybody ever trust Mae? The better you knew her, the less you would trust her."

I'm done now. I head back to the defense table to see if Susan or Aaron thinks I missed anything.

I have been concentrating on Cassity, focusing on getting these questions answered as expeditiously as possible, and as I turn back to the gallery, I am finally able to read the expressions and the mood of shock. No matter how far-fetched it might seem that a father would kill his daughter, there's some logic to the notion that Hardy could no longer stand having his erratic daughter hold his marriage, his job and his political destiny in her hands. I notice that Bea appears to be eyeing me in some alarm, perhaps because, having known Hardy so long, she regards my insinuations as unfair. Or because she never envisioned me being this nasty. But from the grave atmosphere in the courtroom, I realize I have landed a more solid punch to Jackdorp's case than I had anticipated.

Feeling all of that, and despite my inward cautions to myself, I can't help a quick glance at Mansy, right beside his son in the front row behind Jackdorp's table. He's never looked at me like this before. With that kind of righteous outrage. For an instant, just an instant, the feeling enters me of the damage Mae's death and this trial are doing to him. If some doctor told me I was hastening his end, I wouldn't doubt it. I was prepared to lose our friendship, but not to do him harm. There is going to be a moment tonight when I'll be stabbed by guilt and shame. But not now. Now I am defending Aaron. And I'm defending him with the absolute truth.

Aaron, in the meantime, has written a note for me. "My back-pack." Recognizing the unanticipated impact of Cassity's last bit of testimony, as I stand at the defense table, I begin to feel some doubts, fearing that I might have gone too far and opened myself to Jackdorp's scorn in closing argument about the utter indecency and desperation of the defense. Distracted by those thoughts and the sight of Mansy, I can't even fathom the meaning of Aaron's note at first. I had no idea that he'd told Cassity the story about what had happened with his backpack when Mae chased him down. But given my hard-and-fast assumption that Aaron won't testify, we'll have no other opportunity to offer an innocent explanation for why he might have wanted to discard his backpack and sleeping bag, and so, with no time to think further, I decide to put the question to Cassity.

"Cassity, just one more thing," I say. "Going back to your conversations with Aaron about what had happened with Mae, the ones you had when he returned to Mirror on September 16 and after that. Did you have any discussion about what Mae had done with the backpack he'd left behind at their campsite?"

"You mean that Mae had peed on it?"

"Oh my God!" Jackdorp screeches.

After the silence that greeted the revelations about Hardy, the courtroom flips into a disconcerted buzz.

Judge Carrington bangs her gavel.

"You're done, Mr. Sabich. That's enough." I can see from her closed expression that Judge Carrington is upset by what has transpired in the last few minutes, and that this business about the backpack may have made her regret how far she let me go. Furthermore, it's starting to sink in on me that following Aaron's suggestion was stupid and dangerous: stupid because Cassity's answer *is* hearsay—it's meant to show what actually occurred—and dangerous because the first rule of witness examination is never to ask a question to which you don't know the complete answer. Aaron might also have told Cassity about burning the backpack, which would overwrite the gains of the last few minutes. Jackdorp's outraged objection has, unwittingly, given me the chance for second thoughts, and I withdraw the question and make no protest when the judge strikes the answer from the record, treating it as something that was never said. Eager to make the best of it with Judge Carrington, I literally deliver a half bow, and say, "Thank you, Your Honor," and return to my seat.

Although Jackdorp is very much the kind of lawyer who never wants to display a reaction that confirms that the defense made points, he asks Judge Carrington for a minute. He then speaks heatedly with Glowoski. Just watching them conferring at the prosecution table with their heads close, I sense he's blaming her for not interviewing Cassity in more depth, or perhaps is challenging her to recall something that might counteract what has just emerged.

These moments when the jurors are idle in the courtroom are the ones when they are likely to pay the closest attention to the lawyers and the defendant. I try to display an air of confidence, even as I jot a note to Susan asking, 'Did I just fuck up with that stuff about Hardy?' She writes 'No' immediately and follows it with three exclamation points. Aaron, by contrast, when I turn his way, appears less pleased. For the benefit of the jury, I put a paternal arm around him and whisper, "What's up?"

He shakes his head at first, unwilling to answer, but then murmurs, "You're making her a complete crazy person. Like that's all she was. And that makes me look stupid for caring about her so much."

I did not warn him in advance that Cassity's testimony might include Mae's threats to her father, mostly because I was dubious that Judge Carrington would allow it. But I am startled that even in this moment he remains so focused on Mae. Knowing the jurors are watching, I respond with a patient smile, as if Aaron has said something endearing, while I murmur that we can speak more at the jail later.

When Jackdorp stands again for redirect, it's immediately clear that he and Glowoski have decided to go hard at Cassity. I spent some time preparing her for this possibility. She's on guard from the start.

"Now, Ms. Benisch, you said you spoke often with Mr. Sabich."

"I spoke to him when he asked, just like you."

"Well, many of the things you just testified to, you didn't say to me or Lieutenant Glowoski, is that true?"

"Can you be specific?"

"That Aaron, the defendant, told you to tell the State Patrol officers the truth."

"That's what he said."

"But you didn't tell me that, did you?"

"You didn't ask me. She didn't ask me."

"Or any of this business about Mr. Potter. You never mentioned that to me, did you?"

"You couldn't get off the call fast enough, frankly. You had a checklist, and you went through it. And told me not to talk to Rusty."

"But the only time you, Aaron's best friend by your own word—the only time you recalled these things was after you had these long conversations with Mr. Sabich, is that right?"

"I remembered all of it always. Nobody would forget about those texts. I answered the questions you asked me. Both of you. And I didn't hide anything. And I didn't lie to you or the lieutenant or here today. I don't lie. My mother always said to me, 'Don't lie, Cassity, you're not smart enough to get away with it.'" Unexpectedly, the line provokes tremendous laughter in the courtroom, all of it in seeming appreciation of Cassity's candor. Even the judge is smiling down at her.

Jackdorp, seeing he is getting walloped, says he has nothing further and resumes his seat with a sour look.

The judge excuses Cassity. She picks up her purse, and I hold the swinging door in the rail open for her, so she can exit the courtroom. She waves to Aaron, touching her lips for a kiss.

"And my mother was kidding," she whispers, as she passes me.

She didn't need to tell me that.

26

Inside

As soon as Cassity is gone, the judge asks if this is a good time to adjourn for the day. I tell her I have a few matters to raise with her and Jackdorp outside the presence of the jurors. She sends them home with the same instructions as yesterday and, after I say it's no problem, she also dispatches Aaron to the jail. The judge then takes a five-minute recess, meaning a bio break or something in chambers demanding immediate attention. Once the gavel falls, I head to the restroom myself.

I am surprised to find Cassity waiting for me outside the courtroom doors. It's all I can do to stifle the impulse to hug her, but I direct her across the corridor to the small attorney/witness room, a narrow space at the front of the building with an old couch and a desk, reserved for those waiting to testify or attorneys who need somewhere to confer with clients or witnesses. Preparing for the cold, Cassity's put on her parka, unzipped, and a green Wisconsin State stocking cap. The outerwear instantly makes her appear more like a kid.

"You couldn't have done better," I tell her as soon as I close the door.

"I was just telling the truth," she answers.

"That's why you couldn't have done better. Because there wasn't a soul in that courtroom who didn't realize that was exactly what you were doing."

She smiles bashfully. Cassity, I suspect, at this stage of her life, does not get as many compliments as she deserves.

It turns out that she waited because she wants to know if she can visit Aaron, now that she is off the witness stand. I feel vindicated by my instructions to stay away. It's clear to both of us that Jackdorp would have insinuated she and Aaron had used their time together to cook up the favorable portions of her testimony. But now it's fine for her to visit, and given her schedule, I suggest she go over to the jail now, since Aaron's already on the way back.

Before she goes, I apologize to her.

"I'm sorry I had to ask you those questions about Hardy. I know you didn't want to get into that stuff."

She makes a face and issues a heavy sigh, still somewhat pained by the subject.

"Oh, I don't really care about Hardy," she answers. "He's a jerk. I was just afraid that once I started, you know, with the texts, I'd end up having to get into the stuff that could really embarrass Aaron."

I don't understand. "What would embarrass Aaron?" I ask.

Something complex registers on her face then, a fleeting look of recognition followed by an emotion that narrows her eyes and may even border on fear. But she covers that with a hasty smile. She waves her hand, already in a knit mitten that matches her hat, and says, "Forget about it. It ended up okay."

I have an instinct to press her, feeling I'm missing something important, but she's right, it ended up okay, better than okay, and I've pried enough secrets out of this young woman for one day. I grab the doorknob.

"You're quite a person," I say. "Aaron has told me a hundred times how blessed he is to have you."

She blushes again and looks like she might wither with embarrassment. It's she, behind the closed door, who steps forward to impart a quick hug before departing.

I arrive in the courtroom just as Judge Carrington is resuming the bench.

The case is moving into the phase where most of the State's witnesses will be people who were unwilling to speak to Susan or me in advance. Joe will testify next, but he will be followed by George Lowndes, the private citizen who claims to have seen Aaron and Mae quarreling in the parking lot at Harold's Woods. Lowndes hung up on Susan when she tried him. After Lowndes, Jackdorp will be putting on a bunch of state employees—Special Agent Glowoski to testify about investigative details, and forensic experts like the shoeprint person or the police pathologist from Kindle County. They almost never talk to the defense.

Thus, I want to raise a point with the judge which Susan made to me after Charmaine testified, namely, that we have not received any of the investigators' raw notes from their interviews. We made a motion—actually Cap made the routine motion, which was granted at the time of the initial appearance—to have the State Patrol officers and sheriff's deputies ordered to preserve and produce the notes made in meetings with anyone called to testify, so that we could see how those notes compared to the finished reports about those encounters that we've received.

"And I said we would produce any notes that were *Brady* material," interrupts Jackdorp, who said nothing of the kind. Investigators always hate having to hand over their notes, because they're just that, bare notes, which never fully match the written reports that follow. That gives defense lawyers fodder, because they can highlight statements that show up in reports that weren't recorded earlier, or, contrarily, subjects that ended up omitted. Jackdorp is claiming that he said he would hand over notes only if they clearly favor the defense— so-called *Brady* material—but the rule is absolute that prior verbatim statements have to be produced, and the agents can hardly say their notes are anything other than faithful transcriptions of what they were hearing. Jackdorp's claim now is nothing but a thin veil for the fact that he has once again defied the judge.

"Produce the notes, Mr. Jackdorp," Judge Carrington snaps. She continues to seem unnerved, perhaps because she feels she may be losing control of the proceedings. She was mad at me a few minutes ago for going too far with Cassity, but obligingly, Jackdorp has now stepped into the line of fire.

The judge bangs her gavel and leaves the bench. With the day finally done, I am gripped by a mood of assessment. The bad part of jury trials is that you never know until the end how things are hitting in the box. It's a bit like some of the first dates I experienced, after I decided more than a decade ago, with Nat's encouragement, to post a profile online at a couple of over-fifty sites. You think you're making a decent impression, only to discover afterwards that the other person won't even answer your texts. But recognizing that I'm guessing, I still feel satisfied with today, whatever qualms I was experiencing a few minutes ago. My opening went well. The jury may think I pushed too far with Charmaine, or that my implications about Hardy were purely desperate. A prosecutor plays house odds and doesn't take chances. But on the defense side, you have to gamble periodically if you're going to elude the government's methodical advance. If nothing else, I've already proved good to the promise I made the jurors in opening that I would show them that Jackdorp has a less secure grip on the truth than he claimed. His redirect of Cassity essentially admitted as much.

After court, Susan and I sit in a corner of the empty courtroom to confer. I need her help, especially, with the details of Mr. Lowndes's expected testimony, but I can't cut short my visit with Aaron. We agree that she will head to our house to make calls and work on other matters she can handle alone. We'll talk together while we have the dinner Bea's promised to prepare, and Susan will stay over.

When I arrive in the jail reception area, Bea is on the way out, opening the locker where she stored her purse and her phone. I'm surprised to see her. For one thing, it's Cassity I expected, but Bea says Cassity only had time for a quick hello. Bea was permitted back in the cafeteria to see Aaron after Cassity departed.

"I just needed a couple of minutes to see how he was doing," she explains. I told her last night that I owed Aaron a longer visit, and she wants me to understand she wasn't trying to get in my way.

This is the first time we've faced each other since our odd interaction about the rope in the middle of the night. My earlier hope that in the light of day she'd give up the subject was clearly unrealistic.

"I need to talk to you when you get back," she says.

"About?"

"The case. A couple of things." There's something a little cold in her affect. She's back to being put out with me, no matter how much she liked my opening. That means she's going to stand her ground about the rope.

Officer Crawford, with whom I've managed an increasingly cordial relationship, tells me they've got Aaron in the attorney visiting room, and I leave Bea, telling her we can resume our conversation at home.

I find my client in the tiny room in his blue jail jumpsuit. In yet another unyielding part of jail protocol, they make him change back into that outfit in the processing area every night, before he can return to general population. As Aaron was told last fall, the jail runs cold, and tonight I don't remove my topcoat; despite his short sleeves, Aaron seems better accustomed to the temperatures. Then again, I'm often struck that low temperatures seem to bother young people less. Darwin, or something. Make all the old people go to Florida, where they can survive.

"I wanted to get your reaction to things, just to start," I say, and try to reassure him about our approach on Mae. He interrupts.

"I get it," he says. "It's a show."

"Exactly," I say. "It's a show for the jury. Each side presents the evidence in the light most favorable to it, and the genius of the system is that generally the twelve of them find the point in the middle where the truth lies—or at least, where they're convinced it is. So far, I really think Mae is coming off as we want, an extraordinary person, very erratic but also deeply talented and magnetic." Aaron shrugs at that assessment. It's still not his Mae I know.

We then revel in our day's highlight reel—Cassity's loyalty and guts (" 'Is that a pun' " Aaron repeats with rare uncontained delight) and Susan's cleverness, leading to that remarkable moment when the juror turned out to be wearing Nike Air Force 1s. Aaron also makes approving comments about my opening, although not for any reason I might have expected.

"You seemed nicer," he says. "Jackdorp seemed mean."

This assessment strikes me as astute, because it's probably close to the way some of the jurors view things. I may not be ready to open a charm school, but I can count on coming off as more likeable than Jackdorp, who seems utterly indifferent to that kind of appeal. That manner can still work out for him—it has for decades, in fact—but he needs to have a more secure mastery of the facts than he demonstrated today.

Aaron is not inclined to giddiness, but I still feel obliged to remind him of the fundamentals of the case as Damon, the jury consultant, presented them to me: a Black-on-white crime in a rural all-white county, where some people undoubtedly are still uncomfortable with interracial relationships. Damon thought the odds were long against twelve people from this area agreeing to an acquittal. I've never shared that part of Damon's assessment with Aaron. Instead I say, as I have before, that we started this game playing from behind, whatever the judge said about the presumption of innocence.

I wanted this time with Aaron, not simply to gather his reactions to specific developments, but also to observe his general mood after the first three days in Judge Carrington's courtroom. The trial, an event he awaited with both dread and hope, is finally unfolding, but he seems as he has seemed throughout—polite, possessed of occasional sharp observations, but basically withdrawn. It concerns me at moments that I have seen none of the rage that you would think would justifiably engulf an innocent person, but he may be too depressed for that.

Now and then, I have inquired about Joe's assessment of his grandson, since he has visited Aaron the most often, driving the two hours in each direction virtually every day to spend the hour he's allotted. So far as I can tell, most of their time together has been spent playing gin, with a deck the deputies inspect, then lock up. When I asked a couple months back how Joe thought Aaron was doing, Joe in his naturally disagreeable way responded, 'Well, how would you be doing?' I could actually answer that question, since I have been in Aaron's place, if for a shorter time, but the truth is that I let most of it flee from memory. It's like having been to war. You can't really connect the anxiety and humiliation of imprisonment, or its severe boundaries, to what you feel when life as you knew it has resumed.

Generally speaking, jail is not a good time for anyone. Losing liberty, having every second of the day determined by the will of brute authority, shrinks the spirit of any human. As we expected, Marenago has been a better experience for Aaron than the Skageon County Correctional Center, which was close enough to urban areas that it housed a cadre of 'scary dudes.' Here, there was a menacing skinhead type who arrived a few months in. He was charged with a serious assault and battery in a bar, and frequently expressed a desire to mess up Aaron, but he also tangled with the COs and was shipped out to one of the state penitentiaries.

With that exception, Aaron has been well-liked by the inmates and the guards. The jail administration will not let him have his drawing pencils, which they see in their upside-down way as potential weapons, but Bea persuaded the warden that no one could be hurt with Cray-Pas. Aaron has spent a ton of time doing pastels. He has earned a reserve of favors from his fellow prisoners, by using photos to do color renderings of the people at home these men miss—children, wives, girlfriends, mothers. One of the COs here informed Aaron that the state was doing an exhibition of prison art, and he has submitted several pieces, albeit with scant hopes.

The weird truth of jail life is that Aaron is a celebrity inmate. The charges against him, with the potential of life inside, are the gravest faced by anyone in here, which, in this perverse world, commands respect, especially because they carry a warning about Aaron's dangerousness. And he is also the only prisoner in here whose case has earned extensive media coverage, meaning he can't be treated as a dispensable nonentity by the guards. Most have not been harsh with him, due also to the fact that his institutional deportment has been excellent. One of the COs, a younger guy named Diesenberg who was the guard during my first attorney visit when I asked if Aaron wanted me to represent him, refers to Aaron as 'a good guest.'

On the other hand, even after four months of visits in this intense setting, I feel like I've gained little in the way of additional insight into him. Perhaps the only times I've felt I was breaking through have occurred when we've put aside the case, and he has talked to me about his art. He showed up to one of our meetings with a photo of a self-portrait by the

British artist Lucian Freud, whose work I'd become familiar with during an international judges' meeting in London. In return for one of those favors Aaron is owed, a fellow inmate had torn the picture out of one of the few magazines that made its way into the institution. Having the picture, given its source, probably violated several rules, but Aaron treasured it and has taped it to the wall of his cubicle, without any trouble. It was one of Freud's customarily cheerless works, where the artist, in his sixties by then, looks askance, his irregular features eaten on by surrealistic shadows, conveyed in harsh contrasts that might well reflect the artist's view of the unvarnished hardness of life.

Aaron loved the painting, because he felt its depth, and yearned to create something like that himself, even though he freely admitted feeling thwarted.

'It's like being a kid. Do you remember how much you didn't understand? The adults are talking, and you know how to talk, but you don't know what they're saying. And then all the sudden you do understand, or you understand more. And it's like that now for me. I understand more, I can feel more, but I still can't move all of that from my brain to my hands. It gets stuck halfway inside me.'

But much more often I have been impressed by how jail reinforces the isolation Aaron has always felt. His bad behavior years ago was always more in the nature of leave-me-alone than an expression of rage. His fights with his mother—I witnessed several before his conviction—seldom saw him shouting back. He would listen and then do whatever she'd asked him not to. 'Lost.' 'Depressed.' They have always seemed good words for Aaron. 'Angry' or 'belligerent' less so. He was a temperamental little boy, according to Bea, and would storm, resisting any discipline. But after Lloyd moved out, he became morose, and that never really has changed.

Whether it's because of being one of the rare Black kids in Skageon, as Bea believes, or simply the way he came out of the wrapper, there is a pained aloneness at Aaron's core, which I've always suspected was what his drug use was attempting to erase. He connects with only a small group of people. The love for children that Aaron shares with his mother may reflect the fact that in the company of kids he feels free of the reactions that often trouble him in his relationships with peers.

Thinking about Aaron as I worked late one night, understanding how isolated he has always been, I felt a sudden bolt of comprehension about Mae, and why he found it virtually impossible to give her up. He has loved only this girl. And her love for him, like young love always, brought with it the joyous news that there is someone else, a matching soul whose very existence meant he no longer needed to march through the world by himself. They became a universe of their own where only their wants, their rules, mattered. Yes, she capriciously withdrew from him periodically. But she always returned, the thrill tarnished a little, but still elevating and essential to somebody like Aaron. In a world where few desire to remain alone irretrievably, Mae was the one person with whom he had found a bond that changed the fundamental terms of living.

Knowing that, I could take in the depth of the crisis he finally faced on September 14 last year, when he realized that no matter how much he needed or wanted that connection, she was no longer capable of providing it reliably. The best and happiest thing he'd ever known was lost to him for good. And as I sat late at night in the intense beam of a shell light in my office in Mirror, gripping a glass of whiskey in which the ice had melted long before, I was paralyzed, because I recognized the clear emotional logic for Aaron of killing her. It would provide the only avenue for a needed escape, one he might otherwise not have had the strength to make. In Harold's Woods, he may have experienced his choice as perpetual disappointment or a saddened life in which he was nonetheless free.

Yet as I told Bea yesterday, if that is the truth, I can't absorb it. We are all enigmas to each other, but the young man I heard talk about his aspirations as an artist does not seem to harbor that destructive capacity. Then again, perhaps I'm protecting myself from accepting something that could sap some of the zeal needed for Aaron's defense.

I tell him a bit about what to expect tomorrow, then stand up to leave. With that comes the dispiriting thought of what I face at home with Bea, and I realize abruptly that Aaron can solve that problem. I sit again in the molded plastic chair the jail provides, bolted to the floor so an inmate can't turn it into a weapon.

Having only minimal prior experience as a defense lawyer, I have followed the example of Sandy Stern when he represented me. Like Stern, I have never asked Aaron to provide a complete account of what happened last fall. That practice is actually for the defense attorney's protection. Ethical rules prevent a lawyer from putting a client on the witness stand who the lawyer knows is lying, and a client who, after listening to the prosecutor, tells his attorney a different story than the one he told before falls in that category by implication. Thus, I will allow Aaron to give us his full version of events only after he's heard the entire case against him, when we will decide whether he should testify. I will be dead set against that, but it's Aaron's decision in the end.

When I've needed to know particular facts that might require investigation, like why in the world he would go buy a rope, or what happened to his missing sneakers, I've put the questions to him, but our conversations about the proof are deliberately limited. As a result, I've never asked him whether he placed the length of white rope he'd bought in our garage, because I knew the answer and had nothing good to gain. Bea didn't do it. I didn't do it. It could only have been Aaron. Or so I thought until about fourteen hours ago.

"Aaron, I need to ask you one of those questions I've waited on."

"Sure," he says.

"The rope you bought. Did you bring it home and put it in the garage?"

He shakes his head once. "Never."

"Well, where did it go then?"

"I left it with Mae. I mean, come on, man. I bounced without my backpack and my sleeping bag. Why would I grab a big rope I had no real use for by then?"

That explanation rings home at once as true. As I've thought to myself often, Aaron has only mediocre skills as a liar. He's completely matter-of-fact now, looking straight at me, with none of the tics or tells of deception.

"I mean," he says, "I guess that rope in the garage, that's an old one my mom had brought home from school. That's what she told me right before you got here."

High and hopeful a second ago, I hit bottom just as fast. That's

why Bea rushed over here. To plant that story. So Aaron would corroborate her.

For Aaron, like so many other humans, there is no one like his
mother. His loyalty to her naturally far exceeds whatever he feels he
owes me, the more so given the agonies he's caused her the last two
years. If she told him that this was what he had to say, he would. I'm
just not sure he could do it so convincingly.

"Is this true, Aaron?"

"That she told me?"

"No. That the rope on Jackdorp's table isn't the one you bought?"

"Legit," he answers. He looks at me a second longer, studying
him. "Man, why are you stressing on this, Rusty?"

He's a smart kid, and he heard Jackdorp's opening. Is it really
possible he didn't appreciate the significance of what his mother just
announced? But then again, as Susan and I have both often sensed,
the prosecutor's so-called proof may be like someone screaming at
him so loudly that it becomes only harsh sound, with no meaning to
the words.

27

Hardy's Texts

When I come through the front door, Bea again is on the thirdhand sofa with a half-consumed bottle of white wine on the square coffee table in front of her. She clocks my arrival with a dark, inert look. I absorb yet again the loss of the upbeat woman who magically seemed to elevate my serotonin levels. I worry, as I always do now, that with a bad outcome for Aaron that person will vanish for good.

As I step into the living room, I register the still air of the house.

"Where's Susan?" I ask.

"She went home."

"She went *home*? She was supposed to stay over. We have things to discuss for tomorrow."

"I told her I wanted to talk to you. So she decided to leave. She says she'll have the phone thing turned on, and you can call her now or after we eat." Susan uses a fairly remarkable piece of technology, a Bluetooth device that attaches to her helmet and allows her to make and receive calls with surprisingly little road noise. But it's far better for us to talk face-to-face because of the spotty cell coverage in the areas she's traveling through and at her home. It's pure luck to get five whole minutes without the call dropping.

Instead, from the way Bea is describing things, it sounds like she more or less asked Susan to go. I feel a flare of anger about that, but I hold my tongue and retreat to the bedroom to exchange my suit for some sweats. If anything, though, my vexation grows in there. Bea has long realized that she cannot contribute much to the defense, but the one thing she's done is not get in my way. She's never been an obstacle between Susan and me, and has always seemed to follow my guidance not to discuss the case with Aaron, let alone talk about a critical piece of evidence.

While I've been in the bedroom, she has returned to the narrow kitchen, reheating a skillet meal, something with noodles and chicken and veggies.

"I need to talk to you for a second," I say from the doorway.

Bea, too, is in sweats, but given her weight loss, the pants bag on her like clown trousers. For court, she has a stylish blue suit that she bought at one of the outlet malls. Even without paying legal fees to me, the costs for Susan, for my brief consultations with experts, and the expenses for weeks of living out of town, are eating through Lloyd's and her savings, and she's unwilling to spend much on her wardrobe. She tries to vary her look each day with different blouses and accoutrements. Today she wore a big white bow under her chin, which, appropriately, made her resemble an Old West schoolmarm.

She reaches up to switch off the fan in the vent over the stove so she can hear me, then diverts herself to top off her wine. She offers to pour for me too, which, in my current mood, only irritates me further. She knows by now that I don't drink until I'm done working.

"Can you explain to me why you went to the jail and talked to Aaron about you putting the rope in our garage?"

"He told you?" she answers at once, probably the worst response I could imagine. She seems to have startled even herself, and adds, "I asked him to let me tell you. I guess he missed that. But I said at the jail, you and I needed to talk."

"But if I asked him tonight about whether he left the rope in the garage—which was only logical after you woke me up about it—I wasn't supposed to know what you'd just told him?"

Her mouth gapes. She's wounded.

"That's not fair, Rusty. I assumed he told you a long time ago that he didn't put the rope in the garage." That's a good answer—but I'm still not buying it. She turns to face me fully, reading me as always with uncanny accuracy, and says, "Now you think we're both lying to you."

"Bea, think about this, please. No one will believe either of you. There's a video of him buying the rope."

"Then it was a different rope. How unusual is it to buy a rope?"

"All the fibers they collected are the same nylon as the rope in our garage."

"I heard you say that kind of nylon is everywhere." She gives the food a desultory stir, before again eyeing me directly. "I don't lie to you, Rusty. I told you that last night."

"Bea, is there anything you wouldn't do for Aaron?"

She pouts. "What kind of question is that? Every mother would give the whole earth for her child."

"I.e., you'd lie to save him."

"Not to you," she says. She squints, as if it's getting hard for her even to see me.

"Bea, please," I say. "It didn't dawn on you to discuss it with me, before you had a conversation with my client about a pivotal piece of evidence?"

"Your 'client'? Rusty, he's my son. I made this catastrophic blunder in what I said to Dom, and then I compounded it because I was too afraid of how I'd feel if I bothered to look at what was supposedly in Aaron's hands when he killed Mae. And instead, I ended up creating this ridiculous predicament for him. And for you. So I wanted Aaron to know I'd messed this up. And why. I thought he should hear that from me."

I really don't know what Bea looks like when she's lying, because she's right, I can't recall even a minute when I've doubted her in the seven years we've been together. Like Aaron in the jail, she seems convincing—except that the timing will always undermine her credibility, and thus her son's.

I am so thoroughly put out with her that I leave the kitchen and return to the living room. I take a seat in a wing chair across from the sofa with my hand squeezed over my mouth, while I try to manage my anger. I am revisited by the recurring sense of doom about our relationship. And it's my fault in the end, because I knew at the start that no lawyer in his right mind would even consider representing his fiancée's child.

In a minute she follows me in. I expect that she's come to temporize or apologize, to do what little she can to make things better, but instead she says, "Can I ask you about the other thing I wanted to talk to you about?"

I lift my hand, inviting her to go ahead, but with a hopeless air that suggests things can't get any worse. She takes a place on the sofa, leaning toward me.

"Are you serious about this stuff with Hardy?"

Who is this woman? I think, just that plainly. It's incredible that in the middle of all of this it's somehow important to her to come to Hardy's defense.

"What stuff?" I ask her cautiously.

"That he murdered Mae? And that you're going to subpoena his cellphone records to help prove it?"

I've told Bea often that she must display serene confidence before the jury, but when I glanced back at her while Cassity was testifying about Hardy, I was surprised to see her stark alarm.

"Look, Bea. I know somebody murdered Mae—or probably murdered her anyway—and I don't want the jury to believe it was Aaron."

The problem with the prosecution case, when you think about it deeply—and I surely have—is that it makes some sense. And the rope burn around Mae's neck tells it all. It's great to release rabbits, to mention suicide, but that will be a hard sell in the end. The best defense for Aaron is to suggest that somebody else murdered Mae. But whoever it was still used that rope. There are no bullet holes, no knife wounds, because they'd still be manifest on Mae's corpse, putrefied or not. And to strangle a woman as tall and fit as Mae, who continued her MMA training, even amid her drug use, required somebody substantially stronger than her. Which makes it far more likely it was a male, and a male in good shape. Aaron is in that category. But so is Hardy. He will have to be our bogeyman-in-chief, our best alternate suspect.

Bea searches me with an uncomprehending look.

"You never told me you suspected Hardy."

"Bea, honestly, I don't know what I believe right now. I'm doing my job. Do I truly think Hardy murdered his daughter? Probably not. But I'm pretty sure that Hardy is a weak spot in the State's case. He was supposed to have nothing to do with the prosecution, *because* it was his daughter, and I doubt he followed that rule." Since Mansy told me that Jackdorp called Hardy as soon as I discussed representing Aaron, I've taken it that the two PAs are more or less hand and glove.

"Isn't the prosecutor supposed to consult with the victim's family?"

"He's supposed to keep them informed. Not hand over the keys to the car. But I'm going to try to turn that to our advantage. The more irregularities there are in the investigation, the more credible it becomes when I tell the jury there was a rush to judgment. And yeah, maybe any parent wouldn't have been able to restrain himself and keep from getting involved. But that gives us the chance to suggest that Hardy was overstepping because he actually had something to conceal. And today we proved what he wanted to hide. So we're on the right track."

"So you *are* going to subpoena his cellphone records?"

I probably won't. Susan has already told me that the providers don't keep text messages that long, and Hardy, if he had any sense, deleted his messages about Gwen's private parts and like correspondence with other women a while ago. Mae's cell, with its file of old pictures, was locked of course, and as often happens these days, the investigators have failed in their efforts to break into it. Neither the prosecutors or her family have been able to guess her password, although Glowoski, with nothing resembling proof, suggested to Susan that Aaron changed the lock code before returning the phone to Charmaine.

"What's the deal with Hardy's cellphone?" I ask.

The question, to my amazement, seems to stop Bea cold. Her face knots with a look of intense concern, which in the lingering silence sets off a slow-moving cascade of connections. I recall Cassity's remark that she was reluctant to talk about Hardy's texts, not for his sake, but because she could have badly embarrassed Aaron. And what suddenly enlarged Cassity's eyes after saying that was a panicked recognition that she'd inadvertently revealed something to me. She'd been thinking about the problem only in terms of its impact on Aaron. But I could be hurt too.

"Bea," I say then, "is there something in Hardy's texts you don't want me to know?"

And there is. My question seems to deprive her of breath. She can't look away from me, because she has no idea of what should come next. Finally, she shifts her seat on the sofa, moving her bottom from one cushion to the next, looking down at her hands for quite a while.

She finally says, "Yes." She straightens up and says, "If the records go back far enough, there could be some messages I'd rather you didn't see."

My body is instantly lit by the kind of shock that seems to leave even my lips numb. Now I'm the one who needs a second.

"What are you saying to me, Bea?"

"Rusty, I mean, you know this. People have secrets, sexual secrets, and they don't make sense to anybody else. That's why they're secret."

I find that I've fallen back in the wing chair, while I watch her fumble.

"Can you skip the philosophy and be a little more concrete?" I say. "What kind of messages am I going to see?"

"I mean, Hardy and I never quite stopped. After high school?"

"Stopped what? Seeing each other?" I pause, then lay it on the line. "Fucking each other?"

She moves her body a bit, stiffening against an impulse to recoil.

"Both, I guess." She is still looking only at her hands, which are clasped in an aspect not too far from prayer. "I mean, it stopped. Sometimes for years. And it's been completely over for a while now. But sometimes, you know, you find something with somebody else that you don't really want to give up, if you don't have to."

"So, let me follow this. In college, while you were dating Lloyd, you'd still see Hardy on the sly?"

"A little."

"And when you got married?"

"Well, not when I got married. I cut it off then. Except when Lloyd and I were near the end. I actually told myself at that point that I might get pregnant that way, which could save the marriage. How's that for a rationalization?" She laughs at herself, without putting any effort into it. "But I told you, I've always told you. It took me a while to face the fact that Lloyd, nice as he is, was not enough for me. And this was one of the ways. Lloyd was too churchy to ever enjoy sex much. And then I was divorced. And it was my business. But even then, I didn't see him more than once every month or two."

" 'Him' is Hardy?"

She nods.

"I thought you hated Hardy."

"I'm getting to hate him now. But what I've told you is a little different."

"Which is?"

"That I've never really liked him. He's never known how nice people behave. But for the most part, I've just always felt sorry for him. You know, it's like a joke you hear whispered in the teachers' room. What do you do with the child who has an inferiority complex because he's actually inferior? The truth is that Hardy always experienced himself as powerless. He's never felt strong enough to defy his parents. Instead, he was stuck doing what Mark did, knowing he would never do it as well. His looks, bedding women—that's all Hardy has, that's the only place where he feels in charge."

"Well, Sigmund Freud can make excuses for him. I won't."

"It's not an excuse for him—or for me, Rusty. I know that."

"And you were okay being part of his parade? Because he was so great at it? Is that it? It was the greatest sex you ever had?"

"It was sex without obligation, Rusty."

"You didn't answer me."

"He made it interesting."

"What does that mean?"

"Do you really need to know?"

I think about that. I wish the answer were no. But I'll always obsess without an answer.

"Yeah," I say. "I need to know."

"Now and then there were other people, other men mostly. Sometimes another couple. Sometimes drugs."

"Drugs? A lawyer in the PA's office? The PA himself?"

"We were being bad, Rusty. Together. No rules. Or our own rules."

"Wow," I say. My thoughts are shooting across my brain without guidance or control. But I'm beginning to realize that my shock is not merely about the sex. What is world-turning is how much there is about Bea I didn't know.

With the resulting feeling of distance, I find myself perversely impressed. I've never seen enough imagination in Hardy to believe he'd include other men in his sex life. But it means, I suppose, that Bea's always going to be disappointed in me.

"And you enjoyed that?"

"Sure. I enjoyed it. I enjoyed crossing those borders. I was a single mom in a small town, and I felt hemmed in by all of it, you know that. I was entitled to some excitement, Rusty. Everyone is. I didn't have the time or money to go trekking in Nepal. Or to visit Machu Picchu. This was my adventure. But it's been-there-and-done-that. I mean, Rusty, until us, love and sex were always two different things for me. Maybe I wasn't actually in love before. But I never knew the way the two parts fit, the way they enhance each other. I was approaching fifty, and when we got together, I suddenly felt like I'd just landed on another planet."

This at least is something I've heard her say often before. We, us, our relationship—our love—was a turning point in her life. I just had little clue that being Hardy's fuck-buddy preceded that.

"Before us," she is saying, "I was just into sex for sensation. I didn't have much time for dating apps, blundering around, swiping left or right or up or down. I dated. I tried. But I had this backstop. Hardy would always have time for me."

"And how did this work? You'd bump into him at church and plan your next fuckfest?"

She glowers. She thinks she's being open and I'm rewarding that with sarcasm. She's right about that, but were I to respond, I'd say, 'Too bad.'

"I called him. Mostly. Because I didn't want him pestering me. It wasn't often, Rusty. A few times a year, almost always when I was off of school. But yes, I called him, and that was one of the things I loved, that I was in control."

"And why was he okay with that? I mean, I know you're hot stuff, but I don't imagine there was any shortage of other women. What was in it for Hardy beside the ego stroke?"

"Ego, obviously. I always came back. And I guess it gave him a chance to make his case."

"What does that mean?"

"It means he'd spout a bunch of crap he didn't really mean. And that I didn't believe. Or want."

"Like?"

"That Charmaine was going to pass soon and then we'd be together. Or that he loved me and would leave Charmaine the minute I said."

"But you didn't believe that? Or didn't want that? Which?"

"Both. Definitely. Sometimes, I believed *he* thought that. He clung to who he was in high school, before his brother died. He's always been convinced that his life would have been better if I'd stayed with him. Which is nonsense. His life would have been better if he didn't have to take on the weight of trying to be Mark, which he's basically failed at. That had nothing to do with me."

"But you let him make his proclamations of undying love anyway?"

"I scoffed. Always. I told him he wasn't leaving Charmaine, and I had no interest in marrying him—or even being seen with him in daylight. None of it was ever going to happen."

Not only am I learning a lot about Bea in this conversation, but the truth is that much of it is things I don't like. She's plainly discounting the role that Hardy played in the end of her marriage. And, at least in her telling, I feel a little bit sorry for Hardy, because I know damn well there were moments when she raised his hopes.

I sit, just trying to fit the pieces of all this together. There is a taste of iron in my mouth like I'd just finished a run beyond my lung capacity.

"And so you were sneaking around with each other when your children began dating?"

"We both discouraged them. You know that."

"But you didn't worry about the impact on them if they found out?"

"No one found out. For decades. I mean, it was just this harmless secret. Like masturbation." I'm not the one to throw stones, but I don't think either Charmaine or Lloyd would find the truth harmless.

"And nobody else ever suspected?"

"I worried about Mae. I knew she spied on Hardy now and then. She said something to me once—'My father's always going to be hung on you.' And she had this smart-ass smirk. But God knows, I never heard anything from Hardy about Mae breaking into his cellphone."

"And you didn't worry that she'd share her suspicions with Aaron?"

"Sure, I worried. But I'm positive she didn't. He wouldn't have been able to hide something like that. He'd have been completely weird with me." Cassity, clearly, believes that Aaron remains clueless. Which, oddly, offers a further insight into Mae's destructiveness. Cassity's offhand assessment of Mae's misbehavior offered on the witness stand struck me as penetrating. Like people who commit suicide by proxy, taunting the police into killing them, Mae, as Cassity said, wanted people to hate her as much as she hated herself. But Mae's acting out wouldn't give her what she wanted if she wasn't diminished in the eyes of her victims. There would be no satisfaction in telling Aaron about his mother, because his disappointment would focus on Bea. And he couldn't really blame Mae for telling him the truth.

In our conversations about our romantic pasts, Bea has hewed to a line like the one she's struck today. Before Rusty. And after. An epiphany near the age of fifty. But what has crept up on me is that those statements, much as I've liked hearing them, are fictitious in a central regard. Something's been clear since this conversation began, even if I haven't wanted to hear it said out loud.

"And so when exactly did this thing with Hardy stop? You said it stopped. But when?"

She's appeared a bit more relaxed in the last minute, but she goes still now.

"What are you asking?"

"You know what I'm asking."

Again, she looks straight at her hands.

"If you're asking if you overlapped, the answer is yes."

I've heard that term, 'overlapped,' before and always despised it, because it pretends shitty behavior is like some spot on a color chart.

"How long? A week? A month?" I'm only hoping at this point.

"Longer."

"How long?"

"It stopped completely before we moved in together."

"But not before that?"

"Not completely."

"So Hardy and I were sharing you for years?"

"You weren't sharing me. They were two different things."

"But you lied to me all that time?"

"I never lied to you. You never asked if there was anyone else and so I never said."

"Really? You and I spoke almost every day. You mean I never asked what you did the night before and you answered me with some fairy tale?"

"I don't know. I probably said I had a meeting." She stops there for a second, then finally raises those amber eyes to me, now darkened by pain. I'm sure it's obvious that I'm feeling quite provoked. She sighs and heaves and straightens herself up, before again facing me. "I'm being stupid and defensive. And dishonest. I know I need to ask you to forgive me. And yes, for deceiving you. And for not stopping it sooner. For not believing more in us. But I was afraid of ending up with nothing. Being with Hardy was easy. And familiar. And safe for me. I had a couple of hours of pleasure. And I felt wanted."

"But I wanted you too."

"I know. I know. I'm not going to tell you I was right. I was wrong. I was completely wrong. But I was afraid to gamble on you. I was afraid to stop calling him. Because I knew that was the one thing he could never tolerate, me saying 'I have someone else and don't need you at all.' It's too close to the way he felt with his parents when he was growing up. And I was constantly afraid of having nothing when you and I broke up. It's not like you were quick to commit, Rusty. You were holding back."

"I was crazy about you. And you knew that."

"I was afraid. I was reluctant to believe it. You didn't say it, but I knew you felt you'd die from one more disappointment. And if I told you about this, that would have been the end."

"Stop making excuses. You were trying to have it both ways."

"That's true. From the outside. But I'd kept this secret for decades, Rusty. It was part of my life. It was like I was living in two separate realities that didn't touch. But I was wrong. Really, really wrong. You have every right to be furious."

"I am," I answer. I would scream at her if I were less confused. "And what else is there that I should know?"

"Nothing. I mean it. I'm trying to be as honest as I can. Because I never want to have to talk about this again. Assuming you talk to me at all." She peeks up at me. "But, Rusty, the big point is that it's been done for years now. Four."

"Almost four," I answer, quibbling for the hell of it. "Is this why you've been reluctant to get married? Because you were afraid to tell me? Or because you wanted to keep your options open with Hardy?"

She winces at that and sags.

"I know I deserve that, but I've never had any second thoughts about Hardy. I don't want or need any of that now. But I would never feel right marrying you without telling you this. Only I couldn't ever figure how even to start the conversation. I never wanted to make you feel the way I know you feel now." With this, saying this, owning the pain she's causing, her eyes brim and she's finally crying in silence. "But what's really important is that it's done. I made the choice I should have made long before, but I bet on us. I gave up something that at some points felt like it was keeping me alive. And I don't even speak to him now. If I'm in a room with him, I won't look in his direction."

"Because he doesn't stop trying?"

"He's bitter and really angry. As I expected. It flattened him to hear me say that I'd given someone else the total love he always wanted from me. Everything he directs at me now is shitty. Like when we got engaged. He texted me, 'Congratulations. It will never last.' I didn't even bother with 'Fuck you.' "

"That's okay. I'll take care of it for you."

"Please don't."

"I would never give him the satisfaction," I answer sharply. Another thought, important but somewhat off-center, shoots into my mind. "Do you think this is why Hardy is such a jerk to Aaron. To get even with you?"

"Probably. But I don't have anything to confront him with. He supposedly has had nothing to do with these cases, even though it's like you say—I've always had the feeling he's manipulating things behind the scenes." When Aaron got arrested with Mae, Hardy's office insisted that he had to plead to a felony, even though Cap argued there were comparable cases, second offenses, where the prosecutors had agreed to defer prosecution.

I have a bottle of scotch in the kitchen that I resort to late at night. I bring it back and pour myself several fingers. I drink half at once.

Her tears have continued while I was gone, and she wipes her nose on the sleeve of her sweatshirt, before casting me a bleak look.

"And *are* you going to talk to me?" she asks.

"I need to think, Bea."

"Should I move out?"

I finish the whiskey while I ponder.

"Look, I can compartmentalize with the best of them," I tell her. "I'm Olympic caliber. But I can't look at you in the morning and at night and concentrate on saving your son's life. So yeah, it's better if you go join Joe at the motel for a while. Tell him I'm impossible to live with right now."

She nods and stands slowly and heads into the bedroom. I pour another glass of whiskey while I hear her knock around. Her sobs from the other room penetrate the thin walls, and I realize from the way the sound stops periodically that she's trying to pull herself together before she reappears. When she does, her face is red and wet. Her coat is on and she's holding a small leather duffel.

"Can I sleep in the other bedroom instead?"

"Bea, please."

"I'm sorry I was so stupid. I'm truly, truly sorry. Please try to forgive me. Will you at least try?"

I shake my head, not knowing what it means, except that it's too soon to tell.

"Let's get through the trial," I say. "It won't be much longer than the end of next week. How about if we take on one crisis at a time?"

"But tell me you'll try."

"I'll try," I answer. I'm being decent, but even I hear my response as less than half-hearted. A giant bubble of a sob rises through her again. With her hand mashed to her face, she goes out the door.

There is no hope of sleep, even while I'm reluctant to sit and stew. Bea has given me so much to think about, to digest, that I don't feel like I can even begin to take it on.

After another hour, and two more drinks, I find my small emergency cache of sleeping pills, bypassing any second thoughts about the dangers of ingesting them on top of alcohol. I need sleep if I'm going to be anything but a befuddled mess in the courtroom in the morning. And so with welcome speed the heavy hand of the medication drags me down.

But later—with no sense of how much time has passed—I bolt awake. I sit upright in panic. My heart is banging like an alarm bell, and a night sweat has soaked my T-shirt and most of the sheet. I realize I am not thinking well yet, that a combination of the drugs and sudden waking has allowed the nightmare to cling to me and with it, the deep fears that precede reason. It is thoughts of Bea, of course, which have wrested me from sleep. There is more deceit, more vanity and selfishness, even cruelty, perhaps, than I ever recognized hidden in her sunny affect.

But I'd already realized that when I lay down. Those thoughts, sad as they are, don't seem the stuff of panic.

And then, as happens, the layers peel back. What I saw in sleep was a vision of Bea when we first visited Aaron in the Marenago Jail after his arrest, and in anguish she offered to take Aaron's place by confessing to Mae's murder. I ridiculed that idea. But the piece the nightmare recovered was Bea's hard-eyed declaration in response that if she talked about what Bea had done to Aaron, her claim of responsibility would be credible. 'I can be much more convincing than you think.'

And now I feel the way the links of calculation join. If there is a much darker side to Bea than I knew—and there is—and if she believed Mae was certain to drag Aaron back to addiction and ruin—and she did—and if, beyond that, Mae knew a secret Bea never wanted shared with her son and even more so with me, a secret that could upend the life that Bea had finally settled into after decades of a wanting she had been afraid to declare even to herself, a secret that Mae, being Mae, might have occasionally hinted she would expose...

I know I will find some comfort in daylight. Better sense will rinse away these anxieties. How could Bea even have found Mae? Won't there be dozens of people at school to verify her whereabouts every second of the day on September 14? But in the country darkness, shrouded in a moment of chilling stillness when all life beyond my door seems to have ended, I cannot fully shake the logic that says Bea may have murdered Mae.

28

Joe Takes the Stand

February 8

The State's next witness is Joe. He clumps up to the witness stand in a pair of sturdy black oxfords that look like they may be left over from his army days. The old suit he's wearing might have been purchased for Willi's funeral, since the pants are slung low below his belly so he can still get them on. Under the jacket, he wears a crimson dress shirt and a black knit tie, another part of his mourner's outfit, I'd guess, which has formed a knot the size of a pair of socks right below his throat. Behind his glasses, his eyes are squirreling around. He doesn't have to tell anybody he'd rather not be here.

As he settles in the witness box, I turn briefly, even though I know I shouldn't, and glimpse Bea in the first row, who appears to have been waiting to catch my eye. Her nose is as pink as a rabbit's, and with one glance it's clear she got no sleep. She mouths two words, 'Forgive me.' I nod slowly, just to show I register the remark, and then turn back.

Jackdorp arrives at the podium. He had a rougher day yesterday than he expected, and he seems more tense. Even though most attorneys in town, as well as others who know him, speak about Jackdorp reluctantly, I have gradually acquired background information.

The dermatological affliction that has left Hiram Jackdorp with large boils and patches of roseola apparently overcame him in his thirties. He was married then to a kindly woman who was as cheery as he was dour. They had no children, to their mutual despair, but doted on each other. Then, when she was forty-five, she was diagnosed with breast cancer, waged a long fight and died not long after her fiftieth birthday. No one claims Hiram Jackdorp became any nicer in the aftermath. Tim Blanc, Jackdorp's ex-deputy, who clearly harbors no affection for his former boss, believes that Jackdorp takes his looks as an insuperable obstacle to courting other women. Besides, in the saddest aftermath of a happy marriage, he regards his wife as irreplaceable anyway. He still lives on his father's farm, in one of the original Sears houses, which has undergone several additions. His companions are more than a dozen cats who leave the place with the reek of cat litter and fishy foods. At night, he reads weighty volumes of history. His wife was the social person in the couple, and Jackdorp seldom sees other people, aside from the activities required by his public position and his job as county party chairman. Even his visits to church became rare after his wife's death. Despite the sympathy for his circumstances, he remains far more feared than liked. Like many prosecutors I have met, he seems to find that being the engine of punishment provides a perverse outlet for his bitterness, like opening a vein to release acid rather than blood.

Most of our necessary dealings have been conducted face-to-face. In working out issues, he does not tend to negotiate. He decides in advance what he thinks is fair or obligatory under the law and will not budge. As a result, I have accepted that our differences will not be resolved quickly. On the lengthy stipulation, the set of agreed facts that will be read to the jury sometime soon, I made several changes to his draft, listened to him say no and responded like a parrot, 'No.' I got a draft back that accepted exactly half of the alterations I had insisted on. I demanded two more I regard as critical, both about telephone records, to which he is yet to acquiesce.

And I have never gotten onto a first-name basis with him. He calls me 'Judge' and I call him 'Mr. Jackdorp.'

After his experience with Cassity, Jackdorp asks the judge for permission to treat Joe as an adverse witness, meaning he wants to cross-examine him with leading questions. I could object to this, as I did with Cassity, but it's in Aaron's best interests, both emotionally and in terms of the case, to get Joe off the stand as quickly as possible, before he makes an ass of himself as he usually does. Even so, he hunches over as Jackdorp approaches him, placing his hands on the rail of the witness stand, looking like a linebacker ready for the ball to be snapped. On the several occasions when I've tried to prepare Joe for his testimony, I've asked him not to be combative with the prosecutor, but I knew that was futile advice.

Jackdorp makes it as quick as he can, after establishing that Joe had to be subpoenaed to testify. Joe admits buying Aaron the Nike Air Force 1 sneakers ten months before—"real good shoes," Joe adds, in apparent praise of his generosity. Then Jackdorp shifts to the events at Joe's farm the morning after Mae's body had been found. Aaron showed up in the dark, a little after five a.m., and asked to borrow Joe's truck. According to Joe, the State Patrol never asked how Aaron got over there, but I suspect Joe led the police to believe his grandson hitchhiked.

"Did you know," Jackdorp asks, "that he was under a court order not to drive?"

"I knew it, but it didn't really cross my mind at that moment. Here was this boy, just about growed up, and crying his eyes out when he told me that the Potter girl had been found, drugged up and missed a turn and ended up dead at the bottom of this wash."

"That's what Aaron told you?"

"That's what I'd heard in a bar the night before, so it wasn't any news to me when Aaron said it."

"And you say he was upset?"

"Pretty much broke in two," Joe says.

"Did he request anything else?"

"I give him a sleeping bag."

"Didn't Aaron have his own sleeping bag, as far as you knew?"

"Nice one. That was another gift I give him a couple years back."

"And did you ask where his nice sleeping bag had gone?"

"No reason. Seemed like it was something he just thought of, that he might even stay out overnight."

Jackdorp takes a second to stare the old man down. Joe's explanation is apparently an improvisation.

"Is that what he said, 'In case maybe I stay out overnight?'"

"Maybe. That's how I understood him. I warned him that the alternator had been acting up on the truck, but that was old news."

"So he was eager enough to get your truck that he took it, even knowing that it might have mechanical problems?"

I object that he's asking Joe to testify to Aaron's thoughts, which is sustained.

"But this business about Aaron being gone just overnight. That's not what you told the State Patrol special agents when they interviewed you on the morning of October 2, was it? You never told them Aaron had said anything about being gone just overnight, did you?"

"I don't know."

"In fact, what Aaron said to you was, 'I've got to get out of here.' Did he say that?"

"Kind of."

"Kind of?"

"He said it, but not how you're trying to twist it around."

"Judge," says Jackdorp.

Judge Carrington tells Joe, in a kindly way, to answer yes or no when he can. She adds, "Mr. Sabich over there is a good lawyer and he'll ask you to explain, if he thinks that's needed." She shows me a brief puckish smile, realizing that Joe and I must be well acquainted.

"Okay," says Joe to her, "but I thought you were trying to get at the truth in here."

"We are," the judge answers. "But there's an established process. It's been done this way for centuries."

Joe shrugs.

Jackdorp gets Joe to say yes this time, when he asks if Aaron said, 'I need to get out of here.'

"And what about the wilderness area up at Ginawaban? Have you ever been there with Aaron?"

"Yep. Many a time. Taught him all about it. He loved it there in the Northern Moraine," says Joe, referring to a glacial formation, "with the gorges and big hills. That to Aaron, that's like Disneyland, being in wild country."

Jackdorp returns to his seat, saying he has no more questions.

"Mr. Sabich," says the judge, passing the witness.

"Now, Joe," I say, "I notice that Mr. Jackdorp didn't ask you any questions about your background, but let's tell these folks a little bit about who you are." He gets it out quickly: raised as a migrant, picking fruit here through the summer. There is a juror, a quiet elderly man, a retired farmer now living with his wife in Portage, who Joe insisted he recognized from those fields. Today the man goes as Gomes, rather than the Gomez Joe remembers, but the juror seems to give tiny involuntarily nods as Joe describes that time in his life.

I quickly steer Joe through the remainder of his biography—state champion wrestler at Skageon Consolidated Regional High School, Bronze Star in Vietnam, and then work at US Motors and vice president of the UAW Local there. Even this far north, the closing of US Motors is still regarded as an epic catastrophe, like a dam break, and as I move back toward the defense table, I glance over and see several of the male jurors react visibly to that detail in Joe's biography, especially the guy with the Nike Air Force 1s. Although it hadn't occurred to me in advance, it seems as if some of these men take Joe as a local hero.

"Now when did you meet Aaron?" I ask.

"He come to us," says Joe, "meaning my daughter Bea there, and Aaron's dad, Lloyd, when he was about seven days old."

"And do you love him?" I ask.

I am behind Aaron with my hands on his shoulders.

"Like my breath," says Joe. "Like no one else."

I can feel a quiver pass through Aaron.

"And from the time he was about three, where did he live?"

"Well, after Bea and Lloyd split up, she didn't really have nowhere to go, so they moved into a second house, a little place on the back of my farm."

"And did you spend time with Aaron, as a result?"

"Most every day. My wife Willi died sudden, and we were keeping Aaron during the day when his mom was off teaching, so then it was just me. He'd follow me around and help me do everything on the farm. Once he was in school, I'd pick him up and bring him home most days."

"Did you have any occasion to teach him about outdoor life?"

"Oh sure. Boy was like he was born in a canoe. Any kind of fishing—winter, summer—loves to be outside, best of all when he can be by himself. I mean, he was eight or so, and when we camped, I had to bring two tents so he could sleep alone—although he'd usually crawl into mine once the owls starting hooting."

Several of the jurors grin, including every woman.

"Was that Aaron's habit or regular practice, to want to be by himself outdoors?"

"Always like that, yes. Got to be when he was in high school, and he was going through all that stupid high school stuff, like when he'd break up with the Potter girl, which seemed to happen every month, he'd go off by himself. Always been his way."

"And referring to September 29, the morning after Mae's body was discovered, when he came to ask to borrow your truck, why did you say yes?"

"I already said. Cause he was so upset. And I knew that was his way, that he needed to get off by himself."

"Now, you've known Aaron since he was seven days old. And saw him every day for years. Would you say you're familiar with his moods?"

"Like my own."

"And when you told Mr. Jackdorp Aaron was upset when he came to ask to borrow the truck, how did you assess his mood? Did he seem frightened?"

"He was grieving. Pure and simple. He was grieving that girl, not that it made sense to me, little as I liked her."

"But did he appear frightened?"

"No. That thought didn't even cross my mind. He'd just lost a big piece of his world. That was it."

"When he said, 'I've got to get out of here,' how did you understand it?"

"Like he needed to get off by himself like he usually did."

"And he said he was *borrowing* your truck, is that correct?"

"Sure."

"Can you work your farm without that truck?"

"Not really."

"And by the way, is there any equipment you keep routinely in the flatbed of your pickup?"

"Shovel. Work gloves. Hand truck for moving stuff around, especially my hay, since it's just me sometimes and I'm not as strong as I once was."

"And you'd put those items in the truck before you lent it to Aaron?"

"Sure thing."

"Nothing further."

Jackdorp's redirect is obvious.

"You love your grandson, you said."

"I sure do."

"Anything you wouldn't do for him?"

"Nothin," Joe says.

Jackdorp hesitates, then goes for it.

"Lie for him?"

"He's never been much for lying. Clams up, but he's not much of a liar."

"But you, would *you* lie for him?"

"Oh, *me*," says Joe. "Hell yeah. If it was the right thing to do, I'd lie for certain."

Several jurors smile brightly at that answer, including the Nike guy and the hair-curler lady with a sense of humor. Amazingly, Joe has been pretty much a hit with the jury, which proves yet again that a trial is not really a truth-finding process.

Judge Carrington calls a recess before the State's next witness. Bea is standing by the rail, waiting to speak to me. She steps forward but Joe grabs my arm from behind.

"I can sit in here now and listen to this hogwash, right?" The judge's pretrial order sequestered witnesses, meaning all but Glowoski and Susan were excluded from the courtroom before their testimony. Now that he is done, I tell Joe, he may join the spectators, just as Charmaine did yesterday once she was off the stand, positioned in the wheelchair notch in the front row, beside her husband. I went out of my way not to look in her direction when Cassity was talking about the messages on Hardy's cellphone, although I suspect the same is not true of some of the jurors, who hated me a little for putting her through that. But I was wagering their irritation with me was nowhere near the contempt they felt for Hardy. Now that I'm remembering all of that, while I watch the spectators sift out the courtroom door into the hallway, I notice that Charmaine is not here today, which requires no explanation. But I'm taken from those observations by Joe.

"Hey, how'd I do?" he wants to know. It's always vaguely amusing to me that folks like Joe, who act as if they care so little for other people and their opinions, are always so ravenous for compliments. "I did my best not to make it sound too bad for the boy," he says quietly. I cut him off immediately, since that's not something I want Jackdorp and his many spies in the courtroom to hear. Plus the remark is unsettling in itself. It sounds like Joe might have kept to himself far more incriminating details. If Aaron ever hinted to anyone that he killed Mae, it would be to Joe, knowing that his grandfather would fight lions and tigers and bears before sharing that information.

Bea has continued waiting for me, but I just shake my head as I pass her. When I woke up, I realized that Bea had continued to preoccupy whatever part of me thinks while I sleep, but she remains entirely incoherent to me. Out of kindness, I touch her shoulder as I pass, suddenly recognizing that not only have I lost any sure grip on who she is, but that that uncertainty has spilled over into my understanding of myself.

29

George Lowndes

When court resumes after a brief recess, I ask to address the judge before the jury reenters. We still haven't received the notes from the agents' two interviews of the next witness, George Lowndes.

"Well, Judge," says Jackdorp, "the notes concerning Mr. Lowndes turned out to be in Skageon County. An agent is driving them up right now."

"Your Honor," I respond. "Two points. The first is that I am entitled to those notes before I cross-examine Mr. Lowndes."

"Agreed," she says. "What's the second?"

"The second is that you ordered immediate production of *all* interview notes."

Jackdorp jumps in. "He just said he's entitled to the notes before cross-examination. Now he wants it all special delivery."

I have her prior order in hand and read it into the record.

"Okay, let's get on with Mr. Lowndes's testimony. I have the jurors cooling their heels in the jury room. We'll address the other issues later."

Like last night, Judge Carrington seems just a little unstrung. It would be no surprise if somebody, perhaps another judge, passed a remark to her about what she allowed to happen to poor Hardy Potter.

Susan says Cassity's testimony was what passes for big news in Skageon County—headlines in the Como Stop paper, a weekly which
happened to be coming out today, and in the Patch, the online site.

George Lowndes enters through the swinging doors at the back
of the courtroom. He's a stout man, close to six feet, wearing a long-
sleeved patterned shirt and slacks held up by clip-on suspenders.
Above his wire-rimmed glasses, his grey hair is curly and matted to a
scrambled mess. He's probably younger than me, but frankly, doesn't
look it.

Lowndes seems affable, a talker. Like a lot of witnesses, he has
trouble responding only to the question he is asked. He says he and
'the missus' live outside the town of Egan in northern Skageon
County. He farms, and his wife helps keep the books at a local feed
and seed supply. He was at Harold's Woods, he says, because it was
his wife Gina's birthday, September 14. She, he tells us, "is kind of a
nature nut, so that's what she wanted to do, hike around up there, and
it's her birthday, so okay."

Lowndes says their plan was to catch the sunrise on the East Trail,
but their older daughter and two grandchildren stopped by with
birthday cookies before school, so the Lowndeses didn't arrive in Harold's Woods until roughly eight a.m. Then, as soon as they reached
the trailhead, Gina realized she'd forgotten her water bottle and he
returned to the car to retrieve it. When he got to their auto, he saw
two people shouting at each other at the far end of the gravel parking
area. Jackdorp has had a schematic prepared of the car park and gives
Lowndes a marker to make an L, where he was, and an A and B for the
position of the people he was watching.

Jackdorp asks, "Can you describe these people who were shouting
at each other?"

"Well, one was a tall blonde. You know, cutoff shorts and a skimpy
top. Twenty maybe."

"Female?"

"Yes. And the other was a guy. Taller than her."

"Can you describe him?"

"On the thinner side. Darker skin. Same age range."

"African-American?"

"If I had to guess. I mean, he might have been, you know, a Pakistani or a Puerto Rican. Darker. That's all I'd say for sure. He had on jeans and a long-sleeve white shirt."

"And you said they were shouting?"

"It was her mostly. He had something in his hand that he was holding over his head, and she was screaming at him to give it back. He was answering her, not quite as loud. She was jumping up and down to get it from him. Then there was some kind of scuffle."

"Describe the scuffle, please."

"Seems to me he kind of shoved her and she ended up on her keister. Then he walked away."

"Was that the last time you saw them?"

"Her. Not him."

"When did you see him again?"

"Well, Gina and me, we finished our walk or hike, what have you."

"When, relative to when you started?"

"Say two hours. She went back to the car, and I decided to find the men's—kind of at that age, if you know what I mean." Jackdorp has him circle the comfort station on the map. "And as I was coming back from there, I see this car making like sixty through the lot and headed straight at me."

"Can you describe the car?"

"Silver SUV. Late model."

Jackdorp has a photo of Mae's SUV, and Lowndes says the picture looks just like the vehicle he saw.

"And what happened then?"

"Well, like I say, he was headed right at me. So I kind of shouted out, called him a name, to be honest, and jumped aside and he swerved but never slowed down and went tearing right past me."

"Did you see the driver?"

"Same guy I saw before, if you ask me."

"How did you make that conclusion?"

"You know. He was dark. Same guy."

For a second, I hope that Jackdorp is going to ask Lowndes to make an in-court ID of Aaron, to say 'Yes, that's the man,' but Jack is too savvy for that. I'd have a good time boxing Lowndes's ears on cross, if he claimed to be able to positively identify a man he glimpsed for less than a second as he went speeding by. Instead, Jackdorp passes the witness.

I've actually started forward when Susan calls my name to remind me: the notes. We all go to the sidebar at my request.

"No notes," I tell the judge.

"They'll get here," Jackdorp says, like I'm being a pest.

"Are you asking for a recess?" I say to Jackdorp.

"Mr. Sabich," says the judge, "you're entitled to a recess, but I'd prefer you start your cross. I don't want these jurors getting antsy. You never know which side they'll blame. Then we can take an early lunch while you review the notes."

I think about objecting further, but it's serving us well for me to be the good boy in this classroom. I return to the podium, then walk toward the diagram that Jackdorp has up on an easel next to George Lowndes.

"Now, Mr. Lowndes, I want to make sure I'm visualizing this correctly. According to your direct testimony, your car was parked here on this diagram?" I point to the L that Jackdorp had Lowndes mark on the diagram, right near the entry into the parking area. "And when you returned to the parking area to get the water bottle, where you previously placed an L, you saw this couple on the far northern end of the lot, right near the other trailhead, correct?"

He agrees.

"So according to this schematic, you were about 120 feet from them at that time. Does that sound right?"

"I guess."

"Now, Mr. Lowndes, the State Patrol interviewed you twice? The first time was on September 26, 2023, and then nearly two weeks later, on October 8? And on the initial occasion, had you heard or seen anything on the Internet or in the papers or on TV about a young woman being missing?"

"Can't say for sure. I know the troopers mentioned that."

"Well, what I'm wondering, sir, is did you call the troopers or did they find you?"

"Nope, they found me. I asked them how, too, and they told me that they'd collected data from the cellphone towers closest to

Harold's Woods and identified any numbers that had remained in the area more than an hour on a couple of dates. They got Gina's phone and mine that way. So that's how they got to us. Impressed me, I admit. Guess nothing's a secret these days."

This detail will undoubtedly enhance the jurors' impressions of the investigative capabilities of the State Patrol, which runs counter to my theme of a botched investigation. For the one-thousandth time, I learn the lesson everybody knows, to never ask a question on cross-examination to which you don't know the answer. In court, ignorance isn't bliss, but it's often the better alternative.

"And in that first interview, you told them about witnessing this quarrel at the other end of the parking lot, right?"

"Yes sir."

"Now, Mr. Lowndes, is your memory of events more accurate closer to the event or further from the event?"

"Huh?"

I have to go over that a few times before he finally agrees that he generally remembers recent events better than things that happened longer in the past.

"Have you had a chance to review the reports the State Patrol officers made of their first meeting with you?"

"Jackdorp over there showed me something."

"Well, did he ask you if there were any mistakes in what the agents had written down?"

"I guess. I mean, I didn't notice anything."

I hand him the report of the September 26 conversation made by two troopers who were out canvassing the owners of all of those phones that had been in the area on September 14.

"You'll agree with me that in the first report, the agent makes no mention of you saying that the male had pushed or struck the young woman, or even that she'd fallen down."

"Huh," says Lowndes. This time he lifts his eyeglasses to read the report more closely. "Okay," he says.

"Now again, you were looking from a distance of 120 feet, right? And is it fair to say that there were a lot of hands and arms in the air as this couple was quarreling?"

"Okay," he answers.

"Now, the second time you spoke to the agents, they found you at your home near Egan in northern Skageon County, is that right?"

"Right. On a Sunday."

"October 8?"

"Sounds right."

"In fact, Lieutenant Glowoski here was one of the two State Patrol officers who came to talk to you, wasn't she?"

"Yeah, pretty girl. I remember her." He smiles a bit at the lieutenant, thinking that he's given her a compliment she will appreciate.

"Did you know by then that a young African-American man had been arrested and charged with the murder of a tall, blond young woman?"

"Couldn't miss it. All over the news."

"And what you said in the second interview with the lieutenant was that the male 'might have put hands on her.'"

More cautious this time, George Lowndes raises his spectacles again and takes his time examining the report.

I continue. "And did you say 'might'—the male *might* have put hands on the young woman—because you weren't sure, you didn't have a clear memory?"

"Well, they wrote down 'might,' and that's what it means to me, but I don't recall that part, saying that."

"Fair enough. Now before you testified, did you meet with Mr. Jackdorp?"

"Yes. Came up here to see him twice."

"When was the most recent occasion?"

"Last night."

"And by the way, my investigator, Ms. DeLeo over here, she asked to speak to you a couple of times and you refused, true?"

"I didn't see why I should."

"Had Mr. Jackdorp said anything to you about talking to the defense?"

"He didn't want me to. I can't remember quite what he said, but he didn't want it."

I deliberately cast a sideward glance at Jackdorp, who is rolling his lips like he's contending with indigestion. Seeing the same thing I have, Lowndes continues on his own.

"Wasn't telling me anything I wouldn't have done. We've got a nephew who's an officer down in Milwaukee, and he's told us stories. We know how it goes in here." Lowndes circles a hand, meaning the courtroom.

My first impulse is to move to strike the remark, but Susan flashes me a look and a subtle smile, and I realize that Lowndes, as my aunts used to put it, has 'told on himself.'

"Well, thanks for admitting that, Mr. Lowndes," I respond for the benefit of the jury. "But was it while you were talking to Mr. Jackdorp that you became positive the young man had pushed down the young woman?"

"I guess."

"Thank you. Now let's go to when you saw the SUV speeding through the parking lot. We'll agree you didn't mention anything about that, the speeding car or the driver, the first time you spoke with the troopers on September 26?"

"They didn't ask. They were just trying to figure out if we'd seen the girl."

"But we can both agree then, that the first time you told the agents that the driver of that vehicle was the same young Black man you'd seen across the parking lot—the first time you said that was after you read all the publicity about a young African-American man being charged with Mae Potter's murder. Right?"

"True enough, but like I say, nobody asked me until then."

"Okay. So let's go back to September 14. You came back from your birthday walk and decided to use the facilities. Do you happen to remember where Mrs. Lowndes was while she waited for you?"

"Like I said, she's kind of an outdoor person, and you know, to me, outdoors, it's where I work, so I'm like—you know. A lawyer, you don't go to the office on your day off, do you? So she wants to go hiking for her birthday and it's her birthday. Anyway. What was I saying?"

"You were saying, I believe, that Mrs. Lowndes had remained outside."

"Right. She sat on the back bumper of the car and was looking at her phone."

I put a G behind the L on the chart.

"Now, I believe you said when you saw the SUV speeding toward you, you shouted out. Is that right?"

"I called him a name and jumped out of the way."

"And the car swerved?"

"Big time."

"That parking area isn't that wide, right? Twenty feet according to this diagram."

"Seems right."

"So you'd jumped out of the way, but you turned back in time to get a glimpse of the driver?"

"Right."

"And you were looking through the passenger-side window to see the driver."

"Okay."

"And you'll agree that the car windows are tinted dark?"

"Are they? Don't remember that."

I ask Jackdorp for the photo of Mae's SUV and, in a little bit of courtroom theatrics, ask to also mark it as a defense exhibit, before I show it to Lowndes.

"Does that refresh your recollection that the car windows were tinted."

He shrugs. "Pictures don't lie," he says.

"And I notice, Mr. Lowndes, that you wear glasses. What's your prescription for, if I may ask?"

"Oh, about six different things. Bad astigmatism."

"Nearsighted?"

"And how! About 6/20."

"Had you worn your glasses on your hike?"

"Nope, left them in the car. Put on my sunglasses."

"Prescription?"

"No. Polarized, though."

"And you'd gone into the men's room. Did you leave your sunglasses on there?"

"Don't think I would have."

"So when you looked through the tinted passenger window, you didn't have either set of glasses on?"

"Well, not these. Maybe the sunnies. Probably had put them back on."

I've done enough. A man with a strong eye prescription, looking through sunglasses and a tinted window, is telling us what he saw in a fragment of a second as a car sped past him—and now claims he recognized the driver as a man he'd previously seen from 120 feet, something he said only after learning that a young Black guy was charged with the crime. The most delicate art in cross-examination is knowing when to stop, the point at which the jury has learned enough to form their own doubts and where the questions raised can be hammered home in closing argument.

There's just one more point, which Susan made to me last night when I finally called her after Bea left, grateful to have something else to think about for a minute.

"Now, when that car swerved, Mr. Lowndes, if I'm not mistaken, it actually came closer to Mrs. Lowndes sitting on the bumper than it was to you. Is that right?"

He can't really fight with the diagram.

"And her view would be from the driver's side, correct?"

"Okay."

In a stage whisper, I ask Susan for the State's witness list.

"Mr. Lowndes, does your wife use the same last name as you?"

"Only for the last forty-six years," he says. He thinks he's funnier than anybody else seems to.

"Well, I ask, sir, because I don't see her name on the State's witness list. That first interview on September 26, it sounds from the report that the agents spoke with the two of you together?"

"Right. The two agents just rang the bell and stood on the doorstep, wanting to know if we'd seen the girl. Gina was right there and we both explained how I'd seen the boy and her when I went back by myself for the water bottle."

"And was Mrs. Lowndes at home when Lieutenant Glowoski and the other agent came to visit for this follow-up interview on October 8?"

"She let 'em in the door, actually."

"And did they speak to Mrs. Lowndes?"

"I told them not to bother."

I actually draw back. "Can you explain that?"

"Yeah, when they were done with me, they asked if they could have a word with her. I went and talked to her and came back and told them she didn't want to speak to them, which was good by me."

"And what do you mean, it was 'good by you'?"

"Well, look. I'm under oath, right? That woman lives, I mean *lives* to say I'm wrong. I say it's daytime, she's gonna run to the window to check." There is an outbreak of serious laughter in the courtroom. Several of the jurors are chuckling. "It was fine with me she didn't want to talk to all of them."

"And what was it you thought she might disagree with you about?"

He gives his head a solid shake.

"Nothin in particular. I'm kind of joshin here. Just I didn't mind if she didn't want her turn."

"Did you ask her not to talk to them?"

"If I did, she'd have gone charging right out there to see them." Laughter again rises up. I thought the agents' failure to speak to Mrs. Lowndes was going to be helpful to us, a small but added example of a messy investigation, but in his candor, Lowndes is reinforcing an impression that he's a fundamentally honest guy.

I look back to check on Susan's reaction to this. And she's gone. I assume the notes have arrived.

"Judge, I think it's time for that break we agreed on. Lunch perhaps?"

After we recess, I ask Aaron if he knows where Susan is. He doesn't.

I find her, quick-stepping as she reenters the courthouse. She grabs me by the elbow and pulls me back into the attorney/witness room, where I spoke to Cassity yesterday.

"I wanted to give Gina Lowndes a try at work, once I heard him identify that feed store. I thought she might talk without him around. You want the good news or the bad news?"

"Which is there more of?"

"Hard to say."

"Let's hear the bad news first."

"She won't testify. We can get ten subpoenas and a team of horses, she says, and if we get her here, she'll say she doesn't recall a thing."

"You pushed, I'm sure."

"Of course. I told her someone's life was at stake. And she said, 'That makes two of us. I'm not coming into court and calling him a liar. I got two children and six grandchildren, and I need to live with that man till one of us is buried. So I don't remember. What do they say? That's my official position. I don't remember.' And she hung up on me."

I take a second. "She'd call him a liar?"

"Her word."

"About what?"

"That's where the good news comes in," Susan says. "I have the notes."

30

The Notes

Our early lunch turns into a late lunch, when Jackdorp, without explanation, announces that Lowndes won't be available for another hour. It is close to two p.m., however, when he asks Moriah, the clerk, if we can have a word with the judge about scheduling. I suspect he'd like to go back to chambers, but the judge is on the bench instants later.

"Your Honor," he says, "there's been a mix-up." It's the first time I've ever seen him look sheepish. And it's also the first time he's addressed Judge Carrington as 'Your Honor,' so it's clear he's in trouble.

"Your Honor, Lieutenant Glowoski wasn't at the sidebar earlier in the session and she mistakenly thought when we recessed that Mr. Lowndes had been dismissed. He's gone home. We've tried to get him back here, but he had a medical appointment in Milwaukee and can't come back now until tomorrow. It was an honest mistake," he adds.

I actually doubt that Jackdorp was part of that plan. I've seen him lie several times already, when he takes on a simpering pious look. Right now he's pretty clearly embarrassed.

Having seen the notes, however, I have my doubts that Glowoski acted innocently. She adiosed Lowndes in the hope that the judge, already concerned about the jury's impatience, would decline to wait for the witness until tomorrow. I'm actually somewhat fearful that is what will happen. Judge Carrington will say that if it's important to confront Lowndes about something in the notes, I can call him back when we present a defense.

What weighs against that, of course, is that the judge is increasingly aggravated with Jackdorp. She speaks to him sharply when she reminds him that informing witnesses of the court's schedule is his responsibility. He nods while he's being upbraided. When she's done, I ask her permission to confer with Susan, who's already come up with the same idea I have.

"Your Honor," I say, "understanding the court's concerns about keeping the jury waiting, I'd like to propose the following. In lieu of completing my cross-examination of Mr. Lowndes, I'd rather call Lieutenant Glowoski to the stand now."

"*What?*" shouts Jackdorp. "This is ridiculous. We're in the middle of our case. He doesn't get to call witnesses. He'll get his turn when we're finished."

"Your Honor, I am representing to the Court that there has been a serious *Brady* violation regarding Mr. Lowndes's testimony. There is significant evidence favorable to the defense that the State should have disclosed months ago. And the best cure now is to put Lieutenant Glowoski on the stand briefly."

"No," says Jackdorp.

As always, he has nearly perfect pitch for what will inflame the judge.

"Mr. Jackdorp," she says, "you're not making the rulings here. All right, Mr. Sabich. I'll listen carefully. And if I don't hear evidence of a serious *Brady* violation, as you're claiming, I'll strike the lieutenant's testimony. Bring the jury in," she tells the courtroom deputy.

Plainly agitated, Lieutenant Glowoski evens the edges of the files on the prosecution table, rather than face the judge. She forgets to stand when the jury comes in, the normal demonstration of respect, which in the circumstances displeases the judge.

"Come to the stand to be sworn, Lieutenant," Judge Carrington says tartly.

Glowoski cuts a precise figure as she makes her way to the side of the bench. Unlike Jackdorp, I have found Glowoski virtually unknowable. Her appearance is so orderly that it's hard to figure what's behind it. She reminds me of certain female athletes or coaches. Somehow there is a desiccated air to her, scrupulously lean and with her careful blond hairdo lacquered flawlessly into place. She wears a bit of makeup that is always perfect as well, and her jacket and trousers are pressed every morning, which is a trick I haven't mastered with my suits. You see models or high-fashion women in the city who are this fastidious, but in those cases the effort is in service to allure. With Glowoski, it feels like a shield.

Susan has dealt with Glowoski and finds her polite but predictably restrained in all ways. She carries a tiny notebook in her inside vest pocket and, with her nails polished but carefully pared, makes notations with an expensive silver pen. Her writing is tiny and as carefully formed as calligraphy. I'm not sure I'd believe her if she testified to a shortcoming as minor as 'I forgot.' There is nothing that could be called a duty that Vanda Glowoski neglects.

When the jury is settled, Judge Carrington explains that I've been given permission to ask the agent a few questions, because Mr. Lowndes didn't understand the situation and went home.

I am angry but controlled, which is generally a good mode for a defense lawyer. For her part, Glowoski's eyes are lasers, making no effort to hide her hostility.

"Now, Lieutenant, you are what's called the case agent, is that right? You're the State's chief investigator into the murder of Mae Potter. You supervised other agents and county sheriffs' deputies, gave them direction, reviewed their reports. Yes?"

"That's correct."

"Now, you visited Mr. Lowndes, who testified this morning, at his home in Egan on October 8, 2023. And you were accompanied by another special agent of the State Patrol, Alpina Martinez?"

"Also correct. She was with me."

"And Special Agent Martinez took notes of what occurred. And you were ordered by Judge Carrington several times to turn over those notes to Ms. DeLeo and me, including before trial, and you didn't do it, did you?"

"I didn't understand her order that way. But apparently that was my mistake."

"Okay, and going back to your meeting at the Lowndeses' house outside Egan, Mrs. Lowndes admitted you to the home and ended up listening to part of your conversation, is that right? And she left the room eventually?"

"Correct. She left."

"And when she departed from the room, she made it apparent that she did not agree with what her husband was saying?"

"I don't think I would say that."

"Really? Well, doesn't the following notation appear in Special Agent Martinez's notes?"

Susan made a slide with her phone and has transferred it to the computer, so it appears on the monitor to the agent's right. I remove the diagram of the parking lot, which was up on an easel, so the jury can see what's been projected on-screen now:

'[sp leaves—doesn't agree???]'

"And sp stands for 'spouse,' doesn't it?"

"You'll have to ask Special Agent Martinez. She took the notes."

"Okay, well then, we'll do exactly that. Where is Special Agent Martinez, right now?"

From the speed with which the lieutenant changes direction, I suspect Martinez is close.

"Martinez was guessing, Mr. Sabich. That's why the question marks are there. The wife left the room. That's all you could say for sure."

"And was there something in the way she left the room that made it seem she might have disagreed with what her husband was saying?"

Glowoski takes a breath.

"Apparently that was what Martinez thought. I don't know why. And I certainly don't know if she was correct. The wife, Mrs. Lowndes, didn't say why she was leaving, and like George said, she wouldn't talk to us."

"And do you remember what it was that Mr. Lowndes was saying to you that his wife didn't seem to agree with?"

"No idea."

"Well, Lieutenant, you heard Mr. Lowndes testify that Mrs. Lowndes was actually closer to the silver SUV that went past them in the parking area at Harold's Woods on September 14. And according to his testimony, she, unlike her husband, who was jumping up on a curb, remained seated on the bumper, in a position to see this car tearing through the parking lot, right?"

"I don't know what she saw, Counsel."

"Do you agree, Lieutenant, that in your experience as a criminal investigator, people tend to look up to see what the problem is when they hear their spouse cursing a few feet away."

"Okay," she says. She shrugs, accepting this minor defeat.

"And do you see that in Special Agent Martinez's notes, the notation about the spouse not agreeing comes right after she wrote down, 'Black guy was driving'?" Susan puts up another slide, so both notes are visible. "So Mr. Lowndes said the Black guy was driving and Mrs. Lowndes did something to show she didn't agree."

"That's how the notes go," says Glowoski. "To me, that's all you can say."

"And if Mrs. Lowndes didn't think the Black guy was driving, since Mr. Lowndes saw only two people in the parking lot, that would mean Mrs. Lowndes saw the female driving, through the driver's-side window, which is why she differed with her husband?"

"She never said that, that's for sure."

"Now, in the academy where they train State Patrol officers about how to interview witnesses—do they teach you to ask a potential witness's husband whether she's willing to talk to you?"

"Not really."

"Not really," I say. "Don't they teach you to speak to the witness directly, and to do your best to convince her to talk? Isn't that standard procedure?"

"It's the regular way to do it. That doesn't mean you can't ask the husband."

"Is the reason you didn't do more to get Mrs. Lowndes to speak to you because you realized that she disagreed with her husband that the Black guy was driving, and you actually didn't *want* to speak to her?"

"She didn't speak to us. You can guess and I can guess what she was going to say, but in the end, she said nothing."

"But you made no further effort to speak to her, did you?"

"Not really."

"You didn't call her, or visit again, or try to catch up with her at her place of work, where her husband wouldn't be present, or sub-poena her to the grand jury?"

"Didn't do those things. You can Monday-morning quarterback all you want, Counsel."

"Do they teach you in the academy what *Brady* material is, Lieu-tenant? Material that's favorable to the defense?"

"Sure."

She concedes that she knows that the Supreme Court of the United States has said many times that disclosure of *Brady* is an important ingredient of a fair trial.

"And do you think the fact that Mrs. Lowndes expressed in some way her disagreement when her husband said the Black guy was driving—do you think that's favorable to the defense?"

"I don't see why."

"You don't?"

"No. I still don't know what she actually would say."

"Were you here for Mr. Jackdorp's opening statement?"

"You know I was."

"Well, didn't you hear Mr. Jackdorp say that Mae Potter had been murdered while the Lowndeses were on their hike?"

"I heard that."

"So if the female, that would be Mae, was driving the car that tore out of the parking lot, she wasn't dead, was she?"

Loud laughter rolls through the courtroom. From the corner of my eye, I see several jurors taking part. Glowoski glowers at me unwaveringly.

"Well, she's dead now, isn't she?" she finally says, as the laughter dies down.

"Sadly yes, but not because my client killed her. Did you show these notes you don't think are *Brady* material to Mr. Jackdorp and ask him whether he thought that was favorable to the defense and needed to be disclosed?"

"Never did that."

The judge intervenes. "I think we've heard enough, Mr. Sabich. Ladies and gentlemen of the jury, I am instructing you now that the notes of the interview with Mr. Lowndes, and especially the portion wherein they indicate that Mrs. Lowndes might not have agreed with what her husband was saying, particularly because it might be read to indicate a disagreement about the identity of the driver—I am instructing you that, as a matter of law, those notes are evidence favorable to the defense which the prosecution had a constitutional obligation to turn over. At the end of this case, you will be allowed to draw whatever inference from that failure seems proper to you."

The judge tells Jackdorp to call his next witness. He takes a second working around the prosecution table before he tells the judge he doesn't have anyone here. He assumed, he says, I'd be quite a while finishing with Lowndes, and his next witness is the Marenago County sheriff's deputy who arrested Aaron at Ginawaban. They learned over lunch that the deputy had been called to the northern part of the county on an emergency traffic fatality.

All this takes place in front of the jury. The judge bakes Jackdorp in another four-hundred-degree look and then simply turns to the jury box and says, "Well, you heard that." No doubts about who's to blame. With lengthy apologies for calling another recess so soon after lunch, the judge sends them home.

Even while they're on the way out, Jackdorp rushes to the podium.

"Your Honor, if I may," again trying to be uncharacteristically respectful. "Your Honor, what the lieutenant just testified to, that I never saw those notes, I want to represent to the Court that that is true. And Judge, I'd also like to point out that if Mr. Sabich wants to examine Mrs. Lowndes so badly, instead of playing gotcha, he can subpoena her to testify in the defense case."

I saw that one coming. I jump in at once.

"Now that the cake is baked, Your Honor? Now that her husband has testified under oath and she has to come in here and say publicly that he's dead wrong about a vital detail? The time to have disclosed these notes was months ago, when we could have talked to Mrs. Lowndes with the notes in hand, instead of asking her to bushwhack her husband. You could tell from what Mr. Lowndes said that there's a fair bit of tension in that household about who's right and who's wrong."

"The time to have disclosed this," the judge says, "is when I ordered it disclosed. That's point one. And point two, Lieutenant Glowoski, so that we don't have further disagreements about what is or isn't *Brady* material, I want *all* notes from all law enforcement personnel involved in the investigation of this case—I want every single note in the hands of the defense within forty-eight hours. That will be the order." Judge Carrington stalks off the bench without even bothering to adjourn.

We've scored big, this time. Another court officer comes to remove Aaron, but he gives me a thumbs-up as he departs. Glowoski leaves the courtroom in an obvious huff, with no word to Jackdorp. He follows a moment later, looking straight ahead like a soldier at a memorial, and brushes past the three local reporters waiting to get a word with him. For the journalists, the case, with its ups and downs for the prosecution, has been good copy so far.

Whatever my distaste for Jackdorp, I don't believe he simply would have hidden the notes. For one thing, I've read the state supreme court decision Mansy mentioned (it turns out he wrote the opinion), reversing an armed robbery conviction and reprimanding Jackdorp for not disclosing a report that indicated that one eyewitness, among several, described the person with the gun as looking nothing like the man who was ultimately charged. Wendy Carrington was the state defender at the time. More to the point, there are subtler ways for a canny prosecutor to deal with the problem, while disclosing the notes. From Susan's conversation with Mrs. Lowndes, it's fairly clear that if the investigators had actually spoken to her, she'd have said she remembered nothing.

I march up to the three reporters, gathered like a pack of schoolkids, and call the behavior of the prosecution 'shocking and disturbing.' The jury is instructed each night not to look at any reports on the trial on TV or social media or, for those who still recall them, in the newspapers, but the research says that 80 percent of them do anyway, so it's part of trying a case well to offer your side to the press daily.

With that done, I wait for Susan, who's gathering our files, and then ask her if I can have a word. Because of our early recess, the attorney/ witness room has not been closed, and I lead her in there and close the door.

"What's wrong?" she asks. Apparently, I'm wearing my worries and she's startled by my change of mood, especially in the wake of a good day for the defense.

I compliment her for being so dogged about the notes, then sit down with her at a small, worn table and tell her what Bea wants to say about the rope. Susan's an equal partner in the defense and she's entitled to hear this. Because of a rough complexion, Susan wears a lot of heavy makeup that sometimes seems to me to mask her expressions. But not now. Susan finally says, "You're not going to let her get up there and say that, are you?"

I explain that Bea's adamant and, worse, that she beat me over to the jail yesterday and spoke to Aaron, who now corroborates her.

"Well, that wasn't very smart," she says. Susan is one of those no-judgments people who try to go through life without condemning anyone. We all have our stuff, and our reasons. So these few words about Bea are stark.

When I first met with Susan to discuss getting her on this case, her only reservation was that I would be representing the son of the woman I was supposed to marry. I explained the difficulty of finding other counsel, which is why Susan ultimately said yes, but she still characterized the situation as 'like trying to juggle with a live hand grenade.' She has every right to say, 'I told you so,' but doesn't. Yet as we part tonight, I know that's what she's thinking.

But right now, after two successive nights with little sleep, I am too exhausted to worry further about any of this. I walk back to my car, parked in the lot behind the courthouse, grateful for the cold, which seems to revive me enough that I can remain awake through the ten-minute drive to the house.

The saying is that trying cases is a young person's game, and my weariness only goes to prove the point. Yes, you could do it like Jack-dorp, as a nine-to-five job, knowing that in this community you're odds-on to win as soon as you say your name. But to try a case the way

I am doing it for Aaron, with every cell dedicated to the fight, with my mind never at rest for weeks, so that all sleep is incomplete, and with my body in an unrelenting fear state as if it was my life, as much as Aaron's, at stake—I am too late facing the fact that this is a task at the edge of my physical capabilities. Driving home, completely alone, I am overcome by a gust of laughter. Of all the excuses I made to Bea about why I should not be Aaron's lawyer, I never seized on the most obvious and indisputable: I was—and am—too old to be doing this.

Admittedly, I don't spend much time pondering the grim fact that at this stage, I am close enough to see the other shore. But my physical being permits no illusions. My body is like the streets in Kindle County, in a state of constant repair. In the last five years alone, I have had my cataracts removed, dental implants for two failed molars, and knee replacement surgery, with the other knee, my right hip and my lower back all vying to be the next part cut. Every morning, I down at least twelve different pills to forestall what really can't be held at bay, so many of them that I sometimes think of myself as a human maraca. A few years ago, I accepted that I would have to live by the watchword, There is always time to pee. I find it hard, especially after a glass of wine, to retrieve the names of people and places I have known for years. And the legion of souls, once part of my life and often on my mind, who no longer walk the earth is a virtual ghost army.

And yet I was no more ready to say to Bea 'I am too old for this' than I would have been to respond the same way when she takes my hand to bring me to our bed. Twenty-three years older than she is, once I was in love with her, I never wanted to confess we were anything but perfectly matched.

One discovery of being old is that it's not really what I would have imagined. In younger years, I would have thought that, heading for seventy-seven, I would sense my vitality starting to slip away. The truth is that even now, I feel the force of life bounding through me as unequivocally as it did when I was a six-year-old. The maxim is that if things are going well in a family, there will be three generations living fully here on earth. Being honest, I have not enjoyed any stage without reservation—the beginning, the middle or the end. But until Bea sent me ass over teakettle last night, I would still have judged this part the best. What gets called 'wisdom' is in many senses just having seen the movie before, but in this stage of life, the manifold resemblances of the present to the past provide real comfort. No matter how badly Bea stomped my heart yesterday with her news about Hardy, a part of me knows that lovers have done that to one another for eons and will continue as long as humans last. And great sadness, like Mae's, no matter what the distinctive details, is still a dirge I have heard so often that I basically know the tune by heart. In the end, I guess, the greatest solace of being so familiar with these cycles is the recognition that in death you won't really be missing all that much you haven't seen before.

At home, I take off my shoes when I come through the door, and after a few steps fall face down on my bed. I sleep the entire night without taking off my suit, a good thing in some ways, because I was too tired even to set an alarm. I wake within a few minutes of when I am due in court, and only because my phone is buzzing on my night table with a call from Susan, who is over in the courthouse looking for her rawhide outfit.

When I sit up, I think about Bea. The shock settles on me again, and then, like yesterday, I store that grief away. I splash water on my face, and give myself a once-over with my electric razor. Then I examine myself in the mirror. Sleep has restored me somewhat. Enough.

"Come on, cowboy," I say out loud. "A few more days."

31

Deputy Holloway

February 9, 2024

According to what Jackdorp has told me, today, Friday, the last trial day for the week, the prosecution case will begin the shift to the large accumulation of forensic evidence. Before that, the final 'percipient witness,' as the law refers to people who saw or heard direct evidence of the crime, will testify. He is a Marenago County sheriff's deputy named Akira Holloway. Holloway did four years in the army, then used the GI Bill to get an associate's degree in Police Science from Kindle County Community College. He blizzarded the Midwest with job applications in order to get a position in law enforcement, which he ultimately found up here. He's a big guy, at least six four. He's been on the job five years and has been promoted twice. He's careful but not fussy. He's got a broad wedding band on his finger, and you get the feeling that you'd lose the rest of the day if you asked Deputy Holloway to see photos of his kids.

What he says in response to Jackdorp's questions is that he was making a routine patrol through the state preserve at Ginawaban, when two hikers told him that they'd noticed the flash of something in the heavy brush at the base of a steep slope. The slope, Holloway said, is sometimes referred to as a utility road, because it was occasionally graveled to prevent erosion, but it's a natural wash that was cleared years ago so it could serve as a drainage way at the low point of the road leading up to the nearby parking lot for Ginawaban. The preserve proper may only be entered on foot.

After inspecting from the top of the 'road,' Holloway sidestepped down to the heavy undergrowth and trees at its base. Peering in, he saw a silver SUV, and when he lifted a bough from the back, he recognized the license plate that had been in an APB every day for the last couple of weeks. He used a pry bar to get through the brush and, with his flashlight, looked inside. The airbag had first deployed and then deflated, partly covering what he noticed only on second sweep—a bloated corpse. Her body had been thrown over the center console, with her upper torso and head in the dark well under the dashboard in front of the passenger seat. He took it from her clothing, a shrink top and cutoff jeans, that it was a female, but the body was so far decomposed that most of the hair had fallen out.

He immediately called his lieutenant, who asked him to do what he could to make a positive ID on the remains without disturbing the body. Given how long the search had gone on for Mae Potter and the number of agencies involved, the lieutenant didn't want to sound any false alarms. Holloway figured that with the way the body was positioned over the center console, he might be able to reach into the back pockets, and the lieutenant told him to proceed.

Holloway had gloves in his cruiser. The doors to the SUV were locked, but he had a jimmy that he used to help motorists who'd locked themselves out of their cars.

"Did you open the door?" Jackdorp asks.

"I did."

"And what did you notice?"

"Everything, sir?"

"Just a brief summary."

"Well, first, the odor just about knocked me over. I'd never been around a body that had been in the heat that long. Her corpse was bloated and covered with maggots."

There is a groan from the jury box from one of the men. The

testimony of the pathologist from Kindle County will be accompanied by photos, but Jackdorp has decided not to overplay his hand and to spare us all for the moment.

"Then what did you do?"

"I went back to my cruiser for a bandanna that I used to cover my face and came back and reached in as far as I could to her left rear pocket."

"What did you find, if anything?"

"Mae Potter's driver's license and six twenty-dollar bills, and when I pulled them out, there were also five blue tablets."

"Did you recognize them?"

"They looked like fentanyl tabs we'd been picking up on recent arrests."

"Did you make any further effort to examine the remains?"

"Not really. Lieutenant said don't disturb her. I mean, I ran the flashlight over her, but mostly I was looking for a wallet or her phone."

"Did you report your findings?"

"I called the lieutenant and told him this was the missing girl and about the pills. Him and me kind of kicked around what seemed to have happened so he'd have an idea what to report to other law enforcement. From what I found, the best guess was that she'd been, you know, impaired and mistaken the drainage way as the road to the parking lot and then lost control and bounced around without a seatbelt, until the car crashed down into a big oak in the high brush at the bottom."

"And what orders did you receive?"

"Remain at the site. I got a call back in about twenty minutes to say that some State Patrol brass were on the way from Skageon County."

"And how long did you remain on the site?"

"Six hours total, I'd estimate, sir. I got there lunchtime and it was close to sundown when I left. The state police and some of the others had arrived and a few of the forensic people began to process the scene."

"Did that conclude your involvement with this matter on that date?"

"On that date, yes."

"And calling your attention to three days later, October 2, did you happen again to be at Ginawaban?"

4

"Well, yes sir. That was part of my regular patrol, so I swung by over there on my way into the station for shift change."

"What time did you arrive there?"

"Seven a.m., give or take. Sun was just coming up."

"And did you encounter anyone at that time?"

"Well, there was an old Ford F-150 truck, 2013, 2014, FX4, the off-road model, parked on the shoulder, pretty close to where there was now a lot of yellow plastic tape closing off the drainage way."

"Did you approach the pickup?"

"Yes sir."

"And what did you find in the pickup?"

"There was a young guy in a sleeping bag on the flatbed in back, sound asleep."

"And do you recognize the young guy? Is he in court today?"

"Stipulate to the identification," I say.

For the record, the judge notes that Aaron has been identified.

"And after establishing the identity of the man in the sleeping bag, what happened?"

"I called in the info on his driver's license and found out there was a warrant for him for the murder of Mae Cheryl Potter and I placed him under arrest."

"And how close to the crime scene tape did you say he and the truck were?"

"I mean, right there. Five feet."

"And once you had him under arrest, did you observe anything else in the flatbed?"

"There was a dolly, you know, for moving stuff, and a shovel, as I recall."

Jackdorp nods and says he has nothing more.

My turn. Aaron says Holloway was okay and never went hard-guy on him, even after he learned about the warrant. I don't expect him to fight on cross.

"Thank you, Deputy. You say you've been on the job here in Marenago for five years. Have your duties taken you to the southern part of the county?"

"Yes."

"And have you patrolled on the Marenago side of the large state park called Governor Harold State Park?"

"Yes."

"It stretches across the border between Skageon and Marenago Counties, does it not?"

"Correct."

"The part in Skageon is called Harold's Woods, and the portion in Marenago is referred to as Governor's Park, right? But they're both part of one state park with the same forest and the same wildlife?"

"I think that's true."

"Now, in the southern part of Marenago in Governor's Park, do you receive any reports about black bears?"

Jackdorp jumps up as soon as I ask the question.

"Good *grief*, Judge! Is this another theory of defense now, that the bears strangled Mae Potter? And what does this have to do with my direct examination anyway?"

Judge Carrington, whose head is on her palm, lifts a free hand in my direction, inviting me to explain.

"Your Honor, Mr. Jackdorp's probably got a point about his direct, but it's just a few more questions, and I'd hate to have to take the deputy away from his duties again to bring him back here to testify in the defense case."

I have been good to my word when I've asked to be briefly indulged, and she knows that.

"Five minutes, Mr. Sabich."

"I won't need half of that." I ask the court reporter to read back my question about bears, and Holloway answers, "A lot."

"Any time of year more than another?"

"Well, they're in there all year, but especially in the fall."

"Is that because the bears are going to be denning soon and they're hungry?"

"They're hungry. I mean, I never even seen, saw, a bear outside the zoo before I got here. But from what I'm told, they're all over the forest in the fall, because they like acorns."

"Acorns?" That one takes me by surprise.

"Couldn't believe it either. But you know, I guess acorns are good food to a bear. The moms chew them up and spit them out for the cubs. And Harold's Park, all of it, that's a primary growth forest, more than half oak. So lots of black bears."

"And the reports you receive in the fall, are they principally from campers?"

"Campers and hikers. Sometimes in the spring the hikers get between a mother and her cubs and then, you know, we've even had a couple black bear attacks. But in the fall, like you say, most of the reports come from campers."

"And what's the nature of the reports you receive?"

"Well, like I say, the bears are there to eat. So you know, a pack full of food, that's kind of like a Happy Meal to a bear." As often happens, the unexpected wit brings down the house. You can learn a lot about the social aspects of laughter in a courtroom, but everybody finds the deputy's comparison hilarious—the jurors and the judge and the courtroom personnel. Even Aaron, who's more a smiler than a laugher, is sitting there chortling.

"And do you ever advise campers about how to keep the bears away from their packs?"

"Well, like I said, I'm a city kid. But other deputies, they've told me, best to put your pack up in a tree. You can lock it in your car, too, but the bears will scratch up the finish."

"And how do you put it in a tree?"

"General advice is to get a rope and hang your food pack from a limb or a bough that's too thin for the bear to climb out on."

I go to the prosecution table, where the coil of white rope from our garage has been positioned on the corner since Jackdorp's opening. I have asked him several times to put it away, which he does, but it reappears soon after. The rope, as Bea recognized to start, is probably the most damaging piece of evidence against Aaron for many reasons, including because, until this moment, there was no conceivable reason for him to have bought it—except to strangle Mae Potter.

"Have you seen campers use a utility rope like that one to suspend their packs?"

"You mean like white?"

"A utility rope of this dimension. Plastic. Hemp. But a rope of this thickness?"

"Definitely."

"Definitely," I repeat.

I turn to glance back to Bea in the gallery, with no sense of exactly why. I still want to be her Knight Valiant, I guess, although I deserve absolutely no credit for this explanation. It was what Aaron said the first time Susan and I asked him after we'd viewed the video footage from the store where he'd bought it. When he mentioned bears, I gave Susan the side-eye, but she knew it made sense. We've been looking for a naturalist as a defense witness, in case Holloway stiff-arms us. But I was reluctant to preview this for Bea without knowing we could prove it, as we now have.

"All right, Deputy, that will conclude our excursion with the bears. Let me return to the events of September 28, when you found Mae's body. Did you examine her vehicle before you looked inside?"

"Not for long."

"Well, let me show you one of the photos of the scene, Defense Exhibit 7. Do you see any damage to the rear bumper and some marks above? Does it look to you like the Subaru could have been pushed down the road by another vehicle, one with a higher bumper?"

"I can't really say either way." I expected that answer, but it's another theme worth exploring. If Mae's car was pushed down the road, then it couldn't have been Aaron who did that, because the state says he was driving the Subaru.

"Deputy, let me move ahead to my client's arrest on October 2. You said you established his identity, which means you had some conversation with him, is that correct?"

"Yes sir. Quite a bit, actually."

"So I'd like you to tell the folks here about your interaction with Aaron."

"Objection hearsay," says Jackdorp from his seat.

I start to protest about the rule of completeness, but the judge cuts in and overrules Jackdorp before I've said more than three words.

"You opened the conversation, Mr. Jackdorp."

"I assume you woke Aaron up?" I ask.

"Yes sir. Shined my light on his face and rapped on the side panel."

"And after he'd gathered his wits, did you ask him anything?"

"I asked him what he was doing there."

"How did he answer?"

"He said he knew the girl who died here, she was basically his girlfriend, and after he heard she'd passed, he'd been driving around thinking about her and decided to come up and pay his last respects at the spot she'd died. And then once he got here, he found that the drainage way was all blocked off, so he turned around to go but then the truck wouldn't start. He said he'd been having troubles with it, but now it had just conked out. Figured it was the alternator, so he'd taken the mechanism apart and hitchhiked up to an auto supply store by the interstate. They said the alternator was fine but on a 2014 F-150, it was probably the wiring harness, so they ordered a new one and he was supposed to go back and pick it up that day."

"What did you say?"

"I told him my dad owns an F-150 about the same age, and he's had a lot of alternator trouble too. But after I heard all that, I asked him for some ID."

"And did you call your dispatcher with that information?"

"Yes sir."

"What did they say?"

"Well, the first they said was, 'You got him. There's a warrant out for his arrest for murdering the young woman, Mae Potter.'"

"The calls with dispatch are on a recorded line, aren't they?"

"Usually."

"Do you remember how you responded when they told you Aaron was wanted for murder?"

"Not exactly, but I was surprised."

"You said, '*That* guy?' Should we play it for you?"

"I remember being surprised. I'd been off for two days and visiting my sister in St. Louis. I didn't even know it had been ruled a murder instead of an accidental death."

"But you said, '*That* guy?' meaning Aaron didn't come across to you as the kind of person who'd end up wanted for murder, is that correct?"

"I guess."

"So why had you been surprised?"

"Well, you learn in this business, you can never tell about people, but still— He'd been pretty natural with me, and just told me all that stuff cold as soon as he was awake. He didn't come off to me like any murderer. But like I say, you can never tell."

"What did you do after learning about the arrest warrant?"

"I came back and said to him, 'Did you know there's a warrant out for you?' "

"How did he respond?"

"He asked if the warrant was for driving up here. I said 'Driving? It's for murdering that girl.' "

"And what was his response to that information?"

"Well, he stared for a second and then said, 'For murder? That's complete bullshit. I thought she died in a car wreck.' I said, 'Well, they don't think so now.' I asked him to get down out the truck and I handcuffed him and gave him Miranda."

"Was he cooperative?"

"Completely."

"Polite?"

"Well, he kept saying this was completely f'd up, you know, while I handcuffed him, which my mama wouldn't call polite, but I mean, he wasn't cussing at me or resisting."

"Did you draw your weapon to effect the arrest, even though you knew he'd been charged with murder?"

"No. I mean, I frisked him as soon as he got down. But no, I don't like to take out my service weapon, if I don't have to. On inventory, we found a good-sized hunting knife in the glove compartment, but he never got near there."

"You felt he presented no risk to your safety?"

"I agree with that."

"And what happened after you cuffed him?"

"I put him in the back of the cruiser and called the station. Sergeant told me to wait for another unit, and then one of us would bring him in, Aaron that is. I'd told him about the other stuff in the back of the F-150, the hand truck and the shovel and whatnot, and Sergeant said the one who didn't bring in Aaron should look around up there to see if there was anything that had been messed with."

"Did you ask Aaron about the stuff in the flatbed, the hand truck and whatnot?"

"Yeah, first off when I found him. I was just like, 'What's all that?' and he said his grandfather was old and having cancer and he used the dolly to move stuff around. Hay bales, things like that."

"And who was it who checked the scene for evidence of disturbance?"

"Me. Cause I'd been there on nine twenty-eight. Deputy Rennert brought in Aaron. I got the techs' reports from three days before and looked all over the area. Nothing different so far as I could see."

"Any tracks from that hand truck, for example?"

"Not that I could see."

"No dirt recently disturbed with that shovel?"

"No."

"How much time did you spend looking for signs of tampering with the site?"

"A while. I walked up and down the road a few times, and looked pretty careful where the car had been."

I'm ready for my big windup, but both Aaron and Susan are motioning to me. They've got a good point about Aaron's phone.

"I'm sorry, Deputy. A couple of things. You said he was surprised when you told him that the warrant was for murder?"

"I don't think I said that. I said he acted surprised. Whether he actually was, I don't know."

"Fair enough. But did you have any conversation with him about his phone?"

"When he told me he had to go back for the wire harness, I told him to call over there first, and he showed me his phone was dead. He said he'd had two percent when he left home and took his charging cord, but the twelve-volt adapter wasn't in the socket in the truck like usual. He tried to buy another one at the auto parts place, but they were out of stock. That was another thing that was supposed to come in with the alternator harness."

"And you say the car was dead?"

"Yes."

"Did the radio work?"

"I never checked, but it won't work on my dad's when the alternator's out."

"So he had no way of knowing that a warrant for him had been issued?"

Jackdorp objects that it's beyond the knowledge of the witness, and the judge sustains the objection.

"All right," I say. "But as part of your duties, did you find out if the truck could be driven?"

"Well, yeah, the truck ended up impounded, and they had to tow it in, so no, the truck was dead, like Aaron said."

"Thank you, Deputy," I say and head back to the defense table and snap my fingers as if I'm just remembering something. I ask Susan for the copies of two photographs, which she'd long had set aside. "Now you say, Deputy, that on September 28, your lieutenant instructed you to remain on scene, and that he had told you to expect a number of other law enforcement agencies to be involved. Do you remember who ultimately arrived?"

"A lot of people. My lieutenant and my sergeant came, and two evidence techs from our office. An accident reconstructionist. Two FBI agents showed up eventually. And a lot of folks from the State Patrol. Maybe eight of them."

"Anyone from Skageon County?"

"A number."

I show him one of the photographs that had been taken from the top of the drainage way, shooting down toward the bottom. Two all-terrain vehicles are parked behind Mae's SUV and about ten people are gathered in conversation with one another beside the rear bumper. He acknowledges all of that. When I ask if he overheard the discussion, he says that because it was a vehicular accident, the FBI was willing to turn the scene over to the State Patrol. After that, they talked about how the vehicle and the body should be processed.

"In the end," Holloway says, "they all agreed that the evidence techs would complete taking photos, then they'd tow the SUV out of there so they could process the vehicle and the remains where there was plenty of space and better light. Then they'd get the girl a decent burial as soon as they could."

"Now, looking at this photo, there appears to be a black Cadillac Escalade right behind the SUV Mae was in."

"Yes sir."

"Was that the first law enforcement vehicle that was driven all the way down there?"

"That's how I remember."

"And who drove that vehicle?"

"The girl's father."

"You mean the Skageon County PA, Harrison Potter?"

"Yes sir."

"And looking at the photo, is that Lieutenant Glowoski, the woman seated at the prosecution table—is she down there in conversation?"

Holloway looks back and forth from the photo to Glowoski a couple of times.

"I'm pretty sure that's her."

"Well, here's my question, Deputy. Two additional vehicles were driven down the drain way or utility road, whatever we call it. And there are at least ten people I can see marching around down there next to the SUV— Is that how you were taught to process a crime scene?"

Holloway rears back to eye me with suspicion.

"That's kind of a trick question," he says.

"I apologize. That wasn't my intention. Why don't you explain why you think it's a trick question?"

"Well, yeah, the father drove down there. But he was pretty emotional, and you know, he wanted to see his daughter and pretty soon he was talking about getting the body back so they could have a funeral."

"Without an autopsy?"

"I don't think he said one way or the other. But you know, he was a dad, he was being a dad. He wanted to get his child home, so that her mom could be with her one last time. And yeah, looking back, there were a lot of people walking around down there, but man, you know, the reason I called it a trick question is because you said 'crime scene,' and nobody there seemed to be thinking that. It was an accident scene. Even the reconstructionist agreed. He didn't find any skid marks, you know, displaced gravel, but without a seat belt, she'd have been bouncing around on that slope and couldn't get to the brakes. She'd have gone flying down there pretty fast."

"But the footwear impressions, the tire impressions that might have been at the scene—this crowd was driving and walking all over them, right?"

"Hindsight is always 20/20, sir. I'll give you that there was a lot of confusion. The girl had been missing for a couple of weeks, and now she was dead."

"But my point, Deputy, is this: In those first hours you had at least a dozen experienced law enforcement officers involved, and none of them said, 'This looks like a crime scene,' right?"

"That's true. There was some, you know, discussion while I was there, because the crash reconstructionist noticed that the gearshift was in neutral, but she said with a head-on, sometimes a car jumps out of gear at impact. So people were still talking accident all the time I was there. Probably blame me for that. I was the first to say it."

"I'm not trying to blame you, Deputy, for reaching a logical conclusion. I'm making a much different point. Whoever murdered Mae Potter, if she was in fact murdered—whoever did that knew how to fool law enforcement, right?"

Jackdorp objects to the question as argumentative—it is—and the judge sustains him.

I try again. "But the first person to drive down there and trample the crime scene, and the clues that might have been down there—that was Harrison Potter, right?"

"Asked and answered," says Jackdorp.

"Right," I say, "it was," and sit down.

32

Agreed Evidence

After Holloway is excused, Jackdorp and I ask the judge for an early recess for lunch, so we can clear up the last details concerning the stipulated evidence. I know, from having spent years on the other side of these negotiations, that I have all the leverage now, since Jackdorp has not even begun to locate and interview all the witnesses whose testimony is summarized by our agreement. We go back to his office where, for the most part, he sullenly caves on the last points on which I've been holding out. Aside from Jackdorp's visible aggravation with Glowoski after the fiasco with the Lowndes notes, and a somewhat perceptible increase in his level of tension, he's generally maintained a poker face. He looked old to start, but the strain of trial doesn't seem to show in his appearance, and he's no more short-tempered than he's been with me all along. He's all business—the People's business, he would say. There is nothing pleasant about what he's trying to do, punish a guilty man for committing a horrible crime, so no bother pretending.

Court resumes at 1 p.m., and before Jackdorp reads the stip, the judge explains to the jury what a stipulation is, namely an agreement between the sides that the matters noted may be taken as established facts. The judge praises both lawyers for working this out and saving the jurors' time.

From Aaron's side, these are all matters that are not worth contesting, both because we want it to be clear that we're not fighting every point, and also because we don't have much chance of convincing the jurors of anything else in most of these areas. There is, for example, no way around the fact that Aaron's fingerprints are on Mae's key fob and her steering wheel and her telephone, or that his DNA is all over the SUV. As Jackdorp finally agreed to include in the stip, DNA analysis does not determine what kind of cell left the genetic material that's been identified, and thus it might have been, among other things, sweat, spit, sperm or minute flakes of skin, all of which Aaron no doubt shed there.

Nor is there anything to be gained by prolonging the State's proof regarding Aaron's purchase of the white utility rope. Similarly, we have no way to deny that the white nylon fibers were collected at various telltale locations, including from Mae's remains, particularly her neck, blouse and under her fingernails, and from the closet of Aaron's bedroom at home. We were also willing to agree to the substance of a fiber expert's testimony, establishing the chemical composition of the nylon, but after I ridiculed Jackdorp for saying that all the little threads 'matched' the rope from our garage, he engaged a new expert witness, the top person in the field, who will testify and, presumably, put me in my place. That's a troubling prospect, but we won't get the expert's report until tonight, when we'll find out how badly I blundered in my opening.

The stipulation also agrees to the evidentiary foundation for a variety of other proof: screenshots from Mae's Instagram and TikTok accounts, call records from both Mae's and Aaron's cellphones, documents relating to the connections those phones made to various cellphone towers, and the workings of the tollbooth camera, located on the interstate, about twenty miles east of the Ginawaban preserve.

Jackdorp reads the long document slowly in an even tone, in his best Joe Friday manner. This is a harder task than you might think, since trial lawyers rarely read anything straight to the jurors, and when I did it, I always found myself falling into a monotone. The jurors won't get a copy of the stipulation—the logic is that they are not given a transcript of the testimony either. Because of that, stipulating is always a balancing act for the prosecutor, trading the benefit of introducing the proof without contest, versus the downside of the jurors losing track of its significance in the blur of words.

To lessen that risk, Jackdorp next calls Lieutenant Vanda Glowoski to the stand. His plan is to formally move various records into evidence while Glowoski is up there and to use her to provide a narrative framework about the proof, under the guise that she is testifying as a 'law enforcement expert.' The whole growth of expert opinions as trial evidence has taken place while I've been practicing, and I don't think it's done much to improve the process. What Jackdorp wants to do with Glowoski is a good example of why I hate this kind of testimony, since he will gussy up a police officer's hunches and call them expert conclusions, even though it's often the kind of speculation by witnesses that the rules of evidence had prohibited for centuries.

Jackdorp begins by running Glowoski through a chronological account of her role in the investigation, starting with her assignment to the case on September 19, a week after Mae was last seen at home. The lieutenant testifies about interviewing Cassity on September 20, who told them Aaron and Mae had been in Harold's Woods. Glowoski traveled up there the next day with a team of agents, including a couple of evidence techs, and discovering, among other things, the impressions from Mae's and Aaron's shoes and rope fibers in the dried mud—presumably left after the heavy storm on the night of September 12. The troopers also found the items of Mae's that Charmaine identified.

"And in your expert opinion," Jackdorp asks, "what does the presence of those items of Ms. Potter's, the clothing and cosmetics, indicate to you as an investigator?"

"Well," she says, "it would suggest to me some form of hasty departure, or that someone else packed up Mae's belongings for her and overlooked items he wouldn't know were there."

"Objection, Your Honor." I take to my feet. "How in the world is that kind of rank speculation expert opinion? Maybe Special Agent Glowoski can tell us what kind of crime is indicated when I leave my reading glasses where I can't find them."

Judge Carrington stares down at me with mixed emotions. She gets my point, of course, but she knows that I'm grandstanding.

"The jury will determine what weight to place on this testimony, like that of all other witnesses. Overruled, Counsel." She offers a decisive nod as an instruction to me not to try that again.

Jackdorp then asks Glowoski to summarize what various documents reveal about Mae's and Aaron's whereabouts. People's Group Exhibit 6 is images of Mae posted to her Insta and TikTok accounts, beginning on the afternoon of September 12 and continuing through the early morning of September 14, all depicting Mae against various backgrounds from Harold's Woods. The postings ceased on the morning of September 14, coincident with the time, 9:06 a.m., that phone company records show that her cell was powered down, remaining off until Aaron handed the device to Charmaine. By contrast, with a few notable exceptions detailed in the stipulation, Aaron's phone and voicemail remained off most of the time from September 12 to 16.

"Now before we talk further about Mr. Housley's location on September 14 in particular, do you recall Ms. Benisch's testimony that when Mr. Housley called her on September 14, he told her that he'd left Mae and started hitchhiking home?"

"Yes," says Glowoski.

"And does the evidence, in your expert law enforcement opinion, verify Mr. Housley's statement to his friend that he hitchhiked straight home starting on September 14?"

This time I get up shouting.

"Your Honor, there was no such testimony. Mr. Jackdorp told the jury in his opening that that was what Ms. Benisch would say, but she denied that, and said that Mr. Housley told her in a subsequent conversation that he was so upset about Mae when he left her on September 14 that at first he hitchhiked twenty miles or so in the wrong direction."

"The jury may depend on their recollection of the testimony. Overruled."

"Your Honor," I say, "I apologize for persisting, but you cannot have expert testimony about evidence that simply doesn't exist."

Jackdorp tries to save himself.

"Well, Special Agent, did Ms. Benisch tell you when you interviewed her in late September that Mr. Housley had said he hitchhiked straight home?"

Because Cassity never had the opportunity to say whether or not she told the special agent that, her statement to Glowoski is not admissible now, and the judge agrees with me. Her ruling reduces Jackdorp to sputtering, but he goes on anyway to the proof regarding Aaron's whereabouts on September 14. Aaron's phone was first powered back on that day for roughly ten minutes, starting at 12:07 p.m. The retained data shows he was using a navigation app. Seven minutes later, he received a phone call that lasted one minute or less from a number registered to a woman who lives in Missouri, Elaine Harop.

Jackdorp interrupts Glowoski's testimony to read a portion of the stipulation he didn't get to before. A stip is normally read all at once, but I can't figure out a valid basis to object to the piecemeal presentation.

"'Elaine Harop,'" Jackdorp reads, "'would testify, if called as a witness, that on September 14, she and her husband were on their way home from a car trip around the Great Lakes. She does not know and has never met Aaron Housley and does not recognize his photograph. She has no memory of ever speaking to him, but does recall dialing a couple of wrong numbers when she was trying to book a motel room in Como Stop for the evening.'

"So stipulated?" Jackdorp asks me.

"So stipulated," I answer sullenly.

Glowoski then testifies about some of the cell tower records. When Aaron's phone came on at 12:07, it was registered by cell tower 259, located eight miles west and nineteen miles north of the parking lot in Harold's Woods. By the time he connected to Elaine Harop's call, his phone had been handed off to a tower five miles north. On her end, Ms. Harop's outgoing call was completed through a cell tower fifty miles away, near the interstate exit closest to Ginawaban.

The next time a cell tower polled Aaron's phone was at 8:17 p.m. on September 14 when he called Cassity, and then at 9:22 p.m. that same night, when he texted Gert, and then his mother and father (and me, although I'm referred to as Bea's fiancé) after I saw Joe at the VFW. For all those communications, the phone connected through tower 291, which is about twenty miles south and east of the parking lot at Harold's Woods. That location is near the roadside culvert where Aaron has long said he spent the night.

The fourth time he powered up was the next night, September 15, when he phoned Cassity to say he would be home soon. The cell tower that first registered that call was only another thirty miles south of where Aaron had been the night before, indicating the slow progress he was making hitchhiking.

The other piece of evidence that Jackdorp will claim bears on Aaron's location is a photograph taken at 11:48 a.m. on September 14. An image of Mae's SUV was captured passing through a tollbooth on US 843, approximately seventy miles north of Harold's Woods, and twenty miles east of Ginawaban. In all other cases, as the various records referred to in the stipulation have been admitted in evidence, Jackdorp has displayed them on the monitor. The only exhibit that Jackdorp asks to pass among the jurors for their direct inspection is the overhead black-and-white tollbooth photograph of Mae's SUV. The image is focused on the license plate. Within the car, you can see only a white decal high up on the windshield and an indistinct figure whose hands are blurry forms on the steering wheel. Even so, the expectant way Jackdorp watches each juror as he or she examines the photo makes me write a note to Susan that we better look at that picture again. I sense there's something we missed.

I'm sure all this evidence of where Aaron was on September 14 is coming across to the jury as a complete hash, which is no accident. There's a serious problem for the prosecution when you start placing the records end to end, which I'll get to on cross-examination of Glowoski. But the subjects he's saved for last—the shoes, the search of our house and the rope—are far more coherent.

Glowoski, who's come to the stand as damaged goods after the spanking the judge gave her yesterday about the Lowndes notes, is doing her best to appear crisp and proficient. Just as the jury came in, she also made a grand show of delivering to Susan a huge manila envelope of the notes gathered from the investigators who worked on Mae's case.

After the early adjournment yesterday, Susan received several responses to calls she'd made in the last few weeks to acquaintances to gather background on Glowoski. All of those people, figures from law enforcement that she's known over the years, characterized Glowoski as an excellent cop and person. This morning, we also suddenly got Glowoski's 'jacket,' her State Patrol personnel record we'd subpoenaed weeks back, and it showed no serious disciplinary infractions, and an almost endless record of commendations.

One of the State Patrol officers who spent the longest time talking with Susan last night, a neighbor of hers and Al's in northern Skageon, told her that Glowoski, the oldest of seven children, became responsible for all the other kids when both of her parents were killed in a traffic accident. Glowoski was all of fourteen at the time, but with the occasional assistance of an aunt, held the household together. Each of her sibs graduated from high school and went on to college, and only when the last of them was at Wisconsin State did Glowoski follow her own dream of entering the military, serving two tours in Afghanistan. She's close to sixty now, and credit where due, doesn't look within a decade of that.

I have no basis to quarrel with the bona fides of Glowoski's character references, but the timing of the callbacks is obviously suspicious. The unspoken point of the sudden transparency about Glowoski is that we should take it easy on her, and not lodge a separate complaint with the State Patrol Merit Board, the civilian disciplinary agency, concerning the *Brady* violation. I'm not much for after-the-fact revenge, but I told Susan what I can't square is how a supposed standout cop, especially a supervisory officer, would choose to hide the notes— or fail to persist about questioning the wife.

Right now, Glowoski is explaining how the State Patrol traced a transaction on Aaron's debit card to a Home Warehouse store about nine miles from Harold's Woods midday on September 13. The store receipt, a copy of which Glowoski's team obtained, and which is now moved into evidence, reflects the purchase of '50 ft White Nylon Rope' at 2:12 p.m. Jackdorp then introduces the surveillance video from the camera over the cash register and plays it on the monitor. Aaron—with his chartreuse hair—shifts from foot to foot while he pays. He leaves the store with the long loop of white rope hanging from his arm. While the video is showing, Jackdorp stands next to the screen, holding the coiled rope that's been sitting on the prosecution table. Jackdorp has used the rope, probably his strongest evidence, effectively, and the video instills a sober vibe in the courtroom.

"Now, calling your attention to late in the day on September 30, 2023, did you have occasion to take part in the execution of a search warrant on premises outside the town of Mirror where Aaron Housley resided?"

"Yes."

"And did you have occasion during that search to find a long white nylon rope?"

"Yes."

"And what is People's Exhibit 1?" He still has the rope in its thick plastic evidence wrapping in hand.

Glowoski looks it over.

"I find my initials and the date on the evidence label, and so I can testify that it's the rope I found in the garage of the house where the defendant resided."

"And can you describe the circumstances under which you found the rope?"

"Yes, the deputy sheriff from Skageon County who was leading the search team from that agency was Sergeant Dominic Filipini. Sergeant Filipini told me that he'd been acquainted with Aaron's mother, Beatrix Housley, for decades and regarded her as highly trustworthy. He said that when he'd asked about any white nylon rope in the house, perhaps the garage, that she'd told him she was sure there wasn't any rope out there, because she'd been searching through the garage a few days ago looking for a gardening tool. The mother's fiancé, who lived there with her, witnessed the exchange and clearly agreed." This is the testimony I promised not to contest when I entered the case.

Glowoski continues. "Sergeant Filipini wasn't completely sure of how much of the garage his people had searched, so I decided that I'd double-check. After about ten minutes, I found People's Exhibit 1 stuffed in the bottom of a cardboard carton with some ceramic pots and reams of colored paper on top of it."

"And where was that carton located?"

"It was shoved in the back of one shelf in a metal storage cabinet in the garage." Glowoski took photos of the rope in the box and they are admitted in evidence and displayed on the monitor.

"And what was your law enforcement opinion after finding the rope?"

"Well, since the mom and the fiancé were so sure there was no rope in the garage, it seemed pretty obvious to me that the defendant had hidden it out there recently."

Like the surveillance video from the store, Glowoski's testimony, supported by her photos, lands with a significant wallop.

After that, Jackdorp goes on to the various shoeprints, whose admissibility we've also agreed to. The photos taken by the evidence techs in the mud at Harold's Woods, the ultraviolet image from Mae's blouse and a photo of the print at the base of the utility road at Ginawaban are all received in evidence.

"Now when you searched the house where Aaron was living, did you find the Nike 1 sneakers that Mr. Sabich acknowledged in his opening statement that the defendant was wearing in Harold's Woods?"

"No."

In response to Jackdorp's questions, she lists all the places they looked in our residence.

"And after Mr. Housley's arrest on October 2, did you examine the clothing that was inventoried at the Marenago County Jail to determine if he was wearing the Nike sneakers when he was taken into custody?"

"Yes. They weren't there. He had a new pair of Adidas shoes."

"And when you say new, had you encountered Mr. Housley a week or so before on September 23?"

This was the brief meeting in our driveway when I'd told Glowoski to pound sand. She testifies that Aaron had an Adidas shoebox under his arm.

"Now let me turn to other items that were not uncovered in your search. Did you look for camping items you would have expected Mr. Housley to return with after his trip to Harold's Woods? A backpack, for example?"

"We found backpacks that Aaron's mother and her fiancé said were theirs. We did not find Aaron's backpack."

"Did you find Aaron's sleeping bag?"

"No. His grandfather said he'd given Aaron a nice one, but we didn't find it in the house or anywhere else."

"Now let me ask you about the closet in Aaron's room at his mother's house. Under your supervision, the evidence techs assisting you found the white fibers in that location, as stipulated People's Group Exhibit 12-C."

"Yes, they vacuumed them up from the floor there."

"And did you impound Aaron's clothing that you found hanging in the closet?"

"Yes."

"And was it examined for the presence of other white nylon fibers?"

"Yes. There were none."

"And what about the clothes he was wearing when he was arrested on October 2? Were they examined for nylon fibers?"

"Yes, and there were none."

"So what in your expert law enforcement opinion accounts for the fibers on the floor of Aaron's closet?"

"In my opinion, there were several possibilities. Some of the fibers could have been shed from clothing that Aaron had hung in the closet when he got back from Harold's Woods. Or he might have stored the nylon rope there before he hid it in the garage. But in my opinion, they came from Aaron or his possessions."

"Now, given the absence of any clothing containing nylon fibers, the absence of the Nike sneakers, the absence of Aaron's backpack, and the absence of Aaron's sleeping bag, what expert law enforcement opinion did you reach?"

"I concluded that after returning from murdering Mae Potter, Aaron had hidden or destroyed all of those items, which would be evidence of that crime."

"Nothing further," says Jackdorp. His strategy in getting to Glowoski before we break for the week is obvious—and sound. He wants to send the jurors home thinking for days about all the evidence in Aaron's control that has gone missing.

There's no doubt Jackdorp has us in a corner with this evidence, probably a tighter one than he recognizes. I know what happened with his jeans and his backpack and his sleeping bag, and if the jury were ever to learn about that, it's unlikely to help Aaron's defense. We can account for where his Nikes went, but if we do that, the jury will only wonder why we can't explain what happened to the other missing items.

Instead, on cross, I employ a familiar strategy in the face of difficult evidence—I change the subject.

"Now I take it, Lieutenant Glowoski, that as a law enforcement expert, you believe, as Mr. Jackdorp maintained in his opening, that on the morning of September 14, Aaron Housley strangled Mae Potter in her Subaru when it was parked in Harold's Woods and that he soon after drove the car north to Ginawaban, where he hid the vehicle with Mae's body inside at the bottom of that utility road. That's your expert law enforcement opinion, correct?"

"That's my opinion, yes sir."

"But it's a fact, Lieutenant, is it not, that the evidence you just presented, especially the telephone and cell tower records, prove the opposite—they show your theory is wrong, do they not?"

"No sir."

One of the main flaws in the prosecution case, which Susan pointed out to me months ago, is that there is a flat contradiction in their evidence of Aaron's whereabouts after he left Harold's Woods. As Glowoski would have it, Aaron drove Mae's Subaru through the toll station at 11:48 a.m., where he exited the interstate for Ginawaban. But half an hour later, when his phone was repowered so he could use a navigation app, it was polled by towers fifty miles to the south.

I go through all that painstakingly with Glowoski and then get to the jackpot question.

"Doesn't that evidence show that Aaron could not have been anywhere near that highway tollbooth or Ginawaban at noon on September 14?"

"No, I don't think the evidence establishes that. If I can explain."

I could cut her off now and let her offer on redirect whatever unlikely story they've come up with to account for this discrepancy, but Susan and I have a pretty good hunch about what Glowoski has to say. So I lift my hand benevolently in her direction, and she goes on.

"Well, first of all," she says, "the fact that he was using a naviga-tion app, that shows me he was driving, not hitchhiking."

"Is there a law that prevents someone from checking their location when they're hitchhiking?"

"Not that I know of," she says, ignoring the sarcasm. "And the fact that his phone was connecting to cell towers fifty miles to the south, that doesn't mean that's where he was. Phones have completed calls through towers forty-five miles away. That's documented."

That is precisely the response Susan and I were expecting, and for the next five minutes or so, Glowoski has to endure a figurative pommeling demonstrating the complete unlikelihood of that theory. Just to start, although Glowoski has become familiar with cell tower records from her work on several cases, she is far from an expert, as she readily admits. She is unfamiliar with something called a 'drive test,' which would show definitively how far signals travel from a given tower, and which she has to admit was not performed in this case. She concedes that the area between Ginawaban and Harold's Woods contains many steep hills and correspondingly deep valleys, which ordinarily block cell signals. And she admits that the forty-five-mile connection she said was documented occurred about five years ago. As cellphone technology has advanced from 3G to 4G to LTE and now 5G+, cell signals carry more and more information, which reduces how far they can go. That is why the carriers have had to build more towers closer together. In fact, after some jousting, Glowoski agrees that current publications say again and again that over 99 percent of cellphone calls connect to towers within three miles of the phone.

"And finally, Lieutenant, your expert law enforcement opinion is that Aaron supposedly drove from the interstate to Ginawaban, right? Meaning that when Elaine Harop mistakenly called Aaron at 12:14, a half hour after he passed through the tollbooth, he would have been sixty miles from the tower that polled his phone, which would be a new world's record for connection, wouldn't it?"

"If he did like you said and went toward Ginawaban. But maybe he turned back south when he got off the highway."

"And what evidence, Lieutenant, supports the idea that he went south then?"

"Well, it was lunchtime, wasn't it? There's a McDonald's a couple miles south of there."

"So he stopped for a hamburger? That's how come his phone could have connected to these distant towers. Is that what you're saying?"

"I don't know why that couldn't have happened."

"Because according to you he would have had a corpse draped over the center console of the Subaru, which might have made for a tense moment when he passed through the drive-thru, wouldn't it?"

That one brings down the house. Glowoski doesn't like it and reddens. But she struggles to recover quickly.

"I'm just saying he might have had a reason to go back south a little," she says.

"But that's no more than a hope on your part, correct? You have no evidence of that, do you?"

"No."

"Isn't it true, Lieutenant Glowoski, in your expert law enforcement opinion, that what the cell tower evidence shows is a couple of things. First, it corroborates Cassity Benisch's testimony that Aaron said when he left Harold's Woods he was so upset that he hitchhiked about twenty miles in the wrong direction. Because that's exactly where those cell towers—259 and 263—are, about twenty miles north of Harold's Woods, right?"

"That's where they are, but I don't agree with the rest of what you said."

"And the second thing we can tell from the tower evidence is that, just as Mrs. Lowndes apparently thought, it was Mae who was driving the Subaru, not Aaron, which explains how the car could have been fifty miles north of where Aaron's phone was when the woman from Missouri, Elaine Harop, misdialed him?"

"I wouldn't say that. That's not all the evidence on the subject. There's that photo at the tollbooth."

"Are you saying you can identify the ghostly figure in that photograph as Aaron Housley, rather than Mae Potter?"

"I'm not saying that. What I am saying is that you can talk about the drive tests we didn't perform and the normal range of those towers, but the fact is that none of that shows for dead certain where the defendant was located. That's my expert opinion."

"So in other words, Lieutenant, you're telling us that the government has put this proof about the cell towers Aaron's phone connected to between 12:07 and 12:14 on September 14—Mr. Jackdorp offered those records and you testified about them, but as far as you're concerned they prove absolutely nothing? That's your expert law enforcement opinion?"

She shrugs. "Pretty much," she says. She's made an absolute jackass of herself, but there is a lightness to her normally dry persona that alarms me. Looking at her across the courtroom, it comes to me, much too late, that I've just stepped into a trap.

33

The Night

N eed to talk.'

For only the second or third time this week, Aaron has scrawled across my yellow pad at the defense table a note I see when I return at the end of my cross of Glowoski. In at least one regard, Aaron is an all-star client, because he is entirely undemanding, and so I take the note as a sign of important business.

Now that the jurors are gone, the deputies are already approaching to handcuff Aaron and bring him back to the jail, so they can move on to their weekend. It will be a minute before the jail van arrives, and with their assent, I follow Aaron back to the lockup for a word while he is waiting.

"Something quick?" I ask him, referring to his note. The judge is coming back to the bench at Jackdorp's request, so I have only a second. But standing here, I'm struck by the sudden hope that he wants to take back what he said the other night about the rope. I'm not sure how he would explain a change, but if he says something simple, like he was mistaken, I'll accept that and move on. I don't need to turn him into a witness against his mother. But instead, he shakes his head slowly about the prospect of dealing quickly with whatever he wants to talk about. I know the COs won't be happy if I want to make a late visit to the jail on a Friday night.

"Can I come see you in the morning, first thing?"

He's okay with that and I tap him on the shoulder. Overall, he's bearing up. In terrible circumstances. Foolishly or not, I feel proud of him.

Judge Carrington has already returned to the bench when the court officers readmit me to the courtroom. It turns out that Jackdorp wants to make a record about finally having turned over the notes and to admit that in a few instances, investigators destroyed their notes after finalizing their reports. That's SOP, with the clear goal of foiling cross-examination, which is why Cap made the motion for preservation to start with.

"In violation of my order," Judge Carrington snaps. I've gradually come to realize that for Wendy Carrington, too, this trial is a special moment. In terms of the stakes and the publicity, it's the biggest case she's presided over. By my lights, she's an exceptionally good trial judge, smart, disciplined and quick to rule, but it's wearing her out too. I remain rooted to my initial impression of her, formed close to twenty years ago, that she's one of those people in life with whom I would, in other circumstances, form a lasting friendship. I admire and like her. But a case like this, a pinnacle of kinds, is likely to bring on all kinds of questions about her future, since she's no longer waiting for the chance to preside over a 'heater' case whose stakes are appreciated for hundreds of miles in all directions. By seniority, she should be in line to become the chief judge here, but Jackdorp, who has wide sway with the other judges, has blocked that. Wendy has two daughters, one in college, one nearing the end of high school. Her husband is a business guy, who supposedly has done very well, so they don't need her salary. She's got to be asking herself how much longer she wants to deal with Hiram Jackdorp as a daily nemesis.

Since the judge has the ears of both attorneys now, she asks about our schedule next week. How long before the prosecution rests, how much time should be set aside for the defense evidence?

This is one of many subjects that Susan and I will dig into over the weekend. I answer, "Two days," simply as a placeholder. Under her black bangs, the judge hesitates over something, which, I suspect, is inquiring whether the defendant will testify. Pressed, of course, I would say, "God, no," but my answer might shape Jackdorp's decisions for the rest of his case, and so the judge, as usual, has the good sense not to put the question.

I have promised Susan that she can ride home tonight, but we have a lot to discuss now. We wait for the courtroom to empty and take a seat in the back row. Moriah interrupts to show us where the light switches are and asks us to shut them off when we are done. Moriah is an odd presence in the courtroom, more than six feet tall with waist-length straight grey hair. She frankly has the personality of an automaton. Her voice is never anything but a monotone, and my efforts to joke with her occasionally have seemed to simply go past her. Every day, she wears a huge wooden cross, which I suspect a grandchild made for her, perhaps even in a shop class, but when I asked about that, she simply clutched the cross, as if I was planning to steal it. On the other hand, she is very good at her job, an organizational wonder, which is required.

Once we're alone, I confess my fears to Susan that I blundered somehow by ridiculing Glowoski on the cell tower evidence.

"She still looked like an idiot," Susan says, "and that's always good for us."

But with a second to reflect, I understand what was nagging at me. In the end, we want to argue that the cell tower records establish that Aaron was nowhere near Ginawaban around noon, and, thus, couldn't have been in Mae's Subaru when it went through the tollbooth half an hour earlier. As trial lawyers often do with unfavorable evidence, Jackdorp offered the tower documents as part of their case, hoping to create the illusion that what they show isn't all that bad for the prosecution. But I fell prey to the first instinct of a defense lawyer, to counterpunch, to dispute. By supposedly 'forcing' Glowoski to testify that the records prove absolutely nothing, I did a huge favor to the government, neutralizing what we want to rely on as telling proof for the defense. I will get a chance to backpedal in closing argument, but the jurors may see me as contradicting myself.

As I assess my mistake, there are a couple of takeaways. For one, this is the first instance when Jackdorp may have outflanked us tactically. His straight-ahead style doesn't tend to require much guess-work about what he's actually up to. I'll need to tread more carefully.

The second conclusion is even more important. Since Jackdorp wants to ignore the cell tower records, he must intend to rely on some-thing else to corroborate George Lowndes's claim that Aaron drove off in the SUV. That could only be the tollbooth photo. Glowoski in fact called attention to it again when I pressed her on cross about the lack of evidence confirming their theory of Aaron driving the Subaru. I didn't really understand what she was saying in the moment, but was afraid to ask more. Yet Jackdorp chose to pass the picture among the jurors, so, as I noted at the time, there must be a significance to the photo both Susan and I have overlooked. She finds our copy and we hover over it together.

"Oh, fuck," she says first, although we both recognize the same thing pretty much simultaneously. The grainy hands of the driver on the wheel are far darker than the white decal on the upper right corner of the windshield. Jackdorp will maintain in closing argument that the photo shows plainly that a darker-complected person was driving, namely, Aaron.

"That's crap," Susan says at once. "Those cameras don't work like that. They're not made to capture actual contrasts." But, if Susan is right, we need to prove it. She has to figure out who made the camera and then scramble to find somebody at the manufacturer willing to testify to what she's hoping. It's a big task and with a few minutes left before 5 p.m., she wants to get going.

The truth is we both already have too much to do this weekend. She needs to make a first pass through the notes Glowoski finally handed over. I'm sure, in the usual lawyers' trick, they have included as much irrelevant material as possible, so we miss what's significant. Tomorrow, after my visit to the jail, we need to figure out what we might offer for the defense. After that, my principal job will be to pre-pare for the forensic experts, the fiber and impressions specialists and the pathologist, who will close out the government's evidence. I have probably a thousand pages of reading.

I leave Susan and head out to my car, frigid after a day that topped out at 18 degrees. The trial has distracted me from the inevitable discomforts of winter: the dim skies, as if the world was beneath a pot lid, the sense of confinement inside, the dry heat that cracks my cuticles and, when you finally venture out, the Midwest winds so cold and sabering that they seem capable of hindering all thought. Down in Mirror, the changing climate brings us little snow. Several times, after we've gotten a decent accumulation, Nat and Anna and the girls will schedule a weekend trip to come up to snowshoe or toboggan, and half the time the snow's melted even before they can get in the car. In Portage, there's just enough of a temperature difference from our part of Skageon that the snow sometimes lasts longer. Right now it's been reduced to icy hummocks along the curbs, and frozen strips, slippery hazards in the middle of the road, that were left when drivers followed each other's paths through the initial snowfall.

As I leave the courthouse, there is an unshaven old man watching me somewhat suspiciously from across the street. He has on a worn tweed overcoat and walking shorts, and he's out here with his dog, a mutt at the end of a string. He's smoking a roll-your-own of some kind clenched between his lips. In the city there'd be a court order to keep him away from grade schools, but his utter weirdness sends up a spark of recognition in me that I cannot place.

On the short drive back to our empty house, I realize that I'm facing the hours I've dreaded all week, when I will finally have to think about Bea. I stop for another bottle of whiskey and then proceed to a roadside stand nearby for a gyro. It is not a time to resist comfort, and by the time I'm through the front door of the house, I'm deep in the malaise, almost like seasickness, that has been an intense background sensation for several days now.

Nat has called me every other day, and when I spoke to him Wednesday he asked how Bea was holding up. I took a deep breath and said, 'We're having some issues.'

My son took so long to respond that I actually looked at the phone to see if the call had disconnected.

He finally said, 'Jesus Christ, Dad.'

'Yeah.'

'What a shitty time for this. For both of you.' He was plainly battling the impulse to ask more, and I offered nothing further.

My principal reaction to Bea's departure, when my mind against my will has drifted there, has been almost ridiculously beside the point. I'm too old, I've thought. I'm too fucking old to start again. I'll be seventy-seven next month. This is the end for me. I'll die alone, a ridiculous burden to my son, depressed and probably sinking into alcoholism. The troubling shadow of that future has hung over me at all times since I directed Bea to the door.

Twice in as many nights, I've been awakened with dreams of my mother. The daughter of a Jewish labor organizer and a lass from Cork, my mom was regarded as an eccentric old maid—at the age of twenty-six!—when she accepted my father's marriage proposal, offered almost certainly because he needed her savings to open the bakery. She was a timid person, easily cowed, and the perfect match for a sadist like my father, who loved holding her—and often me—in a dominion of fear. Basically agoraphobic, my mother relied on me to make trips with her lists to the corner grocery, or on her sisters, my beloved aunts Flo and Sarah, when she needed adult emissaries in the world. My mother's glory days came late in life. My father had left her by then for Mrs. Bova, a widow whose urgent bearing whenever she entered the bakery would have signaled to someone more worldly than a child about her long-running affair with my father. But for my mother, this arrangement, in which my father still paid the rent, became a kind of liberation. Her interest in the world outside her suddenly increased. She became one of the first of the regular callers on those listener-participation radio talk shows: Tell us what you think about inter-racial dating, legalizing marijuana, who killed Kennedy. She stacked the dining-room table with old newspapers and magazines, pads and index cards on which she made notations, preparing for tomorrow's programs. She even became something of a local celebrity, valued by the hosts. 'Here's Rosie! Let's hear what Rosie has to say today.'

That is the kinship that I felt with the old man outside the court-house. In his oddness, he reminded me of my mom, who's been on my mind. And she in turn seems in my worst moments to presage the future to which I'm now condemned without Bea, a withdrawn and misanthropic old man, confined with my obsessions.

But after I exhaust my reserves of self-pity over Bea, warring thoughts take over. I, of all people, have no right to complain about infidelity. And it wasn't really infidelity, not in her mind. She'd made no actual promises. Yes, she knew I was making assumptions. Yes, she was dishonest in a fundamental way. But after decades of living with this secret, it went into the category of something she was convinced no one else would ever know, and thus a pleasure she had no need to abandon until she was fully convinced her life was on another course.

The image of Hardy crawling over her, which I've occasionally been unable to hold at bay, is agony itself. But what leaves me dizzyingly sick with discontent is how much I didn't realize about her. Yes, I miss her. Yes, I feel as if an amputation has taken place. But it's astounding that after seven years together there was such a significant piece of her I knew nothing about, not just the sexual adventuring, but her secrecy and, when you boil it down, her selfishness.

After a while, the person you love ceases to exist for you in and of herself. She becomes a composite, in which she is coated with all the dreck you've dragged along from your former life, your longings and expectations, and especially the wounds that scream out for healing, that become smelted to that being in your mind's eye and your soul. To me, Bea is no longer the woman with a clever look who beat me to the Sunday paper. She is the personification of steady love, a hitherto unknown experience in my life, which fits my needs as ideally as the right key mates with a lock.

But the recognition of how much about her I've missed revives the anxiety that visited me the other night. Is there, being fully awake, really any chance that Beatrix Mena murdered Mae? I work hard reconstructing my memory of September 14 and finally recollect that Bea wasn't home yet when I went off to find Joe at the VFW. She supposedly was attending the Principals' Roundtable, talking again— again!—about bathroom use for transgender kids. I could call Daria, Bea's associate principal, who I think went to the meeting with her, but how in the world do I explain why I'm calling on a Friday night, when Daria knows I'm engulfed by Aaron's trial?

Yet no matter how much about Bea's character I failed to recognize, it remains beyond imagining that she would ever let her son stand trial for a crime she committed. It is true that the first time we visited Aaron at the Marenago Jail, I lectured Joe and her sternly, telling them all the reasons Jackdorp would never accept a confession from either of them in an effort to take Aaron's place. I said—and meant—that such a gambit stood a good chance of making Aaron's situation even worse. But we live in the physical world, and as I told both her and her father, neither of them at their age and size was tall enough, strong enough, young enough to be capable of overpowering and strangling Mae Potter. Shooting her? Yes, of course. Poisoning her? I guess. One of them maybe could have caught Mae unawares with a knife. But placing a rope around Mae's neck and choking the life from her as she fought back? The laws of physics say that could never have taken place.

Unless I've missed something essential. That's possible, of course. But I've imagined this crime on a daily basis for six months now and still can't envision any credible scenario where Bea committed it.

By now, I have consumed one scotch and most of another and am lying on the full bed that, until a few days ago, we shared each night in a crowded heap. I can think whatever I want, I can process, chew it over, feel dizzy with despair, chastise myself for feeling victimized by conduct that is a lesser version of what I inflicted on Barbara, indulge dark suspicions until they yield, with whatever reluctance, to reason— but none of those is really the ultimate question for me. What I really need to determine—assuming I can eventually accept the piece of Bea that I hadn't recognized—is whether I can recover some of the joy that was fundamental to our life together. And what if the answer is, Somewhat? Should I live with half a loaf?

Right now, another reality is taking hold. Between the whiskey and the rigors of the week, sleep again is coming on fast. I try to hold on to consciousness, because I have important thoughts, and then, blissfully, I am gone.

34

Testify

February 10

I want to testify," Aaron tells me, as soon as we are alone in the narrow attorney visiting room at the Marenago County Jail on Saturday morning.

This declaration catches me completely off guard. I have told him often that I'm going to let him tell me everything before we face the question of whether he should get on the stand, although I have almost always added that we're likely to conclude that's a bad idea. He's seemed to accept that in the same vague way he's nodded at most everything Susan and I tell him.

"Where is this coming from?" I ask.

"Everybody in here is asking me if I'm going to get up."

With effort, I succeed in keeping myself from groaning.

"Aaron, how many times have I asked you not to talk about your case with anyone in here?"

"I don't, but they see the news. Half these dudes come back from visits with questions they're getting from their relatives. I mean, I'm famous." He smiles with his usual appreciation of irony. "I mean the case is."

"Aaron, I hope you don't take legal advice from other inmates. If they had such a great understanding of the law, most of them wouldn't be here in the first place."

"Even the guards say it. Bill Atkinson keeps telling me I ought to take the stand."

This time I can't keep myself from making an involuntary sound.

"Aaron, Bill Atkinson is the one whose brother is a deputy sheriff, right? Hitch Atkinson?"

"Meaning what?"

"Meaning Hitch works with Jackdorp all the time. I'm sure Jackdorp would love for you to take the stand."

"Why?"

"Because once the defendant takes the stand, that's what the case is about, whether or not he is telling the truth. All that stuff about the burden of proof and the presumption of innocence goes out the window. So if a prosecutor has a case that's leaking oil, he'd want the defendant to get up, because frankly defendants usually don't do well."

"Meaning I won't do well?"

"Aaron, the very first thing that jury is going to hear is that you have a felony conviction for possession with intent to distribute."

"Man," he says, and shakes his head. "You don't think they've figured out that this court order thing had to do with drugs?"

"Actually, I don't. Drunk driving, maybe. The fact of the matter though, Aaron, is that in my experience, especially as a trial judge, I found that juries do a pretty good job of coloring inside the lines. If they're told the law says they shouldn't know more about a subject, they don't make assumptions. So no, I don't think they realize you had a drug problem. Which means that if you testify, they'll learn that and worse, that you have a conviction that sounds on the face of it like you were not just a drug user, but a dealer."

The actual research about what happens when defendants testify is far spottier than I would have thought, but what there is tends to confirm what I just told Aaron: It's an all-or-nothing bet. It's true that about 70 percent of acquittals take place when the defendant gets on the stand. But what that statistic doesn't tell you is the number of cases where convictions became more likely after the defendant told his story. The scant research tends to suggest that happens too. And certainly that was the view of virtually every trial judge I ever talked to about this subject. But the one thing that has been studied several times with identical results is that the rate of guilty verdicts increases significantly after the jury learns that the defendant has been convicted before. He's a confirmed bad guy at that point.

"You're going to make their case stronger by testifying, Aaron. And your conviction isn't the only issue. You're going to have to admit that you burned your backpack and all the clothes you were wearing and your sleeping bag. I can't let you lie about that."

"I wouldn't lie anyway. She'd peed all over it. Cassity already said that."

"She said *you* said that. But Jackdorp will argue that was just a clever excuse for what you knew you were going to do. Saying you burnt the backpack and everything in it is one of those things that will never go well on cross."

"Why?"

"'She urinated on it? Haven't you ever heard of a washing machine, Mr. Housley? Or a dry cleaner? Instead, you were out of work and decided to burn up several hundred dollars' worth of clothing and equipment?'"

He stares for a second.

"I was emotional. I admit that. But I needed to be done with her. I didn't want to have to look at that stuff and keep remembering her."

"'You mean you wanted to get rid of the evidence, Mr. Housley?'"

He responds with an eye roll and a chuffing sound. I lean toward him suddenly with a pointed finger, scolding Aaron as I seldom have.

"*Don't* you do that. You do that on the witness stand and the jury will hate you. Testifying well requires epic self-control. You lose your shit for one second and they'll see you as a hot-headed murderer."

We are both a little taken aback by the vehemence with which I just spoke to him. A bit wounded, he says, "It's my right, isn't it? To testify? Isn't that in the Constitution?"

I take a second. I need to talk him off this ledge, but I know enough about Aaron to realize that shaking a finger at him will make him more determined. I play for time.

"It's your right, Aaron. And it's your decision. But let's see how the rest of their case goes. We think we've got some good stuff to poke more holes in the State's case through their experts. Let's decide about your testimony after the pathologist and the impressions and the fibers experts are off the stand."

Clearly, I haven't persuaded him yet. He shakes his head again.

"I've been listening to this bullshit for a week, Rusty. I want those people to hear the truth. You remember what it's like to have to sit through this crap?"

Oddly, I don't, not really. I remember feeling intensely agitated, but I knew I was never going near the witness stand. There were too many questions I had no wish to answer.

"I understand, Aaron. And I realize it's just the weirdest thing in the world to listen to somebody say horrible things about you without getting up and screaming that it's untrue. But we're doing a good job, I think, of showing that the prosecution has made a lot of mistakes. That they're untrustworthy."

"I guess." He seems kind of mopey. "But, you know, sometimes what goes on in there makes no sense. Like with that stipulation today? There was stuff we agreed to that's just a sack."

That alarms me. "Like what?"

"Like how that lady from Missouri called me."

"Oh." I understand. "We weren't agreeing that you had a conversation with her, Aaron. We were just agreeing that if she testified, she'd say she called a wrong number that was apparently yours."

He's still shaking his head.

"Nn-uh," he says. "My phone rang like once. And I turned it off right after that. Because it was Mae who called. And I didn't want her dialing me back a hundred times, which I knew she'd do."

"Mae?" I ask. I'm on high alert again.

"You know," says Aaron, with a sorrowful look, "it was the same old shit the minute I picked up. 'I can't live without you. I'll die. I'll kill myself.' I just hung up, because I couldn't stand to listen to that again, because you know, I always wanted it to be true. And when Mae said it, she probably wanted it to be true, too. But she would never be able to live it. That's what I saw in Harold's Woods. When she called, I was with this Black trucker who'd picked me up outside Ginawaban, and I just pressed the red button on her and sat there in that guy's cab, going sixty miles an hour in what I'd just realized was the wrong direction, and trying not to cry."

As I have listened to Aaron explain, I am slowly sorting out the reasons for my panic, and panic is the right word for what's radiating through me, because I instantly find what Aaron is saying unlikely. First, Mae calling is such significant evidence for the defense—if true, it proves she was alive after he left Harold's Woods—that it's hard to believe Aaron is only now mentioning it, no matter how zoned out he's been or how much I've insisted that I'll ask questions when it's the right time to hear the answers. Beyond that, the report of the Missouri Highway Patrol of their interview with the lady at the other end of the line was completely convincing to Susan and me. On September 14, she and her husband had exited the interstate at a rest stop to enjoy the fair weather. As they ate a lunch they'd packed, she phoned several B&Bs in Como Stop, trying to find a place for the night. It had required a number of calls, because a few were already closed for the season. But she remembered dialing at least one wrong number and reaching a young-sounding man who hung up on her impatiently. The woman, Elaine Harop, had no discernible reason to lie, and her husband, like her, remembered her elaborate apologies to the grouchy young guy she'd misdialed. If Aaron says it was Mae instead who phoned him, Jackdorp will bring the Missouri lady to the witness stand, and her testimony will be corroborated by the records from Aaron's own phone. What he's saying now can't be true.

"Aaron, you had Mae's cellphone."

"So what? I've said all along, man, she had money. Isn't that what Holloway testified to today? She had a bunch of cash in her back pocket. She must have bought a Tracfone, just like I kept telling you guys in September."

This, I see now, is the true cost of Bea's interference. She's injected real doubt into my relationship with Aaron. It's possible that since his mother persuaded him to tell one tale, he feels free to embroider others.

Jackdorp's theory, which he will put to the jury, is that Aaron is one of those quiet, cagey guys, an artful liar, capable of thinking many steps ahead, like telling Cassity—and me—that Mae peed on his backpack, so he had an excuse for burning it. I have recognized none of that in Aaron in the years I've known him. But there's a layer of calculation in his mother that was also invisible to me. Perhaps he's just like her.

I stand up, explaining that Susan and I have several days' work to accomplish in one weekend. I knock to signal the jailer to come collect Aaron, but before the young woman on duty today puts the cuffs on him, he looks at me and says, "I really don't expect to change my mind." He's being discreet in front of the CO, but I know he's referring to giving testimony.

35

Too Much

Susan has already let herself into the house when I return. I am boiling over to share what just transpired at the jail, but she stops me cold, while I'm still removing my pea coat, by asking casually, "Where's Bea?"

I take a long time, debating different responses, including a polite version of 'mind your own business.' My relationship with Susan is very pleasant and happily congenial, even somewhat admiring, but almost never veers into the personal. She is generally unrevealing, as if everything she wants to offer about herself is summarized by her attire. I've learned little new about her that I didn't already know from the time we worked together a decade ago. And so I feel little obligation to be forthcoming now. Instead, I settle for a small portion of the truth.

"She moved over to the motel with Joe."

This news stills Susan. Her eyes stay on me, while her tongue is placed strategically inside her cheek.

"I'm very sorry," she says. Then she adds, "It's got to be a terrible time for her." I'm faintly amused that the first instinct of women these days is to stick up for each other. Not that she's wrong about Bea. Or that females in general aren't right to make common cause out of the special vulnerabilities they share both as part of their social roles and the brute fact—and 'brute' is the word—that men are so often bullies.

One of the most startling and upsetting things I learned in my years of dating after I moved up to Skageon was that almost every woman I got at all close to had a story to tell of having earlier survived some form of sexual abuse. Bea had a professor in grad school who said he'd fail her unless she slept with him. Lloyd, a human mountain, made a trip to campus and introduced himself. The professor admitted nothing, except to stammer several times that he hadn't realized Bea was married, which was an absolute lie, according to Bea. And he still gave Bea a C in the course, the only grade lower than A– she received in twenty years of formal education.

Lorna Murphy had been raped as a college freshman by a senior in her dorm, an incident which she was too mortified to admit to anyone but her mother. And her mother, a prisoner of her times, warned Lorna never to tell anyone else, an injunction Lorna followed until she felt the need to tell Matt on their wedding night.

What might have happened to Susan along this line, I'll never know, although I've long suspected there's something. The truth is that we could probably work side by side daily for the rest of our lives without Susan ever growing confessional, especially about her past. Over time, I've decided there is a fairly fragile core to her. From what little I can piece together, she was a runaway, who was on her own from her early teens, and probably endured plenty on the street. She never mentions either her mother or her father or any siblings, and I think her longtime desire to assist in the defense of young people like Aaron, whom others might deem lost or useless, stems from her own experiences.

I do know that when she was about eighteen, she fell in with bikers and led a pretty wild life, until she encountered Al. I think there was another Mrs. Al at that point, but it's clearly worked well for both of them. They have no children together, but he had two kids by his first marriage, and that son and daughter and the five grandchildren are a perpetual topic of conversation. She seems very bound up with Al and those offspring and the farm creatures they tend together. As for the rawhide and the turquoise, I think she is saying to the world and herself that she has not broken compact with the fearless young woman who felt it was important to present herself to the world this way. Besides, she fits right in on the weekends, when Al and she are riding with a crew who all think of themselves as wild and free.

I've met Al once or twice when he's come to court, but he doesn't say much. The one thing that emerges in the few moments I've been with the two of them is a mood of absolute peace that clearly sustains each of them. Until a few days ago, I thought that's what Bea and I shared too.

"I've been thinking about this whole thing with the rope," Susan says. She's a fine investigator and she clearly assumes that Bea's new tale concerning the rope provked an intense argument that drove Bea out of the house. "What if I go back to the store and see if I can get some more information? If there's nothing to corroborate the idea that the rope from Home Warehouse is a different rope—well, at least we can show both her and Aaron that the State Patrol is going to find the same thing. Give them some second thoughts before they get irrevocably committed."

"Jesus, Susan. You have so much to do already without solving my domestic problems."

She scowls and eyes me sidewise.

"I'm not solving your domestic problems, Rusty. I know everybody at trial drinks their own Kool-Aid, but even so, I think this defense is making real headway—if we don't do anything really stupid to mess it up. So this is about Aaron, frankly, not you."

I take a beat and thank her. Then I say, "Speaking of really stupid." I tell her about our client's desire to testify. She listens with a constricted but pensive expression.

"You know," she says, "in the abstract, he's the sort of guy who'd do well up there. Self-contained. Polite. You wouldn't have to school him about not rambling. Is there any way," she asks, "that Judge Carrington could exclude evidence of Aaron's conviction on cross?"

"We can ask before he gets on the stand. But it's pretty much in stone that if a defendant chooses to testify, then the jury gets to know the significant details of his background in order to assess his credibility. And a felony conviction is pretty significant, at least as jurors look at things."

"Then testifying would go in the really stupid category," Susan says.

"And it gets a little worse." I share what Aaron told me this morning, that the phone call he received during the brief period he hitchhiked in the wrong direction was from Mae, not some woman from Missouri. I can see at once that Susan's doubts are as resounding as mine. Even while what's happening in court seems to be creating doubts there about Aaron's guilt, his new stories about the rope and now the phone call seem to be eroding the faith of the defense team.

Susan says exactly what I did: "He had Mae's phone."

I tell her about Aaron's theory that Mae bought a Tracfone and a phone card.

"Well, what sense does that make?" Susan asks. "Tracfone or not, the incoming call would be reflected in his service provider's records."

"Is there anything about a Tracfone that might keep it from showing up?"

"Not that I know of. I've got a person to ask. But think about this: Aaron wants to say Mae called only him? Not her mother? Not her sister? The first week they were looking for Mae, the deputies must have talked to twenty people who knew Mae, and no one had heard from her. We have all those reports."

"Maybe she bought a card with limited minutes. Or was killed right after she spoke with Aaron?"

Susan is still shaking her head over this new muddle.

"So now we'd be saying there were two phone calls? One from Mae and one from the woman in Missouri?"

"He insists there was only one." But in thinking that over as I left the jail, I've wondered. Upset and bewildered enough to go in the wrong direction, and then even more upset after realizing his mistake, Aaron could have easily forgotten about a two-second hang-up.

"We never spoke to the woman in Missouri, right?" I ask Susan.

We had no reason to look in the mouth of the gift horse. Given the connection on Aaron's end to the nearby cell tower, her call was good news for the defense, since it so strongly suggested Aaron was nowhere near Ginawaban or the tollbooth when Mae's car passed through.

That thought reminds me about the tollbooth photograph. On that front, there is finally a little good news. Susan reached the highway authority last night, which said that all the tollbooth cameras were manufactured and installed by a subsidiary of a big defense contractor, called Northern Direct. With the advantage of the time difference, Susan reached customer service at the headquarters in California. The young woman Susan spoke to seemed to confirm what Susan thought—that the camera focuses on the license plate and is specifically designed so that it doesn't capture identifiable details about the driver, including skin tones. Someone from the General Counsel's office at Northern is supposed to follow up with Susan this afternoon.

We agree that if the call comes in while we're together, I'll field it. Susan needs to triage. If her to-do list gets any longer, she'll be a candidate for *The Guinness Book of World Records*. She's yet to start on the piles of investigators' notes that Glowoski coughed up yesterday. Our hope, of course, is that there's another nugget there like Mrs. Lowndes's apparent disagreement with her husband, but paging through the notebooks and scraps of paper we received will still take most of the weekend. Trying to reach the woman from Missouri will just have to wait.

So will the extended discussion we were planning about whether or not to offer evidence for the defense. As a prosecutor, I always felt it worked to my advantage when the defendant rested without proof. The theory among defense lawyers is that standing up and saying, 'The defense rests,' right after the prosecution finishes, is a dramatic demonstration that the PA had an epic fail in proving their case. My own thought was that it was a tacit admission that the defendant didn't have a damn thing to say for himself.

In our case, we have several options. One idea I've been toying with is calling Hardy as an adverse witness and forcing him to admit under oath all the ways he interfered in the potential case against Aaron. But no matter how much I'd enjoy embarrassing Hardy, given my current vexations, it's a risky ploy. He may come off better than I expect, and the jury's takeaway will be that I'm just piling on a grieving father. On this question, I'll need to rely on Susan's judgment, and right now she's too busy to ponder that carefully. And the better course, just as I told Aaron, is to wait to decide a defense case until we see what kind of headway we make with the government's forensic experts. For the time being, I agree to prepare a few subpoenas we might need and deliver them to the sheriff's office here for service. No witness is ever unhappy when you call later and say, 'Never mind.'

Susan puts herself down on the sofa and spills out all the investigators' notes in order to make a first pass through them. I concentrate on my computer, and various jottings I've made over the months about impressions evidence.

We've been at it a couple of hours when I hear a key scratch in the door. Bea walks in. She and Susan are both clearly startled by the sight of one another.

"I need to get some more clothes," Bea says to both of us. She does not look good. She looks bad, to be more exact. She's drawn and colorless. Her eyes appear shrunken.

"Sure sure," I say and motion her ahead toward the bedroom and turn back to my screen. I can tell she hasn't moved.

"Rusty, can we talk for a minute?"

If Susan weren't here, I would probably say no. I don't feel any need to be cold to Bea, but I really have nothing to say right now and can't afford the time to get upset again.

We leave the house through the back door in the kitchen, so we are facing the acres of dormant bean fields. There was a little snow last night and the thin crust of white lies on the overturned soil, where the stubble of last year's crop, now browned, sometimes protrudes. There's a fierce and frigid wind today, and I came out without a coat so I didn't have to spend long in this conversation.

"What's up, Bea?"

"I just need to say some things to you."

"Okay."

She shakes her head though, like she has no clue what that is.

"Rusty, this has been the worst week of my life. I thought when Willi was killed," she says, referring to her mother, "I thought that was bad. But, you know, having to listen to Jackdorp. And then this. With you. I can't stand myself. Because I'm so ashamed. I feel like tearing the skin off my body, I really do. I can't understand how I was so stupid or selfish. There wasn't a time—and there weren't many after you and I started going out—but whatever it was, a few occasions, and there wasn't one of them when I didn't say to myself, What are you doing, why are you here, you don't even enjoy this anymore. I just need you to know that there was never a moment when I preferred him to you in any way. Not even for a second. I always was so desperate for this to work out that I was frightened about having nothing if it didn't."

She dares to look at me then. One of the things that came to me last night, in all my back-and-forth with myself, was the realization that Bea's clean break with Hardy might have had more to do with circumstances than she now wants to acknowledge. The pandemic, which was why she moved in with me, had also rung the curtain down on casual contact for a lot of people. And by then she and Hardy were probably seriously at odds about Mae and Aaron, each blaming the other for their kid's troubles.

But I don't bother with more cross-examination. With my hands jammed in my jeans pockets due to the cold, I shrug to show I've heard her. She stands there, her mouth slightly parted, clearly hoping for more, before tossing her head.

"If Aaron is convicted and you won't forgive me—Rusty, I can't even imagine what would be left of my life."

The last statement opens the sluiceway. Both hands go to her face, covering her mouth and nose, and she is suddenly sobbing uncontrollably.

"Bea, you're being a little manipulative now."

"I'm in agony," she answers. "Can't you at least understand that?"

"Of course I can. Because I'm in the same kind of pain. I'm completely bewildered, Bea, about who you really are."

"You know who I am. Please don't say that."

"Bea, I'm not trying to fight with you. Or make you feel worse. I just need you to understand that I haven't had enough time to process this. And I won't until the trial ends. The better the case is going for our side, the greater the pressure I'm under. I cannot get distracted or lose time I don't have, because it may literally cost Aaron the rest of his life. So please, just give me some space. It's only a few more days."

"Russ, I'll try to do that, but I need to know that you've taken in how unbelievably sorry I am."

"I have, Bea. I truly have."

She looks at me, spouts of fog emerging from her with each urgent breath.

"Please try to forgive me."

"Bea, I believe that would be the best thing for both of us. I do. But you have to give me time to get there. I can't say it just because it's what you want to hear right now."

"Rusty," she says, plaintively. I understand Bea's emotional state. The combination of shame and anxiety has exhausted all her reserves. She wants this to be over with, to know that we're on the path to recovery. But what she needs reflects no concern about what I require, which, very frankly, is how we got into this fix.

"Bea, just give me time."

"Rusty, you had *affairs*," she says. "While you were married. You've told me that. This was nothing close to that."

I realize that her shift of tactics is largely because she's frustrated, but it still enrages me, this effort to turn the tables.

"This isn't about what I did wrong in my life, Bea. It's a long list, and no one knows that better than me. But it's a shitty defense for you. If I murdered somebody, would that make it right if you murdered someone too?"

Somehow—at least to my ear—there is an undertone of frank accusation in my remark, which she seems to hear as well. It clearly stuns her, but I can't read her response beyond that. Is this simply something unexpected, like a rabbit punch, or is what completely paralyzes her gorgeous eyes the anxiety of being found out?

Either way, I've had enough. I reenter the house and close the rear door behind me to get out of the cold. In the sudden dimness, I'm abruptly visited by a memory that seems wildly inappropriate at first of the last time we had romping good sex—although it's the aftermath, rather than the rapture, that preoccupies me now.

It was while she was on Thanksgiving break, in the middle of one of those languorous days over the weekend. We were just back from Kindle County, where we'd celebrated with Nat and Anna and the girls at their house, a large, happy gathering that included many of their friends and a storm of kids excited by the holidays. Bea and I returned in a state of reprieve. The trial was still months off and the shock of Aaron's arrest had been absorbed. Lloyd had brought his family up to Portage, and his daughters and wife were visiting Aaron in jail for the first time. Bea thought it was only considerate to stay away.

Due to the wall of windows in our bedroom facing the lake, the room can run cold in the winter. Lorna had mounted an electric thermostat-controlled heater above the bed, but once the vents opened, it was slow to shut down and often left the air stifling. When I returned from a postcoital trip to the john, I found Bea lying fully naked on the bed, transfixed in thought as she stared at the overhead fixture. To me, especially now that it is confined to memory, there has always been a resonant beauty to Bea, a matter of body and soul, that I never failed to experience, no matter what the circumstances. It's like attending the symphony and still taking in the transporting power of the music, despite the jerk behind you always coughing and unwrapping his candy. But in this moment, there was something especially arresting in her physical presence, a lovely figure of a woman always, but a pure humanity that radiated from her unguarded nakedness, that thing artists are so often attempting to capture in drawing nudes.

When she registered my return, she suddenly declared, 'There is so much pain in life.'

The remark struck me so deeply that I stopped moving toward the bed.

'What brought this on?' All in all, it seemed an odd response to the shuddering ecstasy we'd both experienced fifteen minutes before.

'I'm thinking about all of us. The Potters. And Aaron. And me. Mae's brought us together.' She snorted bitterly. 'We're all in pain.' I was struck that even after Mae's death, Bea continued to see her as a perpetual source of trouble.

'Did we switch roles somehow?' I asked. 'I thought I'm the pain person and you're the joy person.'

'I'm the joy person,' she said, 'because I've never wanted to give in to the pain. And the joy is real.' She looked to me then with a sweet smile, acknowledging where we just had been. 'But so is the pain.'

She was making sense, but after seven years together, it still seemed she was bowing to something she had never acknowledged before. In the moment, I understood this as a response to Aaron's indictment. And now, with my heightened suspicions of her, when I still have this vengeful wish to find that Bea committed a great crime rather than a small one, I wonder if there's any chance she was talking about carrying the terrible burden of the harm she'd done to Mae.

But overall, stock-still in the kitchen, I am taken by the accuracy of her assessment. I have joined their club. Aaron. And the Potters. And her. There is so much pain in life.

36

Impressions

In an unexpected first, Susan is late for court. She texted about eight thirty: 'OTW from Home Warehouse. Portage by 9:15. Don't wait. Will explain.' When she comes on the bench, Judge Carrington notes Susan's absence, and is visibly relieved when I tell her that we are prepared to proceed, nonetheless.

Special Agent Nancy Merado is then summoned to the stand, the first of the three experts Jackdorp will call to conclude their case. Her field is impressions analysis, examining the prints left behind by vehicle tires and footwear. She has been with the State Patrol for sixteen years now, but received her principal training on foot and tire prints at the FBI Academy at Quantico, and now teaches there occasionally. That means she knows her stuff.

The nature of expert testimony is such that not all the jurors will understand it at first. Too often with circumstantial cases, they simply end up assuming the prosecutors must know what they're doing. Accordingly, we wanted to be sure to seat at least one person in the jury box who could quickly grasp the flaws we expected to point out in Jackdorp's circumstantial case. The man we ultimately accepted, Archer Rideau, was, as far as I was concerned, our biggest gamble.

Rideau is a large heavy white guy, half-bald, who comes to court every day in an old corduroy sport coat and chinos. A CPA by training, he left accounting practice and went into unidentified 'business ventures.' About ten years ago, after his kids were on their way, Rideau and his wife moved up to Marenago County so she could raise horses. He decided to 'do good'—his term—and began teaching accounting courses at Marenago Community College. The most troubling thing that emerged about him, aside from the fact that he never missed a Republican primary, was that he had met Jackdorp, on two or three occasions when Rideau gave speeches to the Portage Rotary, explaining changes in various tax laws. I was inclined to ding him, until, on further questioning by Judge Carrington, he disclosed that he also had some acquaintance with Susan. She was a little startled, but eventually recalled Rideau as a Harley owner who'd taken Sunday rides with Al and her and the herd years ago. Her impressions of him were limited, since he was, she said, the kind who sooner or later turned away and rode off on his own. That pretty much seemed to be his nature. He answered our questions with a bristling confidence that made me wary that he might be unwilling to listen to anybody else during deliberations. But Susan encouraged me to accept him. She remembered him as a thoroughgoing libertarian, the kind who believed that in order to screw in a light bulb, a government employee would take two days to read a manual and then put the wrong end in the socket. Mr. Rideau figured to be naturally skeptical of the prosecution.

Seating him also followed the final advice I got from Damon, the jury consultant. He said that in the end he thought that in Aaron's case, 'you're probably looking for one.' In our state, like most, juries must be unanimous to return a guilty verdict. Thus, one determined holdout can cause a deadlock, resulting in a mistrial, which, on a scale of probabilities, Damon regarded as the best outcome Aaron could realistically expect. A murder charge was likely to lead to a retrial. But Jackdorp might even offer an appealing plea deal, which Aaron could look on more favorably after a majority of the first jury had been prepared to find him guilty.

The risk with Rideau, in my mind, is that he's the kind of strong personality who has 'foreperson' written all over him. If he's against us, he could bulldoze the others toward conviction. As a result, I've tried to keep an eye on him without being obtrusive. He's paid close attention, taken reams of notes, and has maintained a poker face, even containing himself when his colleagues have found occasions for laughter. He had assured Judge Carrington that despite knowing participants on both sides he could be fair, and he seems intent on maintaining a demeanor that reflects that.

As for Special Agent Merado, the impressions expert, she was the only state employee, including the pathologist who will be Jackdorp's last witness, willing to meet with Susan for a few minutes to answer questions. Merado's attitude, according to Susan, seems to be that what she does is science that doesn't by its nature favor one side or the other. Susan described her as a total nerd, wearing a T-shirt that read, 'Try to make a good impression.'

On the stand, she takes her time, even with the questions from Jackdorp that she presumably knows are coming. She is in her mid-forties now, brown curly hair, and not especially interested in appearing fashionable. No makeup, such that I would notice, and no jewelry aside from a wedding ring on one of her slim hands, which don't quite fit the rest of her broader physique. She wears black glasses, with thick frames and lenses.

For this investigation, Merado says she has done analysis of both footwear and tire impressions. Identifying either depends on the same factors. First, there are what are called 'class characteristics,' which generally relate to particular features that are incorporated into the design of specific tires or shoes. Then there are 'mold characteristics,' which arise from microscopic variations in the specific forms used in given factories to stamp out those products. Nike, for example, has 132 footwear factories around the world. The final identifying details about an impression are the unique wear patterns that appear in a tire or shoe over time as a result of the stride or driving habits of the user.

Merado testifies that she was first called on this case on September 21, 2023, when she was part of the forensics team that examined a campsite in Harold's Woods. She found clearly visible shoeprints in a low area, where rain had presumably collected during the most recent storm on the night of September 12 and then hardened to mud. Several prints corresponded to the Timberland hiking boots Mae was ultimately found to be wearing when her body was recovered. The other identifiable shoe impressions found at Harold's Woods appeared to have been left by Nike Air Force 1s, a popular sneaker whose sole imprints are distinctive because of the network of whorls that radiate outward from a circle under the ball of the foot.

Merado is showing photos of the three-dimensional casts she made of those prints, just as Susan arrives. She rushes in, still in her motorcycle leathers, carrying her helmet, but gives me a thumbs-up right below the level of our table so the jurors can't see it. Given the brief distraction she's caused, I decide I might as well get up and offer an objection, which is to remind everyone that we've already agreed that the Nike shoeprints found in Harold's Woods were made by Aaron, wearing the shoes his grandfather had bought him.

Jackdorp is looking at me over his shoulder with a pursed look of irritation.

"Judge," answers Jackdorp, "unless Mr. Sabich is also going to stipulate that Defendant Housley hid or destroyed those sneakers, I'd like to continue with my examination, so that the jury fully understands."

"We are certainly not going to stipulate to that, Your Honor. I expect the evidence to show that Mr. Jackdorp is flat wrong."

"Judge," Jackdorp says sharply, "would you please tell him to sit down and let me get on with my business here?"

Judge Carrington is smiling faintly. She realizes that I'm trying to suck the drama out of Jackdorp's big show and doing pretty well at it too.

"I think, under the circumstances, Mr. Sabich, that's a fair suggestion. But Mr. Jackdorp, the defense is correct that we really don't need an involved presentation aimed at showing those were Mr. Housley's shoes, since that's admitted."

I've done enough that Jackdorp seems thrown off stride as he figures out where to go next. In the meantime, I turn to Susan for some clue about what she's been doing, but she mouths, 'At lunch.'

A second later, she writes on my legal pad, 'Bea was right.' My heart leaps and I have to contain myself to watch the witness. Jackdorp is now cataloging the efforts made to locate Aaron's shoes.

"Did you ever obtain the shoe you were looking for in this case, that is the Nike Air Force 1 Lows that the defendant's grandfather had bought him?"

"No," Merado answers. This falls a bit flat, since I've just told the jury there's more to the story. It seemed effective when I offered that on the spur of the moment, but I realize that I've now more or less committed us to putting on defense evidence after all.

Jackdorp next asks Merado if she had any occasion to make an examination of the utility road at Ginawaban. She says she was first called there on October 3, after Aaron's arrest.

"Were there any prints of interest to you on that utility road?"

"Yes," she finally answers. "If I had to say what ultimately proved to be of interest, I would say there were three impressions, which the photos made by the evidence techs showed had been there on September 28 when the body was found."

Adjacent to the forested area where the Subaru had come to rest after crashing head-on into a large oak, there was a kind of dip where the gravel ended, which presumably had also become muddy after the storm on September 12 and subsequently dried up. This runnel or trough ran across the south half of that road. In that trough was an impression ultimately identified as coming from the right rear tire of the Subaru. Also in that low spot, right behind Mae's car, she found a second impression Jackdorp asks her to describe.

"Well, the area had not been processed initially as a crime scene. So all three of the impressions in that muddy area had been partially run over by vehicles or stepped on, reducing or eliminating the significant detail in those prints. There was enough left of the Subaru tire impression to make it identifiable. The second impression I found, on the northern edge of that little hollow, I observed some remaining detail, including two small spots of concentric circles." She shows a photograph.

"And did you form any initial conclusion about that impression with the concentric circling?" Jackdorp asks.

"Yes. The small areas of remaining detail were consistent with a Nike Air Force 1."

As Jackdorp has anticipated from the start of the trial, that fact seems to make an impression in the jury box.

"Now, was that the last examination you made in connection with this case?"

"No. The following day, October 4, I went down to Kindle County, where the Subaru had been removed and garaged."

In the Subaru she found two clear shoeprints, one on the display in the center console right above the gearshift, and another on the dashboard, just to the left. Merado identified both as coming from Mae's Timberlands. There were numerous other areas of dirt in the car that appeared to be shoeprints from the Nike AF1s, but given that Aaron Housley's fingerprints had been identified, she did no further comparisons.

"Was that the end of your work in Kindle County?"

"No, I had received a call the prior day that in the course of the autopsy, before removing Mae's garments, they had conducted an examination with ultraviolet light and observed what might have been a print on the shoulder of the blouse." The ultraviolet exam was repeated in Merado's presence and she photographed and enlarged what was there. That photo is also displayed for the jury.

"Is that a shoeprint?" Jackdorp asks.

"That's my opinion."

"And could that shoeprint on Mae's shoulder have been made by the same shoe, the Nike Air Force 1 that the defendant's grandfather had purchased for him?"

"Yes, definitely," Merado answers. "It definitely could have been made by that shoe."

"And going back to the impression in the dried mud at Ginawaban, near the Subaru. Could that print have been made by the defendant's Nike Air Force 1s?"

"Yes, definitely," Merado answers again.

Despite the warning in my opening, Jackdorp has chosen to conclude Merado's examination with some high-key advocacy. He is betting that simple dramatics are all the jury will remember amid

Merado's largely technical testimony about mold characteristics and wear patterns.

Given that, I move quickly toward the podium, trying to get there even before Jackdorp has taken his seat.

"Special Agent Merado, I want to be clear to start, given those last questions from Mr. Jackdorp. Are you telling this jury that it is your expert opinion that the shoes Joe, Aaron's grandfather, bought for him left that print on Mae's shoulder?"

"No, that's not what I'm saying."

"That's not your expert opinion, right? Yes or no?"

She stops to push her glasses back up on her nose. "No, that's not my opinion."

"And that partial impression with the concentric circles, which you found in the dried mud at Ginawaban near Mae's SUV—are you telling this jury that it's your expert opinion *that* print was made by one of the shoes Joe bought for Aaron?"

"No, that's not my opinion."

"In fact, is it fair to say that millions—literally millions and millions of other shoes could have made those two prints, the one on Mae's blouse and the one in the mud at Ginawaban, rather than Aaron's shoes?"

"I don't know about the numbers, but many many other shoes could have made the two impressions you asked me about."

I look to the jury box. One woman, who's been coming to the overheated courtroom for the last few days in a sleeveless blouse, has her hand over her mouth. Mr. Gomes's eyes are screwed closed, as he tries to understand. Several others are making notes, and I actually catch Mr. Rideau, Susan's guy, unconsciously shaking his head.

"Thank you. I'm going to come back to those two prints in a second, the one from Mae's blouse and the one from the mud at Ginawaban, but let me ask you something Mr. Jackdorp skipped."

He objects to 'skipped,' and I correct the question to "something Mr. Jackdorp didn't cover."

"You first went to the utility road in Ginawaban after Aaron was arrested, right?"

"Yes. The next Monday. HQ won't let me work overtime, so

that was the first I could get there after the autopsy findings were reported."

"And what was your purpose in going on October 3?"

"The lieutenant asked me to come." She's gestured to Glowoski. "First, they wanted to look at the photographs from September 28 and then go on scene to examine any prints that appeared to be of interest. Second, the defendant had told the arresting officer that he hadn't gone down the road once he found it was closed off by evidence tape. The lieutenant wanted me to conduct an examination to see if I could find prints from the new sneakers the defendant was wearing or tire impressions from the vehicle he was driving, the F-150, since the FX4, that's an off-road model."

"And did you find any evidence that Aaron or the truck had gone down the road, when he arrived there after Mae's body was recovered?"

"No."

"No evidence that he tampered with any evidence at the crime scene?"

"Not in the area I examined anyway. As I said on direct, there was a third impression in the dried mud, and that could have been made by any number of off-road vehicles, including the F-150, but when I checked the photographs from September 28 when Ms. Potter's remains were discovered, that print had been there. And there wasn't much left of it anyway."

I then go on to Mae's shoeprints on the dashboard of the Subaru. Although it takes a bit, Merado agrees that there are no dates on the impressions and that they could have been made when Mae had pulled back her seat at times she wasn't driving and put up her feet.

"Now let's go back to this print that was identified on Mae's shoulder under the ultraviolet light. We've already established that it's not your opinion that that print was necessarily made by Aaron's sneakers. But to be clear, are you even sure that print came from a Nike Air Force 1?"

"No. I'm not sure. It's very faint, that print. You can't even see it without the ultraviolet. And what you can see are just some lines left by the sole. So because they're circular, it looks like a print from an Air Force 1, but there are other models of Nike shoes, like the Air Jordans, and even some copycat models, that might have left that impression, too."

"Thank you. Can you tell what size that shoe was?"

"No, because I don't know what part of the shoe left those outer rings."

"Can you say whether it was made by a men's model or a women's model?"

"Well, I can exclude some of the smaller women's models. But no, I can't say man or woman."

I thank her again.

"Can you say whether that print was made by a right shoe or a left shoe?"

Merado actually sits back in her chair this time. That's not a question she's considered. She takes a second to study the photo in her hand. For better or for worse, the jury is bound to take Merado as somebody laboring to be fair.

"I guess not. Because I don't know what part of the shoe we're looking at."

"In other words, as just one example, the print could have been made by a right shoe pointing forward by the rings to the left of the ball of the foot, or it could have been made by a left shoe pointing behind Mae by rings closer to the outside of the sole? The impression we see would have looked the same in both cases?" Susan has prepared an overlay that I use, showing what I've described.

Watching carefully, Merado nods, and the judge tells her she must answer out loud. Merado apologizes and says yes.

"Now let's talk about how that print on the shoulder of Mae's blouse might have been made—whatever shoe it came from—how it was possibly made. The impression on the shoulder of her blouse is not visible to the naked eye, is it?"

"No."

"So Mae wouldn't have known her blouse was dirty, at least not because of the shoeprint?"

"No."

A bit late, Jackdorp objects that we're now asking Merado to testify about what Mae thought. The judge says I'm getting pretty far afield, even for expert testimony, but she allows the answer to stand.

"And there are no dates on this print either, like all the rest?"

"No, of course not."

"So they could have been made at any time prior to when Mae died?"

"Also true."

"Now, with the shoeprint from Mae's blouse in mind, allow me to ask you if you've ever camped?"

"Oh Lord," moans Jackdorp. "How much beyond the scope of my direct are we going now?"

"If that's a relevancy objection, Mr. Jackdorp," Judge Carrington says, "I'll overrule it. I think I see where this line of questioning is going."

"So, Special Agent Merado, have you gone camping? Slept in a tent?"

"My wife's daughter likes it. So we go now and then."

I'm not sure how the word 'wife' is going to land in Marenago County from a female witness. From the corner of my eye, I think I see the sourer of the hair-curler ladies make a face. But my demeanor with Merado, who is far less confrontational than many state employee witnesses, has been cordial and at moments friendly. I make no effort to stifle the reflexive smile I'd offer anyone if they mentioned their family, whether some of the jurors like my reaction or not.

"Cramped space inside a tent, right?"

"Definitely."

"Have you ever had to get up and go out in the middle of the night?"

"Unfortunately," she says. "But it seems to happen only when it's really cold or raining."

She gets a mild laugh. I keep smiling at her.

"Before you go out, you're groping around for your shoes in the dark?"

"True."

"Have you ever stepped on somebody else's clothing on the way out or in?"

"I don't remember one way or the other."

"Can you say you haven't?"

"Definitely not."

"Could that leave a shoeprint on a garment?"

Jackdorp objects and the judge overrules him. Merado spends a long time nodding before she says yes.

"Now let's turn to the fragmentary shoeprint you found in the dried mud right behind where the Subaru had crashed. That one, you can say was left by a Nike Air Force 1 Low?"

"Low, High, Mid, all the same sole. But I'm pretty sure one of them is what we're looking at."

With my subsequent questions, she agrees that, like the print on Mae's shoulder, there's no telling the size of the shoe that made the print or even if it was a men's or woman's model. Most important, in contrast to the fuller print she cast at Harold's Woods, she can't identify enough of the mold characteristics to say this print came from Aaron's shoe.

"In fact," I say, "your report says, and I quote, 'microscopic examination and superimposition were inconclusive.' And by superimposition, you mean taking an image of the Ginawaban print and laying it over the print from Harold's Woods?"

"Yes."

"Ms. DeLeo made a little animation to represent that overlay process. Please tell me if that's a fair representation of your superimposition test."

I play it, and on the screen, a positive outline of the smaller Ginawaban print swims over the full one from Harold's Woods, and at no point are the lines fully congruent.

"That's the idea," says SA Merado.

"Well, doesn't that prove that these two prints were made by two different people wearing two different shoes?"

"That's quite possible, but it doesn't *prove* that." She goes nerd at that point, detailing factors that might lead the same shoe to make prints that aren't fully alike—the angle the foot struck the ground, the character of the earth in which the impression is made, and even the elasticity of the 'Grind rubber' out of which Nike AF1 soles are manufactured. Wearing the same shoe, someone running leaves subtly different prints than when they're walking. She enjoys displaying her expertise and I don't interrupt her, because she's been so cooperative in general. Besides, by the time she's done, even Archer Rideau has phased out.

"But with all that said," I say, "another very reasonable explanation for why the prints from Harold's Woods and the fragmentary impression from Ginawaban don't line up on the animation is because the two prints were made by two different people?"

"Correct," she says. "That's definitely reasonable."

"And so the question becomes, How likely is it that Aaron and someone else who was at Ginawaban were both wearing Nike Air Force 1s?"

She doesn't understand, and so I try another approach.

"As an evidentiary expert, if someone told you that Aaron was wearing blue jeans in Harold's Woods, and another witness said they saw someone in Ginawaban near the Subaru also wearing blue jeans, that wouldn't tell you it was Aaron, would it? Not given the incredible prevalence of blue jeans as attire in the US, right?"

She says she's not an expert on blue jeans, but I persist and ask for her opinion as a witness familiar with logical inferences. Jackdorp objects and is promptly overruled. These days all witnesses can offer opinions about what they perceive.

"That's true. If blue jeans was all I knew, it wouldn't tell me much. It wouldn't prove he was at Ginawaban."

Overall, SA Merado is being pretty helpful and I have a clear suspicion about why, which goes back to the emphatic answers she gave at the end of her direct. I imagine Jackdorp was irate after my opening—probably because I was right when I said that he didn't understand the popularity of the Air Force 1 design. He may well have blamed Merado for leaving him in the dark. To make the best of the situation, I'd bet that together with Glowoski, Jackdorp browbeat Merado until she agreed to give those 'Yes, definitely' answers about whether Aaron's shoes could have made the prints on Mae's blouse and in the mud at Ginawaban. But she knows those answers standing alone are essentially misleading, and so, whether Glowoski or Jackdorp likes it—and they're pretty much as inanimate as statues as they sit at the prosecution table right now—she's going to do her best to help me clear that up.

"Now I want to assert to you that the coincidence that Aaron was wearing Nike Air Force 1s in Harold's Woods, and the person who was near Mae's Subaru also wore those shoes—I want to assert to you that it doesn't mean much more than two different people wearing blue jeans would in the example I gave."

She shrugs and I go on quickly. Because market reports are exceptions to the rule against hearsay, I spend the next few minutes showing her various articles about the sales of Nike Air Force 1s. She agrees readily that with all the models considered, the Nike Air Force 1 is the most popular shoe ever made and may sell as many as 10 million pairs a year these days. Over the forty-five-plus years the shoe has been on the market, perhaps as many as 200 million pairs have been purchased, about equal to the number of adults in the US. And even acknowledging that the shoes wear out over time, she accepts my estimate that as many as 1 in 7 Americans may have a pair of Nike Air Force 1s in their closet.

"And so," I conclude, "bearing all of this in mind, the coincidence that Aaron wore Nike Air Force 1s and whoever was down the utility road also wore those shoes—that coincidence doesn't tell you much more than my blue jean example would, correct?"

She assumes a long thoughtful pose, her chin shrunken as she ponders.

"I don't think it's quite like blue jeans. I mean, *every*one wears blue jeans. But asking me like you did for my opinion on the evidence, I'd agree that the print on the utility road doesn't go very far in identifying Aaron. For me, my opinion, I wouldn't put a lot of weight on it."

Behind me, I hear a sound that I'm pretty sure is Jackdorp tossing his pen down on the prosecution table.

"Now, I want to end by going back to where you started your testimony, that is saying that Lieutenant Glowoski asked you on September 21 to go to Harold's Woods. And you said she referred to the person who was with Mae as, quote, 'a person of interest.' Is that right?"

"That's what she said."

"And 'person of interest'—does that suggest that the so-called person of interest might have committed a crime?"

"Might have. Yes."

"But it was a missing persons investigation, correct?"

"Correct."

"Mae's body hadn't been found yet?"

"Correct."

"And do you know who, even at that point in time, before Mae's remains had been discovered—do you know who'd designated Aaron as a person of interest, a potential criminal?"

"All I know is the lieutenant said that. Protocol is not to refer to a 'person of interest' unless a prosecutor has signed off on that."

"And do you know which prosecutor signed off on that?"

"Lieutenant referred to the Skageon County PA's office, I believe."

"Did she mention the Skageon PA, Harrison Potter, in connection with designating Aaron a person of interest?"

"I don't recall, sir, to be honest."

"Now you said, I believe, in the photos of the shoeprint in the mud at Ginawaban, you can see that most of the print had been obliterated by a car tire running over it. And was it also stepped on?"

"Right," she says. "The first I got there, it was pretty clear that there had been vehicles and some people marching around down there near the Subaru, because, you know, it was regarded as an accident scene initially, and there was a lot of excitement and sadness, you know, when Mae was found."

"Did you do any measurements to determine what car had driven over the shoeprint?"

"No. That wouldn't have been possible. It had been dry, and windy. There really wasn't enough tread to identify the tire."

"Same answer regarding the shoes that had stepped on the print?"

"Frankly, from the faint outlines, it looked to me like more than one person had walked over it. But that's not a lot better than a guess."

I nod, and Susan illuminates one of the photographs from the night Mae's body was discovered.

"Let me ask you if that Cadillac Escalade is parked exactly where you found the shoeprint partially obliterated?"

She spends a second.

"It's close," she says.

"And do you see the Skageon PA, Harrison Potter, standing next to what has been identified in prior testimony as his Escalade?"

"Yes."

"And what kind of shoe is he wearing in the photo?"

"It's some kind of athletic footwear."

"Could it be a Nike Air Force 1?"

"I don't know what shoe it is."

"My question is just like the questions Mr. Jackdorp asked you at the end of your direct. *Could* the shoes that Mr. Potter has on be Nike Air Force 1s?"

"They could be. I can't say no. I can't say yes."

I have actually said, "Nothing further," when Susan behind me says, "Wait." I go back to our table. Susan has a point and Aaron agrees. Things with Merado have gone so well that I hesitate to do more, but I consider myself outvoted. I ask the judge's permission to put a few more questions to the special agent.

"So," I say, still standing between Aaron and Susan. "You told us that you found three impressions of interest in that muddy spot behind the Subaru. One was from the Subaru itself. One was from somebody's Nike Air Force 1. And last, there was a tire impression on the utility road in Ginawaban that you first believed might have been left by the F-150 Aaron was driving when he was arrested, except you saw on examining your original photographs of the scene that the print was there on September 28 when Deputy Holloway first found the Subaru."

"Right, about three feet to the north of the shoeprint, there might have been a tire impression, but all the significant detail had been obliterated because of people walking or driving over it."

"But it looked like that tire print had been left when the Subaru crashed?"

"Well, sir, you're the one who keeps saying there aren't dates on these prints."

"But to be in that muddy runnel there, it had to have been made after the storm on September 12, but before the ground had dried? Within a day or two of the heavy rain?"

"Assuming that rain would have washed away any prints that were in that low spot before, I'd agree."

"Meaning this third impression was probably left at the same time as that Nike AF1 print we've been talking about. Correct?"

"Seems logical. But there's nothing in impressions science that gives an exact date."

"Did you take photographs of that possible tire impression?"

"Only to show the area. When I studied it on October 3, I determined that I would never be able to identify the impression."

"But you don't think it was left by Mae's car?"

"The outer margins of that impression make me believe it was from a wider tire than the Subaru's."

I'm excited now. Susan was, as usual, right.

"But do you understand, Special Agent, that the government is telling us that Aaron Housley drove the Subaru to Ginawaban? So if another vehicle was down there the night the Subaru crashed, it couldn't have been driven by Aaron, could it?"

She smiles. "I'm an expert on tires and shoes, not drivers."

"But to you as an expert it looked to be the width of a tire print from a bigger off-road vehicle?"

"Like it, yes. But it wasn't enough that I'd want to testify to it."

Since she is in fact testifying, the incongruousness of her remark causes some laughter in the courtroom. Merado gets it and smiles herself.

"But to drive down there and leave that print, the vehicle clearly had to be an off-road model, correct?"

"That's fair."

"Like that Cadillac Escalade?"

"Oh Jesus," says Jackdorp in pure exasperation.

"Stricken," says Judge Carrington. "The jury should disregard Mr. Jackdorp's latest outburst." She gives him another hot look, which as ever he feigns to ignore.

"Like a Jeep Wrangler," says Merado, "like, I don't know, dozens of models of cars and trucks. The larger off-roaders tend to have big wide tires."

Merado is beginning to resist me, because she thinks I'm doing what Jackdorp did, trying to get her to say more than the evidence warrants.

"Fair enough, Special Agent. Thank you for your expertise and your testimony. Nothing more." I smile at the judge, and she smiles too when I say, "For real, this time."

37

Fiber Good and Bad

The judge calls the lunch recess then. I'm eager to hear whatever it is that Susan learned at Home Warehouse, but she needs a minute to herself that will include changing into her usual outfit, which is where I left it, in a plastic hanging bag on a wooden coat rack in the rear corner of the courtroom. She's also famished and will call the Lamp, the diner across the street, for sandwiches, which they've been good enough to deliver throughout the trial. We plan to meet in the attorney/witness room in ten minutes. All she says about what she's going to tell me is, "You're going to be very happy."

I take advantage of the break to head to the men's room. Joe is just clumping his way out with his metal cane and his heavy oxfords. In the contrast of octogenarians from the families this case has pitted against each other, I have to acknowledge that Joe, long withered by disease, looks even worse than Mansy across the courtroom. For one thing, I know he is barely sleeping. He hasn't spent a night away from home in more than fifty years, except years ago when he passed out from drink, and for him the motel might as well be a bed of nails. Like his daughter, he's stopped eating, and his face, already hollowed by his various bouts of chemo, is growing skull-like. Somehow he seems more stooped than when the case started. He's changed his shirt today—now a dark blue button-down—but he's got on the same

suit and tie, what I take as his mourner's outfit. I draw him aside, pur-
portedly to ask what he made of Merado's testimony, but that's largely
a pretext to reassure myself that he's going to survive.

"She didn't know shit," he says. "But she doesn't think Aaron was
there with Mae's car. That's how I took it. Same as I've told you all
along."

I smile a little. I doubt there's a subject which Joe can't twist
around to enhance his own opinion of himself. But at least his pug-
nacious energy seems undiminished. I thank him and head into the
john.

As I come through the swinging door of the men's room, I find
myself inches from Hardy Potter, who is about to exit. This close to
him, I'm impressed by his size and a sense of his overheated masculin-
ity. He's a good three inches taller than me and holds his ground now
that he sees who he's facing. He plainly takes great pleasure in focusing on me with a menacing eye.

"Nice show," he says. "You're putting on a nice show."

"And it has the additional advantage of being true," I respond. I
try to step around him, but he grabs me by the bicep. For a second,
I'm afraid that it's the first move in what will end up as a punch, and I
self-consciously prevent myself from recoiling.

"Do I have to tell you that I didn't murder my daughter?" His
voice is louder than needed, which is clearly intentional. Some of the
jurors also end up using this facility, and I take it he already noticed a
couple of them inside. He's testifying in effect. For that reason, I realize how I must respond.

"Do I have to tell you that Aaron didn't kill her either?"

"That's crap," he says. I break away, but I don't get far. "You think
I don't know why you're doing this, bud?" he asks, and I turn back.
"You think I don't know why you want to grind your heel in my face?
It has nothing to do with Aaron. And I'm not the one to blame. I
never started any of that. All I ever did was say yes, when I got invited."

I know exactly what he's referring to—Bea, of course—but I summon the best actor inside me, an Oscar contender, and put on a mask
of complete incomprehension.

"What in the fuck are you talking about now, Hardy?"

And I sell it. The anger drains from his face, quickly replaced by the swimming uncertain look of the core Hardy, instantly convinced that he's screwed up. His mouth moves, and then he heads out, looking a bit deflated.

Yet I am surprised by what that new affect produces in me. Standing amid the unpleasant sounds and odors, I am suddenly full of what I've been suppressing in the courtroom, my sense of the agony this trial is causing all of them, Charmaine and Mansy and even Hardy. The worst part about murder cases, I always found, is that for the victim's family the clock stands still. Whatever distance and healing the mere passage of time might provide is withheld from them, as they relive the horrible details of the crime and endure the indignity of the defendant's denials. Their grief, their mourning, feels as everlasting as the agony of Prometheus, chained to that rock and having his body parts pecked at and consumed by scavenger birds every day.

In this instant, I would love to go out and tell Hardy, all of them, how sorry I am, how brutal I know this process is and how much I wish it were otherwise. Then I button my heart back into my chest and soon enough am on my way to Susan and whatever must come next.

Dr. Leland Shapera showed up at the top of the three or four lists of possible fiber experts, which Susan and I collected from law enforcement friends. He charged the highest hourly rate of any of the experts we considered, and I ultimately decided he was too expensive, even for an introductory conversation. Not so for Jackdorp.

Rarely challenged in his realm, Jackdorp was seemingly wounded by the many errors I accused him of in my opening, and he's decided to spend freely in hopes of buttressing his credibility with the jury. As I just learned from Susan over the lunch hour, it's not going to work.

And it's probably bad strategy anyway. I always thought the better course, even when I'd made a serious mistake, was to shrug and tell the jury that: 'Yeah, I'm human and maybe not as smart as I thought, and certainly not as clever as the bunch of you guys put together. But because you're so bright, you realize that the issue in this trial is not whether I'm a lamebrain, but whether the defendant has been proven guilty.'

Dr. Shapera is a PhD in chemistry who worked for DuPont for two decades, before returning to academia and a chair with a multimillion-dollar endowment at Carnegie Mellon. He holds that position jointly with his wife, another PhD, who is equally eminent but who never goes near a witness stand. They are now both world leaders in developing techniques to recycle nylon.

Dr. Shapera undoubtedly knows everything there is to say about nylon 6. Unfortunately, he wants everybody in the courtroom to realize that. I find his presentation, during which Jackdorp barely gets to ask a question, utterly snooze-worthy. Taking far too long, he explains the fiber characteristics of the rope located in our garage, and the many ways it corresponds with the various white filaments found in Mae's car and on her clothes and body, and at the campsite in Harold's Woods and in Aaron's closet.

"And is it fair to say," Jackdorp asks in his big windup, "that these many filaments of nylon 6, which you've identified in People's Group Exhibit 1-A—is it fair to say they 'match' this rope, People's Exhibit 1?"

Shapera offers a patient smile.

"As laypeople speak about these matters, it's perfectly fair. Naturally, as an expert, I'd use a different term. But yes, 'match' can be said to be accurate."

"And is the rope found in the garage of the house in which Aaron Housley was living, People's Exhibit 1, is that the source of the fibers in People's Group Exhibit 1-A?"

"Based on the totality of the evidence, I would say that is a substantial likelihood."

Jackdorp of course takes his seat at that point. Again, I just about run to the podium.

"Now, Dr. Shapera, I think you told us that you're being paid an expert fee by the people of Marenago County?"

Jackdorp stands with feigned indignance. "Object to 'people of Marenago County.'"

I respond as Jackdorp would, if the shoe were on the other foot.

"Really, Judge?" I say. "I've passed more than a week listening to Mr. Jackdorp talk about 'the people of Marenago County' whenever he can. If he prefers, I can say Dr. Shapera's bill is being paid by 'the taxpayers of Marenago County.'"

"Enough, both of you," answers Judge Carrington. "The objection is overruled. Mr. Sabich's remark is stricken. Mr. Sabich, you know better than that." References to 'taxpayers' have long been banned as an appeal to the financial interests of the jurors, which may bias them.

"Sorry, Your Honor," I reply.

"Answer, please, Dr. Shapera," she says.

"My fee," he says, "is being paid out of the budget of the Prosecuting Attorney's Office for Marenago County, which was approved many months ago."

"The numbers went by very quickly in your direct, but did I understand your hourly rate for court time, which certainly includes your testimony now, is fourteen hundred dollars?"

"That's correct."

"And so, according to my back-of-the-envelope math, including preparation, you're being paid more than twenty-five thousand dollars for your testimony here today, is that right?"

"I am being paid for my time, not my testimony. I took an oath to tell the truth and that, not any check, governs what I say here."

He's a smooth item. No doubt of that. Shapera is a kind of typical-looking older white dude, curly grey hair, a bit portly, who blinks often enough that I'm sure he's wearing contact lenses for his courtroom performance. He's donned a blue suit and tie. He looks quite professional.

"And am I correct about the amount?"

"I really can't answer. Billing is handled by my office. I pay no attention."

I just stand there smiling at him, giving him the side-eye. I glance to the jury. Mr. Rideau, the CPA, isn't buying that, for sure.

"You testified, Doctor, that there is 'a substantial likelihood' that the rope, People's Exhibit 1, was the source of the fibers contained in People's Exhibit 1-A, correct?"

"That is my opinion."

I take several steps closer to him.

"But there is no scientific basis to say People's 1, the rope from the garage, was the source of those fibers, is there?"

"As I testified, Counsel, my opinion is based on the totality of the evidence."

"Move to strike the answer as unresponsive."

"Sustained," says Judge Carrington. "Please answer the question, Doctor."

He asks for the question to be read back.

"I would say that because the fibers are all nylon 6 and People's 1 is made of the same material, that is the scientific basis of my answer."

"Are you saying, Doctor, that as a matter of scientific certainty, People's 1 was the source of those fibers?"

"I am not saying that."

"In fact, in a case like this, fiber science is unable to positively identify the source of any nylon fiber, correct?"

"It might be. I would need to think about that."

"Again, Doctor, fiber science is not like DNA. You can't positively identify the source of any fiber, to a reasonable degree of scientific certainty."

"I think I answered that."

"I think you didn't. Yes or no, can you identify to a reasonable degree of scientific certainty the source of the fibers in People's Exhibit 1-A, the collection of fibers?"

"As I say, I've answered." He directs a look to Jackdorp, clearly inviting him to object on that basis, and Jackdorp slowly rises to do exactly that. Judge Carrington instructs the court reporter to read the last several questions back. Then nods decisively. She's got it.

"Yes or no, Doctor?" she asks. "Can you identify to a reasonable degree of scientific certainty the source of the fibers in People's Exhibit 1-A?"

"No. Not without considering the other evidence."

Imitating the judge, I nod several times, to be sure the jury gets the point.

"Isn't it true that nylon 6 is a ubiquitous material, by which I mean it's everywhere?"

"I'd agree with that."

"And do you also agree that nylon ropes are a rather common household item?"

"I suppose I would say it depends on the household, but because nylon is waterproof and unusually strong, yes, it's frequently used, especially for outdoor needs."

"And nylon 6 is more or less standard in the manufacture of nylon ropes?"

"It's definitely the most common polymer used for nylon ropes."

"But it's also used for, say, the lining of sleeping bags or for carpeting?"

"It can be."

"And thus, there is an almost unlimited number of potential sources for the fibers introduced in evidence?"

"Not according to the proof in this case. There is only one object in evidence that could have produced those fibers."

"And when you talk about what is in evidence, what are you referring to precisely?"

"The rope. The video from the store surveillance camera."

"That's People's Exhibit 2?"

"I believe so."

"The receipt for that purchase? People's Exhibit 2-A?"

"Yes. I considered that."

"But isn't it a fact, Doctor, that People's Exhibit 1 is *not* the rope Aaron purchased?"

There is a second of pure silence, then Jackdorp rises to object.

"Mr. Sabich knows better than to phrase a question like that without an evidentiary basis."

"I have a clear evidentiary basis, Your Honor, as I'll shortly demonstrate."

Judge Carrington has her hand on her chin. She knows I'm up to something.

"You may proceed, Mr. Sabich, subject to a later motion to strike."

I take the rope from our garage, in its big heavy-duty clear plastic envelope, and place it on the rail of the witness stand.

"Is it correct to describe People's Exhibit 1 as a double-braided rope?"

"It is. That's what I've testified."

"And you testified, did you not, that a double braid is particularly strong, correct? Stronger than, say, a mere twisted-strand rope?"

"In a twisted rope, the two principal strands are simply wound around one another. With a double-braided rope, a braided jacket is wrapped around a braided core. So yes, it's stronger."

"And just to get to what you were implying during your direct, Doctor, someone thinking about strangling his girlfriend would prefer the stronger double-braided rope, right?"

He's a little taken aback by my boldness but smiles and says, "That would be a better choice, if that's what you had in mind."

"Whereas a mere twisted rope would be adequate if you were, say, just hanging something like a backpack from a tree to keep it away from bears?"

"Sure. Unless the backpack weighed several hundred pounds."

"And what is the diameter of People's 1?"

"I could measure, but I'm fairly certain it's three-eighths of an inch."

"Now, let me call your attention again to People's Exhibit 2-A, the receipt for the purchase of the rope Aaron is seen buying in People's 2. The product purchased is described as, and I quote, 'fifty-foot white nylon rope.' Correct?"

"I agree."

"Now to the left of those words there is an eight-character alpha-numeric notation preceded by the abbreviation S, K, U? Do you see that?"

He says yes. Susan has put it up on the monitor beside him now.

"And SKU is an abbreviation for stock-keeping unit. Do you know that, Doctor?"

"That sounds right."

"And it's on the receipt so the store can identify precisely the merchandise sold to a customer. Does that sound right, too?"

"It does."

"Now, Your Honor, with the Court's permission, I'm going to ask Ms. DeLeo to approach the witness with her laptop, which is open to the Home Warehouse website. And I'm going to ask Dr. Shapera to type the SKU number for the fifty-foot white nylon rope into the site's search bar."

Susan makes the wireless connection to the monitor. Wary, Shapera asks the judge's permission, then takes a second typing, looking back and forth to the receipt. What comes up on the screen at once is a picture of a coil of white rope, as expected. Manufactured by a company called Reliant, it's described as half an inch in diameter, with twisted strands, which is obvious in the photo. I make him read that printed description out loud.

"Is half an inch the same as three-eighths of an inch?"

"No, of course not."

"And you've already explained how a double-braided rope differs from a twisted-strand rope, right?"

"I have. But there's obviously been a mistake."

"We agree, Doctor."

"I mean in the inventory system at this company."

"On the contrary, Doctor, will you accept my representation that Ms. DeLeo visited this morning with the merchandise manager at the store identified in the upper right corner of the receipt, People's 2-A, that is Store 83, on State Route 47 in Skageon County, which is thirteen miles from Harold's Woods? And that the manager, a Ms. Heidi Klonek"—I spell the last name for the court reporter, and then make a show of writing the name down on a page of my legal pad, which I tear off and deliver to Glowoski with a flourish—"Ms. Klonek advised, after checking with the national distribution center in Ohio, that there has never been an exception reported about this SKU number: No merchandise returned because the SKU was incorrect, no complaints from the merchandise managers at any of the eighteen hundred Home Warehouse stores across the country about this particular product being mismarked. Will you accept my representation about that, or would you rather return to hear Ms. Klonek called as a witness for the defense?"

Jackdorp rises with a fusillade of objections, including that my recitation is rank hearsay, but Judge Carrington overrules them all. Even if my question is regarded as a hypothetical, it's proper cross-examination of an expert.

"Well, I'm sure you're not lying about that," Shapera says, "but I really don't understand."

"Excuse me, Dr. Shapera, but I think what's happened here is pretty obvious. Since the SKU information about this item has never been reported in error at close to two thousand stores, isn't it clear to you, sir, that this rope, People's 1, the garage rope, is *not* the big loop of rope that Aaron is seen buying in the video that's People's 2?"

He actually takes another few seconds to study Susan's laptop. He's enough into himself that what I've just said clearly had not dawned on him.

"I guess that's possible," he says. "But let me say, I'm familiar with this manufacturer, Reliant, and they use nylon 6 in all their cordage. So I wouldn't be wrong about all those fibers in 1-A."

"But you were wrong, Doctor, weren't you, when you testified that there was a substantial likelihood that People's 1, the rope from Aaron's garage, was the source of those fibers? Is that true?"

Again, he looks to the laptop before answering, "It might not be."

"In fact, Doctor, does this rope, People's 1, discovered in Aaron's garage, have any connection so far as you understand to the crime alleged in this case?"

"Well, there may be something I don't know about."

"You told us you were familiar with the evidence. Does it have any connection to the crime alleged?"

His eyes roll to the side as he again tries to think of a way out, then says, "I can't think of one. Again, assuming all that SKU stuff you mentioned is true."

"Your Honor, I move to strike People's 1 from evidence."

It's another pin-drop moment.

"Mr. Jackdorp?" she finally says.

"Judge, I didn't know a thing about any of this. I have to look into all of it."

"Your Honor, I think he just made my point," I say.

The judge can't resist a tiny smile. "People's 1 will be stricken, subject to the State's right to re-offer it if they can connect it to the crime on trial."

I march with the rope to a trash bin beside Moriah's desk and drop it in the can. Like a moron, Jackdorp runs right up and pulls the rope back out and returns to place it on the corner of the prosecution table. Which provides another opportunity to show him up.

"Your Honor," I protest, "that rope is no longer in evidence and has no business being displayed to this jury."

"Here," says the judge. "Let me have it." Jackdorp for a second looks like he is parting with a child. He hands the plastic package to the clerk, who passes it up to the judge, who drops it under the bench, completely out of sight.

I say I have nothing further and take my seat. So much for People's 1.

Because she has a hearing on a temporary restraining order, Judge Carrington announces that we are going to adjourn for the day. The break clearly suits both sides. Jackdorp doesn't want to do his direct of the pathologist and give me overnight to sharpen my cross. And Susan and I still need time to finish the homework that occupied us all weekend.

As the jury files out, I do my best to look completely pleased with myself about what we did to Shapera. So that some jurors can see it, I bend to whisper another compliment to Susan. Yet the truth is that what Susan learned about the rope, which overjoyed me at first, ended up putting my heart on a seesaw.

Right now, this is very good news for Aaron and his defense, because the prosecutor and his expert appeared to be catastrophically mistaken. But Jackdorp will recover eventually. And when he gives his closing, he will remind the jury that despite the stunts from the defense, the evidence still shows that Aaron bought a nylon rope, and a nylon rope was what was around Mae's neck when she died. And the rope Aaron bought was made of the same material as all the telltale fibers on Mae's body and in the car. That's bad news.

And yes, it was good that this development restored my confidence in Aaron. He was telling me the truth that the rope he bought was never brought back to our garage. But the bad news is that we have no way to account for that rope's whereabouts, unless I give in and allow Aaron to testify. Assuming I don't, that rope will take its place on Jackdorp's long list of items of Aaron's that are conveniently missing.

And yes, it's also good news that Bea had told me the truth about the rope. But it's bad news that the rope in our garage was Bea's—very bad given her many motives to be rid of Mae. Sitting alone in the attorney/witness room after hearing out Susan, I recognized the grim irony that Jackdorp may have been right to start: The rope in our garage conceivably was used to kill Mae Potter.

That possibility seemed to increase substantially when I pondered what Bea told Dom Filipini. From the start, it felt odd to me that she was so emphatic that there was no rope out in the garage. She's rarely in there except to park. But if Bea hid the rope on the shelves of the storage cabinet right after killing Mae, that, very sadly, would explain why she wanted to misdirect the police. For me, today's little triumph may end up being the worst news of all.

38

Pathologist

February 13

Last night's TRO hearing in Judge Carrington's courtroom did not finish. When I arrive, Moriah says that we'll be starting half an hour late this morning, and I return to the attorney/witness room for one last look at the reams of stuff I've brought with me for potential use in cross-examining the prosecution pathologist. That's where I am when Susan finds me, hanging her head around the door.

"Bad time?" she asks.

"Not perfect." I am in that anxious state where I fear that all the pathology I've stuffed into my brain will fall out if I allow a significant distraction. At a technical level, this will be the most difficult cross-examination of the trial, especially since I need to try to keep it uncomplicated enough for the jurors to understand.

"Okay," she says, then hesitates. She's clearly eager to report. "Do I ever get excited?"

The answer is no. Susan is the prototypical even-keeled professional.

"Well, I'm excited," she says. "I got some great stuff after court yesterday. I'm going to speak to Lainie Harop, the Missouri lady, again tonight. And I found something in the agents' notes that might be game-changing. I mean, I still need to button it all up."

I interrupt. "If it's not for sure, then let's put a pin in this. I'm not good with disappointment."

She smiles at my admission, but answers, "Sure sure."

Twenty minutes later, court convenes for today. The jury files in and Dr. Bonita Rogers, the Kindle County police pathologist, who conducted the autopsy on Mae, is called as the State's final witness. Jackdorp has saved what he regards as his best evidence for last. That is not because Dr. Rogers's opinions are unassailable—we have plenty of good questions in my judgment—but because they will be accompanied by gruesome pictures of Mae's unrecognizable body that are bound to disturb the jurors, much as they did me. In the photos Mae is bloated, and her skin has turned into a dusky patchwork of green, brown and black. Most of her hair has fallen out, leaving only a few dried-out spectral wisps, as well as all but two of her fingernails. Most difficult to view, her corpse is covered by flies and maggots that have eaten tiny holes in her flesh.

Jackdorp begins solemnly displaying the photos to the jurors on the monitor beside the witness stand as soon as he has qualified the doctor as an expert on forensic pathology. Interestingly, Jackdorp also made extensive reference to Dr. Rogers's work for a decade now as the Kindle County Unified Police Department's pathologist, highly familiar, as a result, with law enforcement practices. That means he intends to try more of the nonsense he went through with Glowoski, dressing up cop-think as a subject of expertise, which Judge Carrington probably will allow.

Jackdorp does an economical job on the physical evidence, getting into the confusing details of the science only as required. When found, Mae's body was well into putrefaction, a later stage of decomposition, which Dr. Rogers acknowledges makes postmortem examinations more challenging. Nonetheless, in this case the cause of death is clear: Mae died of occlusion of the carotid and jugular veins, due to strangulation. Anticipating a line of cross-examination, Rogers says that although the drugs in Mae's bloodstream may have hastened the time it took for her to expire, there is no question in Rogers's mind that the rope constricted around Mae's neck is what killed her.

Upon her autopsy, Dr. Rogers found no broken bones—not the trachea, the hyoid, or in the spine—but several factors support her conclusions about how Mae died. First, she testifies, basically reading from her report, "There is a black parchmentized line which remains largely visible around the neck, appearing as a horizontal mark above the cartilaginous cage over her vocal cords, then rising upward obliquely along the sides of her throat, until it becomes invisible on the back of her neck as it approaches the knobs of her cervical spine." On microscopic examination of that line, called 'the ligature mark,' the adjoining flesh of the neck, despite decomposition, displays a regular pattern of breaks in the skin suggesting blistering at the time of death, which is in turn characteristic of plastic rope. Finally, despite the decomposition, the body continued to exhibit signs of something called cadaveric spasm, which is generally known to accompany violent death. The hands and forearms are initially locked in the posture of desperate resistance in which they were raised when the victim died. As she rested on the car's floor under the passenger-side dashboard, Mae's head had eventually sagged to the left. Her right arm relaxed a bit, falling over her face, but her left hand was trapped beneath the side of her face, leaving the forearm, hand and fingers in the crippled pose in which they were first frozen as her life ended.

"There is also evidence suggesting a physical struggle preceding the strangulation," says Dr. Rogers, which picks up where George Lowndes left off. Given a few long dirt streaks on Mae's blouse and the putrefied signs of abrasions on her chest, Dr. Rogers believes that Mae was ultimately subdued and dragged some distance on her stomach. The presence of the rope fibers trapped in the hardened mud at a few spots near their supposed campsite suggests that this dragging might have been accomplished by looping the rope under her arms or around her torso. She must have broken away, Dr. Rogers thinks, and run to her car, but before Mae could lock the doors, the murderer was able to jump into the back seat and circle the rope around her neck.

"The physical evidence," Rogers says, "certainly indicates that Mae struggled against the attack. There are rope fibers all over the front of the Subaru cabin, but they are concentrated in the driver's seat area. The same fibers were found under Mae's two remaining fingernails, and there are boot prints on the screen of the center display and on the dashboard suggesting that Mae tried to get leverage to resist her attacker. The murderer was apparently far stronger than she and overcame Mae by sliding along the back seat. He pulled her over the center console and then, probably with his foot on her shoulder, drew the rope taut. Based on the angle of the ligature mark, the killer may have used the headrest on the passenger's side like a winch, winding the rope against it while he stood on Mae and pulled upward with all his might."

At some point within the first hour of Mae's death, Rogers says, the murderer pushed her torso further into the space under the dashboard, presumably so he would be able to drive the car. As a result, given the position of Mae's hands and the fact that the ligature mark becomes attenuated on the back of her neck, the first officers on the scene, careful not to disturb the body, were likely not to notice the black line around Mae's throat.

This chilling scene is augmented by a simple animation that Jackdorp has had prepared to create a literal picture of what Dr. Rogers is saying. The computer-generated figures move robotically, resembling a cartoon, but there's no missing the solemn effect the reenactment has on the jury. After Jackdorp passes the witness to me, the first thing I do is turn off the monitor.

The one expert we thought most seriously about hiring was our own pathologist. At Sandy Stern's recommendation, we interviewed one, quite famous after appearing on various true-crime TV shows, Dr. Malcolm Daner. We paid Dr. Daner to review the file, at the discounted rate of $1,000 an hour, and I then drove up to Minneapolis to speak to him face-to-face. He is eighty-two now and I understood immediately why he was so successful in court. He was genial and warm, the kind of old guy almost swollen with the happiness of living. Long ago, I fantasized about being that kind of person when I reached my dotage, but I've realized in recent years that I am too sour ever to assume his gentle, accepting demeanor. He is patient and wise-looking, with a thick white mustache and white trimmings over his ears, and otherwise bald. He remains clear as a bell.

The most startling thing Dr. Daner had to say came at the beginning of our meeting: 'It's not completely clear to me that this young woman was strangled.'

Before he explained, he added, 'I have a lot of respect for Bonita, and I certainly wouldn't testify that I regard her opinion as wrong. But it should be a bit qualified. Like all of us, she has her shortcomings.'

I said I'd been told she was arrogant and stubborn, and he smiled kindly.

'Well, I'd rather say that her vocabulary is short on three words.'

'And what are those?'

' "I don't know." '

Sandy had spoken about Bonita Rogers more tartly than Daner. Stern cross-examined her half a dozen times and regards her as a formidable witness—very smart, very well trained and widely credentialed. She is also a handsome human being, which is always an advantage in maintaining the jurors' attention. Now approaching fifty, she remains shapely, with hair the orangish-red of an orangutan, and large green eyes that stand out distinctly against her paper-white complexion.

Yet over the years, I have noticed that pathologists, whose 'patients' are, frankly, all dead, are often short on social skills. Rogers, according to Stern, is thin-skinned and haughty, quick to become combative in his view, and in consequence can put off some juries. Beyond that, Stern thinks that after a decade of working for the police department, and making a second marriage to an officer—a lieutenant in TAC—Rogers seems to have installed herself in the Blue Wall, ever eager to defend law enforcement.

Yet for all of that, both Daner and Sandy assured me that Rogers, after some initial struggle, would ultimately concede facts that are well documented in the medical literature. In other words, whatever Daner would testify to, Rogers should reluctantly concede on cross. Yet, as I stand to confront Dr. Rogers, I continue to regret the limits on the Housleys' resources that made us pass on hiring Daner, who, in the courtroom war of impressions, would almost certainly have kicked Rogers's butt. More pertinently, his testimony would have dramatically lessened the pressure on me now.

I start humbly.

"Dr. Rogers, as we both know, I am not a pathologist, so please feel free to correct my mistakes."

She hoods her eyes and smiles in a way that indicates she isn't buying my act.

"Certainly—" She hesitates. "I'm sorry, Counsel, what do people call you these days?" This is a jibe, even if it's one the jury won't understand. Rogers was already working in Kindle County when I was tried for Barbara's murder, and clearly is one of the many law enforcement types that never accepted my innocence. Whether Judge Carrington hears the same undertone, or is just unhappy that Rogers isn't following the protocol the judge set out for how I'm to be addressed, she frowns and injects herself quickly.

" 'Mr. Sabich' is fine here," she says pointedly.

Despite the minor nature of the correction, Rogers immediately justifies her reputation by delivering a sharp look at the judge. For one second, there is a staring contest between the two women. They are off to a bad start.

"Dr. Rogers," I say, "I want to go over only a couple of areas with you. The first concerns where Mae died. I take it from your testimony that you support the government's theory that Mae was killed at Harold's Woods. Her body was then driven to Ginawaban in the Subaru, which was subsequently concealed at the bottom of this wash, which we've all referred to as a utility road."

"I believe the totality of the evidence, including the pathological findings, supports the conclusion that Ms. Potter was murdered in Harold's Woods."

"I am going to ask you, Doctor, to consider a second possibility, namely that Mae died at Ginawaban."

"She didn't," answers Dr. Rogers, lifting her chin slightly to be even more emphatic.

One of the imperatives of cross-examination, especially with a strong figure like Dr. Rogers, is 'controlling the witness,' which means getting her to answer your questions, rather than the ones they wish you'd asked.

"Were you there at the time, Doctor?"

"Of course not."

"What you are expressing is merely your opinion, correct?"

"Correct."

"And what the jury is entitled to know is whether your opinions are well-founded?"

"Of course," she answers.

"Now, regarding Ginawaban as the site of Mae's death. I assume you have looked at the reports and testimony in this case in forming your opinions about the circumstances of the crime."

"I have."

"And because Mae's death was initially taken as an accident, is it fair to say, to the best of your knowledge, no other locations in Ginawaban were examined for clues? You saw no reports, for instance, of troopers looking there for the presence of plastic rope fibers, for example?"

"I don't recall reading reports concerning searches of other areas in Ginawaban. Which isn't surprising. It's a large preserve. And Mae's remains were discovered more than two weeks after her murder, meaning things like rope fibers would have been, as they say, gone with the wind." As a flourish, she adds a quick triumphant smile, amused at how her little joke puts me in my place.

"I'm sorry, Doctor. Did you hear me ask you why other locations weren't examined?"

"If you ask the question, I'm sure the jurors would want to know why something occurred."

I simply look up to Judge Carrington.

"Dr. Rogers," the judge says. "I don't know how they do things in Kindle County. But up here, we prefer that witnesses answer the question they've been asked without volunteering additional information."

Understanding that it's no compliment in front of a Marenago County jury to accuse anyone of acting like they were in Kindle County, Rogers gazes up again at the judge with plain irritation. Again, the judge stares back. I'm beginning to suspect that Rogers testified in that murder case Wendy Carrington tried when she was the state defender. The two appear to have an unpleasant history, and it would be just like Jackdorp to hire the same pathologist, to indicate to the judge that he still believes he was completely right.

"And when you examined Mae's body for autopsy and found those dirt streaks on her shirt, did you suggest a forensic soil study be done in order to confirm that the lines of dirt on Mae's blouse came from Harold's Woods?" I continue.

"I did suggest that."

"And the result was inconclusive, correct?"

"True."

"There was, in particular, more iron in the streaks on Mae's blouse than in any of the samples from Harold's Woods?"

"That's correct. Which might just mean they sampled the wrong places. It's a little bit of a needle in a haystack to guess the exact piece of ground she was dragged over."

"Was any soil from Ginawaban tested?"

"Not that I know of."

"Would you agree with me that as you go north in this state, there is more and more iron in the soil?"

"I don't know that."

"You've never gone north in our state, Doctor?"

Just from the snide look on her face, I sense that she's on the verge of saying that there's not much north of Kindle County she finds interesting. But she recognizes what a mistake that would be.

"I have. At times."

"Have you noticed the soil often gets redder and redder?"

"I guess. But I don't know if that reflects the presence of iron. And I'm not sure I've noticed that as far south as Ginawaban." She's wrong on both counts, which the jurors will know.

"And by the way, when we talk about Mae being dragged, isn't it commonplace when someone has been involved in a physical struggle for their life that they grab their attacker hard enough that some of the attacker's flesh ends up under their fingernails?"

"That's common, yes."

"And was there any foreign DNA—meaning somebody else's DNA—found under Mae's fingernails?"

"No, but I don't think that means much after two weeks of decomposition."

"But it wasn't there, correct?"

"It wasn't identified, no."

"Now, you spent some time talking about the position of Mae's body in the car. Is there anything about the position of Mae's body, and the related pathological evidence, that tells you she could not have died in Ginawaban?"

Rogers, for the first time, takes a moment to think.

"I haven't considered that before, but offhand, I would say no, assuming we're looking only at the pathological evidence."

"On the other hand, doesn't the position of the body make it less likely she died in Harold's Woods?"

"I certainly wouldn't say that."

"But you testified on direct that Mae's remains were moved after her death."

"I said that I believed the murderer pushed her torso further beneath the passenger-side dashboard."

"But her legs were adjusted, too, weren't they?"

I put up a photo of Mae's corpse as it was found, once the deflated airbag was removed.

"Would you agree with me that no one could drive for two hours with Mae's legs between himself and the steering wheel?"

"I assume he pushed them out of the way, but the testimony was that he rushed away from the scene, so who knows?"

"But if he pushed them out of the way in order to drive, that means he put them back when he reached Ginawaban?"

"Apparently."

I don't ask why he would do that, because I'm sure Rogers will answer that he wanted to make it look like Mae died in an accident.

"Now, how long does it take for rigor mortis to set in, by which I mean the natural process in which a body stiffens after death."

"The average is two to four hours, but it's highly variable."

"And do you, as a pathologist, have an estimate of the time of Mae's death?"

"A rough one, yes."

In response to my questions, she goes through the evidence. Lowndes saw Mae and Aaron quarreling around eight a.m. Her supposition is that Mae's murder followed soon after as the altercation turned physical. Mae's phone was powered down at 9:06 a.m., which, since it concealed her location, indicates she was probably dead by then.

"Eight forty-five then for the time of death?" I ask.

"Maybe."

"The Subaru passed through the tollbooth at 11:48. And it's at least another thirty minutes to Ginawaban, correct? So when Mae's remains arrived there, under your theory, rigor mortis might have been well underway. Meaning her body would have moved more or less as a piece. So when her legs were drawn back over the front seat, her corpse would have flipped on its back?"

She smiles like I'm a child.

"Too many assumptions, Mr. Sabich. Rigor can take up to six hours to begin in a fit young individual like Mae, who has high glycogen stores in her muscles."

Rogers and I go around for a few minutes on minutiae—how fast glycogen is depleted in a violent death, and the fact that the drugs in Mae's bloodstream might have hastened rigor mortis—but Rogers won't give ground.

"But you will agree, Doctor, that rigor would not have set in if Mae died at Ginawaban, with her body disposed of shortly after."

"That would be true."

"So if Mae had been placed in the driver's seat of the Subaru soon after her death at Ginawaban, without securing her seat belt, and the car was then pushed down the utility road where it crashed at the bottom, wouldn't her body have ended up in the exact position in which it was found? Wasn't that, in fact, the opinion of the accident reconstructionist who came to the scene on September 28, when Mae's remains were discovered? And doesn't all that make it far more likely that she died at Ginawaban?"

"I've already agreed, Mr. Sabich, that the pathological evidence alone does not establish the site of death. You can spin whatever stories you like to make it possible she was killed at Ginawaban. But there is a lot of other evidence that is consistent with Harold's Woods as the place where she was murdered: The rope fibers in the mud there. Mr. Lowndes's testimony about the driver. And the tollbooth photo that corroborates him."

I pause to shoot Susan a look. We got that one right.

"And by that you mean the black-and-white photo of the license plate on the Subaru from the tollbooth camera?"

"Yes."

"And what is it about that photo that makes you say it corroborates Mr. Lowndes?"

"Well, I see hands on the steering wheel that belong to a darker-skinned individual."

"I see." I put the photo up on the monitor.

"And in your role as police pathologist, have you frequently examined tollbooth photos of license plates?"

She shrugs. "Maybe once or twice."

"Are you an expert on how the tollbooth cameras actually work?"

"No, I wouldn't say that. But I have eyes in my head, Mr. Sabich, and I know what I'm looking at."

I stop and ask the court reporter to mark Dr. Rogers's last answer.

"The cameras on the tollbooths are made by a company called Northern Direct. Did you know that?"

"I have no reason to know that," she says.

"Well, Doctor, would it surprise you to learn that a witness from Northern Direct, a senior vice president for engineering, testified before the state assembly when those cameras were scheduled for installation on our toll roads in 2012? And as background, Doctor, civil libertarians across the political spectrum were very concerned that the cameras might become an avenue for spying on citizens. And as a result, a Dr. Dalbert Fornier was called before the State Assembly Committee on Roads and Transportation and said this, under oath, about what those cameras see and record." I hand her a copy of the transcript that Susan obtained and provide another to Jackdorp, who takes only a second to jump to his feet.

"Judge, I knew nothing about this."

Judge Carrington looks down at Jackdorp, vexed by him as always, but also clearly startled. We're back to where we were yesterday with the fiber expert when Jackdorp tried to use his lack of preparation as some kind of argument against the admission of evidence.

"Mr. Jackdorp," she says, "is that an objection or a confession?"

The last word, 'confession,' is far more stinging than Judge Carrington has allowed herself to be with him previously. Without waiting for him to answer, she does my job for me and explains to the jury that prior testimony under oath is not regarded as hearsay and that the defense is under no obligation to share its cross-examination in advance with the prosecution. "Proceed," she tells me.

I ask to display the Fornier transcript for the jury, and it comes up on the monitor.

"'The G-42,'" I read, "which I represent, Dr. Rogers, was the camera model over the tollbooth near Ginawaban in September 2023, 'the G-42 focuses on the auto license plate. The resulting images do not reliably reflect any details from the automobile interior. Because of the focal length of the camera, all persons within the car appear indistinct and dark, without any marked differences between them. Any variation in the images from a given camera is the result of the time of day and other variables concerning lighting.' Then, under questioning by one of the state reps, Assemblyman Lemeke Brooker, Dr. Fornier answered as follows, 'Yes, Assemblyman Brooker, that is correct. The camera functions so that everybody in the front seat of the car, everyone is going to look pretty much the same. You won't be able to tell the race of the driver, the hair color, the eye color, whatever. It would definitely be incorrect for law enforcement or anyone else to think the license plate image provides any clue about the identity of the driver or passengers.' Do I appear to have read that testimony, given under oath by Dr. Fornier, correctly?"

Still recovering, Dr. Rogers takes a second to agree.

"And your opinion that the tollbooth photo shows a darker-complected driver, because you have eyes in your head and know what you're looking at—you were wrong, weren't you?"

"I was just looking at the picture," she says.

The judge, hugely irritated, immediately intervenes.

"Answer the question, please, Dr. Rogers. You were wrong, weren't you, to say that the photo reflects a darker-complected driver?"

Rogers actually glances back to the copy of the photo she's holding, in a seeming last attempt to avoid admitting the mistake.

"Well?" says the judge.

"Yes, I was wrong," Rogers finally says. On the bench, Judge Carrington shudders in frustration. I'm convinced now that the two have tangled before. I also suspect that Judge Carrington is offended by the racial subtext, the eagerness to blame a Black man without any further investigation. There have been hints before that the judge thinks Jackdorp is a bigot. On the other hand, I know something Judge Carrington may not, that Dr. Rogers's new husband, Hugh Maxfield, the police lieutenant, is African-American. I've learned that from my Sunday readings of the Kindle County *Tribune*, where he's frequently mentioned as a potential candidate to become chief. In my own mind, the lapse involving the photograph—which was really Glowoski's—is less about racism and more about confirmation bias, the readiness with which law enforcement views evidence in a light that makes it fit their case.

"And does that cause you to reconsider your opinion about where Mae died?"

"There's still the eyewitness testimony at Harold's Woods. About the driver."

"Given by a man who was not wearing his prescription glasses, who was looking across the road through the tinted glass of the auto as it raced past him while he was jumping out of the way. And whose wife might not have agreed with him about who was driving. Do you see any potential for error in that testimony, Dr. Rogers?"

"I see it, but I think it's up to the jury to decide what to conclude about Mr. Lowndes." Her sudden deference to the jury will be well received in the box, but is clearly a cop-out.

"Given the quote unquote 'totality of the evidence,' Doctor, it's quite possible that Mae died at Ginawaban and not Harold's Woods, isn't it?"

"That is possible, yes."

"And you were wrong when you unequivocally declared that she didn't?"

She takes a second. "I still think there's a good chance she was murdered at Harold's Woods. There's nothing that shows that she wasn't. But I should not have been so emphatic. She might have been killed at Ginawaban too."

I could stop here. Because the cell tower evidence shows Aaron was nowhere near Ginawaban. But this is where Dr. Daner comes in.

"I didn't say she was killed up here, Doctor. I said she died. Isn't it true, Doctor, that even absent putrefaction—even much sooner after death than Mae's body was found, pathologists find it difficult to distinguish a strangulation from a hanging?"

I've caught her completely off guard. She responds slowly.

"It can be," she says.

"And in the various studies that pathologists have written on this subject, they have suggested when looking at the ligature mark, which I'll call a rope burn for convenience, there are three ways to tell a hanging from a strangulation. If the mark is below the Adam's apple, that suggests strangulation, because, in hanging, the weight of the body pulls the rope up higher on the throat. Is that right?"

"Yes."

"Where's the ligature mark, the rope burn, on Mae?"

"Above the cage of the larynx."

"Which would mean it's consistent with hanging?"

She frowns and doesn't bother with a response.

"The second factor noted in the medical literature is that if the rope burn rises up at an angle—it rises obliquely—that suggests hanging, because a strangler ordinarily would be immediately behind his victim. You've already told us that the rope burn here is oblique."

"Yes. For the reasons I suggested. He'd pushed her down to the floor and winched the rope around the headrest, with a foot on her shoulder."

"But the oblique angle of the rope burn is usually taken as suggesting hanging?"

"It's consistent with hanging."

"And the third way a rope burn can distinguish hanging from strangulation is if the mark is 'discontinuous,' meaning it doesn't completely encircle the neck. Because in a hanging, the weight of the body pulls the rope away very slightly from the slipknot. Is this mark discontinuous?"

"That's what it looks like, but that could be because of the state of decomposition."

"Or because she hanged herself?"

Dr. Rogers again takes a second to consider things, sitting up very straight in her chair.

"I will agree that the ligature mark in this case is consistent with both hanging and strangulation. But there is other evidence that leads me to conclude that she was strangled. The boot print on the dashboard. The signs of a physical struggle on her body, including the abrasions on her chest, and the rope fibers under her fingernails."

I deal with those quickly. Merado acknowledged yesterday that Mae could have left boot prints on the center console when she pulled her seat back and was having a conversation, perhaps at a rest stop. And Rogers agrees that people who hang themselves cannot stifle an instinctive response, and quite often claw at the rope, which could account for the fibers under Mae's fingernails. In fact, depending on where Mae hanged herself, her body could have bumped against something, say a tree, as she was thrashing around reflexively while she was dying, leading to the abrasions. On the last point, Rogers is more skeptical.

"I think that's far less likely, Mr. Sabich. But, frankly, this discussion is silly. I give you points for reading the medical literature, and you're having your fun, but Ms. Potter didn't hide her car at the bottom of a road after she was dead."

She gets a good strong gust of laughter with that one. I remain sober-faced, waiting for the amusement to subside.

"That is true, Doctor, but is there anything in the pathological evidence that disproves the possibility that soon after Mae hanged herself, a loved one came upon her and hid the body so that her mother, for example, didn't know that her child had taken her own life? After removing the rope from whatever it was tied to, that person transferred her to the front seat of the Subaru, cut the noose off her there, and then sent the car down the road with the goal of delaying discovery of Mae's death as long as possible, and making it look like a car accident, if she was ever found. Is that possible?"

"I don't know of any evidence to support the notion of a well-intentioned third party concealing Mae's suicide. That strikes me as a theory conveniently concocted to fit the proof."

"Are you aware that Mae's mother has testified that she suffered from borderline personality disorder and sometimes threatened to kill herself?"

"I mean evidence of this imaginary third person. You might as well say her body was concealed by the Easter Bunny." Someone behind me laughs again at that, but I can't tell if they're chuckling at Rogers's snottiness. Dr. Rogers is turned sideways behind the sycamore rail of the witness stand so she doesn't have to face me and my stupidity. Her plump mouth is fixed in a dismissive frown.

"On the contrary, Doctor, can you name *any* physical evidence that disproves that theory?"

Her eyes shift around as she thinks.

"Without commenting on the likelihood of your theory, I guess I'd say no."

"Since you mention physical evidence, there is one other piece of pathological evidence that is more or less determinative in telling a hanging from a strangulation, isn't there?"

"You obviously have something in mind, Mr. Sabich, so go ahead."

"But it's not occurring to you?"

"Not in the middle of cross-examination." She gets an understanding laugh on that one from somewhere in the jury box—Mr. Rideau, I believe.

"Well, hanging victims, unlike the victims of strangulation, often display hemorrhages in their legs, don't they? Because the heart can no longer pump blood to the head, blood pressure increases dramatically in the lower extremities, leading some of the blood vessels in the legs to burst. Does that happen?"

"Yes, that's right. That happens frequently in hanging cases."

Susan illuminates the next pictures on the monitor.

"Now, calling your attention to your own autopsy photos, these two black areas on each of Mae's calves—could they have been hemorrhages?"

"They could be spots where hemorrhagic blood has putrefied, or simply putrefaction as part of the process of decomposition. As I told you before, no one can say one way or the other."

"Even though they are in the same location on each calf?"

"Same answer, Mr. Sabich."

"But if they were hemorrhages, that would be rather convincing evidence that Mae died of hanging?"

"She didn't hang herself." Unlike her snide declaration that Mae didn't die at Ginawaban earlier in her testimony, Dr. Rogers now sounds like a sullen spoilsport. She again has turned half away from me in her chair.

"On the contrary, Dr. Rogers, doesn't the pathological evidence, including the position of the body, the ligature mark, the hemorrhages, isn't it all consistent with Mae dying by hanging at Ginawaban?"

"I will leave it to this jury, Mr. Sabich, to decide if they find your theory as far-fetched as I do."

"Move to strike," I say, and the judge tersely instructs Dr. Rogers to answer the question I asked.

She straightens up again, attempting to strike a pose of great dignity.

"I will grant that the pathological evidence does not disprove Mae dying by hanging at Ginawaban. Common sense might suggest otherwise. But not the pathology."

The remark about 'common sense' knots Judge Carrington's face in anger, but there's been enough of Dr. Rogers and I declare that I am done.

39

The Game

Jackdorp's redirect of Dr. Rogers is halting. He repeatedly tries to get her to use the word 'speculation' to describe my questioning, but she is clearly upset with him, probably about the tollbooth photograph, and responds stiffly, often with one-word answers. I don't bother with recross and she leaves the courtroom like a marching soldier, head held high, looking neither left nor right, a posture that seems to dismiss everybody here.

Jackdorp then stands and says in his customary gravedigger's tone, "The People rest." The declaration means the prosecution may offer no further evidence, except in response to whatever is presented by the defense. Far more important, he and Glowoski are putting down their marker that the government has satisfied its duty to prove the defendant guilty beyond a reasonable doubt.

Judge Carrington releases the jury for the day, and then says that this afternoon she will hear the lawyers argue the motions that are customarily made when the prosecution concludes its case. Tomorrow morning, we must begin the defense evidence, if there is any. Some of my questioning and comments recently have more or less committed us to calling a couple of witnesses, but the question of whether the defendant will testify is one the judge is bound to ask me soon.

Critical decisions loom. Before this afternoon's session, I need a word with Aaron, who has a right to make a significant tactical call. I tell the court that my client has elected to be present for today's arguments, and she instructs the court officers not to return him to the jail. After we adjourn, Susan offers me a solid fist bump, and strong praise for my cross of Rogers, which is one of the few positive developments for the defense during the trial for which I deserve more credit than Susan. She wants to skip the afternoon of argument—it's all typical, and we both know the outcome—so she can pursue the two open matters she described to me this morning.

She packs up and goes at once, while I knock on the door in the paneling that will admit me to the lockup. When I come in, Aaron is standing over the seatless stainless-steel cloaca, peeing with his back to me. Public excretion is one of the many privations of confinement I never really got used to, and I turn to face the door until I hear the hoarse flush. After washing in the tiny sink, he picks up the bologna sandwich and the Coke he has been given for lunch each day. With the sandwich in hand, he draws close to me beside the bars.

"Can I ask you about the stuff with the police doctor?"

"Sure."

"Do you think that's true? That Hardy found her hanged and decided to make it look like an accident?"

I told Aaron long ago about my visit with Dr. Daner, but he clearly was in the stage where he was overwhelmed by everything and not processing all the information he was getting from Susan and me.

"What do you think, Aaron?" I ask. "Do *you* think she could have killed herself?" Although I've typically avoided in-depth conversations with Aaron in the lockup, for fear of being overheard by the court staffers who might report back to Jackdorp, I saw both court officers step outside to eat their own lunch.

"I kind of panicked when you brought that up with Charmaine. Because, you know, it would sort of be my fault."

"How is that?"

"Because, you know, I hung up on her. And she was saying exactly that. 'I'm going to kill myself, I can't live without you.'"

His reference to the phone call he says he got from Mae on September 14, while he was hitchhiking in the wrong direction, strikes me completely differently today than it did on Saturday, now that I know he was telling the truth about the rope. In fact, his focus on the part of the conversation that in his mind might even make him somewhat blameworthy for Mae's death pretty much convinces me that the call in fact occurred—although I still can't understand how that squares with the phone records. Then again, even the little bit that Susan said this morning about the woman from Missouri makes me hopeful now that there's more to that story.

"You know," he says, "the thing with Mae is she was always saying outrageous shit, and you'd say to yourself, She'll never do that. But then she did. So you know, even though I don't like to think I should have taken her seriously, that actually makes the most sense of anything else—that she hanged herself."

As Dr. Daner first pointed out, the pathological evidence of hanging is significant. But even taking that as a possibility, my guesses about how her body and the Subaru ended up at the bottom of the utility road strike even me as unlikely. Rogers was right that my theory of a benevolent stranger who decided to hide Mae's remains has no real evidentiary support, except for all the shadows I've tried to cast on Hardy.

But right now, I need to draw Aaron back to this afternoon's arguments, because I want to give him a couple of minutes to reflect on what might be a somewhat fateful decision. Both motions that are in my briefcase—albeit on a single page in each case—are ones the defense routinely offers when the State's case is over, made in order to preserve certain issues for appeal. In the first, we will maintain that the State's evidence is so weak as to require the judge to dismiss the case. That is a largely hopeless venture. In considering that motion, a judge is required to give the State the benefit of every doubt. For today's purposes, George Lowndes will have the eyes of a kingfisher, cell towers can receive signals from fifty miles away or farther, and both the suspect shoeprints on Mae's blouse and in the mud at Ginawaban were made by Aaron. Even Judge Rusty Sabich of the superior court, the man I was for close to a decade, would deny that motion after applying the governing legal standards. "The trickier question, Aaron, is whether we press the judge to grant a mistrial."

"What does that mean anyway? I keep hearing the word, but maybe I don't understand."

"It means we scrub this trial and start again, assuming Jackdorp wants to tee it up all over."

"He will," says Aaron.

I agree. Hardy, if no one else, would never accept dropping the case. And it's a hard sell for any prosecutor to tell the voters that he's setting free a person he's said is a coldhearted killer.

A mistrial based on prosecutorial errors, which is what this would be, gives the defense some advantages that don't apply after a hung jury. If delay was what we wanted, we could launch an appeal claiming that Jackdorp's errors were intentional and thus that Aaron's retrial should be forbidden as double jeopardy. Yet that's a steep hill legally, and while I was on the appellate court, we never ruled that way, despite some fairly strong cases. Again, Jackdorp might offer a plea deal, but I can't imagine Aaron would ever accept it, without the stimulus of seeing a strong majority of a jury prepared to find against him.

"I don't know if at the end of the day the judge will grant us a mistrial," I say. "For one thing, if she does, she has to do all the work again, too, and that will mess up her calendar. But there's been enough—all of Jackdorp's stunts and the notes about Mrs. Lowndes—that if I am really strenuous about it, she might say okay. So the question is whether you have a better chance of walking away in this trial or the next one."

Susan has already cast her vote. She is a veteran of the defense wars and accepts the age-old wisdom that it's a triumph for the defense whenever you stop the prosecution from gaining a conviction. The rock for them is harder to push up the hill every time they try, especially knowing the first effort did not succeed. Witnesses like Lowndes may have a change of heart about testifying again, or Mrs. Lowndes might relent and talk to us. And in a second trial, the defense has some built-in advantages. No human ever repeats a story exactly the same way, which means there will be inconsistencies we can highlight.

"But Aaron, we've caught them by surprise several times. And they'll be better prepared. I may have proved too much today. Maybe they'll try the next case on the theory that Mae died at Ginawaban.

And Dr. Rogers will have better answers about why Mae didn't hang herself. Maybe they'll call the shrink who saw Mae to testify that he saw no real evidence of suicidal ideation. Maybe they can document Hardy's whereabouts every second on September 14, so they can show he was never near Ginawaban.

"And we'd have to be really lucky, Aaron, to get as good a jury next time. The odds say we'll never see three people of color in the box. Or somebody who knows Susan. So you know, the basic problem with a mistrial motion is, be careful what you wish for."

"So skip it?"

"No, that's the conundrum. I've got to make the motion to preserve the issue for appeal. It's just a matter of how emphatic I am. Judge Carrington's been playing this game for decades. She can read the signals. If I say we're renewing our motion for a mistrial, but we'll stand on our prior arguments, there's very little chance she'd grant it."

"Well, look," says Aaron. "I'd really hate to have to go through this again. Like really hate it. But nowhere near as much as I'd hate getting convicted. So I've got to follow your advice and Susan's. Tell me what you think."

I explain Susan's point of view.

"But what about you?" Aaron asks.

This is where being a lawyer with a client, an experience I've barely had before, gets really tough, because you're rolling the dice with someone else's life. If Aaron were convicted, I'd kick myself until my final rest for not pressing for a mistrial.

"I think we should go to verdict with this jury. If you disagree, I'll be happy to follow your instructions. And frankly, I may even change my own mind, depending on how Judge Carrington reacts during the first argument. If I thought there was a real chance she'd prohibit a retrial, then I'd push mistrial. But knowing what I know right now, I say, let's go forward."

"Let's go forward," he says. Then adds, "But I still want to testify."

I knew there was a good chance that we'd get back to that.

"We're not there yet," I say.

"Why not?"

"Susan tells me she's developing some great stuff for the defense case."

"Like what?"

I explain that we didn't have time to talk about it this morning, but Susan said she was excited.

"She actually used the words 'game-changing.' By the time we come to court in the morning, she'll be able to brief us both."

"I won't back off, Rusty," he says.

"I understand, Aaron. But we both have to see how it plays out. If she's found someone who wants to come in and confess to Mae's murder, would you still want to testify?"

He laughs. "Okay, you got me."

But somehow my example launches a stroke of fear across my heart, which I understand as I reenter the courtroom. Another dark fantasy. What would I do if Bea came to me tonight to say she wanted to do exactly that—confess? I'd let her, I suppose. But do I really think that's possible? I oscillate, moment by moment, between grave doubts about Bea and times when I am frustrated with myself even for entertaining these thoughts.

I go back to the judge's chambers to file with Moriah the simple motions that I will present this afternoon. She's there but gives me some bad news. Since the judge doesn't expect the hearing on my motions to require the entire afternoon, she's decided to let the lawyers on the TRO—which aims to stop construction of a seven-story commercial and apartment building in downtown Portage—make their final arguments first. I have an extra hour at least.

With the time, I go across the street to the diner and eat a quiet lunch, instead of bolting down a sandwich, which has been my routine since jury selection. Naturally, I can't resist a hamburger and fries, because discipline in this realm seems beyond me, given all the self-control required in the courtroom. I consume every fry even though I know that another pound or two might mean I won't be able to button my suit pants when we get to closings.

When I return to the courtroom, the first set of lawyers haven't finished their presentation to the judge. By the time she's ruled on that case, it's approaching four o'clock. I've stood up to reoccupy the defense table, when my phone lurches in my pocket. I've assigned Susan her own signal by now, and I feel the two quick pulses. Since the judge is back in her chambers signing the orders that will allow the building to proceed, I go out to the corridor to find out what's up. 'Call ASAP,' she's written, but when I do, her line is busy. In response, she texts almost immediately.

> 'On phone, sorry. Great stuff. Go easy on mistrial. You'll want verdict.'

Perplexed by her change of heart, I text back a line of question marks.

She does not have time to provide more than two words in reply.

> 'He's innocent.'

III.

The Defense

40

Brice

February 14

B rice Flynn, the father of Cassity's son, is the first witness when we open the defense case on Wednesday morning. We have no choice about calling him, if we want to account for why Aaron's Nikes are not to be found. Susan explained that there was only a brief window when Brice would be available, but initially, I was reluctant to start the defense with Brice, fearing the impression he might make. The young man I saw with Aaron last September always seemed to read slacker, with his haphazard mullet-like hairdo and his drifting, unfocused look. He was a little soft around the middle in his washed-out T-shirts and he gave the impression overall of being one of those men who grew far taller than he expected and was still not sure about the outer bounds of his body.

Today Brice enters the courtroom in the blue dress uniform of a Coast Guard seaman, with a blue tie and the long coat with gold buttons over matching trousers. They have taught him to stand up straight and to look people in the eye, as he does when the judge swears him in. He has been a seaman for all of a week now, when he finished basic training. His hair is gone, sheared to a stubbly fuzz. He is only briefly available because he is going back for three more months for what is called A School. Then he will enter the Coast Guard Reserve, spending a weekend a month assigned to port security in Chicago, Kindle County or Milwaukee.

"Seaman Flynn," I start, "thank you for your service. You are here pursuant to subpoena?"

He answers yes, that the subpoena was necessary so he could get an additional day of leave.

"Do you know the defendant, Aaron Housley?"

"Yes sir."

"How long?"

"All my life, sir."

"Did you go to school together?"

"We went to the same school, sir. He always liked school way more than me, so he was in a lot more advanced classes, but yes sir, we walked in and out of the same building every day for twelve years."

"And calling your attention to the second half of September in 2023, did you work with Aaron?"

"Yes sir."

"Can you explain?"

"Yes sir. Aaron had a job he really liked, doing graphic design for an event planner in Como Stop, but you know, it's seasonal, and so he got laid off after Labor Day. I had started painting houses for extra money a couple of summers back, and when I got to the middle of September, I had more jobs than I'd be able to finish before the weather started to turn. Below 50 degrees, you can have a problem with some of the paints. So I asked Aaron if he could help me out for a couple of weeks."

"He worked for you?"

"Yes sir. Sort of."

"You said, mid-September. Can you correlate the period that Aaron worked with you to any trips he'd taken with Mae Potter?"

"Yes sir. He'd just gotten back from that."

"How did you know?"

"Well, he told me he was going away with her, and we agreed he'd start painting with me when he got back."

"Did he talk about what happened with Mae?"

"He kind of didn't want to talk about it. He was, you know, pretty bummed. He just said—"

Jackdorp interrupts with a hearsay objection which Judge Carrington sustains. Aaron's out-of-court statements can't come into evidence, unless the prosecution goes into a particular conversation first, as they did with a number of their witnesses.

"And by the way, when you and Aaron starting working together right after he returned from his trip with Mae, did you notice any serious cuts or bruises or other signs that he'd been in a fight?"

"I don't know if he's ever been in a fight. He's kind of a lover, not a fighter."

Someone on the jury chuckles. I glance quickly to find it's Mr. Smith, the African-American farmer.

"But you saw no sign on him that he'd recently been in any kind of physical struggle?"

"No sir. That would have really surprised me, so I probably would have noticed."

"Now, do you know what kind of shoes Aaron was wearing when you and he began working together?"

"Yes sir. He had a pair of white Nikes. Air Force 1s."

"And why do you know that?"

"Well, you know, frankly, you get a lot of paint on your shoes, doing what I do. And I was at Aaron's birthday when Joe gave Aaron those shoes, and I knew he liked them. I told him to wear booties, but you know, he never cared for being up that high on a ladder to start with, and the booties, the plastic shoe coverings, they're a little slippy. He was afraid to move. So he painted in his shoes, and I promised him I'd give him money for another pair."

"What happened to the Nikes?"

"Well, sir, he wore them every day. We worked thirteen days straight until I was sure I could finish the rest of the houses by myself. The shoes were pretty bad by then."

"What do you mean by 'pretty bad.'"

"They were covered in paint, sir, even the soles, all kinds of colors. And the paint, when it dried, kind of shrunk the shoes a little. And a lot of latex paint dried on the laces, too, and in the openings for the laces, so in the end, he couldn't even untie them. He said it was so hard getting his feet in and out, for the last couple nights he actually slept with the Nikes on."

"And when did Aaron stop working for you?"

"It was the Kitniks' house. That was a Thursday. Originally, he said he'd help me for two weeks, but— He's a great artist, you know, he loves to paint on canvas or paper, but you know, house painting, I don't think that's ever going to be his jam. He never really got to like the ladder. So when I was sure I could finish the other houses on my own, I told him, you know, 'If you're sick of this, I'm okay without you.' I didn't have to say it twice."

Aaron, when I glance back, is smiling, amused by Brice's description. He's said that he spent close to two weeks, ten hours a day, completely terrified.

"And what, if anything, did Aaron do with his shoes?"

"While I was breaking down the ladders and picking up the drop cloths, he got an X-Acto knife and cut the shoes off himself. I drove him home barefoot."

"What happened to the shoes?"

"Straight into the trash. We had a garbage can right in the driveway there in front of the Kitniks' house, because we'd had to tear off some rotten fascia board. And he threw the shoes right in it."

"You saw it?"

"Yes sir."

"And do you recall the timing of when he threw the shoes away in relation to when you learned Mae's body had been discovered?"

"That was a few hours before he heard anything about it."

Jackdorp objects successfully to what Aaron had heard.

"How did you hear about Mae's death, Brice?"

"Cassity called me when I got home to tell me to read this article on the Internet."

I show him the item from the Patch, which is labeled 'Breaking News Exclusive.' The dateline is 6:32 p.m.

"And the shoes were thrown away before that? You're sure?"

"Positive. We'd been working hard to make sure we finished that job. You need to be done well before sunset. When the light gets low, it's hard to see how the paint is going on. So we stopped no later than six p.m. And we were done before that, more like five thirty that day."

Prosecutors are often poor cross-examiners, because their opportunities are limited. Most defendants rest without presenting evidence and even then, they usually don't call more than two or three witnesses. Defendants themselves testify even less frequently, since more and more jurisdictions, including our state, have enacted sentencing laws requiring defendants who are convicted after testifying to get more time in prison. The courts have ruled that a longer sentence is not punishment for exercising your constitutional right to be a witness on your own behalf, but rather, for perjury. I haven't explained this part to Aaron yet, but it's one more reason he shouldn't get on the stand.

Jackdorp, however, is much better on cross than I hoped, although I doubt he'll ever approach any defense witness without an accusatory air.

"So you're the defendant's lifelong friend?" he asks Brice.

"Yes sir."

"And you visited with him before trial?" Jackdorp has papers in his hand, which I'm sure are the sign-in sheets from the jail. At Judge Carrington's direction, the jury still hasn't been told Aaron has been held behind bars, which suits both sides. I don't want them wondering what there is in Aaron's background that might have made him a poor candidate for bail, while Jackdorp doesn't care to have anybody in the jury box who's dubious about conviction driven further in that direction by learning Aaron's already endured some punishment.

"Yes sir. Several times. Before I shipped out for Basic."

"Talked to him, of course?"

"Of course."

"Did you talk about those shoes?"

"Sort of."

" 'Sort of'? Did you talk about testifying about those shoes?"

"He said they were important in the case and Rusty would be calling me to be a witness."

"Important how? Did he tell you that he needed to explain what happened to the shoes?"

"I think so. Maybe."

Jackdorp rolls his lips and takes time to deliver a knowing nod.

"Now you've come here and taken a vow to God to tell the truth, is that right?"

"Yes sir."

"And do you know Cassity Benisch?"

"Yes sir. She's my girlfriend." I sit up a little and look to Susan. Like me, she has no idea where this is going.

"More than your girlfriend, isn't she? Isn't she the mother of your child?"

"Yes sir. I was just trying to give you a simple answer."

"And did you ask her to marry you, when you understood she was pregnant with your child?"

"Yes sir."

"You were prepared to make a vow to God and her and your community to honor her and be faithful to her, is that right?"

"Yes sir."

"And did you understand that vow to God and everybody else to be as important as the oath to God you took today to tell the truth?"

"More important, actually."

"And did you regard yourself as bound by that vow even before you had that marriage ceremony?"

"I suppose. Yes."

"And did you honor that vow to honor her and be faithful to her?"

Briefly word-struck, Brice looks at me. I wish I'd seen this coming, and I'm sorry he's being humiliated this way. I think about objecting, but Jackdorp did a clever job of setting up the equivalence for Brice of his commitment to Cassity and the oath he took today. I'll be overruled and look bad to the jury for trying.

"I didn't," Brice finally says with his eyes in his lap.

"And Cassity refused to marry you, didn't she, because you were the kind of man who didn't keep his word in these solemn matters?"

"I don't know why. She was angry. And real hurt. And I've been trying to change her mind for three years now, and I think I have. I mean, that's what I'm doing in this uniform. To prove to her that I've grown up."

Jackdorp gives Brice a long look, dripping with contempt, and turns from the podium. He's started to say nothing further when Glowoski waves to him and whispers a suggestion.

"Oh yes," says Jackdorp, standing over the prosecution table. "To be clear, Aaron still owned those Nike 1s when he went away with Mae?"

"Yes sir."

"And you don't know of your own account what happened to anything else he took on his trip with Mae—his clothes, or his backpack or sleeping bag?"

"I know what he told me."

"No no no," says Jackdorp instantly. He sees, too late, that he's made the classic cross-examiner's mistake of asking a question to which he doesn't know the answer. I'd demand that Brice be allowed to finish his response, but I'm as apprehensive as Jackdorp for different reasons. I don't want the jury to hear about the fire. "No hearsay. I'm saying you didn't witness anything to explain what happened to those items?"

"I smelled his jeans," says Brice.

"Nothing further," Jackdorp says. It's a bad ending for him after a good cross, because he knows I'll ask the next question. And I do, popping back up.

"You say you smelled Aaron's jeans?"

"Yes sir, the first day we painted, he was wearing these jeans that reeked of smoke. I guess there was a storm the first night he was out there with Mae that kept drowning their fire. He said he didn't care about getting paint on them because he was going to throw them out anyway."

Jackdorp interrupts again with a hearsay objection, but Judge Carrington allows the part of the answer to stand about Aaron saying he was going to throw out his jeans. Statements about what you intend to do aren't hearsay, because the out-of-court words don't tell what actually occurred. It's one of those fine distinctions the law draws that's always seemed a little too cute to me. But it works for us today.

"And you said you joined the Coast Guard and are wearing that uniform to show Cassity you're a better person?"

"Exactly, sir."

"Is that uniform important to you?"

"Super important."

"And would you disgrace that uniform by coming into court while you were wearing it and lying under oath?"

"I wouldn't lie under oath whether I was wearing a uniform or not. Because of what happened with Cassity, I've learned a lot about respecting your own word."

Beside me, Susan nods. That's good enough. I say thank you to Brice and resume my seat.

41

Glowoski Again

Once Brice is gone, I say, "The defense recalls Lieutenant Vanda Glowoski."

"Now what is this?" Jackdorp demands. "The lieutenant isn't on their witness list."

I remind him that she's already been called by the defense and that he is not entitled to further notice.

"We're not going to replay that testimony," Judge Carrington says.

"No, Your Honor. But we are going to introduce evidence of a separate *Brady* violation."

"What *Brady* violation?" Jackdorp demands again. "We know nothing about this."

The judge regards Jackdorp with a look seeming to combine affront with amusement. If the prosecution hid evidence favorable to the defense, it goes without saying that they know about it.

Glowoski strides back to the stand, with her impressive military posture. The judge reminds her that she is still under oath, and I establish the foundation, that the State presented us last Friday with all the notes that could be found from the State Patrol troopers and the deputies involved in the case.

I have a stenographer's notebook in hand, with the metal spiral holding it together from the top. I mark it as Defense Exhibit 6 before showing it to her.

"And are you familiar with the substance of this note, Lieutenant, dated October 5, 2023?"

She reads it to herself and says yes. We already know that because Susan spoke yesterday to the young trooper who'd made the note. She said her orders were to inform Glowoski of any calls about the Potter case.

"And whose note is that?"

"It's from a trooper at the Skageon substation who was on the tips line on that date."

"That date was after Aaron had been arrested and arraigned? There was quite a bit of publicity in this area about the charges against him?"

"That's how I remember it."

"Will you please read this note to the jury?"

Jackdorp stands to object, saying he hasn't seen the note yet. He comes up to look over Glowoski's shoulder. Once he's read the note, he looks to the ceiling, then stands right there, as if he's going to whisper answers in Glowoski's ear, as indeed he might prefer. The judge finally instructs him to return to his seat and he nods like an awakened sleepwalker.

By the time he gets back to the prosecution table, he says, "That note is hearsay, Judge."

"Your Honor," I answer, "I'm proving a *Brady* violation, which necessarily involves showing what the State Patrol, and the state government it's part of, knew."

The judge agrees with me. "Read the note, Lieutenant."

"Akylles Parrish." She spells the first and last names for the court reporter. "262-444-1440. Long-haul trucker. Picked up man in papers when he was hitchhiking near Alderville. September 14."

"How far is Alderville from Harold's Woods?"

"A few miles."

"And did you call or visit Mr. Parrish or ask another agent or trooper to do that?"

"No."

"Why?"

"Because I was sure it was BS."

"And what was it about this tip that made you certain it was untrue?"

"Well, first, you get a lot of calls like this when a case has some notoriety. And nine out of ten are just hot air. People are either convincing themselves of something, or just want to get themselves into the limelight. And many are complete nuts. Plus I checked out Parrish and he had a criminal record."

"What kind of criminal record?"

"He had done time for armed robbery."

"And when was that?"

"A while ago."

"Thirty-two years sound right?"

"I don't recall exactly. Like I said. It was a while."

"Did he have any other felony arrests in the last thirty-two years?"

"No."

"Misdemeanors?"

"I don't think so. There were a couple of traffic violations."

"And what else did you find out about Mr. Parrish that made you dismiss this tip?"

"What do you mean?"

"Did you find out his race?"

"That was on his record."

"What race is he?"

"African-American."

"Now, as a State Patrol officer, am I correct that you are familiar with ELD?"

"Yes."

"What is ELD?"

"It stands for Electronic Logging Device. Since 2019 every interstate truck has to have one of these devices on board that records a lot of data every hour."

"Does the data recorded include the date, the time, and the vehicle location?"

"Rough location. It's accurate to one mile."

"And are interstate truckers required to maintain that data?"

"Yes."

"So when you saw that note saying that the trucker, Mr. Parrish, had picked up the man whose picture was in the papers near Alderville, you knew he would have records that could corroborate what he was saying, or contrarily, indicate it was untrue?"

"Like I said, I didn't get that far, because I decided it was crap."

"Without speaking to him?"

"Yes."

"Because he had a criminal record and he was Black, and the Blacks they all stick together?"

"I didn't say that."

"Did you think that?"

"Like I said, there's a lot of worthless junk that comes in at those times, and this guy was a felon."

"So you decided not to investigate further?"

"Right."

"Were you in the courtroom when Aaron was arraigned on October 2, 2023?"

"Yes."

"Did you hear Judge Carrington require the disclosure of all material evidence favorable to the defense, what gets called *Brady*?"

"I must have."

"But when this tip came in three days later, you decided not to inform the defense, is that right?"

"I didn't really decide that. It was just a lead not worth pursuing. This was a major case and as the saying goes, you know, we were drinking from a fire hose. We had too much to do."

"Had you interviewed George Lowndes yet?"

"I hadn't. I think other agents had spoken to him briefly by then. We had the longer interview at his home after this."

"But one way or the other, Lieutenant, you'll agree with me that if Aaron was with this trucker, then Lowndes was wrong to think Aaron was driving the Subaru?"

"I get your point," she says. "But I don't think we knew yet about him saying the guy was driving the Subaru. That came when we interviewed Mr. Lowndes the next weekend."

"But it was always your operating theory that Mae was killed at Harold's Woods, wasn't it? Because you'd found the rope fibers there and Lowndes had already told other troopers about seeing the couple fighting? And because you found signs of a hurried departure, you assumed that Aaron had driven the body north to dispose of it in Ginawaban? That was what you were thinking?"

She appears to take a second to recollect. "I would say that's what we suspected. We didn't think it for certain until we spoke to George—and then got that photo from the tollway."

"And what the truck driver said contradicted all of that, right?"

"If there was any truth to it. But you're not getting the sequence here, Counsel. The tip comes in from this felon. And it's bushwa. And later Lowndes says the guy was driving and we see the tollbooth photo."

"And did you make the decision not to talk to Mr. Parrish on your own and not to inform the defense or did you consult with someone else about those decisions?"

"I did, as it happens."

"Another sworn officer?"

"No."

"Who?"

"A prosecutor."

"Mr. Jackdorp?" Jackdorp's head rises like a dog that's heard its name. From the way he tenses, I believe his instinct is to object until she answers no.

"Someone in Mr. Jackdorp's office?"

"No."

I'm actually stumped. "Who was it?"

"Someone in the Skageon Prosecuting Attorney's Office."

"And may we have that prosecutor's name?"

She is still one second before she says, "Harrison Potter."

I actually make a sound, a groan like I've sustained a minor blow. I make a big show of turning slowly to point at Hardy, who's there beside his wife and father in the first row of the gallery behind the prosecution table. He's been looking down to his hands, but Mansy nudges Hardy and he straightens up to face us. He has that wavering uh-oh expression I saw as he left the men's room.

"That man? The victim's father?"

"Yes."

"And you told him about the tip, and what did he say?"

"I told him what the guy said and what I'd found out. And he said, 'That's BS, forget about it,' which is the same as I thought."

My heart is sort of levitating in my chest. I should have seen this a long time ago.

"Were you previously acquainted with Mr. Potter? Before this case?"

"Yes."

"Did you work investigations with him and his office?"

"Definitely."

"And you conferred with him about the investigation of his daughter's disappearance and later of her death?"

"The same as any other parent."

"Really? How many other parents have told you to forget about *Brady* material, evidence that might help the defense?"

She doesn't answer.

"Wasn't Mr. Potter's public posture that he had turned over the investigation to his chief deputy?"

"And that was true."

"Did you ask her about how to proceed with this note about Akylles Parrish?"

"Probably not."

I got it now. I've got it. I may not be the sharpest knife in the drawer, but I've got it now.

"And aside from work, did you have any other association with Mr. Potter?"

"What does *that* mean?"

"Exactly what I said." I'm trying to figure out what role Glowoski played in Hardy's Fuck Club. I hadn't read her as interested in men, but who knows exactly what happened in Hardy's varied life. I have an instinct, largely inchoate and bordering on the vicious, that I may also humiliate Bea with the next few questions.

I am still calculating, when something hits my shoulder. Startled, I turn back toward the defense table and realize Susan has thrown a pen at me. She waves me over, and I ask the judge for a moment.

"Did you read that email I sent you late Sunday?" she whispers.

I tell her the truth. I haven't read my email in days. For one thing, I've gotten tired of the many vicious creeps following the case online who've figured out how to reach me with messages that include creative uses of the N-word. And for a second, on Sunday, I was neck deep in pathology and tire impressions.

After a second's tapping on her laptop, Susan swings it in my direction, so I can lean over her shoulder and read.

"Rusty. More intel on Glowoski. She served with Mark Potter in Afghanistan. He was JAG Corps and she was some kind of army investigator. She was in the Jeep with him when it hit an IED. She accompanied the body back Stateside. Apparently she moved to this part of the country after her tour to help Mark's widow and his kids. She's considered family."

"Thank you," I whisper to Susan. I was about to step in a deep hole. Half the jurors would never forgive me.

I turn back to Glowoski.

"Let's leave it at this, Lieutenant. You and Mr. Potter have been personal friends for some time, correct?"

"I'd say yes to that."

"And did Mr. Potter, Harrison Potter, ask for you to be assigned to this investigation?"

"I'm not sure if he suggested it. I think I asked to be assigned to the matter."

"Involving the daughter of your friend?"

"Yes. I wanted to be sure it was done right."

"And is hiding defense evidence doing it right?" I expect Jackdorp to object, but he's just sitting there, almost as if he no longer has a speaking part in this drama.

Glowoski says again that she never connected the tip about the truck driver with what Lowndes eventually said.

"And by the way—this decision not to talk to Mrs. Lowndes. Did you discuss that with Hardy Potter as well?"

"Mrs. Lowndes didn't want to talk to us. You heard her husband."

"Did you discuss with Mr. Potter your decision not to try further to interview her?"

"I don't know. I talked to him often, especially when there were significant developments. I might have, I might not."

I take a long second staring Glowoski down, then go back to Susan to see if I've missed anything else.

In the interval, Glowoski, clearly unstrung by the way all this is turning out, decides to speak in her own behalf.

"You know, this thing with the truck driver is just like Mrs. Lowndes. You want to make like she had something great to say for your side, but you don't know that, and I don't know that. Same with the truck driver. You think I stepped out of bounds because I'm friends with the Potters, but I bet you, it's like we thought, and when push comes to shove, the truck driver will never show his face in here and say any of that stuff under oath."

The judge is frowning. "Do you want to strike that, Mr. Sabich?"

"Not at all, Your Honor. I want to ask the court reporter to mark it, so I can read it to the jury again in closing argument."

Jackdorp has his forehead in his hand now. In the other hand he's got the revised witness list I gave him this morning. We've used the same trick he did, including the names of every person mentioned in the reports, including all of the agents. He needs to go line by line to see what's different each morning, but from his posture, I suspect by now he has.

I say I have nothing further, and Jackdorp shakes his head minutely to show he has no cross.

Before Glowoski can even leave the stand, I say what Jackdorp seems to realize is coming.

"The defense calls Akylles Parrish."

42

Akylles

Akylles Parrish—first name pronounced like the Greek hero's—enters the courtroom at an unhurried pace. He seems to be the kind of man who decided a while ago that he was done being scared of anything. He's big, linebacker size, well over six feet, dressed in jeans and a jean jacket over his flannel shirt. He has a thick mustache, and his hair is a little woolly, like he hasn't had time for a cut recently. He's got to be in his early fifties. Jackdorp, naturally, objected that he'd not been given twenty-four-hours' notice about Akylles's testimony, but under the circumstances, with Akylles basically hidden by the government for months, the judge agrees with me that Jackdorp won't be heard to complain. Jackdorp surrenders the podium to me with a resigned air.

"Now, Mr. Parrish, let me start," I say, once I'm past the basics to identify him, "with something that has come up already. Have you ever been convicted of a felony?"

"Yes sir. I grew up in Kindle and I hung out with some guys—some good, some not—and I got pretty high one night and thought it would be a laugh to go out and stick up people with a popgun."

"A popgun?"

"A toy. I took the cork and string off it. But in the dark, it looked real enough to the people I was pointing at for me to get a couple hundred bucks and two watches. I mean, that was real money to me then. No pretending."

"And you were apprehended?"

"Sure. The cops scooped up one of my so-called friends the same night and he give them my name."

"And after you were apprehended, how was your case resolved?"

"I pled guilty. It was some youth provision, since I was nineteen. Was supposed to be that the conviction could be erased if I didn't commit another crime for ten years."

"Was the conviction erased?"

"Yes sir. I hired a lawyer a few years back. If someone asks, like you, whether I was convicted of a felony, I'm supposed to answer, 'Yes, but it's been'—he pauses—" 'expelled'?"

"Expunged?"

"That's it."

"And were you sentenced to prison as a result of that now-erased conviction?"

"Yes sir, I got five years at the youth camp at Rudyard and served two. And I always tell folks I got a couple things out of that. First, I decided I was never doin nothin that might put me back there. And second, I learned to drive heavy equipment. There was a farm we tended in the youth camp, and I learned to drive a dump truck and other farm machinery and how to work on the engines. Which was how I got into truck driving once I was out."

"How long have you been driving trucks?"

"The big rigs? More than twenty-five years. I have my own company now. We have three cabs. My wife and oldest son drive one, and the other, I let out. And I drive the third."

I ask Aaron to stand, then say, "Mr. Parrish, calling your attention to September 14, 2023, did you have occasion to meet this young man, the defendant in this case, Aaron Housley?"

"Yes sir. He had green hair then and something in his nose, but it's the same cat."

"How did you meet him?"

"I was driving a load of transformer equipment from Milwaukee to Duluth. Aaron there was standing by the side of State Route 47 with his thumb out. And I stopped for him."

"Which direction were you headed?"

"Northbound."

"And where you stopped for Aaron, how far is that from Harold's Woods?"

"Four miles, I'd say."

"And what time was it when you stopped?"

"Noon, I'd say."

"What happened then?"

"Well, he was about to step in and said he might not smell too good. Made me laugh and I said, 'Come on, you know, on the road, you can be a few days between showers,' but once he climbed in, him and his pack—well, he'd told me the truth."

"I'm sorry, but can you describe the smell or smells?"

"What he was wearing, that smelled of smoke. I asked him to put his pack in the back of the cab because it was pretty sour."

"Did you ask him about that?"

"Yep. He said his girlfriend had, you know, relieved herself all over it because she was so mad at him for leaving her up there at Harold's Woods."

"And what did you say?"

"I said he better be careful of a woman like that. And he said he knew that. He said he'd been in love with that girl since he was like twelve years old, but it had come to him today that he had to be done with that. He said she was all kind of smart, and all kind of beautiful, but he had to face it, she was never gonna be right, no matter how much he hoped."

"How did you respond?"

"I said, 'Goin wee on your backpack, I kinda see your point.'"

There is a lot of laughter. Everything Aaron said to Akylles is hearsay, and I was prepared to maintain that they were excited utterances, which are exceptions to the rule, but in the event Jackdorp is too staggered by the last half hour to object.

"And what was his mood, as you observed it?"

"He seemed to be a quiet young cat, you know. He was kind of sad and seemed to have stuff on his mind as we drove. We talked a little. He told me that he wanted to go to art school, maybe at the museum in Kindle County if he could ever get the money together. For the most part, he was to himself."

"And how long was he with you?"

"Half hour or forty minutes."

"And what happened then?"

"I don't know, toward the end, he had got his phone out. I could see the screen light up with the apple, so it seemed like he'd just turned it on. And he was poking at it for a bit and finally asked me, 'Are we going north or south?' I said north, and he kind of groaned and said that woman had got him so messed up he'd gone in the wrong direction. I said I'd drop him at the next intersection where he could get to the southbound side."

"And did anything happen with his phone?"

"It buzzed in his hand a few minutes later. He stared at it for a second, then he picked up. I could hear a woman's voice, but he listened only for a second. He clicked off and then turned the phone off again. I asked him, 'That the girl?' and he said, 'Yeah,' but nothing else. We got to the intersection with Baldwin Road a few minutes later and I pulled to the side at the stop sign."

"Did he get out as you'd planned?"

"Yes sir. I held up so he could cross in front of me. He actually ran the last bit because there was a car coming from the north, and he got across and held his thumb out, but the car went right past. I rolled down the window and told him, 'You gonna be out here awhile, son,' and he shouted back that he knew it and he thanked me again and I took off."

"Now what did you mean when you told him he'd be out there quite a while."

"Well, you know, there been enough horror movies about hitch-hikers just to start with, most people won't stop, and you know, a young Black man, not smellin too good—the people in northern Marenago County who'd pick him up would be few and far between."

I try not to wince. Akylles had not been an easy witness to pre-try, meaning rehearse. I only got about half an hour on the phone with him, and he interrupted me often to say he was going to tell the truth, period, he didn't need to trim up anything. With the last question, I'd expected him to say that traffic on that stretch of 47 was sparse, especially at that time of day. I wanted to account for the amount of time it ultimately took for Aaron to get home.

I try again.

"In your experience as someone who is often on those roads, would it be a slow trip if Aaron was heading back to the vicinity of Como Stop?"

"Normally, yes. You can't tell who'd be driving by. Could be somebody like me, but that would be lucky. If I were standing out there and wanted to get back to that area, from where I dropped him, I think he'd be doing well to get back in a couple of days."

"Now, can you tell the people on the jury what ELD is?"

"The federal government in Washington says that interstate motor carrier operators like me and my rigs need to carry this equipment, the ELD, the Electronic Logging Device. It's a little blue box that runs off my USB in the cab and that connects to the electronic control module in my engine, and it automatically tracks certain data and transfers it to the Motor Carrier Safety Administration."

"And what kind of data does it capture?"

"Date, time, location, engine hours, miles driven and driver identity. There's more, but that's the basics. It's, you know, to make sure you don't drive longer than regulations allow and that your rig is operating safely. I can't say anybody likes it, but it's the law. And like I said, I don't mess with the law."

"And how often does the ELD record that data?"

"Regs say has to be at least once an hour."

"And how long are you required to maintain that data?"

"A week at least. But you know, I don't want no trouble, so I always have a month's data on each rig backed up to our server in the office."

Susan hands me a piece of paper.

"And is this a copy of your ELD for September 14, 2023?"

"Yes sir."

"And does it show your location at 11:15 a.m.?"

"Well, it's in geographical terms, you know, longitude and latitude, but I was in Skageon County on State Route 47."

"And at 12:15 p.m.?"

"About forty-five miles north. Same road. Near Alderville."

"And at 12:15, how far were you from what's been identified in testimony as cell towers 259 and 263?" I have Susan illuminate the map that Jackdorp put up during the prosecution case.

"A couple miles."

"And was Aaron with you at 12:15?"

"Yes sir. As I been saying."

"And how far were you then from the tollbooth on US 843 near the exit for Ginawaban?"

"An hour and a half, I'd say."

"And from the wilderness preserve there?"

"At least another half hour. Up to Ginawaban, that's a twisty drive."

I have Akylles mark Aaron and his location at 12:15 on September 14 on the map, and then move our copy into evidence as a defense exhibit. Jackdorp objects again and the judge agrees to withhold her ruling until after cross.

"Now, you said you preserve your ELD records for thirty days. How is it that you still have this record today?"

"Well, say, three weeks later or so, I stopped to eat at a place in Skageon County and the newspaper was sitting on the table. And there's a mug shot of that young man and a story."

"The record will reflect, Your Honor, that the witness has indicated the defendant, Aaron Housley. What did you learn from the article?"

"The article said he'd been arrested for murdering his girlfriend, and that the papers they'd filed against him said he was suspected of killing her in Harold's Woods and then drove her body in her car up to Ginawaban and dumped it there. And I studied on that awhile, thinking, 'Now how is all that possible when that young fella was sitting next to me in my cab?' So I kept the article and went back and checked my ELD and then I called the State Patrol. The trooper I talked to, she thanked me up and down for calling and said to hold on to the records, but then I didn't hear nothin else. So I figured maybe I got it wrong, maybe it was another date. Or the police ain't had time to get to me yet. I just stuck all that there in a file, and kinda let go of it then. Maybe I should have done more, but you know, I'm busy like everybody else. I heard from Susan there a couple days ago and I told her straight out, I was happy she found me."

"And so is Aaron," I say.

With a frown, Judge Carrington strikes my remark. Jackdorp rises to take his turn.

"So you say you know not many people in this part of the world would pick up Aaron, is that right?"

"That's what I said."

"And you said that was because people around here won't pick up a young Black hitchhiker?"

"Here's what I know. There's plenty of time, I've seen a hitchhiker on the side of the road, and drove back the next day and that guy's still out there with his thumb out, and almost all the time that happens, the hitchhiker is Black."

"So you've got an opinion that up here in Marenago we're a bunch of racists. That's what you think?"

Susan grabs my arm to encourage me to object, but I opened this door, and knowing Akylles just a little, I think Jackdorp is pushing too far.

"No sir, I don't think you-all are a lot of racists. I *know* that. I been coming up here for close to thirty years. But that don't mean everybody. There are plenty of folks up here who'll just judge on who you are, too. See, the point is, not many people up this way know a lot of Black folks and there aren't too many who want to start learning by picking up a hitchhiker. That's what I'm saying."

"And what about the State Patrol who you read had arrested Aaron? Are they a bunch of racists, too?"

"The state troopers? They're not as bad as they once were. When I first started driving, I got pulled over three times a week, you know, Black man in a rig. But that's better now."

"And how often do you pick up hitchhikers?"

"Not every day. Now and then."

"But do I understand that you picked up Aaron because you're Black and he's Black, and you thought he'd be standing out there a long time, if you didn't?"

"I think that's a fair way to see it. I hope a white driver would do the same. I work with several guys who might, but yeah, he's Black, I'm Black, yeah, that's true."

"And you took time to come here and testify for the same reason, because you were once a Black young man dealing with the criminal justice system?"

"I was a guilty young Black man."

"But a young Black man—he might be getting railroaded up here in Marenago County?"

"He might be. All I know is what I know. He was in my cab at noon on September 14, 2023. And I'm pretty sure he didn't have a dead body in his backpack either."

The courtroom explodes. Mr. Alvin Smith, over in the jury box, the Black farmer, is nodding to himself. Akylles—hardworking, sane and tough—is his kind of guy.

"Now this ELD log you presented. Does it show you were with Aaron?"

"His name isn't on it."

"Thank you," says Jackdorp. "And these ELD logs—can they be altered?"

"Apparently. But I wouldn't have the first idea how to start. There are some who've gotten prosecuted for doing it, and like I said, I had enough of that thirty years ago."

"But you are a convicted felon. We can agree on that?"

"I've explained."

"The answer is yes, you're a convicted felon?"

"Like I said, I was convicted but it's been—whatever that word is."

"And you know, don't you, that the law says your testimony may be disregarded for that reason alone?"

I object that Jackdorp is trying to state principles of law and, more important, that an expunged conviction does not carry the presumption regarding credibility. I'm vamping here and am not positive I'm right, and neither is Judge Carrington. Judge Carrington reminds the jurors that she will sum up the law at the end of the case and strikes the question.

Akylles doesn't understand and answers anyway.

"Seems to me you ought to judge every person for who he is today, not the dumb kid of thirty years ago. Anyway," he says. "I've said my piece." He turns to Judge Carrington. "Can I go now, ma'am?"

She looks to Jackdorp and me, and then says, "You are free to go, Mr. Parrish, with the thanks of the court."

On the way out, he stops in front of Aaron, who stands to greet him. They have a second eye to eye, then they shake hands and Akylles Parrish claps him on the shoulder and leaves.

43

Lainie

With Akylles's departure, we have reached lunchtime, but I ask the judge if we can bring on one more witness, since we'd like to get her going on her long journey back home.

"And who is that?" Jackdorp asks.

"Her name is Lainie Harrup."

"Spell that please," says Jackdorp, and I do.

"And do you know if she will be your final witness?" The judge is asking in a roundabout way, as she did quite directly last night when the jury wasn't present, whether Aaron is going to testify. I put her off, saying that we're holding the decision until we see how the defense case goes. To testify or not is a constitutional right and so she can't push me too hard. On the other hand, she's said plainly that she won't let us game Jackdorp, either by springing Aaron as a witness at the last second, or by announcing unexpectedly that he won't go on and trying to proceed directly to closing arguments. Whichever is going to be the next step, she's said Jackdorp deserves time to prepare. I tell her we will resolve the issue shortly.

"Okay," she says. "We'll talk more about our schedule after the next witness concludes her testimony."

"Wait, wait, wait," says Jackdorp. "There's no Lainie anybody on the witness list."

"She's there," I answer. We've played Jack on this one though. Our witness list includes an 'Elaine Harop,' as the Missouri State Police misspelled Lainie's last name.

"But we didn't get twenty-four-hour notice of this person."

"Strictly speaking, Your Honor, she's being recalled." I'm being crafty, but accurate, because Lainie's testimony was summarized in the part of the stipulation Jackdorp read while Glowoski was on the stand.

"Recalled?" asks Jackdorp.

"We're all going to take five minutes to stretch our legs," says the judge, "so you guys can talk a little more."

As soon as the judge and jury have departed, Jackdorp asks me, "Who is Lainie Harrup and what is she going to testify about?"

"Jack, did you ever answer that question for me?"

"You had reports. And notes. I got you the investigators' notes," he says, proving how historians make history. I don't bother to answer that one. "Did Susan do any report?" he asks.

Susan is too smart even to take verbatim notes that would have to be turned over. I suspect Glowoski might recognize Lainie's last name, even in a varied spelling, although I'm not sure Jackdorp and she are speaking at the moment. But I finally show an ounce of mercy.

"Jack, go look at the stipulation. You already have a report."

When we finished court last night, I drove to Milwaukee, where I had to wait nearly an hour. Lainie's connection out of O'Hare, the closest thing on earth to purgatory, was late. But I doubt Lainie Harrup has ever complained in her entire life about a routine frustration like a late bus or plane.

Lainie Harrop's superpower turns out to be that she is nice. Not ordinary nice, not even merely Midwestern Nice, but so decent and kind and so committed to those parts of herself that she has a kind of radiance. We had no real way to compel her to make the journey here, since the power of the court in Marenago County does not reach outside our state, but telling her that she was in a position to more or less save a young man's life was enough to propel her. Even Bea, who I used to think of as one of the most positive people I've ever met, is not this eternally sunny. I don't know if Lainie is trying to be like Jesus at every moment, as I suspect, but whatever motivates her, she is entirely sincere. She is an exceptional person.

She was pleasant company, a woman in her early fifties, still a pretty blond, carefully groomed but not a fashionista. We went over her testimony a few times and then turned to other subjects. She is a nurse by training and is thinking of returning to the profession now that both her kids are on their way. She has plenty to do, but she knows that the hospital nearby in Jefferson City, Missouri, is strapped for qualified staff.

'And how did your husband react when you told him you were coming to Portage?' I asked her.

'Oh,' she said, 'the way he usually does. He shakes his head and smiles. He and my kids call me The Saint.'

I go now to retrieve her from the attorney/witness room, but Jackdorp has been clever enough to shadow me and races up and asks to speak to her. She is, naturally, much too nice to decline. Letting him hear it from her directly is better than any report I could have handed him. He stops nodding about halfway through his conversation with her.

She is on the stand a few minutes after that.

"Ms. Harrup, we have heard your name in the evidence in this case before. It was stipulated that in December of 2023, you spoke to the Missouri State Police at the request of Lieutenant Glowoski here."

"All right," she says.

"Now, when you spoke to the Missouri State Police, did they tell you anything about the case for which that interview was being done?"

"They said they didn't know all that much about it themselves. They said they got a written request from your State Patrol here."

"Had you read or heard anything there in Jefferson, Missouri, about the death of Mae Potter?"

"No. Since Susan first called me last weekend, I've been on the Google, but I didn't know anything before that. I don't want to put my head in the sand, but I'm not as interested as some people in the horrible things that happen in the world. There's just too much of it."

"Tell us about your meeting with the Missouri State Police last December, as you recall it."

"Well, they were very nice, but I was flustered. I'm not sure a police officer has ever knocked on our door to investigate anything. They told me that I had made a call back in September to a young man and wanted to know why."

"Did they give you his name?"

"Yes."

"Did you recognize it?"

"Not at all."

"Did they show you a photograph of that young man?"

"Yes."

"Did you know him?"

"Not at all."

"And can you describe the person you saw in that picture?"

"I'm pretty sure it's the young man who's at the table over there."

I ask Aaron to stand.

"Have you ever seen this young man before, except in that photograph?"

"No."

"Is that what you told the Missouri State Police?"

"Exactly. And they said, 'Well, ma'am, you called him. We have the record.' Frankly, the way they said it, I thought they had a recording. So I began piecing together what had happened back in the fall. Phil and I were on our way south after taking a car trip to see the foliage and going all the way around Lake Superior. So beautiful! But now we were on the way home. When we stopped for lunch that day, September—?" She stops.

"Fourteen?"

"Right, September 14, I made several calls to B&Bs in Como Stop, which was where we were headed. We wanted to see Como Lake. So many people talk about how lovely it is. All that going back and forth from one screen with the search results to the phone screen—if you can't copy the number, I never can remember all the digits. So I'd dialed a couple of wrong numbers. I assumed I'd called Aaron—this young man— by accident, as one of those wrong numbers. I did remember talking to a man who was young by the sound of him who was a little irritated and hung up on me very quickly. And that's what I told the officers."

"Did the police officers ask you for your phone bill to verify what you were saying about calling various B&Bs?"

"They did. But we pay our bills online. They asked to look at the record of calls on my phone. I gave it to them, but mine only stores the numbers of the last fifty—that's barely a week for me. And this had all happened two months before. One of them said that if I went online, my service provider would have a record going back a year. That gentleman told me how to do it, and he stood over my shoulder while I used the computer in our living room alcove. But we'd changed providers at the end of October, so I got a message that there were no records available for my phone number. We left it at that. I really don't think they doubted what I was saying."

"I'm quite sure about that," I say.

Lainie smiles. Jackdorp could object to the byplay, but the fact is that the jury can sense exactly who she is, Superpower Nice, and several of them are already smiling at her as she speaks.

"Susan," Lainie adds.

"This Susan?" I'm standing over Susan's shoulder.

"Yes. When we talked yesterday, she said that even if I'm not a customer anymore, they're supposed to have records for twelve months. I called customer service from the old provider, and they said yes, but since I'm not active, someone would have to go to backups and that will take a month at least. I explained it was for court, and they said even with a court order that's how long it would be."

I thank her for those efforts and bring her back to lunchtime on September 14.

"Yes. We'd pulled into a highway rest area just off the interstate. We'd stopped at a grocery earlier and I'd made some sandwiches. Phil loves liverwurst, believe it or not. I dread the stuff, but we have a harder time finding it where we are in Missouri. You have much better liverwurst up here, at least that's what Phil says."

"Do you remember where the rest stop was vis-à-vis a place called Ginawaban?"

"We were near that exit, as I remember."

I give her the coordinates that were part of the stipulation, latitude and longitude for the cell tower that had connected her call to

Aaron's phone. With the use of maps, we agree that it was adjacent to the rest area where she and her husband, Phil, had stopped.

"And while you were at the Exit 73 rest stop, did you have any interaction with a young woman?"

"Yes."

"Can you describe her?"

"Just a beautiful young woman, frankly. Tall. Blond curls. Very striking. Slim. Cutoff jeans, sleeved midriff blouse and hiking boots."

I bring several slides of Mae up on the monitor.

"Did the young woman you spoke to bear any resemblance to this young woman?"

"I believe that's she," says Lainie Harrop.

"And when you spoke to the Missouri State Police, did they show you any photos of this young woman?"

"No, we never talked about a young woman. They just wanted to know about how I ended up speaking to Aaron over there."

"Tell us, please, about your interaction with that young woman."

"Well, she saw me and Phil making all those calls to the places in Como Stop and asked if she could borrow my phone for just a minute. She offered me ten dollars."

"And what were your observations, if any, of her emotional state?"

"She seemed very excited, frankly. Kind of wild-eyed. And talking too fast. Phil said later that it looked to him like she was high—"

Jackdorp objects and Judge Carrington sustains the hearsay objection to what Mr. Harrup said. I ask if, as a nurse, it looked to Lainie as if Mae may have been chemically intoxicated, and she says yes, given what she'd seen years back in the emergency department.

"Something was wrong," says Lainie. "I mean, she was very upset."

"And what did you do?"

"I gave her my phone for a minute. She took it and walked away about thirty feet. We could see her, but Phil was exasperated with me. He always says I trust people too much, and she was either going to call Outer Mongolia or steal the phone altogether. So we kept an eye on her."

"What did you see?"

"Well, when she was close by, she made a call and started to talk."

"Could you hear what she was saying?"

"Not over the highway noise, no. But she started talking and then just stopped and took the phone from her ear and looked at it. She was very frustrated."

"Any impressions?"

"I thought the person on the other end had probably hung up on her."

"And then what happened?"

"She walked further away. Her back was to us, and she dialed several more times. At one point, she seemed to be talking a little."

"And what was your impression then?"

"She might have been leaving a voicemail. That was my best guess at the time. Or talking to somebody for maybe half a minute. I really don't know. She could have been talking to herself, too. She seemed so overcome."

"And then what happened?"

"She was wandering further and further away, and finally Phil got up and asked for the phone back. And she gave it to him."

"What did she do then?"

"She just jumped in her car and drove out of there too fast."

"Did she remember to give Phil the ten dollars?"

"No no. We wouldn't have taken it anyway. She was distressed. Beside herself, I'd say from her appearance. Very upset."

"And do you remember anything about the vehicle she was driving?"

"It was six months ago. I have a vague memory. It was taller."

"So not a sedan?"

"No."

"Color."

"Lighter color."

"And do you remember anything about the make or model?"

"I'm terrible at that. I drive a Camry but I'm not sure who makes that. Toyota?"

I show her the slides of Mae's Subaru.

"Is this the car the young woman was driving?"

"I want to say yes, but it was a while ago and I don't pay attention to autos. I can't say for sure."

I pass the witness.

Jackdorp has had a few minutes to think about what he wants to do on cross, and he confers with Glowoski, their faces close together.

He finally gets up and asks Lainie to concede that she hadn't seen Mae in more than six months when Susan first emailed Mae's picture to Lainie. But Susan had been careful and sent photos of three different young women. Lainie tells Jackdorp that she picked out Mae at once.

"But after six months are you absolutely certain that it couldn't have been another young woman who came up to you at the rest stop?"

"Well," says Lainie, "another young woman who looked exactly like Ms. Potter. As I said, she was very striking. The pictures match my memory."

This line of questioning is absurd anyway. Who else but Mae would have made the call to Aaron's phone? Even Jackdorp seems to recognize as much. He stops himself in the midst of his next question, thanks Lainie and resumes his seat.

44

Jack

After Lainie is off the stand, the judge releases the jury for the night, but keeps Jackdorp and me around to discuss the remaining schedule.

"Well, Mr. Sabich?" she asks me, meaning, Is the defendant going to testify?

I tell her we are having a meeting in half an hour at the jail, when we will reach a final decision. I promise to communicate that to Jackdorp as soon as I leave my client. She's irked with me, but asks Moriah to call the jurors and tell them to come in tomorrow at 2 p.m. That will give Jackdorp time to prepare for Aaron's cross, if he's going to testify. Otherwise, we will hash out the jury instructions and proceed to closing arguments. Judge Carrington asks about the instructions, the summary of the points of law relevant to the case, which she will read to the jurors. There are preestablished forms in our state for most common issues, so the prosecutor puts together a first draft, with the defense lawyer then suggesting changes and the judge resolving any conflicts. Jackdorp says a set is being finished in his office as we speak, and that I'm free to come pick it up right now when we're done. An assistant will also bring a copy to the judge.

As soon as we are finished at the podium, Susan comes up to tell me that Lainie is still waiting to depart. We asked the judge to call her before the lunch break, because it will require some luck with flight connections for her to get back to Jefferson City tonight. Her first plane leaves from Milwaukee, a two-hour drive, at 5:30. Al, Susan's husband, has been kind enough to pitch in today as the chauffeur, albeit in my car. They are an all-bike family. But as it happens, I forgot to give Al my keys.

I run out to the lot behind the courthouse offering mea culpas to Lainie and Al. As she's getting into the Tundra, Lainie again says she's sorry she couldn't obtain the phone records Susan wanted. I laugh off her apology, telling her she did far more than we had any right to hope for and once more thank her emphatically. Lainie steps out of the SUV for a second to hug both Susan and me, as if we'd known her for years.

Given this morning's witnesses, I find myself happily at the place I wanted to be from the start, convinced that Aaron had no hand in Mae's death. But then, who? The reason Susan wanted to get Lainie's call records from September 14 was to find out if Mae in fact had another conversation after Aaron hung up on her, when Lainie thought Mae might have been speaking very briefly to someone else. The phone company records from Aaron's line show that he shut down his voicemail again as he powered off, so Mae wasn't leaving him a message. If Mae contacted someone else, it's natural to wonder if the call had any connection to the end of her life. Did Mae reach Hardy, who came to rescue his daughter and was soon, as so often happened, driven into a senseless rage by her? Or, in the suspicion that haunts me like a persistent goblin, did Mae phone Bea, hoping she had heard from Aaron by now and could get him to come to Ginawaban? Bea would have learned Mae's location that way, answering a question I'd previously counted in Bea's favor.

Yet the truth is that we are unlikely to know any more than Lainie just told us on the stand. As Mae was punching at Lainie's phone after Aaron cut her off, she was at least thirty feet from the Harrups, her back to them and her voice inaudible next to the roaring highway. My best guess is that Mae was simply redialing Aaron obsessively and telling him off for her own sake when he would not pick up.

Last night, my mind finally returned to the possibility, which

I recognized long ago, that Mae's death resulted from a random encounter. Maybe she stopped for a drink. Maybe she tried to borrow another phone. But it's certainly not impossible that beautiful Mae, a natural flirt, caught and rejected the attention of the wrong guy. Or perhaps there was some creep lurking in Ginawaban, awaiting a lone female? One thing I learned as a prosecutor is that when the truth of a crime finally emerges, it rarely turns out that you had imagined all the details correctly. Criminals are that inventive, and life that unpredictable. The reality is that the truth about Mae's death may never be known.

Which makes all the more terrifying the reality that Aaron remains on trial for her murder. Damon's initial warnings about the likely outcomes in this case seem even more foreboding. I know that juries sometimes reach results that are fathomable only to them. I trudge upstairs to the PA's office, where the packet of jury instructions is waiting, and then, on impulse, ask the pleasant receptionist if Mr. Jackdorp has a minute for me. I'm surprised when he emerges to escort me back.

"Am I supposed to buy you lunch?" he asks when we are seated on opposite sides of his desk. This is humor, Jackdorp style, and I force myself to smile. He still has his suit jacket on, even sitting in his desk chair. I've never seen him without it. It's a weird formality in this day and age, but I guess he just doesn't feel right working in his shirtsleeves.

"I wanted to ask you to consider something," I say.

"Shoot."

"I think you should nonsuit this case."

"Dismiss it?" He rears back, with his standard poker face, still looking like he's withstood the stress of the trial better than I have. "You think I'm that afraid of a not-guilty?" he asks. "I've had them before. Last I checked, I was still alive."

"All good prosecutors lose now and then, Jack. We both know that. If you've never had an NG, you're not prosecuting the right cases. Sometimes if you're bone certain the defendant did it, you've got to take a chance."

"Agreed."

"Are you bone certain now that Aaron is guilty?"

He mugs up. "I don't express those kinds of opinions in the middle of trial. Have you done a hell of a job? I grant you that."

"Jack. There is nothing left of your case."

"I really haven't had a chance to ponder on that, Rusty. May I?" he asks, referring to the fact that he's just used my first name.

"Of course."

"Thank you. The girl was murdered. Your client was deeply distressed about her. He bought the kind of rope she was strangled with. That's a pretty good start."

"He was nowhere near the place she died, which was Ginawaban. The evidence is better that she was hanged than strangled. And we don't really need to debate any of that, because how, in your heart of hearts, can you believe you've proved your case beyond a reasonable doubt?"

He's actually listening to me. I notice over his shoulder an old picture of his wife and him on their wedding day that didn't catch my eye the first time I was here, when I was struck by all the shots of him with various important folks. She has on a satin dress that pools on the floor—a pretty dark-haired woman with a sweet face. Today I also look to a side credenza where there are pictures of kids, which, I'm guessing, are grandnieces and nephews. He's laughing like hell with one little boy in one of those snaps, as he snatches him off a swing.

When I glance back to Jackdorp, he's still in thought. Behind every innocence case, in which a defendant unjustly spent years behind bars, is a prosecutor who became his own prisoner and could not accept the fact that the guy they thought was guilty didn't do it. It's catastrophically incompatible with the valiant image prosecutors have of themselves—of someone dedicated lung and kidney to the good and the just—to think they convicted and incarcerated a blameless person.

The suddenly amiable air struck between Jackdorp and me in the last few minutes is a remarkable change, but I realize what accounts for it. Hardy. Hardy directed the investigation that's come a cropper, and even advised Glowoski in some foolish and lawless decisions. In Jackdorp's own mind, he's been absolved. The case is no-lose now. This one will go on Hardy's account.

"Rusty, let's be practical. I can't dismiss this case. Vanda Glowoski's in a lot of hot water already. Not saying it's entirely undeserved, but if I dismiss, that will surely make it worse for her, and because of that, I will rile up the people in law enforcement I rely on to do my job. And what really matters is the Potter family. They're entitled to see this case come to verdict. Unless they've had a change of heart—which is quite unlikely, given their state after Vanda testified this morning. I may have to put Hardy on in rebuttal."

"You wouldn't be that good to me," I say.

"It's what he wants."

"One thing that's been proven beyond a reasonable doubt is that Hardy is not a person of good judgment. He lives in the sway of his emotions. And I promise you, he'll explode on the witness stand."

Jackdorp screws around his face to prevent himself from smiling.

"Rusty, I can't dismiss. Mind you, if I was sitting where you're sitting, if I'd done the kind of job you've done, I'd ask the same thing."

"Lawyers don't make facts, Jack. We both know that. And the facts are a hell of a lot different than you thought when Hardy talked you into bringing this case up here," I say, making my best effort to take advantage of Jack's state of mind, as I've assessed it. "He convinced you it would be a walkover, without telling you he'd screwed the whole thing up. Hardy doesn't deserve to get to make more decisions now."

Jackdorp smiles again in his lukewarm way and gives his grey head a little toss.

"Like you said, we don't need to waste time debating. I could never desert a victim family. It's not in my bones, since you want to talk about my bones. It's just not. They deserve a verdict from twelve honest citizens. I'll admit I've had a lot more confidence in a guilty verdict than I do in this case. But that's my job. On the other hand, if you want a mistrial, I could probably see my way to acquiesce."

He's deadpan, but I can't keep myself from laughing out loud. And miracle of all, Jackdorp laughs too.

"I didn't think you'd bite on that one," he says.

"Jack," I say, "I'd never get the drop on you this way a second time."

"Heh," he says, a mock laugh, although he's happy to be flattered.

I nod and I thank him for listening. He stands again to see me to the door.

"So will he testify or not?" Jack asks.

"Like I told the judge. You'll know minutes after I do."

"You'll tackle him from behind if he actually heads for the witness stand."

"I give advice. I don't get to decide."

"I understand. But I'm going to spend my time until you call thinking about my closing argument." He smiles again. "And I better come up with something pretty good, don't you think?" he says.

Although I'd never have seen it coming even a day ago, when I part company with Hiram Jackdorp we are sharing a laugh.

45

God Save Me from the Innocent Client

God save me from the innocent client.' That is the watchword of defense lawyers. When I was a prosecutor, I never really understood the phrase, except as a smartass expression I heard often from a lawyer on the other side, since they'd usually follow it by saying, 'But God has been good to me in this case.' Yet there is a grim truth in the maxim. The burden of this case has increased enormously in the last few days. It's no longer enough to commit my every fiber to doing my best. I must—*must*—win. Whether or not Bea and I reunite, Aaron's conviction would depreciate my own sense of the value of my time on this planet.

Innocent clients are also harder to represent in a fundamental way. They are unpredictable. Guilty clients will lie, deny, blame others. They have a certain limited register of reactions. Innocent clients, caught in their nightmarish predicament, cannot be counted on to be rational, because they have understandably lost all faith in reason as a governing principle of the social world.

So, prevailing on Aaron to see the foolhardiness of testifying will be difficult. To buttress me, I asked his permission to invite his mother and his father to this session, in which Susan will be included too. For Aaron's sake, I reluctantly offered to include Joe, but even Aaron doesn't think of his grandfather as a reliable person for advice. He'll say yes and no in the same conversation and then insist afterwards that he was right.

Bea is waiting alone in the tiny, spare reception area at the jail when I get there. My heart, of course, surges at the sight of her. I remain dizzyingly in love with this woman, which is becoming clearer and clearer as my outrage starts to subside. The one hump I can't get over is Mae's death, no matter how unlikely I know it is that Bea had any role. Yes, I've realized that suspecting her provides a convenient off-ramp from the more difficult task of forgiving her and committing myself to reconciliation. I would have bet anything that she wasn't sleeping with Hardy or anyone else while she was seeing me, and this—Mae's murder—is the low spot where my new distrust of her has gathered. I have also slowly come to realize that my own history with Barbara is playing a large role here. Psychologists say that unsuccessful second marriages involve making the same mistake twice. There would be a vicious circularity in living again with someone with such dark capacities. I can't.

She stands and takes a single step forward, and then stifles the reflex to approach.

"Am I allowed to say how brilliant you have been?" she asks me.

"I haven't been brilliant. I'm reading the script that Susan wrote. *Susan* has been brilliant."

The technicolor Mohawk comes through the door as I'm saying this. She smiles just a little.

"Go ahead and smile," I tell her. "You're entitled."

Susan then says what I'm already feeling: It's much too early for either of us to be taking victory laps.

I ask about Lloyd, but cold snaps, like the one that's just passed, always create emergencies and high demand for new heating equipment. He hasn't been able to come to court all week, and has been relying on Bea, and sometimes Joe, for reports.

Although she is being included in an attorney visit, Bea is not formally a member of the defense team, meaning she is subject to a full body search. Officer Crawford, whom I've come to call by her first name, Serena, emerges from behind the bulletproof glass partition and directs Bea to a tiny side room, which looks literally to have once been a closet. They are behind the closed door for several minutes. Bea returns finally with an awkward joke. Nobody's touched her like that, she says, in weeks. Susan doesn't want to laugh at what clearly hangs out our dirty laundry. But I smile, recognizing that Bea intended the remark as gallows humor, making the best of a bad situation. I understand how completely overwhelmed Bea has been, how much she feels like one of those movie astronauts whose lifeline gets cut and who just drifts off to die in an endless orbit through space.

Once we get back to the attorney room, I brief Bea. I am careful to maintain Aaron's privilege. I don't repeat my prior conversations with him. I simply explain the reasons not to testify. His conviction. The blaze in the fire pit—which earns a cocked eyebrow. The risk of a longer sentence. And the biggest problem, that the case will suddenly be about whether he is believable, instead of the complete failure of the government's evidence. Testifying will be applying voltage to the metal rods at the temple of Jackdorp's Frankenstein of a prosecution.

Bea takes all that in soberly and then asks Susan if she agrees. I'm pleased that Susan feels no need to defer to me when she answers.

"Rusty and I still haven't really discussed this fully, but I don't see it quite as clear-cut as he does. A defendant who can get up there and do a good job for himself is the best thing to happen to any defense. That's how most acquittals happen. And I think Aaron, quiet and thoughtful as he is, is likely to do a good job. But his conviction? That will hurt a lot. And to me, when you consider our position now, it doesn't make sense to take a big risk. When you're holding pocket aces, you go all in and grab the pot. You don't wait for somebody to hit a flush on the river."

Aaron arrives then. For Bea there is a reward for the humiliating search she went through. For the first time in months, she can hug her son. It brings her to tears, of course. Because this has been one of her stubborn fears all along. If Aaron is convicted, this may literally be the last time that happens for as long as she will live.

Four people fill this tiny room. Even in the usual cold, we can feel the heat of one another's bodies. The jailers can't find another chair and I end up standing. Everybody gets a turn to speak. Aaron, always good at listening, turns to face each of us, his grey eyes intent. I explain the holes we've poked in the hull of the Good Ship *Jackdorp*. And the perils of testifying. Susan repeats what she just said to Bea, including her comparison to Hold'em poker, which Aaron understands. Bea is next. She says, "Aaron, we both asked Rusty to do this. And I know you have to feel the same way I do, that Susan and he have done an unbelievable job. Even I began to lose faith after Mr. Jackdorp's opening, and now, as far as I'm concerned, the two of them, Rusty and Susan, have actually proven you're innocent. I hope you are as grateful as I am."

"I am," he answers.

"I understand that only you can make this decision. And I hope what I'm telling you is said with what's best for you at heart, and not because I want Rusty to know how much I love and appreciate him." She stops then and looks downward until she can continue. "I hope I'm separating things as much as possible. But I think having come this far with Rusty and Susan guiding you, you need to listen to them now. They seem on the verge of saving you."

Aaron takes another moment to consider what he's heard, his smooth face largely expressionless. Then he says, "I'm going to testify.

"I really hear what you're all telling me. I know it's said with love, Mom. And Rusty, man, I mean I can't even believe I'm going to tell you that I know better than you. But let me ask you one thing, Rusty. If I don't testify and I get convicted anyway, what are you going to think?"

The prospect of that is so foreign to my current mindset that the question startles me.

"Aaron, I wish I could make you guarantees, but sometimes juries get back there and a kind of group psychosis sets in. There are some trial lawyers who never talk to jurors after a case, because their reasons for what they did can sound like they were receiving signals from another galaxy. But to answer your question, even so, I'm *not* going to wish you'd testified."

"But what would you *think*, man? What would you be saying to yourself afterwards? 'How did this happen?'"

I ponder. "I'd probably say that the people up here were bigger bigots than I realized."

"Right. That's what I'd think. So testifying, to me it's kind of a Black thing," he says. "Mom, I always remember what you told me when I was little. You must have said this a thousand times. I think the first time was about this girl in preschool, Evangeline. I was so crushing on this girl, I thought she was so cool, she had this tiny voice like a cartoon character and white-blond hair like Mae. I guess she looked like Mae must have looked at that age. But her mom—you remember her?"

"Morris," says Bea, squeezing her eyes shut, anguished by the memory. "Hilda Morris. What an awful woman."

"Right," Aaron says. "She wouldn't let Evangeline come to our house to play or let me go over there, and I liked that little girl so much, I made you call a dozen times, and you finally said to me, 'Aaron, God doesn't think you're different, but there are some stupid people who do. And you're just going to have to accept that and make your way.' And you were completely right. That's what I've had to do.

"And there's no foolin—that hasn't always been easy. It made me feel every kind of way, angry and sad and lonely. There were times I hated to leave our house, because I knew there was that thing out there, like some evil force in a horror movie, and I had to face it every day. And man, it's never *easy* for any Black person, not in this country. But being a Black kid in a white family, I mean, that's a special load, its own thing. I cannot tell you how much I hated the message I was always getting that I was different from you people who loved me and who I loved. I hated it. Until I understood the truth of it. And you know, by now, I kind of think of being Black as God's gift to me. 'Proud' isn't even the right word. It's an *honor* to be able to claim the legacy of what was endured and is still endured by Black folks in America. And since I got sober and started talking to Reverend Spruce, it's the reason staying sober is so important to me, because I have to make something out of the chance I have that so many Black people never got, and so many still don't have.

"But that *thing* is out there. And you know, white folks, there aren't many who won't *scream* when you tell them they're racists. They'll say they go to church and take it fully into their hearts when the minister says we're all alike, we're all God's children. But they'd still feel like their daughter was next to dead if she decided to marry me. And if they have to fill a job, they'll still take white over Black. And Rusty, you and Susan, man, you've defended me against *everything*. Shoeprints and tollbooth photos and even the rope. But you haven't defended me against that, that thing."

I take a second. I am having a little trouble reacting to the substance of what Aaron is saying, because this is, without doubt, the most I've ever heard Aaron say at one time. There is a kind of singsong to his speech, the emphasis falling oddly in the middle of sentences, and that thing that young people have had for a generation now, with their voices rising for emphasis, as if they're asking questions.

I've always believed that Bea was correct when she maintained that her son is a thinking person, but I've never heard him talk about race, let alone this cogently. If it's this person, the young man speaking now, who comes to the witness stand, then it might work. But I'm still not willing to say that out loud.

"Aaron, I wish we could defend you against that, that thing, as you call it. I wish somebody in this country could figure out how. I *will* tell you, if I took you back to the city neighborhood where I grew up, you'd see it's a lot better. But it's still not good. And I knew that before this case started. Did several of those jurors, whether they recognize it or not, walk into that courtroom with a higher threshold to acquit a Black person than they'd have if you were white? Probably. Do I think it would have been better for you if you could have sat in the courtroom behind a screen, so they'd know nothing about you, except the evidence they heard? I do. And I'm an old white guy who's never been the object of the kind of bigotry you have. So forgive me for what I get wrong. But in my view, you're right, most white people, especially the ones the ages of most of those jurors—they're racist, even if it's several levels down in their brains.

"But here's something I've realized: Not all white people are racist in the same way and to the same degree. In a close case, I'd be worried about what you call 'that thing.' But Jackdorp's prosecution is in the dumper. And I don't think many of those jurors believe in convicting innocent people *only* because they're Black. Could a couple of hard-core racists hang that jury? Yep. I know that. But it's more likely that even they will capitulate to a larger majority to get themselves out of that room and back to their lives."

"No, Rusty, I'm not explaining this well. You know, Akylles, man, he is one amazing dude, he's a rock, just like Lainie. I mean, it's a great world that people such as them would put themselves out the way they did to tell the truth. And Akylles said it. Up here, folks don't know many Black people. And that goes both ways. Akylles, he doesn't know that many white people either. Blacks know whites better than whites know Blacks, cause they have less choice sometimes, but Akylles, in him, there's probably a piece that thinks that every white person he meets is a racist, no matter what they say, cause, you know, that's the safe assumption, so he doesn't get caught off guard. That is still the biggest problem in this fucked-up divided country where white and Black don't live all that often side by side. We don't know each other.

"But I do. I had that advantage. I grew up *loving* white people. And I *know* that Akylles is wrong—they're not all racists. There are plenty of white people like Mae. Mae, you know, I was never different to her in that way. I was always Aaron. She knew me for me." He looks down to the table, taking a second to control his emotions. I am struck by how much Aaron's reflex—his posture, the frozen eyes—is like Bea's when she was speaking about me. As for what he's said about Mae, that's been consistent. To her, he's said more than once, his being Black was the same kind of thing as her being blond. Other people sometimes had wacky reactions to those physical facts. But those responses had nothing to do with the essential person each of them was in themselves and to each other.

"And even up here, I know there are some people—I couldn't begin to say how many—but there are probably some people on that jury who are like Mae. But most aren't, they have some prejudice, like you say, whether they know it or not. But it's not all their fault. Because, like Akylles was saying, they just don't know many Black folks. And that's the point. I can't just think the worst of all of them. I *have to* give them the chance to *know* me. I've been talking to white people like the ones on that jury all my life, whenever I've been out by Joe. And I think I can make them hear me, so I'm more of a person to them just like they are people, and not some silent dark-skinned dude across the room who they were inclined to believe the worst of when they first got a look at me. I—*me*—I'm the defense against that *thing*, Rusty. So I'm going to testify."

He looks to each of us for a second. But there is truly no more to say.

46

Hail Mary

Susan and Bea and I emerge from the jail together. I am going to walk back to the diner to eat something, while I wait for Al to return with my car. According to his last message, he'll be back in less than an hour. Assuming Aaron would relent in the end, and that I was most likely to spend the night preparing for my closing argument, Susan was originally planning to join me at the diner, where she would then meet Al and ride home beside her husband. Now she'll spend the night in the second bedroom at our house, so she can accompany me to the jail when it opens at 7:00 a.m. to prepare Aaron to testify. She says she is too tired to eat anyway—I understand the feeling—and prefers to go through our exhibits, making sure we've introduced everything we want the jury to see. After that, she'll turn in.

Bea has stood by on the sidewalk throughout this discussion and offers to drive me over to the diner. It's a ten-minute walk, and the weather has been mild today—about 35 now. But it feels too hostile to simply say no. I settle in the passenger seat of her 4x4 Wrangler.

"What do you think?" she asks, with the key fob in her hand. Obviously, she is speaking about Aaron.

"I think it's a reasonable decision by a grown man who knows what he's doing. I wouldn't balance things out the way he has. But I haven't experienced what he has throughout his life either. What do you think?"

"I stopped believing I could think logically about any of this a long time ago. But I accept his decision. And I'll do what I've been doing for weeks now, and pray it turns out right." She starts the car and then looks back at me. "It was really nice, by the way, to see what a strong relationship you two have developed."

"He's a good man, Bea. You and Lloyd and Joe did a fine job. There have been some bumps, but Aaron deserves the chance I hope he gets."

"Thank you," she says quietly. After a block in silence, she peeks over at me. "It's Valentine's Day, you know."

I can't stifle a huge laugh at my own expense.

"Oh Lord! Talk about tunnel vision. I noticed all this red on everybody's desk all day and never made the connection. Trying a case is living in an altered state."

"I thought maybe it wasn't a good idea to bring you a card," she says, with a cute little smile, as she glances up from the quiet street. I decide it's better not to answer.

We arrive in the center of Portage. Aside from the weak light cast by the old iron streetlights, shaped like chess queens, the only illumination, except for a tavern two blocks down, comes from the Lamp.

"I've tried to give you the space you asked for, Rusty, for the last few days."

"I've noticed and I appreciate it, Bea."

"But I admit I was hoping you might say something to me—you know, about the rope? You didn't believe me, and I told you the truth."

"So you did," I say. I take her point, but this could go sideways quickly, if I reminded her why that can't do all that much right now to restore my faith in her as a truthteller. But I give her what she feels she deserves and say, "I'm sorry."

"I thought I had done a terrible thing to Aaron. But am I wrong to think it's worked out well in the end? The judge even took the rope from the garage away from Jackdorp, because it had no connection to the case. And that's the truth, isn't it? That rope, my rope, has nothing to do with Mae's death, right?"

My heart responds with a sudden bump, and a voice inside me screams, *Say it!* And I do.

"Unless you're the one who killed her." It shocks me to hear the words emerge, a thought so wild and private that it belongs with the weird sexual fantasies that rear up occasionally and are soon forgotten, or some of the deepest secrets of my past that have not crossed the threshold to speech in years. But my tone is neither accusatory nor bitter. To my own ear, I even sound a bit lighthearted, as if the mere notion mocks me in some essential way, as it probably does.

But it is not hard to read Bea's response. The shock, the dismay, whatever I might call it, that inhabits her expression cannot be feigned. For a second, she's totally immobile. The heat in the car has still not kicked in, and the wisps of vapor from her breath completely cease for a short time.

"You're *really* mad at me," she says finally. "To even say that."

There is something oddly reassuring that even now her understanding of me is so quick and precise.

"Admitted," I answer.

Not surprisingly, she still does not seem to have recovered. She looks down to her gloved hands in an effort to gather herself.

"I thought it was over the top when you asked me to leave the house, Russ. But you were right. Because it only would have made everything worse if I had to listen to you say things like that. So crazy. And damaging. And you're a kind person, Rusty. I know you are. Please tell me you don't truly believe that."

"I don't," I answer, and it feels like the truth.

"Thank you."

A jacked-up car with a bad muffler rockets right past us, followed by another. They're racing. Down Main Street. And they're probably not teenagers. Grown-ups, supposedly, and worst of all, likely very drunk. Small-town excitement.

"This case goes to the jury Friday, Bea. We can talk or start to talk then. I want to do that. I do. I'm still incredibly hurt, but I don't want to give up."

"Thank you for saying that, too."

We hang on the edge of moving toward each other, but it's not to be now. She lifts a gloved hand and says good night, and I alight. I watch the Jeep vanish down the street.

In the diner, I call Jackdorp first.

"He'll testify."

Jackdorp is completely silent, and finally thanks me for phoning, before clicking off. Given how consistently we've turned the tables on him, I'm sure he suspects another trick now.

Then I reach Cap Sabonjian. I've kept him apprised of how things are going, and he knew that Aaron might take the stand. He agrees now to come to the jail at noon tomorrow to play the part of Aaron's cross-examiner, so Aaron gets a taste in advance of what he is likely to face.

I have ordered salad with grilled chicken, as an act of recognition that I have a future beyond this trial. But I have little appetite. A pall lingers from my conversation with Bea. I am both guilty and ashamed for telling her what was on my mind, and on the other hand, relieved. If I wanted to, I could remain unconvinced by her denials, but I am getting ready to set that aside.

Whether Bea will forgive me for those thoughts is another matter, but I think I can explain, especially if I'm willing to cross some of the hard lines that I've long drawn for myself. Now that I've finally voiced it to myself, I recognize the degree to which the omen of Barbara has altered my thinking, like the moon's invisible pull on the tides. Bea would understand that, I suspect, once she's over the shock from what I haven't shared before.

But what lies ahead for us as a couple will require some strength on each side, and in this moment, I realize that my calculations about our alternative futures remain correct. If, Lord forbid, the decision Aaron just made leads to his conviction— If he's found guilty, Bea and I will probably never make our way back to each other. The trial will be the time when everything between us unraveled. What I just said to her will be the nadir, not simply because it shows how completely my trust in her has eroded, but perhaps, in her mind, because it's evidence of how fragile that was to start. And in the devastation of a conviction, neither one of us may ever have the wherewithal to reconnect. Instead, we'll each want to turn the page. Contemplating the worst, with the center ripped out of my life in Skageon, I see a very different future lying before me. I'll move back to Kindle to be near my son and granddaughters, the people unlikely to forsake me.

But recognizing the immense stakes of the outcome of the case not just for Aaron but also for me, of the final outcome in this case, I can't simply sing another verse from "Que Sera Sera." The last stone needs to be turned, even if it's somewhat desperate. I pick up my phone again and text Mansy.

> 'I apologize, but is it possible you could give me ten minutes to talk about something very important? Wherever you like.'

He answers just as Al enters in his black leather jacket with my car key. I have my cell in hand and read Mansy's reply. 'The Clay Pigeon at 8pm.' He's added an address. I need to get moving, but I chat for a second with Al.

Al is older than Susan—about fifteen years I'd guess—but he's in peak condition, at least if you don't look at him carefully. He's a bodybuilder, still ripped, with a neck like a pillar and biceps that strain the sleeves of his T-shirts. But he has the wattled visage of a seventy-year-old, along with a salt-and-pepper caterpillar of a mustache over his lip. It's a little like having the body of the Rock, topped off with the face of the guy from the decades-old TV commercials who rose half asleep in the middle of the night, mumbling about needing to make the doughnuts.

I hand him the diner menu, and beg him to order dinner at my expense for himself, and for Susan if she's changed her mind. I also give him directions back to the house so they can visit, after he picks up his Harley in the courthouse parking lot. I encourage him to stay over if he likes, even offering to switch bedrooms so they're more comfortable.

"I'm a homebody basically," he says. "And I love ripping along these country roads at night. Susu says it may all be over Friday anyway. Always good to miss each other a little, right?"

I thank him again, and then head for Mansy.

The entire Potter clan has been housed at a country club with a renowned golf course about twenty-five miles from the courthouse.

Miller's Glen, the club, has suites for the summering rich from Milwaukee and Kindle County, who choose to come up for the weekend, or even longer stays. Through their network of highfalutin connections— and their boundless wealth—the Potters got the club to agree to open those quarters to them for the duration of the trial. The Potters sometimes arrive at the courthouse in Hardy's notorious black SUV, but often there is a second car, Mansy's Lincoln, which is driven back and forth by Ben, who helps Mansy around the house. I've waved at Ben several times when I've seen him leaning on a fender outside the courthouse and he, at least, has delivered a small, sage smile.

The Clay Pigeon turns out to be adjacent to the skeet range at the country club, and unlike the rest of its facilities, the Pigeon remains open all year. It's considerably posher than the usual country tavern, more in the mode of the old-fashioned Midwestern supper clubs with white tablecloths and big leather booths and English hunting scenes on the paneled walls. The inn sits on the shores of a good-sized body of water, Lake Pitsky, one of a network of lakes, all connected by small channels. I'm sure the summer scene in here is like the hurly-burly I've often witnessed in the bars of the two grand hotels, the Morevant and Billingsley's, that sit side by side on the shore of Como Lake. A lot of sunburned boaters, who've moored at the dock below, trudge up the hill hungering for drink—guys in their tailored shorts and logo polos, accompanied by blond wives and girlfriends, all of whom proceed to become too drunk and too loud. But now, in the winter months, there are only a few customers. Mansy is one.

He is seated in a tall brown leather booth, from which he makes a characteristically elegant Mansy gesture, raising a single finger to signal me. He wouldn't believe me if I tell him he looks good. Aging, when you've been forestalling it, can have a sudden and cruel effect once the defenses break down. Two grooves between his lips and chin, as distinct as chisel marks, are now engraved there forever and his eyes look like they've sunk into his skull another quarter of an inch. I realize yet again that he will never fully recover from Mae's death.

As I take a seat opposite him, I say, "I'm very grateful that you'd give me the time."

"I'll still take your word, Rusty, if you say it's important. But let's skip the small talk."

"Sure. Have you been in court this week?"

Except for isolated moments, I have adhered to my practice of not allowing my eyes to roam over to the Potters in the front row behind Jackdorp. I've tried to be as dull to them as I was to the valentine on Moriah's desk, although I did notice that after Charmaine testified, Mae's older sister, Harriet, disappeared, almost certainly to return to her family in Denver.

"I was there," he says. "It reminded me of one of those magic tricks, where the guy with a cape pulls back a curtain and the pretty girl has disappeared. Now you see it, now you don't. Where did that guilty little shit go?"

"He's gone because he was never there, Mansy."

The server comes over, a tall woman in her middle years in a black-and-white uniform, a pro who can take your order without the need of a pad to write it down. I ask for the same scotch that Mansy's drinking.

"He's buying," Mansy adds. She nods in a studied effort not to react to the remark and removes the two menus that are lying on the table.

"You've run rings around Hiram Jackdorp," Mansy says then. "The stupidest thing that man did was when he said he had no objection to you representing Aaron. Even Hardy knew that could be a problem."

"Which is why you tried to talk me out of doing it."

I've caught Mansy there. A flicker of something, embarrassment, crosses into his face and causes a brief retreat from the somewhat truculent approach he's decided to adopt with me. Having set him back a step makes this the right moment to say what I've intended.

"I had a meeting with Jackdorp this afternoon. I think if the Potter family said they'd seen enough, they accept the fact that it wasn't Aaron, he'd dismiss the case. So, whether or not it's a Hail Mary, I want to humbly ask you to consider that."

There's a very tough guy inside Mansy. He was an officer in Vietnam in the war's early days and saw plenty of atrocities he won't discuss. That very tough guy gives me a very harsh look.

"I know you're not kidding," he says. "But that will never happen."

"Because?"

"Because I still think your jerk of a client killed her."

"Mansy, you're much too good a lawyer to believe that. The case against Aaron has collapsed. There's no credible evidence left."

He gives his head a simple shake in disagreement.

"I wouldn't say that." He resorts to the same litany as Jackdorp did this afternoon: Aaron was angry. He bought a rope. And that's almost certainly what was used to kill Mae.

"Mansy, I didn't come here to argue, but if you really believe Aaron is guilty, can you tell me the first thing about how that murder supposedly happened?"

"I don't know the evidence the way you do, Russ."

"Come on, Mansy. After close to sixty years involved with trials, you can analyze the proof in a case almost by instinct. It's like the coding etched on a computer chip. Can you even tell me where this crime supposedly occurred?"

He gives me a low look.

"Maybe it's like you said. Aaron killed her at Ginawaban."

Quick-witted always, Mansy has settled on the only remotely realistic possibility allowed by the evidence. But that's an alternative I've considered at length and disregarded.

"Okay, let's consider that," I say. "How in the first place did Aaron know he'd find her there? Both witnesses, Akylles and Lainie, said Mae's call lasted seconds before Aaron hung up."

"Well, maybe that was what she said before he cut off the call. 'Meet me at Ginawaban.'"

"Think about the timing, Mansy. Aaron's not driving a car, he's hitchhiking, in an area where rides for a young Black man are few and far between, let alone somebody with clothing and a backpack that reek. He got out of Akylles's truck about twelve thirty p.m. The sun set around seven, which was when he had to stop traveling, because he was nowhere near home and needed to find a place to sleep. The cell towers show he spent the night on or near Route 47 about thirty miles south of Harold's Woods.

"So he has six and a half hours to go to Ginawaban, kill Mae, hide the body and the car and then travel back to where he slept. The next day he made it all of eighty miles to Mirror in roughly eighteen hours. But you want to say that the day before he managed to hitchhike twice that distance in one third the time, not to mention murdering somebody and concealing the evidence while he was at it."

"It's not impossible."

"It's highly unlikely. And here are a few questions about your imaginary scenario: How could he have found Mae once he got to Ginawaban? The cell records show he didn't turn his phone back on until eight that night when he'd found that place to sleep along 47."

"Okay, so maybe that's what Mae said before he hung up on her. 'Meet me at Ginawaban in the parking lot.'"

"And he killed her there?"

"There are rope fibers all over the car."

"But there are dirt streaks on her blouse, Mansy, and the kind of abrasions that wouldn't come from being dragged over an asphalt parking lot. She was on open ground when they supposedly had that struggle—which according to every witness oddly left no serious marks on him. But then you want to say he decides to kill her in the car, knowing the parking lot is the one place in a wilderness preserve where he's most likely to be seen by other people.

"And here's the biggest question, Mansy. Riddle me this. If Aaron heard Mae's voice and decided to go meet her at Ginawaban, then why in the world did he get out of Akylles's truck and cross the road to head back south, when Akylles was going north toward Ginawaban in the first place?"

That one stops him cold. He sits back a bit.

"I don't know. I can't answer all these questions on the spur of the moment. Maybe he changed his mind after a while and decided to go up there."

"Well, here's another question you won't be able to answer. If he killed Mae and then headed home, the standard route, because it's far faster, is to stay on the interstate all the way down to Como Stop. But somehow he ends the day still on 47. Isn't the most reasonable explanation for that because Akylles dropped him off on Route 47 and he caught a couple of rides south along that road before he stopped for the night?"

"Maybe he went back to Harold's Woods to get rid of evidence."

"Really? He did a piss-poor job of that. The State Patrol found footprints, fibers and Mae's clothing at their campsite. Plus, the time that cleanup adds to your scenario. Tick tick tick," I say. "Every extra step makes this more impossible. You were right to start. I *do* know the evidence. And the evidence says he didn't kill her—at Ginawaban or anywhere else."

Mansy's pale blue eyes loiter in thought for a second. I let the silence stretch before I speak again.

"But here's the real point, Mansy. No matter what kind of crazy make-believe you want to imagine, it's too far-fetched to constitute proof beyond a reasonable doubt."

"Rusty, to be vulgar, I don't give a loose turd about reasonable doubt, not with what you're asking. I'd have to be one thousand per-cent convinced. And I'm not."

This, of course, is another reason innocent people end up lan-guishing in prison, because the victims' families, having been offered one explanation for a devastating tragedy, cannot let go of it. Their excuses, of course, are better than the prosecutors', whom the fam-ilies often pressure not to back down. For the victims' loved ones, having been promised the only possible recompense—justice and punishment—they now find that even that is about to vanish. It's loss and more loss for them in an increasingly senseless world.

"Mansy, this is about law. Cling to whatever anger and suspicion you need, but I'm asking you to accept that Aaron is not guilty as a legal proposition. You and I have staked our lives on the law. It's not perfect. But it seeks to govern life with reason, rather than submitting to the chaos of the stupid impulses and passions that might otherwise drive us. We both believe in that process intensely."

"I care about my family even more. I told you the truth, Rusty, when I asked you not to handle Aaron's defense. I thought you'd do a pretty good job as Aaron's lawyer, I admit that. But I also knew our friendship wouldn't survive. And it hasn't. You've used my son as a scapegoat. Which would be bad enough, because the insinuation that he killed his daughter is all crap and you know it. But worse, you've done that in public, even while this whole trial has revived the very depths of his grief. I hope you never lose a child or grandchild, Rusty, but there is nothing worse. And instead of hesitating at the boundary of decency, you've aired Hardy's dirty linen and put a rent in his marriage. And ruined his career in the process. He'll be out of office by the end of the year. He doesn't realize it yet. But I do. He's going to lose the primary to Madison, who even you will come to regard as a far worse PA. That's another service you've done to justice."

I have been thinking about Hardy now and then since our encounter in the men's room. Oddly, I have arrived at the same place as Bea, feeling sorry for him. Bea said all of Hardy's actions descend from a sense of powerlessness that often enrages him. That would explain all his bad behavior in league with Glowoski. It's got to be the zenith of impotence to be unable to protect your child.

"Hardy has been a target because he made himself a target," I say. "Even you must be able to see that."

He takes a sip on his scotch and rattles the cubes against the glass.

"He thinks you're getting even with him," Mansy says, "Hardy does."

"For what?"

"He won't say. But I suspect it has something to do with Bea. I always had the feeling those two were not quite done with one another."

I could defend myself somewhat with the facts, say that I'd started trashing Hardy before I knew why I should be looking for revenge. But if Hardy is too embarrassed to tell his father the truth—perhaps because he looks so foolish, moping after a woman for decades who was basically using him as a sex toy and then dumped him in the end—then I won't either.

"Please think about this," I say in reply.

"There's no chance I will. This is about what's best for the Potters, all of us, what will make Mae's death easiest to deal with. And having twelve hicks applaud your circus act and let Aaron go is a damn sight better than declaring the trial never should have happened in the first place. Which would say everything Hardy and Charmaine—and I— have suffered during these proceedings was all for naught."

I haven't touched my drink and I'm not going to. But I will tell Mansy the truth. There's no point in diplomacy.

"You're right. This *is* about the Potters. Because when you really stand back and look at this, the only reason Aaron is on trial is because of them. Hardy decided even before Mae was found that he wanted Aaron in prison. 'A person of interest,' " I say with contempt.

"That's because Charmaine and he were terrified for their daughter, and your client decided not to answer questions."

"He was happy to answer questions, Mansy, but with some legal protection. He was on probation, which prohibited activities he would have admitted to, like driving a car or hanging around with a drug user—namely, your granddaughter. Cap was afraid, with good reason, that even after Mae came back, Hardy would jigger things and violate Aaron, so he could keep him away from Mae for years. I would call Cap's advice sage lawyering, given all the lines Hardy crossed.

"And let's be honest, Mansy. It's not all on Hardy. You've been telling him right from wrong for years. But you decided to put a stopper in your mouth after Mae died. You've known Vanda Glowoski for a long time. You understand the bond she has to your family. You knew damn well that no matter how competent she is ordinarily, she wouldn't lead a dispassionate investigation in this case. Instead, her loyalty to your family would compel her to let Hardy call all the shots. Did you step in and tell him that was dangerous and idiotic?"

"He's my son. He was insane with grief. We all were."

"I grant you, Mansy, that if I had the same power your family wields, and it was my child or my grandchild who was dead, I might not have behaved any better. But having Hardy and Vanda in charge was a recipe for disaster. So no complaints that, lo and behold, that's exactly what it turned out to be, a disaster, a catastrophically closed-minded investigation.

"And once Aaron was arrested, the Potter family—and I know damn well you were part of this—decided Aaron should stand trial in Marenago County, where there was much less chance that Aaron might catch a break because one or two jurors knew Bea or Lloyd or him. So don't beef about Hiram Jackdorp. Because you chose him.

"So yeah, you're right, in the end, it *is* all about the Potters. And this question: Will that family, which has always acted with enormous decency, let the legacy of this tragedy be all their shameful power plays? Or can the Potters be the noble and righteous people they usually are, look into their hearts and say, 'We were wrong, we let sorrow destroy our judgment, and we will now make amends, by not forcing an innocent young man to risk a verdict in an all-white county where his race is the only real evidence left against him.' "

"That's BS, Rusty. The reality is Aaron will walk out of there because Hardy and Vanda made those mistakes. And me too, if you want to blame me for the same errors. *That's* the truth. At least if Aaron doesn't breathe life back into the prosecution by getting on the stand." As soon as Mansy hears his last words, he stops cold and slowly rears back against the dark leather. He emits a low sound, while he lifts his face to see me from the side.

"Oh," he says, "oh, *that's* what this is about. That's why you're thumping your chest and giving me all these pretty speeches about the good and the true. Because your idiot client is going to jump on the witness stand. It's not enough for him to get away with murder. He needs to lie to their faces, too. *That's* your problem, isn't it?" He snorts. "You want me to save that twisted little devil from himself, when you can't."

He's had a napkin on his lap for some reason and throws it on the table as he slides awkwardly to the edge of the banquette he's been seated on.

"And let me tell you one more thing," he says. "This was a wasted trip. Because even if you'd convinced me with all your blather, there's one person who'd never accept it."

I know what he's going to say.

"Charmaine?"

"You're damn right. Charmaine. I haven't even talked about what you've done to her—publicly humiliating a devastated grieving woman who's sick as hell. You've destroyed her life, too, Rusty. There's wreckage everywhere you've gone."

"It's called the criminal justice system, Mansy. It's a slaughterhouse and just about everybody who gets close ends up spattered with blood. People think it's so great to punish bad guys until they're caught up in the grisly business of doing it. And yes, I have thought often—*often*—about the toll this has taken on all of you, the way you've been steeped in pain every minute. But is the right response to cause more suffering? To risk imprisoning an innocent young man for the sake of your family's pride?"

Mansy slugs down everything that's left in his glass and gets up without even saying goodbye. He walks off with his old man's gait, a limp a bit more pronounced on the left than the right. I notice again that the back end of his chinos looks like an empty paper bag.

The truth is that I never really believed I'd lose Mansy's friendship. In the future I foresaw, I'd fuck things up in Marenago and Mansy would end up trying to console me.

But it's as Mansy says. There is blood and loss everywhere. I realize only now that if, pray God, dear God, Aaron is home soon, I will not be exulting. I'll be there with the Potters, still reeling and touching my wounds and dwelling on everything this case has cost me.

47

Testimony

A aron," I begin, "did you kill Mae Potter?"

He is a bit taller than many of the other witnesses and has to lean forward to the microphone stalk on the witness stand to be certain his quiet answer is heard.

"No."

"Did you *ever* deliberately hurt Mae Potter physically?"

"No. Never."

So far so good, I think. He is utterly placid and shows no ragged signs of nerves. Bea has bought him a new shirt—bright white today—and a red tie, and he also appears to have slept well, looking a good deal fresher than his lawyer.

He is the second witness of the afternoon. The first was his Narcotics Anonymous sponsor, Rev. Donall Spruce. Dr. Spruce is an enormous man, close to six eight and probably three hundred pounds, who appeared in a white clerical collar and a black suit. He has a lot of grey in his hair and in the small mustache he wears, and is utterly imperturbable. His sonorous deep voice sounds like God—if God has a gender.

Susan and I thought Reverend Spruce would be a good way to introduce the jury to Aaron's conviction, demonstrating that Aaron turned an ostensible negative, his jail time, into a positive by enrolling in Spruce's program and sticking with it. Dr. Spruce says he also sees Aaron for individual counseling and ministering from time to time, and that Aaron appears regularly for Sunday worship, despite the distance from Mirror to Kweagon.

We were not, strictly speaking, allowed to ask the Reverend if he believes Aaron's sobriety is permanent, but that bears on Aaron's truthfulness, which is what a character witness, like Reverend Spruce, is supposed to address.

He said, "I have great faith in the person he is today as the person he will be, and full confidence in his truthfulness."

On cross, Jackdorp asked a good question, that is, whether in the various programs that Reverend Spruce leads in four different penal institutions throughout the middle part of the state, Dr. Spruce has made mistakes from time to time in his assessments of the character of some of those enrolled.

'Well, sir, I would answer you this way. Yes, but—'

Jackdorp cut him off with a stern 'Thank you,' and I objected that the witness should be allowed to complete his answer. Given the strict control I tried to maintain on cross of the prosecution witnesses, Judge Carrington overruled me. I said that I would just ask on redirect, and Jackdorp, knowing that was only moments away, sighed and said, 'All right, Reverend, let's hear it.'

'As I was saying, sir, I make mistakes. I've even had my heart broke now and then, although I'm always telling myself that their lives are in their hands and God's, not mine. But over the years, there have been some when you just *know* they've made the change. And Aaron is one of them. And, not to boast, but in those cases, I really don't think I've been wrong yet.'

He clearly went down well with the jury, but it's always a question whether character witnesses count for much in the end.

As soon as he was done, we introduced the record of Aaron's clean drug test on the Monday after he returned from his trip with Mae. We made copies for each juror and asked permission to distribute the two pages. Some studied the document, some didn't. Mrs. Liu, who runs Portage's one Chinese restaurant with her husband, seemed to read it over twice. Washboard thin, with her straight obsidian hair and bangs, she has impressed me throughout by her attentiveness. Given her accent and the hesitant way she spoke to the judge and lawyers, we feared at first that she might struggle with legal language but by all appearances her comprehension has been unwavering.

I face Aaron again now.

"And how did you meet Mae?"

"Well, the first I saw her was at a church dance in junior high."

"Do you go to church?"

"Not as much as I should, I guess. But I accept Jesus in my heart." The cross tattooed on his neck is partly hidden by his shirt collar, but we've instructed him to touch it respectfully when he answers this question, so the jurors realize what it is. He lays two fingers there tenderly. "I've always known He was there, since I was four or five. And He's been a big part of my getting sober. Back then, in junior high, I was going every Sunday with my dad and my stepmom and my stepsisters. Lakeside United Congregation of God on 75, between Mirror, where I grew up, and Como Stop."

"And you saw Mae at that church dance?"

"It was a Young Life thing. And I mean, man, I saw her and I was *slain.*"

"Did you speak to her?"

"Man, I was twelve, and she was definitely a snack, even at twelve. Everybody talked about her, not just how she looked, but you know, her family, the Potters. They were the top, they ran everything. I was way too intimidated to speak to her, except to kind of whisper hi."

"And how did your relationship progress?"

"Well, the next year, eighth grade, we were in the same Sunday school class, and I was less afraid of her and we talked sometimes, even on the phone now and then. Charmaine, Mrs. Potter, when she testified, she said Mae and I were going out since then. Which, in junior high, is a whole bunch of nothing. And maybe that's what Mae said. But *I* was just a dumb guy and didn't realize exactly what was happening."

There is some tittering in the courtroom, including from three of the women in the jury box. The other hair-curler lady—Ellmendorf, I believe—who doesn't have much sense of humor, allows herself a motherly smile.

"Please continue describing the evolution of your relationship."

"Well, the next year, we were both freshmen at Skageon Consolidated, and I saw her more often. It was the usual stuff, trying to bump into her walking between classes. But something was going on right away. Her friends were telling me she liked me. She started saying I should come to parties. It happened real fast, the way I recall. I barely knew her and then we were a couple. And then we were in love.

"I know grown-ups kind of smile when you talk about teenagers, young teenagers, being in love. But honestly, I don't think grown-ups *can* fall in love like that. Not how Mae and I fell in love. You're young, a kid, you love your parents and your friends, but you're still alone. And I felt really alone, you know, being adopted, being Black—there wasn't anybody else like me. And then there was this person who *was* me. My soul. It was an entirely different existence. When you're fourteen and in love—everything else kind of falls away. Everything else is just kind of mid, except that person. We were our own world. If we decided there was no gravity, then no matter what anybody else saw, in our minds we'd be flying. Up into junior year, that was the greatest time in my life, being in love with Mae. And she was so outstanding, truly. She's like one of the smartest people who ever lived, and funny, I mean I was *dead* all the time. I loved her so much. And I think she was just as much in love. And truth, man, I've never had something like that with anybody else. Something that intense. That consuming. Someone rent-free inside me all the time? I'll always love Mae. Always."

"And how long did that floating state—how long did it continue?"

"Like into junior year, and then Mae began to get different. I mean, she was always unhappy like at home, always scrapping with her parents. But suddenly everything with her, man, it got dark. Moods. Up and down. Sometimes, like the middle of the night, she'd want to go out to the Cliffs, that's at Como Lake, and jump butt naked into the water fifty feet down below, and then she'd get down and glum, and just hang out in her parents' basement with no lights. And get high. I don't know how to explain this. But there was like Mae with me, and Mae not with me, and Mae not with me was not really somebody I cared for all that much. She was kind of flighty, and stupid a lot of the time. She did mean stuff—like the story Cassity told about the Christmas ornaments. She was like somebody in deep water who thought she knew how to swim and didn't really and was just thrashing every limb so she could float.

"She got into drugs then. I mean, more. We'd both tried some of everything. But you know, she got into coke. I did it with her. I liked it, too, I'm not blaming her.

"And I'd say, looking back, by the time we graduated, we were both addicts, or pretty close to it, really. Mae, you know, she'd say, 'You're not on the hook if you've got the money,' which, even as messed up as I was, I knew was ridiculous. But the coke, I don't think you get strung out like I did on meth. I just really liked the lift it gave me.

"We said we were breaking up when we went off to college, that we'd see other people. Mae started at this great little college in Iowa where her family had gone for like a century, and I went to Wisconsin State, and I was just, you know, miserable. I was miserable without Mae, even though we were fighting a lot while we supposedly weren't together. I was high all the time, and I was on the way to flunking out when the university closed because of the pandemic. And you know, I got cracked the first time then—"

"Arrested?"

"Yes sir. Mae's little college in Iowa had shut down too, and she came up to Glenville one weekend, and I went out to buy stuff from this dude I thought was a college kid who turned out to be an undercover cop. I had, like, five hundred bucks on me, which the police thought meant I was dealing. But I'd gotten the money from Mae. For a while they were saying I was going to get prosecuted as an adult, but eventually I got a juvie adjustment and probation. But when I went back to Mirror, the cops, the Skageon deputies, they had an eye on me. Hardy, her dad, he thought Mae's whole drug issue was me.

"I came back to Mirror then. I can't even tell you what I did for the next year and a half, because I was just absolutely fried most days.

I was just a lowdown dirty junkie. I shoplifted a lot, I stole from my parents. I ended up living in a sketchy apartment with all these sketchy people in and out, and always looking for drugs."

"What about Mae?"

"In the fall, she told her parents her college had reopened, even though it hadn't. She was just hanging out in Iowa when her parents caught her. Somehow, that became something else her parents blamed on me. She moved back then. And for like the next year, we'd meet up and do drugs. We were too burnt up even for sex a lot of the time. And one night I was driving my car—I had an old car Joe had given me—and the cops were just waiting for me and pulled us over, said I was driving erratic, which I'm sure I was, but they were waiting for me anyway.

"So I had on me this baggie full of pills Mae had bought. They were in my pocket because Mae, she always wanted a nice drip, look sleek and smooth, nothing in her pockets but her phone. And this time I was held in the Skageon County Correctional Center, while my case went through court." I make it a point to turn toward the jury, so I can test their reactions to this troubling part of Aaron's biography. And that, frankly, is how they look—troubled. I've noticed that Mr. Alvin Smith, who loved Akylles, has a habit of waving all ten fingers right above the rail of the jury box when he's pondering, and his hands, moving like he's practicing a piano piece, indicate he's thinking hard. Even my good-natured hair-curler lady has developed a narrow squint as she considers Aaron.

"What were the charges?"

"Possession with intent to distribute."

"Did you have any thought of saying that the drugs you were carrying were Mae's?"

"Man, what was the point? It wasn't like I hadn't taken them. It wasn't like I hadn't been driving high. I totally had been. So why snitch her out? The cops knew anyway. But she was the PA's daughter. At one point, she came to visit me in jail and said she was gonna tell her dad the stuff was hers. And I was like, 'Baby, if you get in trouble too, your dad and mom, they're just gonna hate me worse.'"

"And what happened to your case?"

"Well, the four months I was in jail, that wasn't a great time, but

I was like Akylles. I promised myself I was never going back. I got sober. Reverend Spruce came up there once a week to run the program and I got into it, and I trusted in Jesus's guidance. I attended the Rev's virtual meetings every day and went to group at the jail. I'm two years sober now."

"Congratulations," I say. "And how was your case resolved?"

"My lawyer made me a deal, time served if I pled guilty. So I did. I mean, I was guilty, so what else was there to say?"

"Was that a felony you pled to?"

"Right. Possession with intent. I was put on probation for two more years, with all these conditions. No driving. No using. No leaving the county. No hanging with the wrong people. That's the court order we've been talking about. It was part of my sentence."

"And what happened to Mae?"

"Well, by the time I got out, she was gone. Cassity told that story. Her parents were kind of desperate for her to go back to college, but she wanted to do her modeling thing in New York."

"Did you stay in touch while she was in New York?"

"Texts, but she was still using a lot, and that wasn't what I needed."

Although it didn't dawn on me before, there are two people on the jury, the other hair-curler lady and the youngest man, who are nodding now. I don't know their backstories, although you'd guess from their reactions that they have children or spouses or relatives who were users, or perhaps they are in a twelve-step program themselves. We didn't go anywhere near that subject during voir dire, the questioning of potential jurors, because the idea of Aaron testifying was not something we were seriously entertaining, and we didn't care to plant the thought that addiction had any role in the case.

"I had to live with my mom and her fiancé—that was another part of the court order—so they could keep an eye on me. I thought it would be worse than it was. I got a really good job—Brice talked about that—and I actually felt I was getting somewhere. Finally. I got the feel of a regular life, and I liked it. I started thinking about art school."

"And what about Mae?"

"She came back from New York after a while there. One more big bust-up with her parents. I'd heard gossip about what had happened, but I never wanted to, you know, embarrass her by asking straight out. One good thing about New York was that she'd gotten into mixed martial arts training, especially the kickboxing part of it, and she wanted to open a studio in Como Stop, and did for a while. I mean, all this talk that I laid hands on Mae and hurt her? I mean, man, that is *humorous.* That woman, you know, she had some serious moves. She'd bust me up if I got physical, that's the truth. It would have been like fighting a kangaroo. Four limbs of fury, man. That was something she'd say. Watch her hands and then there's a foot coming out of the sky."

There is a good deal of laughter, including from the jury box. I take a second to glance back to the gallery. Nat and his wife, Anna, and the girls are beside Bea and Lloyd and Joe. Nat knows that Bea and I have not patched things up yet, but he still said they, his entire family, wanted to be here for Aaron and for her.

Aaron is testifying in what is called a modified narrative form, telling his story without me waylaying him often for questions. He wanted the jurors to hear him, and Susan and I agreed that this would be the best way. So far, Jackdorp is letting Aaron proceed. In a criminal case, the jurors always yearn to hear the defendant's side, much as they often end up doubting him. Jackdorp is wise enough to realize that they would resent frequent interruptions.

"Did you see Mae during this period when you were on probation?"

"I tried not to. We'd text sometimes. I mean, she was still my friend. She would always be my friend. And she was always hilarious."

"Did you see other women?"

"Sure. But, you know, it wasn't like Mae, nobody was ever going to be like Mae. Not as smart, not as funny. And they never got me the same way. I mean, I'd talk about her to people like Cassity. I'd say I missed her. And they would tell me I was cray."

"So how did you reunite with Mae?"

"There was a party in late August last year at one of our friends'. It was an end-of-summer thing for the kids who were heading back to college, and you know, Mae was there and she was kind of bringing it. It was the first time in forever we'd really talked in person. And you know, for me, talking to Mae was like talking to nobody else. I mean, she *knew* me and I knew her, it was pretty special. And I was really happy being with her. Really happy.

"She knew I couldn't drive, and she offered me a ride home, but we both wanted to talk more—it had been so long. So she drove me around the lake and we parked in the public lot by the boat launch, and anyway, long story short, we ended up in the back of her SUV. And that part was great for both of us, as it usually was, if we weren't zeroed out on dope. And that was when she said, 'Man, we really need to stop fighting this thing, it's you and me, it always will be.' She said the only time in her life she like knew who she was was when we were together. Finally, she said, 'You know, we should just get married.'

"I was like Whaaat? But I didn't say that out loud."

"Did you want to get married?"

"Not then. I always expected I'd get married someday, but you know, I still had a lot to figure out. But I didn't want to just reject her. And you know, she made sense when she said we were never getting over one another. I said I'd think about it, and I did."

"You told us a second ago that people you trusted had already advised you against taking up with Mae again."

"Reverend Spruce—or my mom—they both thought Mae was part of the addiction, that I was like addicted to Mae. And that when I was with her, I'd do whatever she wanted, just like I'd do for drugs. My mom's thing was that Mae got off on messing with me, because she wanted me to be as unhappy as she was. Dr. Spruce, he didn't like the idea of getting back with Mae either. He was like, 'Yeah, but in this life, you don't get to go backwards. You're not fourteen. You're twenty-two. You've seen some ugly things. You've done some ugly things. You won't be in love like that again. It's sad. But you only get to do first love one time.'

"And I really thought about that. But I didn't want to be fourteen again. I wanted Mae because Mae was amazing when she could be herself.

"So you know, Mae and I were talking a lot then, on the phone sometimes for hours, and I told her, 'If you're serious about this, marriage and being together, then there have to be a lot of steps in between.' I thought, you know, if she felt that I was truly with her, committed to her, then she could get back to being herself, the person I knew she could be. 'But we really need to talk this through,' I told her. 'We need to go away and like focus on just us. No phones, turn them off.'"

"And why was it that you wanted to turn off your phones, power them down?"

"Well, obviously, while I've been in jail up here since I got arrested—"

Jackdorp objects instantly and the judge sustains him. Aaron's confinement in Marenago is irrelevant to guilt or innocence, but his reference now was, candidly, inserted on my instructions, so the jurors know he's already endured some punishment, which one or two who doubt he's a murderer might feel he still deserves for things like violating probation.

"I just meant I don't have a phone now," he says. "But from the time I first got one, I'd power it down when I wanted to be by myself. Usually, I'd turn off the voicemail too."

"Why was that?"

"If I didn't get messages, I didn't have to worry about listening to them. I mean, people may not agree with me, but I think it's up to me to decide when I want to be in touch. If I need to be by myself, without other people reaching after me, then I should be able to do that. Alone time—like I said, that's how I grew up, feeling super alone, and sometimes I need to go back to that. It's, like, at the center of who I am."

"And did Mae agree when you said you'd power down?"

"Sure. And I also said no drugs. 'I don't judge,' I said, 'but there can't be drugs. We need to be there, each of us, one hundred percent.' And she was like, 'Yeah yeah yeah, of course.'"

"And what happened?"

"Well, we left in the afternoon of September 12. Because of probation, I needed to stay in-county. So we went up to Harold's Woods, and she seemed super excited to be there at first, but only so she could go stepping around and take selfies against this beautiful background.

I didn't get what she was up to initially. I thought she, like, needed some time just hanging out before we started talking seriously, and I was okay with that, because, I mean, it was big stuff. After the sun went down, we started to make camp and it began raining. I mean hard, like the drops were bouncing off the ground. We put up the tent while it was coming down and got soaked. We weren't in a designated campfire area, but we built a fire anyway, we were so cold. But we couldn't really get it going. And we were just like choking on the smoke, me especially, because I was being like I'm Mr. Survivor, I can make a fire in the middle of a hurricane, and I kept trying. Honestly, I smelled like the inside of a fireplace afterwards. But we had to give up and walk back to the parking lot. We sat in her car until the rain let up some, and it was a good time, just vibing. Me and Mae never really ran out of stuff to talk about. I mean, people sometimes said we were a great match, because she loved to talk and be the center of attention, and I was basically quiet, but with me, she listened a lot too. She really did."

"Did Mae put her boots on the dashboard and the center console then, while you were in the car?"

"Yes. I mean, Mae sometimes would drive for a minute when the car was on cruise with her right boot on the dashboard. I'm not kidding. Anyway, finally the rain let up some, and we were both hungry. So at last I got the fire going and we roasted some veggie dogs on sticks. I mean, Mae was pretty much a vegetarian. She'd do coke and fentanyl, but she wouldn't eat meat." He gives his head a tiny shake at the mystery of that. "I knew cooking there wasn't so smart, but it was like five minutes. But bears' noses are eight times more sensitive than dogs'. They can smell stuff miles off.

"I figured we'd hear them before there was a problem, but we didn't. The rain had finally stopped, and we were back in the tent. It was way more than an hour since we'd cooked, but then we heard the bear pawing through our trash. We were naked by then, and you know, in the middle of things, which is not how you want to be saying hello to a bear." In the courtroom there is another riffle of laughter. Again, I peek over to see several jurors smiling. They are with him, I realize. They're past the drug use and his conviction, and the women especially *love* him. Aaron has paused to smile, as he rarely does. There is a brownish cast to his teeth I've always noticed, but it never dawned on me before that it's a leftover from his meth use. Hiding that may even be part of the reason he generally remains so deadpan.

"I didn't want to make any noise, but we still had to scramble around to get dressed in case we had to run. We had a little rucksack with the food in the tent with us, and I raised the flap and like hurled it. And the bear chased after it. It was like in shreds in the morning. Really. Just strips of cloth."

"Is that when you stepped on Mae's blouse, when you were rushing to get dressed?"

"It might be. To tell you the truth, I don't remember stepping on Mae's blouse. And I know Mae didn't see it, because she was very particular about that stuff, her fit, her clothes. She'd have gone off on me. But with a bear right outside, we were moving fast in a very small space, truly scrambling, so yeah, I could have stepped on her blouse by accident. I mean, we were scared, both of us.

"Afterwards she said she had to take something to calm down— she'd always needed stuff to sleep—and it seemed okay at first, but she must have taken more in the middle of the night and couldn't get up. She was still snoring at noon. I took her car and drove off to get a rope and more food. We needed it and I had no idea when she'd wake up. When I got back, I put the groceries in my backpack and got the rope over a bough of a tree near our campsite, and suspended my pack from that.

"Mae got up around then. And we took a hike, but she was so high, I was afraid she was going to fall off the trail, and all the time she was taking selfies. I mean, two steps and she'd lift the phone and smile into it. So like, I finally said, 'I mean, what the hell?' And it turned out she had this semi-insane plan I'd never heard about to become an influencer, so she could get her own money and her parents didn't have a string on her. But her brain was everywhere. It was a bad day.

"After dinner, when I thought she was coming down, I told her what I'd meant to tell her."

"And what was that?"

"Well, I'd planned this big speech, and I pretty much gave it to her. First off, I needed her to know how great she was, that she'd never be with anyone who realized that more than me. And I could feel her, too, the pain of how far she'd gotten from that person and how much she wanted to get back to that. I mean, I know she wanted to be with me, because she had *loved* herself when we were first together. And she deserved to feel that way, because Mae, the real Mae, she was just an absolute *star*, I mean really, a star."

I'm trying not to stroll too much as Aaron speaks, because I don't want to distract the jury from him. But I do face the gallery briefly, to measure the response out there, as a proxy for the jurors, who I remain cautious about checking out too often. My glance passes over Mansy, who's covered his face with both hands at Aaron's mention of Mae's luminance. Charmaine is weeping silently, and I allow my eyes to linger on her an instant with what I hope is a sympathetic look.

"And I wanted to help her. I was willing to make that commitment, not to get married right now, but to say we were trying to work toward that, to say out loud to everybody—her parents and my parents and our friends—that we intended to be together thick and thin. But there were a couple of things that were kind of had-to-be's for me.

"First off, I wanted her to know that overall, I liked being sober. And I needed to be with someone who would respect that. Because being sober wasn't always easy. I wasn't going to judge, and if she wanted to have a drink now and then, or whatever, okay, but partying every day and living high—that would never work for me. Because that would disrespect me and what I needed.

"And second, for her own sake, there was stuff she had to start setting aside. Like her parents, her dad, especially. She had plenty of good reasons to be pissed at him, plenty, but she wasn't in charge of raising him; he raised her. She wasn't ever going to give him up, so just stop all the wrangling and make the best of it.

"And last, and maybe most important, if she needed help to be herself, then she should accept that. She'd told me before she didn't like the drugs the psychiatrist had given her, because she thought they took the edge off life. If there was another way for her to get a hold of herself besides the meds, fine, but if that didn't work, then she needed to think hard about taking them."

"How did she react?"

"Mostly, she just listened. And mostly I wasn't even sure I was getting through. The one thing she sparked on was the meds. 'So you want me to take *some* drugs but not others?' That was Mae, just so quick and sharp. And I said all of that was up to her, it wasn't up to me. But if she could find a way back to who she really was, that would make both of us so happy.

"After that, you know, we made love again, which was pretty real and tender, and she promised that we'd have a better day tomorrow. We said we'd get up to watch the sunrise, but it was like, you know, Groundhog Day. I could see as soon as we were on the trail that she was high already, and taking pictures of herself every second step. The morning light was streaking the sky in these amazing colors, but it was just a background to her while she was posing and looking at her camera. I was angry at her, and even angrier at myself. I mean, I'd really told her my truth the night before, and this was her answer, making videos of herself for freaking TikTok. I kept thinking of the Bible verse, from Corinthians, 'When I was a child, I used to talk as a child, think as a child, reason as a child; when I became a man, I put away childish things.' Reverend Spruce had quoted that to me.

"And it killed me, but I realized that morning on that walk that Mae was something I was going to have to put away. For years, I felt I could never be who I wanted without Mae. And now I saw, I had it backwards: I could never be that person *with* her. Because whoever or whatever she'd been years ago, something had broken inside her. She just couldn't let somebody love her, not anymore. She was going to punish anyone who tried."

At those words, a single sudden high-pitched sob resounds through the courtroom. I do not have to turn back to know it is Charmaine. Her wail silences Aaron for a second, much as it has briefly frozen everybody here. He looks out toward the gallery and Mae's mother, and then with two fingers reaches inside his jacket and lays them for a second over his heart. The gesture transfixes this entire large chamber, as these two people, Aaron and Charmaine, so long at odds, recognize their connection, both having loved intensely the same young woman, both having suffered her loss, well before last September, when Mae submitted to her own unconquerable demons. It's the sort of instant that arises now and then in trials, about which you say, in retrospect, 'The case was over then.' I finally turn to observe Charmaine. She is positioned in the wheelchair notch at the end of the first row. Small and wasted, she has been abruptly surrounded by her husband, far bigger than she, who has drawn her into himself with his left arm. I'm sure he shares her anguish, but Hardy is also a trial lawyer, who clearly wants to cut short what seemed to be transpiring between Aaron and her.

"I told her that, as soon as we got back to camp. I tried to be nice, as nice as I could be in the circumstances, just like, 'Thank you for trying, I'll always love you, but this isn't going to work.' And she went off on me, you know: I wasn't fair, she'd get it together, she needed me, she'd end it all without me, I was like the key to her whole life. I just shook my head, and lowered the backpack from the tree and started packing my stuff.

"A minute later, I hear her talking, and she has her phone out, of course, and I realize she's making a video of me. She's like doing a voiceover. 'This is Aaron, who says he loves me, abandoning me in the middle of nowhere.' That was the end. The end end. It's right after she said she needed me so much and was going to get a grip, and now she wants to mock me on TikTok, for like a billion users. I was *so* steamed. I just jumped up and grabbed the phone out of her hand before she knew what I was doing and kept walking back down the trail toward the parking lot. I didn't even turn back for my pack. For a second, she was stunned, but then she started screaming and ran ahead of me, trying to block me and grab the phone, but I just stepped around her and held it over my head."

"Where were you then?"

"The parking lot."

"And did you see George Lowndes?"

"No. But Mae was making enough noise to attract a lot of attention."

"Did you hit her or lay hands on her in any way?"

"No. I mean, she was jumping up, trying to get the phone, and stumbled at one point. But she got right up. I never hit her or pushed her. I mean, that was just totally not our way, it never had been. We screamed, okay? At one point, she tried to kick me, but she was so stoned it was like in slow motion, and she came nowhere near me. And even that, you know, that never happened before, so it was like, this thing, us, it's just gone. Anyhow, I walked away. And she was like yelling behind me, 'Where are you going?' and I was like, 'Someplace I can be alone and get over this.' She shouted, 'You don't have a car,' like I was as mixed-up as she was and wouldn't realize that. I just held up one hand with my thumb out while I kept going without looking back."

"Did you hitchhike often?"

"A lot, once I was on probation. I rode my bike anywhere within, say, fifteen miles, when it wasn't insanely cold. When I couldn't bike, Joe, my grandfather, drove me sometimes. But I hitched plenty, too."

"Did you say anything to Mae about going to Ginawaban?"

"Not that I remember. She knew it was my top place. So maybe she figured that's where I was headed."

"And what did you do when you walked out of the parking lot?"

"Well, first off, to tell the truth, after I was sure I'd gotten completely away from her, I found this big rock and sat on it and, you know, cried a little. I was just feeling a thousand things, angry and upset and sad. And this emptiness inside me, like where there'd sort of always been a space for Mae. But I'd faced up to a lot of stuff in the last couple of years, and this was going to be another thing. No Mae. But I could do it. One day at a time."

"What did you do then?"

"I messed with her phone for a second and turned it off."

"Why?"

"I figured she'd go up to some store and buy a burner and call that phone a hundred times or track me, maybe both. I was done."

"So that would have been 9:06 a.m. on September 14?"

"Sounds right."

"And what did you do then?"

"I just started walking. There was almost no traffic coming out of the park, because it was a weekday after Labor Day. I figured I'd have to go up to the first main road, State 47."

"How far was that?"

"About four miles."

"And did you have any further encounter with Mae while you were walking?"

"Not face-to-face. But about an hour on, I heard a car roaring down the road behind me. When I looked back, I thought I saw the Subaru, and I just ran into the brush beside the road. But she'd seen me."

He tells the story of Mae stopping, screaming, and when he would not come out from hiding and return her phone, throwing his pack on the roadside and peeing on it, before tearing off again in her car. The jury has heard fragments of this tale a couple of times now, from Cassity and Akylles, but there is still scattered laughing and a good deal of headshaking in the courtroom about Mae's extreme behavior.

"I thought it was a little funny, until I realized that I'd never get back to Mirror in one day, and I was going to have to spend the night in a wet stinky sleeping bag. And I mean, I was really messed up by the whole situation, disappointed in Mae and disappointed in me. And by the time I got to Route 47, I was completely turned around and on the wrong side of the road when Akylles stopped for me.

"Once I was in the rig with him, I'm watching stuff go by and thinking, I don't remember this, and then I looked up at the sun and thought, Oh shit. Sorry," he murmurs and glances to Wendy Carrington, who lifts her hand with a small smile to wave off the apology. "I turned on my phone to get GPS just to be sure. I groaned out loud and I told Akylles I was going in the wrong direction. He kind of ribbed me, you know, 'That woman got you turned around, young man,' but you know, I wasn't supposed to leave Skageon County, and we were in Marenago by then, and my probation officer could check my location anytime. Anyway, I was dealing with all that and then the phone buzzed in my hand. I looked at it for a second before I answered, but it was a number I didn't recognize. I'd applied for commercial art jobs everywhere in the Midwest, so I thought, Well, maybe I'm getting an interview. But it was Mae. She just said, 'Aaron, I can't live without you. I'll kill myself, I really will.' Mae could be pretty manipulative, and I just felt all this hopelessness and hung up on her and shut down my phone again."

He tells the story of his trek home after leaving Akylles, walking south on 47 with his stinking pack, and spinning around to stick out his thumb whenever he heard traffic coming. He got three rides that day, but there were also two people who stopped, but wouldn't let him in the car when they smelled him. By sundown on the fourteenth, he was no better than thirty miles south of Harold's Woods. He walked along the roadside until he found a wooded area just off 47. There was a dry culvert nearby and that's where he tried to sleep. Around eight fifteen, he turned his phone on to call Cassity, and afterwards finally looked at his texts. He returned messages to his probation officer and his parents, so they knew he was on the way back, and powered off again, mostly so he could save juice.

Rides were just a little better the next day, but he was still thirty miles from Mirror when he ran into a high school friend at a gas station next to a campground he'd sneaked into. He got back to Mirror about two a.m. on the sixteenth. He talked to his mom and her fiancé for a while, then tried to go to sleep. He had put the backpack in his closet.

"Is that how the rope fibers ended up in your closet?"

"Probably. The backpack had been up and down the tree on the rope several times. The fibers could have been on my clothes. I just threw them in the corner of the closet, too, until I could wash them. Which didn't work, by the way."

"And where was the rope you'd bought?"

"It was on the ground under the tree in Harold's Woods, last I saw of it. I had no need for it at that point. I assume Mae took it with her when she packed up the campsite."

Jackdorp objects to the last sentence as speculation, and the judge sustains that.

"And what became of your backpack?"

"I couldn't sleep the night I got back to Mirror. I could smell the backpack across the room, and I couldn't stand the reek. I took it out to the firepit and lit a fire and threw it in. The sleeping bag was cinched to the bottom. I thought about saving it, but you know, it was always going to remind me of Mae, of our last times together, and it hadn't smelled any better than the pack when I slept in it. So I let it burn too."

"And what about your jeans and shirt?"

"I washed them, but the smoke was never coming out. I wore them to paint the first day, but then Brice got me a pair of coveralls, so I threw those clothes in the trash."

"Did you hear Mrs. Potter's testimony, Charmaine Potter's testimony, about returning Mae's phone?"

"Yes."

"Was that correct, as far as you're concerned?"

"Completely. I mean, it was Mae's phone, so I took it back when Brice and I knocked off after the first day. I wasn't stealing it. I just didn't want to be in any more videos."

"Did you realize that day, September 16, when you went to the Potters' house, that Mae hadn't returned?"

"No. I thought she was out, because her car wasn't parked in front. I think I heard from my mom when I got back that night that Mae wasn't back yet, which really surprised me."

"What did you think about Mae not coming home over the next few days?"

"To tell you the truth, I was doing my very best not to think about Mae. Brice and I were working pretty hard, and I really had to watch myself on that ladder, so I tried to keep my mind off her. Which didn't always work. For the first few days, I figured she was just out in the woods staying high, and she'd come back when she finished all the pills she'd brought with her. Then I started thinking she was trying to teach me a lesson, show me how much I'd miss her. Which, you know, I didn't need any lessons to realize that. But I figured she wanted me to go looking for her, which I nearly did."

"Calling your attention to September 28, did you learn that Mae's remains had been found at Ginawaban?"

"That was my last day working for Brice, and my mom and her fiancé were waiting to tell me. I can't describe that feeling. I was just totally bewildered. I really couldn't think. I didn't even feel like I had a body. I didn't sleep. So about four a.m. I got up and went over to my grandfather's and asked to borrow his truck."

"Driving violated your probation, didn't it?"

"I'm not sure I even remembered I was on probation. I was pretty messed up at that point. I just needed to get away by myself."

"And what was it your mother had told you about Mae's death?"

"Well, we all read that news item you showed Brice. And I heard local news on the truck radio. They'd found pills on Mae and assumed she was skulled and crashed after taking a wrong turn. The Subaru was at the bottom of some road buried in the woods."

"And what was your purpose in going away?"

"To be alone. To get somewhere I could feel myself and think. But pretty soon, I decided to go up to Ginawaban, where she'd died."

"Why did you want to go there?"

"For the same reason her father did. I loved her and I wanted to be where her spirit had departed, to kind of feel what I could of whatever little bit of her might still be clinging, you know, to life down here."

"When did you turn your phone off?"

"I didn't turn it off. I got one call from my mom's fiancé when I left the house, but I knew what that would be about, so I didn't answer, because I had, like, three percent on my phone and didn't want to waste it on getting chewed out. I'd grabbed my charging cord. Joe kept a 12-volt charger plugged in in the front of the truck, but I didn't notice it wasn't there until I was on the road. My phone was dead by then."

"When did you arrive in Ginawaban?"

"Late Friday."

"How late?"

"The sun was still up. I saw the evidence tape, but I walked around it and went down the road. I could see that they'd towed the Subaru out of there, which is what the first news item said was the plan. You know, I stood at the bottom and said a prayer and walked back up. And, like I told Deputy Holloway, the truck wouldn't start then. I knew why. The freaking alternator. I slept in the truck, on the flatbed, and once I was up on Saturday, I took the alternator out and then hitched with it to the nearest town, Armont, and found an auto parts store there. They tested the alternator and told me the problem was the wiring harness and ordered the part for me. They thought it might come in Monday. I bought some groceries and hitched back to the truck to stay out there until Monday, which was when Deputy Hollo-way found me."

"When did you learn that the authorities believed Mae had been murdered?"

"When Deputy Holloway told me about the warrant. It happened exactly like he said."

"Did you know there was a warrant for your arrest before then?"

"I had no idea. The radio didn't work in the truck without power. My phone was dead, which, you know, like I've explained, that was okay with me. So no, I had no idea about any of it until Holloway told me."

"Were you fleeing prosecution?"

"Like I've just said, I didn't know anything about a warrant or that she'd been murdered. And even if I heard she'd been murdered, I never would have thought anybody would think I'd done it."

"And do you have any idea who killed Mae Potter?"

For some reason the question seems to catch him short. We'd been over it several times, but I've garbled it slightly, because he hesitates now.

"I didn't kill her. I mean, you say, do I have any idea. I've heard some stuff in the evidence."

"I'm sorry. Do you *know* who killed Mae Potter?"

"No. It wasn't me. That's what I know."

I go back to check with Susan, then pass the witness to Jackdorp.

48

Cross

Because of prosecutors' general inexperience as cross-examiners, I've seen some employ what I can only call 'shtick' in confronting a defendant. John Walsh, who mentored me when I started out as a deputy PA, often refused even to engage. He'd wave a hand at the defendant and sit it out when it became his turn for questions. In closing, he would then argue, 'He's the defendant, of course he says he didn't do it.' Alexander Demetrieff, another senior guy, would basically rage. He'd advance toward the accused on the witness stand in the mincing sidesteps of a fencer, waving a finger and yelling something like, 'You did it, you did it, admit you did it!' They never did.

But unless Jackdorp is reading the room far differently than I am, he is going to have to challenge the core of Aaron's story. With limited time, Cap Sabonjian and I tried to school Aaron that during cross he should err on the side of brief answers, trusting that I will invite him to elaborate on redirect, if longer explanations are required. The hard part of being in 'the bucket,' as the witness stand is sometimes called, is that being effective requires some judgment. At occasional moments when it would only be natural for Aaron to explain himself, he should, if he can do it without appearing silly or defensive. Naturally spare with speech, Aaron might be very good on cross, or simply get tangled up and look guilty, which is, of course, the big risk he's taken.

After Aaron's direct, Jackdorp could have requested a brief recess to get his thoughts in order, but apparently he doesn't want the good impression Aaron made to sink in with the jury. In another boxy dark wool suit, Jackdorp walks forward and stands about three feet from Aaron with his arms folded, silent for an instant as he tries to stare Aaron down, which does not appear to work. Aaron remains expressionless, but refuses to look away.

"You've got all the answers, don't you?" Jackdorp says.

Aaron thinks, then says, "I don't understand that question."

"You've sat here and you've listened to the evidence and *now* you've got all the answers."

I'd rather not object. Jackdorp let Aaron tell his story without many interruptions, and the jurors will expect the same from me on his cross. It's also imperative that I never appear to be coaching Aaron. Yet I have no choice but to stand. I don't have to say anything, because Judge Carrington intervenes.

"Mr. Jackdorp, that's enough. You're on some very dangerous ground. I remind the jurors that the defendant has a constitutional right to hear the evidence against him and to testify at that point, if he chooses. Proceed, Mr. Jackdorp."

"But you've got an explanation for everything, Mr. Housley," he says. "All the evidence?"

Aaron runs his tongue around his mouth.

"That's because I'm innocent. Everything you think shows I did it doesn't show that at all. And that's the point of my testimony, Mr. Jackdorp. So I hope I *am* explaining everything."

Beside me, Susan shoots a quick look. She's far too disciplined to smile broadly in front of the jury, or say out loud, 'I told you so,' but I will have to grant that she predicted Aaron could do well up there.

"Now is it really true, Aaron, that out there in Harold's Woods, that was the first time you knew you had to be quit of Mae Potter?"

"I'm sorry?"

"Your mother, Reverend Spruce, Cassity—they all told you to stay away from her?"

"That's fair."

"You'd tried to end things with her before?"

"Yes."

"But you decided to try again anyway?"

"Yes."

"She had a hold on you, didn't she, Mae Potter, a hold you couldn't break?"

"I wouldn't agree with that. I thought if I could make it work with Mae, I'd have a better chance to be happy than I would with anybody else I'd ever meet. But I didn't feel like she was like some temptress who had me around her little finger."

"But you were out there with her against the advice of everyone you trusted?"

"Pretty much."

"And what you realized out there, Aaron, was that the only way to break away from her for good was to kill her. Isn't that so?"

He takes a second, leans closer to the microphone, and calmly says, "No."

"But you were 'steamed'—that was your word, wasn't it? Very angry because she wouldn't do what you wanted, wouldn't turn off her phone and pay attention to you? That made you very angry?"

"I was angry because she was breaking her word."

"And you said you never laid hands on her, but in order to get that phone, you had to wrestle it out of her hands, didn't you?"

"I grabbed it while she was messing with it."

"You used force."

"Barely. I, you know, took her by surprise. And kept walking with it."

"And you were steamed, Aaron, because she took that video of you packing up to leave?"

"Yes. I felt she was mocking me. She was breaking my heart and then posting about it to like build her following."

"She was humiliating you?"

"I don't think she realized that. She was just being totally into herself."

"But you were steamed and disappointed?"

"Yes. Definitely."

"Because being with Mae, you'd been happier than any other

time in your life, and now you had to face that it was never going to happen."

"Yes."

"You wanted to forget all about Mae."

"I was going to have to."

"Put her in the past?"

"Yes."

"And so you killed her."

"No sir."

"But you say at one point she attempted to kick you?"

"It was like for show. To show, you know, she was frustrated."

"But you were afraid she could hurt you?"

"She could, but like I said, she didn't try in the end."

"But that's why you hit her first, isn't it, Aaron? Before she could put that kickboxing to use?"

"I never hit her, Mr. Jackdorp. Because of stuff my mom lived through as a child, she always told me men don't hit women. Full stop. She said if she ever heard of me beating on a woman, it would just destroy her."

Oddly, although Cap asked almost the same question twice, Aaron never offered this reason. But knowing how Bea feels about Joe's behavior toward Willi, I'm certain this is true.

"But that business about the video she took, that makes a good story, doesn't it, Aaron? It explains why you took Mae's phone."

"It's not a story, Mr. Jackdorp."

"But it isn't true, Aaron, is it?"

"It's completely true."

Jackdorp goes to Glowoski and comes back with the plastic envelope with orange evidence tape in which Mae's phone rests.

"But as a matter of fact, Aaron, that video you claim she took. This is a story you made up later, isn't it? There was never any video posted, was there?"

Jackdorp thinks this is his big gotcha. Aaron remains placid.

"First of all, Mr. Jackdorp, I snatched it from her before she could do it. And it's not on the phone now, Mr. Jackdorp, because I deleted it. Like I said on direct, while I was sitting on that rock, I messed around with her cell. I found the video and trashed it. That was the reason I grabbed the phone to start with. Because it would have been so freaking insulting if she put that online."

"You knew her password?"

The government's forensic investigators have never figured out how to break into Mae's phone. But Aaron shrugs off Jackdorp's amazement.

"She knew my passcode, I knew hers. She used the letters for her sister's name on the keypad. If the phone's battery isn't out, I can open it for you now."

We're at the first real crisis of Aaron's cross, and my body reacts with a throb of alarm. We missed this, all of us, Cap and Susan and me. Taking it as given that the phone was locked, we never asked Aaron what happened to the video or whether he had any idea of Mae's code.

On first blush, it's worked out well. Aaron looks fearlessly honest in offering to open the phone. But it's a perilous moment for all of us, since neither side has any clue what's there. The images of Hardy's texts—including, perhaps, some to Bea—might remain. Yet the whole case would flip upside down, if, for instance, Mae had ever sent a message to anybody saying she feared Aaron physically.

My immediate anxiety is that Jackdorp, realizing the prosecution does not have much to lose at this stage, will accept Aaron's challenge and examine the phone now, or beg time from the judge to let his experts go through it. I've never believed much, when I was preparing witnesses, in setting traps for a cross-examiner. Too often, you're the one who will end up falling into the hole. But from Jackdorp's weighty pause, he seems convinced that's what we did, since it would be logical to forecast that he would confront Aaron with the lack of corroboration for his testimony about the video. I can't really imagine what Jackdorp fears is on the phone, and I suspect he has no clear idea either. But he can't shirk the habits of a lifetime. Prosecutors are supposed to build a case methodically, not swing for the fences. And I'm certain he's always abided by the courtroom maxim to never ask a question on cross to which you don't know the answer. He responds to Aaron's offer with a kind of sniveling smile—You won't get me!—and passes the back of his hand in Aaron's direction.

Instead, he goes sideways onto surer ground.

"But you didn't give Mae her phone back, did you, when she followed you with your backpack?"

"I couldn't just throw the phone at her, because, like, that might break it. And I wasn't getting into another face-to-face with her. I never minded that Mae was smarter than me, Mr. Jackdorp, because she was smarter than everybody. But being Mae, she'd have a hundred new reasons why she was going to change, and I didn't want to listen to that again. It was too frustrating and painful."

"So you left a young woman alone in the middle of nowhere with no means of communication?"

"Mae always had cash in her back pocket along with her license. The money is on the evidence inventory from when her body was found. Like I said, I kind of expected her to buy a burner phone and a phone card."

Because Aaron is so often catching the PA by surprise, Jackdorp's doing a poor job of controlling the witness, cutting him off and demanding yes or no answers. But the second of panic that just passed makes me realize that sooner or later, Jackdorp will score. He'll find some hook to tear at the fabric of Aaron's story. And he's probably saved his best stuff for last.

He tries a couple of other gambits, with less success. Aaron admits that the fact the phone was off when he headed up to Ginawaban kept him from being tracked, but says again that he had no reason to think law enforcement was looking for him.

Glowoski and her State Patrol colleagues have gone through Aaron's debit card records and found that he visited the grocery minutes after the news broke that Dr. Rogers had declared Mae's death a murder. Yet Jackdorp has no way to disprove Aaron's calm denials that he heard that while he was in town.

Jackdorp finally goes where I would have started, with the burning of Aaron's backpack and sleeping bag. Jackdorp asks the questions I first predicted. But Aaron is prepared. He says he's tried washing a backpack before, but it loses shape in the machine, and dry-cleaning the backpack and the sleeping bag would have cost a fortune, which was money he didn't want to spend while he was out of work. More important, he repeats what he told me that night, that he couldn't imagine ever using the sleeping bag after these last few days without thinking about Mae in it, which he was determined not to do.

But Jackdorp is finally more effective when he turns to Aaron's life as an addict.

"Did you steal then?"

I object, but Judge Carrington just shakes her head at me. A cross-examiner has the right to question about prior acts of dishonesty. We'd prepped Aaron accordingly.

"Yes."

"Who from?"

"I shoplifted a lot at the malls."

"What about your family? Did you steal from them?"

"Yes sir. I said that on direct."

"Who in your family did you steal from?"

"From my mom."

"No one else?"

"My grandfather was giving me money. And I couldn't steal from my dad's house, because he has a big security system."

"But you stole from your own mother?"

"Yes sir."

"What did you take?"

"I stole her engagement ring from my father, because she didn't wear it now."

"That all?"

"I stole their TV. Some table silver my mom's fiancé had from his wife who'd passed."

"Did you lie to them about whether you'd done that?"

"Yes."

"So we know you're the kind of person who steals and lies, don't we, Aaron?"

"We know what I was like when I was an addict, yes. But I was never violent, Mr. Jackdorp. I was, you know, strung out and desperate more than once, but I never hurt anybody physically."

That is an answer Cap and I prepped Aaron to give now, or on redirect.

Yet, as was just proved with Mae's phone passcode, Susan and Cap and I have not thought of everything. Nearing the end, Jackdorp finally finds a productive theme that brings home all the risks of Aaron's choice to testify. He gets Aaron to admit that he promised Judge Sams that he'd follow the terms of his probation, but despite that, he'd kept company with a drug user, driven without a valid license and even left the county.

"And your promise to Judge Sams, you made that in court, just like you're now promising these folks, in this court, that you're telling them the truth."

"I don't think going to where Mae died for a couple of hours, when I'd really respected the terms of my probation before that—that's not the same as lying under oath."

"So you get to decide whether or not to keep the word you give in court?"

Knowing he blundered, Aaron takes a second, and his delay does not look good.

"They're both wrong, you know, but one's a lot worse than the other. I mean, to me. I took an oath to God here."

That's a good comeback. But Jackdorp has finally damaged Aaron a bit.

"Now, we know, Aaron, that you lie to keep yourself from getting in trouble, don't you?"

"I'm sorry, Mr. Jackdorp. You're going to have to like tell me a specific thing you're talking about."

"For example, you knew you had to stay in touch with your mother and her fiancé under the terms of your probation, didn't you?"

"I knew that, yes."

"And when you ran off to Ginawaban on September 29, that wasn't the first time that you'd violated that term of your probation, was it?"

"If you mean when I went to Harold's Woods with Mae, I'd also been out of touch, yes, that's true."

"Had your dad and mom and her fiancé been angry at you about that?"

"Yes."

"And even though they'd been angry, you decided to do it again when you fled to Ginawaban, correct?"

"Yes."

"And when you went to the auto parts store with the alternator, you made no effort to recharge your phone, did you?"

"No. I forgot my charger."

"So you didn't think it was important to honor your probation and get in touch with your mom and her fiancé?"

"I was too upset to want to talk to anybody."

"And that's the reason you didn't contact anyone, isn't it? Not because you forgot your charger?"

"You asked why I didn't recharge my phone, Mr. Jackdorp."

"But the truth is you didn't want to."

"I didn't want to."

"Because the police could track you, if you turned it back on."

"That wasn't the reason. I wanted to be by myself."

"And as a matter of fact, you'd lied to your father and your mother and her fiancé after you left Harold's Woods on September 14, hadn't you?"

"No."

"Didn't you text them on September 14 that your phone had run out of juice and that's why you hadn't been in touch?"

I don't quite suppress an open grimace. Susan's head also droops for just a second. We forgot about this one.

"Sorry. Yes. That wasn't true. I wasn't ready to tell my mom I'd been with Mae and that I'd, like, turned my phone off because we'd both agreed to do that."

"But your mother's fiancé had texted you earlier in the day that he was going to have to notify the judge who put you on probation, if they didn't hear from you, hadn't he? Did you see that text when you turned your phone back on that night of September fourteenth?"

"There were a lot of texts that came in when I turned my phone on, especially from my mom."

"But you didn't want your mom's fiancé to notify the judge that you'd violated the terms of your probation, did you?"

"I'm not sure I'd seen that message, Mr. Jackdorp, but no, I definitely wouldn't have wanted him to tell Judge Sams that I'd violated my probation."

"And you knew that was a risk of being out of touch, right?"

"I guess, yes."

"And so you lied that you'd just been unable to recharge your phone, so they didn't know that you *deliberately* had avoided communicating."

"I've already explained why I said that."

"Because you didn't want your mother to know you'd been with Mae?"

"Right."

"And you didn't want to say that you'd violated your probation by being deliberately out of touch?"

With my heart sinking, because we missed this detail, I try clairvoyance, begging Aaron not to fight further. Just give Jackdorp his point.

"I think you're right," he says. "I didn't want to say I deliberately didn't contact them. But I was more worried about them feeling dissed than having trouble with my probation. But it's true. Saying I had just gotten to recharge my phone was a lie."

Good, I think. Better than more denials.

"So we know you lie, Aaron, to avoid getting in trouble, don't we?"

"What I said about the phone wasn't true."

"But that wasn't the only time you lied to stay out of trouble, was it?"

"I can see you've like got something in mind, Mr. Jackdorp."

Jackdorp, finally feeling he's very much in charge, can't stifle a nasty little smile.

"Didn't you tell Deputy Holloway that you hadn't gone down the utility road when you got to Ginawaban?"

Until we began prepping for Aaron's testimony, I hadn't known that he'd ventured to the bottom of the wash. Susan and Cap and I had disagreed initially about whether Aaron should acknowledge that on his direct testimony. I thought if he skipped that detail, there was a good chance Jackdorp wouldn't stumble upon it. But I was overruled by my client, who was determined to honor the full meaning of the oath to God he was going to swear.

'Truth is important,' he told us. 'Telling the truth is how you know who you are.' Assuming I can maneuver it, I expect to ask him to repeat that thought at the end of his redirect.

"I heard Deputy Holloway say that," Aaron says now. "I didn't mention to him that I'd walked down the road late Friday, but I never actually said I hadn't gone."

"But you intended to mislead him, didn't you, about whether you'd walked down the road to the crash site?"

"I didn't want him to know I'd gone down the road."

"Because of what you'd done there?"

"Because there was evidence tape up at the top, and I knew the police had meant to close off the road."

"But you went down anyway?"

"Because I needed to be at the spot Mae died. That was my whole point in going up there."

"What did you remove when you made this little trip down the utility road?"

"Mr. Jackdorp, the evidence techs had searched there when Mae's body was discovered, and at that point, I hadn't been in Ginawaban in years. And Deputy Holloway testified that nothing was removed or disturbed. And by the way, since I'm like defending myself, the only reason you know I went down the road is because I took an oath to tell the whole truth and I admitted that. So if I'm such a big liar, you need to tell me why I would say that, when I didn't have to."

Jackdorp moves to strike Aaron's last remark and the judge readily agrees. Aaron knows I had intended to make the same point with him on redirect, and he finally seems like he's getting rattled and losing command. This is just how Jackdorp wants the jury to see him. If Jack is smart, he'll quit soon, before Aaron recovers.

"Sorry, Your Honor," Aaron says when the judge grants Jackdorp's request. She nods barely. Her body language, too, indicates to me that Jackdorp is scoring.

"But you intended, Aaron, to lie or mislead Deputy Holloway, right?" Jackdorp says.

"Mislead, yes."

"Because you didn't want to get in trouble, right?"

"When I saw the deputy, I knew I was probably going to get in trouble on my probation for driving and leaving the county, and yes, I didn't want to make it worse."

"You lie to get out of trouble, don't you, Aaron? You lied to your mom and her fiancé about the phone? To Deputy Holloway about the utility road?"

"I didn't tell the whole truth. Those two times."

"Are you in trouble now, Aaron?" Jackdorp asks, and without waiting for an answer goes to sit down.

IV.

Judgment

49

Verdict

In life there is probably no other moment quite like the one when a jury delivers a verdict. Our existence also changes dramatically with unexpected events like a fatal car crash or a cancer diagnosis, but a jury verdict is one of those rare times when we as a society have all agreed to the fundamental changes that will happen in the aftermath. It's the defendant, of course, who has the most on the line, prison for years versus freedom. But the stakes are sky-high for so many of us, Bea and Joe and Lloyd and me, and all the Potters. Even for Judge Carrington and Hiram Jackdorp, the verdict in this case will alter the local understanding of their performance of their important public roles. History is about to be made, I thought more than once as I stood to receive the jury's decision.

But for all the extraordinary drama of the moment when a jury speaks, waiting for that to happen is as close as I've gotten in this life to suspended animation. Even compared to the many evenings I've passed hanging around in candidates' headquarters, including my own, on election nights, trying to feign cheerfulness, while the day's votes were counted, sitting on a jury, as it's called, is a special kind of indeterminacy. There have been no polls or professional predictions of the outcome, like a surgeon saying, as he did when Nat was operated on for a perforated appendix as a freshman in high school, 'He's young, I expect he'll be fine.' On top of that, a jury works without a deadline. They could return in an hour or a week. Perhaps because of the blown-out sensation of withdrawing from weeks of adrenaline, I have always experienced a chronic lack of focus that turns my mind into a shooting gallery of random, unconnected thoughts. There is a long list of tasks I have neglected for months now, but I can't begin to summon myself to, for example, answering a message from the hardware store outside Como Stop about a mounting bracket I ordered for the living room TV. Instead, as soon as Judge Carrington finished instructing the jury and sent them out, I gave Aaron an optimistic hug, and proceeded to lunch with Nat at the Lamp. For all my time up here, I still haven't found any other place to eat. On my side of the booth, a large rent in the red faux leather has been repaired with duct tape.

"Can I ask what's going on with Bea?" Nat asks.

"We need to work something out that came up during the trial. I just didn't have the bandwidth to deal with it before."

"Do I need to say I hope you do? You know, work it out?"

I just move my hand. Like anything else of substance, my mind won't go there at the moment. In fact, as soon as we sat down, I ordered a whiskey. Sitting vigil on a jury are the lone times I can recall having a hard drink while the sun was shining.

Years ago, when I was just starting out in the Kindle County Prosecuting Attorney's office, I walked into the office of a couple of much older colleagues, Harry Dunham and Gretl Shortsch, who were waiting for a verdict on a three-week murder conspiracy case. They tried a dozen cases together and spent all their time outside of court laughing. After his wife died, they married, which the outward details might not have suggested. She was quite a bit older than him and he was a head shorter, but even now, well into retirement, they are still having a great time. Before the trial, I often had them in mind, connecting them with me and Bea, as people who found unexpected contentment later in life.

At the moment I walked in while they were awaiting a call back to the courtroom, they were playing cards on the corner of his desk.

'Gin?' I asked.

'No,' she told me. 'Go Fish.'

I have always taken that as the consummate statement of the level at which most trial lawyers' brains operate, while they're waiting for a verdict.

"Your closing was great," Nat says, not for the first time. I'm happy to hear him say it, since I haven't yet given up the usual lashing of myself for what I didn't say or could have put better. The contradictions and failures in the prosecution case were so substantial that it was almost like reading from a catalog. 'It is a sad thing that this trial will conclude without knowing how Mae Potter died, whether she hanged herself or was murdered, and if that, then by who. All you know for sure is that the government did not come within a million miles of proving beyond a reasonable doubt that Aaron did it. What role if any did Hardy Potter play regarding his daughter's death? We don't know. All we can say with certainty is that his behavior was wrong and strange and that he, Hardy, is most of the reason Aaron has been sitting here accused.'

The biggest problem I faced was anticipating what Jackdorp was going to say, since his argument followed mine, and would be the last word, with the defense getting no opportunity for rejoinder. I was unsure how he was going to try to reassemble the pieces of his fractured case, but I didn't want to formulate arguments for him that he might not arrive at on his own. In general, I relied on another tried and true trope of the jury trial, telling them that together, the twelve of them were smarter than any person in the room. Given that, I beseeched them to figure out what I would say in response to any new argument Jackdorp ventured, were I to have that chance. Still, I thought it was likely enough that he would follow in the direction Mansy went and concede that Mae died at Ginawaban. If he tried that, I told the jury, then they might want to bear some questions in mind, and I listed several of the points I'd made to Mansy.

And that, indeed, was what Jackdorp maintained. He never mentioned George Lowndes's name. 'We made a mistake,' he said nonchalantly, 'and they proved it, but that doesn't mean the defendant is innocent.' Yet he didn't bother trying to answer the questions I'd raised in advance, starting with why Aaron would have left Akylles's truck, if he'd decided, after Mae's call, to follow her to Ginawaban.

Now Nat and I end up talking about the girls. Minnie, the older one, is getting interested in boys, and Nat is shocked by his own reactions. He's like some dad in a sitcom who wants to stand at the front door with an ax.

"We might be better off," I tell him, "if human adolescence was passed like a butterfly's in a cocoon. You just come out when you're beautiful and whole and can fly straight on your own."

He likes that. He likes many things I say. The miracle of being treated with love and respect by my son, who was a complete pain in the ass for so many years, is another deeply satisfying aspect of my current place in life. I did some stupid things, cruel things, to Nat's mother, and he knows that. But her responses were beyond the pale. He decided long ago that these were the parents he had, for better or worse, and more important, that we'd both treated him with unflagging love.

We walk back into the courthouse. I am on my way to Judge Carrington's chambers to tell Moriah that I am heading home and to give her my cellphone so she can reach me if the jury issues any communications. Instead, I see the judge hustling in through the back door the judges use from the courthouse parking lot. She's in a lavender shirtwaist dress, probably returning from lunch herself. She catches sight of me down the corridor and stops abruptly to point.

"Don't go anywhere," she says. "I just got a call." She doesn't explain, and Nat and I stay in the hallway outside her chambers door for about five minutes. I finally knock and peek in. The judge apparently forgot we were there. Her assistant covers the mouthpiece on her phone and says, "I'm trying to reach Mr. Jackdorp. They have a verdict." I look at my watch. Overall, they probably deliberated a little more than an hour.

I know the conventional wisdom: A quick verdict is an acquittal. I call Susan, who is running errands nearby, then Bea and Lloyd and Joe. They have gone back to the motel, but will have time to return, since the judge has said she will receive the verdict at 2:00 p.m., about forty-five minutes from now. The jurors are being given lunch in the interval.

"Chinese," Rolly, the courtroom officer today, tells us, which is not what I would have predicted for a meal paid for by the taxpayers.

Nat and I go and sit in the courtroom.

"I told you," my son says.

"We'll know when we know," I answer. But my insides scream that they could not convict that young man and send him to prison for decades, if not for life, with only an hour's deliberation.

Susan comes in then, bright as a penny. "You know what they say about fast verdicts."

I say again that we'll know when we know.

At 1:45, Rolly signals that Aaron has arrived from the jail. I go back to the lockup to see him. I hope it's the very last time.

"Verdict?" he asks.

He says he had just changed back into his jumpsuit at the jail and had to wait while they retrieved his suit.

"You think they'll mind if I don't wear a tie?" he asks.

"Put on the tie, please," I tell him. "I'm insanely superstitious at this point. I promise, you won't have to wear a tie tomorrow."

That's Aaron's kind of low-rent humor and he smiles.

When I come out, Bea and Lloyd and Joe have arrived.

"How is he?" Bea asks.

"More collected than his lawyer. I'm terrified."

"Me too." She reaches down for my ice-cold hand, and we remain that way for a second.

Jackdorp comes through the side door. The Potters won't be here, he says. In the pressure of the moment, I didn't notice that they weren't present for the closings either.

"They've had enough," says Jackdorp, a remark that requires no explanation.

I assume Glowoski is also going to skip it, but she rushes in at the last moment. She is carrying a polished caramel-colored leather hand-bag, an expensive item, which she'd had the good sense to leave behind before when it might have swayed the jurors' impressions of her. Susan and I are still hearing from acquaintances who want us to know what a fine, upright cop she is. I don't really doubt it. If she faces discipline, it won't be because I filed any kind of complaint with the State Patrol Merit Board that handles such matters. What she did for Hardy was stupid, but right now I'm too spent to be indignant with her.

Moriah peeks out to make sure the lawyers are present, and Rolly brings Aaron to stand beside me. A second later, Judge Carrington ascends the bench. There is something about her appearance that's struck me in the countless times I've seen her climb these stairs, which I can finally name only in this abstracted moment. She's short, and her sensible shoes, boxy with low heels, seem a couple sizes too big for her. Clumping upward, she reminds me a bit of Minnie Mouse.

She tells Rolly, "Bring in the jury."

I put my arm around Aaron. "Here we go," I tell him. "Your mom and your dad and Joe and I, we will be here no matter what."

The jurors enter solemnly, but both of the hair-curler ladies look toward Aaron immediately and smile. I know then for sure.

"Madame Foreperson," Judge Carrington says, and Mrs. Liu, the restaurant owner, stands. She has papers in her hand. "I am informed you have reached a verdict," the judge says.

"Yes, Your Honor," answers Mrs. Liu, and without awaiting further instruction gives the sheets to Moriah, who passes them to the judge. With a studied lack of expression, Judge Carrington unfolds the documents and examines each for a moment to be sure that the twelve required signatures appear.

"I have examined the verdict forms and find them to be in order. The clerk will now publish them." Moriah, whose six feet seems taller than ever, stands to receive the papers back and remains on her feet as she reads, in the kind of deadly monotone I've come to expect from her, as if each word means as much as the next.

"Count One. We the jury find the defendant Aaron Housley not guilty of premeditated murder in the first degree."

Aaron sags beside me into his chair, his face in his hands, weeping, while Moriah reads two more not-guiltys. As a stopgap, Jackdorp at the last minute requested the judge to instruct on the lesser included offense of aggravated assault, in hopes the jury, whatever their doubts, might give him some kind of conviction. I had begged them not to compromise, or let Jackdorp reconstruct his case, and apparently they heard me. The not guilty on obstruction is read last.

The judge, with a kindly look, is waiting for Aaron to recover.

I put my arm around him and encourage him to stand so we can finish up. I've handed him my handkerchief, and he mops his face with it as he rises.

"Mr. Jackdorp, shall I poll the jury?" Judge Carrington asks. This is the process by which each juror is asked, 'Was this and is this your verdict?' meaning 'You haven't changed your mind, right?'

"Unnecessary," Jackdorp says. That graciousness I would not have predicted.

The judge asks the jurors to wait in her chambers, in order for her to thank them personally.

"I have watched with admiration the great attention you have shown as this case proceeded. You can return to your lives and homes knowing you have performed a true service for your neighbors and our system of justice."

They all file out the jury room door beside the bench for the last time.

"Mr. Housley," the judge says then. "You are discharged and are free to go. I wish you good fortune as you move forward with your life.

"That will be all," she says. Moriah hammers the gavel and the judge departs, and Aaron and I are swarmed from behind, a melee of hugging. Aaron has embraced Susan, and Bea is hanging on the two of them and then me.

"Oh my God, oh my God," Bea is repeating. Joe is standing there watching but also crying. Lloyd wraps his son in his arms next.

To my surprise, Jackdorp has waited out this scene to shake my hand.

"Well tried, Rusty," he says, and then also offers his hand to Aaron, who I am briefly afraid won't take it. "Good luck," Jackdorp tells him. He motions me to follow him a few steps.

"You know, you've been in my shoes, I *knew* he did it, and then right near the end of my opening, I came over here and pointed at him and the way he looked back— I've gone eye to eye with plenty of defendants, and I'd never seen that before, confident instead of angry. And my heart hurt me for a second, and I thought, Maybe not. Oh, my Lord, maybe not." He shakes his head, claps my shoulder and walks away.

By the time we reach Mirror, the party has already started, thanks to Cassity and Brice, who has unexpectedly gotten another weekend of leave before shipping out for his additional training. Several of Aaron's high school friends have arrived. There is a lot of beer. Still in his white shirt, with his bright tie dragged down from his open collar, Aaron stands in the kitchen, somewhat awkward as he greets the well-wishers flowing in, a predictable response from someone who has gone in a few hours from months of confinement to celebration. Several of Bea's school colleagues are here, including Daria, her friend and deputy principal. A sizeable contingent from Lloyd's church sifts in. Camille comes in later, with all three girls.

"Jeez-o-pete, Rusty," Joe greets me and pounds me on the back too hard. He's got a beer, despite his many proclamations that he's gone dry. But it's Joe. So what else? "From day one, day one, I knew you'd get them to see truth. I *knew* it," he says.

A circle of her former students is around Daria. She is renowned even by grade-schoolers for her sense of humor, but the young adults are inevitably tickled when it turns out she has the vocabulary of a rapper. She steps away from them to embrace me.

"You know," she says, "you nearly had the world's worst fucking witness."

"Who was that?"

"Me. Bea called me on the second day of trial. I'm the one who bought that rope we used to rig the scenery for the Second Grade Sing? She wanted to know if I remembered that and why she ended up taking it home. Which is because Mr. Nicky Neatnik"—she means her husband—"starts checking the net for divorce lawyers when I come home with even a toothpick we don't have a place for. But once Bea explained, I told her, 'Sign me up.' I spoke to your investigator on the phone last week, but she called Monday early to say there was no need. Lucky for you. Try telling me to shut up."

I nod. I'm unsurprised to learn that there was byplay between Bea and Susan that didn't include me. I explain the prosecution's error. Of all their many mistakes, that's the one I know I probably would have made too.

"Then last night," Daria says, carrying on, as usual, under her own conversational momentum, "Bea called me at midnight, to ask if I went with her to that meeting about the damn bathrooms." That was that interminable Principals' Roundtable about transgender restrooms, which took place the day Mae was killed.

"Did you?" I ask Daria casually.

"Hell, yes. Bea had her hand on my knee for hours to keep me from going off. You tell me how the fuck we've gotten to the point in this country that using the toilet is political? Build the damn thing and put up a sign that reads 'Restroom.' It doesn't have to say 'Queer Enclave.' It's a few of the older teachers who need extra privacy who'd really like that. I asked Bea why the hell she was waking me up and she said it might matter to you, but it was too complicated to explain."

As much as Bea loves Daria, she doesn't treat her often as a confidante. It tweaks my heart a little to think Bea felt it was urgent to prove to me she was uninvolved in Mae's death, but I'm glad to have Dar's recollection. I suppose I could have called her myself days ago, if I'd been facile enough to come up with the same excuse that occurs to me now.

"You get paranoid trying a case, Dar. Sometimes a prosecutor who's losing is like a bull that gets stung on his nose by a bee. I was afraid he'd be so enraged at me and Aaron, he'd accuse Bea next."

"Shut the fuck up!" Daria says.

"Honestly, I don't think the thought ever crossed his mind. It was all me. At trial, you get into a mindset like a fighter pilot, looking for incoming from all sides."

I thank Daria for her willingness to help and move off to greet other visitors. The doorbell rings and I hear Bea give a little yelp of joy, as she opens her arms to the visitor, who turns out to be Reverend Spruce. He stays just a moment. He finds Aaron in the kitchen and lays his hands on each of Aaron's shoulders, speaking to him quietly as Aaron looks up at him.

I've been glancing to Aaron periodically throughout the evening. At one point, someone handed him a beer. He took a long draught, then considered the can and put it on the counter. So far as I can see, he hasn't picked it up again. People continue to cluster around him in the kitchen and the living room. He takes all the well-wishing with good grace, lots of nodding, a fixed smile, but he looks often like he is waiting for a chance to pull himself away. At a couple of moments, I see him retreat to the kitchen, standing in the corner beside the refrigerator, eyes down and trying to make some sense of today and the last five months of his life. I wouldn't be surprised if he's thinking most about Mae.

Once Susan and Al arrive on their motorcycles, Bea gathers everyone in the living room and raises a glass to Susan and Aaron and me. "They were magnificent, each of them. But let me tell you, there is a reason people refer to very hard times as 'a trial.'" Those gathered aren't completely sure this is a laugh line and chuckle with restraint. "I thank Susan and Rusty for their incredible hard work, their imagination and their commitment to Aaron's innocence. And I thank God as well. He was with us too."

Her toast is greeted with applause.

Around ten, Aaron says he's going to Cassity's to play games on their new console. Oddly, Judge Sams terminated Aaron's probation on his own motion when Aaron was indicted. He figured the probation office didn't need to monitor somebody in custody. That, in turn, ended the suspension of his license. As a result, Aaron is free to drive. I hand him my car keys.

"Sure you don't want my truck?" Joe asks. "I put that wiring harness in and the thing runs great."

From those who understand the joke—more people than I might have guessed—Joe's line produces affectionate chortles, particularly when Aaron plays along and recoils in mock horror.

After Aaron goes, our place empties quickly. At last, Bea and I are alone in the kitchen. She brings her whole body against me, and I wrap her in my arms. I am virtually shattered by longing and the feeling of how far from whole I have been without her.

She rears back to see me, more tears, which have not ceased all evening, glistening on her lovely dark face.

"Please," she says "please be with me, stay with me, love me, forgive me, forgive me, please. Please. You have given Aaron back his life. So I know it sounds like a lot to ask. But please, please, give me back my life, too."

50

Joe's Sickness

February–March 2024

For the first days after the verdict, Aaron spends the daylight hours paddling around in one of our aluminum canoes. Despite a recent thaw that has brought temps to the upper forties, there are still migrating islands of ice on Mirror Lake. He wears my wetsuit and his own parka over it as he floats without an obvious destination. His former boss has called and offered him his old job back, starting April 15. He'll probably accept, but he also has made plans to go to Kindle County next week to stay with Nat and Anna and the girls. With time to apply before the fall semester, Aaron wants to look at the Institute of Art and Design, which is associated with the county art museum. Although he has no intention of showing up to collect his prize, he received a letter yesterday saying he won third place in the state prison art competition.

In one fairly speculative conversation, Bea asks me what I would think of moving back to Kindle, no matter what happens with Aaron. Right now, she's had enough of Skageon County. She can take an early retirement program that has long made it advantageous for higher-salaried educators to move on, and live out her long-sequestered wish to be a city girl. I am actually warmer to the idea than I expected.

I would be able to see Minny and Bri far more often and also be on standby to provide the kind of guidance teenagers frequently find easier to accept from an adult who's not their parent. Bea and I could still return to Mirror on weekends, or for longer periods if we liked.

More frequently than I might expect, when I'm between phone calls in which I'm reassembling my arbitration practice, I wander down to the shore to watch Aaron on the water. I'm not really spying on him, but it satisfies me to see him out there, drifting and paddling alternately, moving with the seeming impulsiveness of a divining rod.

On the Wednesday following the veridct, as I am in the midst of one of these shoreline visits, my cellphone rings. The caller ID says, 'Carrington, Gwendolyn.'

"Hope I'm not interrupting," she says.

"Of course not, Judge. Life better with all of us out of your hair?"

"I suppose. That was a hard trial," she says. "Hard on all of us."

I tell her that I think she did a fine job, and she murmurs thanks, too professional to wallow in the compliment. But she knows very well that I was a trial judge for many years, so I hope she finds the praise more gratifying than what she hears customarily from winning lawyers.

"Anyway," she says, cutting off any small talk, "I wanted to call because I spoke to the jurors after the verdict. Care to hear what they said? They were fine with me passing it on."

"It's usually Jabberwocky, frankly. Twelve people suddenly pretending they were thinking just one thing, and trying to put reasons on what for some of them came straight from the gut."

"That's true," she says. "But this group seemed to be of one mind. They said they discussed the evidence for about an hour and then took what proved to be their only vote. Apparently one person somewhat favored conviction initially but changed their mind by the time they took a tally."

It's chilling evidence of the perils of the jury system to think that anybody could find proof beyond a reasonable doubt in Jackdorp's shattered case. If the judge knows who the yes-for-guilty was, she clearly won't share the name.

"They said that once they started talking, they just couldn't make

any sense of the prosecution's case. It was like a puzzle where no matter which way you turned the pieces, they didn't fit. Yet they were all
grateful that Aaron testified. They realized he didn't have to, but it
struck them as something only an innocent person would have done,
to get up there and tell his story, despite the obvious deficiencies in
the State's presentation. There's one for you," she adds. They say that
juries are sometimes like children in the way they make observations
that are beyond the lawyers, just as kids sometimes see things the
adults around them routinely miss. I've spent fifty years practicing
criminal law, with the principle that jurors can't hold a defendant's
silence against him like something inscribed on a stone tablet. But
nowhere is it written that they can't treat a willingness to speak as evidence favoring the accused.

"I thought they did a good job," she says, stopping short of saying
she agreed with them, which is beyond the purview of a trial judge.

"You share this with Jackdorp, too?"

"I phoned him, but he hasn't called back yet. We never speak much
outside of court, and I imagine we won't again. He's decided not to
run for reelection in November. I'm not sure that news would have
reached Skageon County. He's a moody fellow. I suspect you could
tell. I heard rumors on Monday and thought he'd change his mind,
but he made an announcement to the deputy PAs yesterday. Apparently, he said he's had enough."

I'm sure our case had some impact on that decision, but it's beyond
me to guess whether it's disappointment or exhaustion that motivates
him. There was a lot about that trial that would give a prosecutor second thoughts about his job.

"Who's going to succeed him?"

"It's too late for anybody to file for the primary in six weeks. So
it will all be write-ins. Jack has said he won't endorse a candidate. I'm
thinking of tossing my hat in the ring. Supposedly, I have a good
chance. I'm the only judge who's interested. And the only female. And
the three or four others who are thinking about it will probably split
the more traditional vote," she says, avoiding a loaded term like 'law-
and-order.' Our trial, I'm sure, ended up providing a lot of favorable
publicity for her and increased her name recognition.

"That would be a great service to your county, Judge. I'll be watching to see how it turns out." With that remark, our conversation soon concludes. I'm impressed that even now, Wendy Carrington and I remain bound by the formalities of our respective roles. She's not being a prig. She wants to avoid any appearance that whatever mutual regard we may feel had any impact in court. It's Aaron's acquittal she's trying not to impugn. For that reason, I don't say what would be natural in Kindle County, that I'll contribute to her campaign, or offer to endorse her. For Aaron's sake, the distance between the judge and me is now permanent.

The next day Joe reenters the hospital for tests and treatment. The news is not good. Bea, never much inclined to woe-is-me, is flattened by the reality of yet another major crisis. Hanging up after her call with the doctor's office, she wilts so completely that I am afraid she will hit the floor.

"I know," I tell her and embrace her. It seems as if we have spent the entire period since the verdict wrapped in each other's arms.

Joe is hospitalized in Milwaukee, which requires Bea to take yet another day from work the following Monday in order to meet with the oncologist before Joe is discharged. I go for support, and Aaron at the last minute decides to come with us. When we see the doctor without Joe, she says that he had a troubling scan about a month before the trial but refused to start a new round of chemo until afterwards. The chances of any appreciable effect on the metastatic disease were not great, she acknowledges, but they wanted to try an older medication that occasionally slows tumor growth and might give Joe a few more months. He did not help his chances by waiting.

The cancer now is in the bones. He is at serious risk for spontaneous breaks of his ribs, in particular. There's a tumor in a bile duct from his liver and there are several lesions in his brain that have grown significantly. The doctor, a short East Asian woman, who has none of the undertaker's personality I might expect from someone who loses patients so regularly, adds that the growths inside his skull have been there for more than a year. She tells us to be prepared for personality changes, especially extreme irritability or impulsive behavior. In response, Bea laughs out loud.

"Doctor, he must have had brain cancer since I was a child. Any chance he'll get nicer, instead?" Bea asks.

The doc, who seems to share Bea's sense of humor, lifts her brow and says, "It's been known to happen."

Aaron takes all of this in with a tight look. I have a sense, although it's entirely of my imagining, that he is wondering if this is the bargain God is exacting in the end, his freedom in exchange for his grandfather.

Joe, for his part, is less morose than he's been on earlier occasions when he got bad news. We greet him in his room, where he's ready to depart. He's fully dressed and his belongings are in a big plastic bag heaped in his lap as he sits in the wheelchair in which an aide will bring him to the door.

"Well, they've given me a couple months before, right?" he says.

That is true, although the prognosis has not been quite as absolute as this time. But he's correct. He's been living under the dangling sword for years now and he's still here. My old internist in Kindle County once marveled to me that it seems to take nasty people longer to die.

Joe does appear even stiffer and more immobile as we ease him into the passenger seat to take him home, but that may be the result of the enforced bed rest while they were giving him the massive starter dose of the chemo. He is his usual garrulous self, reporting on speculation that another atmospheric river may strike California, and complaining especially about the other patient in his semi-private room, who was apparently experiencing near-constant flatulence. Then, as soon as we are on the highway, Joe erupts with explosive vomiting that spatters the window, the dashboard and of course himself. I wrestle off my parka while I'm driving and leave it to Aaron and Bea to help clean him up. As always, an apology is beyond him, and he swears about the doctors and nurses who he says should not have let him eat.

Assured that Joe's passing is not imminent, Aaron decides to proceed with his trip to Kindle County. We eat dinner together the night before he leaves. The trial and Mae have largely gone unmentioned because Bea has begged for no talk of it, especially at the table. Nonetheless, tonight Bea tells us about an interlude with the state superintendent, who was in town. Aaron knows the man too, whom he met when Bea and he were going out. Bea says the superintendent remained silent throughout the whole ordeal, not even bothering with an encouraging message after the verdict, but today he drew her aside as he was leaving. She expected some word of compassion. Instead, he asked her who she thought did it.

"If one more person asks me that," Bea says.

"That's natural," I tell her.

"Everybody in town expects me to dump on Hardy." She shoots me a sudden glance, as if even her uttering his name might upset me. She's right that I experience a qualm I do my best to suppress.

"Hardy's a jerk," says Aaron, "and I'll hate his guts the rest of my life. But he didn't kill Mae." His declaration is so emphatic that both Bea and I react the same way and share a panicked look, as if her son is about to say something awful about himself. "What?" he asks, when he finds us both staring. "I'm just saying it wasn't Hardy. That's all. I don't believe it."

And if not Hardy, then who? I have begun to settle into the state of mind I had to adopt when I experienced the few outright acquittals during my career in the PA's office. Usually, of course, I remained convinced of the defendant's guilt and attributed the verdict to bad rulings by the judge or the entirely quixotic nature of juries. But there were a couple of instances when I had to accept exactly what I told Aaron's jury in my closing—that we just didn't know. 'No one is asking you to deliver a verdict of "Found Innocent," even if that's warranted,' I told them. 'The words on the forms you'll get are "Not Guilty," and that means simply that the government didn't prove its case, that we just don't know for sure how Mae died or who may have been responsible.'

At the start of the third week after the verdict, I drive to Como Stop to pick up the television mount I'd ordered, and Mansy Potter comes out of the hardware store door as I am headed in. Today, out on the street, I notice that he is more stooped. I see his nostrils flare, and his eyes harden when he catches sight of me, but then he overcomes that response and moves a few steps forward and offers his hand. It's a blustery day, in the midthirties now, but cold enough that neither of us will be inclined to linger long.

"That didn't end well, the last time I saw you," he says. "But you said some things I've been turning over in my own mind since."

"It's in the past now, Mansy," I say, meaning to comfort him.

"Having no idea what actually happened?" He shakes his head in sorrow. "The mind craves an explanation, you know? Such a hole in your heart."

"I understand," I tell him.

He takes a step back and says, "I've missed your company, Russ. I admit that."

"Likewise," I tell him.

He nods. Maybe when the swelling goes down, I think. If it ever does.

"And tell Aaron that I wish him well," Mansy adds. "It helped all of us to hear his story. I couldn't believe you put him on, but he did a fine job for himself."

"That's because he was telling the truth, Mansy."

He shrugs. He's not going to argue, and the way he moves his head from side to side suggests he might be moving toward accepting that.

"How much of that had you heard from the start?" he asks, just as he's about to turn away.

"Virtually all of it," I say. That's not true, of course. But I will always be Aaron's advocate. I do believe that if I'd allowed Aaron to give us his complete version earlier, what he said on the stand is exactly what he would have told us.

Two days later, I get a text from Lainie Harrup, who asks if I have a second to talk. I call her immediately. The Saturday after the verdict, I found myself unable to completely disconnect from the trial and was moved to write things down. I sent notes to her and Akylles and Susan, brief words of praise that I felt each of them wholeheartedly deserved. I told Lainie that I hope she was aware of how few people would wrest themselves from their daily lives to endure two days of connecting flights, just to face the ordeal of testifying in a murder trial, even with the hope of saving a young life. In my book, I told her, she is a genuine hero. I said much the same thing to Akylles.

"Oh, Rusty!" she says when she answers, happy to hear from me.

She tells me how grateful she was for my note, then says, "Tell me, please, how Aaron is doing."

She could not be more interested if we were talking to her about her niece or nephew, although she also asks about the Potters, whose plight she says she's thought about often. I'm glad I can tell her about my visit with Mansy.

She finally explains why she contacted me.

"You'll never guess what showed up in my mail this morning: Those phone records the company said they couldn't get to for another month. I know the trial is over, but I wondered if you still wanted to see them."

Do I? I'd still like to know if Mae actually completed a second call with Lainie's phone right after Aaron rang off suddenly. First thing, I remind myself that if she did, Mae didn't speak to Bea, as I once feared, because Bea was with Daria and all the other principals. What is striking, though, is how automatically I retreat, if only for a second, to the atavistic fear that my life is on replay.

Still silent with Lainie, I sort the remaining possibilities. If I had to bet, my biggest wager would be that Mae dialed and dialed but reached no one. But I'd save a few pennies to put on Hardy.

"Yes, I'd love to see the records."

"I'll scan them and email them to you this afternoon. My daughter put an app on my phone, and I just love to use it."

With Aaron gone to Kindle County, Bea and I have been taking turns looking in on Joe, usually a couple of times a day. Medicare sends a visiting nurse who spends about an hour, taking blood and checking other vitals and administering his daily injection of chemo. Yet, given the array of side effects he's experiencing from the medication, he would be better off with care for a longer period. Holding her breath, Bea offered to take Joe into our house, but Joe, as always before, refused, knowing perhaps that that kind of proximity to his daughter would make his last days a turmoil for both of them. Besides, Joe would never admit he requires help. We have been arguing with both the VA and Medicare that they should pay for more nursing, but in the interim, Bea's brother, Fritz, has volunteered to advance the costs of a caregiver. It makes him feel better about his ironclad refusal to return. A trained nurse's aide will be starting later in the week. Even without paying a lawyer, the costs for Susan and our brief consultations with experts, plus the travel and hotel bills for Akylles and Lainie and her own stay, have left Bea with a huge debt to her 401(k), which she will not allow me to repay for her.

I knock and let myself into the 'big house,' as the modest farmhouse where Joe resides is called. He has not changed one piece of the heavy German furniture with which Willi decorated, dark wooden items with lots of carvings, crimson brocade upholstery on the sofa and the easy chairs. We got him a hospital bed, but it's too big for his bedroom, given the presence of the old four-poster in which he slept with Willi. Instead, he has set up camp in his living room, not far from his big TV, tuned eternally to the Weather Channel. The medication causes him to sleep most of the time. A plastic emesis basin is beside the bed, and even with one step inside the door, I can tell it has been used. I glove, then take it to the bathroom to empty it. Once there, I look into Joe's small bedroom next door. He is a surprisingly tidy person, and when I push aside the closet door, his shoes are lined up against the back wall in a perfect row. I pick up one of them and come to sit down on an oak pressback chair that has been positioned beside the bed. I printed out the single page of records Lainie sent last week and have it folded in my back pocket.

I wait a good twenty minutes for Joe to wake, in which I decide for the one hundredth time that I will just leave it be, but, as I expected, I can't quite summon the will to depart.

At last Joe's dark eyes open, as he finally feels the weight of my presence. Lying there beneath the covers, shrinking away now with the disease, he reminds me of a peanut in a shell, especially his withered face.

I don't say anything in greeting, waiting instead until I'm certain he's awake and focused. Then I lift the athletic shoe I've been holding.

"Nike Air Force 1," I say.

"Yeah," he says. "Real good shoe. That's why I bought them for him." I realize that he was clunking around the courthouse in his big oxfords for reasons beyond trying to affect respectful attire.

"So, Joe," I say. "You told me the truth."

"How's that?"

"That first day in the Marenago Jail, you told me you killed Mae. When I asked how you even located her, you told me she called you. Which I find now was true." I reach into my back pocket and unfold the printout of the phone record. I show it to him, and his eyes flick over it, although I doubt he can see much at this stage. "She phoned you after Aaron, thinking you were the person your grandson was most likely to check in with, and that you might be able to get him to call her back or even meet her at Ginawaban."

His tiny black eyes are still and hard as marbles, but he shakes his head.

"I told you I'd say I did it to save Aaron. And you told me, 'Nothin doin, the prosecutor will never believe it.'"

"But you killed her, right? Mae called you, told you where she'd be and begged you to let Aaron know, right?"

He doesn't answer.

"You're bulletproof, Joe. They can't prosecute you. The doctors will tell them that you'll be gone before they can even get the charges on paper."

"Well fuck me anyway, if I'm goin out with everybody standin over my deathbed and callin me a murderer. Whatever peace I can get, I'm takin."

"What would you have done if Aaron was convicted?"

"Well, I hadn't figured that out, but I'd have had to do something, wouldn't I? But it was you who stopped me cold in the jail with all your questions. Aaron had her phone, so how was it that she called me? I had no idea."

"Well, for Godsake, Joe, don't you owe somebody the truth? Mae's murder turned all our lives upside down. The least you could do to make up for that is to let us know what really happened."

"Won't do anybody any good now."

He might have a point about that. Bea doesn't need to feel more rage about her father. She will never resolve the emotional cyclone Joe unleashes, so it might even be cruel to add this. And Aaron—Aaron knew about the shoes to start. And chose to say nothing. I know I told him in an early visit that Joe and his mother had offered to confess. I wanted him to feel the depth of their love, but I explained how incredible their stories would be. It's hard to say how much logical thinking Aaron was doing at that point anyway. Maybe it was Joe he had in mind at some level of consciousness when he told me before the trial started that he knew he'd be walking out at the end.

But Aaron has just started on the business of reassembling his life. It would do serious damage to knock away one of its pillars right now. He knows enough to ask questions in the years ahead, if he's ever ready for the answer. The Potters, on the other hand, might be soothed to know what actually happened. But it will be a while before I can set aside my outrage with them or feel they have any right to the truth after they shamelessly tailored it to fit Aaron.

"Well, how about if I hear it and don't tell anybody else? Let's say you've come to me for legal advice now that I'm done representing Aaron. So it's a secret I can't share. At least until long after you're gone."

He tosses his head back and forth. He looks a mess. His eyes for whatever reason seem to have begun protruding from his sockets, and the liver failure is yellowing them.

"Don't see why."

"Come on, Joe. Cut the crap. She's dead. And you've gotten away with it."

"And seen that boy stand trial for it? I don't call that getting away with it. I was in agony every day. And it wasn't how you're thinking anyway. I didn't rush up there to kill her. It was more an accident her dying, and her fault anyway."

"Okay," I say, "so it was an accident. What's the harm in talking about it, then, especially if you'll never have to face the consequence of anybody knowing while you're around? Come on. She called you. And said, 'Please, please, tell Aaron to come see me at Ginawaban.' Right? And you said you would, so she'd stay put, and you raced up there instead, didn't you? You went to tell her to leave him the fuck alone, right?"

He smiles a bit. Like so many—like Mae—who do so much to push others away, Joe still enjoys it when it turns out the people around him have some understanding of him.

"That's right. She said when she called, 'He's quit on me, Joe, and I need him to change his mind, or I'm going to kill myself, I really will. Call him for me, get him to see me.' Then she says, maybe I can find him on the road hitchhiking and drive him up. I mean, no end of entitled, that girl."

"So you sped up there?"

"Right. Said she'd be along the first trail running northeast from the parking area. And there she is. Not very far in. Got herself in a real pose when she heard me comin. There's this huge brown boulder, you know, the local granite, at least four foot tall, right under a big oak. And she's sittin on top of it like Humpty Dumpty, but with a noose around her neck. Must have been that damn rope Aaron bought, and she's thrown the loose end several times over a low limb overhead. So he can see, like she says, she's ready to do herself in without him. I just about laughed out loud, the kind of show she was puttin on.

"Course, she catches sight of me, and first thing is, 'Where's Aaron?' Not even hello. 'I told you to call Aaron, to bring him.'

"'Aaron,' I say, 'he ain't comin. You say Aaron's done with you and well he should be, sister.' She called me every kind of name. Crying and furious. I give it back to her real good, told her just what I thought of her and how she was gonna use her life to make a misery for everybody else and enjoy doing it. I'm standing right below her, and finally she moves at me sudden, gonna throw a punch or kick me. Only she's too drugged up to recall she's got a rope around her neck, she's like a dog on a chain. And when she jerks back, she falls off the damn boulder, and then she's swinging there, hanging for real, gasping and grabbing at the rope, legs goin like an eggbeater. She wasn't maybe more than two foot off the ground, but that was enough. I just watched her there, swingin back and forth."

"But you could have grabbed her at any second and steered her back onto the rock, right?"

"Coulda," he says. "But she done all this to herself. Ain't my part to save her, is it?"

"Not if you ignore the law."

"Fuck that," he answers. "People been saving that girl from herself for too damn long. I wasn't gonna be another one."

From what I read preparing to cross-examine Dr. Rogers, people like Mae, whose neck isn't broken by the initial drop, live roughly seven minutes before dying from the loss of circulation to the brain. Maybe with all the opioids in her bloodstream, Mae would have gone more quickly, but she would have been dancing at the end of the rope for a few minutes, a hideous sight.

"And you just stood there watching?" I ask.

"Pretty much. Hated that damn girl for years."

"And in all that time with her swinging around there, tearing at the rope and running like mad through the air, she never got her feet back on that rock?"

"She didn't, no." His black eyes are completely still as he looks at me. "Might be I gave her a little shove once or twice to make sure that didn't happen. Might be," he says. Emily Dickinson has a line, 'Zero at the Bone.' That's what I'm feeling, hearing Joe.

"Like you was always sayin," he says, "she ever got her neck outta that noose, she'd have kicked the teeth out of my head before I knew they was gone, beat me bloody. Man in my condition? Woulda killed me. So it was self-defense, I'd say."

He's smug enough to think he's smart.

"Well, I'll tell you the part I don't understand about this accident, Joe. How did she get that shoeprint on her shoulder? Or the dirt and abrasions on her chest?"

"Ah," he says. A smile, fleet as a fox, comes and goes with the memory. "That girl, smart as she was, she couldn't have organized a picnic if she was the only one comin. She's swingin there, making these little gargly noises, and most of the way to dead, when son of bitch if the limb doesn't give way. It was all mostly for show, like I said, her hanging act. Breaks clean off and she comes down in a pile with the rope on top of her. She's not movin, so I can't tell if she's alive or not, but no point I see in chancin that, not for Aaron, not for me."

"For you?"

"How would it turn out for me if she got back on her feet and told that story about me givin her a little poke now and then? It was a done deal by then, far as I was concerned. So I took hold of the rope and drug her out from under the limb, ten feet or so, then I got my foot on her shoulder to keep her put and hauled on that line hard as I could for a while, until I was damn sure the job was done. Probably was dead when she hit the ground, but like I say, I was past the point of takin any chances."

As usual, Joe's story is constructed to minimize his responsibility. It's a favorite law school hypothetical to ask students whether you're guilty of murder for shooting a dead man, and the answer in most states is no—it's not even attempt. But those abrasions on Mae's chest could only have been inflicted while her blood was still flowing. Joe killed her. No question.

"So you know, I got an issue now," Joe continues, caught up in the momentum of his story. "Thing is she called me. I had no idea it wasn't from her own phone, so I figured once she turned up dead the police would come round to ask me questions. Always surprised me when they didn't show up, but I was fixed to tell them she was talkin crazy and I just hung up on her.

"Still and all, they pretty sure woulda given me a hard time. If she was still hangin there, I'da left her. Suicide, clear enough. But layin there with a rope around her neck? Maybe choked, the cops would say. My first thought was to string her back up, frankly, but it was hell to pay, getting that rope over a high-enough bough, and I wasn't sure, with my leg and all, I'd be able to winch her off the ground. Then I remembered that utility road. If they found her a month or two from now, there wouldn't be enough of her left to say it was anything but an accident.

"So I put on some work gloves and got that hand truck from my flatbed and took her back down to the parking lot and stuck her behind the wheel of her own car, which was sitting there with the key in the cup holder, cause what does a rich girl like that care? I actually sat on her lap, believe it or not, while I drove it over. Once I'm lookin down there, I see I might get pretty messed up if I went freewheeling with her to the bottom. I got out and tried to push it, but the car was on a little rise there. So I went back for my truck.

"I was about to nudge that car of hers over the edge, when I remembered, 'Jesus, you better get that noose off her.' Had that knife in the glove compartment of the pickup. Kind of had to saw through that slipknot, tight as it had got. White fibers flying all over. After that, away she goes. Only, when the car came to rest, you could still see the back end plain as day. So I drove down, and pulled some of the broken brush around to cover up. Had to hope my truck would get back up that damn incline. It stalled out twice. But I made it. I was drinking with you at the VFW before the night was over."

"When you fed me your alibi about being in your Harvestore?"

"Fuck alibi. It was good riddance. She wasn't the first person I watched die under my hands. Sixty years or so had passed, but felt pretty much the same. Grateful in a way. You or them and it ends up them? Kind of brings things down to the basic level. Naturally, it all got fucked up to hell, when Aaron got blamed and you wouldn't let me tell what happened."

It's become a story typical of Joe, all mismatched pieces and everyone to blame but him.

"Glad to know that now it's my fault."

"It's her fault, pure and simple. You want to talk fault. I did what needed doing, if you ask me. What happened to Aaron, watching that trial was like dying alive. But her, I haven't given her a second thought. Sorry. So now you know and can't tell nobody, like you said, Rusty."

As always, he thinks he's got the drop on everyone. I ponder whether I should speak any words of judgment. It won't make any difference—except to me.

"Joe, I'll keep my word to you. No one will know now. But you realize who'd be at the top of the list of people who would never forgive you? Your grandson."

"Nnuh-uh," he answers. "He'd know I done it out of love and that it was pretty much an accident and the best for him anyway."

If Joe had ever spent any time being a real parent, he might have learned what comes of it when you try to make decisions for adult children. But that's the least of his failings that's of concern at the moment.

"Joe, let me give you a professional view of this. Free of charge. When you set hands on another living person to cause their death, the law has one word for it. Murder. So don't try that accident bullshit with me. You're just a plain killer. And, I might add for myself, one lowdown fucked-up shitty human being."

I can see at once, just as I expected, that he has no use for my pronouncement. Whatever strength he has remaining is summoned for the sake of fierce resistance, just as he has always refused to bow to anybody's opinion of him.

"Oh sure," he says. "Guys like you, Rusty— Ever think much about what you did with your life? Folks like you, when you actually look, all you do is talk and think your pretty thoughts. But who is it you call for all the hard things that need doing in the name of the law? Who is it you ask to push the button in the death chamber, or slam the cell door shut on some shit-scared kid, or throw some poor bastard and his family out on the street cause he can't afford his rent? Then you need shits like me. That girl was gonna be an everlasting misery to whoever was unlucky enough to love her. Aaron already done a stretch in jail on account of her, and that silly mope that's her father, he'll be looking for a new job soon. She was just twenty-two years old and only getting started. Pain would just fall from her like rain." He shared that view in the immediate wake of Mae's death, but I didn't realize then that he was deprecating her to excuse himself.

"So if your precious law says it was okay for me to crawl into some hole in the ground to choke and beat and stab some poor slope who was down there fighting for his life, just so the Vietcong would make sure his family got a few extra grains of rice—if that was my patriotic duty, then what do you call it when you're protecting a boy, the one soul who ever actually loved *you*? *That's* duty.

"So go on now," he says. He rolls to his side, in order to avoid seeing any more of me. "I'm done with you, and you're done with me. Good for both of us. Go."

I stand over the bed, peering down, but he won't turn back. After a second, he picks up the TV remote to turn the sound up even further on a story about another late snowstorm assaulting the plains.

I take a seat in my car, facing Joe's fields, softened by the rains that have been part of a recent thaw. He rotates his four parcels between soybeans and alfalfa year by year, and in front of me is the wasted brown stubble of last season's crop that will soon be plowed under.

Joe's tale is a lot to digest, of course. Mae Potter was a young person I knew fairly well, deeply troubled but, as Aaron and Mansy believed, still in reach of her potential. The actual details of how she lost her life make that fact seem far sadder, even though I have mourned her at moments for half a year. I know for sure now that Bea has the right idea. After we bury Joe, we'll depart for the city. It's what we need for lots of reasons. Being close to my granddaughters and my legacy is at the top of the list. But deep down, I sense there's a piece of me that yearns to return to where I started, as the right place to finally make my peace with all that went before. And together, Bea and I share the view that we have too much good time left to spend it beneath the shadows of what's transpired here.

As for Joe, oddly, what sticks out for me right now is his harsh judgment on my working life. 'Just talk and pretty thoughts,' he said. Having literally gotten away with murder, he probably feels he has the right to give the back of his hand to the law. Its categories and abstractions don't feel like much against the ruthless plainness of the country, where death and life, the warp and weft of existence, always feel so much nearer at hand, with the birth and slaughter in the livestock barns, the crops that rise and fall and grow again. Mae Potter's killing is, I guess, just another raw fact, part of that harsh cycle, all of which gets swallowed in the consuming silence of the open land, where often you cannot hear even the wind.

But I don't regret my career. Aaron's trial has been, by my lights, a fine coda, a healing balm on the wounds left by my own experience as the accused. Yes, the law blunders along at times like a blind elephant. Even when I was a prosecutor, I realized that we caught only a tiny share of the bad guys. Most got away. Joe marches on as part of an endless phalanx of the unpunished.

But values matter. Ideas matter. Sorting wrong from right, the law's most basic task, dignifies our lives, sets a path that most of us who aspire to see ourselves as good people try to follow, even knowing that there are those, like Joe, whose pasts robbed them of that desire and leave them feeling at heart that crime, and banishment, are their truest destiny.

So yes, Bea and I will move on, but I will go with no regrets or second thoughts about my decade and a half out here in Skageon. Within the profound silence of the country, I have, like Aaron, come to feel more of myself. I have healed. Loved well and been loved. Known regrets, some deep. But best, learned to live as I will live now in the time I have. With gratitude.

Naples
Salem
Evanston

Acknowledgments

Big thanks are due to many of the usual suspects, starting with the pillars of my personal and professional life: my lover—and wife—Adriane Glazier Turow; my agent of nearly four decades, Gail Hochman; and my gentle and astute editor, Ben Sevier. I am grateful for the insights from my cadre of first readers: Adriane, the first of the first; my forever friend Julian Solotorovsky; my beloved cousin, Dan Pastern; my daughters, Rachel Turow and Eve Turow-Paul. The team at Grand Central are always stalwarts. There are too many to name them all, but I am indebted to Kirsiah Depp, for her line edits and other editorial contributions; to my scrupulous copy editor, Rick Ball, and his boss, Mari C. Okuda; and to my longtime publicist at GC, Staci Burt. At home, my two outstanding admins, Kinga Luczkiewicz and Kelley Genne, are ever-reliable guides through the thicket of my own life.

And very special thanks to Michael W. Kaufman, MD, a board-certified pathologist, who, over the course of several books, has done his best to keep me from making gross errors in his specialty area. I am deeply in his debt.

To readers, let me offer my perpetual gratitude and one note to avoid confusion. Like Kindle County, the unnamed Midwestern state in which this novel is set is equally fictitious, partaking of aspects of Wisconsin, Illinois, Iowa, and Minnesota. While I am always happy to hear from you at scottturow.com, there is no need to burden yourself with messages telling me that you can't make sense of the supposed location of Skageon or Marenago Counties. That is solidly—but only—within the peaceful confines of my imagination.

S.T.

About the Author

Scott Turow, a writer and former practicing lawyer, is the author of thirteen bestselling works of fiction, including *Presumed Innocent* and most recently, *Suspect*. Mr. Turow has also published two nonfiction books, including *One L*, about his experience as a law student. His books have been translated into more than forty languages, sold more than thirty million copies worldwide, and have been adapted into movies and television projects. He has frequently contributed essays and op-ed pieces to publications such as the *New York Times, Washington Post, Vanity Fair*, the *New Yorker*, and the *Atlantic*.

For more information, you can visit:
ScottTurow.com
X: @ScottTurow
Facebook.com/scottturowbooks